FAIR HELL

Richard Pendleton Watts

FAIR HELL

ISBN: Paperback: 978-1-7370685-9-4

Disclaimer
This work contains language that reflects the historical period in which it was written. This includes words and characterizations that are now considered offensive and harmful.

Scripture verses from the King James Version Bible. Public domain.

Editing: Joni Wilson

Cover and Book Design: Deborah Perdue, Illumination Graphics
Cover artwork by Tara Thelen

NOTES ABOUT THIS BOOK

This book was originally written in the mid-twentieth century in longhand by Richard Pendleton Watts. It was then typed onto paper pages (imagine an old-fashioned typewriter) by secretaries (yes, that's what they were called back then) who worked in his law office.

The novel is set in a historically accurate setting, complete with names of cities, towns, rivers, and other places, many that still exist. Some of the characters in this story are fiction, but there are also many names that are real people who lived during this challenging time in US history. While the story is not necessarily a true account of what happened to the characters, it is a reasonable rendition of the times and the peoples.

Kentucky is famous for salt licks, which are natural springs rich in salt. Their presence was a factor in attracting settlers to the area. The first state industry was the extraction and boiling of salt from the licks, providing this essential mineral to much of the American population.

Because the author is no longer present to guide the editing process, his son has asked that the book be as true to the original text as possible. This includes language that is no longer used in current style guidelines, but these are the words that were used in that era.

The names of places and peoples mentioned in this book have been reviewed by the editor. Where they differ from current names, an endnote explanation is given. Where noted, further explanation is given about people, activities, and places. Many forts and stations were established in Kentucky during the 1700 settlement period.

Note that the dialogue is presented as phonetic speech, as it would have been spoken at the time by the character speaking. If a reader is in doubt about the words, try saying them out loud.

A reference section has links to various documents and images that cover this crucial historical era. The reader is encouraged to review these references to give a better overview of the Kentucky area, the people who settled the area, and the general history.

DEDICATION

In memory of Robert McDowell and Anthony Foster. Without their excellent research, this manuscript would not have been possible.

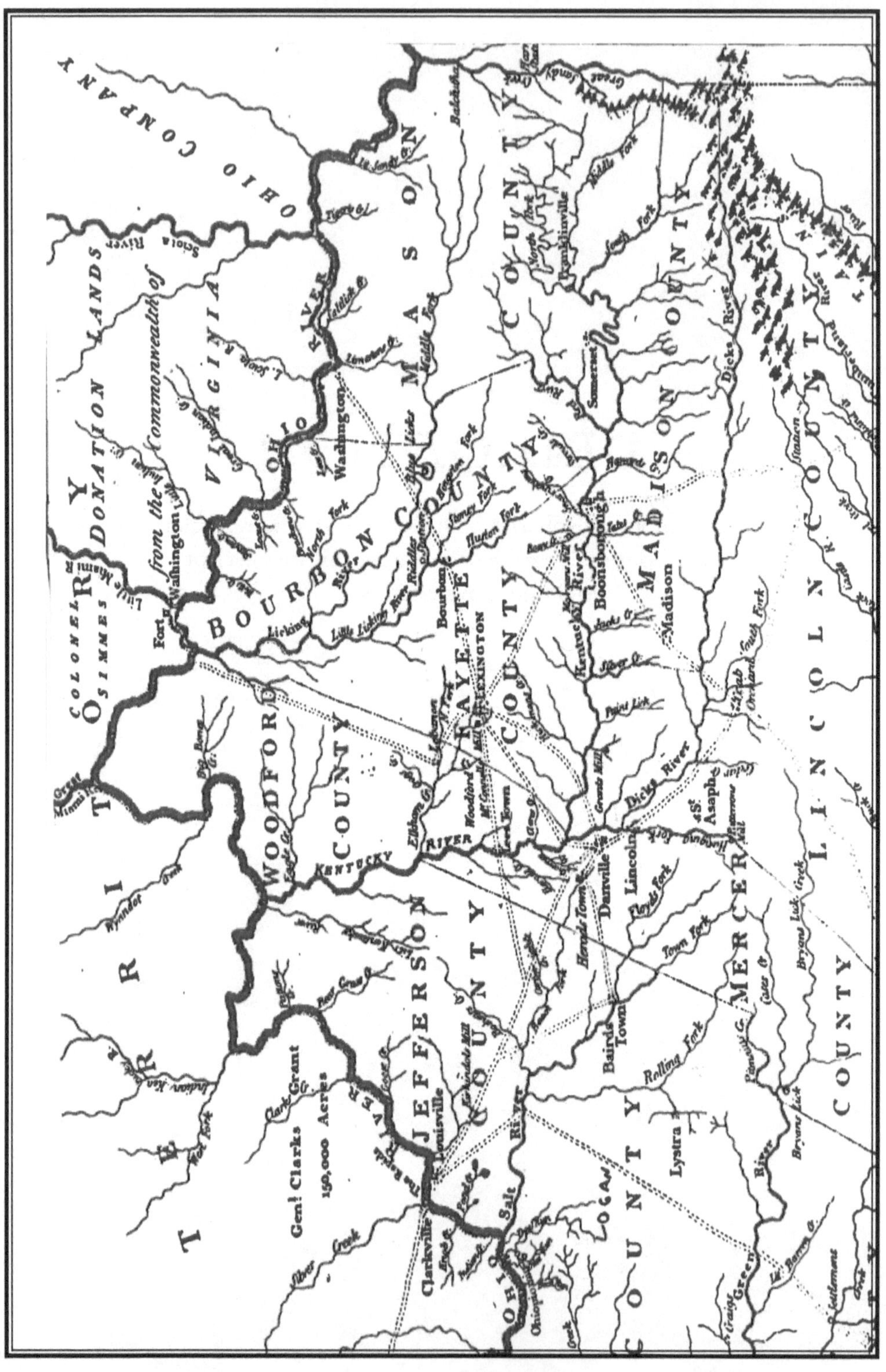

OHIO COMPANY
DONATION LANDS
Scioto River
Lt. Scioto r.
Tygerts C.
from the Commonwealth of
VIRGINIA
COLONEL R.
O. SIMMES
Little Miami R.
Fort Washington
OHIO RIVER
Limestone C.
Washington
MASON COUNTY
Bracken C.
Middle Fork
Licking
North Fork
BOURBON COUNTY
Hinkston Fork
Stoney Fork
Bourbon
Little Licking River
FAYETTE COUNTY
Lexington
Boonsborough
MADISON COUNTY
Kentucky River
Jacks Cr.
Silver Cr.
Paint Lick
Madison
Dicks River
LINCOLN COUNTY
St. Asaph
Orchard
South Fork
TERRITORY
Big Bone Cr.
WOODFORD COUNTY
KENTUCKY
Elkhorn Cr.
Woodfords
McConnels
RIVER
Grants Mill
Lincoln
MERCER COUNTY
Danville
Dicks River
Miami Cr.
Bryndet
JEFFERSON COUNTY
Clarks Grant
150,000 Acres
Gen! Clarks
Louisville
Salt River
Floyds Fork
Rolling Fork
Town Fork
Lystra
LOGAN COUNTY
Clarksville
Ohio River
Bryans Lick creek
Beech Fork
Bards Town
Harpes Town
Green River

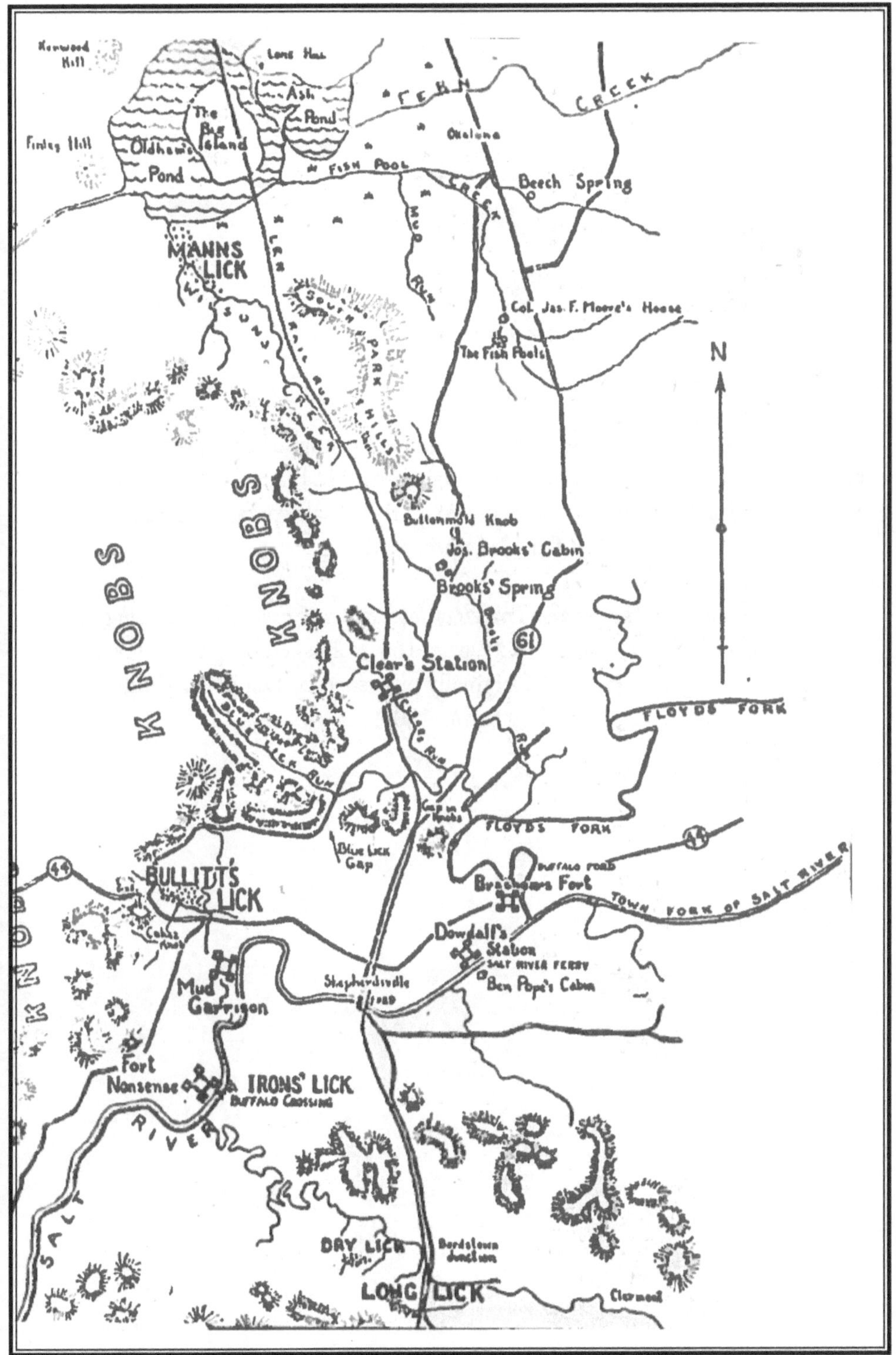

Map of Bullitt's Lick Region by Robert E. McDowell.

After we crossed the river the first house we stopped at proved to be a particular acquaintance of mine from Pittsburgh, (Mr. Haymaker), who treated us with kind hospitality, advising us not to go to the saltworks; for, said he, "it is a fair Hell upon earth."

A Narrative of the Life and Travels of John Robert Shaw, The Well-Digger, Now Resident in Lexington, Kentucky, page 165. Published by George Fowler, Louisville, Kentucky, 1930. Originally published by Daniel Bradford, Lexington, 1807.

CHAPTER 1

He had followed the buffalo trace from Bairdstown[1] since late evening of the day previous. True to the information he had received before starting on his journey, he found he had reached the bank of a wide stream, which he reasoned must be the river that had been described to him—Salt River.

Thus far, the moonlight had guided him along his way, but before him the path sloped sharply downward and was completely darkened by overhanging branches except for an occasional hazy filtering of moonbeams through the leaves. He moved with difficulty; stumbling over stones and limbs; falling frequently. At last he neared the end of the trail. He could hear the water as it rippled along its rocky course. This was the rapids—the fording place the buffalo had discovered long ago. He unslung his pack and determined to rest before continuing on to Bullitt's Lick.

The bite of the air, plus the dampness, caused an involuntary shivering, and he decided to risk a small fire. He tilted his powderhorn and poured a little powder, preparatory to its ignition by the flint of his rifle. A slight movement in the tree directly above alerted him. Grasping his knife firmly, he thrust its blade quickly upward. There was a weighty impact, and he was borne face down to the wet, sandy loam. He rolled as he fell; the taste of earth in his mouth. The motion carried his body away from his attacker, but not before the latter had stabbed and missed. He slashed at his unknown adversary, and a wild, eerie cry of pain rang through the stillness of the early morning. He attempted pursuit, but whoever it was splashed his way across the stream and made his escape. There was a dull clumping of hooves on the far side, and all was quiet again—all except his pounding heart and the excited breathing it induced.

He returned to the other shore and kindled the fire. When it was blazing, he seated himself, determined to wait until dawn before resuming his way. He thought back upon the events immediately preceding his departure from Bairdstown . . . Only Dracie Claycomb had known when he was leaving and his destination. He was certain he had not been followed, for had he been, he felt he would have been set upon long before—there had been many places more favorable for an attack than the present setting. Probably his assailant had lain in wait for any chance victim who passed the way to the ford. Robbery and murder had undoubtedly been the plan. Bullitt's Lick was measuring up to its dubious reputation, even before he reached there. By his best reckoning, founded upon that which had been told him, he must be yet four or five miles southeast from the settlement itself. If he was correct in his thinking, Dowdall's Station should be about a mile upstream on the north bank of the river. When daylight came, he would soon know the exactness of his deduction. He kept his vigilance, despite the drowsy invitation of the warmth of the lively flames.

Daybreak was heralded by the awakening of the birds, whose clamorous outcries were as intense, concentrated demands that the night raise the murky fringes of its curtain. Their chattering ceased with the coming of light, and he arose and stamped out the last flittering sparks of his fire. He shouldered his pack after taking from it a chunk of dried venison. The morning had brought a sharp appetite, and he chewed the tough meat vigorously. Reaching for his rifle, he saw the handle of a knife, its blade embedded in the earth. Here was the reason his attacker had fled so quickly—the lost weapon had made escape imperative. He turned it in his hands, noting the unusual shortness of the blade and that the handle was much wider and thicker than any he had seen elsewhere. For want of a better place, he slipped it inside his pack.

The water at the crossing was little more than ankle deep, and he made his way to the other side without incident. He climbed the rather steep ascent and reaching its crest, noted that the path diverged: One offshoot leading to the east and the other, a seemingly more traveled way, to the northwest. Since he had kept his prescribed course, the former trail must lead to Dowdall's Station, the latter to the salt licks on Bullitt's Creek.

The faint streaming of the spring sun only seemed to accentuate the chill he now felt in his bones as he looked eastward and noted a nebulous rising of smoke. The folks at the station were starting upon another frontier day—a day similar to those that had gone before, but yet of its own, dissimilar in character; a distinction discernible only to those who lived their lives in the open.

He did not pause for long but moved briskly on his way. Thoughts of yesterday crowded upon him, bringing in their wake a rise of passion as he recalled the contrasting comfort of the warm body of Dracie Claycomb under the covering of buffalo wool they had shared, and the near frigid atmosphere in which he was traveling today. Again he sensed the tinge of guilt, which was always lurking when he reflected upon his association with her. Though he could all but dissolve this dark coloring of his mind, he could never quite erase the feeling that they were wrong in consorting in an unmarried state. He sought to soothe the hardened rule of society with the acknowledgment that frontier people did not condemn the practice if the ultimate intention was honorable. With the same absolving vein, however, ran the admission that while they did not condemn, they yet did not approve. The best standing of such a relationship was but an ambulatory one hovering between that which was considered absolutely right and what was undeniably evil. Even the mental balm supplied by the fact that there were few ministers serving this new wilderness, furnished, in its most favorable aspect, only mitigation and nothing of justification. The neighbors at Bairdstown had been most charitable and tolerant, though the raised brows of some had shown a strained acceptance of a situation involving a young widow and an unmarried man. Back in Williamsburg, this would have been prime scandal—would be such—if and when the tongue of the gossiper set it loose upon the streets of that city; a happening he hoped to circumvent by marriage prior to his return.

His thinking entered the realm of dead possibilities. If Gabe Claycomb had not been murdered on his way to Bullitt's Lick; better still, if Gabe had not married Dracie and brought her with him on his ill-fated adventure; again, if instead of sending Gabe, he, himself, had come to Kentucky, he would not have lost his heart to her for the second time. For the second time? That was not true. His heart had remained hers even after he had met Neicia Warren and had become engaged to her. The subsequent breaking of that engagement by Neicia had only freed what he later realized had been a chained love for Dracie. But yet, unpremeditated as had been his act in sending Gabe on his fateful journey, he nevertheless recalled David and the Hittite, Uriah. The result was the same. As David had Bathsheba, so he would have Dracie.

He realized that David, the sweet singer of songs and ruthless exterminator of the inhabitants of a whole city—men, women and children—was favored of the Lord; that he was an instrument of God's will. But as he thought upon it, he concluded that so are all men—those of evil and those of righteousness. For God rules the lives of the willing, as well as the unwilling.

Lost in theology, his unilateral debate suddenly ended. A man lay sprawled in the road ahead. He hastened forward and found the fellow was a peddler. The wares scattered upon the uneven way made this clearly evident. As he helped the fallen one to his feet, he observed him to be a little man, whose smiling apple cheeks were deceiving, imparting to his face an innocent, youthful look.

There was no thanks immediately forthcoming for the aid rendered. Only after the last article had been placed in the oversized pack did the little man express his appreciation.

"Much 'bleeged to yew, stranger. Lost m' footin' in that damn hole there. M' name's Johnny Littelby. Little Johnny, folks call me, an' yew kin do th' same. Whut's yore's?"

He answered the direct inquiry, noting the appraising glance that accompanied it. "Mercer—Barth Mercer."

"Where yew from?"

"Virginia—Williamsburg."

"Hmm. Don't 'member seein' yew at Dowdall's last night. Yew stay up to Brashear's Station?"

"No, I came on from Bairdstown—traveled the trace."

"Where'd yew say yew come from?"

"Williamsburg. Why?"

"Heerd of a feller whut lives in Virginny, with th' same name; had a lotta land—wuth considuble. Yew eny kin?"

Mercer crossed the question with one of his own. "I noticed a knife you just picked up a moment ago: Had a wide handle and a thick blade. Where'd you come by it?"

"Oh, yew wanna buy one, eh? Usta have quite a passel of 'em, but I don't git 'em much no more; not sence I quit goin' to North Car'liny. Used to trade fer 'em down there. Yew want to buy this here one? It's th' last one I got, but I'm willin' to sell it to yew—sell enything in thet there poke of mine."

All the while he talked, Mercer was thinking, *Could this man have been his attacker? With that heavy pack, he would have had the weight, and he had the same kind of knife. Wait a minute. How would he have gotten that pack up a tree? And the man who did it had a horse waiting on the other bank.* The thoughts vetoed any suspicion Mercer might have entertained concerning the little peddler.

"Whut yew studyin' 'bout?"

"Nothing. What time did you leave Dowdall's?"

"Jest as soon as them damn fellers opened th' gate this mornin' to let th' damn cattle out."

"You going to Bullitt's Lick?"

"I'm stoppin' there for a spell—jest long 'nough to try an' sell some of them damn saltmakers suthin'. Then I'm goin' on to Falls of th' Ohio—Louisville, they calls it now. This yore fust time 'long this way?"

Mercer acknowledged with a nod of his head. "Yew goin' to Louisville too?"

"No, to Bullitt's Lick."

"Stranger—I mean Mr. Mercer—I reckin it ain't none of my bizness, but I'm goin' to give yew some advice jest th' same. Whutever yew got to do there, git it done an' then git away. They's folks there that'd cut yore throat jest for yore boots."

"Your advice is most welcome, but it's a little late. I've already had a rough introduction to one of the throat-cutters." He recounted his experience at the ford.

When he had finished, Johnny whistled. "Whut do yew think of that! Mighta been eny one of a dozen people whut I kin think of right off, an' a couple dozen more I could pick with not much more thinkin'." He scratched the narrow line of whiskers that ringed his jaw from ear to ear, digging through their full length. "Ain't nuthin' ornusal 'bout it though—happens all th' time 'round here. If he had got chew, he'd a pushed yore body downriver where it's deeper, weighted yew down, an' let yew bloat. By th' time anybody woulda found yew, if they ever did, yore body'd bin in sech bad shape they'da jest buried yew to git rid of th' stink."

"Do you think that's why he picked the ford to jump me?"

"Naw. That's jest a spot where folks has to pass if they wants to cross th' river. Did make it sorta easy for 'im, though, didn't it?" Before Mercer could answer, he continued. "Whut chew carryin' on yew theta body might want? Enything speshul?"

Mercer sensed he was thinking again about the Mercer back in Virginia. "No, nothing special; just what I need."

"Hmm," mused Johnny. "Yew got money? I got enything yew want to buy?"

"I believe not. Not now, anyway." The light of anticipation died in Little

Johnny's eyes as his prospect failed him.

"Where did you say you are from, Mr. Littelby?"

"Didn't say; 'sides, I done told yew, yew kin call me Johnny."

"All right, then. Where are you from," Mercer hesitated before adding, "... Johnny?"

"From Pennsylvania—Philidelphy. Yew heerd of that place, ain't yew?"

"I've been there numbers of times. You don't talk like you were born and raised there though."

The little fellow sharpened his tone. "Didn't say I wuz borned there—that's jest where I come from." He came back with a query of his own. "Whut's yore fust name agin?"

"Barth." Mercer suppressed a smile as he recognized the purpose of the question was to shift the inquiry to himself.

"Barth—Barth Mercer, huh? Well, we can't be standin' in this damn place all day. Let's git movin'."

Barth found Johnny to be a wellspring of news and listened intently as they trudged along. The little peddler was flattered by his attention and talked the more freely. By the time the first cabins of the settlement were seen, the two had established a friendship. Because of the wide range of knowledge, which his companion seemed to possess concerning Bullitt's Lick and of those who lived there, Mercer decided to seek his aid.

"Johnny, you know so many of the people who live at the Lick, I was wondering if you could tell me some that I could trust, and arrange for me to meet them."

"Hell, thet's easy; nobody, thet is, 'cept'n me, an' if there's money in it fer me, I ain't allus so damn trustful, myself." He laughed, and his laughter drew a hearty chuckle from Mercer.

The road had straightened now, and Johnny informed him this was the main, and only, street of the settlement. Taking an opportunity to rest, Johnny dropped his burden with a sigh of relief and braced his back with his hands as he straightened. Pointing to a chain of knobs at the far extremity of the road, he said, "See thet there hill standin' out from th' rest? Thet be Kahaz Knob.² Th' licks scetters out from there fer about a mile. Damn ground's got a funny white color, an' yew kin see where th' gullies is bin hollered out from th' tongues of all th' damn buffalo an' th' rest of th' critters whut used to lick it fer th' salt. Bullitt Lick Crick runs through there," he described the direction by a winding movement of his hand and wrist, "an' on over to th' river."

Barth gazed toward the distant hill, and as he did so, the same foreboding feeling, which the attack upon him had inspired returned. Johnny brought him out of his mood, saying, "I got to be gittin about m' bizness. I ain't fergot yore wantin' to meet someun yew kin trust. That's a hard one fer me to answer, sence I jest don't trust nobody. Thet way I ain't never gonna git fooled. Tell yew whut— yew meet me down there where yew see all them people movin'—thet's Ben Skinner's store—meet yew there," he squinted at the sun, "long about noontime."

"Suits me fine, Johnny. Oh, before you go, you ever hear of a man named Mace Hardin?"

Johnny pulled up in his tracks. "Whut-ut in th' hell did yew say! Feller, yew better lissen to me—wait til I meets yew afterwhile."

"I'll do that, Johnny."

"Yew shore better do it—if yew know whut's good fer yew."

Barth watched him as he struggled to lift his pack. Once it was on his back, he walked with unbelievable ease. Mercer's eyes followed the little man and his bobbing appendage until his figure became lost in the crowd, far down the street. He watched, but his mind was not on Little Johnny's progress. His concern was with Johnny's reaction to the mere mention of the one he was most interested in contacting: Mace Hardin. It had seemed that the easiest and quickest way to meet this man would be simply to inquire about until he found him. Yet there was something in the manner in which Johnny had spoken the name that made Barth decide to follow the advice he had been given so spontaneously.

He walked the length of the road on the one side, sauntering along. Half tempted to proceed to the knob, he now knew to be called Cahiz, he abandoned the idea after he had considered the deceptiveness of the open. Objects, which appeared to be relatively near, so often were found to be actually quite far away. He came back on the opposite side of the thoroughfare, the south side, as he traveled eastwardly, determined to mingle with the folks grouped in front of the store he had bypassed previously. He noted the irregularly situated cabins of accustomed one-room construction. He did not need to go inside to know their interiors—a fireplace, earthen floor, bare furnishings, and one window, next to the door. An animal's intestine, stretched and dried, would cover the window during the day in fair weather. A boarded covering, whose outer surface was of rough logs would be fitted into place, filling the opening at night and in winter or on inclement days. His nostrils had inhaled the heavy air within such a confined dwelling on many occasions. But though this settlement appeared to be the same as numerous other settlements he had visited or traveled through, its atmosphere was entirely different. Here, all seemed to be bustling. The place breathed vitality. The faces of its people, particularly those of its male inhabitants, had a set cast upon them, which bespoke more than seriousness. A decided suggestion of cruel selfishness—countenances of those who would cheat, rob, steal and kill to satisfy their greedy desires.

Cleanliness was entirely absent; refuse littered the spaces between the cabins and the street itself—a street in name only—a widened, rutted path. Evil-looking, vile-smelling puddles were frequent in their occurrence. Filthy were the habits of those who lived in this settlement. He wondered as to the existence of diseases here, the causal relationship being so thoroughly established. And if sickness was as common as would logically be assumed in such environment, what of medicines, or a man of medicine? A doctor in such a place as this? One might just as well expect the visitation of a saint. This sacred reference illuminated his thinking. He had found the complete description of

Bullitt's Lick in one all-embracing descriptive—the violence of Godlessness. This was truly its ethos.

He met stragglers, coming from Ben Skinner's, and the objects in some of their hands advised him that Little Johnny had been busy, and successfully so. He imagined the wrinkling of Johnny's nose when he said, "Yew wanna buy anythin'?" The little fellow had an unusual personality, but was sharp enough underneath the smoothness of its contagion.

He was meeting more people now, and some gave him tight-lipped greetings that he acknowledged just short of stiffly by a nod of his head or a flip of his hand. Soon he had entered the gathering in front of Ben Skinner's place—a store built after the fashion of the familiar frontier trading post.

He was completely unprepared for the next instant's happening. As though quickly passed from person to person and thence to him, he sensed a magnetic charge of the unusual. Then it happened. A massive figure stepped from the stoop in one gigantic stride, holding a little man by the collar much as a large dog would carry a smaller one by the nape of its neck. Recognition came swiftly. Little Johnny was in trouble.

Barth pushed his way through the throng and inside the open circle that had quickly formed. The big man uttered one blasphemous oath after another, and still holding Johnny aloft, hit him so hard the little fellow was turned around by the blow. To Johnny's credit, he was game. He kept trying to reach and strike his captor, squirming and jerking in a hopeless bid for freedom.

The big man was just that—a veritable mountain of bone and muscle, bent on destruction. Bald save for a fringe of hair at his temples, his face was as thoroughly malevolent as any Mercer could recall, even including the hardened features of the indentured criminals the Crown had permitted to leave its prisons and come to this country. A vivid scar, lashed red by his rage, made the left side of his face unforgettable. His ire was at its zenith as he said explosively, "Damn yer! This'll larn yer ter try to cheat me—wantin' so damn much fer thet wuthless suthin'!" The blow that followed to Johnny's side caused the terrified little peddler to retch violently; the spasms made the more difficult by reason of the tightened garment about his throat.

Resolve came before reason, and Barth suddenly found himself confronting the combatants. "Turn loose of Johnny! You've punished him enough for any grievance you may have against him!"

"Whut th' hell yer mean, turn 'im loose? I hain't done with th' li'l son-uv-a-bitch yet, but if'n thet's whut yer wants, I'll be pleased ter 'blige yer—if'n yer wants ter take 'is beatin' fer 'im." He dropped Johnny like he was a sack of meal and moved toward the newcomer.

Mercer ducked well underneath the vicious swing aimed at his head and brought his own right fist upward and into the lowered jaw of his opponent as the latter, slightly off balance, extended forward with the missed blow. The crowd became hushed from its former noisy enthusiasm as the big man dropped to his hands and knees. A singular, "Glory be!" was the only vocal expression. The fallen one shook his head woozily.

Johnny had scurried free at the first opportunity, but, just as amazed as the spectators, he lay on the ground a safe distance away and watched for the next development.

Barth stood with clenched fists, looking down at the fallen giant. To the astonishment of all, he used words instead of his feet or his knife. "Is that enough fighting for you, or do you want to continue?" His voice was cold and firm, and his antagonist looked at him out of the corner of one eye as the meaning became clear to him.

The reply was action. Mercer's whole body shook from the impact of his back and shoulders against the hard ground. Now his opponent towered above him, holding him by his knees, one on each side of surprisingly narrow hips. Emphasizing his advantage, he said roughly, "Yer a pore dumb son-uv-a-bitch, fer shore, hain't yer? Yer hed yer chanc't ter do me in, but yer jest hed ter make thet purty speech, din't yer? Wal, yer a dead son-uv-a-bitch now!"

The crowd made up for its earlier quiet, urging the big man to finish the stranger. They called his adversary's name, but its sound did not register in Barth's mind. He struggled to marshal his wits, recognizing that if he were to get out of this situation, he could only do so by surprise—by a quick move such as his foe had made to gain the superiority he now enjoyed.

Clamping Barth's knees even tighter to his sides, the big man pulled him well off the ground and attempted to snap the suspended body as one would crack a whip. Barth anticipated this and raised himself from the waist, for the moment foiling the maneuver. He realized that the next move by the man holding him would be to swing him in a circle, but he could see no way to prevent this action. He considered twisting himself sideways so as to be in position possibly to seize hold of an imbedded rock or perhaps secure a stone or piece of wood that might be in the road. He discarded these thoughts almost as they occurred, since if he twisted in any way, his body could be snapped to the right or left, according to the way he turned.

Little Johnny's apprehensions mounted at even pace with the swelling of his features and the pain from his battered ribs. The moment of hope, when Mercer had the big man at his mercy, had quickly faded. Through enlarging lips, he muttered to himself, "Th' pore, trustin' sonofabitch is goin' tew where th' dogs can't lick 'im." Had his physical condition permitted, Johnny would have long been in flight. But as it was, all he could do was to await Mercer's end, and his own.

The big man began a step with his right leg. Barth was acutely aware of the beginning as he felt the muscles rippling in his opponent's thigh and tried to pull himself up. Suddenly the now implanted foot seemed to slide along the ground as if on a roller. Perhaps it was a loose stone beneath the sole. Whatever the cause, there was a loosening, ever so slightly, of the hold on his right knee. The big man stumbled forward and in that split second, Barth twisted to his left; the big man came cracking to the ground as his right leg tripped over Barth's arm and shoulder. Quickly, Barth swung on around, freeing his left leg from the grasp, which had held it, and bounded to his feet.

Both men were upright now, and they circled each other warily.

His antagonist made the first move—an attempt to cup his hand behind Barth's neck. Agile as he was for his size, the big man was still too slow. As he grabbed for him, Barth ducked and again caught him with a hard left. This time, to the exact point of his jaw. He fell and he was prostrate, his right cheek flat against the ground. There was a moment of awed silence. It was clear now, he wasn't going to get up. Water splashed in his face, and he stirred. Shakily, he got to his feet. He did not look at his conqueror but lumbered back inside Ben Skinner's store. The fight was over.

The astonished onlookers finally drifted away. At Johnny's direction, Barth helped him to the one refuge the little fellow knew in Bullitt's Lick—Rosie Tindall's.

CHAPTER 2

Across a table at Widow Tindall's, Johnny talked to Barth through lips that had puffed grotesquely.

"Yew did yerself proud; real proud, yew did! Of all the folks yew had to tie into, yew had to pick Mace Hardin."

Barth mused, "So that was Mace Hardin. It's rather funny."

"Damned if I sees enything funny 'bout it. Why, he'll kill yew shore; an' if he don't, some of his family folks'll do it fer him—like Jed or Hawkstraw, or one of them. Yew best clear out, an' I mean right now. An' don't come back here no more."

"I'll say one thing, you sure are an appreciative cuss. Maybe I should have let him kill you instead of spotting myself."

"Aw, hell, yew know I'm thankful—I was in a bad fix; but I'da got out somehow. Mebbe not. But yore as good as dead, an' now they'll probably git me enyhow, figurin' we must be speshul friends if yew was willin' to risk yore neck fer me."

"Let me worry about it. I've a hunch everything will be all right, though it would have been better to have met Hardin in another way. Now I'll have to really watch him. How are your ribs feeling? Wonder he didn't break all of them instead of just a few, the way he hit you."

"Well, I could feel lots better," said Johnny, "Yew ain't got a mark on yew— shore pack a wallop, don't yew?"

Barth smiled. "Now, tell me how this started, and who are Jed and Hawkstraw?"

"Well, one thing at a time. I wuz in Skinner's, there, an' I had a drink—a couple of 'em, in fact. Mace come over an' started goin' through my poke. He found some beads an' he asked me how much they wuz, an' I tole him a fairer figger than they wuz wuth, 'cause I didn't want to sell 'em anyways. Yew see, I wuz savin 'em fer a lady friend of mine. Well, Mace kept a-tryin' to git me down, and I wouldn't lower th' price none. Finely, he gits mad; an' yew knows th' rest."

"Was he drunk? Doesn't seem logical that he would try to kill you for just that."

Johnny looked at Barth through mere slits in his face. "Don't know whut logical is, but he wuzn't drunk—never drinks much in th' daytime—he jest is a feller whut gits whut he wants, all th' time."

"Well, what about this Jed and Hawkstraw?"

"They's two of his younguns, his only real children. He's got another—a girl—but she ain't really his'n. Her step-pa gave her to Mace an' his wife fer three bushels of salt an' left here, fast, like yew oughta do. Whut's th' matter with yew, enyhow? Damndest fighter I ever seed! Too damn perlite! A man's tryin' to kill yew, an' yew follers all th' nice rules. Yew ain't gonna last long 'round here, an' I mean it, fer shore!" Johnny looked at him and shook his head. "Ever heerd 'bout gougin'?"

Mercer shook his head.

"Didn't think so. Thet's th' kind of fightin' they does 'round here. When Mace grabbed fer yew, if he'd got holt of yew, he'd a helt yore neck in his arm an' then he'd a gouged yore eyeballs out with his thumb an' fingers. He's did thet to many a feller. They says he has chewed off a lot of pore sons-a-bitches' noses an' ears. Thet's th' way they fights here. An' yew, a-standin' over 'im a-talkin' nice-like!" He shook his head again, this time sadly.

"Well, he didn't get a chance to do any gouging today. Now, forget about him. What about Jed and Hawkstraw?"

"Well, if'n yore pinnin' me down to it, I'll hafta tell yew." Johnny coughed and spit a patch of blood. "This Jed, or Jeddy-Boy, as Mace calls 'im, is the mean-est critter I've run up agin, enywheres. Mace's mean, but thet Jed is ten times wusser; gits pleasure, real pleasure, outa doin' harm to enything er enybuddy. Seen him shoot a deer one time; carved the critter's eyeballs an' tongue out 'fore he finely kilt it. He wuz drunk, of course, but thet ain't no 'scuse.

"Yew know suthin?" Johnny said, spitting more blood, "He probly knows about th' fight right now, and he'll be after both yew an' me. Yew won't see him though, nobuddy ever does. But yew jest turn 'round real quick-like, and he'll be there with thet damn knife of his'n. Wust family I ever knowed fer knives. Thet's how Mace got thet scar of his'n. His ole lady carved him up. Heerd today, they hadda 'nother scrap. They say she's got a nice cut on the same side of th' face as his'n."

"All right, now tell me about Hawkstraw."

"Wait'll I finish tellin' yew 'bout Jeddy-Boy—damn him. He ain't quite so tall as Mace—Mace is 'bout six foot four."

"You don't have to tell me how tall he is. I had a real good opportunity to judge his height; and I mean from the ground up."

"Now, yew want me to tell yew, or not?" Johnny was becoming exasperated.

"Go ahead; but tell me about the boys, not Mace."

"All right, all right, I'll jest let yew fine out 'bout Jeddy-Boy yoreself. Wal, this Hawkstraw's really a queer-un. Thet ain't his name, of course. The whole family's queer-uns, if yew ask me."

"I'm not asking you; just tell me about this Hawkstraw," Barth said impatiently.

"Well, Hawkstraw's about twenty year old, I reckin. He's 'round five or six years of yore age, I jedge; say, twenty-seven."

Barth nodded in affirmation. "I'm twenty-eight."

"Wal, his real name is James. They give him his nickname 'cause he wuz allus gittin' straw an' feathers an' sellin' 'em for beddin'. Did thet when he wuz a real young'un. He'd git firewood an' sell it too. He wuz allus doin' this, so finely they jest up and called him Hawkstraw. Funny thing, he'd sell all thet stuff, an' never say a word."

"How could he do that?"

"Fer a good reason," Johnny laughed. "He can't talk—dumb as a stone. But he kin hear a dog bark ten mile away. Back when th' Injuns useta come 'round more oftener than they does now, folks would take Hawkstraw along fer pertection, an' he'd hear enythin' enywheres near clos't. Reely knews these parts 'round here better'n enybuddy, 'cept'n mebbe Abe Foster."

"Who's Abe Foster?"

"Wait now," said Johnny, feigning complete exasperation. "Yew wanted to know 'bout Hawkstraw. Yew want ter talk, or yew want me to tell yew?"

Barth smiled. "You go right ahead."

"Wal, this Hawkstraw's about yore size—six foot, 185–190 pounds, I'd say."

"You'd say right. You're a good guesser."

"There yew go stoppin' me agin."

"I'm sorry."

"No, yore not a damn bit sorry—yew jest wanna learn everthin' 'bout everbody at onc't—an' yew or nobuddy els't kin do thet. Git yoreself kilt, bein' in sech a damn big hurry one of these days."

"Go ahead, Johnny." Barth was half laughing now.

"Damn if I do. Thet's all I aim to tell yew, leastways fer now."

Barth laughed. "Well, get this drink past those big lips of yours if you can see well enough to do it through those eyes. My, but you really are swollen good. And you are starting to blacken up too."

Johnny interrupted Barth's chuckling. "Jest gimme thet drink an' shet up, an' then let's git outa here. I ain't too proud fer enyone to know I knows yew."

Barth started to reply, but held his words when a young woman sat down abruptly across from him.

"How do you do, Miss." Barth rose as he spoke.

Johnny, straining to see, asked, "Where yew goin' now? Bet it's thet Abby Tindall. She's allus meetin' eny new feller thet comes here."

Barth felt uncomfortable. "Johnny, you clod-headed fool, the young lady is right here at our table."

"Oh," said Johnny.

Entirely at ease, the young woman said, "That's all right. No one pays much attention to what Mr. Littelby says, thinks or does. However, I heerd Mace Hardin paid him some attention today. Pity he didn't fix him so's he couldn't talk for a while. Maybe folks would have had some peace for a spell."

"Git on away from here, yew smart talkin' wench, 'fore I tells yore maw to tie yew up with them horses out in th' back!" Johnny's offended dignity hurt more than anything Mace Hardin had done to him.

"I'd just soon be with them horses as around you," she said heatedly. Then once more aware of Barth's presence, she explained, "Of course, I'm only talking about Mr. Littelby, sir." She renewed her tirade against Johnny. "Them horses never smelt half so bad as you does. Bet you ain't washed or aired yourself or them buckskins for a year."

"Jest git away, git right on away. They ain't no one asked yew here enyways!" Johnny flicked his hand in a manner of disdain.

At this moment a pleasant looking woman in her late thirties approached the table. "Abby Tindall, I told you to find out if these gentlemen wanted anything else."

"Mamma, there ain't but one gentleman here."

"Now, Abby, mind your manners. I declare; every time Mr. Littelby comes here, you go out of your way to start a ruckus. Now you stop your baiting him."

"Mamma, I believe you are sweet on Mr. Littelby."

Mamma's face flushed. "Get about your business, Abby!"

Abby, recognizing the tone of authority, threw her head back and walked away.

Waiting a moment for Johnny to introduce her but to no avail, Mamma decided to do so, herself. "I'm Rosie Tindall, sir. That bad-mannered young lady is my daughter. You'll have to excuse her; she's sixteen, but she tries to act like she's thirty."

Barth rose. "Sit down, ma'am. I'm Barth Mercer. I believe you know Little Johnny better than I do."

Rosie flushed again. Johnny smiled weakly.

"That's a puffed-up smile, if ever I saw one!" Barth laughed at his own remark as he sat down.

"Yore th' real funny one, ain't yew, Mr. Mercer?" Johnny lowered his head in genuine disgust.

Rosie, once introduced, took over the conversation. She had been a widow for the past three-and-a-half years. Her late husband, John Tindall, was killed by the Indians up near the mouth of Floyds Fork where it runs into Salt River above Brashear's Station. Since then, she had sewed, taken in sleepers, and finally, began selling food and drinks. She classed her home as half a tavern. She hastily added that she hadn't always been among these rough people. Before her husband's death, they had lived at Brashear's. Before coming here, they had lived, first, in Philadelphia; then at Redstone Old Fort and Falls of the Ohio. John Tindall had been a good provider, and they were getting along fine until the Indians attacked and scattered the saltmakers. For the next year, no one ventured to produce any salt except for personal and community use, and everyone lived at Brashear's Station. But the quarters there were crowded, and it was not long before it was decided that a garrison should be built nearer the licks. Accordingly, Mud Garrison had been erected—a double row of pointed timbers, filled with earth and gravel covering about half an acre. Kentucky was receiving more and more settlers, and Bullitt's Lick was becoming the focal point to which they journeyed. The need and demand for salt was ever increasing, and the price rose out of sight—as high as $700 a bushel in inflated paper currency.[3] This brought the saltworkers back to the licks in droves in the spring of 1780. They moved into those cabins already standing and built new ones when the former were all occupied.

She had not intended to remain, but with her knowledge of the needs of the settlement, she found herself and her services in such great demand that she decided to stay for a spell.

For herself, she did not mind; but her present desire was to take Abigail with her to the Falls, at Louisville, to live. There they could find a larger measure of safety; the threat and fear of Indians were with her constantly. They had taken all but Abby away from her. She was determined they would get no more of her family. Then too there would be some added convenience of living there, and the possibility of another marriage for her. She was forthright; a woman was meant to be with a man. More than that, on the frontier a man was a necessity. She had made John Tindall a good wife, but he was dead. She'd take the right man if he came along. She looked at Johnny when she said this, and he averted his gaze. Noticing this, she abruptly changed her course. "How long will you be here, Mr. Mercer? For a spell, I hope. You'll pardon me for sayin' this, but not many like you comes around here. Just once in a while. Mostly, it's nothin' but that rough bunch that stays here."

To stem the flow of Rosie's discourse, Barth seized the opportunity to answer. "It all depends, Mrs. Tindall." Rosie beamed at his courtliness. "I'll have to have a place to stay, though I guess I could camp out. Don't reckon I'd get much sleep in view of what's happened today. Could you put me up here?"

"I'd like to, but I don't know where it would be." Her eyes suddenly lit up. "Oh, yes, I remember now! Of course! You could have Jim Trench's bed—he's gone up to Clear's Station. Why didn't I think of that right off? He won't be back 'fore tomorrow evenin'—maybe th' next day even."

"That would be fine, but I just happened to think—what about Johnny?"

"Oh, Johnny has a place here. He always stays with us when he's at the lick." And again Rosie beamed at Little Johnny.

"Ain't nothin' hi-falutin', yew'd better know thet. Jest a bag of straw on th' floor yonder. So when Rosie sez bed, thet's th' kinda bed she means. Johnny looked at Rosie as he said this and Rosie wasn't beaming—she was embarrassed.

Barth eased her discomfiture. "Why, Johnny, that's all I expected."

"Glad yew did, 'cause that's all yew'll git. Whew! Thet shore hurts when I breathes." Johnny had his hand on his sore side. His eyes were practically shut.

"Here, you poor thing. Let me help you." She moved toward him. "Oh, I just thought of somethin'! Them Lillards has left—his wife died a few months back and he took his younguns back where he come from. Left th' day 'fore yesterday. Maybe you could get their place. It ain't much; just a bare cabin."

"Well," drawled Johnny, "while yew air rememberin', better remember that Mace Hardin owns thet there hut, an' I know he'd jest love to let it to Mercer."

"That's right," gasped Rosie. "Still he really don't own it—just has charge of rentin' it for the owner."

"Same diffrunce," said Johnny.

"That'll be fine," Mercer said. "I'll see Hardin ,about it the first thing in the morning—have to see him anyway."

Rosie and Johnny looked at Barth as he said this.

Johnny recovered first, "Whut in th' red-ringed hell is th' matter with yew? Yew ain't really thet crazy, be yew?"

Barth smiled. "It'll be all right."

Rosie's eyes were still wide, and Johnny shook his head sadly. "Glad I ain't gonna be 'round here much longer. I'm gonna pull outa here tomorry night, shore. Hope I never meet another 'un like yew. Yore—yore a damn fool!" Johnny sputtered as he said this, and the pain brought an exclamation and an oath from his puffed lips.

Barth only relaxed his mouth into that quizzical smile, which Johnny had already recognized as being characteristic, but which was also already a source of irritation to him.

Abby came to the table, close upon the heels of her departing mother. "Mr. Mercer, you've just got to tell me all about yourself. Honestly, I think you're just the best lookin' man I've seen around here for a long, long time."

"Damn yew, Abby, git!" growled Johnny.

Barth started to say something to relieve his own embarrassment when he felt a firm hand on his shoulder. Turning his head, he looked up toward a man of his own approximate height and who obviously had had too much to drink. He invited him to sit down, but the invitation was declined.

"Stand up, damn you. I ain't never hit a settin' man."

Bewildered, Barth arose, wrenching his shoulder free of the tight grip upon it. As he turned, he drove the heel of his hand into the man's chest, sending him sprawling across the room.

Instantly, onlookers, evidently friends of the man, seized him and took him forcibly out of the place.

Squinting more than ever, Johnny asked, "Who wuzzat? Who wuzzat? . . . Sounded like Tom Chism."

"That's who it was," said Abby, and in the next breath, turning to Barth, she continued her quest. "Thank you so much for protectin' me, Mr. Mercer."

"Believe me, ma'am, I honestly was thinking more about protecting myself."

Abby's cheeks flushed a deep crimson and she lowered her head.

"Yew hev did it agin." It was Johnny, straining the words through his lips. "Thet there Tom Chism mighta hepped yew, but not now—no, sirree—not by no damn site now."

Rosie was back at the table and Abby had once again been dispatched. "Oh, Johnny, Tom won't even remember this tomorrow—he was drunk." Rosie seemed to be trying to convince herself of what she was saying.

"Drunk—huh! Yew jest wait and see if he don't come a-lookin' fer my friend here, the very fust thing in th' mornin'."

Barth broke in. "Who does Mace work for?"

"Nobuddy said he worked fer enybuddy," Johnny responded, glumly. "Course ever'buddy knows the works ain't Mace's."

"Well, whoever owns it can't be gettin' much out of it," said Abby, speaking from behind her mother's shoulder.

"Abby, I do declare! When will you ever learn to keep thoughts like that to yourself. It's not safe to say things like that. You couldn't prove a thing—no one could. What if Mace Hardin heard you were talking like that? Like as not Jeddy-Boy or Hawkstraw would come a-callin' on you." Rosie's reference to the Hardin boys silenced Abby quickly, Then, a fear-laden question. "Oh, Mamma, do you think they would really do that?"

"If they did, you'd never know anything about it til it was too late." Arising, Rosie brushed away some imaginary crumbs from her dress before saying, "Gentlemen, it's time for me to get about my chores—soon be supper time." Rosie suddenly had changed the subject. Then, aside to Johnny, so low Barth barely heard, she whispered, "Here comes Jack Doniger."

Rosie was gone, and Johnny was feigning sleep, when Doniger entered. He came straight to their table. Grasping Johnny by the shoulder, he shook him roughly. "Wake up! You hear me?"

"I hear yew—hev to be deef, not to," Johnny said.

"Well, lissen good. Mace says you'd better be gone from here 'fore sunup. That's the message. I reckon you got it."

Barth stirred. Johnny caught the movement and put his hand on his arm. "Steady now," he said. Then, to Doniger, "I got whut yew told me."

Doniger turned and went out the door. "Who's Doniger, Johnny?"

"The worst Judas in Kentucky or anywheres else. He's like a jackal. He's fer hire fer eny kind of a job 'cept th' kind thet calls fer work. Mostly does errands like this-un fer Mace. He's sly an' dangerous. Thet scar 'cross his forehead'll tell yew he played awful rough one time an' got away with it."

"I believe he's the dirtiest looking man I've seen around here," Barth interjected.

"Well, they's a sayin' 'bout han'some is as han'some does—remember? Well, he's dirty as he looks. They run him away from th' Falls—caught 'im robbin' drunks."

"You leaving tomorrow, Johnny?"

"Yew bet I am, an' I ain't comin' back enywheres soon."

Barth studied a bit. "Johnny, you were pretty brave there with Mace today. I didn't think you'd scare so easily."

"Brave, yew say!" Johnny coughed a bit. "I ain't no damn bit brave. I wuz fightin' to git free when Mace had me. I don't figger on doin' thet enymore. Next time I'd feel a knife in my back an' thet'd be it. I'm leavin' 'fore sunup."

"They'll probably get you along the trail somewhere, Johnny. You're safer right here."

Johnny thought a little. "Mebbe yew are right, at that."

"I know I am, Johnny. With that pack of yours you'd be easy game walking alone."

"Din't figure on walkin' or bein' alone. I wuz aimin' to go along with thet pack train of salt thet's leavin' tomorry."

"Pack train?"

"Yep, some of Tom Chism' s men are takin' it to the Falls."

"Perhaps you'd be safe at that."

"Nope, believe yew wuz right the fust time. Jeddy-Boy'd git me soon as we stopped. Nope, reckon I'll stay here a spell longer. Mebbe Mace'll run into suthin' new that'll take his mind off'n me."

"Just don't worry about Mace, Johnny. It'll be all right, I promise you."

"Aw, shet up, Mr. Mercer. Yore promisin' a lot fer someone I don't know nothin' about, and never knowed wuz even livin' 'fore today. I'm gonna git some sleep, if I kin."

"Wait, Johnny, don't you want to eat a little?" Barth's words were wasted. Johnny moved away, calling Rosie as he did so. Barth saw her meet him, and the two of them go through the doorway into the next room.

Rosie was a good cook and Barth felt fully sated when he lay down on his bed on the floor.

"Not much sleep tonight," he told himself.

Rosie came by shortly afterward. "Everyone is gone now, Mr. Mercer. The place is locked good and tight and you can rest easy. Are you comfortable?"

Barth nodded affirmatively. "This bedding is really soft. I ought to get some good sleep."

"Glad you like it. It's some I took off of Johnny's bed. He's got another; hope he doesn't miss this one."

As she spoke, Johnny hollered from the other room. "Rosie, where in the red-ringed hell is thet other feather kivver?"

They both laughed. She went to pacify him. Barth turned on his side and despite his assertion to the contrary, was instantly dead to the world.

CHAPTER 3

There was a stinging sensation in his buttocks. Barth turned over quickly and was fully awake. There stood Johnny. And if his face bad been swollen yesterday, it was nothing to what encompassed his features today. Barth could hardly make out what he was saying. He sounded like someone with afflicted speech.

"Git up, yew! Gonna sleep til yore dead?"

Barth smiled the smile that nettled Johnny and instantly there was the quick response.

"Yew an' yore damn smile!"

Barth laughed as he arose. "What's wrong with my smiling? Someone ought to be happy around here, don't you think?"

Abby was close at hand. "How did you sleep, Mr. Mercer?"

Johnny answered for Barth. "How in the hell would yew think he did? Damn fine, I kin tell yew. He had my feather kivver fer beddin'. Why'nt yew ask me how I slept?"

Abby strove to control herself. "It isn't yore mattress, Mr. Littelby, it's my mother's; and I didn't ask how you rested because I figured all jackasses slept the same."

Johnny fumed, at a loss for words. Then inspiration came. "Say, mebbe I ought to marry yore maw. Then I'd be yore step-pa an' I'd whale th' tar outa yew."

"I'd say you are taking a lot for granted, Mr. Littelby. I'm sure my mother would never consider lowering herself to marrying up with you."

"Oh, she wouldn't, wouldn't she? Yew jest fetch her an' we'll see 'bout thet!"

"Careful, Johnny, that'd be a proposal, you know," said Barth.

"By jingoes, yew are right! Whew! Best watch whut I'm a-doin'."

"Someone want me?" It was Rosie. "Did I hear you tell Abby you were going to ask me to marry you, Johnny?"

Johnny sputtered for all he was worth. "A frame-up, thet's whut it is. A damn frame-up! But I'm tew smart fer sech traps!"

All but Johnny were laughing heartily.

"Johnny, I don't want no man unless he wants me." Rosie was serious and Johnny knew it.

"Aw, Rosie, thet she-kat of a daughter of yor'n jest gits me upset. Makes me say things whu' I don't mean a-tall."

"Well, that's settled and forgotten now," said Rosie. "Let's have something to eat and we'll all be the better for it. How would you all like some turkey hash, hot biscuits, currant jelly, eggs and a bit of ham?"

Their stomachs took over, and even Johnny smiled at the thought of such a breakfast. "Yew know," he said, "mebbe I might—I said might, mine yew—ask yew to marry up with me sometime."

All were still eating when there was a sharp knock on the door. Rosie was up quickly and opened it.

Tom Chism, red eyes and jaw set, came straight to the table. Johnny was up in a flash. "Now, Tom, we don't want no trouble." Johnny's words came like bubbles from his battered mouth.

Chism burst into a roar. "Johnny, you're the funniest thing I ever seen. I ain't looking for no trouble. I jest want to apoligize to Mr. Mercer for last night. Guess I was lucky after what they tell me he did to Mace Hardin yesterday."

"No apology is necessary." Barth's sincere manner made a quick, deep impression.

"Here's a man I can really like," Tom said to himself. Then, to Mercer, "Besides, maybe I was the lucky one last night, not you."

Johnny was beside himself. "Whut the green tarnation yew mean by bustin' in on folks when they's eatin' their vittles? Jest no damn considerashun—not a damn bit."

Chism was unaffected by the outburst. "You know, Johnny, I don't know why folks call Damn Ye Johnson by that nickname. You got him skinned all holler."

Barth said genially, "Have a chair, there's plenty here, and it's really good."

"Mighty damn free with a widder's vittles, ain't yew?" After saying this, Johnny lapsed into silence, laboriously and painfully chewing each mouthful.

Rosie went through the formality of introducing Barth and Tom to each other.

The food was excellent—so much so that there was scant conversation. At length, Barth pushed his chair from the table.

"Well, if I'm going to see Mace Hardin, I'd better be getting over to his place."

Astonishment was instant on their faces as he said this. And Johnny all but choked on a hash-covered piece of cornbread.

"After yesterday, you are going to see Mace Hardin?" Tom's question was one of doubt as to whether Barth was a man he wanted to like after all.

"Yes, I want to see him about getting that Lillard cabin."

Johnny was in it now. "I tole yew, yew wuz crazy. Hell, thet ain't no word fer it, yore jest a plain damn idgit! What in the red-ringed—

Barth broke in. "Johnny, it's my business and my hide, you know." With that, he excused himself and started for the door.

"Yew won't find Mace at his place. He's been up long ago. He'll be around them salt kittles er mebbe out checkin' on th' firewood. But he won't be at his cabin, yew kin bet on thet. So yew jest as well wait til noonday, when he'll likely be up to Ben Skinner's."

"Nope, Johnny, I'll find him now."

His ears must have really burned as he walked away, for those at the table all started talking at once. Finally, Tom Chism got control of the discussion. "I felt in my bones that Mercer was my kind of a man. Now, I don't know what to think. It don't make no sense for a man to whup a feller like Mace, an' then go back to see him. Guess I had him pegged all wrong." Speaking directly to Johnny, he asked, "You knew this feller long? Maybe we best all steer shy of him."

Johnny explained his meeting with Mercer and admitted he knew little about him. "I got my idees all right, all right, but I ain't a-sayin' nuthin'. But one thing yew kin count on, Mercer's a straight-un—yew kin shore take thet fer certain. He's plumb crazy an' don't act like enybuddy 'round here, but he's all right, I tell yew, an' I ain't been wrong on nobuddy yet. I can't 'ford to be."

Rosie followed quickly. "He's a gentleman, and that's for sure. I don't understand his going to see Mace Hardin though. Maybe he's like Brother Flinden—just too good and forgiving."

"Brother Flinden's a idgit too, but thet's his religion This ain't no religion that's got holt of Mercer. I got my idees, I tell yew."

"Let's hear 'em, Johnny," said Tom.

"Sometime, mebbe, but not now. But one thing—don't yew git eny wrong idees 'bout Mercer. He ain't no Judas, an' he ain't afeerd of no one."

Rosie checked further talk. "Well, if you all are done, I'd best set things to order." She started to clear the table.

"Hey, woman! I ain't lettin' thet last damn biscuit go to waste." Johnny grabbed for it as she started from the table. "Yew shore kin cook, Rosie."

Rosie smiled. "I've got other virtues too, Johnny, that go to make up a good wife. I'm mighty handy at other things besides cooking."

Johnny caught the lightly covered meaning, and blushed. Tom, seeing it, laughed and said, "Let's get out of here before she starts showing you."

As he walked along, Barth's conclusions as to the people at the licks were certain. He was sure of one thing: The few he had met were about the best there. He stopped quickly. Here he was, going to Mace Hardin's, and he had no idea where he lived. He deliberated a moment upon the wisdom of his asking someone for directions and quickly ruled against so doing. If Johnny knew this, he'd really prove his point as to the advisability of his visit. Barth could hear him now, "Hell, yew wants tew see Mace, an' yew don't even know where he lives." He was approaching Ben Skinner's. The answer still not clear, he went inside. As he entered, there was an apparent lowering of voices—some stopped talking altogether and just looked toward him, then quickly resumed their ways, glancing now and then to see whether he was still there. It was an uncomfortable situation, which Barth needn't be told—he sensed it thoroughly. Just then a young barefooted girl ran past him. Barth heard a low voice to his left. "There she goes. She's a sharp 'un. Bet she's going right home to tell Mace."

Barth made his exit as commonplace as possible despite his desire not to lose sight of her. As he reached the road, she was a few hundred feet ahead. He kept as close as he could without attracting her attention. It proved a longer trail than he had imagined, but finally, she made her way to a cabin, well removed from the settlement. The house was something like Ben Skinner's—two stories on the back of the one floor front. He saw her enter and quickened his pace. He reached the door, which was open, just as she was starting to come out again. Seeing him, she ran back inside the dwelling.

He hesitated a moment, then entered. The room was musty—deep—as though it could be felt with the hand. Directly in front of him was a short, stocky woman. Her tousled, thick hair was matted and fell sloppily about her head and face. There was a fresh wound from her left ear to her chin, a chin that was all but indistinguishable due to the folds of fat, which gave her the appearance of having little or no neck. She was clad in buckskin, and there was a strong stench about her that overrode the odor he had first noticed.

The woman said nothing, aggravating the silence. He thought of leaving and of trying to see Mace elsewhere. He looked at her face again. The pupil of one eye was off center. Dark, bushy brows emphasized the piercing depth of her eyes.

If the devil has a wife, thought Barth, this must be the woman. He roused from the reflection. "I want to see Mace Hardin."

"Him not here—what you want 'im for?" The tones were guttural.

"When will he be back, or where can I find him?"

"What you want with 'im?"

"That is my affair and your husband's," he said firmly.

He saw the quick movement of her hand and spoke before it reached her knife.

"That's not necessary—I'm here on friendly business. But if you draw that knife, I'll handle you like you were a man—even if it means killing you."

She stopped abruptly. "Nancy, go get Mace."

Barth had not seen the child when he entered the room. A rustle behind him at the woman's command caused him to turn his head. He saw her as she put away her knife—a short-bladed, thick-handled weapon. She had been right in back of him. Only then did he realize to what danger he had been exposed. He'd never let his back be unprotected again.

But a young girl—who would have even guessed peril from that source?

Nancy scurried away. For some moments after, neither spoke. They still stood facing each other, as though both were transfixed.

Finally, the woman broke the silence. Her words came slowly and evenly in the manner of a curse, though their meaning was entirely unrelated to any malediction.

"You here for cabin. You no get."

Barth cleared his throat, but did not reply. How could she have known? Did Mace have informers everywhere? He wondered how much more Mace knew about his actions since coming to Bullitt's Lick. Probably everything except what took place this morning. He stopped his thinking and made his belated reply to her blunt assertion. "That's one of the things I want to see your husband about; but that isn't all I have to discuss with him."

"Discuss you want! Be little talk, him come! Him no forget you trick him yestiddy. You smart, you leave 'fore he come back."

"I'll wait outside," he said, welcoming an excuse to breathe fresh air again. His lungs were stuffed almost to suffocation.

"Him got two sons. You see 'em soon. They fix you for what you do to father."

"I've heard of them."

"You hear more."

She was trying desperately to incite anger in him. He sensed the motive—to get him to renew the trouble of yesterday by attacking Mace when he returned. He refused to let her do this and walked a piece from the door.

He saw Hardin coming—blood in his eye. Before Mace could say or do anything, he called to him. "I am Barth Mercer, son of Malcolm Mercer, of Williamsburg, Virginia."

Mace acted taken back—his entire manner undergoing an abrupt change. Pointing to a spot a few hundred yards away, he said quietly, "Let's go on ter thet grove yonder, an' set a spell." Then to Nancy, "Run on inside an' see if yer kin hep yer maw."

They sat on stumps, which suggested this used to be their common purpose and the reason for their not having been dug up.

Mace spoke first. "Enyone cud claim he wuz th' son of Malcolm Mercer."

"I grant that to be true."

"Whut proof yer got?"

As Mace questioned, Barth pulled out a sheaf of papers and handed them to him. "You can read, can't you?"

"Enough," said Mace, "ter git by an' a little mores. How does I know them papers be good—mought be made out like as they wuz, an' still be no account."

"Look at the seal . . . More than that, look at whose name certifies their worth."

Mace read aloud, "Patrick Henry."

"Those papers prove my title to the works here. I left Washington's Army when my father first became ill. I handled all his matters until his death. As you will notice, I am my father's sole heir."

"If'n thet's th' truth . . . an' I ain't saying I doubts yer . . . how kum yew walked inter Bullitt's Lick? A man uv property wud have rid here, an' with men ter guard hisse'f."

"I have a horse back at Bairdstown. It pulled up lame, and I wanted to come on. I have no men with me because I don't figure I need any. I took care of myself in the war, against Indians and white men alike, and I reckon I can still do it."

"How'd yer happen ter kum here?"

"Because there have been no returns from this property. With salt scarce everywhere, these licks should pay handsomely."

"Yer means th' money ain't bin gittin' ter yer?"

"Precious little of it."

"Wal, I knows some uv it mought not hev got ter yer, 'cause some uv them thet wuz carrying hit wuz kilt an' robbed, an' some never come back after they left. But I figgered they'd stayed in Williamsburg with yer pa."

Mace wasn't too convincing. Barth didn't know how much he could believe, if any of it. "That's why I'm here, anyway. While I am here, I want to learn all I can about the operation. I'll need a place to stay. I know you have been told I would see you about the Lillard place. Your wife told me that before you got here. I'll move in there today. Tomorrow, I want to inspect everything."

Mace showed his discomfort when Barth mentioned his wife's information about the Lillard cabin. However, he readily assumed the role of an employee. "Hope they's no bad feelins about yestiddy, Mr. Mercer. This here's a rough place an' things will happen liken thet, an' they has ter happen, hit seems. Frum here on, though, yer tells me whut yer don't like or whut yer wants did an' I takes care uv hit m'se'f."

"We'll get along," said Barth. "But just one thing. I want you to tell no one who I am . . . no one, you understand. That's your first order from me, and one you'd better remember if you want to stay on here."

"I'll hev ter say suthin'; mought be a lot uv talkin' when folks sees yer an' me tergether after yestiddy."

"I'm coming to that. To everyone but you, I am an Army officer sent here by the Continental Army to check on the salt production at this lick. Not only my own works but also all the operations hereabouts."

"How yer aims ter back thet up?"

"I have the necessary papers to prove my authority. The government did request me to do this, and I am an officer in the Army on leave. My rank is captain."

"How 'bout me seein' them papers?"

"You don't need to. I have showed you all that's needed. I want to get along with you, but you're in my employ, and I don't have to explain or prove anything I do."

Mace reddened. "Guess I jest as well start ter callin' yer Cap'n—mought as well git m'se'f used ter it."

Barth knew Mace didn't relish this particle. "I believe that would be best."

"Cap'n, I kin git yer better quarters then thet Lillard place. Knowin' who yer be an' all, yer oughter hev suthin better then thet. Besides, mought be th' smallpox, or suthin' jest as bad, in thar."

"Thanks, but I want the Lillard cabin. I'll chance whatever might happen. What time will I meet you tomorrow?"

"I starts out at daybreak—meet yer wherever yer sez."

"Make it right in front of your cabin."

"As yer sez, Cap'n. As yer sez."

Barth turned and began the long walk back to Rosie Tindall's.

CHAPTER 4

A lot had happened in a short time. About an hour, all told, as best he could reckon. He was certain Mace was only pretending fealty to him. He wondered concerning Mrs. Hardin; but mostly, he thought about the girl. If what he had heard about her was true, how fast she had become one of the Hardins. His thoughts used up his steps and he was back at Rosie's door.

Inside, Johnny, Rosie and Tom had been wrapped in conversation ever since Barth's sudden departure.

As he entered, Barth heard Johnny's muffled voice saying with conviction, "He's either checkin' these here diggins fer hisself or fer one of th' owners. He's too damn set in th' way he's stickin' his nose inter things. Mercer's got a reason 'fer bein' here—ain't no doubts in my mind 'bout thet."

When Barth came in, there was a startled quiet that wasn't broken until he spoke. "You're right in a way, Johnny. But be careful about what you say. It's all right now; there's nobody here that I mind knowing my reason for being at Bullitt's Lick. I must ask you all, though, to keep what you think to yourselves when outsiders are around. Briefly, I'm a captain in the Army on leave to check the production and operation of all the saltworks in this region."

"Hev' a cheer, Kepteen." Johnny pointed to a stool and attempted a curtsy as he said this.

"All right, Johnny, never mind the foolishness; and don't call me captain. It'll get out fast enough."

"Yew kin laugh at me, but yew don't take it too good yoreself, do yew?"

Barth ignored Johnny's sarcasm.

Tom Chism, one leg up on the table, looked at Mercer for a moment. "So that's the reason you went to see Mace Hardin. You had us all a-going for a spell."

"That's right, Tom. I also got the Lillard cabin. Ever hear of any smallpox there?"

Rosie, fearing the question might bring back sad memories to Tom, answered quickly, "Not that I can remember. No, th' Lillards was th' first to live in it, an' none of them had no sickness like that. Mrs. Lillard died in childbirth—both her an' th' baby."

The cloud was over Tom's features, but he shook it off. "I think it'll be all right. That ain't too far from my place. Most of 'em around there works on halves; that is, they pay half of what salt they makes for the use of the kettles and the water."

Abby came in breathlessly. "Guess what, Mamma? Mr. Mercer and Mace Hardin were—"

The sight of Barth froze Abby in her tracks. "Oh, Mr. Mercer, I-I-I-I'm sorry."

Barth smiled. "It's all right, Abby; these folks know all about it." Turning to Tom, he asked, "Tom, how come you're here this time of day? Mace claims he starts at daybreak. Is something wrong at your works? I'm asking this with the best of intentions. If anything's wrong, maybe I can help."

Tom relaxed from his first repugnance at Barth's meddling in his affairs.

Johnny broke in, "Mebbe yew'd best wait til someun asks yew fer he'p."

"No, Johnny, it's all right. I believe Mercer means well."

"Army officer—kepteen—humph! A damn keptccn runned me away from some soldiers at Fort Pitt jest when I had sold ever' damn thing I had in my pack. Got beat outa all of it."

Barth had to laugh. So did the others, and Abby laughed the loudest.

Johnny was beside himself. "Tom Chism, yew don't know how lucky yew be. If yew marry up with thet she-ket, yew'll be sorry til th' day yew die. Best thing could heppen were for her tew marry th' kepteen. Thet'd be a good match—serve 'em both right."

All continued to enjoy the mirth; all except Abby.

"Mr. Littelby, it's hard to remember how nice things was here before you come. Why don't you leave right away so we can see how nice it was again?"

"Humph! Damn right I'm leavin'; soon as I git rid of them things whut I got left. Looks like I ain't welcome here no more."

"You might try paying for something once in a while; maybe your welcome would be better," Abby said icily.

"Abby, you go to the back and stay there! What in the world gets into you, I'll never know. Get, I said, before I punish you, big as you are!"

"Never mind, Missus Tindall. Didn't know I wuz expected to pay—not that I ain't been 'willin' tew. I won't be a-botherin' yew no more."

Rosie was heartsick. "Oh, Johnny, don't call me Mrs. Tindall. You are welcome, I love"—she faltered—"to have you here, you know that. Think how long you been coming here."

"Tain't no use, woman. I'm gonna be a hermit from now on. Yew jest can't count on no damn female. I know thet now."

Tom and Barth were convulsed with laughter. Johnny glared at them. "Yew two shore fine things funny, don't yew? Damn sneakin' kepteen, and a drunk overseer. Go on laffin'—damn the two of yew!"

And laugh they did, until their insides hurt.

"You know," said Tom, "if Brother Flinden was here he'd probably quote the scripture to us. Something like, 'For even in laughter the heart is sorrowful; and the end of that mirth is heaviness.' Ever notice how true that is? You feel real good; so good that something inside you says you ought to be careful. All this pleasure ain't meant for one man? I kinda had that sort of a feeling when I had my family." Tom grew sad.

Barth sought a diversion. "Tom, you quote like you might have more than glanced at the Bible."

"Used to read it a lot," he paused, "when I had my family. They'd have services up at Brashear's Station every Sunday. Sometimes a visiting preacher would come through, but mostly it was Brother Flinden that'd do the preaching."

"You all have mentioned Brother Flinden so much I'd like to know more about him," Barth said.

"I'll tell yew 'bout him," said Johnny, relieved that the merriment at his expense had ceased.

"I asked Tom, Johnny."

"Yes, sir!" said Johnny, "No offense meant, Kepteen." He gave a mock salute.

"Well," said Tom, "I don't know much 'bout him 'fore he got here, but ..."

"See, yew shoulda let me tole yew—I knowed 'bout him in Pennsylvania, where he come from. Damn if I tell yew now."

"Go ahead, Tom," said Barth, ignoring Johnny.

"His first name's Aaron. Owns around 500 acres on the south side of Salt River. Guess it's about two miles, maybe not that far, from here. Got a lotta cleared land on his place. He's a good, sincere man, but a little mixed up. A lot of that is due to his wife, Ursula. She runs him ever' step of th' way."

"What's he, a little man and she's real big?" asked Barth. "I've seen that combination a lot back in Virginia."

"Funny thing, it's just the opposite. He's as straight and strong as they come, and she's a little old dried-up lookin' somebody."

"How old would you say they were?"

"Oh, he's around thirty-five; guess she's close to forty—older'n he is, anyways. Reckon that's the trouble; probably married him when they were real young."

"Doesn't make much sense, does it?" said Barth. "Her dominating him like that, and him so big."

"Well, Brother Flinden is just too good a man. He believes in peace and wisdom; in fact, he says they each mean the same."

"I take it his wife doesn't follow the same belief."

"No, she takes his following of his faith as a sign of weakness, and she's after him all the time. Even interrupted him when he was conductin' services, one time."

"How's he live?" asked Barth.

"No trouble there. He can do almost anything, and does. He's a good farmer, cooper, carpenter, bookkeeper and hunter. Guess he's a better carpenter than anything else though. He says that the Master was a carpenter—a builder of earthly things—before he taught of the structures of heaven."

"He's a damn ole hypocrite!" interjected Johnny, who felt he'd been left out long enough. "Yew don't know nuthin' 'bout him. He b'longed to thet there

Sassiety of Friends. His old woman tried to run it, and they kicked him out back in Pennsylvania. All he ever says is thee this and thee that. I allus thought they's suthin' funny 'bout him."

"You're in league with th' devil, Johnny. Couldn't expect you to see the man as he is," laughed Tom.

"In league with th' devil, am I? Why, yew—yew—yew!" Johnny almost sputtered himself out before his thoughts collected themselves. "Who in hell air yew? Saint Thomas Chism, I reckin, huh?"

Just then, four or five people came in and Barth remarked, "Well, we'd better get about our doing."

Catching the implication, Tom agreed. "Got a lotta things to tend to myself 'fore th' day's out. Incidentally, Mercer, I was up 'fore dawn this morning—had to go a piece with my pack train. Sent some salt to Falls of the Ohio. I left them just this side of Clear's Station. So, you see, I got up ahead of Mace. At least, I did this morning."

"I'm sorry," said Barth.

"It's all right. I got to move on. See you later."

"Well, Mister Nosey, smart alek kep—" started Johnny, before Barth pushed him outside.

"What did I tell you about calling me captain in front of other people? Now, damn you, let that be the last time!"

"Yes, sir," said Johnny in a subdued tone. Then, muttering to himself, "Folks thinks I'm sech a great cusser—bet this Mercer could do some hisself."

They walked along for some distance, neither, saying anything. Then Johnny spoke up. "Where we goin'? Yew know I got to work a little myself. I wanta get through here an' get up to th' Falls."

"That's one of the things I want to go over with you, Johnny. I want you to stay on here with me."

"Wait now—wait a minute. I bin traipsing all over Pennsylvania, Ohio, Virginny, and these parts for a long time. Folks all look fer my comin'. Besides whut I sells, I brings 'em news. Yew know, they's folks in Pennsylvania whut'll never get here, but they knows all 'bout things at this here lick; even about Mace Hardin."

"I know you're an important person, Johnny," Barth was using flattery now, "but I have something important I want you to do for me. I'd like you to be my assistant, sort of."

"Yew mean I gits to wear a badge an' order people around?" Johnny asked hopefully. "Had a uncle onc't whut wore a badge. I allus wanted to be a person with some 'thority ever since."

Barth smiled. "No badge, Johnny. And not much authority. I want you to do things like checking and investigating for me."

"No badge?" asked Johnny, a little crestfallen. "How'll people know yew got the right to do whut yew sez yew want to do? How'll they know yew be whut yew sez yew are?"

"Can you read, Johnny?"

"A little, I reckin."

"Well, here's an official paper—notice the seal. This gives me all the authority I need."

"Best wait til we gits where—say, where are we goin'?"

"To the Lillard cabin. We're going to stay there if you decide to be my assistant."

Johnny liked the word. It sounded real big to him, and he reckoned he could tell a few people what an important man he had become.

"Well, I'll have to read this here writin' first—but I can't do too well, bouncin' along, an' with my eyes still squintin'!"

"All right, we'll wait til later, then." Barth knew he had an assistant right at that moment.

"Looks like Mace ain't worrying none 'bout me still bein' here, don't it?" asked Johnny as they reached the cabin.

"I told you that I would take care of things. You have nothing to worry about on that score."

"Yew know," said Johnny, "for onc't, I believes yew."

Inside the cabin, what was there was in orderly array. But what wasn't there was more significant.

Johnny said, "Hell, I'd druther be back at Rosie's."

"Thought you were done with her."

"Oh, shucks, I jest said thet. Didn't mean it, an yew knowed it at th' time."

Johnny looked at Barth who was feigning shock. "Whut's th' matter with yew?"

"I don't know, but it seems like I heard you say something without using hell or damn in it."

"Aw, ain't yew cute? Clever as hell, yew thinks yew are, don't yew?"

Barth laughed. "Say, Johnny, you know you could do worse than to marry Rosie. I think she really loves you."

"Love, bah!" said Johnny. "Lemme tell yew whut I thinks 'bout love. Come over here to the door so's yew kin see out good. See thet manure pile out yonder?"

Barth nodded his head.

"Now, yew see thet wild rose bush back behine it?"

Again Barth nodded.

"Well, love is jest like a butterfly. It's jest as liable to light on thet there manure pile as on any rose on thet there bush."

"Let me see if I understand you. The wild rose is Rosie; the manure pile must be . . ."

"Not by no damn site," broke in Johnny. "Yew don't try to unnerstand a-tall. You're jest makin' fun of me."

Barth roared.

"Thet's the last time I'm gonna talk 'bout love to yew. I don't call yew kep-teen, and I don't talk no more, an' yew don't talk no more 'bout love to me. That's agreement. An' stop thet damn laffin'."

"You're quite a philosopher, Johnny, you know that?"

"Hell," said Johnny. "I ain't never seen one of 'em—whut they look like."

Barth, seeing Johnny was serious, merely said, "Oh, I was just talking, forget it."

At that precise moment, a head stuck in the doorway.

"Anybody home?"

"Oh, it's you, Rosie. I couldn't make you out at first, coming in from the light outside."

Not only Rosie but also Abby was there.

"Now, we want you men to go sit over there," Rosie said, pointing to a spot a little distance from the cabin, "and make yourselves comfortable. Abby and I are going to make this place livable."

"Yew might start," said Johnny, "by getchin' them there feather kivvers from yore place, fust thing."

"Don't you mind about that, Johnny; they'll be here."

Johnny sighed with satisfaction, and he and Barth moved as Rosie had directed.

Some two hours later, she called them to come back inside "This really looks nice," said Barth. Johnny smilingly agreed.

There was something about Johnny's smile. Something juvenile and mischievous, yet a little puzzling in its intent. Barth had noticed it long before, but had not yet fathomed its depth. But every time Johnny smiled Barth found himself trying to peer inside his curling lips.

Rosie was smiling too; the smile that comes to one's face after doing something good for someone else. It was the evidence of the unselfishness that filled Rosie's heart, and her reward, though none was desired, was the sincere appreciation of Barth—and Johnny—for her efforts.

Abby, tired like her mother, felt only that Mr. Mercer might be favorably affected in his consideration of her. She loved Tom Chism, but she wasn't above making a good impression on another man.

"It's a pity," said Rosie, "that we couldn't have furnished it better for you all. But there's some food, some candles and feather covers for both of you."

"Smells a lot better'n it did," commented Johnny.

"Won't for long," said Abby. "Mr. Mercer, I don't see how you're going to stand it, bein' cooped up there with him. Honestly, if some people would only wash themselves once in a while."

Johnny stormed. "Rosie, yew kin jest take all thet there stuff out of there. Damned if I'm gonna use eny of it. Hit wud make me plumb sick, knowin' thet female had tetched it."

Rosie saddened. "Abby, you have hurt Johnny's feelings. Apologize this minute!"

"Oh, Mama, his feelins get hurt too easy."

"Do it, I say."

Abby, much against her will, yielded to her mother's insistence. Johnny accepted just as grudgingly.

Rosie and Abby made their goodbyes, but not before Johnny, with a wide grin, told Rosie, "I'm the kepteen's assistant—mighty important work we're gonna do. Whut about thet?"

"I think it's wonderful, Johnny. That means you'll be around here for a spell. 'Course, yore an important person, anyhow, Johnny; least ways you are to me."

The embarrassment of the last of Rosie's words was dismissed quickly by Johnny's feeling of greatness, and he cast a contemptuous but patronizing glance at Abby.

After they had gone, Johnny and Barth went inside the cabin. The late evening breeze was still tinged with sharpness.

"Have to get up early, Johnny. Guess we had best eat something and then bed down."

"Right yew are, Kepteen."

CHAPTER 5

It was quite different over at Mace Hardin's. There was an air of nervousness in Mace's words, and in his every movement.

"I wish th' hell they'd git back here."

His wife, in answer to his statement, merely grunted.

"Sounds jest like the sow yer are," he exploded.

Knowing better than to make any retort, she kept busy with what she was doing.

"One thing I'd like ter know," he said, "ez how yer got thet cut on yer face. Don't make no sense the way yer sez it happened."

She started to reply, but he cut her short. "Yeah, I know. Nancy seen it happen—so yer sez. Nancy'd say th' Angel Gabriel wuz here, if'n yer told her to."

Again his wife started to answer, and again, before she could say anything, he was talking.

"I don't see how he got here. Jeddy-Boy wuddn't fail his pap—an' if'n he did miss him, how'd he git by Hawkstraw? It'd be diffrunt if I hadn't planned it so damn good. I knowed when he wuz leavin' Williamsburg even. An' when he hit th' Gap."

His conversation was meant to be one-sided and his wife knew it. He continued thinking out loud. "An' who git whut tried ter git him at th' creek? Mebbe it wuz thet damn Doniger, double-crossing me. Mebbe it didn't happen to him a-tall. Mought jest be Mercer's made thet up. Damn! Why don't Jeddy-Boy an' Hawkstraw git back here?"

As if on cue, the door opened and in they came. Jeddy- Boy, his curly black hair wet with perspiration, and Hawkstraw just a step behind him. An almost violent contrast existed between the two. The one, dark of hair and coloring, reflecting in a rough, handsome way the Indian ancestry, which was his on his mother's side. Hawkstraw, sandy-haired and gaunt. Where Jeddy-Boy perspired, Hawkstraw's parched-looking complexion showed not a trace of sweat. Where the one was boisterous and self-proclaiming, the other was quiet as his silenced speech and lived thoroughly with himself. The extrovert and the introvert. These were the sons of Mace Hardin.

"Mammy, git some vittles cookin'. We're starved most ter death."

His mother moved mechanically at Jed's request.

"How'd yer miss him?" Mace's words were firm and even. "How'd he git by you?"

"Wait'll we gits done eatin', Pap, and I'll tell yer all about it."

Mace's open hand smacked flush on Jeddy-Boy's cheek. "Tell me now!"

"Pap, one uv these times . . ." Jeddy-Boy's words were bitter, but he didn't finish. He shrugged his shoulders and began his explanation. "I picked 'im out at Logan's Station an' I follered him over ter Bairdstown, but I never had no chanc't ter get him—they wuz a party uv 'em travelin' together. I follered him at Bairdstown ter whar he stayed. They warn't no chanc't there, neither, so I made up my mine ter git him liken yer tole us to, if we hadn't got him by then. I crippled his horse by drivin' a stone inter th' frog. Thet horse sure cried like a humin when I done hit." He smiled as the satisfaction he had enjoyed at the animal's pain came back to him. "But somehows he got away frum me, an' I lost 'im."

Mace could control himself no longer. "Yer a damn bunglin' fool! How did Hawkstraw miss him, then? Thet plan wuz shore-fire!"

"Yer'd best ask him yerself, Pap. Best I kin make out frum his signs, he wuz spectin' 'im ter be ridin'. But he sez th' only person whut passed 'im wuz thet li'l pedlar."

While Jeddy-Boy was talking, Hawkstraw's eyes were fixed steadfastly upon him.

Mace faced Hawkstraw squarely. By laborious use of his hands and fingers, he conveyed his questions. Hawkstraw answered by deft, sure movements, but even so, it was slow and tedious. And Mace, beside himself with impatience, could not speed the flow of this strange form of communication.

At length, Hawkstraw finished his story. Repetitions had convinced Mace that he understood the meanings his son had conveyed to him. He turned toward Jeddy-Boy. "Yer din't tell me all thet happened. Hawkstraw sez he waited fer yer, an' yer failed ter meet 'im like I tole yer. He sez he went back ter Bairdstown a-lookin' fer yer an' found yer tryin' to get after some woman that—th' Claycomb womern, th' best I kin make hit out. He sez yer hed been drinkin', though he needn't hev tole me thet. I knowed thet, the secont yer comes in thet door. Yer'd best talk fast."

"Pap, don't get yerse'f enymore worked hup. I tole you I missed thet feller Mercer at Bairdstown—don't know how I done it, but somehow I jest missed 'im. Mebbe when I wuz a-fixin' his horse, he seen me, an' jest left. I wuz tryin' ter get thet Claycomb wench ter tell me if'n he wuz really gone, er if'n he wuz a-comin' back, an' I jest had a couple uv drinks. I don't see whut yer raisin' tarnation fer, enyhow. I kin git him, an' hev him burried, 'fore sunup termorry."

Mace had regained his composure. "Lissen ter me, Jed, an' lissen good. Yer too Hawkstraw, an' you, ole womern, an' Nancy too. I hain't fooled none by Jed's talk 'bout th' Claycomb wench, an' his drinkin'. I know whut heppens when Jed drinks. But thet's all done now. I wanted Mercer ter be found dead miles away frum here. Then, nobuddy cud say Mace Hardin hed enything ter do with th' killin'. Now, 'stead uv killin' 'im, we got ter be sure nuthin' heppens ter him fer quite a spell."

He then related to his sons the events of the past two days. He spared none of the details, including the beating Mercer had given him.

"Pap, how long 'fore we does him in?" Jed questioned.

"Not til I sez so. An' I'm warnin' ever'buddy, if'n eny harm kums ter Mercer before then, him whut does it will git th' same frum me. Is thet unnerstood?"

Even Nancy nodded her head.

Certain he would be obeyed, Mace continued. "One thing I din't know 'bout, wuz thet bizness uv Mercer's app'intment frum th' Army—thet cud be damn trubblesome."

"Pap," said Jed, "they's suthin' else yer missed on. Some uv them fellers whut kum inter Logan's frum Richmond sez they hain't gonner be no more battles— thet Yorktown wuz th' last. They claims they hain't bin no more fightin' 'ceptin' skirmishes. They all sez th' colonies hez won they freedom. If'n thet's true, th' Tories'll all be gone ter Canada 'fore yer knows it, and them whut yer dealin' with won't be no more good ter yer."

"Jed, the Crown ain't gonner let thet heppen, an yer knows it. They'll be the biggest damn army uv Indians an' British thet ever wuz."

"But, Pap, they wuz a feller there whut said he knowed a treaty wuz in th' makin'—thet th' French wuz helpin' th' Colonies more'n th' Tories 'spected 'em ter do, an' thet th' Crown cuddn't fight 'em both. He said thet he heerd thet over in England, th' people there wuz tired uv th' war an' thet it wuz costin' 'em too much, with th' taxes an' all."

"Jed, it's too damn bad yer din't pay as much 'tention ter me, as yer did ter them over ter Logan's. If yer hed, we wuddn't be bothered with Mercer. Yer let me do th' damn thinkin'—yer jest follow orders."

His wife spoke up. "No raise price uv salt. No make money like yer think."

"Kin't be hepped now. Git th' damn vittles, womern, I'm hungry, m'se'f."

To the stench of the cabin was added that of the hot grease, which Massalene Hardin used in profuse quantity.

The meal prepared, everyone fell to eating. Nancy sat on a cobble stool, which just allowed her the height of the crude table. Jed and Hawkstraw seated themselves on a rough bench, and Mace and his wife on the only two chairs in the room.

If Mace had justly called his wife a sow, then all those at the table were kindred swine. Anything that wasn't palatable or eatable was thrown on the floor. Greasy hands were wiped on garments, and when two hands went for the same morsel, there followed a series of violent oaths, but other than this, there was no conversation. They were there to eat.

Mace pushed himself from the table. Emitting a belch that came from his heels, he arose. "Gotter be gittin' ter sleep. They's a hard day a-comin' hup. Jed, yer an' Hawkstraw better do th' same. Mind yers, I don't want yers crossin' my path termorry—an' remember: No trouble, no matter whut!"

With that, he put the ladder to the opening in the ceiling and climbed upstairs. Once there, he called down, "Ole womern, you kum on hup hyar too.

Bin a long time sence yer an' me hez rid th' mare, an' I'm a-feelin' like hit now. Yer don't hurry, an' you'll miss hit. I'm thet tarred."

Ole womern puffed her way up the rungs of the ladder.

Downstairs, Nancy and Hawkstraw were seated together on the bench. She had cleaned the puncheon floor of the leavings from the recent meal, and, as always, when he was home, she sought Hawkstraw's company. She never failed to address him as James, rather than by his nickname. The two seemed to be able to understand each other with a minimum of explanation. Whenever, and it was seldom, his meanings were not clear, Nancy would endeavor the harder to show her what he wanted to tell her. Shortly, she would turn her palm down, and he knew she understood.

Usually, in the evenings, they would go for walks out from the settlement, into the forests, down along Salt River, over the flat lands whose trees had long since vanished in the feeding of the fires under the salt kettles. There were wonders everywhere, and they drank of them all. Sometimes they would go upriver to Brashear's Station. If the big gate was closed, they would walk around the fort, pretending they were attackers, looking for a weak spot in the timbered armor. If the entrance was clear, they would go in and visit with the residents—a few of whom worked at the licks.

From Hawkstraw, Nancy learned all about the other settlements: Falls of the Ohio, Fort Pitt, and the village that was engulfing it called Pittsburgh; the big cities in the east and in Virginia proper, as distinguished from its almost severed part, Kentucky, which some called Kentucke, Kaintucke, or just Kaintuck.

On some occasions they had traveled the course of the river far down from the fort, almost to where the Salt River was joined by the Rolling Fork, and Salt River became the more mighty—a smaller Ohio. Pioneer saltmakers from Fort Pitt had quickly noted the resemblance and named the place where the two streams met Pitts Point. From here, when the river above was low, the salt was shipped downstream to the Ohio and from thence to the north and the south.

Hawkstraw had told of the Indians and their many tribes; of the birds and beasts of this virgin wilderness; of the buffalo traces, which always ran to water at what were convenient places along their way; of how the traces ran into Bullitt's Lick like the spokes of a giant wheel, all meeting at its hub or center. He described, ever so vividly, the abundance of deer, buffalo, bears and small game at the licks when first he came there to live. And how the animals continued to throng there and be killed for some time after the arrival of the settlers. Finally, in their peculiar way of communication, the licks became identified with danger and death, and they no longer came. Hawkstraw and the little girl often mused on what new trails the beasts were now blazin'.

Frequently, Little Legs, as Hawkstraw called Nancy, would become weary, and he would come home carrying her upon his back. Her slumber would be unbroken when he placed her gently on her pallet on the floor, and the next morning when she awoke, it would seem to her as though she had all dreamed it all.

The lateness of his return ruled out any walk this day, so he and Little Legs just sat on the bench, while he told her of the trip he had just completed. He said nothing about the purpose of the journey, but gave account of the animals encountered, the birds he had observed, and the many new people he had seen coming to Kentucky.

She leaned against his shoulder and listened intently—almost reverently. The only interruption came when the peculiar noise upstairs grew louder until it finally ended with a crash.

"Sounds like both them riders fell off'n thet thar mare, or els't th' damn bed's broke down agin," Jed commented from his chair by the fireplace.

As the ride ended, so did Hawkstraw's story. He kissed Nancy and saw her bedded down. Then, motioning to Jed to follow him, he climbed to the loft, which divided the far end of the cabin.

CHAPTER 6

The sun was in its first struggle with the leftover gray of the night as Barth and Johnny made their way to Mace Hardin's. Even as they approached, they discerned Mace's huge form outside his cabin door. A few more strides and they were there.

"How yer feelin' this mornin', Cap'n?" asked Mace, in an apparent effort to show Barth he had not forgotten his instructions of the day before. If he had any feeling of distaste that Johnny was along, he concealed it admirably, although he asked, "Ez Johnny included in this, Cap'n?"

"Johnny's my assistant; sort of an aide," Barth replied, and Johnny's chest swelled and his roguish face beamed, despite its still swollen fullness.

Mace appeared not to notice. "Cap'n, I reckin it'd be best ter guv yer th' whole pitcher—less'n yer thinks yer knows it a'ready."

"Mr. Hardin," Mace winced at the emphasis Barth employed, "I want you to tell and show me everything there is that you know or think is connected with the operation of these works, just as though I had never even seen a grain of salt."

"Yes, sir," said Mace.

Little Johnny couldn't get over it—Mace—terrible Mace—had 'sirred' a man. Mace had said it with Johnny looking right at him, and when it dawned on him that Johnny was impressed, one corner of his mouth turned into the faintest trace of a snarl. Mercer's voice ended this. "You lead the way, Mr. Hardin," followed by Mace's repeated but still incredible, "Yes, sir."

As they walked, explanation and description matched every step. The beauty of the early morning, the sparkling dew on the fresh leaves, the trills of hundreds of multicolored birds, and above all, the clean, crisp breeze that enveloped them filled Barth with exuberance, though the others seemed impervious to this sweet assault of spring. Even the animals rejoice in this change of season, Mercer thought, but not these two.

Mace broke into his reverie. "In most places, hit's the cleared land whut's wuth th' money. But out here, hit's th' timbered ground whut's th' most val'able." Remembering Mercer's directions, he continued with the reason for the difference. "Thet's 'cause them fires eats up th' wood fast as hit gits ter 'em."

"How does it get to the furnaces?" interjected Barth.

"We carts hit thar, an' thet hain't so good; speshul, with th' trees gittin' so fur away. Lose lotsa time an' workers thet way. Don't see no way ter help it none—got ter hev th' wood."

Crossing the open ground, Barth saw oxen straining at their yokes as stumps were being uprooted. There was no waste so far as the timber was concerned. Wisps of curling smoke reached his nostrils even as he saw their heaven-bound spirals.

"Them's th' furnaces over yonder. Want ter go on over?"

He thought a moment before answering Mace's query. "No, let's get to the wells first." Then to Johnny, "How are you holding up? Think you can take a full day of this?"

"Yes, sir, Kepteen!" came the strong reply. Barth noted this and also the fact that Johnny had been unusually quiet.

"Guess you are used to walking long stretches, aren't you, Johnny? I wondered about you carrying that pack on foot, the first day we met."

"Oh, I don't walk, usual. I had me a horse back at Bairdstown. He went lame on me, an' I sold him fer a good figger. Wuz aimin' to git me another, soon's I seen one at th' right price."

"My horse went lame over there too," said Barth, reflecting. "Well, if you're not used to walking, maybe you will have a hard time of it."

"Well, now, ain't thet suthin'. Why, I kin walk yew right into th' ground." Then remembering, Johnny added, "sir."

Barth had his first laugh of the day.

Some eight or ten of the wells lay scattered between the base of a prominent knob on the north and Salt River on the south. Where Barth had breathed only the spring air before, he now inhaled industry. Men scurried all over the area. Much like ants, each with seeming duties to perform.

The water in these wells looked to be almost black as indigo. Did this affect the color or taste of the salt? What was the cause? Could it be that down there, ever so deep, the water passed through beds of coal? The latter appeared the best surmise.

Mace confirmed Barth's speculation. "Wait'll yer gits over ter th' furnaces. Yer kin smell hit when hit biles."

He explained to Barth that a good many of the wells were dug and operated by independents, as he called them. They gave half of all the salt they made for the privilege of using the wells. "Don't know but whut thet thar ez th' best way ter run this whole works. Oney trouble ez, they gits inter too many scraps."

Mace showed him the construction of the wells about thirty to forty feet deep, the inside walls being staked. Generally there was an overhead covering to keep out rain and snow, and deep trenches were dug around the top of each wall to run off excess water so that it did not enter the opening.

"We hauls th' water ter th' furnaces in casks. Tried makin' sluices, but it din't work as good," Hardin explained.

"Maybe we might make some wooden pipes and run them from the wells to the furnaces. That would do away with hauling the water," Barth observed.

"Wal, thet'd work all right 'cept in cold weather; an' anyways, them bastards would be allus runnin' over 'em with them damn wagons an' a-breakin' 'em."

"It'd be a simple thing to dig ditches and run them below the frost line."

"Cap'n, I believes yer right. Mought guv it a try."

All the while Mace and Barth were talking, Johnny had said nothing, but he wasn't missing a thing—spoken or seen.

They moved on toward the furnaces. As Mace had said, it was easy to tell that coal had impregnated the water. Fumes of sulphur and of the coal itself, greeted their nostrils, along with that indefinable, satisfying fragrance of wood burning in the out of doors on a clear spring morning.

This sensory perception recalled to Barth not only the spring but also the autumn mornings back in Williamsburg. There is a definite kinship between the two seasons, he thought, and the strongest link is the soul-filling smell of smoke from fires in the open air. Memories and smoke are of the same substance, he reasoned. Nothing you can put your hand on, but real, nonetheless.

"Wut yew studdin' 'bout, Kepteen?" Johnny asked.

"Oh, I was just giving a little thought to a matter, Johnny; nothing important."

Mace had walked a bit ahead of them and Johnny used the opportunity to confide in Barth. "I'd shore feel lots better if'n we hed badges, to show our 'thority."

"Don't worry about that, we won't need them. A good man makes his own authority."

"Kepteen, them words kin all be true, but them damn fellers up ahead don't know 'bout 'em, an' if'n they did, they ain't gonna b'lieve nuthin' til a body makes 'em. Damn if I don't think I'm gonna resign, right now."

This was more like Johnny. Barth was glad at his return to character, and he laughed aloud.

Mace turned upon hearing him and asked, "Whut's th' fun, Cap'n?"

"Just something Johnny said that kinda tickled me a little."

"Oh," said Mace and continued on.

They crested a little rise and the furnaces were in full view.

"We got fifty kittles down here. Keep them fires a-goin' day an' night, rain 'er shine, summer, an' most uv winter. Course, hit's best in dry weather fer th' makin' uv th' salt." Whatever Mace's faults, a dislike for his work was not one of them. His voice and countenance made that positive.

"You mean you keep fires under all the kettles all the time? Do you have men working all night?"

"Yes, sirree, we does. Oney times them fires dies is when hit's snowed er iced up orful bad."

Barth continued his questioning. "How many men you keep here at night?"

"Usual, 'bout ten. Course, come nightfall, we got th' wood stacked real clos't. Allus keep 'nough more men for guards."

"Indians?" asked Barth.

"Naw, we gotta watch fer thet damn, thievin' Tom Chism an' his bunch," he replied fiercely.

Johnny looked at Barth, but Mercer gave no outward indication of resentment. Inside was a different matter.

"Injuns hain't no trubble now. Hain't been for almost three y'ars. Too many people here now. Oney scrappins we hez with 'em comes frum scoutin' parties, an' they never hez more'n twenty in 'em—usual 'bout twelve. Yer know, they's high as a hundred settlers coming here a day? Course all uv 'em don't stay; but lots settles somewheres 'round here. Naw, they hain't gonner be no bother with Injuns—jest frum them bastards uv Chism's." He spat, and then renewed his discourse. "Injuns hardly never comes through this here in big numbers. Thet's 'cause they all thinks Kentucky is jest a huntin' place an' 'cause it's s'posed to be a sorta holy territory. Not thet they hain't done a lot uv fightin' 'twixt theyse'fs— but them wuz jest heppened meetins where diffrunt tribes runn'd cros't each other." He reconsidered a moment before saying, "Course, hit hain't none too safe out frum th' settlement aways."

They were right at the furnaces now, and Mace's mind jumped to work. "Hey, you lazy, no good son-uv-a-bitch," he hollered at a man sitting near a pile of logs. "Gitcher ass off'n thet ground! Whut you think yer doin'? Hatchin' salt? Gitcher ass on th' run, damn yer!" He heaved a large chunk of wood directly at him.

The unfortunate man ran away.

"You drunk son-uv-a-bitch! It ain't goin' ter be good fer yer when I ketches you. An' yer knows I will, you bastard!" As an afterthought, he called to the fleeing man, "If yer wants ter git drunk, go work fer thet damn Tom Chism! He won't know th' diffrunce!"

Barth sensed that these references to Tom Chism were for his benefit and were leading to something, but he determined to bide his time until they took full form.

"Thet don't heppen offin," Mace apologized, "but hit kain't be holped. This here's a rough job, an' yer kain't allus be too choicey 'bout whut kind uv men you gits."

Mace now gave a detailed explanation of the furnaces and their construction: Long trenches, walled with slate and mortared with clay. The fires were at the front; the flames being drawn along under the kettles, which sat on top of the trenches in long rows and out a chimney at the other end. Overhead, a roof ran the entire length of each furnace pit, furnishing protection from the elements.

Barth observed the massive kettles. He learned that each held around twenty-five gallons of water. A few of them belonged to the Commonwealth, but most of them were privately owned.

Now came the description of the actual operation of making the salt. The water was boiled for a day, or less, depending on the dryness of the weather. From the kittles, as Mace called them, the water went to a cooling trough. The blackness of color had long since vanished. After cooling, the clear brine was drawn off and poured back into the kettles once more where it was boiled until the crystals began to form. As soon as this occurred, the fires were slackened a bit, though the water continued to boil. The salt was then dipped out as it formed and put into baskets where it was allowed to drain. Nothing was wasted. The drippings were returned to the water in the kettles. The process was repeated over and over until the leftovers became charged with impurities. Then the kettles were emptied and the cycle started anew.

Barth noted the number of fires, each the symbol of a salt furnace. Where he couldn't see the actual blazing, he counted the various streams of smoke. There were between sixty and seventy. He estimated the number of men engaged in their operation at around two hundred. This force, he knew, was augmented by coopers, carpenters, storekeepers, wood choppers and hunters. In addition to these, he knew there were bound to be a number of guards posted beyond his sight.

Mace explained that it was cheaper to move the furnaces near the stands of timber than to haul the wood to the fires. Barth could readily ascertain that this was true, since in the latter operation, the wood had to be cut, loaded, transported and then unloaded. By the former method, it needed only to be cut and stacked near the furnace.

As they talked, Barth tried to figure the total output from the works in terms of bushels, tons and the resultant monetary value. He looked to his right just in time to see a figure at a pit some fifty yards away in the act of striking one of the kettle tenders.

Instantly, all the men around there joined in a free-for-all. Curses of all hues and descriptions filled the air. Men from adjacent furnaces were leaving their work and running toward the brawl.

Without a word to Mercer, Mace hurried to the scene. Grasping two of the principals by their belts, he lifted them from the ground, still swinging at each other. Dropping them, he gave each several vicious kicks, and they withdrew quickly to places of refuge from his wrath.

Barth stood by, marveling at the strength and courage of Mace Hardin. One of the combatants, taking advantage of Mace's turned back, gave him a resounding blow between his shoulders with a large club. Mace turned quickly and gripped his assailant by the throat with a hand and the man's face turned blue. He was through fighting.

Mace moved with awful precision, impervious to blows that would have stopped most men in their tracks. He seized two of the battlers and bashed their heads together. Another, he simply caught by an arm and flung him yards away.

The remaining brawlers became conscious that there was a terror in the fray. "Look out for Mace," one of them shouted, and the battle ceased.

Mace then proceeded to punish every one of those who had been involved in the disturbance; much as a mother bear cuffing her disobedient cubs. This he followed with a series of the strongest, vilest and most forceful oaths Barth had ever heard.

Order returned without a request ever being made for its restoration. The "dirty, bleeding, son-uv-a-bitch scum" were working intently at their tasks, and there would be no resumption, at least this day, of the quarrel.

As they walked away, Barth asked, "What brought on the trouble?"

"Mought be enythin'; but prob'ly it wuz over them damn Dusenberry whores, back at the settlement. They sells their favors, and these here dumb bastards gits j'alous. Mix that with a little corn squeezins whut they drunk last night an' yer gits trubble. Hell, hit's allus sumthin' heppens. Them sons-uv-bitches! Them dirty bastards from hell!"

"Who are the Dusenberrys?"

"I kin tell yew, Kepteen."

Barth gave Johnny a harsh look, and he closed his mouth.

"Them's twin whores. They duz a right pert bizness. Ain't nuthin' so bad 'bout them; hit's whut them bastards make uv it after they's been with 'em. I like 'em m'se'f." Mace's features broke into a good-natured grin that gave an arc to the scar on his face.

"If they cause so much trouble, wouldn't it be better to move them away from here?" Barth did not say the words in a condemning manner. He was thinking only of their alleged effect on the men.

"Hell, no! Beggin' yer pardin, Cap'n. If'n they wuzn't no wimmen, them scum wud do it with each other, the dirty, low-down, no-good bastards."

Johnny interrupted the conversation with an excited, "Look over there!"

Another melee had broken out at the far end of the line of furnaces to their left. Barth and Mace ran toward the latest outbreak. Johnny brought up the rear. They reached there too late to prevent a bare-waisted, bald-headed water drawer from striking another with what looked to be a kettle bar, used for lifting the kettles on and off the trench. The impact was sickening—the unmistakable sound of bone being broken.

Mace knew the sound well, and he shouted, "Git Roller to Doc Grainger, an' don't waste no time a-doin' it!"

Mercifully unconscious, but moaning piteously, Roller was borne speedily away in a wagon half filled with fire wood.

The bald-headed man turned around at Mace's command and walked toward him.

"Hit's you agin! Tain't been a week sence yer crippled Morgan. Whut'n hell are you tryin' ter do, put me out uv bizness? Whut's th' 'scuse this time? Hit better be a good un', er I'll lamb yer ter death."[4]

"Wait a minute, this man's been hurt bad," said Barth. "Look at his eye."

"Hurt, hell! He wuz hurt all right, but Roller ain't th' one whut did it. Thet there horbal injery wuz don by one uv Tom Chism's sneakin' cutthroats."

A horrible injury it was; regardless of when or by whom it had been inflicted. The eye was gone, leaving an empty red socket, now festered throughout the rim of its circumference. Insects settled quickly on the round sore like vultures upon their prey.

"C'mon, Smith, whut in tarnal started hit?" Mace was striking his palm with his fist. "Le's hev it."

"Thet thievin' scum stole two Louis d'ors[5] from m' pouch. I ketched 'im with his damn hand right on it." Smith's one good eye was shifty, and played first on

Barth, then on Little Johnny and last upon Mace. As he looked at Mace, his thin lips turned up at the corners forming a wry smile.

Before what next happened, Barth knew he was lying. But even as the thought entered his mind, someone rushed at Smith. Barth saw the latter's hand go to his hip. The noon sun flashed on the blade as it came from its sheath. Smith slashed at his oncoming attacker, who yelled as he grappled with him, "That's a damned lie! You ain't never had two louis d'ors in yore life."

Mace stepped between the two, and each backed off.

Smith's knife had found its mark. Blood gushed from a cut on the top side of the victim's left forearm, from his wrist almost to the elbow. Some of the blood dripped into one of the kettles.

An onlooker said facetiously, "Thet'll shore pure the salt in thet kittle."

Doctor Grainger had another patient.

"Thet's all fer you, Bad-Eye," said Mace in a, matter-of-fact manner. "Git on ter th' storehouse an' wait fer me. I'll ten' ter yer proper." Then, as though nothing had happened, he said, "The rest uv yers git back ter your work."

"Does this brawling take place very often?" Barth asked in an incredulous tone.

"Cap'n, these ez all rough, devil-lovin' suns-uv-bitches. They hain't no day goes by, but whut they ain't some fightin'. An' if'n they drinks at night, hits even badder then in the daytime. Now, mebbe you kin unnerstan' why I whipped yer fren' thar." He pointed to Johnny. "Yer jest kain't take no chances with none uv 'em 'round these parts. Saltsburg is jest plain full uv wild-ass, fightin' bastards. Most uv 'em warn't no good whar they frum, and they hain't a damn bit better hyar. Th' words out, fur an' wide, that thar's money ter be hed fer th' takin' at these here licks, an' th' scum comes a-runnin'."

This was the first time Barth had heard the use of the name Saltsburg to describe the settlement. Thinking further, he wondered if Tom Chism had the same trouble with his men.

"Kepteen, ain't we seen 'nough fer today? 'Sides, ain' t it 'bout time fer some vittles?" Johnny was tired and showed it. His still-puffed features moved Barth to say, "I guess we have had plenty for the time being. Reckon we have covered this pretty well, except I did want to look at the records. But I can do that the first thing in the morning Then, after we finish, we'll go check on Tom Chism's works."

Mace shifted his weight. "Records, Cap'n? Whut records yer simin' ter see?"

"You have been keeping records of how much salt you've been making, how much you had to pay out and what you took in, haven't you?"

Mace swallowed before he answered. "Oh, shore—shore. We got 'em at thet storeroom whar I sent Bad-Eye. Unnerstan' they hain't fancy-kept. I hed a good 'un with figgers, but he took off 'bout year ago; hain't hed no one sence. But we does th' best whut we kin."

"I want to see them tomorrow, Mr. Hardin. Get them in as good order as you can by that time."

Johnny's spine still tingled when he heard Barth say, "Mr. Hardin."

"By the way," Barth turned back toward Mace, "What's Smith's first name? I heard you call him Bad-Eye."

"Don't rightly know, Cap'n. That's all I ever knowed him to be called by." As Mercer and Johnny moved away, Mace said, "Cap'n, if'n yer ain't too proud, I kin hev my woman, Massalene, fix yer some eatin's. Be closer'n goin' back ter th' burg. That is, if'n you don't mind a lotta grease in th' cookin'. She's hell fer th' grease."

Remembering his brief confinement with Massalene the day previous, Barth was quick to decline the invitation. "No, thanks, I've got to attend to some things back in the settlement and we'll eat there."

Mace nodded as they walked away.

"That's strange," muttered Barth.

"Whut's strange, Kepteen?"

"If Tom Chism's men knocked Smith's eye out, it must have happened before Smith came to the licks."

"Howzzat, Kepteen?"

"You heard Mace say that Bad-Eye was the only name he had ever heard Smith called, didn't you?"

"By jingoes, yew are right, Kepteen; but I could've tole yew thet none of Tom Chism's bunch didn't do that. Th' way I heerd it, it wuz a Injun whut hit 'im with his tommyhawk sideways."

"I knew Chism or his men didn't cause that injury, but I was surprised that Mace tripped himself up. Somehow, I thought he was sharper than that. I suppose be just wanted to make Tom Chism look as bad as he could, and he just overdid it."

"Yew don't bleeve eny of whut Mace said 'bout Tom Chism?"

"Not a word of it, Johnny."

"Yew mought be right, but yew air still too damn trustin' fer yore own health an' money bag to be safe 'round here."

Barth just smiled.

The butt of Johnny's rifle dragged on the ground behind him. Barth was a stride or two ahead. "Where we gonna eat? Rosie's?" Johnny's question hopefully envisioned some of her cooking.

"We're not eating right away. I want you to take me to this Doctor Grainger's place. I want to see how Roller made out and how badly that other fellow was cut."

Johnny wasn't a bit pleased with Barth's decision. "Hell, all I done all day wuz to foller yew an' Mace like a damn puppy dog. Whenever I wanted fer to tell yew suthin', yew allus shet me up good. If'n this here's whut yew call bein' a depity, damn if I'm so damn proud of bein' one! I thought I'd have me a lil' 'thority enyhow." Johnny's growlin' stomach was companion to his sulking disposition. "Hell, thet feller, Roller, an' thet one whut wuz cut, ain't gonna be no worser if'n we don't see 'em fer 'nother hour. Don't see why I have to go enyways.

Prob'ly wouldn't let me tell yew nuthin' I knew, if there wuz eny good I could do there."

"All right, Johnny, I'll go myself; just tell me where I can find Grainger—is he really a doctor?"

"So, yew finely wants me to tell yew suthin', does yew? I ain't tellin' yew a damn thing. Whyn't yew go ask Mace or Tom Chism? No, sirree, I ain't givin' yew no more chanc't to tell me to shet up."

"Johnny, you numbskull, this isn't any time for you to be acting up. If I hurt your feelings today, I'm sorry, but you must understand that there's a method in what I do, and in what I did today. Can't you understand that I wanted Mace to talk, for him to give me his version? Then, later, I could ask you what you thought when we were alone and compare what he said with what you know."

Johnny pushed his coonskin cap way back on his head. "So thet's it, Kepteen?"

"That's the way it is, Johnny. Now will you tell me about Grainger and how to get to his place?"

"Why, shore, shore." Johnny cleared his throat and was once more the proprietor of discourse. "Grainger wuz a damn fine doctor, in th' east. Thet damn woman of his'n, Drusilla, is th' cause of him a-bein' in this damn place. He learned his medicine 'crost th' waters. He was a real good un. Wuz a ship's doctor too, in the Navy. Thet's when th' trouble started. This Drusilla got herself lonely like an' moved all 'round in differunt pastures. Grainger foun' out all 'bout it when he come back from duty one time. Loved her so damn much, 'bout driv him outa his senses. Finely, he made up his head. T'warn't nuthin' to do but to get 'way from where ever'body knowed 'em. He shore got 'way, 'way from folks, when he come here from Redstone Old Fort, there on Monngehely.[6] Been here nigh two year, now."

"His wife doing any better?"

"Far as I have heerd, she's stayed in his stable; but she don't seem none too heppy, near's I kin make out when I sees her."

"Outside of being a good doctor, what is he like as a man?"

"Damn fine feller. But thet wife of his'n worries him to death."

"Grainger's quite jealous, I take it."

"He's that a'right. But it's thet quiet, even way of his, whut hides it."

"Does he drink much?"

"Not thet I ever knowed."

Without any direction, Barth would have known they were approaching Doctor Grainger's. Terrifying, soul-rendering shrieks, each one more horrifying than the one before, came in staccato sequence.

"My God, my merciful God! Don't do it, Doc—My God! My God! My God!"

Suddenly the cries stopped. Johnny led the way around the far side of the house, explaining, "Grainger's got a keepin' room whut he uses to keep books an' his doctorin' tools in. It's suthin' like a office."

Barth had noticed the dwelling this morning as he came out of Rosie's place.

He had wondered then as to who lived in the two-story house sitting apart from the others and how he had failed to observe it yesterday.

The doctor looked to the door when they came in. Mrs. Grainger, or so Barth took her to be, was by the side of the prostrate Roller who was stretched out upon what looked like a rectangular, thinly padded table placed in convenient fashion near an unusually large window.

Grainer's greeting was sharp. "What's on your mind? You'll have to be quick about your business. I've got a bad one here. He just passed into unconsciousness when I told him I'd have to take his arm. I'm letting him be for a little while, but he might come back any moment."

"Thet happens to be our bizness, Doc. This here's Kepteen Mercer, an' I'm his depity. Th' Kepteen wants to fine out 'bout Roller. Mighty 'portant bizness I kin tall yew, Doc."

Grainger's politeness hid his irritation. "I'm pleased to meet you, sir. May I present my wife, Drusilla." Barth bowed, and Mrs. Grainger gave a slight nod; but for one fleeting second, her eyes hung on his handsome features.

Barth noted her brief appraisal of himself but did not permit his recognition to be conveyed to her. Instead, he asked the doctor, "You think there's no chance of saving his limb?"

"None at all; and if I don't act quickly, I may not be able to save him. He must have received a tremendous blow. Three of his ribs were also broken on that side. If I delay too long, it may result in putrefaction, which would surely mean his death." Grainger spoke deliberately, and his deliberativeness was doubly accented by his grave manner.

"What about the other man whose arm was cut? Have you attended him?"

"As best I can. He has a nasty wound, which I am fearful may have touched a tendon. How much, I'm not certain. I've cleansed it as much as is possible and I've sutured it. If it isn't clean, he'll have a great deal of pain and trouble with the arm. If it's free of inner defilement, he should recover without any incident save that of pain. If the tendon is involved, the use of the arm and possibly the hand might be affected."

Roller came to suddenly. "Don't do hit! Don't cut off my arm! In God's name, don't . . ." the shrieking died as he again lapsed away.

It was then Barth first noticed that Roller was tied to the table. Then too he observed the other wounded man, his arm in a sling, seated in the far corner of the room.

Although it was light by the window, the rest of the interior was illuminated by large homemade candles, set in beautiful silver sconces—sumptuous evidence of the former gracious life of the Graingers.

Other than the one glance she had given Barth on their introduction, Mrs. Grainger kept her eyes steadfastly on the patient.

Grainger cautioned, "Quiet, now, he's starting to come back."

There was no repetition of the previous outbursts. Roller looked at those gathered about him. Deep fear came into his eyes, as a wild light into darkness, but he uttered no sound. He recognized Johnny, and in an almost inaudible voice said, "Did 'ya git m' Jew's harp?"

"Hell, yes, I got it—it's right in m' pack, but I ain't brung it with me." Then aside to the others, Johnny said, "I promised I'd git 'im a Jew's harp 'fore I left outa here, las' time."

Roller's expression was relaxed. "When will ya bring it to me?" he asked feebly.

"Why, jest as soon as the Doc cuts that no good arm off'n yew. I'll git mine an' we'uns'll hev a dueyet."

Johnny's words were the tinder for the fuse. "No, by God! Yer not gonna take my arm, ya damned high-toned butcher! They ain't nuthin' wrong but hit's broke—you ain't gonna cut me none! I'll kill ya, ya son-uv-a-bitch, fust!" Roller's bonds were weakening, but they held.

Grainger gave Johnny a look of direct contempt. "Get me the whiskey. I want to fill him as full as I can. It will help some."

At first Roller resisted all efforts at this enforced intoxication, but weakness overcame him and he no longer spat the liquor, or caused it to run upon the floor, but swallowed it slowly.

His struggles had triggered his bowels and his kidneys, and the stench of the mixture of whiskey, excrement, urine and blood was terribly nauseating.

"I'm gittin' outa here," said Johnny. "The son-uv-a-bitch has went an' pissed an' shit all over hisself."

Barth helped him outside with a vigorous shove through the door. The doctor and Mrs. Grainger ignored the incident, but Barth felt impelled to make some sort of explanation. "I feel I should make excuses for Johnny; he didn't want to come, but I . . ." Before he could finish, Grainger waved his hand, both commanding and conciliatory in its conveyed meaning.

Johnny sulked wearily along. He looked for all the world like a tired-out little boy, with the accompanying ill humor of infancy under similar physical and emotional stress. His rifle, grasped by the upper barrel, was dragging again, the butt bouncing along over the uneven ground. His powderhorn was askelter and his coonskin cap was in its familiar position on the back of his head. His belt had sagged, causing the seat of his britches to droop.

A hurt, discomfited soul was he, and he was traveling the road to solace, or so he confidently and expectantly thought. Ahead lay Rosie Tindall's; she would understand. Damn fine woman, Rosie. It's good I got me one friend enyhow, he thought, as he neared her place. He would eat, have a little drink and Rosie would make over him as she always did. Then he'd sleep right there. "Damn th' Kepteen! He kin take care of hisself. Whut th' hell do I want to be a damn depity fer, anyhow, if I ain't got no badge? Them rowdys 'ud beat me to death, if I ain't got nuthin' to show 'em fer my 'thority." He mumbled his feelings to the rutted ground.

Walking with his head down, Johnny didn't see Rosie and Abby, in their best linsey-woolseys, standing outside the door in the late afternoon sunshine. But they saw him, and as he came within hearing distance, Abby said to her mother, "Mamma, is that Daniel Boone, or is it his brother, Squire? Whichever it is, he looks mighty tuckered."

"Hush, Abby, he'll hear you. Now be nice to him, for once, for my sake. The poor thing is dead tired."

Rosie's quiet words were in vain, for Johnny had heard Abby's vibrant voice, and his ire forced new strength into his weary body. "Rosie, I can't b'leeve thet she-ket be really yor'n. I ain't in no feelin' fer no smart talk frum her. If th' sun's as tarred as I am, it won't be no use in nobuddy gittin' up tomorrow. It'll be pitch black all day."

"I was afraid this might be too hard for you, Johnny, soon's I heard you all was out together." Rosie took his cap from his perspiring head. "Come in and rest and I'll fix you somethin' good."

Johnny smiled blandly. Rosie's th' real one, he thought.

Abby couldn't let things be peaceful, or Johnny have any ease. "Mamma, you know, I thought this was our lucky day. When we heard a man got his arm broke, I was sure Mr. Littelby was the one. I figgered he broke it tryin' to shoot that gun he was carryin'. Seems we just ain't lucky, I guess."

Johnny's blood pressure hit the boiling point, but before he could explode, Rosie had chased Abby away. Seeking to divert him, she asked, "Will Captain Mercer be along shortly? How did it happen he didn't come with you?"

"Damn th' Kepteen!" exclaimed Johnny, "All he hez done all day wuz to hev me foller him 'round like a puppy dog. He ain't aknowin' hit, but me an' him's 'bout through!"

"Don't say that, Johnny. You know he's a good man. He's a gentleman, and he likes you."

"Gentleman is he? Humph! Guess all yew wimmin is th' same! He's so damn 'portant! Hell, I'm 'portant too!"

"Of course, of course, Johnny. But you mustn't get mad at him. He can make you a big man if you let him."

"He kin make me a big man! Why, damn his hifalutin hide he ain't never gonna see no day when he's big as I am, right now. Don't chew reckin' people knows me everywheres? An' me tarred? Hell, I bet he ain't never walked from Philidelphy down here, or up from N'Orleans, like I has!"

"There, there, Johnny. Don't fret your poor tired self no more. Drink a little of this." Johnny complied and a warm glow spread throughout bis body.

"Now, tell me why are you mad at Captain Mercer?"

Johnny explained in detail and at length. When he finished, he asked, "Why'd they all git so all-firin' mad at me? I jest meant to be comfortin' to Willie Roller. All I sed wuz, thet soon's th' Doc cut his arm off, we'uns could play a dueyet on our Jew's harps. An' when he done thet all over hisself, I can't see no harm in tellin' how I felt."

"Johnny, it's all right to talk plain to me—I ain't no lady, like Mrs. Grainger. You prob'ly embarrassed her. An' you ought not have reminded Willie that th' doctor was gonna cut off his arm, when they was tryin' to keep him quiet. I know you didn't mean no harm, but it wasn't exactly the right way to do."

"Humph!" said Johnny. "Yew don't know no ladies, much, if yew are callin' thet Drusilla one. She wuz a damn slatter in fancy riggins back where they come frum, an' I heerd it fer th' truth. 'Sides, Doc treats all 'em scummy bastards an' they talks lot's worser'n I does. So I know I didn't say nuthin' new fer her damn, dainty lady ears, if that's a-worry yew."

She shook her head, despairing of making him realize his lack of propriety. "Well, Johnny, you just set there an' I'll fetch you some real good vittles."

Johnny propped his feet on another chair and waited comfortably for his supper.

Back at Grainger's, the door opened when Johnny made his forced exit, remained ajar, giving some relief to the atmosphere within. Roller was as far under the influence of spirits as he would ever be, and Grainger prepared to operate. He had tied a black band around Willie's head, covering his eyes. His instruments ready, he began the grisly task.

Hardened as he was to human suffering, and to witnessing the wounds and tortures endured by men at war, Barth yet winced when the first contact was made by the blade with the bone, and the grating sound of the instrument sawing its way set his nerves on knife-like edge. All the while, Roller raved, and struggled at his bonds.

After an eternity, Mrs. Grainger carried away the severed portion of the limb. The bleeding was limited, but what blood flowed dropped into a wooden bucket placed precisely beneath the stub that remained. Grainger had tied a tourniquet about four inches above the severance. He spoke for the first time, quietly. "Please get me the firing iron." Drusilla returned quickly and transferred the padded end of the rod to the doctor. There was a hiss and, with its blood-made steam, the overpowering odor of burnt flesh. As the white-hot iron touched him, Providence decreed the end of Roller's consciousness, and he had fainted.

Barth helped the doctor and his wife move Willie to a more comfortable bed. The ropes were secured once more about his body to prevent self-injury when he next awoke.

Barth bade the exhausted pair goodbye, and started back to his cabin.

When he reached there, he found it empty, and surmised Johnny had gone to Rosie's. Spent as he was, he welcomed company and decided that he too would go to Mrs. Tindall's.

CHAPTER 7

There were ten of them, Mace's selected furnace bosses, seated on the stumps in back of the storehouse. Mace alone was standing as he talked to them. The sinking sun was almost behind the knob in the distance. The chill of evening was upon them, and those who were bare-waisted were beginning to become uncomfortable.

"This hain't bin no bad day," said Mace, "An' it hain't gonna be no bad night, neither." He laughed, and they guffawed with him.

"Tomorry morn, when the great Cap'n Mercer comes ter look at them records whut never wuz, they's gonna be all burned up, an' this here storehouse with 'em." More hearty laughter ensued.

"No sirree, boys, this 'twarn't no bad day. Yer fellers played hit jest right. Cuddn't no bunch uv stage actors done no better. 'Does this brawling'—git thet—'take place very off'n?' he asks me, an' I tells him hit does, 'cause yer sech a low-down bunch uv scurvy sons-uv-bitches, er some sech words." Turning toward the storehouse door, he called, "Bad-Eye, come out here fer a spell."

Bad-Eye came, wearing the embarrassed grin of one who is expecting to be complimented or praised for some unusual exploit.

"Whut's yer real name—yer fust name, thet is?"

"Boss, thet don't make no matter." Bad-Eye became more self-conscious than ever.

"Hain't cher got one?"

He nodded his head affirmatively.

"Whut es hit, then?"

Bad-Eye bent his head as he whispered, "Cuthbert." He wished he was miles away after the chorus of gruff hysterics that followed.

At length Mace, after wiping his eyes with the back of his hand, motioned them to be still. He put his index finger to his nostril and blew his nose. "Boys, Cuthbert here"—a renewed series of laughs filled the air but stopped short as Mace continued. "I mean Bad-Eye—wuz the best uv th' whole damn shebang. He gits rid uv thet damn Willie Roller an' almost takes care, complete, uv Davey Middleton. Them two orter never uv left Tom Chism, an' I orter never uv tried ter git 'em ter jine we'uns."

One of the listeners spoke up. "Mought be trouble when Willie gits fixed up."

"Willie hain't never gonner be fixed up like as he wuz. That left arm uv his'n es buried behine Doc Grainger's already. A feller wuz tellin' me he heard 'im pleadin' with Grainger not ter cut hit off. A one-armed feller hain't gonner last long 'round these here diggins."

They all nodded in assent.

Bad-Eye was grinning again, as Mace directed his words to him. "You gotter get 'way frum hyar, Bad-Eye. I told Mercer I wuz gonner deal with yer proper. Now, we wants him ter think thet I run yer off, an' thet ter git even with me, you burned this damn storehouse down. Course, after whut yer done ter Willie an' Dave, hit'd be lots healthier fer you ter git some space 'twixt yerself an' them. So here's whut yer gonner do. You sets th' fire good an' fine, long 'bout three in th' mornin'. Then yer takes off fer Kahaz Knob where you kin hide out frum Mercer an' th' rest. Then yer best go on up ter th' Falls fer a spell. Four er five months an' yer kums on back. By thet time, we won't be bein' bothered none by no Mercer. Howzat 'pear ter yer?"

Bad-Eye didn't like the idea of exile and started to protest, but Mace gave him no chance to do so. "Most fergot suthin'. Th' guards all gits drunk—no imatashun—an' I guvs th' likker, free."

Instantly, all ten volunteered for guard duty. Mace laughed. "Yers ez bosses; ain't no boss kin be a guard."

Bad-Eye, facing banishment, grew bolder and did not address Mace as boss. He merely said, "Ya knows I'll hev to hev a little money."

"Shore yer will. Here's 'nough ter tide yer fer a bit. Yer gets some more later." Turning to the rest, he said, "No speechin' 'bout this, now, an' yer," talking again to Bad-Eye, "set thet fire right, an' when I tole yer to."

Certain that the plan was fully understood and would be carried out as he had ordered, Mace waved his hand and walked off in the dusk.

*

Standing beside the bed, Dolly put her hand on the shoulder of the sleeping Jeddy-Boy. She shook him vigorously, at the same time saying harshly, "Jed, wake up! Yore snorin' fit to wake th' dead."

Jed's only response was to suck on his lips and run the top of his tongue back and forth against his palate.

She used both hands this time and shook him harder, urging him in a louder voice. At this, he struck out savagely with his arm, freeing himself of her grasp. The force of the blow all but caused her to lose her balance. He was awake now.

"Whut in tarnation's th' matter with yer?" he yawned.

"Nuthin's wrong with me; but ya best be gittin' up. Yore paw'll be lookin' fer ya, an' ya knows what that means."

"He kin go ter hell an' keep a-lookin'!"

"I can see ya tellin' thet to him."

"Look," he was getting angry, "I don't need no damn whore tellin' me whut

I gotter do; so shet yer damn ugly mouth."

"It ain't been so damned ugly all day—ya been kissin' it off'n on since mornin' an' it's clos't on to four in th' afternoon now. Sure took you a long time to find out how bad it looked."

"I'm payin' yer, hain't I? I kin say whut I wants ter; I'm a-payin' fer th' doin' uv it!"

"Ya ain't paid me yet! An' ya ain't payin' fer all th' bitin' ya does or th' scratches ya made in m' skin. Lovin's one thing; but you goes at it like a animal."

"Yer gits yer pleasure, same as me."

"Pleasure like th' pain of gettin' a beatin'! I been with many a man, an' all kinds of 'em—gentle ones an' rough ones; but yore th' roughest an' th' meanest I ever laid with. Why ya git pleasure out of hurtin' a body? When ya comes this mornin', I tole ya I wuz tired from last night; but you says ya been burnin' fer two days, so I 'commodates ya. An' how does ya repay me? By smackin' my buttocks til' they aches, pinchin' m' bubbles til' they's sore ter touch, chawin' m' shoulder so's it bleeds an' pullin' my hair 'most out of my bead. An' ya calls that pleasure? Just don't give me no more of it, if that's what it is!"

"Shet up, you damn bitch! Yer knows I had ter be hard put fer a warmin', when I kum here."

"Git up an' git yore riggins on, an' git 'way from here, ya damned half-breed son-of-a-bitch! I may be a whore, as ya calls me, but even a whore's got some feelins."

"I jest think I'll do m'se'f a little carvin' on yer with m' knife." Jeddy-Boy lunged for her, but she eluded him.

"Ya does that agin, an' I'm callin' Molly. She knows you're here, an' she's got a gun she can shoot! Now git on out!"

Dressed now, Jed pulled open the door. "I'm a-leavin' fer now, but I reckin I'll be back soon. You damned flat-assed Dusenberry whores hain't heerd th' last uv me! Call me a half-breed son-uv-a-bitch, will yer?"

"Talk yore damn fool head off, but what about my pay?"

"I hain't givin' yer a damn thing! Twarn't wuth nuthin' nohow. Yer shud be a-payin' me—look at th' tricks I larned yer."

"Ya don't pay me an' I'll tell ever burnin' son-of-a-bitch what comes 'round here 'bout ya."

Jed's hand went for his pouch. He flung the money on the floor.

"That ain't but half what yore s'posed to pay me."

"That's all yer gits; I guv yer lots more'n I orter. I hopes yer belly gits big with two half-breed sons-uv-bitches jest like me." He walked on outside but did not close the door.

The thought of her becoming pregnant by Jed panicked her. She dropped to her knees, her lips moving in fear-filled supplication. Suddenly she heard the cries—wild, weird shrieks of one agonized in mind and body. She ran to the road in front. Others all about had done the same. Soon the news reached her ears—"That's Willie Roller—Grainger's gonna cut off his arm!" She went back inside and closed the door securely.

*

Mace entered his cabin and immediately dropped into a chair. At the same time, Massalene was descending the ladder from upstairs. As she reached the floor and was in the act of moving the ladder, Mace spoke to her. "Ole womern, whar's Jeddy-Boy?"

She turned her back to him as she replied, "No see 'im sence mornin'." She had braided her hair, Indian fashion, and this served to soften somewhat her otherwise ugly features The wound on the side of her face was crusted and was not as vivid as it had been. A thin smear of bear grease ran its length.

"'Bout time he's gittin' here. He's gittin' plumb outer han'. 'Pears like I never sees 'im no more."

"You say him stay way frum soldier feller."

"Hell, yes, I done thet. But I din't mean he wuz ter be shy uv ever'body. Whar's Hawkstraw?"

"Him an' Nance take walk."

"Ole womern, 'twuddn't s'prise me none if'n they's doin' a mite more'n walkin' when they's gone. Nance's gittin older, y'know."

"Devil talk in you—they no do bad."

"Mebbe yore right, ole womern; 'sides, I don't reckin' Hawkstraw's 'clined like thet, nohow—don't 'spec he's ever had a womern. Hain't like Jeddy-Boy, no sirree! If'n he wuz, whut a pair uv boys they wudda bin!"

"Hawkstraw good boy."

"Mebbe, but I shore wisht he wuz like Jeddy-Boy; ternight enyways. I shore got a job ter be did. But thet Jeddy-Boy's gittin' jest like them damn Shawanese—kain't count on 'im fer a minit." Mace spat on the floor.

Massalene's eyes narrowed when he mentioned the Shawanese and her lips tightened as he continued. "Damned Injuns fust fit with th' Frenchies agin th' English. Now they's done changed sides."

"Indians good people. Shawanese good Indians."

"Whut yer mean, good? They fits fer th' best price. An' them Wyandots! Them's th' wussest uv all! I heerd yer, jest then, a-talkin' like they does. Thet's 'bout th' trouble with Jeddy-Boy; thet Injun blood's thicker'n th' white."

"Him grandfather great chief." She was on the verge of losing control of her emotions. Her blood lines embraced the Wyandot and the Shawnee.

"He wuz a horse-stealin' bastard an' th' oney sculps he ever took wuz off'n some pore critters thet'd been dead fer so long they wuz beginnin' ter smell."

These taunts were too much for Massalene's pride. She came at him like a lumbering bear, knife in hand. Mace sidestepped and struck as hard as he could, the blow catching her on the side of her face and reopening the cut afresh. She raised herself from the floor, making no move at retaliation, but hatred was in her black eyes.

"Now, git 'bout yer bizness—fix me some vittles, an' damn quick."

She shuffled about silently, the blood coursing down her face and neck. The meal prepared, she placed it before him. Then she went to a chair in the rear of the room and sat down and folded her arms. The blood still ran.

As Mace finished eating, Jeddy-Boy opened the door. Wiping his mouth with his sleeve and his hands on the side of his deerskin jacket, Mace got to the business at hand without any greeting. He explained the plan, after telling of the day's earlier events. When he had finished, he sought assurance from Jed that he understood.

"Now yer knows whut yer s'posed ter do? I wants yer ter start out after th' fire, say half-hour. Bad-Eye's goin' ter Kahaz Knob—let 'im hev a li'l lead on yer—don't push 'im none er he mought change direction and head somewhere else. Yer orter fix hit so's yer ketch 'im some place past th' middle uv th' knob. After yer kills 'im—then sculp 'im, so's they thinks th' Injuns done th' killin'. An' then yer gits th' money off'n 'im an fetches hit back here ter me. I know 'zackly how much hit shud be, so see thet I gits it all."

Once again, he asked Jeddy-Boy. "Yer shore yer knows yer job?"

Jed nodded.

"Then yer best eat an' git tar sleep. Yer been drinkin', an' I wants fer yer t'be cl'ar in th' head kum mornin'."

Massalene brought Jed's food to the table. "Whut's th' matter?" Jed asked. "Yer face is a-bleedin' agin."

She nodded her head toward where Mace was sitting.

"He done it agin?"

She moved her head slowly up and down.

Mace and Jeddy-Boy were both asleep shortly thereafter, but Massalene did not move or change her position until Nancy and Hawkstraw came in. The candlelight hid the evidence of Mace's fury from the one, but when Nancy kissed her goodnight, she noticed the turned cheek, and Massalene, sobbing softly, told her what had happened. Nancy took a wet cloth and wiped away the carmine stains. She waited until Massalene was asleep on the pallet on the floor before she blew out the candle's flame. Upstairs Mace snored heavily.

CHAPTER 8

The smell of the cooking told what they were eating before he reached Rosie's, and the knowledge only served to whet further his already starved appetite. Men who spend much time in the open seem to draw something into their bodies from the atmosphere that sets up a strong craving for nourishment, and lots of it. Add to that a stomach empty since early morning, and it typified Barth's condition. There will always be but one anodyne for the pang of hunger—food.

He opened the door and walked inside. They were seated on the far side of the room: Rosie, Johnny, Abby, Tom Chism, and a man whom he did not know. The table was rectangular, with benches on either side for seats. Tom, Abby, and the stranger sat together, and opposite them, as was to be expected, Rosie and Johnny.

Rosie was up to greet him instantly, insisting he join them. Barth needed no persuading. As he reached the table, Johnny climbed over the bench.

"If he's eatin' here, I ain't. Damn if I'm gonna hev my eatin' ruint by settin' next to him."

Barth was taken by complete surprise, and for the moment, said nothing.

Abby, seizing what was too good an opportunity to miss, exclaimed, "Thank heaven, you come Captain Mercer! I was findin' it hard to eat—it tasted good, but it smelled like I was eatin' deer skin full of sweat."

The blood rose in Johnny's face up to and above his temples. "Why yew, yew—yew—yew—" Unable to collect his wits, he stormed over to a chair near the door and sat down.

"Abby, you'll be th' despair of me yet." Rosie shook her head sadly. "Why you're all th' time badgerin' him, I can't guess."

Abby giggled in girlish glee. "I reckon I know how Hilda Tressel felt that time after that family of polecats finally moved out from under their cabin."

Johnny sneered at her and turned his face. And when he did so, she only laughed the more, as did Tom and the other man. Rosie and Barth were silent. Rosie, because of her sympathy and embarrassment; Barth, out of ignorance of the cause of Johnny's action.

Rosie went over to Johnny and pleaded with him to return. He stubbornly refused, shaking his head, and stared at the floor. Seeing that he would have to ride out his sulking spell alone, she came back to the others. She seated herself and then said, "Captain Mercer, I'd be pleased for you to meet Jim Trench. You 'member when you was here last, he had went over to Clear's Station."

Barth reached his arm across the table and shook hands.

They had just been seated when the door opened and Doctor Grainger entered. With the most formal of recognitions, he walked slowly to the last table in the room where he sat down facing Rosie and Barth.

Not a word had been spoken since his lonely entrance. Rosie caught the significance of such silence and quickly asked, "How did you find things over at Clear's, Jim?"

Not so tactful as Rosie, Jim asked blankly, "Huh? I tole ya all I know. They hain't no more whut's new."

Recovering, she said casually, "I know, but Cap'n Mercer wasn't here then."

"Oh," said Jim, "Fergot thet. Wal, fer th' one thing, they's signs uv Injuns movin' about there agin. Two diffrunt parties wuz scouted 'bout five mile away. One wuz Cherokee, t'other Shawanese. They's th' fust ones in a heap uv time. Heerd tell they's been a mought troublesome, further over."

No one was listening, and Jim Trench, observing this, concluded, "Don't reckin they wuz up tuh anything er we'd heerd 'bout hit by now, fer shore. Heerd they wuz a ruckus over at th' furnaces t'day. Heerd Willie Roller got hit bad."

"It was terrible," exclaimed Abby. "I declare, that ole Mace Hardin oughta be shot."

"Mace didn't do it, Abby," corrected Rosie.

"I didn't say he did; but I wouldn't put it past him none to have had it did."

"I heerd he hed to hev his left arm took off'n him," said Trench. "Willie wuz one uv th' best uv thet whole Hardin bunch, shore wuz too bad. Heerd too that Davey Middleton got hisself cut on his arm. They know who done it?"

"Captain Mercer was there when it happened, Jim," said Rosie.

"Warn't no accidents, I take it," he asserted.

Barth related what had taken place. When he had finished, Tom Chism said glumly, "I'm sure sorry. I hated to lose Willie and Davey to Mace Hardin, but he promised 'em so much, I couldn't hold 'em. Them two an' Herman Tressel an' Martin Willerhorst went over to Mace at th' same time. They are all honest men. Just never could understand how they expected to get along with that crowd of thieves."

"I take it you'd like to have them back," said Barth.

"That I would; even Willie with no arm could work for me."

"We'd best stop th' talkin' an' git to eatin'," said Rosie. "Y'all can thank Jim Trench for what's on th' board tonight. Brung it fresh killed to us."

A full board it was: turkey, grouse and venison. Jim Trench was chewing on a greasy morsel, which Rosie quickly identified as being bear meat, explaining that Jim hadn't shot it that day. It was part of what was stored on ice at the spring. Bear meat was his favorite, so she had cooked some for him. Then there were biscuits and gravy, wild greens and peach preserves.

"I notice you seem to have plenty of peach preserves," said Barth, "Where did you get them?"

"Why, Captain, we grows peaches 'round here. Got lots of peach an' apple trees—started bearin' last year. They all come from th' McAfee brothers, over near Harrodstown.[7] They was planted about th' same time as theirs was."

"I've heard of the McAfees. They're good men," said Barth.

"Don't know how they ever come through th' winter of '79,[8] if it was as cold here as it was at Pittsburgh." Rosie shuddered at the remembrance of that bitter season.

"Must have been quite cold this year, if you were able to cut and store ice. I heard you say you had Trench's bear meat kept at the spring." Barth glanced toward Grainger's table. The doctor returned his involuntary stare.

"Oh, it wasn't real bad, but we did have ice, for which we're thankful. B'lieve it'll last us nigh through th' summer," Rosie said hopefully. She excused herself, showing off her manners to the gentlemen, and returned with some peach brandy.

As they finished drinking, ending the meal, Grainger came over to the table. Addressing Barth, he said, in low, well-modulated tones, "I would be honored, sir, if you would join me for a moment."

Barth accepted the invitation and excused himself. He and Grainger walked together to the doctor's table and seated themselves.

Johnny, who had been straining his ears, though seemingly indifferent to the goings-on, was up like a jack-in-the-box to retrieve the seat he had surrendered earlier. He fell to with a vengeance, stuffing his mouth as though making up for lost time.

Barth was the first to speak. "How did Roller make out after I left, Doctor?"

"It was quite an ordeal for him and for all of us. I suppose my manner still reflects it. I must admit to a degree of nervousness that I have seldom felt during an amputation. Somehow, this one was different from all the others, and I have had my share of such operations," he said, with an air of professional pride. "This poor fellow, Roller, couldn't believe his arm was gone, even after I had taken it from him. I had to have Chate, my negro manservant, bring it back into the room. I think what happened then is what has affected me so. The wretched fellow asked to hold the severed member. Chate gave it to him, and he grasped it, bringing its hand to his mouth. He kissed it, time and again, crying as he did so. It was as a mother, kissing a child that had died in her embrace."

Barth paused before saying anything, to be sure the doctor had finished, then asked, "Do you think he'll pull through all right?"

"I don't know. He's a strongly constituted man, and he should recover. After healing, which will take considerable time, he'll have about a five-inch stump below his shoulder. Of course, there is always the danger of mortification. If that begins, I may have to take what's left of his arm. Should that develop, I don't know whether he could last it, strong as he is. It is pitiful; he still claims that he has feeling in the whole arm, even though it's all but gone." Catching himself and in a measure of professional defense, he added, "You understand that I'm not maudlin in any degree. I was highly esteemed in the east as an excellent surgeon, both in ability and in temperament. I say this in all modesty, lest you arrive at the wrong impression of me."

"I understand and believe you fully." The sincerity of Barth's acknowledgment was evident to Grainger, whose relief was etched plainly upon his features. Grainger cleared his throat. "However, Captain, that is not what I invited you here to discuss. You met my wife today I believe."

"I did that," said Barth. "She is a very pretty woman."

"And she knows it, as do all women of beauty," he interjected.

The slight rise in Barth's continuing words served notice upon the doctor that he thought the interruption in bad taste. "Where is she tonight?"

"She and Chate are still watching over Roller."

"Begging your pardon, sir, but isn't that exactly where you should be?"

"I know my business, sir." Grainger's voice seethed a bit. "I will be by my patient's side from my return until I am satisfied he is out of any immediate danger."

"My respects to you, sir," said Barth, and he started to arise.

"No, hold on, Captain. I beg you to make allowance for my late experience. If I have offended you, I offer my sincere apologies."

"I don't think apologies are in order, or necessary, Doctor Grainger, realizing what you have undergone. I can well understand that your nerves might well be on edge. I will remain, if you so desire."

"Please do, and I assure you I will keep my voice under gentlemanly control for the rest of our conversation." Continuing, he slaved his discourse. "Captain, the surgeon who delays making an incision, after he has deemed one necessary, is a poor surgeon. I have never so stayed my hand. You know I did not ask you here to talk of Roller's operation or of my care of Middleton, who, by the way, is doing nicely—no leaders are affected and there is no apparent permanent damage to his arm. But in order to come to the verbal incision, which I feel I must make, I must tell you something of the background of my wife and myself.

Barth emphasized, "Doctor, you are staying your hand."

"I assure you, sir, it is not pleasant for me, but without this background you may not comprehend the need for this verbal surgery at all."

"In that case, continue, Doctor."

"I am now forty-three years of age; my wife thirteen years younger. We married when I was thirty-three and when she was twenty. I know that in the settlements and on the frontier, caste or social position, by themselves, never secure a person's respect. But in the more civilized east, they are most important; at least they were so, prior to the revolt of the Colonies. After this war is ended, whoever is the victor, as fortune may determine, it will be as it was before.

"My wife and I came from families of similar antecedents. We appeared ideally situated for marriage, in every respect. I had established myself as a promising surgeon. Drusilla had made her mark in society, so fully had she mastered all the social graces. On both sides of our family were inherited fortunes. At that time, there seemed to be no obstacle to a successful, love-filled marriage. Our wedding was attended by only the most prominent personages. Few wedding ceremonies in this New World, before or since, attracted such attention as did ours." Sensing that Mercer was beginning to show a trace of ennui, he digressed. "I'm sorry. I don't suppose you are interested too much in that portion of my preparation for surgery."

"Your supposition is entirely correct, Doctor."

"I can appreciate that your lack of understanding of such matters is undoubtedly due to your never having been a part of them," Grainger retorted.

"I don't believe that, by any stretch of imagination, your so-called verbal surgery requires or dictates a comparison of our pedigrees, but if that should be true, mine would compare most favorably with yours!" Barth checked further words, determined to contain himself. It was becoming evident that Doctor Grainger had not administered all of his stock of whiskey to Willie Roller.

"I'll not debate the point, Mercer. Suffice to say, your pedigree is important. Indeed, it is the raison d'être for this operation, however presuming it may be on my part to make you a captive listener."

Mercer did not answer, and he continued. "Well, to make this narrative germane, we were married, and we were very happy together those first years of our union and until my services became in such demand that I was required to be absent from our home in Boston for more or less extended periods. I had no fear for Drusilla's safety or her care while I was away for I knew that Chate would tend to her wants completely, and that he would protect her with his life, in the extreme. I did miss her terribly. And I am sure, during the earliest of my medical excursions, that she grieved for my company. The warmth of her greeting upon my return and its profundity assured me of that. But later on, returning from addressing a society of surgeons in Philadelphia, on one occasion, her attentions impressed me as being forced. So obvious was this quality that I asked her what was wrong, and despite all of her strong assertions to the contrary, my fears would not be allayed. This happened after each successive trip I made thereafter. At length, I planned a journey and at the last minute cancelled it, hoping that this might force her hand to disclose any knave of hearts she might have been holding back from our game of love and marriage, for such it had become . . . that was a nice analogy I made there; about the knave of hearts, I mean."

Barth made no comment and any complimentary expression, which Grainger may have anticipated from him, was not forthcoming.

Undismayed, the doctor continued. "I thought perhaps Chate might be able to inform me concerning Drusilla's actions, but I might just have well consulted the Great Sphinx of the pyramids. His loyalty is equally divided between the two of us—an exact balance on the scale of affection. You know, Mercer, we are cognizant of Chate's birth into bondage, but we have never considered him as a slave. If more of you people would trust your Blacks in that fashion, their lot would be far less severe."

"Doctor, you are digressing again."

The firmness of Mercer's tone had its desired effect. "As I was saying, I uncovered nothing of any affair that Drusilla was having. I needn't have tried, for as it turned out, she, herself, told me of her first lover—a gentleman lately come from England. I confronted him forthwith. I challenged him to meet me on the field of honor, and he accepted. I let him fire first, a miss. Then I shot him directly in his adulterous heart. I can see his prostrate form lying there, this minute, with the mist rising about it in the dawn." Grainger paused in retrospect. "Then this confounded revolution broke out. I was resolved to remain neutral and I wished to offer my services to both armies, but His Majesty's officers preempted them. There followed days when I would seldom see my wife, and truthfully, since I had killed my adversary in the duel, she cared but little whether she saw me or not. She never said anything about it to me, but I knew that while I had killed her lover, I had not killed her love—that's another nice selection of words, don't you agree?"

His solicitation again fell on deaf ears. It was clear that the liquor had indeed taken something of the doctor's discretion.

"My future life was decided not too long after my service began as a surgeon for the Crown. I learned that Drusilla was having an affair with one of my former colleagues—a Doctor James Lansdowne, of noble lineage by the way. He had not deigned to avail his medical services to either side, so he was free to use his time in other matters. In other more enjoyable pursuits, shall we say?

"As before, with the first one, I accused him, and he denied the charge with all vehemence. He could not refuse me satisfaction, and he did not do so. I killed him as I had the other, and saw the blood cascade over his lying tongue and lips onto the green turf where lay his head. This happening caused great friction, both in the society in which we moved and among the fellow members of my profession. Lansdowne was quite popular and it followed, logically, that it was seen to that I was ordered elsewhere by the military. I saved some peace of mind by insisting, and having my demands met, that Drusilla and Chate be permitted to accompany me wherever I was assigned."

Barth noted that this portion of his narration had a sobering effect upon the doctor.

"But with Drusilla, it was the same thing all over again. If they were not serious affairs, they were strong flirtations And the realization came to me that I could not kill or even flog every man in whom she showed an interest. Still, and as I am yet determined, I would not give her up. I cherished her and hoped for her eventual renunciation of her ways. Finally, I came to the decision to leave His Majesty's service. We moved on out into the settlements: Chambersburg, Bedford, and to those between and beyond, until we reached Pittsburgh. There again, there were gentlemen moving about. There, again, were flirtations and affairs. I had just about despaired of Drusilla regaining her self control and my love. You know, Mercer, there is a vast difference between the words cherish and love. It was then that I became convinced of the truth of Rochefoucauld's philosophy: 'In her first passion a woman loves her lover; in all the rest, she loves only love.' I don't believe that quotation to be verbatim, but that is its substance.

"At Pittsburgh, I first heard of Bullitt's Lick, or Saltsburg as some have denominated it. I felt that in this faraway place, so fully populated with the lower element of society, that maybe my wife could save herself. She is a proud woman, Mercer, and would never allow herself to become interested in anyone but a true gentleman. That is the only safeguard left her; the only ideal that she still clings to and respects. Anyway, we went to Redstone Old Fort on the Monongahela, and from there we traveled by boat to Falls of the Ohio. We followed the trace from there to the licks. We have been here for almost two years, and if they have not been happy years, there at least has been none of the torment that I suffered before we came."

"And what of Mrs. Grainger? How has she been?" Barth asked pointedly.

"We have come to the point of incision, Captain. The knife is in my hand. You remember a little while back in my conversation, you made brief mention of your pedigree and doubted its pertinency?"

Barth now caught the full import of the verbal surgery and nodded his head.

"Well, I will begin the operation. You are the first person, approximating at least, if you don't fully meet Drusilla's standards. Others of your standing may have passed through here, or she may have seen them, but you are the first she has met in formal fashion."

"But, Grainger, there was no outward incident connected with our introduction. You, yourself, made it."

"I know, I know, Mercer. Perhaps there was nothing unusual in your actions at the time, but I caught the look in her eye as she acknowledged meeting you. It was a spark from all those fires of the past. I know it was ignited at that moment because she has asked that I invite you to dine with us."

"I assure you I would decline any such invitation, Doctor."

"I want you to accept, Captain Mercer. I believe you would not encourage her after hearing the case history in this operation."

"Do you think that your talk of the killing of those two men would act as a deterrent?"

"Frankly, Mercer, I do not. It might have done so with others I could have told this story to, but not with you; not if I have sized you up correctly."

"I am pleased that you at least have given me my due in that respect, Doctor. We might have saved all this baring of the past life of your wife and yourself had you come directly to the point. I still say, you stayed your hand. I'm no doctor, but I don't find it requisite that I tell you of my past life; for, sir, being just as frank as you are, I'll tell you that it's none of your damned business. And I say that, and mean that, strongly enough to face you and your damned bragged-over ability with your dueling pistols."

The veins in Grainger's temples were swollen and his fists clenched so tightly that the blood drained from his fingertips.

Barth ignored the doctor's arousal and sped the flow of his speech. "I want no part of your troubles with your wife; I want no part of being an actor on your confused stage. I have a woman whom I love dearly and whom I intend to marry in the not-too-distant future. Your wife may be a goddess to you, and that is as it should be. What I would have done, had I been in your boots, is not for me to say. And if it was I would not be interested enough to say it! Good night, sir!"

Grainger remonstrated, but before he could rise, Barth walked away, back to his former table.

Johnny saw him as he came and promptly went back into his self-imposed exile.

As Barth seated himself, Rosie exclaimed, although in an undertone, "I thought for a while there was goin' to be trouble 'twixt you and Doctor Grainger! What was he sayin' to you?"

"It was rather provoking; I'd rather not say anything about it." Barth's answer left her curiosity in a strictly ambulatory state, but she accepted his words, resignedly.

Abby's inquisitiveness was less restrained. "Captain, we were all so excited! You've jest simply got to tell us. Was it somethin' 'bout Mrs. Grainger? I'm 'fraid I'll bust wide open if you don't tell me!"

Barth noted Abby's full bosom, and contemplated the effect were she to actually do so . . . Chuckling at the thought, he merely said, "Reckon you'll just have to go ahead and bust."

Rosie gave Abby one of her sternest glances, and she subsided.

Before anyone else could say anything, Barth asked, "What in tarnation is the matter with Johnny?"

Rosie explained it all. When she had finished, Barth laughed, as he said, "Isn't that just like a little boy?"

Johnny couldn't hear all that was said, but he surmised he was the subject of discussion, and this only seemed to deepen the feeling that be had been shamefully wronged.

Barth was talking to Tom Chism. Inadvertently, he raised his head at the same time that Grainger was leaving his table. The latter walked straight toward them as though he intended to say something, but changing his mind, turned and walked out of the place.

Rosie pulled a check-rein on the night's affairs.

"Hate to end this pleasant evenin', but we all best be gettin' to th' feathers. It's gettin' late."

Barth called to Johnny, asking if he were coming with him, and Johnny stubbornly shook his head.

"Well, Tom, I guess you and I will have to brave the great outdoors by ourselves," Barth joked.

Johnny made another wry face and turned his head.

As they walked along, Barth asked, "Tom, you might be able to tell me something. Have you ever observed Mace's operations—particularly, have you seen him ship any salt, say, in the last six or eight months?"

Tom studied. "His wagons an' packtrains go out, same as ours. Of course, they have canvas covers over th' tops, but so far as I can tell, they have moved right regular. I heard tell he ships some down Salt River on boats, or so them that works for him claims he does. 'Course, I have never made no point to check 'im."

Barth mulled over this. If the salt had been shipped, what had become of the money? He didn't believe for one second Mace's explanation when he had questioned him on that score. He was certain that the records he would see in the morning would reveal nothing. There would be records kept from here on; he would see to that. As he gave the matter of bookkeeping further thought, he tried to think of someone who could handle the work. Of the few persons whom he knew here, only Rosie might be able to do it. She seemed intelligent, and from his few conversations with her, he believed she could be taught what she was to do and how it should be done. There was an obstacle, however. That of one woman being among such a rough bunch of men.

Tom, aware of Barth's silence, asked, "What you thinkin' about? That matter with Doc Grainger?"

Shaking his head, Barth told him of his concern about keeping accurate records, and of his inability to come up with anyone for the job except Rosie.

"Rosie Tindall ain't th' one. She might could handle it, but she wouldn't last five minutes if she was to try it, which I doubt."

"Well, do you know of anyone who could do that kind of work?"

"There's one feller could—if he'd do it."

"Who's that?"

"Aaron Flinden. He can do most anything. He's honest and he'll mind his own business; same time, he'll take good care of your'n."

"Good. Do you think you can arrange for me to meet him and talk to him about it?"

"It won't be no trouble for that. When was you reckoning to see him?"

"The sooner the better. I had figured on meeting you tomorrow and checking your operations, after I had examined the records at Mace's."

"'Fraid I can't 'commodate you tomorrow. I got salt movin' out."

"How about the next day then?"

"That'd be fine. An' after we have done enough lookin' to suit you, we can go see Brother Flinden. By th' way, how's it come that you are gonna get th' bookkeeper for Mace's works?"

Barth, recognizing the apparent inconsistency, covered as best he could. "Why, that comes under my authority from the Continental Army."

"You mean, because of that scrap of parchmint you showed me, you would do that at my place if you took a mind to?"

"That is about it, Tom."

"Well, I'll tell you one thing for sure, Mercer: I hope you don't try it. You'll need the Army to help you do it."

Sensing the hostility that had been aroused in Tom's mind, Barth decided to chance it. "Tom, I like you, and I believe you're far and above the rest of the men at these licks. I think I can trust you, and that you won't betray my trust. You are dead right in what you just said. The reason I'm so interested in those records at Mace's is that those works belong to me. Now, you have the full picture."

"Well, I'll be damned!"

"Now you know why I want a good man for that job."

"Brother Flinden's th' man, if, as I said before, he'll take it."

"Just one thing, Tom. Keep this a secret; I mean, about my owning the works."

"You've got my word."

"That's good enough for me."

They were nearing the place where their paths must part.

"Roller and Middleton will do all right, I hope," said Barth.

"Since the works belong to you, you can make sure of that."

"You're forgetting, Tom, that they don't know that fact, and I'm hoping they won't know about it for some time to come."

"You can depend on me. I mcan it."

"I'm certain of that, but I don't think Roller or Middleton want anything more to do with Mace. They wouldn't work for him again, assuming that he'd take them back, which, of course, I could arrange."

"I see what you mean. How are they gonna live then? Grainger told me it'll take a month 'fore even Davey Middleton can do anything. No tellin' how long it'll be, 'fore Willie can be any good—if he makes it."

"Tom, I want you to hire the two of them—pay them every week."

"Wait now! I feel for them two, right strong—more'n anybody else, mebbe; but I just can't pay none that don't do no work."

"I understand that, Tom. I'm going to pay their hire, but you'll give their pay to them. It's up to you to figure how you can get them to take the money. I don't know the two of them, but it's my opinion they won't be very willing to accept any charity."

"That's right, Cap'n. That's th' way they are."

"Well, you see what you can do about it. I'll see you, day after tomorrow."

"Good night, Cap'n, and say, I'm glad there's plenty of business for us all."

"Good night, Tom. I'll see you later on."

Aa they parted, Chism said to himself, I was sure right about Mercer.

Barth pushed open the cabin door and lit a taper. He missed Johnny, not being there with him. Funny how you can get attached to anyone in such a short time, he thought, and as he looked at Johnny's feather kivver, he smiled, and the words ran through his mind: So old the man; so young the boy.

CHAPTER 9

The time was at hand. The guards had taken true and full advantage of Mace's no imatashun and free likker. The two of them near the storehouse were stretched out, fan shaped, upon the ground. Most of the salt stored there had been moved, leaving just enough for effect. Bad-Eye carried a brand from one of the nearest furnaces and started a small blaze in each corner of the room. The dry firewood he had ignited soon surged into tangent fires. As he opened the door, the draft shot the flames to the ceiling rafters.

He ran hurriedly from the storehouse, as fast as he could for a while, and then dropped into a dogtrot.

Ahead lay Kahaz, and temporary sanctuary. At length he slowed to a fast walk, and finally, at the first light of false dawn, he reached the base of the knob, where he sat down and rested. A light drizzle had begun sometime back, but had not since increased in its intensity.

Jeddy-Boy had obeyed his father's instructions with but one variation: he did not follow after Bad-Eye, but instead arrived at the knob ahead of him. His keen ears had picked up instantly the sound of Bad-Eye's approaching feet. Soon thereafter, he made out the moving form of his victim.

When Bad-Eye stopped to rest, Jed was but a short distance away to his left. It would have been a simple matter to have killed him where he sat. But that would have been too easy. Jeddy-Boy wanted to have some sport with him.

Smith sat there until he felt rested; then he arose resolutely and picked up his rifle and started the ascent.

The knob was timbered heavily all the way to its top. There was no trail to follow, and the new foliage of the trees prevented little of the semi-light of the early morning from reaching the ground. Heavy, tangled undergrowth, dampened by the still falling rain, added to the difficulties attendant any passage. Bad-Eye's progress was one of stepping forward and slipping back, of vines winding themselves about his feet and legs at the same time and then alternately. Finally, he worked his way near to what he judged to be about midway. There were hunters' lean-tos up there somewhere, he knew, for he had been there last fall with one of Mace's hunters. If he could but be sure, he would be more at ease. A little farther on, he came upon a small clearing.

Now he was certain he knew his way. Again, he rested; this time with his back against a large chestnut-oak. It was dry there, and he stayed longer than he intended.

He thought back to his previous trip up Kahaz Knob, or Cahill's Knob as some called it. Here he was, with his back resting on a chestnut-oak, which might well be the same one the Wyandots had tied Cahill to, after they had blackened his face for death. Those dead pitch-pine branches might have been part of the very ones the savages had piled at Cahill's feet, preparatory to burning him. Cahill had been saved when some oxen, let out to graze, wandered through the underbrush. The Indians heard the noise and under the belief that more white men were coming, ran away. Cahill quickly freed himself from his bonds and escaped.

The sound of movement to Smith's immediate front alerted him. Was this more oxen? Indians? Pursuers? What or who was there?

He jumped up, rifle in position, his back to the tree. His heart was racing, and he strained his one eye to its utmost, trying to see anything that might betray the slightest movement. Though day was coming on, the little light allowed him was only a haze. His throat was tight; his lips were dry. He held his breath in spurts, in an extreme effort to sharpen his hearing, but the pounding of his heart lessened any added keenness he might have hoped to gain. His arms suddenly felt heavy and his legs weak and trembling. Absolute fear enveloped him.

Now the chorus of the morning chirping of the birds was so loud he could hear but little else.

Maybe it was Willie Roller or Davey Middleton or both of them! Here reason took over. Roller might not be dead, but if he wasn't, he was not up from his bed nor was Middleton. "I fixed them two sons-uv-bitches, good!" He startled himself when he spoke the words. Finding the effect reassuring, he continued speaking his thoughts. "I'll do real good, I will. Mace thinks I'm a'comin' back here." Bad-Eye laughed. "Thet bullyin' bastard son-uv-a-bitch'll hev hesself a hell uv a long squat, if he sets an' waits fer me to ever come back to thet stinkin' rat hole."

"Mebbe hit hain't gonner be fer as long as yer a-thinkin."

The words came from out of nowhere, from no distinct direction; but he heard them. Someone was somewhere out there but where in the hell was he?

To bind what little courage he had left, Bad-Eye spoke to himself again. "Yore jest 'maginin' heerin' them words. Hain't nuthin' er nobuddy anywheres near yuh."

"Near 'nough ter kill yer."

Bad-Eye lost all control of his nerves and fired wildly, sending the resultant echo on its redundant course. Forgettin' the security of his position, he struggled blindly up the inclined way, tearing loose from the hindering growth, falling over unseen logs, but returning upright as though the fear itself was a spring pushing him up. Now, he stopped and tried to listen above the tumult of his heart and brain. But his ears were filled with the humming noise inside. Then the voice came from squarely in front of him.

"Guv me yer money bag, Bad-Eye!" The playing was over; the sport was about to end.

Through the maze of his fear-instilled confusion, there filtered through to Bad-Eye the recognition of the voice. "Hit's you, Jeddy-Boy! Hit's you! Hit wuz yore voice all th' time! You shore hed yore fun, di'ntcha? A-scarin' me 'most to death!" And as calmness returned a little nerve, he asked, "Whut's th' matter? Mace change his mind—wants me to come on back?"

Jeddy-Boy, the light now a little brighter, moved toward him, fingering his knife with both hands. "Mace don't want ter see yer, no mores—never. He had me ter kum follerin' yer, ter be shore uv thet."

Bad-Eye made his arms raise his rifle, screaming, "I'll kill you, ya murderin' bastard!" He pulled the trigger only to hear it snap with a dull, empty click.

"Fergot yer fired back yonder, di'ntcher, Bad-Eye?" Jed laughed, gleefully. "Now, han' over yer money-bag."

Selfishness was strong where courage was weak, and took its place in Bad-Eye's makeup. "Yuh'll hev to take it frum me, damn you!" He made a desperate effort to draw his knife, but it caught in its sheath.

The next instant, Jed had hold of him. "Yer din't heer me so gud, so I'm a-goin' ter jest slice off thet damn left ear uv yern—open hit up some. If'n yer wuz livin', yer mought cud heer better; but yer hain't goin' ter be."

Bad-Eye's face was drained of all blood; the ghoulish white standing out in the half light. His one eye stared straight ahead, seeing nothing. This, coupled with the empty, darkened socket of the other, and his sagging jaw, made out a living skull. He struggled backward, tripped and fell. Jed had to release his hold in order to keep his own balance.

Bad-Eye did not move, and when Jeddy-Boy cut off his ear, he made no sound. When the tomahawk cleaved his skull, and Jed took his scalp, little blood flowed. Bad-Eye had cheated Jeddy-Boy; he had died of fright.

The murderer forced the pouch from the dead man's hand. He emptied it and counted its contents; then he turned and leisurely made his way down the hill.

There lay Cuthbert Smith, born in the squalid, crowded slums of London. Now, at the end, dead on a tree-covered hill far across the sea and miles inland from its shore. The heart, which had performed so valiantly to feed his brain and move his limbs in other times of stress and danger, at last had failed him. The heart that had sustained him through a thieving youth, the gauntlets of arrests, trials, and imprisonments in England that failed to weaken when he murdered, which moved him on from Newgate and Old Bailey prisons to freedom in the New World as an indentured criminal, that spurred his cunning to steal his Carolina master's savings and make his way to Pennsylvania and Fort Pitt, that heart, which had carried him safely past the alarms of Indians to the comparative safety of Bullitt's Lick, now pulsed no more.

CHAPTER 10

At the first glow, the furnace tenders left their fires and rushed to the storehouse. There was nothing they could do. Bad-Eye had performed his task well. Acknowledging this, they went back to their own fires and watched the structure burn.

The heat was so intense as to cause the drunken guards to rouse themselves and stagger away; their incoherent minds, forgetting that the burning had been planned, cautioned them only to save themselves. This having been accomplished, they slept as before.

A light breeze wafted the billowing smoke toward the settlement. In a matter of minutes, the cry was passed: "Fire! Fire at th' licks." Soon it resounded from Mud Garrison, nearly a mile away. The settlers were rushing to the scene like a poorly trained army in a charge, their weapons in hand, on the off chance that this might be an Indian raid.

Barth first heard the rumble of running feet, then sensed the smoke. Finally, he became fully awakened by the panic-breeding alarm. He dressed rapidly and joined the hurrying throng. As he gained his first, far glimpse, he was relieved to note that there appeared to be but one structure aflame. Drawing nearer, he saw it was the storehouse. Fortunately, it had been built well out in front of the line of the other buildings—the farrier's, cooper shop, stables, the firewood shelter and several others whose use was as yet unknown to him The flames were being carried in an almost opposite direction by the wind, now up a little from formerly.

Mace was storming at everyone within the sound of his voice when Barth reached him.

"How'd it start?"

"Don't rightly know yet, less'n hit wuz thet Bad-Eye; he hain't 'round nowheres. Must uv bin set, this un. Cuddn't no place go up all at onc't lik'n this'n done."

"What about the guards? When did they first notice it?"

"Cap'n, them ornery, drunken bastards hain't knowed uv hit yet. They's still a-sleepin' out yonder." He pointed in their general direction.

"How about the other buildings—they safe?"

"They be all right, I b'leeve. Jest in case, tho', I got men a-drenchin' down th' sides an' roofs."

""That ought to be good enough, unless there's a shift in the wind; then I don't know. Better have a bunch lined up with extra buckets, on the ready."

"Yes, sir, Cap' n."

No sooner had Mace gone to carry out Barth's directions than Barth felt a tug on the sleeve of his jacket. As he turned, he saw that it was Johnny.

"H' ya, Kepteen? Howza fire?"

"I'd say it has been a pretty good one, Johnny."

"Yew mad at me, Kepteen? Be I still yore depity?"

"I thought you quit last night, Johnny. You know a man can't be worrying about whether or not he has a deputy. He either has one or he doesn't. If he has to spend half of his time cajoling him, he'd be lots better off without him.'"

"Yew mean yew don't hanker to hev me as yore 'sistant, no more?" The brightness of the fire revealed a downcast Johnny.

"I didn't say that exactly. I'm sorta going to put you on probation. We'll see how you do for a while. You understand?"

"I shore does, Kepteen! Jest one thing tho'. Whut does kajolin' an' probashun mean?"

Barth turned his head away from him and laughed. Recovering, he said, "Never mind about that now. You scout around and see what you can pick up about how this thing got started."

"Yes sir, Kepteen," said Deputy Littelby.

The fire had simmered down, although there were still hungry arms of red enveloping the lower part of the storehouse—all that remained of what had been a story and a half of construction. Watching as it burned itself out, it reminded Barth of the back logs in a huge fireplace. A snatch of flame and a sputter; another attempt and the crimson streak took hold again; then it would disappear only to come back as before.

Rain began to fall, in almost caressing fashion. The red arms struggled the harder against their one master. Each drop produced a hissing and resultant vapor. The fire would cause no further trouble or damage.

"Reckin' thet's as fur as she'll go, Cap'n." It was Mace again.

"Find out anything more?"

"Yep, Cap'n, hit 'pears I wuz right th' fust time. One uv them furniss tenders say he seen Bad-Eye runnin' an' then th' next thing he knowed, the fire wuz a-roarin'.'"

"Why would Bad-Eye want to burn the storehouse down?"

"Dunno, less'n hit wuz 'cause I wuz a li'l rough with him, after whut he done ter pore Willie Roller an' Davey Middleton yestiddy. Now hit seems I remembers 'im sayin' as how he'd git hisse'f even with me." Mace scratched his head. "He knowed these here works hain't mine—kain't see how he'd figger he wuz hurtin' me none, does yer?"

"There's no accounting for some men's motives," Barth replied, looking him straight in the face.

Mace attempted to ignore the inference, but was not wholly successful.

"Reckin there'll be no checkin' uv th' records, now, will there, Cap'n? That damned Smith, him a-settin' thet fire after me a-workin' gettin' them records shipshape. Damn thet ornery hide uv hiss'n clean ter hell."

"The fire took care of the records, Mr. Hardin, regardless of how it was started."

""Thet's fer shore, Cap'n; thet's fer shore."

"One thing. Wasn't there some salt stored in there? Did it burn too?"

"Yer know, Cap'n, hit's a funny thing, but I hed th' men load most uv whut wuz in there, figgered yer'd want ter git it shipped outer here."

"Well, that's one piece of good news at least."

"Got yew some more good news, Kepteen," Johnny had rushed up at the tail end of the conversation. "I heared one of th ' men sayin' he seen thet one they calls Bad-Eye a-runnin' frum th' storehouse a minit 'fore th' damn thing started a-burnin'. Thet's purty good, ain't it? Leastways, we know whut one done hit."

"Good work, Johnny. That coincides with what I've learned."

"Whut's thet mean, Kepteen?"

"Means it's the same thing I found out from Mr. Hardin here."

"Oh, shore," said Johnny.

The echo of a distant rifle shot rolled to their ears.

Mace was the first to speak. "Sounded like hit kum frum over 'roun' Kahaz Knob." He pointed northwesterly.

"Injuns!" Johnny exclaimed.

"Hardly, Johnny. What do you make of it, Mr. Hardin?"

"No tellin', Cap'n. Mought be one uv th' hunters; but I kain't figger them bein' out this hour uv th' mornin'." Noticing someone passing them just then, Mace said, "This hyar light hain't as bright as 'twuz 'fore th' fire let down, but I'm thinkin' thet's Abe Foster as jest went bye."

"Thet yer, Abe?" Mace called after him.

"Yup. Who's a-callin'?"

"Me, Mace Hardin."

"Whut yer wantin'?"

"Kum back a spell."

As Mace had observed, the light was none too good, and about all that Barth could glean of Abe Foster when Mace introduced him was that he was a big man with a deep voice.

"Yer heer thet gun sound, Abe, a minit back?" Mace asked

"Yup."

"Whut yer thinks hit wuz? Reckin' hit's a hunter?"

Abe Foster shook his head. "Tain't none uv mine, an' I doubts as it's eny uv yores."

"Hain't mine," asserted Mace, "Mine's most all 'roun' this hyar fire."

"Who yew reckin' it is?" asked Johnny.

"No tellin'," said Abe, and passed on into the mingled groups of settlers who still watched the fading flames.

Barth thought a moment, then said, "Mr. Hardin, get these people back to their homes. It's beginning to get light, and we've got a right smart of cleaning up to take care of."

"Hit's all done, folks. Th' cap'n here says hit's time yer wuz gittin' back to whar yer comes frum. Le's git movin' now!"

They withdrew, reluctantly, with mumblings against the order. Only then did Barth realize that this fire was about the closest thing to a community gathering that they had ever experienced. It was an event that would be as much discussed and commented upon hereafter as was the bad winter of '79. The fire would become part of the history of the Lick.

Just then Johnny, Rosie, and Abby approached him. Unthinkingly, Barth asked, "Is Tom Chism with you all?" Catching himself, he answered his own question. "No, I reckon not. Not with the way he feels about Mace Hardin."

"Thet's kerrect, Kepteen, he ain't." Johnny was full of his 'thority again. "I bin a-showin' 'em th' fire."

"Ain't it grand about Johnny's findin' out for you that Smith done th' settin' of the fire?"

Barth put a concealing hand to his mouth. "Johnny's been a big help, Rosie, a real big help to me. I'm sorry, but I have to break away from you folks. Johnny, you see that they get home and then you hurry right back here. There's lots of work to be done."

"Yes, sir, Kepteen. Y'all come 'long now."

As they drew out of earshot, Barth managed to hear Johnny say, proudly, "Yew heer whut he sed 'bout me, Rosie?"

Only a few scattered groups remained when the true light of dawn broke through what at first had apparently prophesied a gloomy morning. The rain had ceased shortly before. Mace was trying to convince Barth that Bad-Eye should be pursued.

"Mr. Hardin, Smith is probably miles from here now. He might have gone in any of a number of directions. Frankly, I see no point in following him; he'll certainly not come back here. This would be the last place he'd return to. I hate to see the storehouse destroyed, but catching Smith is not going to rebuild it. I want it replaced right away."

"Course, Cap'n, an' I'll hev it back, all done 'fore three days frum now; facts ez, I done guv orders fer th' startin' uv hit, already." He glanced to Barth for approval of his foresight, but none came, and he continued. "But whut yer over-lookin', Cap'n, beggin' yer pardin, uv course, is thet if'n Bad-Eye gits 'way with thet burnin', ever mother-hatin' son-uv-a-bitch'll be tryin' ter see whut he kin do, an git away with. Why, them bastards'll be stealin' th' salt, th' next thing we knows."

"That's your job, to see that they keep in line, Mr. Hardin."

"Thet I knows, Cap'n, I'm oney a-sayin' this ter hep me keep 'em thet way. With thet rain whut fell, we cud pick up Bad-Eye's trail in no time. I'd git Abe Foster an' some more an' if'n they kain't fine him, then it'd be jest as yer says, oney th' rest uv 'em 'ud be knowin' if'n they done suthin', they'd be follered. If'n they fines Smith, thet'd be th' more better."

Barth remained of his original opinion, however, one thing intrigued him. Mace seemed too anxious to track down Bad-Eye. This finally led him to give his consent. "All right, we'll see if we can catch him."

Mace gave a slight smile of satisfaction.

"Who all will be in the party, Mr. Hardin?"

"Abe Foster, Martin Willerhorst, Herman Tressel, Albert Prather, Virgil Mallory, Justin Gibbs an' a few mores! 'Course, I 'speck yer'll want ter go too, won'tcher?"

Mercer noted the rapidity with which the names rolled off Mace's tongue. He was convinced that Mace had a purpose for pushing the manhunt. "Isn't Abe Foster Tom Chism's chief hunter? How do you figure to get him to do this for you?"

"Thet's jest hit, Cap'n. I figgers yer cud hev li'l Johnny run git him ter guv his 'greement ter do hit, you bein on guvmint bizness an' all."

"I see," said Barth. "I'll send Johnny to talk to Chism about it."

Johnny no sooner returned than he was dispatched to Tom Chism's. Sitting beside the driver of the wagon, he looked like nothing less than a general at the head of his troops.

Meanwhile, Mace got hold of Abe Foster and told him to wait, pending the granting of the desired permission. The others named to complete the search party were hastily gathered. A short time later, Johnny was back with Tom Chism's sanction for the use of Abe Foster's services.

Still striving to follow the straw directly into the wind, Barth asked Mace, "Mr. Hardin, where do you believe is the most likely starting point?"

"Cap'n, I leave thet hup ter Abe Foster. He knows hit all when hit kums ter trackin' critters er hoomans. But I 'speck if'n I wuz a-doin' th' sayin', yer unner-stan', I'd make me tracks fer th' Kahaz Knob out yonder. Yer 'members we'uns heerd thet shot, back a time this mornin'?" Barth nodded, and he continued. "I hain't a-sayin' thet's whar he be, but it be good 'nough ter try fust."

Barth was certain now that Bad-Eye, if he wasn't still on the knob, surely had passed over or around it. Mace had told him that much.

"What do you think of Mr. Hardin's idea, Mr. Foster?"

"'Twon't be a-doin' no harm ter try that, fust. Yer needn't call me no mister, Cap'n. I be jest plain Abe."

"All right, Abe."

This nettled Mace. It required all of his self-control when Mercer addressed him as Mr. Hardin. The time was soon coming when he'd make Mercer wish he'd never heard of that Mr. Hardin. This consolation alone kept Mace subject to his own discipline.

"Mr. Hardin," Barth's tone was curt. "Mr. Littelby is my deputy, and while I'm gone, I want him respected as such. I've told him a few things I want checked. See that your men cooperate with him."

Mace all but blew up; his face reddened, and he clenched his hands into fists. All he said, however, was, "Yes, Cap'n."

Little Johnny swelled up like a bloated toad. 'Thority, at last! And th' kepteen had called him Mister Littelby! His features still showed the effects of Mace's beating; but they never looked happier than at this moment.

The manhunters moved off. Abe Foster and Barth in the lead, the others behind them in a straggled file.

Mace called the furnace bosses together. Standing to the right and behind Johnny, he said in a serious manner, "Men, this here's Little Johnny, er I means Mister Littelby." Johnny didn't like the way Mace accented the mister, but he stood there, clothed in all his 'thority, as Mace continued. "Th' cap'n's 'struct-shuns wuz thet he's ter be considered th' same liken we does him." Mace gave a knowing smile and winked at his men. "Y'all git thet straight now?"

The bosses made it clear that they understood, some smiling openly.

"Wal, sence they hain't no wonderin' who's th' boss," Mace winked again, "I got ter git ter my place fer a spell. See thet yers guv Mister Littelby whut's kumin' ter him as th' cap'n's dep'ty."

Jeddy-Boy was waiting for his father and met him outside the cabin.

"Didjer take keer uv im, proper?" were Mace's first word.

"I done hit jest liken yer tole me."

"How I know yer did?"

"I figgered thet mought be yer thinkin'. Here's his damn sculp an' his ear ter prove hit ter yer."

Mace fingered the ear and looked closely at the scalp. "Wal, fer onc't I reckin' yer done whut I tole yer. Thet's Bad-Eye's hair, a'right. Y'know, he wuz damned near balded enyhow, shuddn't a-bothered him none too much loosin' thet li'l patch uv hair whut went with th' sculp, yer reckin?"

They both laughed, but Mace sobered quickly. "Whar's th' money?"

Jed was evasive. "Whut were hit, Pap—how much yer guv 'im?"

"Han' me th' poutch, Jed, afore I guv yer this hyar." He doubled his fist.

"Now, look, Pap, I done whut yer tole me, din't I? I got th' moneybag, but they's more'n whut yer sed yer guv 'im. Seein' as how I done hit, I figgers whut's over orter be mine by rights."

"Wal, han' hit over, an' I'll let yer hev th' leavin's."

"Don't want no leavin's, Pap. I wants whut's over whut you guv 'im."

"Ha'right, I guv 'im twenny pieces uv sharp silver."

"Yer a-lyin', Pap. They wuzn't thet much on 'im. Yer told me afore, yer guv 'im eight."

"How much, then?"

"Yer will hev ter tell me, Pap."

"A'right, Jeddy-Boy, but I hain't fergittin' this here high-hand stuff uv yer'n."

"How much, Pap?"

"Eight pieces, an' they's all good an' cl'ar, ever' damn one uv 'em."

Jeddy-Boy selected eight coins and handed them to his father.

"How I know them's th' cl'arest an' th' sharpest uv th' lot?"

"Y'don't, Pap, but I'm a-willin' ter leave yer look at th' rest uv 'em."

Mace put out his open hand, but Jed wasn't through talking. "Fust, hand th' ones I guv yer back."

Clutching the eight silver pieces lightly in one hand, Jed handed the pouch to Mace, who promptly emptied it. Five coins fell in Mace's palm for his scrutiny.

"Guess yer did guv me th' best, at thet, Jeddy-Boy."

"Course, Pap. Yer knows I wuddn't cheat yer, if'n yer wuz a-lookin'." They both laughed.

"Jest one more thing, Jed," Mace was in earnest again, "Burry thet damned ear an' th' sculpt right aways. Hit'd be jest like yer ter be a-foolin' with 'em in frunt uv Mercer er someun els't. Right now, yer unnerstan'?"

Jed nodded his agreement, and Mace said, "Heerd a shot, back a time 'fore I set 'em after Bad-Eye. Seemed ter kum frum Kahaz—yer heer hit?"

"Thet wuz Bad-Eye, Pap. He wuz a mought nerviss, I reckin."

They both laughed again.

CHAPTER 11

Abe Foster strode easily along. Barth tried his best to match his stride, but had difficulty in keeping up with him. There had been no talk between Abe and himself, although the others in the rear kept up a running line of chatter, punctuated by frequent guffaws. It was apparent to Barth that if there were to be any conversation with Abe, he would have to start it. Just as he had determined to take the initiative, Abe spoke, halting the party as he did so. "Hyar's whar we'uns split hup. Me an' th' cap'n'll be together. Th' rest uv yers git out on th' sides uv us. Spread yorese'fs, so's ter kiver th' most yer kin."

They were at a point just beyond the last of the salt wells, moving toward the knob. Barth took this opportunity to talk to Abe. "How many of those men do you think can track anything?"

"That mought be a few uv 'em kin, Cap'n. Course, they's all woodsmen uv sorts, ya know, but fer real trackin', none uv 'em shapes hup."

"I had it figured out like that."

"Whut fer yer ask'n'? 'Tain't gonna make no diffrunce. I'll prob'ly fine th' tracks m'se'f. Course, hit ain't no bad idee; jest in case thar mought be Injuns about."

"That's true," Barth replied.

The sun was out now, and the day was clear. Kahaz Knob loomed before them like a vast, green hump. The breeze brought a strong odor of pipe smoke pungently to Barth's nostrils.

"Who's smoking that strong bowl?"

Abe grinned. "Prob'ly Herman Tressel. He's th' farrier fer Mace; kin do other things too. He kin cooper, handle horses liken he war one uv 'em, an' he kin use a adze with th' best thar be. Thet thar pipe he's a-smokin' is suthin' too. He war kotched by th' Injuns onc't an' they kep' him nigh onter a year til they wuz a pris'ners 'change. Him an' th' Chief got ter be frens, an' when he got 'im free, why he guv 'im a piece uv gold fer a present. Reckin' he'd a guv 'im a tommyhawk in his head, if'n he'd a-knowed Herman had stole his peace pipe." Abe chuckled, then shouted, "Keep a-lookin' sharp thar, men."

"You mean," Barth asked, "that pipe he's smoking was the peace pipe?"

"Yup, th' same. 'Cep'n he cut th' stem down some. Uh-oh, whut's this I sees?" Abe was all tracker now.

Peering closely, Barth could discern nothing of any significance. But Abe's keen, experienced eyes were not to be fooled.

"See hit? See hit?"

Barth still saw nothing but the ground. Abe sat on his haunches and pointed with his finger. "Thet thar's a fresh mocksin print. Wuz Bad-Eye a-wearin' mocksins?"

Barth didn't know, but another of the group answered.

"He wuz wearin' boots; thet ain't his'n."

Off to the right, Albert Prather called. "Abe, I b'leeve I picked 'im up."

Prather proved to be correct, and as Abe rose after verifying the find, he said to the others, "Now, we divides up inter two bunches; half goes 'long with th' cap'n, an' th' rest with me. Th' cap'n'll foller this hyar boot mark, an' I aims ter track th' mocksin."

The trail that they followed was simplicity itself. First, the owner of the prints had traveled rather fast. Then, as he tired, his feet made deeper marks, at last evening off to where the pressure on the earth was constant. When they passed through grass, the path was clearly visible, and the prints stood out immediately upon their again reaching barren earth. If they belonged to Bad-Eye, they disclosed an utter disregard for concealment. The only conclusion to be drawn was that Bad-Eye, if indeed he had left this trail, expected no pursuit, or in the alternative, he thought that he would cover as much ground as he could earlier in his flight, and then later he would use the many hiding places that nature had provided in the wilderness ahead. Now the footsteps began to show signs of dragging feet. At length, they ended in front of an old, fallen chestnut trunk. Barth signaled his men to rest while they waited to hear from Abe Foster.

The report wasn't long in its coming. Abe hallooed to them, a scant piece from where they sat.

As he drew near, he said to Barth, "Them marks I wuz a-follerin' wuz made by a real-size man. If'n he's a Injun, he's a big'un. They stops here fer a spell, then goes on inter th' brush."

"Good, Abe. Now rest awhile and we'll go on again."

"Rest? Whut fer, Cap'n? We'uns ain't hardly got ourse'fs a sweat hup. Them with me ain't even beginned ter smell yet." Abe's black whiskers opened in the middle as he roared at his own witticism, then he concluded, "Wal, lemme know when yore ready."

Both groups resumed at the same time. Again, the paths taken by each were traced: the one in moccasins and the other in boots. The latter's forward progress appeared to have been a trial indeed. The undergrowth had been torn, broken and pulled along in snarled heaps. Here and there, the fallen leaves from previous seasons had been scooped in furrow-like patterns, indicating slips and falls. The climbing was arduous, even to these men who were in no haste, and they all welcomed the sight of an open space above them, where the sun's rays were now penetrating.

The boot trail led to a chestnut-oak in the clearing, and Barth saw the place where a man had sat recently with his legs and feet straight out from the base of the tree. He again ordered a break in the pursuit. Hardly had he done so when he heard the approach of the other party, culminating in Abe's coonskin-covered head breaking through a thicket.

"Wal, 'pears them two met hyar, er they trails cros't. If'n one wuz a-follerin, this hyar's whar he finded 'im."

"Ach der lieber!" The man laughed. One said, "What's yore trouble, Motty?"

In a humorous, yet pathetic, mixture of German and English, they learned the anguish that can only come from sore, aching feet. Their laughter raised when poor Motty ended his dissertation with the painful plea: "Blees, cut off der foots!"

Barth cuffed the tears of merriment from his own eyes. Between recurring laughs, he asked Abe, "What's Motty's full name?"

"Th' same as when he hain't a-drinkin'." Again the red expanse of Abe's mouth forced the black covering to give way, as new peals of full-throated appreciation followed his trite reply to Barth's honest inquiry.

When the mirth had subsided once more, Abe answered the question. "Martin's his fust name; last is Willerhorst. Motty is jest his nickname." Looking at Willerhorst, Abe continued. "He's a good man, 'cep'n fer his foots." This renewed the previous enjoyment and it was some time before the last chuckle died away.

"Let's finish our work, men." Barth rose and picked up his rifle; the others followed suit.

The footprints were staggered backward; the deepness of the heel marks evinced that fact. Then as they reached the edge of the clearing, they were reversed. The parted brush gave unquestioned witness to the direction from that point on. It was easy to determine that whoever it had been was in full flight. Here he had tripped over a log and sprawled upon the ground; a little farther, he had whirled about in a circle, then tore forward.

It was Albert Prather who first spoke. "Thar he be, Cap'n. Hit's Bad-Eye, all right. He's bin sculped."

All eyes focused on the body, its left arm flung out at an angle, the right lying along its side with fist closed. The cleft of the tomahawk was a gaping one, emphasized by the absence of the scalp.

"Der left ear, ain't," Herman Tressel observed tersely. The aura of horror was deepened by the white face, the small, puggish nose with its wide nostrils, the gaping mouth and the dropped jaw. But the chief contributors were the vacant eye socket and the full, wide-open eye that stared straight on.

At that moment, Abe Foster's group came through the brush. Abe said slowly, "I kin see he got 'im. Sence we left th' clearin', 'twarn't no question ter me whut wuz a-happenin'. This'un we'uns follered shore took his time an' eased along; hardly busted a leaf." Abe ran his hand around his whiskered jaw. "Shore done 'im in, din't he?" Bending down, he ran his hand inside the dead man's jacket. "Hain't no pouch thar, if'n he hed one on 'im. Wal, 'speck thar ain't nuthin' left fer we'uns ter do but to burry th' pore, sculped son-uv-a-bitch."

Barth took a closer look at Bad-Eye's body, then arose and said to Abe, "You notice there's not much blood on him?"

Abe sat on his heels and turned the lifeless head with his hand. "Demme, if'n thet ain't right. Whut yer make uv hit, Cap'n?"

"I can't rightly say, Abe, but my guess would be that he was dead before he was ever hit with that tomahawk, or whatever it was the killer used."

"'Pears like he mought've died from bein' scairt, don't hit? Jedgin' by thet open eye, an' 'is jaw a-settin' thet away?"

"We'll never know, Abe, just what did happen. Reckon, like you said, we'd better bury him."

"Enybuddy want his boots?" one of the party asked jokingly.

"Not after them stinkin' feet uv his'n has been in 'em," another replied, setting off a new charge of laughter.

Barth stopped the gaiety. "You men ever stop to think this might have been one of you? I reason the proper thing would be to say a prayer for his soul. You never can tell—you might be saying it for your own."

The spirit of Saltsburg would not be long repressed. "Cap'n, whiles yore a-sayin' a prayer fer 'im, liken as not, Bad-Eye's done stole half uv hell frum th' devil." Who said this was of no importance; the whole party, except for Barth and Martin Willerhorst, whose feet forbade it, whooped at what was said.

So they dug a shallow grave for Cuthbert Smith and buried him. Barth said a short prayer, interrupted by a momentary lapse during which he himself had a mental picture of Satan chasing Bad-Eye through the flaming caverns of hell. The moist soil of the hillside was dropped loosely over the body, and the last part to be covered was the stark, staring eye unclosed by death.

They traced the murderer's course down to the base of the knob, from whence it ran to the west. Barth called a halt to any further pursuit, and the trackers, their mission accomplished, headed back for the licks. Barth and Abe again led the ragged procession. Martin Willerhorst trailed behind barefooted, carrying his boots in his hands, the stock of his rifle under his armpit and the barrel in the crook of the same arm. Every now and then his feet would scuff on hidden stones, and he would give forth with anguished German curses.

Abe looked back at him and hollered, "Motty, why'ncher sing thet tune I teetched yer?" Motty made no reply, and Abe decided he'd sing it for him. This he did, in a deep, bellowing off-key bass.

> "Oh, jest scratch yore ear.
> An' then scratch yore ass.
> Jest set still an' let hit pass.
> Fer pass hit will, yer knows hit will.
> So git yore jug, an' drink yore fill."

It was purest doggerel, but the others warmed right to it and joined in—all but Barth, who yet had to smile at the nonsense of it all, and Martin Willerhorst, who couldn't scratch his ear or his bottom, as his hands were otherwise employed with his foots and rifle.

CHAPTER 12

Immediately after Mace left the saltworks, Deputy Littelby began testing his newly bestowed 'thority. For the ensuing hour, he went everywhere, his back straight as any man-at-arms. But the seat of his buckskins still drooped and he still walked in a half-sitting position with his legs markedly bent at the knees. Perhaps *trooped* would describe more accurately the manner in which he moved about.

At first, the workers humored him, even to the point of obeying his command that he be ridden into the settlement to check on the condition of Roller and Middleton. "Th' kepteen would 'speck me to do that," he had explained. Actually, when he reached Grainger's cabin, the doctor, fortunately, met him at the door and averted his patient's being upset further. Thus Johnny was free to spend a little more time on what he had really come for—to display his pride before Rosie. He did not overstay his visit with her and left with a businesslike, "Wal, I got to be leavin'. I got work to do."

It was during his absence that they had conspired and had perfected their plans to plague him upon his return. As the wagon came to a stop, one of them stepped forward and offered an arm to him. Johnny leaned over, resting his weight on the proffered limb. Suddenly, the support was withdrawn, and Johnny hit the ground in a dead fall, knocking the wind out of him. The pain in his already injured ribs was as severe as it had been when he was first pummeled by Mace Hardin. They gathered about him and made out that it had been an accident. Poor Johnny believed their protestations. Then they began their campaign in earnest. One furnace boss would call him and he would troop over there. No sooner had he arrived and answered some inconsequential question than he would be hailed by another, quite a distance away. Soon they overdid it, and Johnny realized that they were having sport with him, much like young boys are wont to do, using the cap of the victim as bait for the chase. Like the boy who pursued his cap in vain, Johnny lost his temper, but his fury drew only ridiculing laughter. Finally, swinging wildly, he lashed out at his tormentors. They caught hold of his arms and legs and carried him to a kettle whose contents were just short of boiling and lowered him into it so that his buttocks barely skimmed the water. He shrieked so loudly his voice left him. Then they raised him quickly and turned him loose.

The wet buckskins held the heat and stuck to his rump like a plaster. He dropped his britches to his ankles and stood there in agony.

One of the pranksters placed a lighted sliver of wood in the crevice formed by the sole and the side of his boot. This burned speedily and at the contact of the fire and leather, he leaped into the air, trying to yell, but no sound would come from his open mouth. He fell, and as his seat hit the ground, the impact of that blistered portion of his anatomy caused him to struggle and free his feet of the entangling britches so that he could arise.

He stood there a few minutes, a pitiful picture of sullen vehemence that terrified no one. Rather, all that it induced in the surrounding circle was added laughter. Finally, his voice returned a little and he said in a croaking utterance, "Yew damn, son-uv-a-bitch bastards has had yore fun. I'll have mine when I tells th' kepteen whut yew have did to his depity. Yew heared how he sed yew wuz to treat me like I wuz him."

"Thet's whut th' hell we'uns did, yuh li'l banty-legged bastard. But whut yuh got ain't nuthin' tah whut we aims tuh do to yore damned cap'n, soon's th' time comes tuh do it."

"Yore a-talkin' awful brave, Mitch Strickler. Lessee if'n yew does th' same when th' kepteen gits back."

Strickler shrugged off Johnny's threat, but he did stop laughing. He was a younger prototype of Mace Hardin, and he fancied himself as Mace's some-day successor, with or without the latter's approval. Goaded by Johnny's words and desiring to squelch the implication that Mercer could administer punishment to him, he replied hotly, "Thet son-uv-a-bitch don't scare me none. If'n I wuz th' boss, he'd done bin gone frum here th' day he come. 'Pears liken ole Mace be a-slippin', don't it, boys?"

No one seconded his thinking, and too late, he saw that he had said too much. Sensing he should say something in a different, more agreeable vein, he bellowed, "Le's let this li'l fart see whut's in thet last shed yonder."

The saltmakers willingly agreed with his suggestion, but it was a calmer mirth that they showed. With Strickler leading the way, hoisting Johnny in front of him by pulling his trousers seam tight up into his crotch, they followed to the ox shed where Johnny was flung headlong inside, landing face first in the crusted droppings of the oxen. Mitch barred the door and the fun was over.

It was a tired crew that returned to the licks from Kahaz Knob, Mercer in the lead and Motty Willerhorst still in the distant rear. Abe Foster had left the party earlier and returned to Tom Chism's.

Their arrival brought a rush of inquisitive men from the furnaces who greeted the returnees as though they had been gone for months. The details of the hunt were recounted fully by all except Willerhorst, who had seized the opportunity to rest his belabored feet.

The lurid descriptions having been finished, Barth asked, "Where's Mr. Hardin?"

"He hain't hyar," one of them volunteered.

"Who's in charge when he's gone?"

"I am."

"What's your name?"

"Mitch Strickler."

"Do you know where Mr. Hardin is now?"

"Thet's his bizness, I'd reckin', but I 'speck he's tuh home."

Barth ignored Strickler's insolent manner, asking, "Where's Mr. Littelby, my deputy?"

The men looked around at each other, no one daring to answer him. Finally, Strickler, figuring that he might suffer loss of face among them, replied, "Th' last I seed uv him, he wuz in thet ox barn, yonder." As he finished, he mustered a sly grin.

"You men get about your work," Barth ordered, as he struck out to find little Johnny.

He looked all around, but Johnny wasn't to be seen. Then he called, "Johnny, you around here?"

There was an immediate rattling of the door of the shed nearest him, and Johnny's voice came from within. "Thet yew, Kepteen? Git me outa here!"

Mercer unbarred the door, and Johnny, covered with dung, came out into the sunlight.

At first, Barth laughed, but he ceased when the full appreciation of Johnny's predicament became apparent to him. "What happened to you, Johnny?"

"Kepteen, they has treated me fearful. I tole yew, an' tole yew, I needed me a badge, but yew wouldn't pay me no mine."

"How would a badge have helped any, Johnny?"

"Aw, yew wouldn't unnerstan'. But I shore bin humulated suthin' orful, an' my ass is so damn sore, I don't reckon I'll ever set down no more even if I lives to be a hunnerd."

It was then that Barth saw the huge rolls of inflated blisters on his buttocks. "Tell me all about this, Johnny."

Johnny, his pride crushed completely, his eyes filled with tears, told him the whole sad story of the sport the others had enjoyed at his expense. When he had finished, Barth said, through clenched teeth, "Let's go."

Eager as he was for a champion of his grievances, Johnny shrank inwardly from the scowl on the kepteen's face. *Some'un's in fer hit shore,* he thought, and then added mentally, *an' they shore has it comin' to 'em.*

Mace was waiting for them when they came up. "Yer lookin' fer me, Cap'n?"

"I surely am, Mr. Hardin!" Iced water was never so cold as Barth's voice. "Who's this Mitch Strickler?"

"Why, thet's th' one's in charge when I ain't here 'bouts. Whut's he gone an' did?"

"When I left here this morning, I told you that Johnny was taking care of things for me while I was away. You remember that?"

Mace nodded his head.

"And that he was to be respected the same as I would be, if I were here."

Again, Mace nodded.

"Then what in the tarnal hell do you mean by letting them do the things that they did to him?"

"I wuzn't here, Cap'n."

"That's no excuse! Don't your men carry out your orders?"

"Shore they duz," Mace bristled. "They tole me they wuz jest havin' a little fun with 'im."

"It wasn't fun, Mr. Hardin. They intended to hurt Johnny and they did it; all to show that they were treating him as they would like to treat me."

"Cap'n, yer tole me not ter say enything ter 'em 'bout yer real persition here. If'n yer hed uv let me dun thet, they wuddn't been no goin's on liken this."

Johnny heard, but was puzzled by Mace's words.

"That makes no difference, Mr. Hardin. You failed to control your men."

"Cap'n, this here hain't no army. Yer knows thet."

"Get me this Mitch Strickler!"

Mace had him summoned at once.

Strickler stood there, a contemptuous smile working the corners of his mouth. This only served to bring Barth's ire to a full boil. "Mr. Strickler, do you know that I can have you before the authorities for what you've done to Mr. Littelby, my deputy?" He all but shouted. "You knew his position, yet you deliberately sought to debase him in front of all the workers. You even enlisted their efforts in your plan to humiliate him. I know that you were striking at me, and I intend to see you punished for it!"

Strickler's countenance did not change as he said, "Whut yuh aim tuh do 'bout hit? We be free damn men, an' we ain't beholden tuh yuh, er th' damn law, er th' whole damn Continental Army, er nobuddy, nowheres. If'n yuh tries tuh do enything tuh me, yuh will hev tuh whup ever damn worker at these hyar licks. An' big as yuh tries tuh be, yuh ain't thet big."

"I'm jest big enough to tell you that you're through working here. Ask Mr. Hardin, if you doubt me."

Before he could do so, Mace broke in. "Cap'n, I knows ye a mought riled up 'bout this here doin's, but men's hard ter git here, as yer knows, an' I asks yer ter try an' ca'm yerse'f."

"This is not a time to be calm, Mr. Hardin. I doubt that you would even punish him if he were allowed to stay on here."

"How'd yer want 'im punished, Cap'n?"

"By giving him the hardest, lowest form of work you've got at these works."

"Cap'n, I kain't do that. This here's a good man. He kin handle them bastards 'most as well as I kin."

"I heerd 'im say to them men yore a-talkin' 'bout, thet yew wuz slippin' an' gittin' old. I heerd him tell 'em thet he'd a got rid of th' kepteen th' day he come here."

Johnny's recollection struck home. Strickler's expression changed instantly.

"He sed thet, did he?" Mace was a raging bull. "Cap'n, looks liken yer wuz right, all er long. Here, me tryin' ter hep this damn traitorin' son-uv-a-bitch, an' him a-tryin' ter git my men agin me. Kum hyar, yer back-bitin' bastard!"

Strickler didn't advance nor did he retreat. The workers had again left their tasks and encircled Barth, Mace, Johnny and Strickler. The latter, with all those whom he hoped some day to boss looking on, couldn't back down; he had to face it. The young buck had to lock horns with the old stag or forfeit his hope of leadership.

"Stan' back, Cap'n, an' yer, Mr. Littelby. Yer asks kin I handle my men? Wal, I aims ter show yer thet I'm still the boss uv one uv 'em, enyways!"

Barth and Johnny dropped back into the bordering circle.

"Wal, kum on, yer scummy bastard! Yer wants ter run the hyar works, lessee if'n yer man 'nough ter do hit."

Strickler said nothing, but stood his ground.

"Yer dunt seem so damned anxious ter take over now, do yer?" Mace taunted him. "Wal, sence yer wunt kum ter me, I'm a-comin' ter yer."

Strickler didn't move, but as Mace rushed at him, he unleashed a vicious blow, which failed to reach its mark, thudding loudly, but harmlessly, off his adversary's barreled chest.

Mace retaliated with a murderous swing, catching Strickler flush on his mouth. The blood gushed and three teeth were spat upon the ground. From then on, it was not much of a contest. Strickler tried his utmost. He had courage, but he was not the equal of Mace Hardin. He was a good brawler; he knew all of the dirty, sly tricks and tactics of frontier free-for-all fighting. But Mace knew them too and knew them better.

No man could have stood up under physical punishment such as Mace meted out to his younger adversary. It was brutal, with all the running gore that the human mind associates with brutality. Beaten to a helpless pulp, Strickler finally toppled over. He made one last effort to pull himself up, then collapsed, Mace kicked him and, but for Barth's quick intervention, would have stomped him.

Restrained by Mercer, Mace roared to the onlookers, "Enymores uv yer underhanded bastards want ter take his place?"

There were no takers. Instead, they all turned and went back to the business of making salt.

Mace calmed down gradually. Freed of Barth's encircling arms, he said, "Cap'n, I kin tell yer one thing: We won't hev no more trubble with 'em fer a whiles. I'm aimin' ter see ter hit thet they respecks you an' yer dep'ty."

"I hope that's true, Mr. Hardin," Turning to Johnny, Mercer said, "Better get you to Doctor Grainger's, I reckon."

Johnny stood up in the wagon all the way to the doctor's. Alighting, Barth rapped on the front door.

Mrs. Grainger was sincerely surprised upon seeing them standing there. "Why, it's Captain Mercer! Won't you come inside?"

"How do you do, Mrs. Grainger? We're looking for your husband. Is he in?"

"Just one moment, and I'll call him. Chate, see that the gentlemen are seated."

"Thank you kindly, Mrs. Grainger, but that's the reason for our being here. Mr. Littelby has, shall I say, great difficulty in sitting." Barth smiled as he said this. Johnny's face became glummer.

Puzzled, she went into the next room. Grainger soon came in alone. "Mrs. Grainger seems confused about the reason for this visit, Captain."

Barth could not have failed to note the absence of any greeting, and the doctor's studiously affected professional manner. However, he made no comment, but explained the nature of the call.

Grainger pursed his lips. "Let's look at him."

As the doctor examined Johnny, Barth took note of the house and its furnishings. It was unbelievable that the interior of any dwelling in the wilderness could so approximate that of the stylish and tastefully decorated homes of the East but this room did so. Everything in it bespoke discernment.

His perusing ended only when Grainger finished his examination. "What do you think, Doctor?"

"I think it most strange, Captain Mercer, that you would presume upon my indulgence by coming to this house for professional purposes after you had so firmly, and almost insultingly, declined my invitation to enter it socially. You also know that I use another room in this house for professional purposes."

"I believe you could understand my reasons for not accepting your hospitality if you would but let yourself do so. Johnny here is in great pain. I didn't think to take him to your study. I just forgot, and I offer my apology."

Grainger said tartly, "I do not accept either excuse."

"I'm sorry, Doctor, that you feel that way."

"Damn how eny of yew feels! My ass is a-killin' me! If yew wants to talk, take keer of me fust!" Johnny exclaimed in suffering.

Grainger looked at him sharply. "I don't think I will treat you. I've about come to the limit of my patience with everyone at this settlement. There's no reason for me to worry and exhaust myself with you or any like you."

"Doctor, you know that I am able to, and will, pay you whatever your fee may be for seeing after Johnny." Barth's tone was solicitous.

Grainger answered angrily. "Do you think for one moment that I have practiced my profession since I came here for the meager fees I have been paid? Paltry worn coins, all but worthless Continental currency, game, salt—is that compensation for a surgeon of my reputation and professional standing? I have no need of such things. The sole and sufficient reason for my engaging in practice here has been that I someday hope to return to the civilized east and take up where I left off before this damned silly revolution disrupted my life."

"Oh, my ass!" wailed Johnny.

"Doctor, doesn't your professional oath demand that you minister to all such as are in pain to the best of your ability?"

"Captain Mercer, my oath is a reasonable one and not to be interpreted in the extreme."

"I would think that the extreme would be the true test of the obligation, Doctor."

Grainger paused, then with an involuntary, "All right, I'll do what I can for him," pushed Johnny toward the light, roughly forcing him to bend at the middle, his broiled buttock thus being the more clearly exposed.

The bending stretched the blisters and Johnny howled.

The doctor straightened himself. "He's got about as bad a buttock condition as I ever have seen."

"To hell with th' buttock condishun! It's m' ass I wants yew to fix," yelled Johnny from his awkward, doubled-up position.

Even Grainger's set lips loosened at Johnny's remonstrance. "You can straighten up for a bit while I check your ribs."

Johnny raised himself with appropriate exclamations attendant his travail.

The doctor's probing fingers brought an expostulation. "Them things is sore, Doc, can't chew be a mought easy?"

"He has some fractured ribs too. I think I felt more than one break in one of them."

Barth told Grainger of the previous injury to the ribs. "Time and rest are about all I can prescribe for the ribs," Grainger said. "As for the blisters, I would hesitate to puncture them—too much danger of infection. I'd rather try some soothing medication—bear grease or deer suet perhaps, although you should let the air get to them too as much as possible. Certainly you should not put those buckskins on, except where modesty demands that you do so."

"Yew means I has to be half-nekkid, til them damn blisters is cured?"

"That's about what the doctor means, Johnny. You don't want to risk the danger of infection."

Johnny looked helplessly at Barth. "How yew gonna git along without no depity?"

"It'll be hard, Johnny. But it'd be better that way, for a while. If your rump were to become infected, I might not have a deputy at all."

"Yew mean it could be thet bad?"

"That's right, Johnny."

The patient dressed painfully. When he had finished, Mrs. Grainger reentered the room, followed by Chate, who carried a tray with cups and a pot of tea. "Do favor us by taking a bit of this before you go, Captain."

Barth thanked her and accepted the offered cup. Johnny aped Barth's words and actions. As the hot liquid passed his lips, he gulped it and exclaimed, "If this here's part uv th' treatment, I'd druther hev th' damn blisters on m' ass."

Mrs. Grainger attempted to hide her embarrassment with little success. Barth could think of nothing to say, and the silence thickened oppressively.

It was Johnny who brought equanimity to the situation, which his uncouth expression had created. "Th' doc says Willie an' Davey is gonna make it."

Grainger made ready grasp of the opportunity for further relief from the disconcerted atmosphere. "I advised Littelby earlier today that, barring the unforeseen,

I thought Roller would have a fair chance of recovery. He has a lot of reserve strength in him, that fellow. Of course, it will be a good, long time before he will have recovered. The other man, Middleton, seems to be doing very well indeed."

"Where are they, Doctor?" Barth inquired.

"Middleton's cabin. His wife is looking after both of them. I understand they have been fast friends. I plan to see them each morning and evening, for a while anyway. They were both in excellent spirits today. It seems that Chism, for whom they formerly worked, is going to reemploy the two of them when they are able to return to work and is giving them a part of their future earnings as advancements. You know, Captain, it's heartwarming to find that there is one man, at least, among all the low element that abides here, who has a real consideration for his fellow man."

Coming from Grainger, Barth couldn't help but consider the incongruity of the man. For one whose very presence here was motivated by the strongest kind of selfish jealousy, it was strange indeed that he should be appraising others who had never had the guidance of learning or the advantages of higher birth. This man, who a short while before, was refusing to aid one of the unfortunates, had the biblical beam firmly within his own eye.

"Captain Mercer, I wish you could honor us with your presence here some evening." Mrs. Grainger's voice was as appealing as her face and figure. So influential was the combination that Barth found himself answering, "I would be a most impolite man were I to refuse so charming a woman." He hastily added, "Especially since her husband has been so kind to my friend here."

His "friend here" chimed in immediately. "Yew means yew wants me to come with th' kepteen?"

Grainger began a reply, but his wife's words flowed first. "Why, ah, of course. We'd be delighted to have you."

Barth came to the rescue. "You're forgetting one thing, Johnny. You'd have to wear your buckskins, and you'd have to be seated most of the time you were here."

"Whew!" exclaimed Johnny, at the mere thought of sitting. "I reckin' I couldn't do thot, Miz Grainger, not for a long spell."

Her relief gushed into sound. "I understand. Perhaps some other time, when you are feeling better."

"I'm a-feelin' all right now, 'cep'n fer this ass uv mine. But I shore couldn't set on it. Damn, no!"

Mrs. Grainger blushed to the roots of her hair, and the doctor twitched nervously. Barth took Johnny by his arm and moved toward the door.

"May we expect you then, Captain—shall we say Sunday, two evenings from this day, at nightfall?"

"I will be most pleased to be here."

Drusilla wore a triumphant, satisfied smile. Barth wondered if the doctor had told her of his earlier refusal of his invitation. He could now comprehend more easily Grainger's frustration. She was beautiful, and she was beautifully alluring. Raven hair, light blue eyes, which could dance or move solemnly, and a complexion of pink roses placed gently upon alabaster; a nose of dignity, with an impish tilt at its tip that made an arc to the lips, full red, but yet delicate in their boldness; a slender neck, suggestive of strength and not thinness; shoulders that sloped smoothly, framing the well-proportioned bosom above her waist, and hips that tended to the youthful masculinity that was most pronounced in her limbs; and lastly, the slender hands, with their colored nails, so like opals set in exquisitely wrought silver. This was the picture of Drusilla Grainger. This was the image which had raced Barth's heart and drew from him his acceptance. This is what Richard Grainger treasured. This is what had cost the lives of two lovers.

The doctor recognized his contemplation, and it was he, rather than Chate, who showed them to the door, saying as he did so, "You seemed transfixed there for a moment, Captain Mercer."

"Believe me, sir, I was." Barth bowed respectfully, and the portal closed behind him.

The recollection of the ornate furnishings caused him to look back briefly at the house. Its exterior was unusual only because of its size and the twin chimneys at each end.

It was the interior that intrigued him. How had they managed to get all those things to Bullitt's Lick?

"Git me to home, Kepteen. My ass is 'bout to burn off'n me!"

Johnny's impatient words ended Mercer's contemplation of the Grainger home. He drove rapidly until they reached the cabin, where he assisted Johnny from the wagon. When they were at the door, and as Barth started to leave, Johnny remarked, "Thet Miz Grainger is shore a purty suthin', ain't she?"

"She is all of that, Johnny. Well, I've got to get back to the licks. See you tonight." With that, Barth climbed on the wagon and was gone.

CHAPTER 13

With Strickler ousted as a furnace boss, Mace's ten were now nine. As he stood talking to them, Mace fingered his chin. "'Pears like we mought hev ter do suthin' 'bout Mercer ahead uv time. Dunt know as how I kin keep a-bowin' ter him much longer." Resignedly, however, he added, "But I reckin we'll hev ter do hit, fer a spell. Kain't 'ford no trouble with th' likes uv Patrick Henry."

The men grumbled openly and Mace raised his hand. "Thet's the way hit'll hev to be, boys; 'tain't no use dangerin' our plans right now. Jest as well make yore mines up ter thet. We'll hev ter let th' salt we're a-makin' now be shipped outer here liken he wants. They hain't no choice about hit." Changing abruptly, he asked, "Whar's Jack Doniger? Seems liken I hain't seen 'im fer a day or more'n."

"Prob'ly in there with thet Dolly Dusenberry," one of them said.

"Hell, it dunt take 'im all thet time ter hev 'is fun, do hit?" They all laughed heartily. "Kum ter think uv hit—hit mought be th' truth, he's a scrawny-assed as they kums."

When the merriment from Mace's joking had died down, he said seriously, "If'n yer sees 'im 'fore I does, tell 'im I wants ter see 'im." Then he said suddenly, "Better scatter, boys. Here kums Mercer yonder."

Barth tied the reins to the footboard and jumped to the ground. Dusting himself with both hands, he asked, "How long before we'll have enough salt for a good shipment, Mr. Hardin?"

"Cap'n, I figgers thar'll be 'nough in 'bout three, mebbe four days. Whar yer aimin' ter send hit?"

"To Falls of the Ohio, Mr. Hardin—all that we can get ready and what anybody else around here has on hand."

"Th' Army needin' all thet salt, Cap'n?"

"It's to be delivered to the Army—Colonel Mason will receipt for it. Then he'll apportion it. Some for the military and the rest to be divided among the colonies having the greatest need. You don't have to concern yourself where it's going or to what use it will be put. You just see that it's ready, Mr. Hardin."

"Yessir, Cap'n."

"I'm going over to Chism's works and I don't expect I'll be back here the rest of the day. I'll be back at daybreak tomorrow, however." Barth noted the change in Mace's expression when he uttered Chism's name. As he walked away, he called to him, "I trust we won't have any fires tonight, Mr. Hardin." Mr. Hardin replied, "They won't be no more fires. I'll be a-seein' ter thet."

*

He ran his fingers lightly through her hair. The myriad circlets, which had presaged the now gently falling rain, made her small, doll-like face the more appealing. Turning on her side so that she faced him, she said, "Jack Doniger, you pleasures me; ya knows that, don'tcha? With most of 'em that comes here, I pleasures them; but you pleasures me, honey, suthin' wonderful. I'm a-thinkin' that's 'cause ya loves me like I loves you. Ain't that right?"

Jack Doniger had heard the alarm spread by the settlers a short time before; but the cries of a fire at the licks did not move him when he had his own private conflagration here with Dolly Dusenberry. Damn Mace and the rest of them. He'd face up to whatever might come as an aftermath of his truancy. In this cabin he was somebody; out there he was nothing. And although Dolly flattered all of the men who visited her, he knew she was sincere with him. She made him experience the fullest degree of adequacy. She magnified into strength those things in his makeup that were so lacking in virility. In turn, he delighted in pleasing her, thus increasing his sensation of mastery. She trusted where others doubted; he responded with fidelity and tenderness. This was the unfathomable way of a man with a maid—the way of Jack Doniger with a magdalene of Saltsburg.

Her voice became insistent. "Ya do love me, don'tcha, honey?"

His answer was a smothering kiss and a crushing embrace. Her lips too were active, and her arms encircled his body, cementing her breasts to his chest and her stomach to his.

At length, their physical forces spent, they lay upon their backs, still coursing in the ensuing nebulous afterglow, and talked dreamily to each other. "Jack, honey, I knows th' goodness in you, an' if ya loves me as you claims, why don't we get away from here? It can't come to no good end, if you stays on at this place, doin' ever' wrongful thing that Mace Hardin sets ya to."

He renewed the gentle twisting of her dampened curls. "I know you're right, Dolly darlin'. But it ain't that easy like. For th' one thing, there's Molly, a-gittin' worser ever' day. I knows you too well to 'speck yuh to leave her and them two young'uns of her'n. An' when we does get from here, we has tuh get fast. Mace ain't gonna be happy with me slippin' away owin' him like I does. We'd have tuh go without her, honey, an' thet we can't do. Don'tcha think it ain't hell for me, darlin', with all them sons-of-bitches jokin' an' laffin' 'bout layin' with yuh. It just sickens me nigh tuh death! An' what in the worldwide hell can I do? You sees things in me that I doubts is there, but yuh makes me feel like they is. But to them bastards, I ain't no part of a man. I can't match their strength, so I gets by with my wits." Here the depressive mood lifted a bit. "I'm stronger that way than they all is, 'cludin' Mace, hisself."

"Mebbe I could stop havin' them other men. Mebbe, if we got married, we could do good here, without leavin'. If you thinks it's hell, what about me, an' them animals a-usin' me, an' me lovin' you like I does?"

"Th' marryin' part is in m' heart, darlin', but it just can't be. Why, them bastards would laugh from mornin' tuh night. If that wouldn't be bad 'nough—how'd we live? An' where? Mace'd have yuh outa this place the first time ya didn't pay 'im. An' then there's always Molly to be a'thinkin' of."

"Mebbe things'll change some, with that Cap'n Mercer bein' here an' all."

"Don'tcha get your hopes up on that, Dolly. Mercer ain't gonna live for long. Mace is just a-waitin' til th' time's right, an' when it is, Mercer's gonna be th' deadest man that was ever killed."

"Someone oughta warn him."

"Don'tcha get no such thoughts in your mind, Dolly. 'Sides, I don't reckon Mercer would leave, if he knowed it was gonna happen to 'im."

A persistent, racking cough came from the adjoining room. "Seems she gits ta coughin' more each day, honey. I'm 'fraid for her; 'fore God, I am. It's suthin' left from th' sickness she took at Bedford. This valley don't help her none neither." Dolly's eyes moistened and cut into him.

"I don't know how we'll do it, but th' lot of us is gettin' out from here. I don't know when, but we're all gettin' out."

"Where'll we go, honey?"

"There's a place that I been a-holdin' in my heart since th' first time I was there—th' gap out from Harristown. Th' air's th' sweetest a man ever drawed into his soul, an' there ain't no Injuns tuh pester a body. It would hep Molly an' it would hep us all. It's a fur piece over in Pennsylvania but, God forgivin' all we has done that ain't been right, we'll get there."

"Oh, Jack, I hope so, I hope so, I hope so." They were the words of a visionary, bolstered more by their utterance, than by any real faith in their realization.

"Just you have patience, Dolly darlin'. We're a-goin'. That's m' promise."

"If it could only be soon. If it wuz today. If it wuz 'fore that Jed ever come back an' used me agin'. I'm feared of him, Jack. I'm real feared of him, honey."

She told her love all about her experience with Jed and it hurt. It brought so strongly to him his own physical weakness and his consequent inability to protect her. He sought to assuage her dread with words he knew to be untrue. "Jeddy-Boy prob'ly done fergot all 'bout it. Bout got hisself drunk and didn't 'member nuthin' when he sobered up. You know Jed, as well as I does."

"I knows 'im, a'right. He ain't never fergot enyone he made a threat to, if he wuz drunk or sober. An' you knows that too, honey."

"Well, he ain't goin' to bother yuh non while I'm 'roun' here, darlin'."

"I b'leeves that; but he's like a wolf. He'll come when a body's alone an' in th' blackest of th' night." She shuddered as the thought ran through her mind. "An' if I wuzn't here, he'd 'bout go after Molly. Oh, good Lord, don't let that happen!"

"You're gettin' y'self all worked up, darlin'. Maybe like I said we can get away from here soon."

His hopeful words did not move her. "I knows ya means well, Jack, honey, but yore hopin' is a-makin' ya say things you knows can't happen, an' yore a-sayin' 'em jest to comfort me."

He dropped his eyes. "I ain't just sayin' it, Dolly. I really aims to try tuh do it. I know it seems like it couldn't happen, but I sure am goin' do my best tuh make it. Til we either does it, or don't, it's up tuh me to protect you. An' someways I'm goin' to do it."

She was moved by earnestness and, leaning above him, showed it by taking his head between her hands and kissing lingeringly his mouth and face. He responded with a touch, soft as velvet, undulating from her ear, down her neck and shoulders, thence to her breasts, over her hips and down her thighs. Her mouth sought and found his again, and their lips met rapaciously. She murmured in ecstasy, "Jack Doniger, you pleasure me . . . you pleasures me so."

CHAPTER 14

He's in that hut, yonder." Barth thanked his informer and found Tom Chism inside, an open ledger before him.

"Counting your money, I see."

Chism looked up, surprised. "Oh, it's you, Mercer. I'll have to watch you, in case you don't always come friend like." He smiled as he spoke the words.

Barth's features lightened and he said, "If I don't come friendly like, I won't come at all."

"I believe that, but I can't believe what you told me before. You said you was comin' early."

"It's this way, Tom. I figured the fire was more important than you," he said laughingly. "Thanks for loaning me Abe Foster this morning."

"He help you any?"

"He surely did. I think he's one of the best trackers I ever came across, and I think I know enough about tracking to be qualified to give that opinion. Why, he saw a moccasin print that I still can't convince myself was there."

"You're right about him, Mercer. There's only one thing he does better'n trackin'."

"What's that?" asked Barth.

"Drinkin' without never gittin' drunk. You wouldn't never believe me, if I was to tell you what I've seen 'im down an' not show no signs of havin' swallered a drop. He claims he sweats it out of him. An' you know somethin'? I think he must. But, drinkin' or not, he's a real man."

Barth nodded in complete agreement. "He seemed quite friendly with Tressel and Willerhorst. I wondered about that since they work for Mace Hardin. I suppose they got to be friends when they were working for you."

"That's right; then they lived over at Mud Garrison together too. In fact, them an' their families is th' best over there. Th' rest ain't much, at all. Never could unnerstand why they ain't never moved from there, less'n it's 'cause them up at Brashear's Station ain't got no time for their foolishness. They're always playin' tricks on each other. Most of 'em is on Motty though. Then, they drink together, an' they get to singin', an' I don't think that'd set none too good with the folks at Brashear's.

"Herman can carry what he drinks purty fair, but he ain't never learned that Abe can do better. Hilda Tressel, that's Herman's wife, like to beat th' wind outa Herman over that once. 'Course she didn't hurt him none—Herman just laughed at her."

"They're really something. Hilda an' Motty's wife, Gretchen, can't speak much English, or don't want to. I don't know which, but whatever's th' reason, they talk German all th' time. They can sure make you laugh when they all get together. Th' only way it could be funnier, would be for Abe to get married." Tom paused. "Well, I could tell 'bout them all day, but I'm sure I'd best do it some other time. Want to get started on your inspection?"

Barth shook his head. "I don't think that's needed, Tom. You can tell me what you've got; your word's enough for me. I would like to see your works, out of curiosity, later on, if you don't mind my doing so."

This assertion of confidence impressed Tom, and he answered, "You are welcome whenever you want to do it." To show his own trust in Mercer, he added, "I'll tell you something. I'm going to give you a real run for this salt business any day now. Soon as th' Ohio's up, I'll have some more kettles comin' up Salt River from Louisville. Don't say nothing about it though. I want to keep it kinda quiet."

"Good for you," Barth answered good-naturedly. "The more kettles you have, the more salt you'll be able to make. Now, I'll tell you something I've been thinking about doing." Barth described his plan to run the water to the furnaces.

"Damn if I don't believe that might work! When you figurin' on tryin' it?"

"Soon as I can find the right men to do it. What do you think about Tressel and Willerhorst? You think they could handle the job?"

"I expect they could."

"Well, if they can, I'll see that they show you how it's done."

"That's mighty fine of you, Mercer, and I appreciate it. Maybe I can give th' favor back to you sometime."

"Don't worry about doing that." Barth waved off his intent of reciprocity. "I would like to see Aaron Flinden this evening, however, and I'd be most grateful if you would take me to his home."

"I told you I'd be glad to do that."

"I know, but I thought you were busy right now working on your ledger."

"Ain't that busy. When yu want to go?"

Barth thought a bit. "Guess we'd better eat before we go, don't you think?"

"'Pends on how long you are figurin' on stayin' there. I'd better warn you: Ursula Flinden will be talkin' more'n Brother Flinden will, an' longer."

"That'll be all right. All I'd want you to do would be to take me there. You wouldn't have to wait for me. I could return by myself."

"I'll take you, an' I'll come back with you."

"What about Abby? Won't she be expecting you this evening?"

Tom scratched his head. "I almost forgot that. We could go there an' eat early, an' I'll tell her where I'm goin'. She'll have to get along 'thout me tonight."

He smiled at his mock display of egotism.

"You do that, Tom. Meet me at my cabin, if you will, when you are finished."

"Ain't you goin' to eat with us?"

"Can't do it, Tom. Little Johnny's at the cabin. Doctor Grainger said he ought to keep clothing off his buttocks for a few days. He'll be looking for me—says he'll do the cooking for us." Barth chuckled as he continued. "I'm little worried about whether I'll be able to eat what he cooks."

"Don't blame you none. Maybe you won't meet me after all." It was Tom's turn to laugh.

Barth retorted, "If you don't see me standing outside, come on in; you'll probably find me stretched out on the floor."

They parted on this note of humor, Tom striking up a whistle as he started on his way. Barth remembered the words that went with the tune: "Jest scratch yore ear, an' ..."

CHAPTER 15

"Mamma, I'm a-gettin' older each day; if I don't marry someone soon, I'll never get married."

Abby's expostulation fell on deaf ears. "The way you carry on, a body would think you was in your thirties, 'stead of just bein' sixteen. Now, just you busy yourself so that dust in th' corner there don't get no thicker."

"Oh, Mamma, you get me so mad sometimes, I declare I feel like runnin' away somewheres. And I would, if there was any place I could go to."

Rosie sighed. "There's Bairdstown, Cox's Station, Harrodstown, Falls of the Ohio—oh, there's plenty places you could go."

"Oh, Mamma, you know I mean some big city." Abby's tone was tinged with curtness.

"There's men at all them places I just said. You say you want to get married? Well, I 'magine there's men there that feels th' same way."

"Mamma, you're mak'n' fun of me. You know I just said that. But I don't see why you won't let me an' Tom Chism get married."

Rosie wiped her brow with her wrist. The days were warming now, and the linsey-woolsey she was wearing emphasized the slight discomfort she was feeling. "Abby, we'll have to change into some lighter things afore long."

"Mamma, you're talkin' 'bout somethin' different on purpose. You always do that when I say anything serious 'bout Tom and me. It'd serve you good if I never got married to no one an' you had to have me on your hands th' rest of your life."

"The Lord would never be so unkind as to add that to all my other tribulations." Rosie made a gesture of mock despair, which served to infuriate her daughter.

"I-I-I wish I was like the Dusenberry sisters, then you'd be sorry, I reckon."

"Yes, Abby, I would be most sorry." Abby had at last succeeded in making her mother serious. "That poor Molly. I took her some broth today. She's beginnin' to waste away; this valley ain't none too good for her. I never heard such coughin' like she does. An' them two little children of her'n sweet as angels. When I think of all th' goin's on their poor little eyes has saw, it 'stresses me plumb sick."

"Mamma, they're too young to know what's a-happenin. Just like th' time I was little an' was walkin' along in that meadow an' I saw that man an' woman a-lyin' there. They was both laughin' an' carryin' on, but it didn't come to me that they was doin' somethin' wrong."

"Maybe they wasn't. They was most prob'ly married," said Rosie, with austerity. "However, I notice that you still remember seein' them."

"Course I do. But I didn' think they was married then, an' since I've growed older, I know they wasn't. I've saw too much of such goin's on."

Rosie's despair was now unfeigned. "Let's just stop a-talkin' about it."

"Mamma, you started it by talkin' 'bout Molly." Abby loved to tease.

"Makes no mind who started it. I'm a-endin' it right now, you understand?"

"Yes. Mamma. Now, let's talk 'bout me and Tom gettin' married. How many children you think we should have?"

"Thinkin' an' children is opp'sites; if there was thinkin', lots of times there wouldn't be children."

"Why, Mamma, you embarrass me." Abby placed her palm upon her cheek and turned her head.

"Stop actin' silly. Molly—I mean, Abby! An' we'll have no more talk of marriage!" Rosie's slip of the tongue rushed the blood to her face.

"I'll bet you didn't talk like that when you wanted to get married to Papa."

"That was diff'rent."

"I know it was. You said you was just fifteen years old."

Her mother's voice rose. "Abby Tindall, I said stop it!"

Whenever Rosie added Tindall when she spoke to her, Abby knew she was truly angry. This realization made its mark and the lightness of her conversation now changed to petulance. "Mamma, you at least ought to give me a reason."

"If your mem'ry's so short, you can't remember Tom Chism gettin' drunk, it don't do much good to give you no reason."

"Mamma, he'd quit it, if we was to get married. Have you noticed he ain't been drunk since Captain Mercer came here?"

"He was drunk that very night."

"But he ain't been since. I do believe that Captain Mercer's changed him. He's just lonely, an' if a man could change him, think what a woman could do! Some'un to cook for him an' ...''

"Never mind your describin' any more of th' things a woman can do for a man. Captain Mercer ain't gonna be here forever, you know. An' then he'll be a-gettin' drunk ever' night, or ever' other night, anyhow." Rosie vented her spleen on a chair that was out of place, slamming it into its proper position.

"Mamma, if Tom was to promise you he'd atop drinkin', or getting' drunk, how about it, then?"

"Abby ... my patience is a-wearin' awful thin."

Abby caught the sharpness of her mother's eyes and they roused her to a spirit of retaliation. "I'm. goin' over an' talk to Molly an' Dolly, an' I'm goin' to ask them all about everything." She walked stiffly out of the house.

Rosie started after her but before she could even call to her, Jim Trench and some others came in.

"Whut's troublin' yuh, Rosie?" Jim asked.

"Oh, it's nothing, just Abby."

Trench laughed and sat down on a bench. "Yuh know, Rosie, Abby oughter be gittin' married. She's plenty old fer hit."

"Now, see here, James Trench. Don't you go a-startin' on that."

Her severity impressed Trench and caused him to mutter to himself man's oldest observation: "Wimmen jest hain't predickuble."

As she walked, Abby's ankles turned on the ruts in the road, serving to take her mind from the frustrated state in which the vain arguments with her mother had left it. She began to have misgivings about her determination to talk with the Dusenberry sisters. Feminine tongues wagged with celerity about the slightest happening out of the ordinary. As with Eve, the woman still imparted things best unsaid to the men.

And where women gossip in hushed tones, men loudly proclaim only choice bits of savory news. Where women giggled, smiled or simpered, men laughed uproariously. Her visit might be the talk of the settlement before nightfall. But, if that be true, how about Rosie's visits? There was never any gossip about them. This reasoning vanquished all hesitancy, and she walked most naturally toward Dolly's door, almost colliding with the hurriedly departing Jack Doniger. He appeared not to notice her, and she felt relieved.

Dolly's door was open, and Abby called to her, resulting in an immediate, "Come on in. I hope ya won't be mindin' th' mess things is in."

When Dolly saw that it was Abby, she was most upset. "Land sakes alive, Abby! What're you doin' here? I reckined it wuz yore ma, kind soul that she be. Y' best git from here, honey, fast, 'fore ever' damned bitch—I'm sorry, honey—I mean woman 'round here starts talkin' 'bout ya. Girls like you just don't go a-vis-itin' women like me an' Molly. Don't ya know that?"

"Mamma comes here, an' nobody talks."

"That's diff'runt. She's an older person."

"Just 'cause a body's older, don' mean she couldn't be bad." Abby quickly regretted the twin implication. "I didn't mean you're really old or bad; it just kinda come out. 'fore I thought."

"That's all right, honey. I understand. That's what ever' one thinks 'bout us. We break one commandment an' we're branded th' rest of our days. A heap of them what brands us, breaks all th' rest of th' Lord's commandments, 'cept th' seventh. An' they thinks they's good. Even them as steals an' cheats ain't thought as bad of as we be. It don't matter none that we don't hurt nobuddy; that we means be kind an' peaceful, er that somebuddy else started us down th' way we are a-goin' or that none of them good people never tried to help us a speck. We be just th' bottom of th' heap, an' there we stays. Now, you git on tuh home, like I told ya."

"If people arc gonna talk 'cause I come here, it's too late; I'm already here, an' leavin' ain't gonna stop it. Them that knows I come here'll tell it anyhow. Maybe I won't be a-comin' back, but I'm havin' this one visit, that's sure."

"I reckon, you're right 'bout that, Abby." Dolly's shapely bosom fell with a sigh as she surrendered her views. "Whut wuz th' reason yuh come tuh see us? 'Fore yuh answer, does yore ma know ya come?"

"I told her I was goin' to."

"An' she said ya could?"

Abby's slowness in replying gave Dolly her answer. "I hopes she won't be mad at we'uns. She's been good to us—real good."

"If Mamma blames anyone, it'll be me, so don't you worry 'bout that none."

Suddenly, Dolly was acutely aware that her visitor was still standing. "I'm turrible sorry. Set in that chair. I 'most lost m' manners."

As Abby seated herself and looked around, she was disappointed. This wasn't at all as she had thought it would be, or as the Bible had described the furnishings of such a place. There was no covering of tapestry, and the bed was most unattractive. There was no fragrance of myrrh, aloe or of cinnamon. In their stead, she caught the strong odor of foul sweat—a man's. She glanced at the still rumpled bed, and she felt a wave of uncomfortableness sweep over her, filling her with abhorrence. It was a shameful way to exist, no matter how truly the other nine commandments were observed.

Dolly sprawled upon the bed, raising herself upon an elbow. "Now, honey, sence yore here, what do ya want to ask me about?"

Summoning all her courage, Abby was just as direct as Dolly. "I want to find out about men, 'bout all th' facts."

"Yore ma's th' one to tell you them things. Ain't she done it?"

"Some, but ever since what th' Injuns done to our family, Mamma kinda took to shieldin' me, all ways."

"Yore askin' me ta tell ya suthin' you got no bizness a-knowin'. If I wuz to do it, then yore mind would be th' same as mine, even if what I told ya never wuz put to no use."

Abby was disappointed. "I just ain't askin' from curiosity; 'fore I get married, I want to know something."

"Time to find out them things is after th' marriage, not before."

"I don't believe that. Look at Mrs. Grainger. She an' th' doctor wouldn't be as unhappy as they be, if she'd knowed 'bout things 'fore they got married. Both their lives would have been different."

"That ain't so. A woman can enjoy herself nigh ta heaven with a man, but if she's that kind, she'll be a-wanting others. It's th' mind, more'n th' body."

Abby was blunt. "Is that your way?" Again she sought to soften the harshness of her uttered thought. "I mean . . . uh . . . What I wanted to say, was—uh . . ."

"I know, honey. No, that ain't my way, nor Molly's neither. Sence we got started talkin', I just as well tell it from th' beginnin'!"

Abby discerned that she had pulled a thread leading to a skein of unpleasantness, and she regretted it. "It was silly for me to ask you that. Let's talk about somethin' else. Is Molly any better?"

Ignoring Abby's maneuver, Dolly continued. "No. I think maybe I'd be repayin' yore ma for her kindness if I wuz to tell you all about it. Yes, I b'leeve that'd be th' best thing I could do for ya."

Abby made one last, feeble gesture. "Maybe Mamma wouldn't like yore tellin' me."

"I'll hafta chance that."

Abby reconciled herself to the unavoidable.

"Molly an' I wuz born back in Cumberland, an' th' early part of our lives wuz happy. Our ma, rest her soul, wuz a good woman an' teached us right, long as she lived. Pa wuz a good father to us, an' he worked hard. Things was so peaceful then." The wistfulness for the past was pathetically apparent. "I never knowed no man, an' never had no heartache til after my ma died. I reckin' I wuz 'round fifteen year old. With Ma gone, a-buried in that one grave on th' hillside of our farm, they wuzn't nary a soul ta look out fer us—Molly an' me. Folks use to think we wuz twins; we looked that much alike, but I'm two year older'n Molly.

"Pa took to drinkin' some, but he kep' a-workin', an' he couldn't teach us like Ma would've done, so it weren't strange that we got ta doin' pretty much what we wanted to do. If they'd been some'un lookin' after us, I prob'ly never would've done what I done with Bobby Williams." Nostalgic regret bore a lengthy silence, as Dolly's thoughts carried her from the licks back to Cumberland.

Abby waited patiently until she renewed her narrative.

"Bobby wuz a sweet one. I honestly b'leeve he's th' only one I really ever loved, til I met Jack."

"Who's Jack, Dolly?"

Dolly snapped from her dreaming to a sense of alertness. She evaded the inquiry, saying, "Oh, he's just one of th' men I knowed. Maybe you are right, Abby. Maybe it's best ta go on home."

Abby's curiosity having been aroused, it would not now be halted. "I'd like to hear th' rest; I honestly would."

Again, Dolly's bosom rose and fell. "Well, like I told you, we practically growed ourselves. Bobby Williams's pa and his family wuz our nearest neighbors, an' Bobby would be over playin' with us most of th' time. One day him an' me wuz pickin' daisies an' he set down ta rest a spell. Somehow, my dress got caught when I tried to set down too. His eyes got big as saucers, an' 'fore I knowed it, or could stop him, he run his hand up under m' dress an' hugged me with his free arm, a'kissin' me all th' whiles. It wuz suthin' new to me, but it pleasured me. My heart was a-poundin' an' th' blood was a-rushin' to m' face an' head. It's funny, me not a-knowin' a thing 'bout anything like that, but still I wanted him, an' I knowed what I wuz a-wantin' him ta do."

"Didja, Dolly? How'd ja know it!"

"'That's th' hardest thing to 'splain. Facts is, I don't rightly guess enybuddy kin 'splain how a woman knows that. Ya just knows it, an' that's all."

"I hope I'll know when th' time's proper for me, I mean."

"You will, Abby, have no scares 'bout that; but just be shore you be married when it happens."

"Uh-huh," said Abby, thoroughly entranced.

"'They wuzn't a dry cloud in th' sky that day. It wuz spring, like now, an' th' breezes wuz just as dainty as could be."

Abby wasn't interested in the weather. "Dintcha have a sorta feelin' 'bout it bein' wrong to do such things?"

"None in th' world. It just seemed to be th' natcheralest thing to be a-doin'. I guess it wuz wrong, but I never even thought about it that a way. I 'member both us took off'n our clothes, an' we wuz there' just like Adam an' Eve."

Abby blushed mightily, and Dolly was quick to notice it.

"See, Abby, you be just too nice ta be a-hearin' such talkin'."

Abby swallowed hard before she replied. "Don't mind that. Just keep a-tellin' me."

"Well, 'fore that pretty day wuz done, I knowed all 'bout a man's body. An' if Bobby didn't know afore that, he knowed all about a woman's. After that, we met all th' time, an' each time we'd be together, it seemed it wuz new, all over agin."

"How old was Bobby?"

"'Bout a year older'n me, but he wuz kinda bashful like, an' I felt like I wuz th' oldest one."

"He didn't seem bashful that first time."

"'That's right. Guess he just got hisself carried away. Seein' bare flesh in th' wrong places can do that. I knows that, fer shore."

"What do you mean by that?"

"'That's just suthin' else you'll find out after you are married."

"Oh," said Abby.

"Finely," continued Dolly, "young as we wuz, we wuz in love. I knowed it then, an' I know it now."

"Did you get married?"

"'That's th' heart-breakin' part of it. No, we didn't. 'Bout that time, Bobby's pa died from th' same thing that kilt my ma, an' his ma sold their place an' they moved away."

"Didja ever see 'im anymore?"

"Just a few times after that. Then he didn' come back no more."

"Why didn't you go to see him? I never would've given up if it'd been me."

Dolly smiled. "I did try to, honey. But it seemed like nobuddy knowed where he wuz. Ya see' they moved somewheres else."

"Oh," said Abby, satisfied that Dolly had at least made an effort to find Bobby.

"Well, Molly'n me bein' so close t' each other an' by ourselves so much, I had told her all 'bout what Bobby an' me wuz a-doin'—that is 'fore he moved away. That wuz bad jedgment on my part. I know that now. But then, it wuz diff'runt—just sharin' secrets like, y'know. Still it would have prob'ly passed from her mind after a while, if it hadn't been fer Pa."

"He died?" anticipated Abby.

"No, but it would have been a blessin' fer me an' Molly if he had. He took to drinkin' worser an' worser, til finely we'd have to put him ta bed. Then, durin' th' nights, he'd git up an' come an' try to lie with us. Him bein' without a woman ever sence Ma died, an' drinkin', it made 'im no mind that we wuz his daughters. We saved him from hisself, but it got ta happenin' so reg'lar, me an' Molly had to run away from home an' leave him by hisself. Many's th' time I wondered 'bout him, an' hoped he got hisself another wife. Wonder if I'll ever know." Her sad recollection occasioned a pause, before she continued. "Well, from then on, til now, it wuz trouble, an' nothin' else, fer me an' Molly. We worked as barmaids, an' in th' inns as chambermaids, an' whatever we could lay our hands to' that wuz honest an' good. But th' damn men we kept a-meetin' wouldn't let it be that way for long. Molly fell in love, an' th' son-of-a-bitch—I'm sorry, honey, but he wuz one—told her he wuz gonna marry her; so she gave in to him. He got her big, an' th' day he had promised her he'd marry her, his wife come after 'im with five kids an' marched him away. Poor Molly like to have died, an' almost lost her baby." Pointing to the little boy who had come into the room, unnoticed by Abby, she said, "That's him there. He's a sweet one, he is, but I shore hopes he takes after Molly."

Abby felt sorry for the child, and he was nice looking, but she was more interested, just now, in hearing Dolly's story. She simply gave an approving nod, ignoring the little boy's appealing, inquisitive gaze.

Dolly helped the situation along. "Bobby, you run on to yore ma." After Bobby's bare feet had pattered from the room, she said, "Time kinda has a way of makin' people fergit what they promises ta do when they's in trouble. Molly swore she'd never have nuthin' no more to do with no man, less'n he wuz her husband. But after a while, th' pleasurin' mem'ries of bein' with a man come over her strong, like they has me an' all women, an' it wuzn't long 'fore she wuz a-skippin' aroun' agin. Me, I wuzn't no diff'runt; 'cep'n I never got big—don't know why not though. I shore took plenty of chances."

"Well, we finely made our mistake—a bigger one than th' rest. What we had been a-doin', up til then, wuz to purely pleasure ourselves or 'cause we wuz fond of th' men we wuz a-goin' with. But one time we wuz partyin' with some officers an' we both had a awful good time. After we wuz done, them damn soldiers give us money fer our favors. From then on, we sold ourselves.

"It wuzn't long 'fore th' good women of th' town, whose husbands had been visitin' us, run us out from that place. Right here, I want to tell ya one thing, Abby. When ya gits married, take care of yore man. If you ain't in no pleasurin' mood, act like you are. Do it anyway. Refuse yore husband enough, an' he'll find hisself another pasture ta romp in. He'll finely git so likin' th' grass there, that he won't be a-botherin' you at all no more."

Abby nodded sincerely. "I'll sure remember that."

"See that ya does. Well, they ain't much more to my story. What happened in that town, happened ever'wheres else; 'cep'n sometimes it wuz th' 'thorities what made us move on. You know, one time th' mayor of one place told us we had to leave his town' an' just th' very night before, he wuz with me til 'most daybreak. If he hadn't dropped his boots when he sneaked in his house, Molly an' me might still be there." Dolly's mouth opened wide, as she laughed at the episode. "You know, he wuz awful sorry when he told me about it an' he give me a big purse, he did, when we left. But like I wuz a-sayin', there's few women knows how to care for a man. Mos' thinks so long as their faces is still pretty, they be all right. They pays no mind to gittin' fat or lazy, an' they wants their husbands only when they feels like it. It don't work that way, Abby. Just remember, it's harder ta keep a husband than it be to git one."

"Oh, golly, can it be that hard? Looks like I ain't never ever gonna get one."

Again Dolly laughed. "Don't ya worry none, honey. You' git one 'fore ya knows it. But when you does, remember how hard it wuz ta git 'im an' how easy like you can lose 'im." She paused momentarily. "Where wuz I? Oh, yes. Well, we kept movin' ever so off'n, an' th' only way ta move wuz tuh th' west, til, well, here we be."

"You didn't tell Ma all of it."

Abby's assertion startled Dolly. "What you mean, honey?

"Well, Molly has two children. don't she?"

"Abby Tindall, yore shore suthin' ain't ya? Molly had the other one along th' way. Th' only diff'runce betwixt th' first an' th' last wuz that she didn't promise that she wouldn't give in to th' next man til she married him, like she done th' first time." Dolly laughed heartily as she said this, then calming somewhat, she went over to where Abby was sitting, leaned down and placed her hands on her shoulder. "Abby. I hopes you gits married soon. Ya shore better."

"Why, what you mean by that?"

"Honey, I seen th' look in yore eyes, an' I heerd ya speakin' thick-like. Yes, sirree; I hopes you meets yore man, real soon."

Abby, too stunned by the truth of Dolly's observations to make any reply, sat there speechless. Dolly straightened up and turned from her just in time to see Jed remove himself from her doorway. Sudden panic came over her, but she tried not to let it betray its presence to Abby. How long had he been standing there? How much had he heard? Would he return before she could tell Jack about it?

Heavy coughing commenced in the next room. Then Molly's voice was heard, calling for her sister. Dolly seized the opportunity for a casual exit. "Honey, Molly wants me. I really liked yore comin' an' I wish you could come back, but I knows better. Ta just be shore you remembers what I told ya, an' you mind yore ma; she's a fine woman."

Abby had not seen Jed, and there was nothing in Dolly's voice or manner that reflected the terror that had struck her. "I'm forever beholden to you, Dolly, an' I sure hope I see you again." Abby waved goodbye and entered upon the street. Had she looked back, she would have seen the cabin door being hastily shut. Had her ears been so attuned, she would have heard these words of fearful prayer from Dolly's lips. "Oh, my God, protect me!"

As Abby turned toward home, she reflected. She had learned some of the things she wanted to know this afternoon, but what she really had hoped to learn, even Dolly had been too discreet to tell her. The wicked atmosphere of the bare

Dusenberry cabin had made a lasting impression upon her, however, and while she was still most desirous of delving into the mysteries of sex, one thing was clear in her mind; she would, as Dolly had so earnestly cautioned her, find out about them after she was married, not before. One other prudent determination was present also. She was going to marry Tom Chism, and soon, despite any objection on the part of her mother.

Rosie was waiting for her. "Abby Tindall, where have you been all this time? You know I can use some help this time of day."

"Over to see Dolly and Molly," she said calmly, adding Molly's name only that the purpose of her visit might be construed mercifully.

"You didn't!" Rosie raised her arms, the palms of her hands open—the gesture of complete helplessness. "Whatever will people think?"

"Prob'ly th' same as they thinks 'bout yore goin' over there."

Rosie had forgotten the presence of others in the room.

Now fully conscious of their open ears, she altered her voice and manner. "Oh, yes. Well, how was poor Molly?"

Abby did not miss the significance of the change in her mother. "'Bout the same; she really 'preciated th' broth you took her."

"That's nice. I'll ask you more about her, later."

Abby caught the implication instantly, and busied herself with the many chores attendant to serving supper.

"Abby."

"Yes, Mamma?"

"Tom Chism just left 'fore you come in; said to tell you he might not get back in time to see you tonight. Him an' Captain Mercer is goin' out somewheres together—said if he did come, it would be late."

"Now, that's something. I wanted to see him 'special tonight." Abby was perturbed, no end.

"I'm sorry, Abby, but all I can do is to tell you what he said."

"Thanks, Mamma."

CHAPTER 16

"That wasn't too bad a meal, Johnny." Barth wiped his lips before continuing. "You know, I just might decide to give you a full-time job as my personal cook. How would you like that?"

Barth's smile was anathema to Johnny, and his wry face was all-answering. "Yew has et yore fill, so yore tryin' some of thet damn funnin' stuff on me, ain't chew? Fer bein' a smart feller, yew ain't so damn smart; thet smile o' yores be like a damn idjit's."

The affronting facial expression persisted, and it so irked Johnny that his face became a lively red. "Jest fer thet, I ain't goin' to tell yew 'bout th' s'prise I bin a-keepin' fer yew."

Barth humored his mood. "I'm sorry, Johnny. I'd like to hear about it."

"Thet's whut yore allus a-sayin'—'I'm sorry.'" Johnny mocked him so perfectly, Barth had to smile in spite of a mighty effort not to do so.

"Thet is it! Damn if'n I ever tells yew nuthin' agin; never, no more, no sirree!"

"Well," began Barth, evidencing mock resignation, "if you feel that way, guess I'll just have to miss hearing about it."

This made Johnny a little uneasy; he had been waiting a good part of the day to tell Barth the news. He stewed a while, then he said, condescendingly, "I reckin' 'twouldn't be right not to tell ye, sence I'm yore depity an' all."

Barth nodded affirmatively without changing his assumed expression of seriousness. This was most difficult, as he was thinking of a reference to Johnny and himself, which he had unintentionally overheard earlier. Thet Cap'n Mercer an' his fried-ass depity.

"Yew'd never b'leeve hit, Kepteen! Would jew?"

"I can't answer that, until you tell me what it is."

"'Course. Well, whiles yew wuz gone, g'ess who wuz here a-visitin' me?"

"I've no idea; who was it, Johnny?" Barth was truly inquisitive and a little anxious. "Wasn't a woman was it?" Dracie Claycomb was in his thoughts.

"Shecks, no!" exclaimed Johnny in profound disgust. "Yew 'spectin' a womin? Who be she?"

"A particular friend of mine, Johnny, a real close friend."

"Hmm, how come I hain't never heared of her 'fore this?"

"You will, Johnny, a lot; but what about your visitor?"

"Oh, shore, shore. Well, 'twuz Mace Hardin hisself! And he wuz real consarned like—said thet nuthin' like thet wuz gonna heppen agin; thet when I wuz able to git back, them fellers would respeck my 'thority. An' without no badge, neither! He wuz shore nice. Jest shows yew how yew kin mistake yoreself 'bout someun', don't it?"

"When the devil appears merciful or friendly, you'd best be mighty careful. You're already two steps toward hell, without your knowing it."

"Whut yew mean by thet, Kepteen?"

"Simply, that you had best watch your step. Mace must have had some reason for coming here."

"Kepteen, thet ain't no way to look at it. He shore 'pressed me as meanin' whut he said. Demme if I don't make them fellers jump, an' without no badge. Like yew says, Kepteen, th' badge ain't so damn 'portant."

Barth thought to reason with him, but abandoned the idea. Johnny was too high in the clouds.

Johnny walked to the open door and stretched himself. His jacket rose with his arms, baring the entire lower half of his body. Viewing him led Barth to comment, "You sure don't look like any Apollo, do you?" He had to chuckle at the sight of Johnny's thin, knobby conformation, which emphasized his half-erect posture. "Good thing we don't have any near neighbors, with you standing there almost nude."

"Whut in th' red hills of hell do yew mean by thet? I hain't never heared of no damn Apollo, an' as fer them neighbors, if'n they wuz eny, I reckin they has saw nekked people 'sides me."

Before Barth could answer, there came the sound of approaching horses. Johnny scurried back inside. "Looks like thet's some of them damn neighbors yew bin talkin' 'bout."

Barth went outside and was pleased to find it was Tom Chism, seated on a big bay and leading a handsome chestnut roan with a blaze face.

"Who was that standin' there without no britches?" Tom's tone was teasing.

Johnny bent the upper part of his body around the side of the door and fired at him. "Who in th' hell do yew think it wuz? Jest one of th' Kepteen's wimmen, thet's who! One thing fer shore, it ain't off'n a feller gits to see two horses thet has each got two asses." The cabin door slammed shut.

Barth had to pause a bit to quell his laughter. "That Johnny, as he puts it, is really 'suthin'." Reining in alongside of Tom, he added, "I didn't expect you for a while. Did Abby run you off early?"

"She wasn't even there. I told Rosie to tell her I didn't 'spect to be back tonight."

Their proximity was such that Barth couldn't escape the heavy odor of corn whiskey on Tom's breath. Seeking to pass it off lightly, he asked, "What's the celebration?"

Tom understood. "I'm just feelin' low again, Mercer, an' I'm askin' you not to make no mention of it to Rosie."

"Of course not, Tom. But if you are really considering marrying Abby, don't you think you ought to stop drinking? You understand, it's all right with me."

"You drink, don't you?"

"That I do; but I also know my limit and keep within it."

"You're lucky. I ain't never been able to know mine."

"That's why I say you ought to stop it. Frankly, some men were never meant to drink. They don't enjoy the taste itself; just the effect it has upon them. Not really liking it, they take too much so as to be sure of getting the effect."

"That sounds like me all right. I get so damn lonesome and down in spirit that I try to perk myself up. Then I wind up drunk. Abby'd make me a good wife an' I love her, but her ma ain't gonna let me have her."

"If I could believe you'd stop drinking when you married her, I'd try to convince Rosie and obtain her consent."

"Would you, Cap'n?"

""That I would, if you could convince me first."

"Cap'n, I'll take a oath—a true oath—on it!"

"I don't believe in taking oaths, Tom. Your promise would be good enough."

"Cap'n, I can't do that this evenin'. I'm too far started, but come daybreak' I'll make that promise."

"Good enough. Now tell me a little more about Brother Flinden and his wife. By the way, how far is it to his place?"

"Well, I'd say we have covered about a mile or so; prob'ly six—seven miles more, I reckon."

They were nearing the river. A melodious strain interspersed with loud, coarse voices floated to them, seemingly from the stockade half obscured in the dusk, to their far right. Barth recognized the tune as German, but the name escaped him. "What's that over there?"

"Mud Garrison, one of th' first built hereabouts. That's prob'ly Herman Tressel playin' th' music."

"What is the name of the song? I've heard it before but I can't place it."

"I can't think of it either."

"Sounds a little like it was being played with bells, doesn't it?"

""Tain't though. That's Herman playin' on his glockenspiel."

"That's what it is. I recognize it now."

Their pace picked up a bit, Barth following Tom's lead in spurring his mount and the music faded rapidly behind them. The cleared ground over which they were passing was soft and yielding to the horses' hooves. The smell of the river was clean and pleasing to their senses. Approaching the stream, Tom directed their way parallel to its course.

"Cap'n, you'd never think that two year ago this was all forest, would you?"

"It's hard to imagine, but I've seen how those furnaces eat up wood."

"Sure do that. That idea you was talkin' about will sure help. Ever'one's goin' farther an' farther for logs." Suddenly recollecting the matter of Brother Flinden and wife, he said, "You asked 'bout Brother Flinden and Ursula. Well, there ain't much to tell, more'n I already told you. He's peculiar in lots of ways, an' you most has to find 'em out for yourself. I'm tellin' you one sure thing though; if Ursula's around, she'll be doin' most of th' talkin'. 'Stead of your learnin' 'bout them, she'll be finding out about you."

"That doesn't sound too much like a good Friend's wife.[9] Usually, they are fairly subservient to their husbands."

"Don't know nothing 'bout what subservient, or whatever it was you called it, means, but Ursula ain't no usual wife. They say she's part of th' reason why they're here."

"I've heard that before. I think Johnny mentioned it to me."

"That Johnny! He knows something about most ever'one. Take a little heed, Cap'n, he ain't allus right about ever'thing."

Barth mentally noted that he himself had the same suspicion. "He does have quite a bit of information concerning a lot of folks here though."

"He does that; but he sure ought to. He's about th' most curious man I ever saw—sticks his nose in ever'wheres."

Passing over this, Barth asked, "How does it happen that folks call him Brother Flinden? Every Friend of my acquaintance is addressed as mister—by other than Friends that is."

"I don't rightly know 'bout that, 'cept, maybe there's Presbyterians an' Methodists 'round here, an' they might be th' ones to have started it, an' th' rest just called 'im th' same."

"Whoa, now." Tom slowed his horse and Barth also pulled his reins as Tom advised, "Th' ford's just ahead."

The bank sloped gently to the stream and they splashed across; the water just touching their boots. The ascent at the other shore was a bit steeper and required a little urging of their steeds to reach the top. Tom cautioned, "We won't be able to go as fast as we been goin'; there's a woods up in front a short piece." It was dark now and the moon was up fairly bright.

"Might have been better to have come in the daytime," observed Barth.

"This is a hell of a time to think of it," laughed Tom.

"That's right, but I didn't want to take you away from your work." Barth sensed that the whiskey was beginning to tell on his companion, but made no reference to the fact. He did consider the impression that might be conveyed to Aaron Flinden. Particularly if Tom remained after guiding him to Flinden's cabin. He determined to circumvent this.

"Tom, after we get there, there's no need for you to stay. I can find my way back without any difficulty."

"'Twon't be no trouble, Cap'n, if you want me to stay."

"I'll be all right, and you might get back in time to sit a while with Abby."

"Not tonight, Mercer. I'm feelin' what I already drunk too much for that. And after tonight, I'm gonna make that promise. I mean it."

"Good for you, Tom."

They were moving slowly, in and out of the trees. The flittering moonlight brought back to Barth his experience at the creek on his way to the lick. It seemed a long time ago. A lot had happened in the few days he had been here.

Now they were on cleared land again. In the distance to their left, the moon showed the faint outlines of a dwelling.

"That's Brother Flinden's over there, Cap'n."

"I see it."

"Take it kinda easy when we git closer. He's got some plantin' 'roun' here, somewheres."

"I'll watch out for it. How about our cutting for those trees ahead on the right? Then we can circle around with them to the house."

They dismounted and tied their horses to a hitching rail in front of the cabin. The heat generated by the ride was unnoticed by them, but thin vapors were rising from the flanks of their animals.

CHAPTER 17

Tom rapped on the door, calling to Flinden as he did so. Barth stood discreetly by his side. When no one answered, Tom rapped harder and called louder, producing the desired result when a woman's pitched voice exclaimed, "Thee must be a most impatient person. Will thee allow me the chance to open the door, before thee breaks it down?"

"That's Ursula," said Tom knowingly.

From inside, the voice came again. "I will admit thee, but first, thee must tell me thy name."

"Tell Brother Flinden, it's Tom Chism, from over at th' licks."

"Be thou alone or in company?"

"I have a friend with me. His name's Cap'n Mercer."

"Thou should know that we have nothing of interest for, or in, soldiers."

"This has nothing to do with no soldiers. He's just a friend of mine, and he wants to meet Brother Flinden."

"Thou could much better meet him in the morning. Why doth thee creep up on us in the night?"

"We can't come in th' morning, an' we didn't creep up on you; we rode our horses here." Aside to Barth, he said, "You still think you're going to get to talk to Brother Flinden?"

Barth smiled. "It's not going to be easy. I can see that."

"Be thee still out there? I don't hear thee talking."

A man's firm tones came from within. "Ursula, where be thy charity? These be travelers at our door. Wouldst thee deny them comfort?"

She responded. "Thee might be fooled. They might be savages. Thou knows their powers to speak English."

"'Twould be the exceptional savage who could last thy conversation. Prithee, stand aside, that I may let them in."

The door, massive in thickness, swung open, revealing an exceptionally well-lighted interior. Barth marveled that not the slightest ray had been visible from without. Brother Flinden's cabin was actually airtight, so perfect was its construction. The room itself, of larger dimensions than most he had seen, other than that of the Graingers, furnished additional evidence of painstaking effort, so typical of the patience of the Friends. Even the ladder to the upstairs chamber was of careful workmanship and highly finished. All around were pieces of furniture, which bespoke fine craftsmanship. All of this Barth took in with swift glances while Tom was exchanging pleasantries with Aaron Flinden.

Tom now sought to get to the purpose of his visit. "Brother Flinden, this here's Cap'n Mercer. He has something that he'd like to talk to you about."

"I am pleased to make thy acquaintance, sir. This is my wife, Ursula."

Barth bowed as he acknowledged the introduction.

"What doth thee wish to discuss with my husband, Captain?"

"With all due respect and deference to you, madam, I expect that's something I had best address to Mr. Flinden."

Ursula's tongue became caustic. "Thou'rt like all the military. We have moved the greater part of the past five years under the surveillance of soldiers. We thought to have seen the last of any semblance of war, or its preparation, when we did come to this wilderness."

"Madam, I assure you I have no intention of even talking about anything pertaining to the Army, or war, save should your husband raise the subject."

"Thy words are most familiar. 'Tis but the same ruse th' others have employed. Such talk first took us from Philadelphia, through Pennsylvania and thence to Winchester and Staunton."

Barth remembered now. Had the Flindens been part of the exiled Pennsylvania Quakers? He had always considered their treatment most unfair, but he fell short of sympathy. He could not but feel that they lived because of the deaths of others, that their bodies were whole because others had bled from gaping wounds.[10]

Ursula interrupted his meditation. "Thee pauses. Is it for the reason that thou be conscious of the truth?"

"Mrs. Flinden, I can only say that you are entirely wrong in your opinion. I recall hearing of the sad experiences of the Friends and which it has apparently been your misfortune to have shared. However, I don't recall mention that there were any women among those in Virginia."

"I doubt that thee has appreciation of the sadness of our confinement. We did not have to leave Pennsylvania ourselves. We moved out of sympathy for others who had to do so and to give them company. 'Tis also a matter of doubt with that thee has read the Book; if thee hath, thee would remember Ruth. Like unto her, I did not have to go; indeed, I was restrained. But follow, I did."

"That is greatly to be admired, madam."

"Admire all thee wants, but I be not fooled; of that I warn thee! Thy companion reeks of strong drink. I suspect that were I closer to thee, I should smell the same."

Aaron Flinden had listened as long as he was able. "Ursula, thee exceeds discretion and good reason. Thou are to the ugly point of insulting these gentlemen. I must bid thee apologize for thy faults and excuse thyself."

She did not comply immediately and Tom, welcoming this interval as a good moment to leave, engaged Brother Flinden in conversation designed to lead to that end.

Barth used the time to study Ursula, now striving so mightily for her self-control. He saw her altogether a plain person, perhaps a little over five feet, fair and fraily inclined, straw-colored hair, high cheek bones, pale gray eyes, a priggish nose and firm, set lips above a pointed chin. These observations he made quickly, before she obeyed her husband.

"If I have offended thee, I am sorry." Without waiting for any acceptance, she added in a voice shaded with defiance, "Thou has heard my words. Thee knows as to their truth or falsity." With that, she gathered her skirts and ascended the ladder.

After again seeking assurance that his presence wasn't further necessary, Tom bid them goodbye.

The two were seated at an easy angle. Barth's chair was most comfortable and reminded him of one that he liked especially at home in Williamsburg.

At what was the vertex of the triangle, made by their positions with it, was a beautiful oak writing desk. Numerous books, some opened, gave the impression their pages had been turned recently in study.

Barth became aware that study was being pursued at this instant, and that he was its object. Aaron Flinden was making his own estimation of him.

Hesitant to open any conversation, and mindful that Flinden was peculiar in lots of ways, Barth waited for him to initiate any discourse. However, he regarded his host in a completely unobtrusive manner. Flinden's frame was big; his whole being proclaimed strength. He was quite tall, perhaps three inches above six feet. His features were most benign, to a conclusion of absolute handsomeness. His lengthy hair, rich brown in color, rolled in waves, which seemingly shaped his face. The thought came to Barth: Johnny had seen Apollo without knowing it. But of all that he noted about Aaron Flinden, Barth centered upon the keen, clear eyes of a depth of blue that was almost purple, and upon a pleasing mouth, which at the same time appeared capable of laughter or of sorrow, without the slightest movement of its lips. The resolute jaw served only to set off these chosen features.

After what seemed an indeterminable silence, Flinden spoke. "Thy friend had partaken of drink, but thee hath not."

"His heart was heavy; mine was not. Nor did I feel ready to perish."

"I see thou has read the Book."

"From my youth. My father gave me a Bible when I was a boy, and I used his gift."

"Friend Mercer, I find that most commendable. 'Tis too bad indeed, thee did not comprehend fully its spirit."

"I don't understand what you mean, Mr. Flinden."

"'Tis simple, friend Mercer. Had thee understood, thou could not have engaged in war or in the preparation for war. Thy hand would have rather guided the plowshare than the sword."

"Do you reconcile Armageddon?"

"Vengeance and battle belong unto the Lord. I do not question his will."

Barth weighed carefully his next words. "Mr. Flinden, I have found many admirable virtues in the Friends' practice of their faith; but on some points I must confess I find them to be most selfish and self-preserving. Here they have a land where there is freedom for the pursuit of their belief. Yet when that freedom is threatened, none will raise a hand in its defense. Surely, the history of persecution under British rule cannot have been forgotten so soon."

Aaron Flinden's brows creased. "I recall no such persecution before the revolt of the Colonies as we have suffered by order of the Supreme Executive Council of the Commonwealth of Pennsylvania. Nor, from my experience in Virginia, can I distinguish between Whig and Tory."

"'He who is not with me'—" Barth began.

Interrupting, Brother Flinden completed the biblical quotation. "—'is against me.' But thy thought is confused, and what thee intended is a strong argument against thy very reasoning. The Lord's way is the way of peace, and the contemplation that thou think and move as he does. Thou cannot take his words and use them out of their meaning to please thine own desires."

"Then the world would lose much practical guidance, if your understanding be correct."

"The Word is to be followed, not used, friend Mercer. For that purpose do we all exist."

"Exist, you say, sir? The spirit leaves when the body dies and existence ends."

"Only for the body, which returneth to the dust."

"That points out another one of my objections to the blind following of your belief. Suppose all Quakers were to die, how would your faith be propagated?"

"We all shall die, friend Mercer."

"I mean, at the same time. As of this moment, for example."

"Thee strives to show thy logic. What are thee leading to?"

Barth leaned forward in his chair as he spoke. "If no one fought or contained the Indians, they would slaughter Friends as well as others."

"Then 'twould be the Lord's will. However, I know of few Friends who have ever died at the hands of savages."

"Purely because they are seldom in their way."

"Thee are wrong there, friend Mercer. 'Tis because the Redman knows that we are men of peace. As thee must have noticed, I live some distance from the settlements and any neighbor, but no Indian has troubled me."

"Not yet," Barth replied. "But consider for a moment your home in Pennsylvania. Did it ever occur to you that you lived there because others had shed their blood and given their lives to wrest that ground from the Indians?"

"They need not have done so. Had peace been in their hearts, they might have lived there, and the Indians also. Think, friend Mercer, how glorious that could have been, redeeming the savages in peace! The entire country could have thus been won to God!" Caught in this spiritual surge, his eyes rolled heavenward.

"Think rather, Mr. Flinden, of the bloody and torn scalps of women and little children, of mutilated bodies, of torture at the stake. Have you ever witnessed any of these?"

"The Lord hath spared me the sight of such happenings."

"Spared is the true word, Mr. Flinden. I have seen them. I have heard the anguished cries. I have smelled the burning flesh. Can you read the Book, sir, and not remember the wars that are waged on its pages? The freedom of will that God gave to man ensures that there will be wars and rumors of wars. All history establishes the fact. Wars are prime examples of man's imperfections."

"It is our faith to change that, friend Mercer."

"You are such a small handful."

"Christ was but one. The faith will spread."

"It can't spread if the Quakers spend their time largely in gainful pursuits. I have seen few Friends who were destitute."

"We have those who go among the heathen savages also, friend Mercer."

"A negligible few. And on that point, all Indians are not heathens, as you term them. They are like the White people. Some groups are good and believe in a Supreme Being while others have no faith and do evil. Do you know that some of their beliefs are similar to those of Christian peoples?"

Flinden shook his head.

"Have you ever heard of a Mingo chieftain called Logan?"

Again, Flinden answered negatively.

"Then I'll acquaint you with him, by reciting from his message to Lord Dunmore, who was then royal governor of Virginia. 'I appeal to any white man to say, if ever he entered Logan's cabin hungry, and he gave him not meat; if ever he came cold and naked, and he clothed him not.'" Barth paused before continuing. "What do those thoughts suggest to you?"

"They are indeed Christlike."

"My father thought likewise. It was he who obtained a copy of the appeal for me in the late years of his life. I committed its contents to what I hope is steadfast memory."

"'Tis to be approved, friend Mercer. But one charitable savage, or a few of them, doth not constitute their races as God-fearing peoples."

"I haven't finished, Mr. Flinden. It is religious legend among them that this continent, the world to them, was once but a small island. One day, a baby squaw was found floating in a canoe made of reeds. This baby grew to be a great prophetess, endowed with powers that linked her to the Great Being, in whom they believe. By her supplications, this Great Being caused vast numbers of water tortoises and muskrats to bring large quantities of mud, sticks and other materials, adding then to the island and thereby increasing greatly its size, so that there was more room for the Indians to live thereon. It is upon this quaint theology that they base their claim to this land. Their great-grandmother, the prophetess, made the land for them; therefore, the white man should not take it from them."

Brother Flinden was impressed, nodding his head and pursing his lips as he listened.

Still on the alert for Flinden's peculiar ways, Barth made sure there was abiding interest in what he was discussing. "Do you find anything reminiscent of the Bible in what I have just said?"

"To be sure. I am reminded of Moses in the bullrushes and, in a crude, aboriginal way, of the Word, as to the world's creation."

"Exactly." Barth determined to continue. "They believe in what correspond to our angels, heavenly subjects who visited their forefathers and who taught them the manner of prayer and how to appease their Great Being, when there had been offense, by the art of sacrifice with burnt tobacco and the bones of certain animals. As in the case of Old Testament taboos, they were forbidden to use the bones of some animals for sacrificial purposes. There are also multitudes of lesser deities who assist in the management of the universe and in watching over the actions of men and in regulating their affairs.

"Certain fowl, such as the eagle and the owl, are thought by them to be bearers of intelligence to heaven. When these birds are seen in their proximity, they offer the prescribed sacrifices. I have known of attacks that have been stayed or ended by the appearance of an owl in a tree along the route of march.

"Just as there are good angels, as they might be termed, so there are also bad angels or evil spirits. These are inhabitants of the lower regions who work constantly in direct opposition to those of heaven.

"You will recall, I am sure, that Saint Paul said any worship of a Supreme Being who bears a name different from that by which we call ours does not mean that those so believing are to be deemed by us nonbelievers. As he said, the Romans worshiped Jupiter, and the Greeks worshiped Zeus. The recognition of an omnipresent, omnipotent being is the mark of faith."

Uncrossing his legs and leaning forward, Brother Flinden inquired, "But did the savages, or do they, believe in the great life to come?"

"That is, as it is with the Whites, a matter of opinion among tribes and individuals. Some do so believe in such a future state, while others deny any afterlife, contending that when dead, a man no longer thinks or lives."

A voice, not of heavenly quality, interrupted them. "Aaron Flinden, be thy company unmindful of the hour! It grows into the night. Advise him to take his rest with us or leave, as he wills."

"It is not that late, Ursula. Seek thine own rest."

"'Tis easy for thee to say; but thou knows that we are quiet persons, given to early retirement."

"Mind thy tongue and thy manners, Friend wife."

The mode of address had the desired effect; she did not reply.

Barth considered leaving and postponing his mission until another time. "I guess Mrs. Flinden is right. I may have presumed upon your indulgence."

"'Tis not so, friend Mercer. However, upon reflection, we have talked at length and I yet know not thy purpose in coming here."

Barth recited quickly his need of Flinden's services. That his efforts were faced with disappointment became evident from Flinden's features even before he had concluded.

"I could not do what thee asks of me, friend Mercer."

"But I understood you were excellent with figures and with books."

"I do have ability in that regard. I was a successful merchant before retirement in Virginia. But I will not use my talents in the service of such a man as Mace Hardin nor associate with those who work for him."

Barth noted he did not say friend Hardin, and that his tone bordered on harshness.

"Before I converse further with thee, I must ask: Art thou in his employ?" Brother Flinden's eyes narrowed.

"On the contrary, sir. He works for me. I had hoped to say nothing about my ownership of the land at the licks. I ask sincerely that you keep my confidence."

"Confidence and Hardin cannot be said to go hand in hand."

"I know that, Mr. Flinden. Believe me, sir, I have a purpose far greater than any embraced by self-interest." Barth then explained the need for salt by the young, aspiring nation, some of whose members were Quakers, as he expressly pointed out. He told of his commission and of his intention to discharge Hardin, once the emergency had lifted or eased.

"I can sympathize with thy concern, friend Mercer, but I could not bring myself to be among such blasphemous heathen I would have to hear cursing all the day and would not be able to bewray its utterance. Why my very body would be in gravest danger. Thou'rt but lately arrived here. Does thee know that those heathen ruffians broke poor Tom Allen's arm because he objected that they had cut and removed timber from his land; that they mocked and reviled him so much thereafter that he removed himself and his family to Virginia?"

Barth sought vainly to ease his fears. The only answer was a slow, determined shaking of Aaron Flinden's head. "I will not accede to thy entreaties, friend Mercer. It is not hard for me to believe that a goodly number of Satan's fallen angels are among those making salt for you. Mud Garrison is but a cavern of hell, friend Mercer, and life among those devils is fair hell itself."

"Mr. Flinden, if I were not in desperate need of your services and aid, I would not ask you to reconsider your decision, as I am now doing. I'll ask you, sir, directly: What is your opinion of me? Do you believe me to be an honorable man?"

"While I have but met thee, and I could be grievously wrong in my judgment, I would say, yes, thou'rt honorable."

"If I promised that I would see that no harm came to you, that you would have no contact with the workers, including Mace Hardin, would you then believe me?"

Flinden's fingers bluntly touched his nose, then dropped to his lips as he sifted the question. At length he replied, "I would believe thee, but I would not agree to enter into thy employ."

From upstairs, Ursula thundered raucously, "If thee doth agree, Aaron Flinden, I shall leave thee; faithful wife though I be to thee."

"I forgot, sir, that there might be another listening to our conversation."

Flinden's ears reddened. "I'm most sorry, friend Mercer; I am truly sorry."

Barth decided to make one last attempt. "I need an honest, educated man, Mr. Flinden. Finding an honest man around here is task enough; only your presence keeps it from being impossible. It will not be for long ... won't you try it for a day or so? If it doesn't work out, you are at liberty to leave and I'll still be greatly indebted to you regardless."

"Aaron Flinden!" Ursula screamed.

Her husband did not answer her immediately. When he did, he said in a calm, firm voice, "That will be enough, Ursula." For some time, he did not say another word, but sat in deep meditation. Interrupting his thought, he asked, "How could I be free of talking with or moving among them?"

"I have a man that I trust who will bring you all necessary advices. Your duties would confine you to the new storehouse being built to replace the one destroyed by the fire."

"I heard of it," Flinden acknowledged.

"I am most interested in the safety of the records to be kept and perforce in the person who has their custody. No harm shall befall you."

"Who is this person whom thee hath faith in?"

"A Mr. Littelby. You may know him as Little Johnny. He was a peddler before he came with me."

"Thee really trusts him?"

"I do most certainly. Had he your intelligence, I would have my man in him."

"What guarantee would I have as to my remuneration?"

"Whatever you might require, even to payment in advance."

"That part is attractive. How much doth thee intend paying?"

"I would leave that to your Quaker conscience, Mr. Flinden."

More silence ensued, during which Barth shifted his position numerous times. Aaron Flinden did not move until he said, "I shall try and help thee, friend Mercer. Now to the terms."

The discussion as to the amount was brief and agreement reached quietly. Barth learned that while Aaron Flinden's faith was tightly confined, his Quaker conscience was most elastic as to monetary consideration.

From the room above, Ursula railed down at him. "Thou will make me an early widow, poor and defenseless, that will I be! Thou has forgot the Script and the examples of Friend Fox and Friend Penn![11] Thou are deserting thy faith. Thy steps turn willingly to evil men!"

Disregarding her linguistic salvos, Flinden asked, "When am I expected to assume my duties?"

"Next Monday, your first day, the day after tomorrow. I shall serve in Mr. Littelby's stead the first week or so. I shall meet you at the ford about the hour of eight on that morning."

"I am most pleased to hear that. Is Mr. Littelby indisposed for some reason?"

Barth sought fast thinking. "Why, yes, he is a trifle uncomfortable at present, but it is nothing serious."

He held his breath, fearing another question as to the cause of Johnny's indisposition might put him right back where he had started. But no further inquiry was forthcoming. Upstairs, Ursula's railing became louder.

"'It is better to dwell in a corner of the housetop'—" began Brother Flinden smilingly.

"—'than with a brawling woman in a wide house.'" Barth finished the proverb from the Bible, and then added, "Good night, sir. You have made me most happy by your decision."

That was the extent of the goodbyes. Ursula's voice filled the room as the door was being closed behind him.

CHAPTER 18

The roan's blaze was reflected silver in the moonlight and its feet moved nervously, as though impatient to move homeward. Barth mounted easily and wheeled around in a half circle to his left. Only after he had completed the turn did he realize that he had used only a leg aid, without any action of the reins. This was his usual manner when riding his gray sagitta, and he had done it from habit. His respect grew for the horse he had borrowed; it was sound and well trained. As he thought back on the ride to Brother Flinden's, he remembered the steed's comfortable, easy, yet sure-footed gait. He would like to own this animal.

He had crossed the open space, now bright as the day under the moon's illumination, and entered the darkness of the woods. The hooting of an owl caused him to tighten his reins, but he relaxed as the bird fluttered from its perch and flew away. What had been only an owl on this occasion, might be an Indian signal the next time he heard it. Vigilance meant life; its absence meant death.

Once the ford had been crossed, he made for the eastern edge of the settlement where cabins appeared as shadows. The visibility was wonderful, even Kahaz Knob's contour could be discerned. Soon the silent shadows became houses and he headed for Rosie Tindall's, where his animal was to be stabled, according to a prearrangement with Tom Chism.

He noticed a light in Rosie's place, unusual for this late hour.

The horse bedded down, he came around the side from the rear, to find a worried Rosie standing in the doorway. "You're up late tonight. I thought you would be asleep long before now," he said to her.

Rosie hesitated, then greeted him joyfully. "It's you, Captain Mercer! Thank heaven, it's you! I ain't never been so glad to see anyone in my whole borned life!"

"What has you so upset, Rosie? Just calm down a bit and tell me about it."

"Oh, Cap'n, it's Abby! She has been after me all evenin' to give my consent to marryin' Tom."

"Is that all? You shouldn't allow yourself to go to pieces over that, Rosie. You get some rest, and it'll be better come morning."

"You don't understand, Cap'n. That girl's actin' like she had to get married to him this very night. He left word he wouldn't see her this evenin' but she waited for him to come anyway. Finally, she went out to see if he was at his cabin."

"How long's she been gone?"

"She run out of here just a few minutes before you come 'round th' side of th' house."

"Good. I'll go right after her. Now, you just settle down. Everything will be all right. I'll have her back in no time at all."

"God bless you, Cap'n!"

Barth decided against saddling the horse. With such a slight start, Abby couldn't have gotten very far.

He ran swiftly for a while then slowed to a jog. Just as he began to wonder if she might have taken another way, he caught sight of what he believed to be her a few hundred yards in front of him. As a sense of relief began to come upon him, he saw that there were two figures there now. A man and a woman. Perhaps Tom was with her. No, that wasn't likely. He recalled Tom's determination to avoid Abby until tomorrow.

Drawing nearer, he saw that the two were struggling. Then they disappeared suddenly, somewhere between the cabins.

Barth hurried after them, veering into the space he thought they had entered. One side was in deep shade, the other in the brightness of the moon. Cautiously, he explored the darkness, step by step. There was no sound whatsoever. Just as he was about to give up and search elsewhere, he heard a muffled cry. Rushing in its direction, at what seemed the edge of the light and dark, he caught a glint of steel—barely in time to move with its arc and to grasp the hand that held the weapon. Locking the wrist, he forced the knife from the grip that held it, but he was unable to hold its owner, who twisted violently to his freedom.

Abby, if it was her, had fairly flown past him toward the road, in an opposite course from that taken by her attacker.

Starting to follow her, Barth's foot kicked the knife into the open glare. He retrieved it hastily and reentered upon his pursuit of the fleeing girl. He caught her shortly, sobbing hysterically. At the sight of the blade in his hand, she fainted dead away. Carrying her in his arms, he was met by Rosie as he neared her home.

It was Rosie's turn to be hysterical, and he found himself in a true dilemma. Fearful he might drop Abby and yet having to use one of his arms to fend Rosie, who, in her hysteria, imagined Abby dead. He finally made it inside and laid his burden gently upon the floor. No sooner had he done so, than Rosie was there also, holding her beloved daughter's head upon her lap, sobbing softly, while shedding copious tears.

He secured a wet cloth and, kneeling beside Abby, placed it upon her frightened brow. Shortly, she opened her eyes, and Rosie gave vent to a shriek of joy, which thoroughly awakened most of her lodgers. Barth went quickly among them, settling them back to their rest.

Now a bit composed, Abby arose with her mother's help and the two seated themselves on a table bench, with Barth across from them. In a faltering tone, she brought herself to describe the happening. "I was gonna go to Tom's, when sudden like this man grabbed me 'roun' m' waist. I was too scared to remember his face, but I 'member him sayin' he'd heard say I was wanting a man."

Abby raised the level of her hushed voice and continued, between racking sobs. "Oh, Mamma. I knowed what he was a-figgerin' on doin' to me, an' I knowed I deserved it; I acted shameful all day."

Rosie comforted her. "That's all right, darlin', just pass it from your mind."

Abby's words quieted when she resumed. "I tried to scream but he clapped his hand over my mouth, an' I scratched at him, best I could."

They looked at her hands. There was dried blood on her fingertips. Whoever had attacked her had some battle scars.

"I reckon he heard you comin', Cap'n, 'cause he twisted around behind me an' drug me in to th' dark. I could tell he was gettin' to his knife an' that's when I tried to give a warnin'. When I got free, I just run, fast as I could. Then when I saw you comin' after me, I seen th' knife in your hand and I thought you was him, and it scared me so, I just dropped right there."

Speaking softly out of consideration for those asleep nearby, Barth asked, "Then you couldn't describe the man at all?"

"Only what I just told you. I didn't have no chance to see him, after he got hold of me from behind."

Reaching to his belt, Barth pulled the knife and placed it on the table as he moved the lighted tallow closer to him. The weapon bore no unusual marks, but it was instantly familiar. Now he had two identical souvenirs of his encounters at Bullitt's Lick.

"This is the same kind of knife someone tried to stab me with, the first morning I came here. Maybe, it was the same person, but, again, it could have been almost anyone. It seems a lot of people around here own knives like this one."

"One thing I'm sure of, Captain Mercer. I won't be goin' out like that no more. An', Captain, I sure thanks you for savin' me."

"And you know I'm most thankful, Captain, and that I'll never forget you for what you done." Rosie's mouth quivered as she spoke.

"That's nice of you," Barth said modestly, "but let's see if you can't stop thinking about it for a while. It's late and I'm tired, so if you all don't mind, I think I'll be on my way. I don't think a little rest would hurt you two either."

All three arose at the same time. As Rosie raised up the bar, preparatory to securing the door, he heard Abby say to her, "It was fearful, Mamma. but I'm still going to marry Tom."

Barth laughed away the first part of his walk home, thinking of Abby's determined spirit. She was frontier stock for certain.

Further along, he noticed a weariness in his legs. The experience had been physically trying.

Ahead of him, a group of the villagers chatted excitedly. Lights shone from open doors. It was the place of the attack.

Passing them, he heard one say, "Ask him if he saw anyone."

Another immediately replied, "He come from up there, a ways. I been watchin' him. He won't know nuthin' 'bout it."

A nasty-tempered Johnny unbarred the door for him and then was back to snoring seconds later. Barth's exhausted frame soon sank into complete repose and, had there been a listener, he could have told him in the morning of the awesome "dueyet" rendered by their noisy breathing.

CHAPTER 19

The men were milling busily around when Barth arrived at the licks. Mace was there ahead of him and as he greeted him, he said, "Yer a mought late, this mornin', Cap'n."

"Yes, I am. Guess I just had too hard a day yesterday."

"Thet Tom Chism guv yer eny trubble?"

"None at all, Mr. Hardin. Why do you ask?"

"Wal, I seed yer ridin' off with 'im last evenin', an' I jest wondered 'bout hit." Changing the subject, he pointed to the storehouse. "Hit's damn nigh done, Cap'n. 'Twon't take no more'n anuther day ter finish it."

"That's good work, Mr. Hardin. Do you mean another day, after today?"

"Naw, sir. I means hit'll be done by nighttime."

The two walked over to the reconstruction and Barth studied it intently. "Looks like a good job, Mr. Hardin. Have you had to lose too many men from the salt operations?"

"Hain't slowed a mought, Cap'n."

"Do you still think we'll have enough for a good-sized shipment soon?"

"Liken I tole yer. I figgers roun' Monday they orter be 'nough fer a real load."

"That's fine. Maybe Chism'll be ready for a shipment at the same time."

"Yer hain't gonna ship our'n with his'n?"

"If he's got enough ready to go."

"Beggin' yore pardin, Cap'n, but does yer think hit's smart ter do thet? A lot uv men an' bosses kin 'tract lotsa 'tenshun. With all thet salt, th' Injuns 'ud be roun' liken buzzards."

"There's always that danger, Mr. Hardin, whether there are few or many. I believe, however, that the larger the group, the more safe it will be. From what I understand, there haven't been any sizeable bands of Indians along our route for some time. I know this is the time of the year for them, but I doubt that there will be any more than raiding or scouting parties to contend with, if at all, and they won't number more than eight to twelve, at most."

"I hopes yer right, Cap'n. They's been lotsa talk 'bout trubble 'roun' Harrodstown and at McAfee's Station an' over at Bryan Station, futher up."

"I've heard that too, Mr. Hardin, and they may be right but the Indians that cause the trouble over there can come down the Miami and Scioto, cross the Ohio, down the Licking or some of those adjacent smaller creeks. It's easier for them to transport their artillery that way."

"I don't think we need to worry too much about any large-scale attacks where we are traveling. General Clark just about put an end to that danger when he captured the forts at Cahokia and Kaskaskia, almost four years ago."

"You know, until Clark's campaign, the savages could cross in great numbers from the Indiana Territory to Kentucky. There wasn't a settlement or garrison within sixty or seventy miles. But the general stopped that when he went in and smashed at their own towns. There's' been talk of his leading a large army into the Big and Little Miami territory. If this were to be done, it would stop, or at least slow down, the attacks by them northeast of here."

Mace nodded. "I heerd uv thet. I mean 'bout them other battles he hed up in Indiana Territory, but this is th' fust I knowed they wuz a-plannin' ter go over on th' Miamis. I still sez, hit'd be a bad thing ter be a-sendin' a lotta men on thet shipment, beggin' yore pardin, agin, liable ter draw them Injuns right ter us, liken back in '77."

"Were you here, then?"

"Jest got here; damn near had ter leave, soon's I kum. Injuns 'bout run ever'body away frum these here parts. But when they's money ter be made, folks'll keep after hit so, liken th' rest, I kum back."

"I heard of that trouble; but if something should happen as you fear it might, it will be my responsibility."

"Thet hain't gonna hep them as gits kilt er shot up."

"That will be my concern, Mr. Hardin!"

Barth's words were final in tone and Mace said nothing more.

"One thing, before I forget it, Mr. Hardin. I've arranged for Aaron Flinden to work for us, keeping accounts and such. I've pledged him that no harm or discomfort will come to him, and until Mr. Littelby is able to return, I am going to see that he is not molested or bothered in any way. I expect you to see to it that your men let him alone."

"Yer kin count on thet, Cap'n."

"All right for that then. Now I want to talk to Tressel and Willerhorst."

"Want me ter sen' fer 'em?"

"No need of that, I'll go see them myself."

"As yer wants, Cap'n."

Barth found Herman Tressel hard at work; the abbreviated peace pipe clenched between his teeth. He explained to him his plan to run the water to the furnaces, and Herman agreed that it might be possible. They discussed the best woods for the project and decided upon the use of gum and sassafras.

Tressel assured him that Motty Willerhorst and himself could see to the hollowing of the logs and to their joinder, but they would need men to help them; the exact number to depend on how soon the job was to be completed.

"Der day, so long, ain't; und fife arms, I don't got. Diss vork und dot iss too much, by vun man," Tressel complained.

"I know it will keep you busy; but after it gets started you would only have to check it, from time to time."

"Gute, but keep in der mind, fife arms, I don't got." Herman released the leg of the horse whose hoof he had now finished shoeing. He wiped the palms of his hands on the thick growth of black hair on his barrel chest. Barth noted that specks of gray were beginning to appear.

"How old are you, Mr. Tressel?"

"Vorty-dew, und a zegret I'll tell you—it feels dot I'm ziggedy." He added hastily, "Budt, der work I do, like der boy."

Barth smiled. "Do you think you and Mr. Willerhorst can take charge of this, and see that it is done properly?"

"Vait der second; vot about der boss? Vrum him, der money comes."

"I've already talked to him, he'll tell you about it himself."

"Den, I see der Mr. Willerhorst." Tressel laughed, as he gave emphasis to the mister. "Budt vork, he von't, shudt I call him mister. Giff directions, he vudt; budt vork, nein."

"Well, you see Motty, as you call him, and go over the matter with him. Then get busy on it the first thing in the morning."

"Der morning iss der Sabbath."

"Are you going to worship?"

"Nein, budt der rest, I take."

"All right, get to it Monday, then."

"Ven der boss says das der time. Vrum him comes der money."

"He'll see you today and tell you it's all right."

"Dot's der vay; vrum der boss der money comes."

His words proved an informal goodbye, as he positioned himself to shoe the animal's left rear hoof.

Like the Hessians, Barth thought, Tressel served and obeyed only the one who paid him.

Recognizing that "der boss" would have to give his sanction, before the work would start, Barth found Mace Hardin and told him what he wanted done.

As they talked, one of the men, who Barth recalled had been in the party in the search for Bad-Eye, came up to where they were standing.

"Mace, they's some'un at th' Widder Tindall's who's a-askin' fer th' cap'n."

Barth's heart jumped. "Is it a woman—a young woman?"

"Nope, it's some feller what's with some more thet's on their way tuh th' Falls. They asked me wuz I knowin' yore where'bouts, an' when I tole 'em I did, this feller sez fer me tuh tell yuh tuh come right away—sez he's got some uv yore b'longins."

"Jest don't stan' thar restin' yore damn lazy ass! Git a wagon an' drive th' cap'n over thar."

Spurred by Mace's order, he was gone before Barth could stop his flight.

"Mr. Hardin, I could have taken the wagon myself. There's no need to take his time."

"Beggin' yer pardin, Cap'n. They mought be suthin' he kin hep yer with."

"Hadn't thought of that; there might be some help he can give me. Thanks for your thinking of it."

In no time, it seemed, the wagon was there, and he was on his way. His heart was racing within him at this unexpected summons. His thoughts were confused, fearing that something might have happened to Dracie. Maybe she was ill, or worse, maybe she was dead. Rough as this place was, he should have brought her with him. Instead of living with Johnny, she could have been sharing his cabin with him. Then he tried to reassure himself; perhaps the man had brought a letter from her. It would be like her to insist that it be delivered to him personally. He wished fervently that he was free to go back to her, but he knew that was impossible until he had straightened out everything here.

From a distance, he saw people gathered up ahead. And as the wagon drew nearer, he could see that the small throng was in front of Ben Skinner's.

"You sure that I'm to go to Mrs. Tindall's?"

"Thet's whut he sed."

"Wonder what so many people are doing at Ben Skinner's."

"Hain't yuh heerd, Cap'n? Ben's done got real winders in th' store—real glass. Yuh kin see ever'thing out here. Them's the first real winders some uv 'em's seen. I went an' looked both ways. Been so long sence I saw glass in winders, I most fergot whut they wuz like."

They slowed some to avoid running over any of the curious; but even so, two or three had to jump out of the way of their vehicle.

"Bet a lotta folks'll be a-gittin' glass from Old Ben, don'tcha reckin'?"

Barth's anxiety would not allow him to answer the driver's question. Instead he said, "Those people up there must be the ones you were telling me about. Slow down a little."

Something was wrong. Before he could be directed to the man who sought him, Barth saw his horse, the gray Sagitta. A lone traveler holding him by his bridle.

Leaping from the seat while the wagon was yet moving, he nearly lost his balance when he hit the ground.

Sagitta saw him and whinnied sharply, nostrils quivering, trim ears forward.

His holder spoke as Barth hurried toward him. ""Tain't no use to ask who you be; the horse has done told me that. But just to be sure, an' carrying out the young lady's instructions, is your name Mercer—Captain Barth Mercer?"

"That's right."

"Mrs. Claycomb asked that I see that you got your horse and your things—they're in that pack behind the saddle. Oh, yes, she wanted me to deliver this letter to you."

"Thank you most heartily. To whom am beholden for this service?"

"I'm Ephraim Mentz, Captain."

"What happened to Mrs. Claycomb?"

"She's gone on to Harrodstown. I 'magine she'll tell you all about it in her letter."

"I'm ever so much obliged, Mr. Mentz."

"Glad to do it."

Appreciative as he was of Mentz's kindness, Barth found it difficult to compose himself and listen to his benefactor's detailed story of his trip thus far and of its purpose and destination. Ordinarily, he would have been most interested in conversing with him at great length, but not today. He was too concerned with what Dracie might have written.

Sagitta nudged him gently, and he stroked the animal's nose and head with evident affection, as Mentz continued what fast became a monotonous monologue.

Barth's patience was all but gone, when someone yelled, "Hey, Eph, here's a fellow that knows Jess Bowman!"

The shout caught Ephraim Mentz with his hands in the act of an emphatic gesture. He stopped abruptly. "Scuse me, Captain. I'm going over there for a minute—be right back; got some more to tell you." With that, he shouldered himself through the constantly enlarging group.

Barth broke the seal after noting the graceful open script above it. "For Captain Barth Mercer, Only, Bullitt's Salt Licks." He opened the letter and prepared to read its contents. Just then, a squatty, bow-legged individual hailed him. "Hey, mister, yuh wouldn't be knowin' a little feller, 'bout as tall as me, who's s'posed tuh be 'round here, would yuh?"

"That isn't much of a description to go on, my friend," Barth answered bluntly.

"Aw right, but yuh might be neighborly 'bout it. He wuz a pedlar; claimed his name wuz Littelly, er suthin' thet sounds liken it."

"Yes, I know him. He's still here but he's laid up for a while. What do you want with him?"

"Want with 'im? Laid up, yuh sez? I'll lay 'im away, I will, if'n I jest but gits my hans on 'im!"

"What did he do?"

"Never mine thet. Jest lead me tuh 'im!"

"Wait a minute. Suppose you take hold of yourself and tell me what he's done."

"Whet he's done, yuh asks? Why, thet sneakin', thievin', mother-robbin' scoundrel; thet rascal; thet-thet-thet . . ." running out of base descriptives, the denouncer added, limply, "He stole my money."

"He stole your money? I don't believe it!" Johnny was no thief, of that Barth felt certain.

"Same as stole it. He sold me thet damn jackass over yonder. I brung it tuh here tuh git m 'money back, er make 'im eat th' damn thing, hide an' all."

Barth looked at the object of this opprobrium. What he saw convinced him that there was the most miserable creature he had ever seen on four feet. In all the animal kingdom, there couldn't be a more disconsolate, decrepit-looking member than this one. Barth remembered Johnny telling him he had sold his horse and that it had brought a good price. He also recalled that its color was gray. Well, Johnny had almost told the truth. That he had made a good sale was evident from the purchaser's present protestations. And it was gray, whether that was its normal hue or whether age and condition were responsible was a matter of purest conjecture. But Johnny had stretched the truth a mite when he had called this lop-eared, broken-down, pathetic thing a horse. The only equine resemblance was that it did have four legs. Where in the world had Johnny gotten hold of this old mule, Barth wondered. Mules were exceedingly rare. This one looked like it had been the first one in America.

The disgruntled buyer renewed his harangue. "Thet damn feller swore thet thet there jackass hed racehorse blood in 'im; thet he wuz gentle as could be; thet he wuz real 'telligent an'—"

"Just a minute now. You looked at him before you bought him, didn't you?"

"Shore I done thet, an' I noticed how he stood on them three legs most th' time; but thet little cheat tole me they hed bin a stone wedged in th' frog of thet foot. I sez tuh 'im, 'Thet mule 'pears tuh be in putty bad shape.' Know whut he sed? 'Jest tarred, thet's all.' Thet's whut he sed. Sed he rid him hard on 'count he'd bin chased by Injuns fer three days 'fore he could rest up eny. Claimed them Injun ponies wore theyse'fs out tryin' tuh ketch 'im. Oh, thet lyin', no good little thief! Wait'll I gits hold uv 'im. C'mon, where is th' varmint?"

"This here feller botherin' yuh, Cap'n?" It was the driver who had come up meanwhile.

"No, no. It's all right."

"Yuh goin' back soon, er yuh want me tuh wait fer yuh?"

"Suppose you go on down to Ben Skinner's and wait for me there." Then, addressing Johnny's disgruntled vendee, "Go get that bedraggled mule and bring it over here. Wait a minute," he called, and both men turned back. To the bow-legged one, he said, "Not you; go ahead and get the mule." To the other, "I want you to tie my horse and that mule to the wagon and watch them for me."

"Right here?"

"No, down at Skinner's."

The driver moved to take hold of the mule's reins as its dissatisfied owner drew near.

"Oh, no yuh don't! Yuh touch thet mule an' I hollers fer help. Yuh two ain'ts robbin' me in broad daylight, if'n I kin help it."

"Shut up, you idiot! I'm going to give you your money back."

"Jest m' money back? Whut 'bout all th' feedin' an' care I guv this critter, an' th' doctorin' an' all whut I done?!"

"Forget about it then." The letter stilled burned in Barth's hand.

"Jest a secont. Yuh aimin' tuh pay me in good coins? I ain't takin' no Army paper."

"In good money. How much did you give for the mule?"

"Fifteen pounds."

"Look, man, this is your last chance that I'm giving you. There's really no reason why I should do it, or why anyone should, for that matter. You bought that animal after you looked at it; you just made a bad buy."

"Whut 'bout all them promises he made me 'bout its condishun?"

"You expect that when you buy a horse or a mule. You have to exercise your own judgment. If it's bad, you have to suffer for it."

"What's yore int'rust in this deal?"

"The man who sold it to you is a friend of mine; in fact he works for me."

"Don't 'pear yore as smart as I be. I jest had one dealin' with 'im, an' I knows more'n tuh trust 'im. Friend! Yuh sez! He's th' kine uv a friend whut'll cut yore throat best chance he gits."

"I can do without your advice. How much for the mule? Better tell me exactly what you paid for it; you know I'll find out. And if I find you've lied to me, I'll find you and scalp you, so help me!" Barth drew his knife and ran his finger along its edge.

"Eight pounds, six shillings, an' thet's th' truth! Thet's whut I guv 'im fer it."

"You'd better be tellin' me the truth. Here's 'your money." Barth counted it carefully, then handed it to him.

"Thet's all right, thet is. Now sence yuh has guv m' price, I'll tell yuh suthin'. Watch out fer that three-legged bastard. He's a mean son-uv-a-bitch! He'll kick hell outa yuh!"

As Barth reached for the mule's reins, he asked, "What did you say your name is?"

"Didn't say yit. Whutcha wants to know fer?"

"So I'll know whose throat I'm going to cut, if you've lied to me about this."

The bow-legs seemed to bend a little more as he answered nervously, "Samuel Hawkins is m' name."

Barth looked at his purchase and then exclaimed, "Why, anyone could tell at a glance that this animal is half-blind in its right eye!"

"Naw, he ain't. It's jest a natcheral glass eye."

"Whoever told you that?"

"Yore friend," Hawkins stressed.

Barth forced open the mule's mouth and examined its teeth. "Why, he's every bit of twelve years old."

"Yore wrong agin. Yuh dasn't b'leeve them tooths. They looks theta-way 'cause thet there mule thought he wuz chewin' on a corn cob onc't, oney it turned out tuh be a iron bar. Leastways, thet's whut yore friend sed caused 'em tuh be thet a-way."

Barth made no comment on the spavined condition, so readily apparent, but said only, "That stone must have really been wedged in that frog."

"Yuh best see yore friend 'bout thet," said Sam Hawkins as he waddled away.

The wagon, with the contrasting pair of grays tied securely behind, was soon on its way. Barth now sought a place of seclusion that he might be rid of the bedlam of endless information about friends and neighbors, which was being constantly exchanged between the travelers and settlers: births, deaths, marriages, Indians, the war, the hoped-for treaty, happenings in the various cities and settlements, the fashions (though none were dressed in more than linsey-woolseys, homespuns or buckskins) and, of course, that universal topic—the weather. An intent, persevering listener could be apprised of what was going on in most of the colonies from the Atlantic to Saltsburg. And generally the news would be relatively new—never older than six months. It was from this confusion that Barth was now extricating himself. Any other time, he would have stayed on, but today, Dracie's letter was his only interest.

He saw Abby Tindall coming in his immediate direction and he avoided her just in time. He thought of Rosie and went inside.

Here too there was a lot of people, of the same makeup as those outside. The only noticeable difference was that the ones inside were much noisier—their tongues the more loose from the drinks that had been consumed.

He located Rosie and spoke confidentially into her very ear, telling her he had something of great concern to him, which he desired to read privately. She ushered him to her room in the rear and as she left him, she told him to bolt the door after her.

His hands trembled as he unfolded the paper and read.

> Barth, Dearest,
>
> Because of the deep feeling of unrest within me, and of my fears for the safety of my person, I have decided to accompany Mr. James Sumner, his wife and others to Harrodstown. They are leaving this morning and there are fifteen in the party, including myself.
>
> I do not know, at this writing, how long my stay will be there, but I am sure it will be at least three weeks.
>
> You need have no worries about me; I am in good health, and will be well protected, as you know, while I am there.
>
> Lucy Harmon (you remember her) and her family live there, so you may be assured I shall not lack companionship or entertainment.
>
> I know you must be wondering, as you read these lines, as to the cause of my decision to leave here. If I were not leaving, I would not now tell you, since it would be a source of worry to you, if you knew, and I yet remained.
>
> Shortly after you left that morning, I was disturbed greatly by someone trying to gain entrance to the cabin. I called and asked who was there, but there was no reply. After a while, the noise ceased and I fell asleep.
>
> When I awoke, I dressed and thought to go to my neighbors, the Murrays, and inquire if they had been so troubled.
>
> As I opened my door, a man waiting there tried to grab

me and to force his way inside. I succeeded in closing the door and barred it against him, but I couldn't stop his vile language. Dearest, he said the most horrible things that I have ever heard. Then, finally, after what seemed hours, he left; but I was so terrified I did not venture out for a long time afterward.

Before I did go, I packed most of my things in my portmanteau and then went to the Murrays and asked Mr. Murray to help me. He carried my things to their place and he insisted that I stay with them.

This would be all right were it not for the fact that Mary (Mrs. Murray) is about ready for her baby, and I would most certainly make the place too crowded were I to stay on with them. I felt myself imposing upon them by being there these few days. They have a six-year-old son, Charles, and a daughter, Edna, who is twelve. The latter should be of great help to her mother with the baby, as she is a gentle and intelligent girl and is quite strong for her age.

Dearest, I still thrill at the memory of our last night together. I sometimes awake and imagine I can feel your strong, protective arm across my bosom. I can hardly wait until your work at Bullitt's Lick is finished, and you can fulfill your promise to make a good wife out of me.

The Rev. John Wyeth, a minister of the Church of England, is at Harrodstown now. Wouldn't it be wonderful, if he were to be in this vicinity when your work is through? We could be married before we returned to Williamsburg.

I wonder what Neicia Warren would say then? It surely would serve her right; she had her opportunity to marry you, but instead she chose that miserable Allen Stockton—just because of his father's money. (I know you will say that wasn't the reason, but it was strange she didn't marry him after he was disinherited.)

You may be sure of one thing, dearest, she'll not have a second chance while I'm alive to prevent it.

Here I have rambled on and on, and I haven't said what I most wanted to say. I love you, love you, love you, dearest, now and forever.

Do you love me? You never say you do—at least not as much as I would like to hear you say it.

Dearest, I must hurry. Mrs. Sumner has just called me, so I'll have to stop.

Please, take care of yourself, and answer this as soon as you are able. I'll write again from Harrodstown.

All my love, always
Dracie

Mr. Ephraim Mentz, who is traveling to Falls of the Ohio—I think it is called Louisville now—has kindly consented to find you and deliver this to you, and I have entrusted Sagitta to his care. He (Mr. Mentz) is of good reputation and is most trustworthy.

Love me always.
D.

Barth read the letter again and again, as one sipping slowly of some sweet liquid of great refreshment. At length, his thoughts at ease, and the present sated with vivid memories of past enchantments, he opened the door and went back into the main room. He eased his way among and through the many who were there. Rosie saw him and inquired as to the character of the news, whether good or bad and, upon being assured of its pleasant portent, returned to her customers.

Just as he stepped outside, Ephraim Mentz hailed him. It was all right now; he was in a mood to listen. The two were soon in rapt conversation; discourse not destined to end until they had thoroughly exhausted all of the news known by each of them.

CHAPTER 20

The windows continued to intrigue the citizenry, and the curiosity they aroused was paying off for Ben Skinner.

Those who were the least timid, but who wanted to look through them from the inside, accomplished their desire by the simple pretext of making some slight purchase. Others merely went in and gazed out at their friends, often making silly grimaces, which were returned in kind. The whole effect was the lighthearted spirit of a carnival. Everyone was in good humor.

Abby Tindall had taken an ungranted respite to examine the new wonder of Saltsburg. As she entered, one of the hangers-on greeted her. "Hev ya opened fer bizness yet, Abby? I'd shore like tuh be yore first customer! I seen ya comin' outa Dolly Dusenberry's a while back."

Abby flushed the deepest crimson, and her scalp burned at the hairline, as the ribald jest drew an avalanche of masculine guffaws. Other than her fiery blushing, however, she managed to keep her composure and quickly retorted, "I always suspected you was faithless to your wife, Jim Mosely, an' now that I knows it's th' truth, I'm gonna tell her!"

The echo of the other mirthful avalanche swung back at the bewildered Mosely, whose turn it now was to redden and swelter. Approving voices were quick to congratulate her for her decisive repartee. Straightening to her full height, she ignored them and walked, stick-like, to the window.

For her, the embarrassing episode had ended in triumph and respect; for him who had sought to taunt her, his creation would continue to react upon him whenever and wherever the settlers gathered—at work or at rest. The story would be told to newcomers; it would be retold a thousand times, and then, thought dead, would yet revive and be a source of vulgar enjoyment. Worse than this was the danger so readily apparent to Jim Mosely that his wife might hear of the happening and distrust him. And when her anger was aroused, Delia Mosely was a woman to be reckoned with. If that were not enough, some of the women who had heard the exchange of words would gossip wildly, putting a gleam of covetousness in his eye, replacing what had been a mere, mischievous spark. Certain it was also that one of his cronies would admonish Delia. "Yuh'd best keep a sharp eye on Jim; he likes th' young 'uns."

Too late, he realized the fullness of the happy state he had enjoyed before those hapless words were uttered. The loafers lost one of their number; a dejected Jim Mosely left for home.

"Thet thar Abby is some gal. Hit'd take a heap uv doin' ter make her turn tail an' run." Abe Foster glanced admiringly in her direction as he spoke. "If'n I wuz a mought younger an' han'somer, I'd marry up with her right now."

A lead pellet he had been fingering dropped to the floor. Stooping to retrieve it, he emitted a tremendous passage of wind, terrific in its resounding report, which resulted in the immediate consternation of every woman present. They rushed as one for the door, leaving an all-male audience in their wake. Freed of any threat of affronting feminine delicacy, the men laughed until tears rolled and stomachs ached. At length, one stifled his mirth to say, "Looks liken yuh misjudged thet Abby, Abe. She wuz th' fust tuh leave outer here."

Abe, choking upon the new surge of merriment that had engulfed an unfinished laugh of the old, finally survived the attack. Wiping the tears away, he observed, in a philosophic vein, "Belchin', sweatin', cussin' an' fartin' are a man's rights; cain't 'spect no womin ter 'preciate 'em."

Ben Skinner broke in to say, "Seein 'yuh drap thet shot lead, 'minds me yuh ain't paid me fer it."

"Jest hain't runned 'crost no fitten-lookin game thet yuh'd want, Ben. I'll take keer uv it in th' mornin'."

Skinner snapped his words when he replied, "See thet yuh does."

It was well past noon when Barth decided he had garnered all the news of any import and bade the travelers godspeed.

They were not leaving, however, until Monday; the morrow being the Sabbath and there being those among them who deigned it a violation of the commandment to travel on that day.

He did not expect to see them before they left, as he intended availing himself of some rest. It had been a hard week. He remembered his Sunday evening invitation of the Graingers to sup with them, and he now regretted his impulsive acceptance. However, he had said he would come and he would keep his word.

At Ben Skinner's, he noted the absence of women in the now dwindled group, most of whom encircled Sagitta, admiring the animal's trim conformation. Sagitta was the purest of thoroughbreds, not only in blood lines but also in keenness of equine intellect and in gentleness of disposition. They raised his legs, petted him, measured him, opened his mouth and examined his teeth, sometimes without proper consideration in their handling of him, but he remained completely docile. On sensing Barth's approach, however, he lent himself to a bit of excitement, neighing, moving his head up and down and pawing the earth with his forefeet. With his master's reassuring pat, he was at once entirely settled.

The driver from the lick roused himself from his nap and inquired drowsily, "Ready tuh go back, Cap'n?" On being informed by Barth that such was not the case, he settled contentedly back again in the seat.

Inside Skinner's, Barth spied Abe Foster and hailed him. "How're you, Abe?

Where's all the women who were around here when I passed earlier?"

"They's whut yuh mought call undisposed." The gathering took up Abe's reply and laughed heartily at its reference.

"Jest soon's I finish this hyar game uv loo, I wants ter talk ter yuh, Cap'n."

"Don't hurry," said Barth. "I'll just watch you a spell. You any good at the game?"

"Th' best thar be," said Abe.

It didn't take long for Barth to reach the conclusion that while Abe Foster might be the ace of nimrods, he was the lowest deuce when it came to "cyards," as he called them.

It also didn't take long for the bushy-faced Abe to acknowledge he might be just a bit wrong in his own estimation of his gambling prowess. But, as with all who lose at cards, he didn't place much of the fault upon himself but only shrugged his immense shoulders as he left the table, saying, "Beats all how a feller kin git sech damn cyards." Then to Barth, "Wal, they hain't nuthin' holdin' me in hyar; let's git outside."

Barth remembered the driver. If he and Abe were going to talk, it would be best that one of Mace's men not be there when they did. Speaking softly, he said, "Abe, you wait just a few minutes before you come out."

The teamster stretched himself out of his lethargy as Barth unhitched the two diverse grays from the rear of the vehicle. This done, the wheels stirred the dust as the wagon rolled into a fast start toward the lick.

Barth tied the mule and Sagitta to the hitching rail and waited the prearranged time until Abe met him. He was now the only one in front of the place. It was time to eat, and past, and the stomachs of those who had been so interested in Sagitta a short while before had since directed their owners' feet to paths that led to food.

Abe ambled up to him. "Reckin it's th' thing ter talk hyar?"

"I believe it'll be all right. Sometimes it's easy to be inconspicuous simply by being conspicuous."

"Whut in th' b'ilin' hell d' yer mean?"

Barth laughed. "Just that if we are openly seen together in a public place, people are likely to think that there's nothing secret in what we are discussing."

"Whyn't yer say thet in th' fust place? Y'know, they hain't much use uv talkin' an' usin' big words, less'n th' feller yer a-speakin' ter unnerstands them big words, an' I be one uv 'em thet don't."

"You're right, Abe; I'll watch myself. Now, what's the news you have for me?"

"Wal, I wuz out early this mornin'. Actual, I wuz gonna shoot some game fer Ben Skinner ter pay 'im fer th' shot lead I got off'n him. I wuz trackin' soft-like, gittin 'ready ter shoot a big turkey gobbler. He wuz a real big un, an' I wuz bein' extry quiet so's not ter frighten 'im none."

"I wuz workin 'my way in closeter, when I heerd talkin' down by th' river. Hit wuz jest past break uv day, an' I cuddn't figger who'd be down thar. If'n I'd heerd it in th' flat, I wud prob'ly a-took it ter be hunturs, same as me. But liken I sez, hit don't line up with my aim thet they'd be down thar a-talkin' so loud, thet early. I edges m'sef til I cud see 'em an' mebbe git cl'ar whut they wuz speakin 'bout. They wuz two uv 'em, an' d'rectly they turned they heads an' I knowed 'em both: Ben Skinner an' Blackie Vermin! They's suthin' shore boun' ter be a-gonna heppen, Cap'n, when sech as them gits thar damn noggins tergether."

Barth whistled through his teeth. "You're mighty right, Abe. Something is in the making, and it's all bad, I'd say."

"Yer heerd uv Vermin?"

"Who hasn't? Black Lester Vehrmon! He's stirred up more Indians for the British than anyone I've ever heard of. They tell me he'd get tribes together to fight for the Crown that were blood enemies to each other, and when no one else could muster them, he'd be the one to do it. For some unknown reason, he has power over them that even some of the chiefs don't have. Next to Benedict Arnold, I'd class him as the worst renegade I've ever known, and presently, the more dangerous. You can be sure of one thing, Abe. If he is planning trouble, it won't be small, it'll be big." Barth was wrought up and showed it.

"I 'grees with yer, Cap'n."

Calming, Barth asked, "Where does Ben Skinner fit into this?"

"Cap'n, he's one uv them damn Tories; leastways, he sides with 'em, same as yore Mace Hardin does."

A faint ray of mental light began playing on Barth's brain. There was some connection—some big relation to his works here at the lick—in all of this. It was just the faintest beam, but he would keep it searching until the significance became evident.

Abe was still talking. "Th' war hain't made too much diffrunce hyar 'cept ter make money, but if'n sides wuz ter be chosen, ever damn one uv Mace's men wud be with 'im."

"I might have something to say about that!"

"Damn little, Cap'n. Damn little."

Recognizing the digression, Barth asked, "Did you hear much of what they said?"

"Not much, Cap'n. They wuz 'bout done. Vermin sez suthin' 'bout th' territory over by th' Licking River, but thet part warn't cl'ar. I cud ketch they voices, but not th' sense uv whut they wuz sayin'."

"They say anything about salt?"

"I heerd 'em sayin', but liken I sez, I cuddn't git th' straight uv it."

"You sure that it was Vehrmon?"

"If I twarn't 'im, 'twuz 'is twin brother."

"He has a brother, I understand."

"Naw, Cap'n, thet wuz Blackie Vermin, I seen 'im afore this, more'n onest. Th' fust time, he wuz s'posed ter be with th' Whites. Then I wuz in a scrape, an' he wuz leadin' th' Injuns agin us."

"This is bad, Abe, all bad. Just this morning, I was talking with some of that party going to Louisville, and part of what they said backed up what I heard before I came here. People think the British have given up, that Yorktown ended the war, but they're wrong, Abe. There may not be any more big battles with all this talk about a treaty that you keep hearing, but you can bet all you've got that the British will keep the Indians riled up, and that British officers will be leading or directing large attacks all along the frontier. More and more settlers are coming here, and unless the Indians strike hard at the larger settlements, and increase the raids against the smaller places, it won't be long before Kentucky will be lost to them. But to hear people around here talk about it, you'd think the Indians were never coming back."

"Think we oughter warn 'em 'bout whut I seen, Cap'n?"

"I believe they should be warned, but in a general way. It might tip our hand if Skinner found out about you having seen him with Vehrmon. It would be well, of course, for you to tell Tom Chism, but caution him to keep the information to himself until our plans are certain."

"Enything more yer reckin we kin do right now? Seems liken suthin' oughter be done quick-like." As he said this, Abe picked at his left ear and then scratched his rump.

"You might just finish it by singing that song of yours, Abe. Looks like you're doing part of what it says, anyhow."

Abe caught on quickly and smiled broadly. "Yer mought be right 'bout thet, Cap'n, jest so's I don't hev ter sing hit too long."

"I hope I'm not wrong, but I believe they are planning something that will take a while before they are ready with it."

"I hopes yer is thinkin' right sartain."

As the two parted, Barth admonished Abe, "Tell Tom I'll see him the first chance I get. And be sure that he tells no one else what we've learned."

Abe nodded his understanding. Holding the mule reins in his right hand, Barth mounted his horse. Obedient to his master's direction, Sagitta moved forward. As he did so, Barth was almost pulled backward out of the saddle. The mule had refused to follow. Barth's arm and shoulder felt as though the one had been jerked from the other. He had started to dismount when Abe came to his aid. "I got me th' best mule starter thar be."

Remembering Abe's vain boast at the game of loo, Barth watched dubiously.

Throwing his full weight on his left foot, Abe swung his right in a powerful upward arc, connecting at a well-directed spot on the rear of the stubborn beast.

There was a noise like the clap of thunder, but the mule's action was backward, not to the fore. Dropping its spavined leg so the hoof barely touched the ground, it kicked back viciously at Abe three times in rapid succession.

Standing clear of the rear attack, Abe explained, "Thet fust one wuz jest th' warmup; this next one oughter git 'im—they's a half side uv hide in each uv m' boots."

Taking careful aim, Abe swung again. Once more, there was the colossal thump as boot met hindquarter.

Even the dumbest ass knows when it has been kicked enough. The mule jumped quickly forward.

Barth waved Abe his appreciation as he moved on his way, the lop-eared nondescript trailing begrudgingly alongside Sagitta's flank.

CHAPTER 21

Approaching the cabin, Barth circled the open door, hoping to catch Johnny unawares. Calling to him in a falsetto tone he said airily, "Mr. Littelby, are you there?"

The answer was an immediate slamming of the door. Barth could hear Johnny mumbling to himself. "Damn female oughta know bettern' to sneak up on a man. But thet's th' way they ketches 'em, I reckin." Then in an audible voice, honeyed in its sweetness, "Be there in a minit, ma'am."

Astonishment changed instantly to ire when a fully clothed Johnny opened the door and saw Mercer standing there.

Wrinkling his nose as was always the case whenever he pronounced "you," he said, "Yew thinks yore purty damn smart, don'tchew? Whyn't yew try to be a acter—thet'd be 'bout whutchew oughta be a-doin', enyways."

Feigning offence, Barth said, "That surely is a nice way to thank me for what I brought you."

"Thet's diffrunt—whutchew got fer me?"

"I brought an old friend to see you."

"There yew go, actin' smart agin."

"No, I'm not, honestly. Look over there."

Johnny looked at the two grays tethered to the right of the cabin. "Say, thet horse is a pretty one, but thet other son-of-a ..." His voice failed as he recognized the mule. Then it came back and he continued slowly, "Thet other one ... is Wallingford. How in th' blue-ringed hell didja ever git holt of him? Yew got yoreself stung fer shore if'n yew paid more'n six pounds fer 'im, and he ain't even worth thet."

"I know that, Johnny. I bought him from a man named Hawkins. He was looking for you with blood in his eye. He claimed you misrepresented the animal's condition."

"I mought hev praised 'im a lil extry, but thet's allus done. Yew oughta hev sense 'nough to know thet. If yew thinks I'm gonna give eny money back to yew, yore shore crazy."

"I'm not expecting you to give me anything back."

Johnny scratched his head. "I jest don't git it. Wait'll I gits these damn pants off'n me, so's I kin think peaceful."

"So that's where your brains are. I knew they weren't in your head." Barth laughed.

"Thet's hit! Damn if I ain't a-movin out! Yew an' yore damn funnin'! An' don't be tellin' me yore sorry neither."

"All right, Johnny. But why don't you say hello to . . . what did you call him?"

"Wallingford. I named him thet after a fren' of mine who wuz as hard-headed as they be."

"Well, why don't you see if he remembers you?"

Johnny, sans the irritating trousers, walked over to the mule who, on seeing him coming, started twitching his ears, first one and then the other.

"Hawkins claims you said he was gentle."

"Why he shore is. He's gentle as a . . ."

Johnny paused as he raised his arm to pat the animal's nose. Wallingford was in no mood for petting, however, and showed it by trying to bite the proffered hand. Fortunately, Johnny withdrew it in time to escape injury, but not fast enough to prevent Wallingford's taking a bit of the leather from his buckskin sleeve.

"You say he's gentle as what, Johnny?"

"As a damn she wildket!" Circling, he kicked the mule in the exact spot where Abe's boot had hit.

Wallingford forgot he was spavined and that he was past the prime of his years. In rocking chair fashion, he bounced up and down, kicking with both rear feet simultaneously. All the while, he emitted a strange mixture of vociferous sounds—bawls and hee-haws—a series of shrill and frightening outcries, classic in their range.

Johnny retreated warily from the onslaught but not before the enraged mule noticed him and changed from a rear to a frontal attack.

Twice around the cabin they went. Wallingford, a murderous glint in his eyes, bent on deadly retaliation. On the third trip, Johnny ducked inside, bolted the door to his sanctuary and sank down exhaustedly, uttering a faint cry when his blistered afterpart touched the floor.

Barth was at the point of collapse. Excessive mirth can weaken a man far more quickly than can hard labor. Gradually however, he felt stronger, despite several relapses suffered when he saw Wallingford standing in patient fury beside the door, waiting for Johnny to make the mistake of coming out again.

An axe was conveniently placed against the cabin wall. With it, Barth fashioned a stake, which he notched and drove deep into the ground. Following this, he moved stealthily on the mule's sight-troubled side and, in a quick movement, secured the loose reins.

Wallingford balked for a moment, but evidently seeing Barth's sturdy boots, decided he'd had all the thumping he wanted, for he moved tamely to the stake, where he was tied securely.

Barth called to Johnny who cautioned him to jump quickly inside before the mule could get in.

After Mercer's reassurance all was safe, Johnny came outside in his curtailed apparel. His first words were an expression of reproof. "Why in th' hell didjew buy thet son-of-a-bitch back fer?"

"I didn't want to, Johnny, but I had to."

"Damn if I wuddn't hev let thet son-of-a-bitch Hawkins shot me 'fore I'd took thet gray bastard back."

"It wasn't that, Johnny. I felt that if word got around here about the transaction, with Hawkins claiming he was cheated, it might give us a bad name. Maybe there might be someone who wouldn't trust us in other, more important matters."

"I git th' idee, but whyn't yew jest let 'im hev th' money an' keep thet damn fool Wallingford too?"

"It's too late for hindsight now, Johnny. Can you fix me something? I'm right hungry."

"Hominy?"

"Not again, Johnny! We had that this morning."

"We're plumb out, Kepteen. We et th' last of our fixin's fer breakfast."

"Make it hominy then, Johnny. I'll have to get some game for us, but I'm too tired to do any hunting today."

"Whyn'tchew go up to Rosie's an' eat? Then yew could bring me suthin' back."

"I'm pretty worn out, Johnny. I don't know whether to go or rest. Besides, a lot of those people who are going to the Falls will be there, and I'm not feeling too much like talking to them."

"Shore wisht I could git outa here an' git some of th' news. I wuddn't be a-settin' 'roun' here, I kin tell yew thet."

Sensing that lassitude was more compelling upon the kepteen than was appetite, Johnny played his trump card. "They ain't gonna be no more'n hominy agin tonight an' tomorry less'n we eats Wallingford, an' I reckin he'd be a mought hard eatin, th' ole, gray son-of-a-bitch."

"All right, Johnny, you win. Just let me stretch out for a spell, then I'll go back in to Rosie's. By the way, looks like she forgot about you today, didn't she? But then I guess she hasn't had much chance to get away."

"Reckin so. But when yew goes in there, see if'n yew can't git Jim Trench to git suthin' fer us. He's most liken to be there now or a li'l later on."

"I'll do that. If I had thought about it, I just left Abe Foster; he could have taken care of us I'm sure."

"Whut yew an' him bin a-doin?"

Barth was moved to tell Johnny all about the startling disclosure Abe had made to him, but thought better of it.

Instead he said, "Abe helped me get Wallingford moving when he balked."

"I'd shore like to know how he done thet. Many's th' time I jest got m'self so damn disgusted thet I walked away an' left him—jest like I done to Joe Wallingford hisself."

"Where did you buy that mule?"

"Over in North Carolina."

"Who'd you buy him from?" Barth yawned sleepily.

"From Joe Wallingford, thet no good, stubborn son-of-a-bitch!"

Johnny talked on, until he noticed his listener had fallen asleep.

About two hours later, Mercer awoke, tidied up a bit and said goodbye to him.

As he mounted Sagitta, he glanced over at Wallingford and laughed. The mule turned his head and returned his gaze. The mule was 'telligunt, as Johnny had claimed.

Instead of going direct to Rosie's, Barth rode toward the licks. Hunger, overpowered by his earlier weariness, now began to reassert itself, and with its new inception, he decided he wouldn't pay more than a cursory visit to the works.

His mind reverted to Ben Skinner and Black Lester Vehrmon and to the inhibition that had kept him from disclosing the matter to Johnny. This, in turn, brought on a searching of their friendship. Had he made a mistake in forming his sudden attachment for the little fellow? What had promoted it? Was it the ever-present quality of humor about him that persisted, no matter how serious his mood? Humor was a necessary ingredient for endurance in the settlements and in the wilderness. It was an essential, the same as was salt, although not, to be sure, as requisite. Was the tie due to the fact Johnny was the first person he had met here, and one who appeared capable of loyalty and trustworthiness?

Johnny was vain and needed to be looked after. He was ambitious, in a small, pathetic way; he was a good companion and that was about the sum of it all. Barth, himself, didn't approve of cursing, but Johnny was always so amusing when he did it that the objectional words lost their meaning.

Casting back upon the whole of his thinking, Barth reflected that his experience in recent years in the Army and on the frontier had been that if friendships were not formed quickly, they weren't made at all. He either liked a person or he didn't; and some who he knew would make good friends had been killed before the opportunity to cement their friendship had fully presented itself.

He considered the settlers who had arrived this morning. They would be taken into the homes of those at Saltsburg, fed and entertained as best as the hosts' resources afforded. To be sure, there would be a few who might not be liked in each group, both host and traveler, but it would never be evident from the treatment of the one by the other. The uncertainty of existence did not allow leisurely appraisal of any person newly met. Thus, newcomers soon lost their identities as such and were counted friends.

Despite all his reasoning, prudence refused to concede that he might have informed Johnny of what Abe had told him. And in Barth's mind there rang the words, "I, prudence, dwell with wisdom." He would continue his caution.

CHAPTER 22

True to his word, Mace Hardin announced the completion of the storehouse as Barth rode up. After his inspection of the new building and the inventory of the salt now stored there awaiting shipment on the coming Monday, he ascertained next that Mace had given instructions to Herman Tressel to begin work on the water conveyor system. Barth then asked Hardin, "I need some game for food at my cabin. Would you have one of the hunters provide some for us? I'd rather have fowl, I believe, if that can be arranged."

"No trubble a-tall, Cap'n. I'll make it m' bizness ter see thet it's at yer place 'fore sundown."

"That'll be most appreciated. What about tomorrow, will the work go on, or do the men rest on the Sabbath?"

"Not much restin' here, Cap'n. Jest a few uv 'em don't work, but most all uv 'em'll be here. These here fires don't know nuthin' about hit bein' Sunday."

"I can understand that, however, I won't be over here tomorrow."

"She'll run jest liken she's been a-runnin', Cap'n. So don't worry none on thet account. I aims ter hev all th' salt I kin git ready ter to git on Monday."

"Have you decided on how many men you're going to send along, Mr. Hardin?"

"Yup, I figgers 'roun' ten. I got 'em picked a'ready."

Barth thought a moment. "If that party going to the Falls, which came here today, was to leave early enough, they could all go together."

"Beggin 'yore pardin, Cap'n. But I doubts thet's wise. Them settlers won't move along near so fast as our boys wud. I'm a-feared they'd be slowed down, if'n they wuz ter jine up with 'em."

Barth acknowledged this logic to be sound. "I expect you are right about that, Mr. Hardin. We'll travel separately."

As Barth prepared to leave, Mace asked, "Meanin 'no offense, Cap'n, but yer missed a good chanc't ter git some game a while back this afternoon."

"How was that?"

"When yer wuz a-talkin' ter Abe Foster, yer shudda got him ter do some huntin' fer yer. I don't hold none with thet Tom Chism, but I got ter say he's got th' best hunter in these hyar parts."

Covering the surprise that rose with the question, Barth answered matter-of-factly. "I didn't know we were needing anything til I got back to the cabin and Johnny told me."

"Oh, I sees. Wal, 'twon't make no diffrunce. I'll hev it ter yer place, liken I sed."

"I'll see you early Monday morning then, Mr. Hardin."

When Mercer was almost out of sight, Mace called to Jack Doniger. "Git a-holt uv one uv them hunters uv our'n an' tell 'im ter git me some birds an' ter make it right sharp."

Within an hour, Mace's order had been filled, and he was knocking on Johnny's door.

Johnny, rousing himself, answered roughly, but softened his voice upon learning the identity of his caller.

"Shore glad to see yew. Whutchew got there in that sack?"

Mace opened the bag so that its contents were readily seen, then said, "Jest a few turkeys fer yer an' th' Cap'n."

"Thet shore is nice uv yew, Mace." Johnny couldn't bring himself to call him mister. "Come in an' set a spell with me."

Their talk was general at first, til Mace said, "Yer know suthin'? I warn't so smart or I'd uv saw how smart yer wuz 'fore th' Cap'n did."

"Aw, yore jest a-funnin' with me."

"Naw, I hain't, I mean hit. He's shore lucky to hev got hisse'f a 'sistant liken yer. Bet he tells yer all th' important stuff in his mine, jest so yer kin tell 'im if'n he's right er wrong."

Johnny, awed by his admiration, beamed. The accompanying blush lightened the black and blue hues, which still discolored his face. "He don't tell me ever'thing; jest whut's 'portant, like you said."

"Yes, sir, I reckin a feller thet owns these here licks has got ter be orful keerful 'bout th' man whut be his depity."

"Owns these here licks? . . . Oh, shore, shore. He couldn't 'ford to take no chances with jest enbuddy, yew know."

"Thet's right, a-right. Whut's th' latest big things he's tole yer?"

Johnny strove not to betray his ignorance. "Ain't nuthin' too much. Course they's some doin's I'd best not say about—the kepteen wants 'em to be secrut, kinda."

"Uv course, uv course. By th' way, th' Cap'n say anything 'bout meetin' hup with Abe Foster today?"

"Jest thet he hepped 'im to git thet damn Wallingford a-goin'."

Here was a new name for Mace. "Who's this here Wallingford?"

"Jest a damn, stubborn son-of-a-bitch."

"I sees yer don't keer fer 'im—whut's he doin' 'roun' here?"

"Nuthin', 'cep'n eatin' his damn fool head off, I reckin'."

"Friend uv th' cap'n's?"

"Hell, no! I reckin' I got yew mixed up some. Wallingford's th' name of my mule—thet jackass over there."

"Yore mule! I thought yer wuz talkin' 'bout a real person." Mace's antici-pation fell flat. Weaving again into his determined plan of discourse, he said, "I hates ter see th' cap'n so close't ter thet Tom Chism an' 'sociatin' with his men, liken Abe Foster."

"Oh, they's all right; hit's jest thet yew don't know 'em as good like we does."

"Thet mought be hit, but ever sence I caught thet Tom Chism a-stealin' from me—frum th' cap'n really—course thet wuz 'fore I knowed these here works wuz his'n, wal, I jest hain't hed none ter much use fer 'im."

Mace had said it again. These licks belonged to th' kepteen! An' th' kepteen ain't never said a word about it to me. If he told Mace, why ain't he told me? Johnny's mind was bewildered. He asked Mace cagily, "Th' kepteen tell yew he owned this bizness, er did yew jest find out about it?"

"Shore, he tole me; said ter keep it secrut, uv course. Knowin 'yer so close't ter 'im, I dint figger hit'd be wrong ter tell you, y' unnerstan'? Course, I hain't tellin' enyone els't."

"Shore, shore." Johnny was hurt by this slight of Mercer's but he masked his feelings. "Hit's all right to tell me. Th' kepteen wouldn't mine thet a-tall."

"Thet' s whut I reckined."

"Did Chism really steal from yew—th' kepteen, I mean—from we'uns?"

"He shore did. Th' drunken son-uv-a-bitch! Yer know, yer cud do th' cap'n a big favor—kinder unbeknownst ter 'im, if'n yer follers my mine."

"Howzzat?"

"Well, when he's plannin' suthin' with thet bastard, yer cud tell me, an' yer an' me cud go over hit 'twixt ourse'fs. Thetaways, we'd know fer shore whut wuz th' best thing ter be did. I heerd tell, thet two mines kin do better'n one."

"I heared thet too."

"Wal, th' next time he, th' Cap'n thet is, tells yer suthin' yer feels is 'portant, yer calls me an' I meets yer, an' if'n I kin hep yer eny, I'll be right glad ter do hit."

"Thet's real nice of yew, Mace. I'll shore 'member thet."

The seed had been planted and more confidence gained. With proper atten-tion, it would sprout, and the plant take root. "Hope yer likes them turkeys. Yer 'member whut I sed."

"I shore will."

Mace left. The startling information he had conveyed was all consuming. It first troubled, then angered, Johnny. What purpose could the kepteen have had in not letting him know? Didn't he trust him? Maybe, and this was the most humiliating of all his thoughts, the kepteen just wanted him around to make him laugh once in a while. Pride forced this idea from further consideration. The kepteen wouldn't make no damn jester out of him. But, if that wasn't so, why did he tell Mace an' not him? The unanswerable fact could not be covered or denied.

Things fitted together a little bit in Johnny's mind. He could understand now why Mercer was so sure he could get the Lillard cabin and that Mace wouldn't bother him further. "He's jest makin' a tool outa me til he gits whut he wants.

Thet's whut he's a-doin'!" Johnny spoke this conclusion.

Then the question as to where Mace entered into the picture came in for studying. Thet Mace Hardin mought be jest tryin' to find out from me whut he kin. If'n I learns enything thet 'mounts to suthin', I'm gonna hev to be shore how much of it I want to tell 'im. Course, could be thet Mace meant whut he said 'bout me; but he's still th' son-of-a-bitch bastard thet damn nigh kilt me. One thing's shore, if'n I ain't gonna git suthin 'outa this fer m'self, I jest better git my pack an' git back to peddlin'.

Back he came again to Barth's failure to tell him that the licks were his property. Johnny talked to himself. "I mought jest ask 'im, kinda 'roun' 'bout, if he knows who they b'longs to, then if he don't claim 'em, I knows fer shore he ain't bein' fair an' square with me. Wait a secunt! How does I know thet thet damn Mace ain't a-schemin' to pizen m' mind?" This possibility occasioned deep deliberation before his decision. "Nope, 'twuddn't be thet. Mace'd be takin' too big a chanc't thet I'd ask th' kepteen about it. Thet there idee ain't right." Redundantly, it returned. "The kepteen shudda told me; me bein th' onliest one he really knowed here. Th' kepteen's up to doin' suthin' 'thout me bein' 'cluded in it an' they ain't no call fer him not 'cludin' me."

The birds had been cleaned and ready to cook when Mace brought them. Johnny engaged the smaller of the two on the hook hanging in the fireplace and started a fire going. The other would have to be cooked soon also or it would spoil. Johnny's stomach had made the selection, since the big one would take longer to roast, and he was getting an appetite.

As he spun the hook from time to time so that the turkey would cook evenly and without charring, he kept rehashing matters. I'll be dumb—jest like a fox, I will. I'll jest bide m' time, til I sees a way to git suthin' fer m'self. Th' kepteen's takin' damn good keer of hisself; I'll do th' same damn thing fer me.

At length, he swung the arm from which the hook was suspended free of the flames and tested to see if the meat was thoroughly roasted. Finding it well done, he allowed the arm to remain as it was.

He was in the act of cutting a leg off the bird when he heard Wallingford braying outside. He left the partially severed member and went to the door.

"Whut in 'ell yew fussin' 'bout, yew ole, gray son-of-a-bitch?"

Wallingford gave a few practice kicks to show that he knew who was talking to him.

"Yew'd shore like to kick me, wuddn'tchew now? Yew 'speck me to worry 'bout yew, after th' way yew done me this afternoon?"

Wallingford brayed some more.

"I knows yew wants water this time of day. I oughtn't to git yew none, but I will, on 'count I ain't holdin 'no grudges, leastways, not against yew no how."

The mule's wants having been answered, Johnny went back inside to satisfy his own.

*

Sagitta's gait was easy on his rider, whose mind was profoundly preoccupied.

Mace's casual yet pointed revelation that he had knowledge of the meeting with Abe irritated him. While anyone might have seen them, it was still peculiar that their being together should reach Mace's ears so quickly. It was now clear to him that Mace was covering his every movement, however slight or meaningless.

The Tory aspect troubled him also. If it were true that Mace and Ben Skinner were hooked up together, it would be difficult indeed to finish here as soon as he had planned. He could afford no mistakes; he must be sure of every step, of each inch of his ground.

It was comforting that Dracie would be safe and provided for once she reached Harrodstown. He tried to estimate the distance from Bairdstown to that station—he guessed it to be about fifty miles, maybe a little less than that. He had felt relieved when Ephraim Mentz told him that there were no reports of Indians having been seen between the two forts recently. If her journey had been without incident, she and her party should either be there, or almost there, by now.

Mentz's tidings as to the Indian situation had not all been favorable. The savages were raiding and stirring about. A war party had met and defeated Captain Estill and his men at Little Mountain, which was northeast of Harrodstown, around the middle of the past March.[12] There was a general feeling among the settlers in that section that there was grave danger of concerted attacks in the not-too-distant future. The Indians at the battle of Little Mountain had been Wyandots. There had been no scalping or mutilating of the bodies. The next band of warriors would follow the rule, rather than the exception, and the scalp halloo would be sure to ring through the forests and roll over the open fields.

Lester Vehrmon, Skinner and Hardin; Hardin and Skinner; Skinner and Vehrmon. What roles did they play, and would they act in all of this?

Vehrmon, to be sure, but how did the others come into the picture? Were they active counselors or were they more passive in their relation to the scene? Salt was a part of the whole, but could it be more than a minor, though necessary, segment?

Sure-footed Sagitta broke pace as he entered the gullied way, which served as Saltburg's street.

Momentarily, Barth recessed his thoughts. The purple haze of an early dusk partially enveloped those moving about the road. Lights were showing from windows and open doors. Voices, some spirits inspired, were raised in good-natured exchanges. At this moment, Saltsburg was at peace. The setting might well have been any one of a hundred small towns whose common characteristic was equanimity.

How favorably impressed must the travelers be in this calm twilight hour, he mused. It would be difficult indeed for them to reconcile this uneventful evening with all the tales that had been spread far and wide about Bullitt's Lick. Not until they resumed their journey and various of their members discovered pouches missing, or when they unpacked at the Falls and were unable to find some valued possession, would they be convinced of the evil nature of the place where they had rested. Some mother, two months later would come upon her sorrowing little girl and discover that her baby was pregnant by that nice-appearing young man where they had stayed at the licks.

Most all of this was certain to come to pass, and if the serenity of the night were to be erased by the brawls so apt to break out at any time, with their attendant obscenity and bloodletting, the favorable opinions of the travelers would be altered the more quickly. In any event, these voyagers would soon have their own stories to relate.

Barth did not unsaddle Sagitta when he reached Rosie's. He did not expect to be there very long, so he just tied the reins to the rail, rather than put the animal in the narrow confine that served as a stall. By coincidence, the blazed roan was also hitched nearby. He made a mental note to take some provender with him when he left for home.

Surprisingly, there were few people inside. Rosie greeted him warmly and asked about Johnny. He joined Abby, Tom Chism and her and ate with them.

When they had finished, and while Abby and her mother cleaned the table, he and Tom discussed the day's development. Abe had already conveyed the details to Tom, and the latter was visibly agitated. They both agreed that the only procedure was one of wariness. There the matter rested as Rosie and Abby returned.

The trend of the conversation bent quickly to matrimony and there the needle of discussion was fixed. Barth could see that the subject had been dwelled upon before his arrival, for Rosie was subdued in her manner and reasoning. The faint traces of resignation were apparent when she answered their arguments favoring their marriage.

For a while, Barth was just a discreet listener. When the moment seemed opportune, he added his urgings to those of Abby and Tom. The threefold cord was not easily broken, and Rosie finally consented, upon one condition. Tom must not take a drink for one month, at the end of which time she would give her final consent.

Abby hugged and kissed the three of them. The most fervent kisses, naturally, were those she gave to Tom.

When her elation had subsided, Barth begged his leave and soon was homeward bound. Only when he reached the covered lean-to adjacent the rear of the cabin did he think about the forgotten food for Sagitta. Disgustedly, he opened the door to the little stable after unsaddling and removing the bridle. He patted his steed's back quarter and stepped in behind the animal. Then he noticed that there was fresh straw on the floor, and he could hear Wallingford munching hay and oats to his immediate left. He barred the door and went around to the front of the cabin.

A sleepy, cranky Johnny admitted him, and though Barth endeavored to talk to him, be received no answer.

Under his breath, Johany muttered, "Thet sneakin', deceivin', son-of-a-bitch."

Barth's fatigue overcame him and he slept.

CHAPTER 23

Mace's snores were full and deep, marked by frequent snorts and grunts. He slept late this Sabbath morning, having been convinced that Mercer would not be at the licks, and if he did go there, that the men had been well posted as to what they were to say of his whereabouts.

His previous night's meeting with Ben Skinner had lasted until the faint rays of the day, and when he came to bed, he had told Massalene he was not to be awakened; that he wanted to sleep until he roused of his own accord.

The coarse, loud vibrations of his snoring lost little of their tonal qualities in their transition to the floor below. They were actually awesome at times, as though they came from some slumbering ogre of ancient lore.

To his family, the turbulent noises were commonplace; even young Nancy had long since ceased to shudder when she heard them.

The early meal was finished and the night's fast broken. Massalene slithered about in her moccasins, the barefooted Nancy in her wake.

Outside, Hawkstraw had gone to relieve himself, and Jeddy-Boy was sloshing his face in a pail of fresh water. He grimaced as the cold rivulets coursed the numerous scratches, causing them to smart sharply. One in particular, near the corner of his left eye, was a source of steady annoyance, since it was constantly irritated by the movement of the eyelid.

He had explained the presence of the marks to his mother by saying that his horse had shied into a thorn bush. She had not accepted his account, saying, "Mebbe, woman." She had been sullenly reticent with the members of her household ever since Mace had struck her, mellowing only to Nancy's endearments.

Little Legs came through the door as Jed reentered. Taking hold of her wrist, he glanced at Massalene stooping to the floor, her rounded rear obscuring the forward portion of her body. He drew Nancy to him, whispering as he attempted to kiss her, "Hit's 'bout time I made a woman out uv yer."

She pulled as far away as she could, her arm taut, and her feet spread and braced.

Toying with her determined resistance, he inched her body toward his. As he tried to force his lips to hers, she suddenly slapped him. The blow partially brushed his eye. Uttering an oath, he loosed his hold and she pulled free. Touching his cheekbone, his fingers felt the fresh blood from the reopened scratch.

He caught her a short distance from the cabin. Grasping her hair, he jerked her head back viciously, holding his hand over her mouth. He moved his face into position above hers and withdrew his hand. Dropping his head, his angular chin grazed her lips. Instantly, her teeth closed upon it and held fast, biting deeply. A stifled, anguished cry caused the hot air from his throat to enter her nostrils and spread about her cheeks and into her eyes. Instinctively, his hand found her breast, the weakness in her feminine physical armor. With viselike grip, he closed his thumb and fingers around the nipple.

Nancy screamed wildly but the maddening pain only increased.

Her agonized yells were not unheeded. Jeddy-Boy struggled to breathe, crushing hands encircled his neck, the thumbs shutting off his wind. Tighter and tighter drew this band of muscle and bone. His eyes saw only a bubbling, yellowish-purple haze, then blackness. He felt his body floating to the ground.

Hawkstraw doused the contents of the unemptied pail upon his brother's face with the force of a cataract. Jeddy-Boy stirred, feeling his throat with his hands. His eyes opened and he stared blankly, like the one-eyed Smith had done on Kahaz Knob.

Vision returned, and with it a measure of strength. He got up shakily to face his white-lipped strangler. Anger increased his virility and he advanced to renew the conflict, but halted abruptly when he saw Massalene rushing up, an axe in her hands.

Hawkstraw and Nancy both restrained her as she shouted, "You my flesh! My blood. But you hurt Nancy! I kill you!"

Massalene voiced her prophecy of destruction. Hawkstraw, denied the power of speech, had already evidenced his intention.

Jeddy-Boy knew not which of the two he feared the most, but he recognized his fate, should they ever learn he had molested the young girl. At that moment he knew, as did the still trembling Nancy, that he would trouble her no more. He hurried past them at an angle, procured his cap, powderhorn and rifle from the cabin and saddled his horse. Only when he had ridden away did Nancy and Hawkstraw release their holds upon the maddened Massalene. As their hands eased, she said, "Him bad, no should live!" The blood of a thousand Red fore-bearers again controlled her thoughts. To her savage mind, there was no complete punishment or remedy for wrongdoing, save death.

So light upon her feet at other times, Massalene now plodded back to the house.

Hawkstraw followed but returned soon, bearing Nancy's moccasins and a deerskin bag. He saw her feeling her breast gingerly, and in his silent tongue inquired as to her comfort.

The pain was still there, but she made light of it, lest it interfere with their planned trip up the river.

The dew skipped ahead of them in little sprays as their feet skimmed through the grass and wild pea vines. They broke the little gossamers, themselves ladened with tiny beads of moisture. Chipmunks scurried from their paths and a host of crows cawed noisily in raucous protestation at being disturbed from their carrion feeding.

Above, the sky was the flimsiest blue, a color even now being put in pleasing contrast by a family of jays swooping by, intent upon pestering the last of the departing crows.

The sun was still behind the distant trees. The morning rested in all its holiness.

They reached the bank of the river and proceeded upward along the water's edge. In the stream, the fish made a multitude of concentric circles as they struck for insects. A rustle nearby caused Hawkstraw to place a staying hand on Nancy's arm. Relief from their vigilance was immediate, a group of bewhiskered otters stared at them for an instant, then scampered playfully, one after another, to an earthen groove, down which they slid upon their bellies, feet stretched to the fore and rear, and zoomed into the water.

The two watched the animals' amusing antics, marveling at the seemingly effortless movements of their bodies. Oblivious of the presence of these humans, the otters raced up the sloping shore, chasing a leader, then back down the slide and its immersing end. Again and again, the game was repeated. Finally, tiring before their entranced watchers wearied of them, they loped away.

As if by signal, Nancy and Hawkstraw moved on. The fullness of their understanding needed little complement. There were moments, however, when she would speak, as when a stately elk discovered them and bounded swiftly away. Hawkstraw then answered, moving his hand with the palm down, in lilting fashion. To her, the meaning was clear; he thought the animal beautiful and graceful in its fleeing strides.

A brief span, and they were at the river's falls or rapids, shallow and inconsistent with its broad majesty downstream. Here they rested, her head in his lap.

The sun's warming rays played upon them and they arose to renew their excursion. Shortly, voices floated to them, heralding their approach to Dowdall's Station, built about two years before, when Brashear's Station had become too crowded. Unlike Brashear's, which was almost half a mile from the river, Dowdall's was on its bank, a mile downstream from the former.

A group of children were outside the station, darting to and fro, playing follow the leader just as the otters had played a little while before.

Despite the day, a few women were washing clothes at the river's edge. George Grundy's ferry was securely docked on the station bank of the stream, which meant he was in the fort, or on this side, since his cabin was south of the river, about three hundred yards from its shore.

The ferry was well located, traversing a deep pool. Its use enabled travelers following the trace from the falls at Louisville to continue on the buffalo path that ran along the south side of Salt River on to Cox's Creek, where a ford was easily made at the mouth of Rocky Run, and thence along the creek's east fork to Harrodstown. Before its advent, a difficult crossing, far upstream, had been mandatory for those who used the trace to the north of the river.

Passing the open gate, Nancy and Hawkstraw paused momentarily and looked inside. It was apparent that many of those bound for Louisville had not availed themselves of the hospitality of Bullitt's Lick. Loaded wagons, their shafts empty, were bunched in the center of the compound. Unfamiliar faces appeared and strange voices were heard.

Hawkstraw's attention was focused on a surveyor's instrument standing on its three legs just beyond the entrance. At its base were piled various belongings and articles of equipment. He recognized their use, having served as a lookout the last time a surveying party came through here. He had also hammered the stakes as directed by the rodman. The whole business was a wondrous puzzle to him. By looking through the telescope, men were able to draw lines on paper and show how much property was embraced within their confines, and where one man's property ended and another's joined it. The surveyors spoke of angles, minutes, degrees, rods, links, poles, chains and feet. He could understand the meaning of feet, but he could not comprehend the interrelated mysteries of the other words. He hoped he could work for these men, whomever they might be.

Nancy tugged at his arm, asking what occupied his mind, and though he did his best to describe the use and purpose of the instrument, he could not, for once, make her understand. Perhaps, this was because there was so much that he himself was not cognizant of. He was intrigued but was helpless to pursue his enticement to any simple explanation. Maybe, if he was hired by the head of this party, he would learn more. Then he would be able to tell her all about it.

They veered northwestwardly from Dowdall's, bypassing Brashear's Station, which he had also heard called Salt River Garrison, intending to stop there on their return.

Weaving their way through the trees, they stopped at length when Nancy complained of something in her moccasin. The offending substance proved to be a small piece of bark, which her solicitous companion removed and then ran his fingers gently around and under her foot to be sure there was no other adhering irritant. They took advantage of the halt to rest again.

As they prepared to continue on, she directed his attention to a pile of white bones off to his right. He examined the heap closely, then illustrated his finding to her. A wolf had attacked a smaller animal. What kind, he did not know. The larger beast had so stretched its jaws as to cause them to lock and then catch between the ribs of its victim. Hawkstraw pointed to the teeth still held in the position, which had resulted in starvation for each.

Nearby, some carving upon the trunk of a large beech tree stood out in bold relief. He traced the indented letters with his forefinger, and though he could not read what was recorded there, he did not need to do so. He knew what it said. "H. Gordin, May 1779—Injuns Killed All." It had been shown to him and translated by one of the party of which he was a member and which had pursued the savages. The base of the last letter was elongated and in a downward slant. Gordin had died as he finished the inscription.

He recounted the bloody massacre and the ensuing, fruitless pursuit of the Indians.

Her eyes were wide, and she clung to his arm the more tightly. Seeing her fright, he soothed her fears, telling her that soon they would reach the open space where the trace paralleled the forest.

He had seen this expression upon her face many times. Usually, it was there when he acted out the legend of the barbarity at Fort Duquesne, now Fort Pitt, following Braddock's defeat.[13] Her impressionable mind pictured vividly the gauntlet, the naked soldiers with their faces blackened for death, the immense pile of scalps, and the savages filling the air with their weird halloos, themselves clothed in parts of their victims' uniforms. She could visualize the tortures at the stake, and she hated the fort's commander because he had not interfered. She would close her eyes and cringe when Hawkstraw showed her how pine splinters had been stuck all over the unfortunate bodies, even in the eyelids, and then set afire. Sometimes she would burst into tears. But the horrendous happenings held a strange fascination for her, and after the terror had faded from her memory, she would request to hear it again. The story was authentic; Hawkstraw had heard it many times from the lips of Abe Foster and Herman Tressel, each of whom supplied any details omitted or unknown to the other. They had been prisoners of the French at the time the event occurred. Both had been youths when they were captured, to which fact they credited their own survival.

They proceeded, perhaps a mile and a half, until they neared Lost Knob; so named because there was a gap through which the trace ran separating it from the chain of knobs to the west. Two miles before them was Clear's Station, on a creek which bore the same name, that of the man who had settled there a few years before.[14]

While it was still forenoon, they decided against continuing on to Clear. If they were going to stop at Brashear's on their way home, they had best turn back now. Besides, for some reason he could not explain, Hawkstraw felt insecure, once he had passed beyond the knobs. It was as though, as long as he remained to the south of them, they would protect him. Not that he was not constantly on the alert, for he was; but he somehow believed things to be safer inside the encircling hills. He carried no rifle, being armed only with knife and hatchet. For himself, these were weapons enough, but not with Nancy along. He reflected that they should not have ventured beyond Dowdall's, and he was relieved that they were not going farther.

Whether due to their exertions, or because the warmth was unseemly for the time of year, Nancy nevertheless perspired freely, although Hawkstraw appeared unaffected by the heat. They both, however, welcomed the known springs along the return route. At one of them, they partook of the victuals—vittles—which he had thoughtfully placed in his bag. The rough hide lent its odor to the taste of the food but this did not deter their sharpened appetites.

Their pace was more leisurely, and while they had traversed the same path the previous fall, there were now new delights for their engrossment. Where before the grasses had been brown and the leaves had fallen, leaving the trees bare, now all was verdant. Flocks of beautiful birds enthralled their vision and hearing.

They left the forest and entered upon the clearing that lay in front of

Brashear's Station. The earth was soft under their feet, giving them a sensation of lightness.

After passing through the gate, Hawkstraw and Nancy were welcomed by the few among the residents whom he knew. These bore him no ill-will or disrespect, as did they the others in his family: his father, mother and Jeddy-Boy. They appreciated his industry and his mute straightforwardness in his dealings with them.

He gestured excitedly as he saw Ethan Belden, who had also helped the surveyors when they were here before. With Nancy's aid, he told Belden of the presence of the new party at Dowdall's and exacted a promise from him to investigate and, if more surveying was planned locally, that Belden would try to secure him a place in the crew. His face radiated at his friend's assent and Nancy shared his joy, wondering at this stranger manner of work, which could please him so greatly.

Using Nancy as an interpreter, the conversation flowed smoothly. So easily did it move, that before they realized its happening, the gate had been closed, as was customary when religious services were about to be held in the fort.

For the moment, the two experienced the panic of trapped creatures. Hawkstraw beseeched his friend, Belden, to aid them in getting out of the garrison.

Before the latter could act, a kindly voice called to them. "Prithee, stay with us and hear of the glory of God." Aaron Flinden asked this imploringly.

They looked toward the voice and saw him, standing so tall and erect upon a low table, which served as his dais. As they had sought and found the source of those serene tones, so also other eyes viewed them, those of the gathered worshipers, some of whom peered at them through curiosity, but most of whom cast benign glances of fellowship. Thus encouraged, the two timidly found themselves places on the fringe of the assembly.

The residents of the station held their services regularly. If they were so fortunate as to have available the talent of an itinerant ordained minister, the occasion was truly noteworthy and they would observe two periods of worship on the Sabbath. Otherwise, there would be just the single session of devotion. Usually, this took place in the morning, but sometimes, as was the case today, there would be a postponement until the late afternoon.

Those who lived at Brashear's were of various denominational faiths, hence, no thought of inconsistency was present in the selection of Flinden to lead this day's celebration. Next week, an Anabaptist might preside, and a Presbyterian might follow him. Had the Catholic tide of migration been flowing at this stage of Kentucky's history, in due turn, one of their number would have been chosen. There had been occasions when their leader had been one who subscribed to the beliefs of no particular church. The only requirements demanded were those of sincerity and adherence to faith in God. They were Christians all, though some might differ in their chosen routes to heaven.

Brother Flinden began slowly and deliberately. He spoke with clarity born of a firm belief in what he was saying. His voice was of wonderful quality and gentle in its reception.

His listeners were rapt in their attention; even the little children in the assemblage, though they understood not what he said, were charmed into quietness.

No less were Nancy and Hawkstraw swayed by Aaron Flinden. For each of them, their presence in such a setting was their first. While they loved and reveled in all the wonders of nature that surrounded them, they had accepted the marvel of existence with no thought as to its source. Now, this man was disclosing to them their maker and his handiwork.

He spoke of the Diaspora—the scattering of the Jews; of their hardships and their enemies; of Christians and the persecutions, which they had endured and were still suffering. He drew deft analogies with the present: The Christians burned by Rome's centurions had suffered agonies the same as those settlers who died upon savage stakes.

There were tear-dimmed eyes when he related the crucifixion of the one who gave his earthly life that others might be saved. The one who had demonstrated by his miracles that his was a willing death; that he did not have to die.

Brother Flinden delved into the miracles: the restoring of sight, hearing and speech. "All this can be done unto thee, if thee but have the faith."

Nancy heard and understood little else of what he said. If James believed, he could talk with his mouth! Oh, James must believe! He must! He must! He must!

She looked up at Hawkstraw. He too was thinking. If I but learn more of this one called Jesus, I will be able to speak as other men!

The meeting over, they waited patiently until the others finished talking with Brother Flinden and then approached him hesitantly. The kind warmth of his manner dispelled their diffidence, particularly that of Nancy, and her tongue loosened. She told him of their mutual desire for the granting of the power of speech to the mute man by her side, whose eyes and silent lips tried to add his own plea to her earnest words.

Aaron Flinden was himself enraptured by the appearance of the two. He caught the glow upon their countenances; the unmistakable desire for the light.

"What is thy name, little friend?"

"Nancy Hardin, sence I been livin' with Mace an' Massalene."

"They are not your true mother and father then?"

"No, they hain't. My really papa died, an' then my mama kum an' got me an' I lived with her an' Mr. Weston til she died an' then he jest leaved me with Mace an' Massalene an' I ain't saw 'im no more."

"Does thee remember thy true father's name?"

"Jes seems liken it wuz Landers—Jesse Landers, but I ain't so shore 'bout thet."

"Where did thy father live before he died? Doth thee recall?"

"Mama sed in Reading, in Pennsylvania."

They were in the midst of a miracle of their own. Flinden had known her father and mother. Indeed, they had been members of the Society of Friends, until Elizabeth Landers had deserted her husband and their only child, this young girl whom he had just met in this wilderness. After Jesse's death, Elizabeth had come back for Nancy and had taken her away, despite the objection of the child's grandparents. That had been some six or seven years ago, to the best of his recollection.

"I knew thy father well. He was a good man, a learned man. Did he not teach thee thy letters?"

Nancy shook her head.

"'Tis the great pity."

There were perplexing emotions within her, which she could not fathom. This man telling her about his knowing Papa brought all the memories, once grown faint, now rushing back upon her in heartbreaking detail. Tears rolled upon her cheeks.

Both men were instantly administering to her. Their attention served its need and her crying ceased.

Hawkstraw suggested to her that it was best that they leave for home.

With the speed of lightning, her mind reached back for the ethereal thoughts that had filled it so thoroughly a few minutes before. Looking steadfastly at Brother Flinden, she said, "Th' promise yer made when yer spoke, be it true? I heerd yer say thet God kin make James able ter talk, same as yer does."

Hearing Jesse Landers's daughter address him in the coarse language of the Hardins pained him, but he shut off this feeling and answered her. "It is most certainly true—if he will but have enough faith."

"How wud he know when he hed 'nough uv thet?"

"When he is able to speak, and his faith is rewarded."

"How does yer go 'bout gittin' it?" Flinden's answer had been a riddle to her and had left her confused.

"First, thee must believe in God, that he is the only God. And that Jesus Christ is his only son, and that he gave his life that thou might be saved. Then, if thee so believe, thou must have the faith that what thee asks of God, in Jesus' name, will be granted thee."

He endeavored to answer further her query as to the amount of faith required to accomplish this miracle, by a practical illustration. "Thee's built a fire, hasn't thee?"

Nancy nodded in the affirmative.

"Thee builds a small fire, first. Then thee adds wood unto it until thou hast a larger one. The more thee build on it, the bigger thy fire becomes."

She began to understand. "How kin I make th' little fire?"

"By believing in God and in his son Jesus."

Turning to Hawkstraw, she said determinedly, "We will b'leeve, won't we, James?" Receiving an enthusiastic nod, she asked, "When does we start ter hev faith?"

"You have started; you have built your little fire."

The novitiates were beside themselves with joy.

She asked, "Now, whut's th' next thing ter do?"

Flinden smiled. "You must learn his commandments and keep them, always." He explained briefly the divine demands, but even his simple explanation proved too complex and their faces plainly showed their inability to grasp any understanding.

"If thee could but read and study these laws of God, 'twould be a great help to thee." He said this more in meditation than in direct discourse.

Eagerly, Nancy asked, "Cuddn't yer larn us ter read?"

The Lord answered for Aaron Flinden. He would attempt to teach them not only to read but also to write. But they would have to be willing to come to his place if he were to do so. The late afternoon would be the hour, and they would have to apply themselves diligently to the task.

They assented as he uttered the last of his provisos.

The sun was down and the Sabbath was over. The residents had long before shifted from the pursuit of the spiritual to the material. Aaron Flinden regarded the closing of the day and reluctantly bid his new found disciples goodbye as the timbered gate closed behind them for the night. At home, an indisposed Ursula, her rasping tongue made the more sharp through its enforced inactivity, would be upon him for his tardiness. He would partake of a cold supper.

So great was their elation, Nancy and Hawkstraw scarcely felt their feet touching the ground as they moved toward home. For them, the entire universe had changed since morning. They walked, hand in hand in silence, yet each heard the other's thoughts. Along with God into their lives had come hope.

Nancy fell to the ground, tripping and falling upon the soft clay. He helped her to her feet, but she had struck her tender breast and she winced.

He carefully assisted her in lifting her arm up and out of the loose-fitting linsey-woolsey, dropping the one side so that her injury might be examined. He let the breast lie gently in his palm. He noted that it was badly discolored as he probed lightly for any lump that might have formed.

She suffered not the slightest embarrassment. Instead, there was a soothing feeling, which persisted along with the pain, a sensation that changed to a different form of pleasantness, strongly akin to that she had experienced when Jeddy-Boy had first put his hand under her dress and fondled her, before she had sickened of his touch. Impulsively, she pulled her face to his and kissed him, her own lips slightly opened. She yearned for him to embrace her, but he merely smiled and aided her in guiding the sleeve along her arm as she recovered herself.

Why couldn't he see in her the change that was so apparent to the despicable Jeddy-Boy? When would he realize that she was growing out of childhood, that she was no longer Little Legs, that womanhood was calling within her, that she wanted to be loved in a new way?

Adult as her thoughts were fast becoming, her body nevertheless retained many of its outgrown, childish characteristics. With the advent of the deeper shadows, her eyelids closed and Hawkstraw hoisted her upon his back. This time, however, when his hands felt the bare flesh of her under-thighs resting upon him, there was an urge within him, which welled when he realized the copious kiss of a little while before. The sensation lingered until he forcibly expelled it from his mind. If the kiss and the touching of her body had been closer in sequence, he could not have exercised this self-control. Someday, they would follow too closely, the one upon the other.

CHAPTER 24

Johnny and Barth both greeted the Sabbath at a rather late hour. The morning passed in a strained atmosphere, and though Barth did his best to entice him from his surly mood, Johnny would not respond.

Barth thought back upon the happenings of the previous day, but he could remember no instance that might have provoked such an extended stay of hostility as Johnny was evidencing. Finally, he decided to let the spell wear itself out and busied himself by going over some previous surveys of the licks, which had been among the effects that Ephraim Mentz had delivered to him yesterday.

Noon came and Johnny's disposition seemed to have worsened instead of improving. The two ate without a word being spoken. After the table had been cleared, Barth resolved to make another effort at pacification. "Tom Chism's planning on having some of his men stay at Falls of the Ohio after they get there with his salt."

For a moment, it appeared that his attempt had been in vain, as Johnny made no reply. At length, however, Johnny's curiosity overcame him, and he asked, "Whut fer?"

"He's figuring on them bringing a boat down the Ohio, soon as it is high, then up Salt River to here."

Again there was the indeterminate pause, and the subsequent yielding to his inchoate interest in what Barth had to say. "Whut's he gonna hev on it?"

"Oh, kettles, mostly. I'm not real sure of what else he's planning on."

"Humphf." Johnny's interest and curiosity ended simultaneously and he lapsed once more into his studied state of unfriendliness. Th' tricky son-of-a-bitch shore tells me a lot of important things—about a boatload of kittles! Thet is shore some news!

Noting that Johnny had resumed his glum expression, Barth determined to go over to the licks and then on to the river and bathe. It would be his first bath since he came here. Might make the air smell better over at the Graingers tonight, he mused.

There was no response when he told his pouting friend goodbye.

Sagitta enjoyed the canter as much as he did and seemed a little disappointed when his master dismounted and tethered him at the storehouse.

Barth inquired casually of one of the men there as to whether Mace was around, and he made no comment when told that Hardin had just left a few minutes earlier but would be back soon.

A hasty check proved to his own satisfaction that there would indeed be enough salt for the morrow's shipment. Thus satisfied, he remounted and rode toward the river.

The water was cold and he exposed himself no longer than was necessary to accomplish his purpose. He let the breeze play about his naked body until he was dry. And after clearing the mud from his feet with some leaves, he donned his clothes.

The air had been chilly after he had climbed up the river's bank and before he dressed, but by the time he reached his cabin, perspiration had gathered upon his brow.

Johnny was no more friendly than when he had left him earlier, so he again pored over his maps. He kept at this until the daylight commenced to grow weaker. He then washed his face and hands and shaved.

He put on the less wrinkled of the clothes that Dracie had sent him and without saying anything to Johnny, he departed to keep his engagement of the evening.

Barth had no sooner gone, than Mace Hardin was there. "Enybuddy ter home?" His question was an idle one, as the open door made such a query needless.

"'Course they's somebuddy here," said Johnny before recognizing the voice, then, "Oh, hit's yew, Mace. Come on in. I'd come out there, but, well, yew knows th' reason I can't."

Mace laughed. "I understan' th' Cap'n's bin alookin' fer me. Ez he aroun'?"

"Naw, he ain't. He jest took off right 'fore yew come up."

"He tell yer whut he wuz a-wantin' with me?"

"Didn't say a damn thing 'bout it, if'n he wuz."

"Whut's th' latest big news yer heerd?"

"Ain't nuthin'—oh, shore! Th' kepteen did say suthin' yew mought be int'rusted in. Ain't 'portant, but yew would prob'ly want to hear it."

"Whut wuz hit?"

"Nuthin' 'cept thet damn Tom Chism—"

Mace interrupted him. "Yer hed trubble with th' no good, son-uv-a-bitch?"

"Naw, not yet, enyways."

"Then wut'd he do?"

"Ain't done nuthin' yet, it's whut he's figgerin' on doin'."

Mace strove to control his impatience. "Tell me all 'bout it."

"Well, th' kepteen says thet Chism is gonna have some of his men stay at th' Falls, after they gits th' salt up there, to bring a boatload of kittles an' suthin' else down th' Ohio to here."

"Thet so? When's they plannin' ter kum down th' river?"

"When it gits high enough. Don't see whut thet had to do with it; but thet's whut th' kepteen says they're gonna do. Ain't much to thet news, is they?"

"Not much, but I sees yer keeps yer ears open; yore a real smart 'un."

Johnny beamed. "Th' kepteen tells me ever'thing."

Having drained his source of information for the time being, Mace bade Johnny a quick farewell and was off to Ben Skinner's. As he rode away, he said to himself, "Th' li'l fart don't know suthin's 'portant when he hears it."

Johnny began to perk up. Mace surely seemed to respect him. But he still didn't figure on telling him anything that was of any consequence. Mace would have to find out for himself.

CHAPTER 25

Before Barth could alight from Sagitta, a little colored boy in livery of resplendent scarlet, who had evidently blended with the shadows, appeared as if by magic and took a firm hold of the bridle. The lad could not be more than eight years of age.

Barth surprised, then amused, asked him, "What's your name, little man?"

Back came the respectful reply. "I'se Jason, suh; ah takes kah of y' hoss."

"Aren't you rather small to handle an animal like this one?"

"Naw, suh; th' hosses all likes me, an' ah likes all th' hosses."

Barth's fingers found a small coin, which he gave to him upon dismounting. As he did so, he said, "Jason, here's something for your trouble." Reflecting that his host might not approve of this act, he cautioned him, "Don't say anything about my giving you this, you understand?"

"Ya, suh, ah unnerstan', an' no, suh, ah ain't gwine tell 'bout it." Jason's white teeth marked the path of his appreciative smile.

Before he could knock, the door opened and the stately Chate ushered him inside, requesting him to please be seated while he announced his presence to his master and mistress.

Barth had taken only a few steps, but he had traveled a thousand miles. He had stepped from Saltsburg into a drawing room in Boston. Everything, from the lush floor covering beneath his feet to the gorgeous candelabrum with its sculptured ophite base, was in perfect keeping with those of a dozen magnificent homes in the east, which it had been his privilege to visit in the years before the war.

He hastily ran his hand across his eyes. This must be some fantastic illusion, and little Jason must have been part of the sorcery that had produced it. But it was real, and at Bullitt's Lick, for even now, Doctor and Mrs. Grainger were welcoming him to their home.

"So nice of you to come, Captain Mercer." It was Drusilla who gave the first greeting as she extended one of the slender hands that had so fascinated him before.

He hesitated. Should he kiss it or merely allow it to rest in his own palm? He decided upon the latter as being the more decorous.

She eased any effect of a breach of manners on his part by permitting her fingers to remain lightly for an instant and then quickly, yet delicately, withdrawing her hand to her side.

From Doctor Grainger's expression, Barth gathered that he was relieved that he had not touched his lips to his wife's person. His welcome was most cordial and his handshake vigorous, an unusual indulgence for one who was surgeon and who undoubtedly guarded his hands from any possibility of the slightest injury, with the same zeal pursued by other members of his profession. Even a slight sprain or a bruised knuckle could conceivably be the difference between life and death for some patient.

Seated on a plushly upholstered chair, Barth drew laughter from his hosts by remarking, "That saddle is going to feel mighty hard when I leave here this evening."

The next instant, Chate was at his side with the wine.

Drusilla immediately proposed a toast, insisting they remain seated, as they started to rise. Something in her manner, in its fleeting second of recognition, told Barth that she had already partaken of several solitary toasts before his arrival.

"To the men," she began, her eyes lit by the traces of the sun that had shone on a foreign vineyard and now were liquified in her lifted goblet. "May they all be as handsome as those who are my present company!"

The wine's fragrance was exceeded only by its taste.

Where had it come from, and what was its vintage? Barth dared not ask his hosts for the answers. Instead, he exclaimed, "Never have I tasted such a wine as this!"

If the doctor had been prone to relate its place of origin or its age, he had no opportunity to do so; his wife barred any such sequential description with her suggestion that Captain Mercer now raise his glass in a tribute of his own.

Barth caught the significance of her request. Her vanity was affording him an opportunity for reciprocation of her compliment which, of necessity, had included her husband.

He did not disappoint her. "To woman, whose beauty and grace make man forgetful of his miseries, mindful of his blessings and hopeful of her continued love."

"How delightful," she responded. "Now, Richard, it is time for yours."

"And time it shall be." He cleared his throat before beginning. "To time, with its haunting yesterdays, its taunting todays and its vaunting tomorrows." He lowered, then reraised his glass. "To time, the vital component, without which woman could not admire the handsomeness of man, nor he praise and lavish his affection upon her."

"Perfectly brilliant, Richard!" She arose and went to his side. So quickly and unexpectedly had she moved, Grainger did not have a chance to arise. Bending down, she bestowed a kiss upon his bulging forehead, letting her eyes play invitingly from their corners at her guest. In the same maneuver, her breasts tilted precariously, as if to spill from the low neckline of her brocaded gown.

To camouflage his momentary confusion, Barth averted her flirting and addressed the doctor. "That was indeed an excellent composition. Might I inquire as to whether or not it was original with you?"

Pleased by the captain's question, Grainger acknowledged it was his own.

Drusilla appeared capable of starting another round of wine when Chate opportunely announced dinner.

Escorted by the two gentlemen, she hugged their arms closely to her body. Barth, on the right, felt the snugness of her breast against his arm and the firmness with which the fingers of her overlapping hand held his wrist. Her hair was heavily scented, its aroma hovering above a perfume that seemed to rise, as a mist, from her emerald necklace. This, plus the effect of the recently consumed wine, combined to produce a sensation of lightheadedness, which threatened his perspective. An impulse struck to pull her arm to his side. With the greatest of tension, he resisted this passionate inclination.

The dining room was no less wondrous than the chamber they had just left. As he took in its magnificence, he wondered at the privation they suffered when they looked out of their windows at the reality of Bullitt's Lick, and how much greater their discomfort must be when they actually ventured out into the settlement.

He was seated opposite Mrs. Grainger, the doctor occupying the chair at the head of the table.

With Chate in a position of constant surveillance, a comely, light-skinned colored woman performed the serving of the viands. Chate reserved the pouring of the wine unto himself.

Barth learned the woman's name when Drusilla, disregarding the canons of propriety, spoke to her. "Callie, these biscuts are most delicious."

Richard Grainger frowned, then cleared his throat, but if this was admonitory, Drusilla paid not the slightest attention.

"Callie is Chate's wife. They have the cutest little boy by the name of Jason. You must see him before you leave."

"You are forgetting that he took my horse when I arrived here this evening."

"To be sure, that completely slipped my mind. Isn't he precious?"

"He is all of that," Mercer responded.

Grainger ended the cross-conversation. "Drusilla, I do not believe our servants, or their child, to be proper subjects to discuss with a guest at our table."

"I'm sorry, Captain Mercer. Richard is quite right. I beg your pardon for so doing."

"I enjoyed your expression of interest in your domestics," Barth said, minimizing her offense.

She appeared to be seated unusually close to the table. A moment later, he knew the reason. The toe of her slipper was playing upon one of his ankles.

There was a minimum of talking during the rest of the meal.

If anything, she held his arm more tightly when they returned to the drawing room than she had when they had left it.

Had his host been less severe in his observance of formality, Barth would have uttered profuse praise of everything that had been placed before him this evening. Judging Grainger correctly, however, to consider the repast as being an accustomed, and not an extraordinary, incident of their station and manner of living, he contained his true approbation of the repast.

The incongruity of this setting in the midst of frontier life kept hammering at his reasoning powers. Sipping his brandy, he considered every moment wasted since he had departed from the comforts of Williamsburg.

Acting in a spirit of congeniality, he made a mistake, which was to deliver the rest of the evening to Doctor Grainger, his casual inquiry as to the condition of Willie Roller.

"It's too early to say. I believe he is doing as well as could be expected."

If the doctor had stopped with that simple answer, it would have been well. However, he drained the last of his liqueur and, settling deep in his chair, took up the thread of his reply. "You know, Captain, the operation I performed on Roller was done without practically any of the present-day refinements. I trust you understand that necessity dictated that I amputate as I did using whiskey instead of opiates and firing the stump after the severance. While Mrs. Grainger was of great aid to me, she is not trained as a nurse or surgeon's assistant."

"I recognized all that the day the operation took place. I thought you did an admirable job, and while I knew that Mrs. Grainger was an emergency choice, I considered that she too had handled her unfamiliar duties in an excellent fashion."

The host and hostess were flattered by Barth's words of commendation. The latter showed her appreciation by carelessly dropping her lace kerchief, which her gallant guest retrieved instantly and placed in her hand. Her fingers exerted a knowing pressure upon his own.

Doctor Grainger, for his thanks, entered upon a learned treatise that covered his training in Edinburgh, Vienna and Paris; the great esteem in which his proven talents were held by surgeons all over the worlds of renowned figures whose doctors had called him into their cases and of past operations he had performed. He paid no attention to his wife but directed his discourse toward his considerate male companion.

Once, he paused and Drusilla snatched a brief bit of talk from him. "Captain, I can't comprehend how you, a perfect gentleman, could adjust yourself to the low rabble that lives here. I know you must do so, or at least you feel that you must, but ... Well, you are just too nice a person to have to associate with them."

The doctor answered for Barth. "Drusilla, when you are in the Army, you have to follow orders, the captain does it all in the line of duty."

Drusilla continued heedlessly. "I'd like to see you in your uniform, Captain. I imagine it would be most becoming to you."

"Yes, yes. I'm sure it would." Grainger was so intent on picking up where he had left off that the import of his wife's words did not register. "You know, Captain. I believe of all the operations that I am called upon to perform, I think I prefer the removal of a leg, about midway between the knee and the hip."

Barth did his best to follow the ensuing surgical description. He listened to a maze of details covering the proper equipment: a large and small knife, a saw, the tenaculum, nippers, stiff ointment, a tourniquet and on and on. His eyes drooped, but he tortured himself into keeping them open. The doctor was beginning the first incision. "I make a swift, deliberate cut, obliquely and upward, taking the knife around the leg in a constant course."

He realized his eyes and ears had closed again. Grainger's voice intoned, "Great care must be taken to avoid tearing the muscles from the bone."

Barth nodded, hearing faintly, "Now, we come to the actual severance."

He alerted himself and bent forward placing his hand over his forehead, that the doctor might think it a position of contemplation. "The saw strokes should be short, cautious and light. This is human bone we are going to cut through, not a tree limb."

The listener stirred himself and glanced at Drusilla and found her eyes centered upon him, her lips forming a lascivious smile—the countenance of a woman willing to wait patiently for the bed and the satisfaction of her desire.

When the fullness of the thought dawned upon him, his drowsiness departed and he was seized with the striking opposites in the personalities of the two, the husband, made shallow by his deep, surgical training and knowledge, obsessed by his profession only for purposes of his own self-exaltation, and to which end everything and everyone else in his life were mere incidents for use or toleration, and the wife, a slave to her own beauty and passion and who would acknowledge love only if it came to her in the guise of a true gentlemen. Certainly, no surgeon's gloved hand could satisfy her amorous instincts nor could his forceps extract her enduring affection.

"Do you follow me, Mercer?" It was the doctor reassuring himself of his audience.

"Yes, I do, sir." Barth's mind hurriedly searched for, and fortunately found, a recent item of his host's discourse by reference to which he could prove his attention. "You mentioned the retractor. I would like to know a little more about its use."

Satisfied as to the captain's interest, Grainger's voice, devoid of inflection, once more pursued his favorite subject. "The retractor? Oh, yes. That's simply a piece of leather, which is fitted around the bones. Its main purpose is to prevent any unnecessary injury from the action of the saw. Now, after the limb has been severed, the bone nippers come in to play their part, the bloody extremity is cleansed with a sponge and warm water, and we pinch off any rough points of bone, then ..."

The guest's mind wandered again, although he now controlled his napping tendencies. For the first time, he was conscious of the pendulum strokes of a clock somewhere within the room. There was that stillness present, which tells one the hour is late without advising its exactness.

Drusilla still looked at him, and the coy movements of her hands, lips and eyes let him know her expectations were undiminished. Sitting there, she was as a fluffy kitten, purring contentedly in a favorite chair, knowing that sooner or later its fur would be stroked with affection and that it would then be picked up and caressed by loving arms.

The doctor droned away. "The tenaculum's work is finished once we have tied the end of the femoral artery. For that, we use ordinary shoemaker's thread—well waxed, of course. Then we let out the tourniquet a . . ."

At this point, three were each engaged in three different subjects of contemplation. Richard Grainger, in his vain display of his learning and skill. Mercer, first, as to how much longer the doctor was going to continue; second, how many of those who had attended the lectures, of which he had boasted, remained awake at their conclusion. And finally how Drusilla would conduct herself when he, at long last, would be permitted to bid them both good night. Drusilla, imagining the physical appearance of the captain in his uniform and then visualizing his bare shoulders and chest.

"The patient must be watched carefully. He should not be fed anything except the lightest of foods. Broths are ideal for a while, then, when he is a little stronger, he can be graduated into his former eating habits. That ends all aspects of the operation. Now as to the postoperative care of the limb." Grainger paused, as Chate thoughtfully provided him with his pipe. Lighting it for his master, he stood by until sure it was fully lit.

The atmosphere had been heavy enough, without this added clouding. Barth became resolute. It was time to leave, before his host got fully started on another forensic foray.

"Doctor, I am afraid I must make my departure. The lateness of the hour might suggest that I have already presumed upon your generous hospitality." He had risen as he said this.

Grainger had just settled back in his chair. "Nonsense, nonsense. I don't know when I have enjoyed myself as I have this evening."

Drusilla added her plea that he remain in their company. "Captain, you cannot imagine what relief you have provided by coming to see us. We have no friends here and but few acquaintances. We live with ourselves. We would so like for you to stay a little longer." Her head was turned to the candlelight, her eyes dancing invitingly, saying, "Please." Her effort had not been without its effect. He wavered an instant, but then said quickly, "I know you are both sincere, but good manners make it imperative that I do not impose further upon your kind indulgences."

Her face plainly showed her disappointment. Her husband, however, sensing his guest's determination to leave, said jokingly as he arose, "I believe Captain Mercer just wants to get home and dream of that young woman he told me about."

Barth smiled in good humor. But Drusilla's lips tightened and her eyes snapped. Her mood mellowed instantly as she and Grainger escorted him to the door. Chate appeared from nowhere to open it.

Glancing at a mahogany writing table to the left of the entrance, Mercer spied an opened dueling chest, its pistols in place. Well, the doctor hadn't any need for them, this time anyway, he thought amusedly.

Grainger grasped his hand. "I meant it when I said that I had enjoyed your company. I hope you will come back soon."

"Thank you, Doctor, and you, Mrs. Grainger. This has been a most pleasant occasion for me also."

As they passed through the doorway, Drusilla found his hand, and he felt her fingers gently squeezing his own. They exchanged formal farewells, with Drusilla having the last word, saying, "I'm sure we will see each other again."

She said this with certainty, not hopefully. She was confident of her charms, and at that moment, Barth was not too sure her confidence wasn't without some justification.

Chate alone remained. The doctor and Mrs. Grainger had reentered the house. In even, courteous tones, which despite their brevity, yet impressed Barth by their pleasing qualities, he said, "Jason has your mount, sir. I wish you good evening."

There was Jason on the outer fringe of the ring of light from the door. Sagitta neighed nervously.

As he came up to the boy, the latter said to him in a quavering voice, "Suh, my papa say ah should give de money back to yo' an' thank yo' foah yo' kineness."

Barth was nonplussed. "Why in the world did he say that? I wanted you to have it."

"Ah knows dat, suh, but papa say fokes who hab a job ter do ez paid ter do it good, an' it ain' no need ter give 'em enythin' extry fo' th' doin' of it." The lad almost gave way to tears.

"You tell your father, for me, that he has my admiration and that I think he has a mighty fine son."

"Thank yo', suh."

As Barth threw his leg over the saddle and took the reins from him, the little boy ran off around the side of the house where he could cry unashamedly. It had been the first money he had ever received, and he couldn't keep it.

The hurts of childhood are often deep and insidious, creating wounds that never fully heal. Jason would never forget his lost coin, and no matter to what abundance he might thereafter attain, he would never be recompensed.

*

Barth's thoughts rolled with Sagitta's gait. Vast as were the differences between Bullitt's Lick and Boston, they could not equal those existing between the Graingers. She, warm and effusive, he, cold unresponsive and taciturn, except for his obsession with his profession. They shared but one common characteristic, and that too differed in its course. Vanity controlled their lives.

With even a minimum of foresight, he reasoned, these two persons could have known they were mismatched, that their marriage was ill-fated from the time she had accepted his proposal. While it was purest conjecture, though based on his acute personal observation, Barth pictured the erroneous union as having been consummated solely on selfish premises. Drusilla, young, radiant and ambitious for what her society would appraise as a successful marriage, and the sexual enjoyment she so strongly hoped for with one who knew so thoroughly the workings and needs of the human body. Richard Grainger, moving on toward middle age, desiring a pretty, talented wife of proven lineage and resources, who would be a willing partner whenever his infrequent physical urges called for satisfaction of their demands.

How insane it had been, Barth thought, for the doctor to have ever left Boston with her, seeking a panacea, which could never exist. It was Grainger's own, insatiable pride that was responsible; he had not the bolstering arm of religious belief, which might have directed such a course, But, why did she go with him so willingly? Barth could not answer this, unless it was because of that entwining branch of vanity, which seeks the air of respectability, even if there is no desire to breathe of it.

He wondered about the course of their lives if they had been able to have foreseen their unsuitableness for each other, but he soon digressed into the ifs in his own life thus far. The world and one's existence, he concluded, were but a realm of ifs, whose shadows danced behind and beyond, regardless of the path one followed.

As he expected, the cabin was dark. He rapped vigorously a number of times, before a sleepy-eyed Johnny unbarred the door, saying to himself as he groped his way back to his bed, "Th' son-of-a-bitch musta had hisself a time."

Barth was in the bunk above Johnny in a matter of minutes. He slumbered readily, dreaming, as Doctor Grainger had so jocularly speculated, of Dracie, and of another, quite outside the boring doctor's imaginary perception, the audacious Drusilla.

Throughout his subconscious meanderings, he rolled and tossed, mumbling incoherently. The aroma of wine from his breath filled the little room and soon reached Johnny's nostrils. Unable to resume his rest after his recent awakening, Johnny muttered aloud, "Th' son-of-a-bitch is drunk."

CHAPTER 26

Barth was up with the first light of the morning. This was to be another busy day for him: seeing the shipment on its way, going for Aaron Flinden, checking the progress of Herman Tressel and Motty Willerhorst on the construction of the conveyor pipes and meeting with George May and his party of land locators and surveyors, whose presence at Dowdall's Station had been related to him by Ephraim Mentz.

The aroma of bacon and eggs brought Johnny to the table. Barth greeted him cordially and received in return only a recalcitrant nod.

He had been patient long enough; it was time this foolishness ended. "Johnny, I have no idea what is bothering you, but whatever it is, I'm tired of putting up with it. Now, you either change your manner or one of us is leaving here." He found it easy to speak in this fashion. He missed his lost sleep, and he was not accustomed to doing so.

Johnny didn't respond for a while. Inside his little round head, there was a lot of cogitation being sparkened and generaled by his scheming little brain. 'Twouldn't do fer me to git m'self sep'rated from 'im; still, he's sech a tricky bastard . . . better make out like I'm makin' up with 'im. His reflection completed, Johnny's voice and disposition changed forthwith. "I'm sorry, Kepteen. Jest bin suthin' abotherin' me, lately. I apologize fer actin' thet-a-way."

Barth too changed and he smiled, saying, "That's lots better, Johnny. What is troubling you? Can I help you with it?"

"I'm a-feared not, Kepteen. This is suthin' I'll hev to work out by m'self."

Wallingford greeted him as Mercer came from the cabin, leaving the door ajar.

"How did you get out of your stall?" He asked the animal, as though it were capable of answering his question. He remembered that the mule was in the little shed when he had last stabled Sagitta, and he distinctly recalled having shut the door after he had done so.

Wallingford did answer, in the only way possible for him. He hee-hawed loudly.

Sagitta was still in there, despite the fact Wallingford had kicked the door down sometime during the night.

"I may not have slept long, but I surely must have slept soundly," he said laughingly.

After Barth's departure, the mule eyed the partially opened door. This constituted an invitation to man and beast alike, so Wallingford, accepting it, ambled inside.

Johnny, back in bed, looked up expecting to see Mercer. When he saw that it was his old antagonist, he bounded forth like a shot from a gun and grabbed the first thing he could put his hands to—an iron skillet. He moved in close to the animal's side and whacked its hindquarter, the same one that had received so much unwelcomed attention the day before, cursing Mercer all the while for having let the creature loose.

Wallingford made no attempt at retaliation this time but tore out of the cabin and around to the stable.

Johnny followed and soon ascertained how the mule had gotten out of its confinement.

"Th' son-of-a-bitch didn't let yew out, after all, did he? I tole 'im he shouldn't hev brought yew here. Now, I got to git m'self busy an' fix this damn door, yew damn, ornery bastard."

If Wallingford understood, he paid no mind, but stood there on his three legs, munching contentedly away.

*

Mace was talking to him. "Cap'n, I don't hold none ter much with yer loadin' them wagins an' sendin' 'em ter th' Falls."

"Why not, Mr. Hardin?"

"Wal, fer th' one thing they's soft places 'long th' trace, an' hit'll be one helluva job ter keep 'em rollin' through them spots."

"Your men know the route, don't they?"

"Good as enybuddy does, they does, but hit still strikes me that it be smarter jest ter ship th' salt by th' pack-trains. Yer wud make hit faster."

"I want the wagons, Mr. Hardin."

"Wal, all right, Cap'n! Thet's th' way hit'll be."

"How far is it to Louisville?"

"Eighteen ter twenny mile, som'eres 'roun' thet. Cap'n, sence yer set on sendin' th' wagins, mebbe we mought jest let them men stay on at th' Falls fer a spell after they gits thar." Mace was thinking of Chism's men and the kettles.

"For what purpose, Mr. Hardin?" Barth's tone was demanding.

"They cud bring some things back with 'em, Cap'n."

"I expect that to be done anyway. There's no reason why they shouldn't be back here by tomorrow evening anyhow. That's the latest I want them back. Is that clear?"

"Yes, sir, Cap'n."

"Who have you picked to be in charge of our men?"

"Virgil Mallory, Cap'n."

"I figured he'd be the one," Barth said.

"Enything wrong with 'im, Cap'n?"

"No, I reckon he's as good as any. Where is he now?"

"Over there by th' storehouse. They's loadin' th' last uv th' wagins. Want me ter send fer 'im?"

"No, I'll ride on over myself."

A keg tumbled from one of the vehicles, splitting open when it hit upon a rock and spilling its contents. Barth bent over and idly picked up a handful of the salt. He was about to scatter it upon the ground when something stayed this action. He took another look at the salt and noted its color seemed a little different than he thought it should, and it was less lumpy than the rest he had seen earlier. The splintered staves of the case appeared to be fully seasoned, eliminating the possibility that it had been one of the few saved from the fire. It strengthened his belief that it had been stored elsewhere, for some period of time. While the place of storage was unknown to him, it had to be away from the works. He now knew what was in every building at the lick. Ben Skinner's store might have been the depository. Mace and Skinner were close, according to Abe Foster. But wherever the keg had come from, the salt had been put into it long before this morning.

He checked the rest of the shipment and found a number of containers whose wood looked well aged in contrast to the freshness of the others in the wagons. Small wonder Hardin had been so certain he would have enough salt ready for today. It was available whenever he had need of it.

Barth kept his discovery to himself. Alongside of Virgil Mallory, he rode in the lead of the party, skirting the knobs on the trace to the north of the set-tlement for about a mile until they came to Blue Licks, where by their previous understanding, Tom Chism and his men, with Jim Trench as their leader, were to meet them.

Tom was there ahead of him. He and Mercer reviewed the details of their plans, then each instructed his own group. Following this, Barth called Mallory and Trench together, emphasizing to whom they were to report when they reached the Falls, how much they were to receive and the manner of payment.

They were both to sign for the money paid them. Trench for Chism, and Mallory for what he believed to be Hardin's interest.

Barth cautioned his men, Mallory in particular, that he expected them to be back no later than sunset the next day. That four of Chism's party with their equipment were to accompany them on the return trip, and that if anything happened to any of them, he would hold Mallory responsible.

Mercer and Chism traveled with the party as far as Clear's Station. At this point, they turned back. Shortly thereafter, when they had passed through Blue Licks, the two separated, Barth leaving to keep his meeting with Aaron Flinden, and Tom retracing the path he had taken to the gap.

*

Flinden was at the ford below Dowdall's, when Mercer got there.

"Been waiting for me long, Mr. Flinden?"

"Just a little while, friend Mercer. I would rather be a bit early than to be late." Flinden's tone was most cordial, but as they rode off, Barth detected a nervous quality in his manner.

"Anything wrong, Mr. Flinden? If you're worried concerning your reception at the licks, you can put that out of your mind. I have instructed the men as to the manner in which they are to treat you, and I will be there to see that my orders are carried out."

"'Tis not that, friend Mercer; 'tis my wife. She has been at me since last thee were to my house. 'Tis truly said, 'A continual dropping in a very rainy day and a contentious woman are alike.' 'Tis not the men who worry me this morning. Indeed 'tis a relief that I go there today."

"I'm sure she'll accept your decision, once she realizes that you mean to follow it through," said Barth encouragingly.

"'Tis not only my determination to aid thee, friend Mercer, but also there is the matter of the young girl who lives with the Hardins."

"Why should that concern Mrs. Flinden?"

"'Tis right that she be troubled, even as I am, but I see nothing that I can do to remove her from that place."

"I must confess, I don't see any connection between your wife and yourself and the Hardin child."

"That's the very point. She is not their daughter."

Flinden related his meeting with Nancy and Hawkstraw and his discovery of her true identity.

"Now, Ursula keeps after me to get the girl away from them."

Barth thought a moment. "There's no way that I can see to do it, the only answer would be by the use of force."

"Thou knows I cannot follow that course."

"Yes, I am aware of that fact."

"So is Ursula, but she keeps after me to do something about the matter, and there is nothing that can be done, except to wait on the Lord's will."

"I wish I could do something, Mr. Flinden, but I'm helpless under the circumstances."

"Thank thee, friend Mercer, I understand. 'Tis up to the Lord to save this lamb."

Thinking back upon his only meeting with the girl at the Hardin cabin, Barth said, "I don't doubt but what the Lord is the only one who can arrange her release from Mace Hardin, but I can tell you this much, Mr. Flinden. He won't be saving any lamb. Nancy is she-bear's whelp, maybe, but no lamb." He then recounted his experience with Massalene and Nancy, stressing the knife in the latter's hand and his own unguarded position at the time.

"That is the exact danger of her remaining with those people. Now my alarm is truly increased!"

"There's no good in your fretting, Mr. Flinden. The Lord is the only hope you have. You'll just have to wait upon him."

"May he move swiftly, friend Mercer."

They were in sight of the licks and of its hearing. Boisterous voices, whose every other word was a curse struck their ears as they approached. Barth feared that this greeting might dissuade Aaron Flinden even before he started on his job. He said nothing, waiting anxiously, but once they were past the furnaces on the lower side, the objectionable sounds diminished and soon were heard no more. They dismounted at the storehouse and went inside.

It took only a little instruction before Brother Flinden understood the full scope of his duties. He had thoughtfully brought along some quills and writing fluid, along with a ledger. Seeing his foresightedness, Barth said, "You needn't have bothered bringing those things with you, I have already provided everything you'll need for your work."

"I thought it best that I be prepared, friend Mercer."

"'Twill do no harm, Mr. Flinden. I can purchase what you have there, if you wish to sell them to me."

"Thank thee, but if they are not needed, I will take them home this evening."

"As you wish, Mr. Flinden. I'll be back shortly to see how things are going with you."

Barth's next stop was with Herman Tressel and Motty Willerhorst. He found them busily engaged in joining the sections of pipe after others had finished boring them. Some sections they banded together with metal. Others they simply interlocked with a slight overlapping of the wood. The banding was employed at each end of a series of such joinings aggregating approximately twenty feet.

There was no conversation other than the inquiry as to how the work was progressing. However, as Mercer started to leave, Tressel looked up at him and wiped his brow with his forearm, saying, "Der digging iss by der Irishers. Ve buildt; dey dig."

"That's a bargain, Mr. Tressel. You get the pipes ready, and I'll see that they are put in the ground." If there were any Irishmen around, Barth could not remember seeing them.

The morning sped quickly by. Then, just as he prepared to leave and go into the settlement, he saw a number of men coming his way. The folded tripod told him they were the surveyors from Dowd's Station. It was thus that Barth met Hawkstraw who, along with his friend Ethan Belden, was a member of the crew.

Mercer and George May, who headed the party, talked at some length. From him, Barth learned that he had come from Cox's Station and that his purpose was to make a resurvey of the land grants in this area, above and below Salt River.

The war had brought about changes in the ownerships of many patents. A veteran of the French and Indian Wars might have received land in recognition of his services to the Crown, as had Malcolm Mercer, however, should that veteran, or those holding title by succession, continue to have honored the Crown in the recently subsiding conflict of the revolution, ownership would, in all probability, be lost, and the land revert to the Commonwealth of Virginia, for new grants by that sovereignty. Hence one reason for the resurvey. Again, errors were constantly being discovered in old plats and maps, or interlacing entrys brought the parties into court for a judicial determination as to what the true lines should be.

May promised to copy such of the surveys for Barth as he might wish, when and as the same were completed. In return, the land locator and agent was to receive all necessary provisions for himself and his party during their stay in this locality.

No sooner had the surveyors gone, than there were other visitors—traders, merchants and individual settlers who traveled here together for their mutual protection. Their points of origin were usually widely scattered, but all came for the same, driving reasons to procure the precious salt.

More and more, Mercer realized how accurate had been the hearsay concerning Bullitt's Lick. It was truly the roughest and busiest place in all of Kentucky.

*

The light of the morning did not enter Drusilla Grainger's bedchamber until near noon. It would not then have illumined the room, but for Callie's drawing the drapes, which covered the windows, now glassed like those at Ben Skinner's. No sooner had Chate brought the doctor the news, than the glass had been purchased, cut and installed.

Today, as was his custom, Richard Grainger had arisen early, and set about his methodical daily life: an inspection of his house and its appurtenances, breakfast and thence to his surgical tomes.

Drusilla stirred but slightly when Callie placed her hand gently upon her satin-covered shoulder. Calling to her in a well-modulated voice, Callie insisted, "Wake up, honey, it's gittin' on late."

Her mistress responded by raising her bare arms above her head and stretching them to their utmost length and then rolling over on her side in a futile effort to avoid the brightness from without. Her white shoulder seemed to gleam against the green of her comforter.

The awakening process followed its usual course: a toe, an ankle, the calf and then her knee emerged from their covering, a pause, more stretching of the arms and a delicious scratching of her scalp, a momentary closing of her eyes, their reopening and the inching of her body to the edge of the bed. At last, like the mythical goddess slipping the folds of the emerald sea, she arose. Like that feminine deity too, her hair was her only adornment.

To Callie, though she saw this same conclusion with only slight variations each day that she awoke her, the scene was always climatic.

"Oh, Miz Drusilla, yo' ez got th' beau-fullest body th' good Lord done ever give a womern!"

"Well, at least that makes two of us who think so," laughed her mistress in true, but lighthearted vanity.

"Bet yo', wuz mine ter be like yores, I'd hab me 'lebben chilluns by this time," Callie chuckled.

"If that were true, Callie, your body would no longer be like mine."

"He-he! Thass right, honey, sho' ez!"

"Callie, after last night, I believe I might truthfully say that there is one other who admires my body.

"Shush yo'se'f, honey. De doctah's downstairs, he kin hear a piller drap on de flo'. Yo' means dat hansome Cap'n Mercer?"

"Who else? Any man who can last through one of Richard's wearisome dissertations without falling soundly asleep has to be deeply interested in something other than my husband and his boring display of self-conceit. I'll tell you what, Callie. Captain Mercer will be back soon. You just wait and see."

"Honey, yo' ain't done gwine got yo'se'f in love wif him, has yo', honey?"

"Completely, Callie. And I'm happier than I've been since we left Boston, oh, so long ago. When we went to bed last night, Richard's back touched mine, and I imagined it was Captain Mercer there in bed with me. I was so carried away, I almost turned about and began loving him wildly."

"Dat th' truf, honey, did yo'?"

"I said, I almost did so. Thank goodness, my imagination isn't that compelling."

"Honey, yo' best ca'm yo'se'f. Don't yo' be fo'gettin' dem pistels downstairs."

"You know, Callie," she said, as she stepped into an undergarment, "I'm not the least bit worried about Richard's dueling pistols, and I don't believe Captain Mercer is either."

*

Mace tossed a twig in the river and watched the current sweep it rapidly away. This was no idle act on his part, the flow of the water carried a singular significance. When the Ohio was high, it would back up into Salt River, neutralizing the downstream force, thus easing greatly the labor required to propel a raft or keelboat up to the licks. By observing the cessation of the movement of this stream, he would be informed as to the approximate time when Chism's men would leave Falls of the Ohio. When that happened, he would put his plans into operation.

Sitting with his back resting against the base of a large sycamore, Jeddy-Boy called to his father. "Pap, hit looks liken it'll be a spell yet, 'fore we hez ter git busy, don't hit?"

Mace nodded his head, seconding the thought.

"More damn waitin'!" Jeddy-Boy got up and brushed the seat of his britches. "Looks liken all we duz is ter set aroun' an' wait."

"Jest as well git yerse'f used ter it," his father said crisply.

"Pap, I'm a-missin' thet money I used ter be a-gittin' when we wuz handlin' the salt our way."

"Yer'd still be missin hit'. Yer spends it fast as yer gits hit."

"Wal, I'm missin' hit more now. Things cost me sence I ain't a-stayin' ter home."

"Nobuddy runned yer away." Mace was gazing absentmindedly toward the licks.

"I kain't rest easy thar no mores. Thet damn Hawkstraw an' th' ole womern wud fix me right in m' sleep'. Jest don't make no sense ter me. Them, my blood kin, a-consarnin' theyse'fs 'bout thet damn orphant girl. She's jest ripe an' ready fer th' pickin', an' if'n I don't do hit, some'un else'll do hit fer me."

"Thet's why yer allus runnin' short uv money, foolin' roun' with ever damn womern yer sees. Thet, an' th' corn an' th' whiskey yer drinks."

Jed settled down to serious talk. "Pap, shore 'nough, I needs a little suthin'. How 'bout guvin' me some on account?"

"On account uv whut?" Mace snapped his question.

"Pap, yer knows I'm good fer hit. Later on, they'll be things yer will be a'wantin' me ter do fer yer, liken a few days back, when I took keer uv Bad-Eye fer yer."

"A hell-uv-a-lot uv takin' keer yer done fer me then. Th' boys tells me Bad-Eye died hisse'f." Without thinking, Mace spat in the wind. A spray came back in his face and he wiped if off with a matter-of-fact brush of his hand.

"Pap, least I got yer money back fer yer." Jeddy-Boy was pressing his claim.

"Yer kept all thet wuz over whut I hed guv 'im too. Remember? Thet paid yer real good fer whut little yer done. I ain't fergittin' how yer helt me up on thet."

While they had been talking back and forth, they failed to notice another's approach. He had come stealthily, when his keen ears had picked up the trap that Mace had set for Bad-Eye Smith. Fearing the consequences were he now to show himself, he remained in his concealment until such time as the father and son would move away.

Mace precipitated this action when he said, "Jeddy-Boy, I hain't a-guvin' yer a damn thing! Yer jest hez ter make out th' best way yer kin, til suthin' heppens an' I needs yer ag'in."

"Mebbe I won't be 'roun' when thet heppens."

"Mebbe, yer damn well better be! Le's git on back ter th' licks. Thet son-uv-a-bitch Mercer is probably got his ass spread a-ready, a waitin' fer me."

Doniger stayed until he was sure it was safe to venture forth. He had intended telling Mace that Mercer was about the licks. Instead, he had obtained information, which properly used when the occasion presented itself, might be the key that would open the door for the fervently desired escape from Bullitt's Lick. Until the time was propitious, however, he would have to continue to do Mace's bidding.

Circling around Hardin and the disgruntled Jeddy-Boy, he waited until the latter mounted his horse, which had been tied along with Mace's, a good distance from the river. When Jed rode off, Doniger delayed his own approach until Mace was astride his own mare, then he arranged to meet him as though he had come straight from the licks.

Mace reined to a halt. "Whut yer doin' here, Doniger?"

"I come tuh tell yuh that Mercer's at th' works, like you told me tuh do."

"How long's he bin thar?"

"Fer a good spell, him an' Flinden was in th' storehouse when I left."

"Yer shore dint break yore damn neck gittin' here."

"Boss, I ain't got no horse, like yuh has. 'Sides, I weren't sure which d'rection yuh was in."

"I'll go see if'n th' son-uv-a-bitch wants enything. Yer come on an' be handy in case I needs yer."

The walk back to the licks was pleasant for Jack Doniger this day. He had a little bit of hope stuck deep within his heart. He began to lay his plans.

*

The sun was all but behind the knobs when Aaron Flinden said wearily, "I believe I have finished the accounts balance."

Noting his air of exhaustion, Barth said to him, "This was a hard first day, wasn't it? It ought to be easier from here on, now that you have the books set up properly."

"I have enjoyed myself, nevertheless, friend Mercer. What do I do with the money that came in today, and the pelts we took in trade?"

"I've got the best man and the safest place anyone could find for their keeping." He stepped to the door and called, "Mr. Hardin, will you come inside?"

Mace obeyed promptly. "Whut yer want, Cap'n?"

"I have instructed Mr. Flinden to turn over to you the day's receipts, consisting of money and furs. He will do this at the close of each day. It is your responsibility to see that nothing happens to them."

"I unnerstans, Cap'n. They'll be taken keer ov proper."

After Mace's departure, Brother Flinden asked, "Where will he keep them?"

"I imagine right here. Things will be safe enough. Frankly, were anything to be missing, I know it would be taken at his bidding. This way, with them entrusted to his care, his hands are tied by the mere fact of his accountability."

"If the thief be the guard, 'twould be most easy to steal." Brother Flinden was skeptical.

"Not if the thief thinks he might be stealing from himself."

"I do not follow thee, friend Mercer."

"It doesn't matter, Mr. Flinden. It's my risk, if any there be, and I'm satisfied."

Flinden pursued the subject no further as Barth asked, "You about ready? I don't want your wife to be upset because of you getting home too late."

They set off at a brisk canter and were soon passing Mud Garrison, from whence reverberated sounds of revelry, unseemly for the twilight hour.

"Satan's work is being done, this evening!" Brother Flinden sadly shook his head.

Barth smiled inwardly, but made no reply to this outspoken meditation.

A mist now began to rise from the river nearby and to roll over when it reached the top of the banks, spreading thinly before them. At first clinging to the ground, it rose slowly, until it gradually obscured their vision as they rode toward the ford.

Sagitta's ears pricked forward as they neared the crossing place. A whinnying came from up ahead. The uneasy feeling it incited was soon dissipated, however, when they were able to make out the horse, standing motionless, and bearing two riders, a large form and a smaller one. Seconds later, Hawkstraw got off the horse and assisted Nancy to the ground.

Neither Barth nor Flinden alighted as the young girl made this unnecessary by coming to where they had stopped.

"We-uns is ready fer more larnin'. We kum, liken we sed we wud." Her manner was casual, yet direct and demanding.

Brother Flinden acknowledged her unusual greeting. "How are you and James this evening?"

Hawkstraw smiled his answer, aroused partly by the fact that another besides Nancy addressed him by his given name. It sounded strange, but it pleased him.

Nancy was more forthright. "We be fine, by God."

Flinden didn't know quite how to receive her reply. His brow furrowed and then relaxed as he gave her youth the benefit of the doubt in his reasoning. "This is my friend, Mr. Mercer." Even the title of one who was a part of the symbol of war did not pass his lips.

Although James nodded his head in response, Nancy ignored the introduction, saying, "Hit's a-gittin' on ter dark, and we ain't et nuthin', so's ter meet yer an' larn suthin' more from yer."

Brother Flinden continued. "Mr. Mercer is seeing me home. Get on your horse, and we'll ride together."

Nancy shot back. "Yer don't need him. James an' me kin see yer ter yer place." She had instantly recognized Barth when she first saw him alongside Brother Flinden.

The latter, missing the barbed import of her words, said to his companion, "The child is right. There's no need of thee going farther with me."

Before a reply could be made, she interjected, "Yer don't need th' likes uv him, damn 'im!"

Despite the failing light and the whisps of fog, Barth saw Flinden's forehead line again, and this time there was no easing of the wrinkles in his brow. "Thou can not learn, if thee thinks and talks like that, Nancy Landers!" Of his companion, he implored, "Forgive her, friend Mercer, 'twas but her lips that spoke the thoughts of the Hardins."

"I feel no offense, Mr. Flinden. However, since you say you'll be all right, I'll be on my way. You just shepherd that little lamb you have there. I'll meet you here in the morning." Waving goodbye, he urged Sagitta into a full gallop.

He found a most welcome surprise awaiting him at his cabin. Rosie Tindall had sent supper for Johnny and himself.

In seeming good humor following the meal, Johnny inquired as to the events of the day, and Barth told him of everything that had taken place.

The conversation lagged after a bit, and the little fellow walked to the open doorway and stared at the lighted cabins in the distance. His shirttail covered him to a point midway between his knees and hips. Though his appearance was now commonplace to Barth, the latter still had to occasionally stifle an errant chuckle.

"What's the matter, Johnny, getting tired of sitting around?"

His words were intended to be helpful, to allow Johnny to unburden himself of the problems that beset one when there is nothing to do, and no way to do anything if opportunity did present itself.

"Hell, no, I ain't tired from settin 'roun'. Yew knows damn good an' well thet I can't touch nuthin' to m' ass er hev anything touch it neither. Whut th' hell do yew think I eats standin up for? An' I don't sleep on m' stummick 'cause I 'magines they's a womin under me neither. Am I gittin' tired from settin' aroun'? Of course I ain't! I'm thet way from all th' sassiety visits I bin a-makin' to Doc Grainger's, er didn't chew know 'bout thet?" He cast a supercilious glance at Mercer, whose face, for once, did not betray the mirth this tirade was engendering.

Barth started to say he regretted asking the question, but feared it would only get another rise out of him.

Johnny wasn't through, however. "An' thet son-of-a-bitch Grainger! Why, I wouldn't let him docter my pisser, if I wuz full clean to m' ears. Next time he docters my ass, it'll be Wallingford yew kin bet on thet. An' I ain't so damn shore I'd let th' son-of-a-bitch work on him even."

"Sounds like you're getting well, Johnny, the way you're going on."

This statement brought on another withering look of disgust. " Gittin' well, my ass!"

"Raise your skirt, I mean, your shirt, and let me set your rump." Barth had to laugh at his unintentional slip of the tongue.

"Thet's right, go ahead and laugh, thet's all yew kin do! So now yore a ass inspector, air yew? I wonders how damn happy yew'd be, if'n yew wuz to git yore own ass blistered to hell an' back!" Johnny threw himself, belly first, onto his bunk.

"Careful of that woman under you, Johnny," Barth quipped.

Johnny sputtered an unintelligible reply and turned his head, his face to the logged wall.

"Come a week from today, you'll be up and about. It won't be so long now. When that time comes, you can take over what I'm doing."

This sounded important to Johnny and he switched his head, reversing its position. "Yew means I'm to run the whole licks?"

"Not exactly. I've promised Brother Flinden you'll take my place, so far as he's concerned."

"How fur is thet?" The importance of the position seemed to be diminishing.

"Mr. Flinden is doing a most necessary job for me, and he won't do it unless he has someone to protect him from the workers."

Johnny thought, Th' son-of-a-bitch thinks he's a-foolin me. B'leeve I'll jest tell 'im I knows all 'bout his ownin' th' works'. Thet's suthin' big fer me tew be a-doin'—nursin' a growed man!

He caught hold of himself, however, and answered, "Ain't th' son-of-a-bitch big enough to take keer of hisself?"

"You know Flinden. I don't think he'd raise his hand if someone were about to kill him."

"Don't go puttin' no idees in m' mine, Kepteen." Johnny flipped his head back to its former position.

Barth unrolled the maps, using two candle holders, their tapers lit, to hold papers flat on the table. Their rustle caused Johnny to once more turn his head and look in the direction of the sound.

"Whutchew allus a-lookin' at them maps fer, Kepteen?"

"I'm looking for something."

"Whut's thet?"

"I'll tell you, when I find what I'm searching for."

"Oh, shore." Johnny looked at the wall again, carrying with his turning head a renewed belief that the kepteen was intentionally slighting him, that he wouldn't tell him about anything that really mattered. He lay there for perhaps an hour, trying to think of the best way to get even with him. He rejected the first measure of vengeance, which came to his fretful mind, that of working with Mace. Lying on his belly, his mending ribs would not let him forget he had a score to settle with Mace also. A little longer and he was asleep.

Barth's eyelids grew heavy shortly thereafter. He put his maps away and barred the door.

CHAPTER 27

For Mercer, the rest of the week passed with an unbelievable celerity. The men returned from Falls of the Ohio with the proceeds of their sales intact. Their leaders reported that the trip had been without incident, except for the expected miring of the wagons in the marshy ground on the approaches to Louisville. They also advised that the travelers who had left the lick after their own departure had arrived safely.

For Mace Hardin, the time was one of patient observation. Each dawn had found him on the river's bank, seeking the telltale lessening of the current.

Tom Chism had a surer way of knowing when the rest would leave the Falls. Amos Wilkins would return with the news, the evening before the embarkation was to take place. The time passed slowly for him, waiting on his courier, and on this part of the probationary period fixed by Rosie Tindall.

Nancy and Hawkstraw pushed each day over into the next one, so avid was their desire to acquire learning. The sessions were proving to be productive, and Aaron Flinden did not regret his decision to teach them. His pupils were both apt and industrious, and Ursula lent her enthusiasm to what she declared was the Lord's work.

With Drusilla Grainger, one day was as another. She rather enjoyed the suspense and its attendant anticipation. It would make realization the more sweet when Mercer at last came to her.

Abby Tindall desired something greater and fuller than Tom's kisses and ardent embraces. Only the memory of Dolly Dusenberry and Bobby Williams held her desires in check. She had determined one thing in her mind. Her mother's consent had better be forthcoming when the month ended.

Dolly feared most the early hours of morning, although each day found her growing more apprehensive. Jed would be back, only the time of his terrifying return was uncertain.

Rosie had passed the interval reflecting upon her decision, always ending in regret. Tom was a good man, excluding his drinking proclivity, but even if he corrected that habit, he was still so much older than Abby. This latter misgiving troubled her, though not to excess, such disparity in ages was not uncommon in marriages on the frontier. What worried her most could not be assuaged. Abby was not only marrying Tom Chism but also she was marrying Bullitt's Lick. Rosie hated this place, though she bore her existence here with characteristic fortitude. She felt that all her bright hopes for her daughter's future would end at the exact second she became Tom's wife.

Dracie Claycomb hoped in vain for an answer from Barth. However, she was appreciative of his situation and though disappointed, she was not alarmed at not hearing from him. Had she been able to have known Drusilla Grainger's plans, she would have joined the next party of travelers bound for the Falls. As it was, her friends at Harrodstown had welcomed her so warmly, and had so extended themselves in their hospitality, these first few days of her visit there, she found little time for herself and her thoughts. There was, however, always the end of day, and the darkness in the room about her. When the pleasant good-night chatterings ceased, her yearning for her absent lover asserted itself, and her bed seemed much too large.

Sunday came, at last, for Johnny. It was almost a novel experience, the act of again putting on his britches. There was but the slightest discomfiture, and so elated was he that even 'th' tricky son-of-a-bitch', as he now alluded to Mercer, noted his joy and was pleased that the little fellow's disposition had changed for the better. Wallingford also shared in this grand moment of recovery. Instead of cursing him, his master had patted his head and scratched the base of his ears when he had saddled him, preparatory to testing the effectiveness of the cushion Rosie Tindall had made for him. He found the pillow to be satisfactory as long as the gait was even, when it wasn't, 'hit wuz 'bout as comfitable as a bear's ass caught in a damn snaggle-tooth trap.

Of all the persons living in the world during this past week of May, in the year 1782, all were happier, and none were sadder, than an obedient, friendly little colored boy named Jason. The silver piece had been so shiny, and it had made him feel so proud and important during the short time it had been his. He couldn't believe his ears when his father had directed its return. He had obeyed but oh, how he wished he might have disobeyed, just that one time. For the first two or three days after the captain's visit, he had tried to pretend a little slick pebble was really the coin he had received that night. Pretending even has its limits in the minds of children, when an unexpected blessing is given, and then is suddenly taken away without hope of its restoration. This Sunday night still found tears on Jason's cheeks.

CHAPTER 28

Johnny had received his instructions. He was to meet Brother Flinden at the ford shortly after sunrise. He would then escort him to the licks and remain with his charge throughout the day, returning with him to the crossing just before sunset.

Aaron Flinden waited with all the patience so thoroughly a part of his being. He was at the ford ahead of time as usual this morning, and he was spending the interval before his escort's arrival in meditation. This concerned itself largely with Nancy's impatience for the miracle to happen to James. They had attended the morning service at Dowdall's yesterday, and upon its conclusion she had insisted that the mute one ought to be able to at least speak his own name, after the week of learning and of the faith they both professed so strongly. When he had counseled her to persistence, her answer had been a question. "If th' Lord made th' man in th' Bible able ter talk th' very second he believed in Him, why ain't James cured after a whole week?" When he had cautioned her that perhaps James had not reached the fullness of faith that the other afflicted one had achieved, she had shocked him by replying, "I know damn well James b'leeves jest as good as thet other son-uv-a-bitch did!" And she had dragged a hesitant affirmation from James to prove her point.

"The Hardins have done their utmost to trade her soul to Satan." He gave voice to the result of the terrible association that had so influenced the child.

The depth of his thoughts allowed Johnny to come upon him unawares.

"Good mornin', Brother Flinden."

The words shattered his trance but he looked at Johnny silently.

"Guess yew didn't hear me. I'm th' kepteen's depity. He wants me to look after yew fer 'im."

"Ah, yes, how are thee, this morning?" Flinden took a good look at Johnny. Why this is a little fellow. I hope friend Mercer hasn't made a mistake, he thought to himself.

"Wal, m' ass is a mought better, but hit still don't feel none too good."

Mr. Flinden was about to ask what ailed the animal when his eye caught the pillow on the saddle and straightened the reference.

"Mr. Mercer told me you were ailing, what was your trouble?"

"Le's git goin' an' I'll tell yew all 'bout it on th' way to th' licks."

Aaron Flinden soon regretted his inquiry, for Johnny's description of the cause and effect of his injury was frequently interspersed with cursing and caused a tide of indignation to rise within him. He would not listen longer to this swearing.

"Thou has not told me thy name as yet."

"I shore thought th' kepteen had done told yew thet, seein' as how he done made all th' 'rangements fer me to take keer of yew. I thought yew knowed who I wuz. I'm th' kepteen's 'sistant—him an' me's big people 'roun' here. Why, they ain't nuthin' whut heppens thet we'uns don't have suthin' to do with hit."

"If Mr. Mercer told me thy name, I have forgotten it."

This was not the appropriate thing to say to anyone as important as a deputy. Johnny resented it deeply and sharpened his words. "Th' name is John Littelby. Depity Littelby, to yew!"

"Thank you for the information, sir. I shall not forget thy name again."

"Thet's better. Yew gotta hev respect fer men like me, if'n yore gonna keep on a-workin' at th' licks. Why, ever' damn son-of-a—"

"That's enough, Mr. Littelby. It was my agreement with Mr. Mercer that there'd be no cursing around me, if I consented to help him."

Johnny was quite taken back by Flinden's censure. As a consequence, the two rode with their own thoughts, the deputy fuming at his rebuke, and Flinden, doubting his own wisdom in accepting this employment and, at the same time, building up a resolve within himself that it must end.

The two dismounted in a silence, which ceased only after the Quaker had entered the storehouse and entered upon his duties. It was then that Johnny gave vent to his pent-up feelings and muttered, "This is all thet son-of-a-bitch Mercer's doin's. Givin' me sech a job as this'n, nursin' a growed man who's big 'nough to be a-takin' keer of hisself—th' church-goin' bastard! Mercer shore figgered suthin' big fer me to do!" He sat upon his haunches and began whittling on a piece of wood whose charred tip bore evidence that it had once been a part of the old structure the fire had leveled.

It wasn't too long before he wearied of his carving. He sat there idly for perhaps an hour, his mind dwelling on his travels prior to the day he had first met Mercer. He had been an important person then, he mused, leastways people were always glad to see him, not only for the wares he had to sell but also for the news he brought of frontier and civilized happenings. He missed the attention he used to receive, just a short time ago. If the kepteen didn't appreciate his worth to him, damned if he wouldn't go to Rosie's and get his pack and leave the son-of-a-bitch to himself. He'd show the bastard!

So, thinking, he stretched his cramped legs, hoisted his britches and got on his mule. The thought came, weakly, that he was disobeying Mercer's orders in leaving Flinden unguarded, but he swept this suggestion from his mind saying, "Them two sons-uv-bitches kin go plumb to hell, fer all I keer." His heel kicked Wallingford's ribs, and he was on his way.

He rode past Ben Skinner's place at an easy lope. Something in the manner of the few persons outside the store arrested his attention. Then he became suddenly aware of what it was. He turned about quickly and made for the door.

His eyes now saw fully that which had registered but faintly a few seconds before, another peddler was in Saltsburg! He scooted from the saddle, anger bristling to the tips of each whisker on his unshaven face.

The unsuspecting hawker, small of size like Johnny, opened his pack as the latter approached. Rubbing his hands together, he said expectantly, "You vant enything? I got lots to sell. Look insite."

Johnny reached into the bag and withdrew a piece of blue crockery.

"Ver' priddy, you t'ink? Neffer you see barg'ins like dis. China from a emperor's palace!"

The emperor wouldn't have approved of what happened to this bit of his alleged former property. In one motion, Johnny jerked off the fellow's cap and smashed the earthenware upon his bushy head.

"Stan' up, yew dumb son-of-a-bitch, an' fight! Stan' up straight!" Johnny circled around him, his fists cocked, holding his arms in the manner he had seen other fighters use.

The poor peddler, completely stupefied, rubbed the particles of debris from his hair and followed his antagonist's moves with bewildered eyes.

"Vy you do dis?" he asked of him imploringly.

"Vy yew do dis?" Johnny mocked. "Why, yew dirty thievin', shit-pot seller, they hain't no room in this here place fer th' likes of yew! I'm th' onliest pedlar whut's got a right to be here! An' here yew comes a-sneakin' into town. Yew kin jest git yore dirty jew-ass out of here, an' right now too! I thinks I'll jest 'rest yew fer trespassin' my rights!"

The fear of arrest and imprisonment aggravated the jew's confused state of mind. He pleaded, "Pliz, I do nutting wrong."

"I'm a depity, an' I kin cause yew all sorts of trouble, an' I'm a-startin' it now. This here's a rough place, an' enybuddy like yew, whut's lookin' fer a fight, kin shore fine it. Stan' up, damn yew!"

The jew was bent over for a reason obvious to all who had gathered at the first cry of "fight!" He was a hunchback, whose gibbosity was most pronounced.

"I stand straight like I can, but I dont vant fight." He still could not comprehend why Johnny had singled him out for this abuse.

This happening was rare sport for the onlookers. It had an element of comedy in it, plus the possibility of bloodshed. As a consequence, there was no waiting of encouragement that the fracas continue.

"Give hit tuh 'im good, Johnny! Bust 'im a good 'un!"

Johnny looked to see who had said this and first became conscious of the encircling audience.

"Yew are damn right, I will!" As he uttered the words, he clouted the hapless hunchback on the side of his head, causing him to double up almost into a ball. Still, he clutched the tip of his pack.

Blows now rained upon his back from Johnny's fists, but he would not uncurl himself. At length, his maddened adversary kicked him squarely on his buttocks, sending him sprawling and freeing the pack of his grasp. He lay there, wailing, while Johnny took charge of his wares. Digging his hand inside the bag, Johnny started handing out its contents to those about him. Thus engaged in this vengeful activity, he was startled to hear a woman scream angrily, "John Littelby, you get ever' one of them things back an' put them in that poor man's sack!"

Johnny hesitated. He knew who it was, although she was behind him. It was Rosie, and she was burning mad. His own anger cooled before the onslaught of her steaming ire.

For that moment, his thoughts stayed any further action on his part.

"Get yourself movin', John Littelby! Get all them things back this instant!"

Mechanically, he obeyed Rosie's command. The crowd snickered and made insulting remarks as he collected that which he had distributed so freely just a moment before.

Rosie busied herself comforting the victim. She helped him to his feet, telling him she would protect him. Seeing that Johnny had finished his collection, she took the pack from his hands, shouldered it and with her free arm supported the battered newcomer as the two headed for her house.

The dumbfounded Johnny, as confused by this sudden turn of events as the jew had been earlier, could only stand and watch them move away from him. He did not hear the derisive remarks thrown at him by those who, minutes before, were urging him to stomp the fallen peddler. His mind just would not function.

Instinctively, he walked toward Rosie's. The induced exertion brought on reflection, and in it he could see one certainty. Rosie's wrath was not for the time being; it would be enduring. She was through with him.

His pack thrown on the ground outside her door confirmed his sad conclusion.

"Why th' red-ringed hell should I keer?" he asked himself. But he did not answer his own question.

He rode Wallingford slowly back to the cabin. When he got there, he tried not to think and to forget at the same time. Through his confusion, there seemed to him to be but one determination. He would take his pack and ride out to Bullitt's Lick, and he would not return.

*

Brother Flinden's decision was made. This would be his last day at this work. Had there been any trace of equivocation on that score, it disappeared the instant he heard about Albert Prather.

His first intimation as to what had happened came when Jack Doniger suddenly thrust his head inside the storeroom door.

"Know where Mace is?" Doniger's words were hurried and anxious.

"'Tis not my duty nor desire to follow his movement," Flinden answered abruptly.

"Look, damn yuh, I got tuh get holt of Mace Hardin, quick. If yuh knows, tell me, if ya don't, just say so."

Brother Flinden sensed something grave. "I have not seen Mr. Hardin recently."

"If yuh sees 'im 'fore I does, tell 'im thet Prather jest got himself kilt. Has Cap'n Mercer got back?"

"Mr. Mercer is still out with the surveyors, I believe. What happened to—?" Before Flinden could finish his question, Doniger was gone.

He received his answer perhaps a half hour later when Albert Prather's body was placed outside the doorway.

There had been an argument, nothing out of the ordinary, as the narrator explained. Just a few blows had been exchanged, but one of them had caught Prather off balance and he fell. "Almost dove head first into one of the kettles. That was all there was to it—'peared to be a accident."

Brother Flinden looked at the distorted features, swollen to hideous and grotesque proportions. The misshapen face was still a dulling pink in color, almost the bright red it must have been at death.

The impact of tragedy sometimes travels strange avenues in the minds of men. Brother Flinden's thoughts were of colors—the contrast between the face of Albert Prather and that of a little blond-haired boy who had drowned years ago in Pennsylvania. His body had been washed upon a little island and covered with silt. The spring rains had cleaned this covering from him, and his light, tousled locks had directed his still-searching parents to where he lay, face downward in the moist soil. (Men and boys always drown face down, women and girls drown face up, he recalled.) When the mother and father had turned him over, the little boy's face was just a rounded ball of black. There was nothing to show where his eyes, nose or mouth had been. Aaron Flinden, himself, was but a child when he had seen this, but it was a sight which was never to be forgotten. Now, there were two colors he would always remember.

*

Mace finished his meal in customary fashion, the swipe of his sleeve across his lips. He wiped his knife on his jacket and put it in its sheath.

Picking his teeth with a fingernail, he mumbled at Massalene, "Thet damn bizness uv Nancy an' Hawkstraw a-goin' ter thet preacher-feller's house hez got-ter stop. Hit's gittin' so thet damn girl ain't good fer nuthin' no mores. Look at her thar, a-piddlin' away with thet burnt stick." He pointed through the opened door at Nancy squatting above a thin flat piece of wood, which Brother Flinden had given her, and upon which she practiced writing, using the charred end of the stick as a pen.

"Hit's time she wuz actin' more growed up, 'stead uv playin' 'round with sech damn things. Don't know but whut Jed's right, she orter marry up with 'im. She'll keep foolin' along with Hawkstraw an' th' fust thing we knows, he'll hev her bigger'n hell in her belly an' we'll hev anuther damn idjit on our han's."

Massalene said nothing but her eyes were black beads.

"Well, I'm a-endin' thet damn foolishness right now." Mace went outside.

Intent upon finishing her name, Nancy did not know he was near her until he had shoved her backward and snatched the writing board from her surprised hands. He broke it into strips and scattered them upon the ground. "Thet's all uv thet damn silly doin's, yer unnerstan'?"

She was on her feet instantly. "Yuh dirty, skunkin', son-uv-a-bitch, I'll cut yer—" Brother Flinden's words bore fruit, this time, and she did not take the Lord's name in vain, finishing, "—damn dirty throat, soon's I ketches yer asleep."

Mace smacked her so hard the blood ran freely from her nostrils.

Massalene was upon him in frightful fury. She bore him to the ground and drew her knife from her waistband. His stronger hand forced the blade from her own and he escaped her hold. Before she could rise, he pulled her to her feet and struck her. The force of the blow propelling her through the open door of the cabin.

She came back quickly, waving an axe. She threw it at him, narrowly missing her target.

He had started toward her, when he caught a movement in the corner of his eye. Nancy had the gun leveled upon him. "Yer dirty bastard," she said. "Hit wuddn't hurt yer none ter git some larnin's yerself, an' I'm gonner larn yer suthin' now!" There was a spark as Mace jumped aside and the lead went aimlessly past. He moved after Nancy, now sprawled upon the ground as a result of the kick from the weapon.

Massalene thwarted this effort on his part. He saw her ramming another rifle. Once she had finished loading it, he would be in real danger. She was a good marksman. Shouting to her, he said, "Ole womern, yer'd best be keerful. If'n yer misses me, I'll kill yer shore. Whyn't us jes' ferfit this whole bizness?"

She shook her head saying, "Massalene no miss."

Mace acknowledged the truth of her simple assertion by running around the side of the cabin and vaulting onto his saddled mount. He circled wide and made for the licks.

*

Brother Flinden was in the midst of turmoil. The men were quarreling over which one was to search Prather's clothing for money he might have had upon his person. Try as he might, he could not bring reason into the dispute.

Mercer ended the turbulence. No one knew of his presence until he thundered, "Let the poor fellow be. I'll see what he has on him."

The order brought grumblings, but it served to end the argument as to who would do the searching. Barth's prying hand coursed the warm flesh under the jacket. A little more feeling around, and he produced the pouch.

"Now, who gits whut's inside? I sez, let's share it up!" It was Justin Gibbs who said this.

A chorus of assent greeted the proposal.

"Nay, 'tis wrong to take from the dead. Let it be buried with the body!" Brother Flinden exclaimed sacredly.

"A foolish thought for you to have uttered, Mr. Flinden. They'd dig him up and take it anyway." Barth's tone was chiding. "The only logical solution is to do as they have suggested." He emptied the purse in their full sight. Albert Prather, a saving man, had saved for prodigals.

So, another grave was dug, and, once again, the loose dirt rustled down upon deerskin, and a body was lost from the light of day.

As they walked back to the storehouse, Aaron Flinden informed Mercer of his decision, "Friend Mercer, I fear thee wilt not like that which I must tell thee."

"Why not? Have there been other disturbances? Have you been troubled?"

"Not as of this hour, but 'tis sure to come to pass and were I to be wrong in my impression, I still could not continue to work here. 'Tis all in the Devil's kingdom, and I will not be his subject."

Barth shook his head sadly. Then it dawned on him that Johnny wasn't around. "Where's Mr. Littelby? Hasn't he been here as he was supposed to be?"

"'Tis another thing, friend Mercer. How could thou believe he might protect me, if he were unable to protect himself? He told me about that which happened to him."

"That was before I straightened the men out as to my authority, Mr. Flinden. You would have been in no danger. How long has Mr. Littelby been gone?"

"Since shortly after our arrival this morning. I delighted in his absence, friend Mercer. His tongue is coated from his cursing."

"You are sure you won't reconsider your decision? I need you badly."

"Believe me, friend Mercer. I have labored in my mind and conscience. 'Tis a regret to me on thy concern, but I must be either with the Lord or against him. I cannot stay on here."

"Will you stay the rest of the day?"

"If I be not rash, I should like to leave now. The work has been light, and there will not be too much change in the books."

"I am most sorry at your decision, Brother Flinden. I'll see you home."

"'Twill not be necessary, 'though I do thank thee."

Barth insisted on accompanying him, however. The two of them mounted and rode away together. There was no conversation. Aaron Flinden's thoughts were of Mercer's disappointment, and he prayed silently that a substitute might soon be found. Mercer's mind was on the same problem, as he ran through the few names he knew of those who might be able to perform the task that Flinden was leaving. Rosie Tindall was the only possibility he could think of, and she wouldn't do. Perhaps Tom Chism might know of someone.

When they reached Flinden's cabin, Barth bade him goodbye, refusing politely his offer of hospitality. However, instead of turning back, he continued riding to the southeast.

CHAPTER 29

Barth had traveled some three or four miles, before he noted a number of deer grazing on the flats ahead. He moved downwind from them, primarily out of curiosity as to how close he could approach without discovery.

Having dismounted and secured Sagitta, he crept quietly along the edge of a thicket. A stag raised its head warily, slowly twitching its ears to catch any stray sound. Its keen senses having allayed any fear of danger, it bent its head to the earth with the rest of the herd.

He was now within fifty yards of them. He watched their movements intently. Suddenly the realization swept over him that the animals were not eating the grass or wild pea vines. They were licking the ground!

The discovery came none too soon. A shift in the light breeze carried his scent to them and they sped away.

Hastening to the spot from whence they had fled, he bent down and tasted the soil. It was heavy with salt!

Astride Sagitta, he covered all the adjacent terrain. All landmarks of any significance he committed to memory. If an entry had been made by anyone, there was no evidence of its having happened. There were no carvings on any trees, no cabins, nor were there any token improvements to hold the land, such as small structures two or three logs high, nor had any of the trees thereabouts been ringed or deadened.

From the survey maps he had been studying, he recalled no plat that contained this parcel of land. Could it be possible it had been overlooked by the surveyors? He would check the maps again. Perhaps, and it must be true, it would be disclosed by them as being part of a previous grant or entry. Maybe he just hadn't ridden far enough.

Spurred by this thought he rode about two miles to the east and a like distance to the west. He noted Aaron Flinden's boundary on that side. He memorized some of the unusual physical features that lay to the east. A few seemed familiar to him, but he dared not trust his recollection of the maps. His elated desire might be influencing his powers of memory.

He rode about a mile to the south and found an immense grove of beech trees. His hopes rose, this was one landmark of which he was certain. This was no trick of memory.

He followed two small, interwinding creeks north to where they entered the Salt River. Then he started back to Bullitt's Lick. If the map did not show these branches, he would know for a certainty that this stretch of land had been overlooked and belonged to no one. Tension built up within him, but he told himself he must be sure that there was no real cause for anxiety. He reasoned only he knew the land and its salt were unclaimed, if such were true. It was not likely anyone at Bullitt's Lick had any immediate interest in it at this precise time. He loosed the reins slightly and his mount responded with a faster pace. He knew his mind would not rest until he had found George May and looked at his survey again. He knew not at this instant what reason he would give for his request to examine the map, but when the time came he would have a logical excuse for so doing. Time and chance proved to be his. When he dismounted at the storehouse, May was there, talking to Mace Hardin.

Getting rid of the burly Hardin was no problem. He said to him, "Mr. Hardin, check with Tressel and Willerhorst and let me know now much longer it will be before our conveyor system is ready for use."

Mace nodded and was gone.

"Where you been all this time?" George May's question was put in friendly fashion. "I been here over an hour. You can't expect to get a day's pay without giving a day's work."

Barth smiled. "I've got a good crew working here, George. I suspect there's more done when I'm absent, than when I'm around." Jokingly, he said, "Come to think or it, I could use a good man. You ought to be good at figures. My storekeeper just quit and I have to find another one right quick."

May laughed. "I don't know what part you're sayin' is in truth and what part is in fun. But, takin' no chances, I ain't the man for you."

"Of course, I was fooling about you taking the job, but now I'm really serious. I do need a man. Do you think any of your crew might be interested, once you've finished here?"

May studied a moment. "Sure, I know one I believe might do. Might take a little trainin', but I reckon he's sharp enough. You 'member Ethan Belden? I think he'd do all right. He lives 'round here, at Brashear's or Dowdall's, one of the two, so he won't be leaving with us. Got another feller that will be able to do it someday too. That's the dummy. The one they call Hawkstraw."

"Him?" Barth was incredulous.

"Yes, sirree, he's a smart one. He can just 'bout run a transit himself. Studies all th' time. I understand someone's teaching him his letters in th' evenin'."

Barth remembered Nancy and Hawkstraw when they had met Flinden and himself at the ford. "I know who's doing the teachings, the same one who was my storekeeper."

"Well, whoever he is, he's doin' a damn good job of learnin' him. You keep your eye on him. You might find use for him."

"I can use him right now. If I can get Belden to take the job, Hawkstraw could be his assistant."

"Good idea. I'd sure try it, if I was you."

"Say, now that you have taken me to task for leaving the lick, I might ask you a question." Barth was mockingly serious. "What are you doing here at this time or day? How does it happen you can find time to loaf around here?"

May chuckled. "Thought you'd be askin' that. We got our work pretty well in hand. Another week and we ought to be done here. Just got to check up on a few stray lines, nothin' to amount to much. We aim to sorta ease to the finish. Thought I'd bring you some more maps. Th' rest of my party has quit for th' day anyway."

"That's mighty nice of you," Barth acknowledged. "Do you figure on doing any more work, south and east of the river?"

"That ain't called for, 'cording to our instructions. That's all supposed to have been resurveyed last fall. Why do you ask about that?"

Barth met the test. "There's a lot of good timber over that way. You know, we're planning on carrying the water to the woods and building our furnaces there. That way we can save a lot of time."

"And make a lot more salt," May added.

"That's right. So you can see why I'm interested in more free land."

"I can understand that all right, Cap'n. But it looks like you got plenty on west of here, without worryin' none about goin' across th' river."

Barth had a ready answer. "That's just it. We don't want to go too far downstream. Rather stay closer to the lick and the garrisons."

"That makes good sense," agreed May. "You can look on th' copy of th' survey I gave you'. It'll show there who's got th' title."

"How about my seeing the original? Then I'll be sure I've got it right."

"No need of that. I made those copies myself. They're exactly alike."

Certainty was slipping through Barth's fingers. He must stop it. "You know, George, I'm just enough of a cynic to doubt any man's being absolutely right in his work all the time. Tell you what I'll do—just on a hunch, mind you—I'll bet you a jug of good whiskey against a jug of corn, that I can find some difference between the two plats, the original and the copy, of that land over to the east of, and including, Aaron Flinden's property. What do you say to that?"

"I'd say that if I could go 'round makin' wagers like that all day, by nightfall I'd have enough whiskey to last me th' rest of my life. It's a bet!" He ended his exclamation by grasping Barth's hand and shaking it vigorously to bind the proposal.

"Well, now that you think you've got an easy mark hooked good and proper, when do you intend settling this?" Barth was prodding him as forcibly as he could without overplaying his hand.

"No time better'n th' present!"

"Fine. When will you get your maps?"

"See that roll in back of my saddle? Well, th' maps are all in there. Now, I'll ask you when will you get your copies, or th' one you're interested in, anyhow?" May laughed at his being able to place the onus of proceeding upon Mercer.

"Mine's over at my cabin, I'll have to go over there. You'd just as well come along. No point in my going over there and coming back here again."

"Guess you're right 'bout that. It'll save me makin' another trip to your place for my whiskey." May nudged Barth with his elbow.

"You better be thinking about how far you'll have to ride to get that corn for me, instead of being so cocksure. By the way, I just bet a jug of whiskey. I'll pay for it, but it'll be up to you to get it, providing I lose, and I don't expect to do that."

"We'll see 'bout that soon enough," said the surveyor, as they got on their horses.

*

Johnny heard them coming. He was disappointed when he saw Mercer had someone with him. He had finished his brooding. He intended to leave, all right, but first he was going to tell th' son-of-a-bitch what he thought about him. Let him know he hadn't fooled him none, that he knew who owned th' licks without Mercer telling him. Now he'd have to wait until the other bastard left.

Barth called to him. "Johnny, bring me my maps."

Instead of complying, Johnny asked, "How th' red-ringed hell did jew know I wuz here?"

"I figured you were when I saw Wallingford out here."

"Oh."

"Now, bring those maps like I asked you to."

Johnny started to tell him to get the maps himself, but thought better of it and brought them out to him.

"This is my assistant, Mr. Littelby. Johnny, I want you to meet George May."

"I done met him," Johnny said sourly and walked back into the cabin.

"Your assistant, as you call him, must have been drinking vinegar." Eyeing Barth in playful suspicion, he asked, "You ain't going to try and pass any vinegar off on me for whiskey, are you?"

"Nothing like that," Barth smiled. "Let's compare the maps."

"No sooner said, than done." May began unrolling his platted surveys.

Eagerly, Barth placed the master surveys side by side, the original and the copy. These maps showed the boundaries of every tract in the area, together with the names of the owners or those claiming title.

His heart rose in his chest as he traced Aaron Flinden's east line on the original work. His eyes caught the descriptive notation: "Big beeches." He noted anxiously that the beech grove appeared on the map as a southward extension of Flinden's boundary. The landmarks he had so carefully committed to memory were laid out on the map as being coincidental with those of Brother Flinden. The whole tract containing the new licks was omitted entirely!

Masking his excitement, he said casually, "All right, now let's look at the copy."

"It'll be th' same as th' one you just checked," said May confidently.

"We'll see about that." Barth quickly located his points. They were the same.

"Well, you ready to admit you owe me a jug of good whiskey?"

"Not quite. Before I concede I've lost, I want to look at the smaller plats. After all, if a mistake was made, it would likely be in the plotting of the area on the large map from the map of the individual tract itself. If the original and the copy are the same, I'll admit I lost the bet."

Again the comparison, and, once more, there was absolute identity.

"Ready to give up now? I knew you'd lost your wager the minute you made it." May was boastingly exultant.

"I lose, there's no doubt about it. I'd like to drink a toast to your accuracy, and that of your men, when you get the liquor."

"Not out of my jug." May laughed in self-satisfying humor.

Barth wanted to ask him point-blank about the land, which he knew lay between the boundaries that appeared as but one on the maps, but he dared not do so. The question he had hoped to answer from the surveys was still unanswered.

"No use studying those maps any more, they ain't going to change none."

"I know that, George, but I was just thinking—not about any particular tract, you understand, but just generally—could it ever happen that a part of what some surveyors had done would be left out when it was put down on the maps?"

"It could happen, I reckon, but it didn't happen on the ones you just looked at. What makes you ask that?"

"Nothing that concerns your work." Barth was truthful because May had not performed the survey of the lands. He had but copied it from the earlier records.

"If it will ease your mind any, I can tell you that whoever owns the land as shown on those maps is the owner, and that's all there is to it. 'Course th' names might change some, if there is any lawin' about any of th' tracts. Now, Cap'n, let's settle th' bet."

"As I told you," Barth said, "I have no whiskey here, nor corn either, for that matter, but I figure twenty-four shillings ought to buy you a jug of the best whiskey you can get." He reached inside his jacket and brought forth the money.

"I'll be thinkin' of you when I drink it, Cap'n. Thanks a lot. Y'know, I got to get on, but before I leave I want to tell you one thing."

"What's that?"

"Never bet a man on his own business."

"I'll remember that, but it was worth it. I still say that a man can't be right all of the time. Maybe, if I checked the rest of the maps."

"You want to make another bet?"

"I said maybe, George. One lost bet a day is enough for my sporting blood."

"It's too much, if you ask me. You keep it up and you won't have any blood to sport with."

While he was talking, May had moved to his horse and mounted. As he did so, he said, "I'll be around for a spell yet, see you 'fore I leave."

"Fines. You do that."

May wheeled around. "You want me to say anything to Belden about what you asked me? I mean, about th' job?"

"Sure do. Tell him I'd like to see him."

"First thing in th' mornin'. If he suits you, you can have him right away. I won't need him any longer." He waved his hand in farewell and headed in the direction of the settlement and Ben Skinner's. He'd have his whiskey soon.

Barth decided against going to the licks. Hardin could see to it for the rest of the day. He unsaddled Sagitta and stabled him.

Johnny did not look up when he entered the cabin.

"I've got something I want you to do for me, Johnny."

Receiving no reply, he repeated his words. Johnny grunted and said, "Guess hit's suthin 'portant, ag'in—like takin' keer uv a growed man, er maybe this time, yew'll hev me lookin' after thet Dusenberry whore's brats."

Barth leveled his gaze upon him. "See here, Johnny, I ought to be angry with you. You failed me in the job I gave you with Brother Flinden. That was important to me. I needed him. He quit, but fortunately, I believe I may have someone to take his place. Now, do you want to help me or not?"

"I'm lissenin'," Johnny replied, adding under bis breath, "yew sneakin' son-of-a-bitch."

Barth swore Johnny to secrecy, then told him of his discovery.

Johnny thought to himself, I almost lost out on this. 'Nother minute an' I'da told th' tricky bastard I wuz leavin' 'im.

"What d'yew aim fer me to do?"

"Here's what I want, Johnny." Barth got out his map. "You see these marks and boundaries? Well, as I just told you, instead of them being on the same line as Brother Flinden's, they're really about two to two-and-a-half miles to the east. That grove of beech trees is actually on a curving line to the southwest, at the southern end of this tract I'm talking about. You take this map with you when you go over there so you can be sure of where you are. When you get there, I want you to carve my initials and the date on about twenty trees at different distances on the inside of these boundaries."

Stopping momentarily, he asked, "You can carve, can't you?" Receiving assurance on this score he pored over the maps before saying, "Well, after you have done that, I want you to build part of a small cabin—just the walls—about four logs high. Might ring some trees around there too."

"When d'yew want me to do all of this?"

"Within the next day or so. Then I'll have a map ready, showing the land I claim, and I want you to take it over to Cox's Station and register it in my name with George May." The corners of Barth's mouth turned up and into a full, involuntary smile. "He'll sure be surprised. Wonder what he'll think about the whiskey then?"

"Whut d'yew mean, Kepteen—about th' whiskey, I mean? I unnerstans th' rest."

"Just that when two men bet, sometimes the loser wins and knows that he is winning, while the winner thinks he has won but really didn't win at all."

"Thet shore clears things up. Whut in th' hell air yew talkin' about?"

"Doesn't matter, Johnny. You think you can do what I've asked you?"

"Shore kin, Kepteen. When am I s'posed to register th' land?"

"I'm expecting to go to Harrodstown soon. You can do it while I am gone."

"I'll take keer of it, Kepteen, an' proper too."

"I'm sure you will, Johnny. You know how important it is. One more thing. No one must know about this except the two of us."

"Yew kin count on me to keep a tight lip, Kepteen. Yew knows thet, don't yew?"

"I'm depending on you, Johnny. Remember that."

Barth busied himself with the maps, studying them more intently than before. When he drew his plat, it must be correct in every particular.

He worked until nightfall. Then, after a supper that Johnny prepared, he threw himself on his bed. A lot had happened this day, and his tired mind yielded readily to sleep.

Not so with Johnny. Barth's revelation had given his avaricious brain the food it needed. The base of a scheme came with the expression or the trust that was to be placed in him. He had warned the son-of-a-bitch the first day he had met him that he wasn't to be trusted if there was any gain to be had by his not being trustworthy. Well, here was gain aplenty, and he intended to get it. He'd register the land all right, but it wouldn't be in Mercer's name. Hell, no! He'd carve initials on the trees, all right, but they'd be his own, not Mercer's.

Johnny weighed the possibility of his plan being uncovered by Mercer. He was certain the latter would not return to the newly discovered licks. To do so might attract attention—the one thing most to be avoided. No, he wouldn't go back there before the tract had been registered. When Mercer came back from Harrodstown, if it didn't happen before then, he would have his hands full with Mace Hardin and the saltmakers. He had heard enough of the undertalk that was being said here of late to know that it wouldn't be too long now before Mace had a showdown with Mercer. And when it was over, there wouldn't be no more kepteen to worry about.

Of course, he'd have to figure on protecting his land from Hardin. But he reasoned he could get Strickler to pull away from Mace along with a few of the others. If he couldn't do this, there were lots of new people coming through Bullitt's Lick every day. He'd get him a good bunch in no time. Promise them shares, if he couldn't persuade them otherwise.

One big obstacle constantly disrupted the evenness of his scheming. He had no money with which to start his operation. But surely this problem could be easily solved by a loan on the land. Anyone would loan money if it was secured by salt licks. Hell, he might even sell the damn ground.

His conniving thoughts led on into fancy, and he envisioned himself in the attire or a gentlemen, and a gentleman he would be! Such damn people as Rosie Tindall and that smart daughter of hers! He could see them now, bowing as he passed. He could hear them telling others that they once knew him, and bemoaning the fact that they had lost his friendship. Damn sorry they'd be, and it would serve them right.

It was on such wings of elegance that he was carried into slumber.

CHAPTER 30

At the river's edge this early morning, Mace raised somewhat from his crouching position as he tossed a sprig of maple into the stream. It circled lazily, then moved slowly upstream. The time was here. He rode to tell Ben Skinner.

Not too long after daylight, Abe Foster and Tom Chism were at Barth's cabin. Their greeting was lacking in its accustomed enthusiasm. Before they spoke, Barth knew that something of significance had occurred.

"Abe here says he run acros't a lot of moccasin prints yesterday evenin'—says they was from at least four different tribes."

"Thet's right, Cap'n. Hit whar 'bout seven or eight mile downriver. Shore looks liken they's up ter suthin' big."

"Skinner and Vehrmon!" Barth spoke his first thought.

"I think th' same. Abe says, best he can size 'em up, they might be 'round forty to fifty of 'em." Tom Chism was a worried man.

"The tracks all fresh?"

"Ever damn one uv 'em, Cap'n." Abe was emphatic, "An' all on this side uv th' river. Th' current is movin' back stream, whut little they is. Most uv hit is just dead as water in a pond. Yer knows whut thet means, don't cher, Cap'n?"

Chism didn't wait for Mercer's answer to Abe's question. "It means my men'll prob'ly be on their way down th' Ohio. If them Injuns sees 'em, they're gone for sure."

"Maybe they won't leave the Falls today," Barth said hopefully.

Chism shook his head. "I sure hope not, but if Jim Trench has things ready, he'll be on his way by now. Might have left last night, or 'fore daybreak this mornin'. Still, if he was leavin', Amos Wilkins should've done been here with th' news." Taking renewed hope from this reflection, he conceded, "Don't reckon they has left yet, but it prob'ly won't be very damn long 'fore they does."

"I hope you're right," said Barth.

"Same here," added Abe.

"Once they reached the mouth of Salt River, how long do you think it will take your men to come upstream?" Barth asked.

Chism was vague in his estimate. "Hard tellin'. There won't be no current, but it'll still be slow goin'. Reckon they might make two mile a hour. They'll be right smart tired 'fore they gits there after comin' all th' way from th' Falls. 'Course they'll have th' current with 'em on th' way down."

He studied a while. "I just can't say."

"How far is it from the Falls to Salt River?"

"Best I can figure, Cap'n, it's nigh on eighteen to twenty mile. Don't rightly know for sure, y' understand."

"I know that, Tom, but say it is twenty miles, what speed do you think they'll make an hour on the way down?"

Abe Foster broke in. "I kum down when she whar high onc't, kum on a flatboat too. My idea is they oughter make four, ter four-an'-a-half, mebbe five mile. Hit all depends on how fast th' current's a-movin' 'near th' shore, thet is. Yer cain't ride th' fastest part, yer knows."

Barth made a hasty calculation. "If the Ohio's flowing four miles an hour, and we figure the distance from the Falls at twenty miles, which would mean they should reach the mouth of Salt River in about five hours with the current alone. Now, how far is it from the licks to the Ohio?"

Abe supplied a ready answer. "Hit's right at fourteen mile."

"That would mean it would take them another seven hours."

Chism observed, "You're forgettin' they'd prob'ly rest a spell comin' up here. 'Sides, all that damn figuring ain't worth nothing unless we know when they leave th' Falls."

"You're right on that, Tom. But it will give us a pretty good idea, once Wilkins gets back. Then we can move to meet them along their way up from the Ohio," said Barth.

"'Pears liken we uns kinder has got off some frum whut we wuz talkin' about. Them Injuns is 'round these parts somewheres. Whut we aim ter do 'bout thet? They hain't gonner wait on we uns ter do suthin', y' knows thet." Abe dug his nails deep into his beard and scratched viciously. "Must hev a damn louse in thar some'eres," he observed sagely.

"Whatever is to be done, best be done quick," Chism commented tersely.

"There isn't any question about that, Tom. No telling what the savages are planning. One thing we can be sure of, Ben Skinner'll have a hand in it, and Mace Hardin too most likely. I believe we ought to set someone to keep an eye on' the two of them right away. Of course, the people should be warned, first thing. As many of them as can be persuaded ought to go to the garrisons for safety. Then we better count noses and see how many men we can round up to defend the licks."

"You needn't speck no help frum Hardin's men. Them bastards will do just what Mace wants 'em to do, and y'know whut thet'd be."

"Maybe I can get a few of them, Abe. Like Tressel, Willerhorst and some of the independents," Barth replied.

"Wal," said Abe, "Yer best git ter stirrin' an' quit jawin'. Hit's plumb daylight. I'll git m'se'f ter Skinner's. Th' way I sees hit, he's th' one they'll be a-seein'. 'Member hit wuz him an' Blackie Vermin whut hed they heads tergether. I'll git th' word ter Tom, soon's I larns suthin'."

Tom Chism nodded his head. "I'll get about twenty-five of my men, maybe thirty." Directing his words to Barth, he said, "I hope you can get some help from your bunch."

Barth pledged his best efforts to this end and the three separated. They were to meet at Tom's place at noon.

*

It wasn't long before Chism heard from Abe. He had alerted the settlers and reported that almost all would go to Brashear's and Dowdall's. Doctor Grainger would see to this, though he had expressed his desire to accompany the expedition against the savages. The most significant part of Abe's message was that a stockade was being erected around Ben Skinner's store and that Skinner himself was overseeing its erection. It seemed that if there was to be a raid on the settlement, he was making sure his property wouldn't suffer. Abe said that he figured this was a precautionary measure in case the Indians made a mistake, they wouldn't attack Skinner's place intentionally.

*

Barth confronted Hardin squarely. "Mr. Hardin, there's danger of trouble with the Indians. We know they are somewhere between us and the Ohio and in large numbers. I want you to get all of our men and as many of the independents as you can and have them meet me here at the storehouse within the next half hour."

Mace, raising his brows and tilting his head back a bit, did not answer immediately. "Cap'n, beggin' yer pardin, don'tcher reckin yer mought be some hasty. Eny Injuns they be wuddn't be no closer'n fourteen ter fifteen mile uv us. Shore, they's Injuns over on th' Ohio. They moves up an' down th' river, but they hain't no danger to th' licks frum 'em, I kin promise yer thet. 'Tain't no use ter git yerself worried none on thet score."

"I have accurate information, Mr. Hardin. There are Indians not too far away, and I believe they will try and attack us. How many men do you think we can raise?"

"None too many, Cap'n. Them thar selfish bastards will all look ter they own hides. They won't be interested none in holpen nobody else't. Makin' salt don't mean fightin' no Injuns, less'n they's kotched off'n they guards. If'n yer a-figgerin' on goin' out after them savages, won't but damn few uv th' men jine up with yers."

"We'll see about that, Mr. Hardin. You just get word to everyone that I want to see them right away."

Mace shrugged his shoulders. "As yer says, Cap'n, as yer says." He called Virgil Mallory, Justin Gibbs and a few others and dispatched them in different directions.

Less than one hundred men answered Mercer's summons. He stressed the danger to be averted and his intention to go out and try to attack the Indians rather than to wait for them to invade the licks. This plan met with the intense disfavor of the workers. As a result, only twenty-one agreed to help him. Among these was Herman Tressel. Motty Willerhorst refused to go after the savages but did offer to help protect the licks and the settlement. Barth recalled Motty's bad feet and understood his refusal. What surprised him most was the zeal displayed by Mallory and Gibbs. He hadn't expected them to volunteer at all, much less to show the marked degree of enthusiasm that they exhibited.

Counting Hardin and himself, there were twenty-three whom he could count on. Actually, there was one less, since Hardin would have to see to the protection and safety of the licks by those workers who had not volunteered.

Tom Chism showed his anxiety. When Mercer and Abe Foster arrived, they found him pacing back and forth. Abe cautioned him, "Hain't no damn good, yore a-doin' thet. Yer jist'll wear yoreself ter nuthin'."

Tom looked at him, but continued his aimless walking. Then he said, "It's all right for you to be a talkin'. If them Injuns ain't taken care of proper, it will be a year, maybe two, before these licks'll be workin' again. An' if they happens to run up on that flatboat of mine, it'll be hell, sure 'nough."

"Hey, Tom!" The exclamation caused them to turn their heads simultaneously. It was Amos Wilkins who hailed them. Almost as he alighted from his horse, Chism had his hands upon his shoulders and was shaking him. "Where in th' hell have you been? I about went out of my senses, worryin'." Chism continued shaking him as he said this.

Barth attempted to calm Tom, saying, "Hold up, and let him talk." Chism released his frenzied grip.

"Got here as soon's I could, Tom. Jim wuz figgerin' on leavin' th' Falls sometime this mornin', if'n ever'thing went right."

"How long ago would that be?" Tom's question was demanding. "How long ago?"

Wilkins could sense that something unusual was in the offing. "Whut's heppened since we left?"

Tom could only repeat his own question. "How long since they left th' Falls?"

"I can't say, prob'ly a hour, mebbe, 'fore noon. Whut's th' diffrunce?"

Tom looked at him helplessly. "Why you stupid son—"

Barth stepped between the men, exclaiming, "No need for that, Tom, I'll tell him about everything."

Briefly and quickly, he recounted the events leading up to the present situation. When he had finished, Wilkins whistled through his teeth. "Thet shore ain't good."

"Wal, yer all gonner be dead bastards, if'n yer jest sets thar an' talks 'bout how bad hit be." Abe spit a gob of tobacco juice that made a squashing sound as it hit the ground. With his forefinger, he wiped the yellowish-colored spittle from the corners of his mouth, whence it had oozed over his beard, and then probed his teeth for remnants of the weed before he continued. "I sez, let's all git busy."

This ended the discourse and the group moved away in concert.

Had they waited a while longer, they might have seen the returning Deputy Littelby. He had been busy. The trees had been ringed and deadened, the little enclosures erected and the date and lettering carved. The initials cut into the trees were J.L. The date alone was true. Shortly, he would perfect his perfidy. He would take the plat that Mercer had drawn, but not signed, to George May at Cox's Station and register the claim to the new licks in his own name.

CHAPTER 31

To Jim Trench, the bustle that he found at the Falls was most pleasing. He liked this village, which was being recognized more and more by its corporate name of Louisville. He liked the name too, for he was one of those who valued the aid of Louis XVI to the struggling colonies.[15] It was with good reason that he was grateful—a French detachment had rescued him from a Shawnee stake at the precise moment that a flame had been thrown into the brush piled at its base. This he could not, and would never, forget.

An air of newness prevailed about this settlement, along with a companion feeling of security. There seemed to be a dedication among its residents that everything done should be pursued with the idea of permanence, that they were building a city, which would endure and become great. This was no mere stopping-off place. This was their home.

If one man could be said to be responsible for this town, he would have to be General Clark. To be sure, many had aided him and were still doing so but it was his courage and vision, combined with his ability as a leader, which had brought this about. He it was who had raised the men for the Army he led so successfully against the Indians and the British, forging the elements of surprise and faith, and then welding them to hunger, cold and weariness to produce the needed weapon to conquer Kaskaskia,[16] Cahokia and Vincennes.

Jim Trench had been a member of Clark's sturdy band. He had waded the freezing creeks; he had starved and he had suffered all of the other hardships so consistently encountered on these campaigns, but at their conclusion, the Northwest Territory had been wrested from the Crown and its domination of this portion of the country ended. With the razing of Indian villages along their route of march, and the killing and scattering of their inhabitants, the danger of sustained attacks by the savages had been greatly lessened. To Jim Trench, the two real heroes of the revolution were George Washington and the man whom Thomas Jefferson had made a brigadier general in the Virginia militia in Kentucky: George Rogers Clark.

The activity at Louisville was not as pronounced as it was at Bullitt's Licks but its character was entirely different. Here, all was clean and orderly. At the licks, greed, violence and filth were ever attendant. Only upon one consideration was Bullitt's Lick more desirable. The presence of numerous ponds and swamps around the Falls combined to produce an unhealthy atmosphere, sickness—cold, chills and fever—were a constant threat to the lives of the residents. Calomel and plasters[17] were the best available remedies, but often, too often, they failed, and men, women and children died. Winter was a God-given pacifier, but with the advent of spring, the ponds would lose their coatings of ice, the marsh lands soften and the later seasons of the sun would bring on sickness. If the winter happened to be mild, there was no respite from illness and death. Even now, Jim noted that there were many people ill, and there was talk of the possibility of an epidemic. Doctor Moss, whom he had met through his friend, William Faith, had given him a written message to deliver to Doctor Grainger when he returned to Bullitt's Lick. He did not know its content, but he was certain it had something in it about the increasing number of people who were taking to their beds.

Jim Trench was sorry he must leave Louisville this day. Earlier in the morning, he had dispatched Amos Wilkins with the information as to their intended departure. Like himself, the men in his party had all enjoyed their stay here. They had been quartered in the new fort erected on the river plain. Some two hundred soldiers were now garrisoned in this fortification that General Clark had named Fort Nelson in honor of the governor of Virginia,[18] and which he had established as his headquarters. The old fort, the station on shore, had been built on land higher, and farther downriver, and still provided a home for some settlers. However, many had moved into the new structure. Fort Nelson was an imposing sight, a magnificent frontier defensive achievement. Not the equal of Fort Pitt, it nevertheless made one mindful of that outpost. Occupying an acre of ground, it was of rectangular, though nearly square, dimensions and was set upon a raised earthen foundation, enclosed by a water-filled moat eight feet wide, whose center line was split all the way around by a palisade, ten to twelve feet high. At its rear, a bridge leading from the gate crossed over its course. Four huge bastions, one at each of its corners, loomed menacingly, breathing defiance to all whose interests might be antagonistic to the young nation whose defenders were stationed inside. Like a mother in front of her young, Fort Nelson faced the Ohio, and the confidence engendered by her presence was reflected in the numerous cabins and houses erected in the town outside the protective wall of the old and new garrisons.

While the saltmakers' visit had been enjoyable, it was one of intense labor in preparation for the journey down the Ohio. The nights had been the period of relaxation. The days filled with varied tasks. Although two Frenchmen named Honore and Tardiveau had offered to help pilot their raft over the falls, with which the latter were thoroughly familiar through previous experience with its rapids, and although Chism's instructions were to wait until the river had completed its rise and to then traverse the falls, Jim declined to take the slightest chance of losing the cargo he and his men had so painstakingly assembled. The suggestion had been made to take the empty craft over the falls, first, and then load it about a mile downstream at the end of the treacherous passageway, but this was rejected, with thanks. Trench felt he could not risk the possibility that the boat might be destroyed or damaged, in which event a new one would have to be built. It was imperative that he leave when the flooded Ohio was at its crest. And any unusual delay on his part would meet with Tom Chism's displeasure. The men were needed at the saltlicks as soon as they could accomplish their mission. Accordingly, a large flatboat, with a sweep oar at its after end, was constructed at the base of the falls and the cargo portaged tediously over the approximate two miles of rough country to that point. Of their entire cargo, ten kettles had occasioned the greatest difficulty in transportation. However, at last all appeared in readiness for sailing. Their preparedness had been completed the evening before, when they had worked until well past sundown, arriving back at Fort Nelson just a shadow's space in advance of darkness.

Honore and Tardiveau were on their way to New Orleans with a load of the finest furs Jim had ever seen. History was being made by these traders and trappers, theirs was to be the first commercial venture downriver from Pittsburgh to New Orleans. The river trade would thus begin.

Despite his determination to leave before noon, Jim Trench was unable to do so. Michael Humble, a fine gunsmith, had promised to have the new rifle he had ordered ready for him by daybreak. Unfortunately, the weapon when finished was found to have a slight defect. Jim offered to waive this and take the gun at the price agreed upon, but Humble would have none of it. His pride in his workmanship would not permit him to do so. So, it was just short of noon when Jim returned to Humble's shop for his purchase. He paid Humble with a receipt given him previously by John Sanders, who operated a keep on the high bank just above Beargrass Creek, where it emptied into the Ohio.

Sanders's keep was a strange place of unique origin. In the great flood of 1780, Sanders, a woodsman and hunter, had moored his boat to a large tree to prevent it being damaged by the rampaging waters. When the river receded, the big craft was left high aground. The ingenious owner boarded it up, put in windows and doors, covered it with a good roof and made it into a place of business. His method of operating was simple. He gave negotiable receipts for skins and hides brought in by the hunters and trappers. A beaver skin was established as a unit of value or currency. These receipts were subject to redemption, and often passed through countless hands before finding their way back to the keep. Sanders always paid when due, consequently, his receipts were greatly preferred by settlers and tradesmen not only at Falls of the Ohio but also along the frontier. They were even honored upriver at Pittsburgh and at settlements far downstream.

It was understandable, therefore, that Michael Humble gave a sigh of relief when he received his payment in John Sanders's paper. He expressed his gratitude to Trench, saying, "I feared you might be payin' me in that sky-high currency. You know it takes a pile of that printin' to buy anything. A while back, my youngest got took with a bad cold. You know what th' doctor—Doctor Harrt—charged me? Two hundred and forty dollars, that's what he did. All that money for four doses of calomel and four plasters. An' if that don't be bad enough, th' British has copied th' printin' of good paper, like Virginny's, and give it away by th' wagonload. Time you find out you been skinned, him that gives it to you is gone. You know how much one Spanish dollar brings in exchange? One thousand of that printin' press paper!"

Jim nodded understandingly. The story was the same at Bullitt's Lick and throughout the frontier. Expressing his pleasure at being able to buy such an excellent rifle, he was saying goodbye when Humble asked incredulously, "You mean, you're not going to stay for th' hangin'?"

The question refreshed his mind. The big topic of conversation this past week had been the trial and conviction of an aged Negro slave by the name of Cato Watts for the killing of his master, one John Donne Sr.[19] The execution was to take place at midday.

"Where's it gonna heppen?"

Humble pointed up the street, looking out of his window as he did so. "In front of the jail. That's where that crowd's going now. Must be about time for it. Wait just a bit and I'll go up there with you. You can just leave your rifle here and get it when we come back."

CHAPTER 32

Jim was indecisive as to whether or not to watch the hanging. His men would have liked to have been witnesses, he was sure, and if he alone saw the happening and told them about it, they might not feel too kindly about their exclusion. Besides, he had sent word by Wilkins that he was leaving well before noon. Chism would undoubtedly have a party scouting down Salt River to meet the boat. Of course, if everything proceeded smoothly, and there were no further delaying incidents, it wouldn't make too much difference if he passed an extra hour or so in Louisville. So he walked alongside Michael Humble on their way to watch a poor, unimportant, colored man breathe his last.

Humble's words were uttered excitedly. This was a most unusual event, the first legal hanging ever to be held at the Falls. Both men were anticipating the coming execution. Neither was possessed of a sensitive nature, too many killings went unpunished. There had been too many murders where not the slightest effort was ever made to apprehend the murderers, for these two pioneers to be swayed by any feeling of sympathy for a slave condemned to die for the slaying of the one who owned him. Nevertheless, Humble did say, as they neared the now thickening throng, "Funny thing about Cato, he never caused no trouble 'fore this. He always seemed to be th' happiest man in th' settlement; never stole nothing and th' children loved him."

"Thet's th' way with them Black bastards sometimes. They plays it along til th' time's jest right fer th' doin' uv hit. I don't see none too much diffrunce in killin' a bear er a nigger. [20] They's both black er brown." Trench laughed after he said this.

"Can't say as how I feel like you about that," replied Humble. "There's them that claims th' Blacks got no soul, but I don't know 'bout that either. I know one thing for sure though, th' law is weak enough as it is, and if the ones who break it ain't punished, there'd be as many killings here as they tell me there are at your place, meanin' no offense, you understand."

"Yuh speaks th' truth, when yuh says thet, Humble." Trench was in positive agreement.

Speculation centered on the site of the gallows. One feminine voice whispered, "They're bringing th' scaffold from th' jail. I heard them hammerin' on it early this mornin'."

A man nearby disputed her statement. "They didn't build nothing in th' jail. They're gonna string him up on that tree over there." All eyes in the gathering focused upon a large oak across the street. One stout limb had been recently sawed off. It was a likely support for the rope, but it did not hold their attention for long. They now looked expectantly toward the jail: a rough, one-story structure, sufficient for its purpose and no more. Soon now, surely, the door would open and they would bring the murderer before their eyes. Would he have to be dragged, or would he walk out with them? Would he have to be beaten to make him move to his doom?

"Bet he's so damn scairt they'll have to carry 'im," ventured one of the spectators.

"Well, it can't be too long now before we'll know," said another.

But it was longer than they had supposed. An hour had passed and the impatient murmurings were reaching a crescendo. "Maybe, they have postponed it!"—"Maybe, they already done it!" A contrariety of opinions arose from all sides.

Jim Trench was nervous. The men would be wondering why he wasn't at the foot of the Falls. They might even have already sent someone to ascertain his whereabouts. If that happened, the chances were that person would first go to Fort Nelson to look for him. Then there would be confusion and delay, and all the while, time would be passing. Maybe Honore and Tardiveau, who were to meet them after their own craft had made the trip over the falls, would tire of waiting and disregard their agreement to follow them down the Ohio.

He decided to forego the witnessing of the execution, and told Humble of his decision.

He had moved only a short distance when a tremendous roar announced that, at long last, Cato Watts, dragged or willing, was beginning his last walk on this earth. Trench hurried back, forcing his way through the jammed, intent assemblage to the gunsmith's side. "Won't miss it, after all," he said thankfully.

As it turned out, the two men has positioned themselves in the best possible place to view the proceedings. The jailer's appearance had been the occasion for the clamor that had induced Jim's return. The official walked deliberately across the street to the oak tree. A familiar voice exclaimed exultantly, "I told you that was where it was goin' to be!"

Jim didn't turn his head, but he recognized the voice from behind as being the one he had heard earlier.

Two men carried an empty box, about three feet square, and placed it directly beneath the shortened tree limb—the gibbet. The man acting as jailer stepped upon it and addressed the gathering, admonishing its members to restrain themselves in their words and actions; that the hanging was not the result of a mob decision, but was to be an execution of a judgment and sentence of a court of law. He concluded his remarks with a warning that any unruly conduct on the part of anyone present would be met with appropriate punishment. As he stepped down from the improvised platform, he removed his hat and wiped his perspiring brow.

The day was warm, and the sun was at its noonday zenith. Replacing his head covering, he ordered crisply, "Bring Cato out!"

At these words, the crowd moved as one person to the tree, forming a half circle, equidistant around its focal point, the fateful little box. Obeying the previous orders given them, the spectators were careful to keep themselves at a reasonable interval from the gallows, roughly twenty feet.

Despite the warning against any demonstration, there was a mild chorus when Cato Watts came through the door. The noise subsided quickly, however, and an opening was voluntarily made in the throng, permitting the condemned man, guarded front and rear, to pass unmolested through their numbers.

The prisoner, blinded at first by the brightness of the out of doors, now lowered his protective hand from above his eyes. Shuffling reluctantly along in his bare feet, he looked only at the ground before him. White, kinky tufts of hair, like puffs of cotton above his large ears, thinned as they extended upward and ringed his balded pate, now glistening with watery beads. His red-stained eyeballs bulged beneath hoary brows. He didn't have the appearance of a killer, but a killer he had legally been declared. And now he must satisfy that judgment with his only possession other than his old fiddle, his right to live.

His attitude was one of complete disbelief. When they told him to step upon the small platform, he obeyed, just as he always did when White men told him to do something. When the rope was thrown over the limb above, and its knotted noose swayed behind his head, touching it in rhythmic fashion, he said nothing and stood motionless. They couldn't really mean to hang him. They were just punishing him by frightening him. They couldn't do this. He hadn't killed his master, it had been an accident, just as he had told those men and the judge, but they had acted as though he hadn't told the truth.

The reflective mood of Cato's meditation was shattered. "Let's get on with th' hangin'!" The jailer frowned at the man who had made this exclamation, causing the others to hold their tongues.

Perceiving this rebuke, and believing it to have been made out of consideration for himself, Cato turned his head and said, "Ah thanks yo' kinely, Mistuh Jack."

Mistuh Jack replied by frowning at him. Holding up his hand to ensure quiet, he began to speak. "You all know what this is all about, but the law requires that I tell Cato here what's goin' to happen to him." He then read from a paper, and though Cato did his best to follow and understand all of it, he could comprehend only a few words of what he said, until the very end, when Mistuh Jack read, "On said day, you shall be taken from the jail and hanged by your neck until you are dead. May God have mercy upon your soul."

He was going to die! They really meant to kill him! The realization was inescapable now. Frantically, his eyes moved over the breadth and depth of the assemblage. Surely, there was some one among all those White folks out there who would stop what they were trying to do to him! He could hold no gaze from anyone whom his eyes touched. Mistuh Charlie turned his head; Mrs. Linton closed her eyes; others glared at him and some just laughed at his pleading expression. His cavernous nostrils heaved like the flanks of a winded horse. His stubby fingers raced along the piece of hemp around his waist that served to support his patched and tattered britches. Perspiration streamed down the sides of his rounded face, along the straining cords of his abbreviated neck and onto his well-proportioned chest, itself fully exposed by his ragged, open shirt. Wave upon wave of nausea swept over him. This couldn't be happening to him! It was just a bad, bad dream! He knew all these people. He liked them, and they all liked old Cato. All those children out there, he always played with them. He must be dreaming. None of his little friends would want to see any harm come to him. Faintly, he heard a voice tell someone to be ready to pull the rope. Hazily, he knew that the noose had been dropped about his neck. When his arms were jerked behind him, his powerful muscles reacted involuntarily, freeing his limbs and bringing them forward again. The crowd surged toward him. "He's trying to break loose! Jerk th' rope!"

Mistuh Jack and his deputies quickly restored order. "Any more of that, and you all will have to leave! Now, get back and stay back!" He turned to the terror-stricken, brown-skinned man standing on the box. "Cato, there's no use you fightin'. I don't like this job, but I got to do it; it's my duty. I want to make this as easy as I can for you."

Make it easy? How could dying like this be made an easy thing? But Cato did not speak his thoughts.

Again, it was Mistuh Jack. "We are going to tie your hands behind you, and then we'll tie your feet. This will keep you from kicking and fighting when the rope tightens on your neck." He said this calmly and in a soothing tone.

At last, Cato's mouth opened. He asked, "Whuffo' yo' wants ter do dis ter Ole Cato, Mistuh Jack?"

"I just told you why, Cato. Try to control yourself. It has to be done, and it will be, even if it takes every man here to do it."

All was lost. He had done as the White man wanted all his life, ever since he was brought to this country as a child. He would do so now. Obediently, he thrust his arms behind him, clasping his stubby fingers together tightly. "That's th' way, Cato. I'll try to make it quick," Mistuh Jack said.

Before the leather thongs could be tied, a voice raised itself above the din of the multitude. "You're forgettin' one thing, Jack. He's got th' right to speak his piece." The jailer quickly searched the crowd until he located the speaker. It was Michael Humble.

Instantly, there was a bedlam of critical comment, all directed at Humble. "Cato had his chance to speak at his trial." "A nigger ain't got th' same rights as a White man; if you let him speak, that'd be th' same as sayin' he's got th' same rights we has!" "You've fooled around long enough! Get it over with!"

Humble was undaunted. "You know I'm right, Jack. Ask him if he wants to say anything before he dies."

The raised hand of authority once more restored quiet. "Thank you, Michael, for calling it to my mind." Addressing the condemned man he said, "If you have anything you'd like to say, you can do it now, but make it short."

Make it short? He was going to die. What would happen when he died? Would he be carried in the arms of an angel to the throne of the Lord, like the preacher man had said he would if he believed? He believed, he had the faith but still he was afraid. Not of dying, but of the unknown that lay ahead of him. By talking, he could delay his leaving for a little while, a sweet little while. And Mistuh Jack said, "Make it short!" Can't he understand that the longer he talked, the longer he'd be alive?

The jailer put his hand on his shoulder. "Don't you want to say anything? If you don't, put your hands behind you."

Cato clenched his fists and held his arms close to his sides. "I'se thinkin', Mistuh Jack, I'se gwine ter talk." The tears were flowing freely now, following the courses set by the many wrinkles in his stubble-covered features. The thick lips quivered, then opened, flashing the contrast of red mouth and ivory teeth. He began his last words. "De fust thing ah wants fo' ter say ez, ah ain't nebbah huht nobuddy, an' ah didn' kill po' Massa John. It heppen jes' lak ah tole it ter th' jedge an' them genelmens whut wuz dar dat day." He scanned the crowd for a moment and then continued. "Yo b'leeves dat dean yo', young Massa John? Yo' knows Ole Cato ain' nebbah bin nuthin' 'cept'n kine an' good ter yo', all yo' bawn days."

John Donne Jr. did not reply, or acknowledge that he heard the words. He just folded his arms. He was not impervious to the slave's plea, however, as the muscles in his jaws flexed nervously.

When he was satisfied his importuning had been repelled by "his family," Cato resumed his funereal discourse. Goaded by the thought that talking was his only hope of salvation, he repeated to himself this redundancy: talk and live, live and talk, talk and live. Thus spurred, his speech came quickly. "Ah don' zackly know how ole ah ez. Yo' see, ah wuz fetched ter dis country when ah wuz jes' a li'l fella; but ah does 'membahs dem White fellas a-comin' wid dey guns an' all. Ah kin see ter dis day, m' mammy a-fittin' wid dem, an' ah sees her dar wid her haid all a-bleedin', cayse she doan do whut de White man he tole her ter do. An' h 'membahs dat ole ship a-crossin' dat oashun, an how pohly we all wuz a-spittin' un ouah insides on ouah se'fs, an' not bein' able ter clean up de mess we wuz a-makin', cayse ebbuddy's han's dey wuz tied behine dem, jes' lak Mistuh Jack wuz gwineter tie mine 'while 'go. Ah rec'lecks how bad hongry we gits, an' de tubble thust fo' de mens finely fotched some watah fo' us. Nex' doin's ah 'membahs, we wuz all a-stan'in' in de squah in Cah'lina, an' dey's a-sellin' us. Cain' nobuddy do nuffin ter perteck theyseffs, cayse dey's all in dem big chains ah fo'gits ter tell y'all 'bout dat dey puts de chains on ouah han's an' foots when we wuz on de oashun, cayse dey wuz some whut gits free fum dere tyin's. Dey sole us all, eb'one. De las' time ah see m' mammy, she cryin' an' a-tryin' ter git ter me, but de man whut buy her, he jes' take dat big black whup in his han' an' whup her wid it. Den dey finely gits her in de waggin wit de rest ob dern whut de man he buy, an' driv' off. Ah sees m' mammy a-lookin' back ter me; she wuz cryin' an' callin' ter me, til dey's out ob sight 'way down de road."

"You goin' to let him talk all day?"

Mistuh Jack spoke softly to Cato, in response to the challenging question hurled from the crowd. "Hurry along with it, Cato. We can't wait forever."

They couldn't wait forever, but it was to forever they were trying to hasten him. Cato used his tongue to catch some of the salty liquid that wet his cheeks and used it, in turn, to moisten his parched lips. He must think of something that might yet make them stop this terrible thing. Then they would just say, "Yo' cain' hang ole Cato. Tuhn him loose!" But what could he say to them that would accomplish this?

"You all done now, Cato?" It was Mistuh Jack, prodding him on to eternity.

"Naw, suh, Mistuh Jack. I'se still got a li'l moah."

He faced his impatient audience and resumed where he had left off. "Dar ah wuz, all by m'self ah fogits ter tell yo' dat m' pappy, he done bin sole too, but ah doan know who buy him. A nice, kinely genelmun he say, 'Ah buy dat li'l fella' (dat wuz me). He say, 'He be jes' 'bout de size ob m' boy, Willie.' So, he buy me, an' dat's how kums an' gits de name ob Cato Watts. Massa John, he hab de same fust name as Massa John Donne. I doan hab jes' two Massas, an' bot' dey fust names ez de same, an' dey bot' good Massas ter Cato—"

"Dija kill the other one too?" The harshness of the tone and its implication startled him, and the tears, which had momentarily ceased, poured forth anew as he protested again. "Cato doan kill nobuddy!"

Fearing a further prolongation of the execution might lead to violence, the jailer sought to discourage him from saying anything more. "It's not going to do you any good, Cato, to keep on talking. Hurry and get through now."

But the spark of hope was still alive within his breast. Before Mistuh Jack could exercise any further effort to dissuade him, his lips began to move again. "Massa John Watts, he growed me up long sides ob Massa Willie, til poah li'l Massa Willie, he die fum de sickness. Kotched de feber, he did; shake hisse'f plum ter death. So dey wuz jes Massa an' Cato dar by deyseffs. Den Massa, he go ter jine li'l Massa Willie. Ah fogits ter tell y'all, de missus, she die when Willie an' me wuzzn't growed. So dey hab ter sell Cato, cayse Massa John Watts, he doan lebe no kin fo'ks, 'cep'n some cuzzins in some udder place ah doan 'membah de name wha' it wuz. Den Massa John Donne, he buy me, he do. Kums de time, Gin'ral Clark, he wuz a cunnel den, he ax Massa John do he want ter kum ter de Falls, an' he say, 'Sho' do,' an 'fore long, us ez all on Cawn Island,[21] yondah." He turned his head and looked in the general direction of the first settlement, then faced his unwilling listeners to continue. But his slight pause resulted in the jailer saying sternly, "That's enough, Cato, you've had your say now." Mistuh Jack started to tighten the noose, to adjust it so that it would fit snugly, but Cato's prying fingers and his pathetic, terrified countenance won him yet more talking time.

"Mistuh Sam, ah sees yo' out dar. 'Membah de day yo' br'er Ahron, he die, an' Ole Cato hep yo' burry 'im? 'Membah how lots ob fo'ks, dey dies, an' Ole Cato, he de oney nigguh heah den, he dig dere grabes fo' dem? It wuz de hahdest diggin' ah done ebbah do. Dat winter, three y'ars ago, wuz de wustest ah done seed in m' whole life." Here and there, heads nodded in affirmation, and Mistuh Sam was pensive. Cato was quick to catch the significance. They were thinking with him, rather than against him. He seized upon this slight bit of corelated favor he had gained. "'Membah, kums Chris'mus, an' eb'buddy done kum ter de station on de shoah—dat Foht obadere, whut Mistuh Chenoweth, he buil' so fine an' dey wants ter hab some dancin'? An' whut does dey do? Ah sees lots of y'all out dar whut knows whut dey do—dey calls Ole Cato, an' dey—y'all say, 'Cato, us needs some musick so's ter dance by de chune. Git yo' fiddle'!"

His face was relaxed now, and he laughed, though the noose interfered a little with his larynx and added a roughened tone, uncommon to his usual laughter.

Those who had spent that first Christmas together remembered, and they too laughed at the remembrance.

The folks were happy; they wouldn't kill him now. Somebody would say, "Tuhn Ole Cato loose, us b'leeves hit wuz a axidunt!" They wouldn't hang him after all. But while they still laughed, the pardoning words did not come, so he decided to play further on their mirth.

"'Membah, ah gits m' fiddle, but dey's oney one string, an' de Lawd know ain' nobuddy whut kin play de Vuhginny Reel on jes' one string, so whut heppen? 'Long kums dat French fella, dat Johnny Nickel, whut jes' heppen ter drap in dar, an' he say, 'Y'all want de musick? Ah makes it.' Oney he say, 'Ze museek,' lak dem French say."

The audience was enjoying the show. Even those who had been most insistent the hanging be promptly accomplished now were glad it had been delayed. Cato's imitation of John Nickel's speech and mannerisms evoked gales of laughter. The actor, himself, was being carried away by memories. He was entertaining the White folks just as he had done so many times before. His thoughts formed into words with the rapidity of rifles fired in an ambush, and when the laughs thinned to chuckles, he continued. "Wal, yo' 'membahs dat Johnny Nickel, he play de minniet, an eb'buddy try ter dance ter it, but dey cain' do it, cayse it so slow. Dat musick, it wuz jes' skinny lak one ob dem ghostes whut de folks talks 'bout. So, finely, Johnny Nickel, he see he ain' pleasin' de fo'ks, 'speshul, atter one man he say, 'Ah done huhd fastuh musick den dat at m' aunt Sally's burryin'. Let Cato play dat fiddle ob yoahs!' But ole Johnny Nickel, he say back ter de man dat he 'fraid mebbe ah busts it, an' so he say he jes' give me de loan ob dem strings whut ah needs, so he do, an' ah play de Vuhginny Reel, fust thing, right off; den de Highlan' Fling, an' den all dem chunes whut fo'ks laks, an' eb'buddy ernjoy deyse'fs."

A sudden inspiration struck him. "Bet yo', wuz ah ter hab dat ole fiddle ob mine right now, ah plays y'all a chune an' dances at de same time!"

The pulse of the crowd's merriment had begun to slacken, and when Cato said this, the picture of him playing the fiddle and dancing with the rope still around his neck brought forth the inevitable, audible observation. "The only dancing you're going to do is at the end of that rope around your neck, an' you'll finish it in hell tonight!"

Cato heard, and the remark froze his heart and the blood it had been pumping so furiously. He grasped at another straw. "Dar's ma li'l friends: li'l Massa Freddy, an' Robby, an' Danny. Does yo' want Ole Cato ter mak' yo' laugh some moah?"

Firm parental hands on their little arms and shoulders told them the answer was, "No." There were no smiles upon their faces. Cato could only say weakly, "Ole Cato play wid yo'; many de time he rock yo' when yo' gets sleepy-haided." Their faces remained expressionless. Cato felt the chill, which a tired and disinterested gathering hurls back to one who has ceased to entertain it. Mistuh Jack was on the box with him again. The jailer had not enjoyed the performance, but he had waited patiently for its conclusion. He knew what he must do and, at last, the time had come to do it.

No tears came to Cato's eyes. His confused emotions were too ensnarled. He heard Mistuh Jack say, "When I raise my right arm, get ready. When I drop it, Martin, you pull hard and quick on th' rope. Jackson, you and Miller move this box out from under him at the same time. Then Martin, you tie your end of the rope around the tree trunk. Make sure that it doesn't slip."

Cato heard these directions, though the words failed to register in his brain. But when the jailer pushed his chin up and slipped the knot tightly against his jaws, he pleaded, "Doan do it, Mistuh Jack! Doan do it!"

The jailer answered, "It has to be, Cato; it has to be." Mistuh Jack sought to bind his wrists together, but stopped when Cato implored him, "Please, Mistuh Jack, ah done bin boun' all mah life; doan bine me ter de death!"

Mistuh Jack acceded to his wish, and them asked him, "Do you want me to put a cloth over your eyes, Cato? It might make it easier for you."

"If yo' pleases, suh, lemme see de daylight, foah as long as ah kin. Ah thanks yo' foah tryin' ter hep Ole Cato, Mistuh Jack."

Mistuh Jack just couldn't understand, could he? Ole Cato just couldn't die easy for a wrong he did not do. He tried to utter his thoughts, but though the words came, they were too faint to be heard by anyone except the jailer. "Wuz Gin'l Clark ter be heah, he stop dis. Foah de Lawd, ah didn' kill Massa John. White man brung me to dis lan'; now he takin' me 'way. Oh, Lawd, deah Lawd, hab mercy on poah Cato." The words trailed off into nothingness; their gossamer conclusion leaving his lips just as Mistuh Jack's arm dropped like a shot. The toes of Cato's callused feet were as fingers, trying so desperately to hold on to the box as it was jerked away.

The rope had slipped. Cato, who had lived without receiving any mercy, now was dying the same way. The powerful neck that had held his head high throughout his many adversities, had now served him ill. It had not snapped, and he was slowly strangling to oblivion. His arms and legs flayed about as though the rope was the string of an amateur puppetmaster, and each violent movement served only to further constrict the precious air from his lungs. His face, at first the color of the reddest clay, was slowly being drained of blood, and an ashen gray began to creep over its contorted features. His eyeballs strained from their sockets, and his tongue, carmine against his pallid lips, inched slowly outward.

The macabre scene still held most of its former watchers, though some had sickened and left hastily. Mrs. Linton asked, "Do you think he's sufferin' much?"

A neighbor replied, "I don't think he ever knew what happened. Them's just his muscles causin' that dancin'."

Dancin' . . . an ill-used word.

As his spirit wrenched itself from his tortured body, the twisting became spasmodic. His limbs hung limply, his toes just skimming the ground. That which had been Cato Watts swung slowly, turning by degrees to one side, then rolling lazily back to the other. The right leg jerked slightly, and the body turned a little faster. When this happened, three little boys, now freed momentarily from their parent's supervision, gathered small pebbles in their hands and cast them at the swinging object, laughing gleefully when the rocks hit their target. The odd twist of words, Cato had rocked them. Now they rocked him.

"When you goin' to take him down?"

The jailer turned his head to see who addressed him, then replied, "Don't know, Adam; in about an hour or so I guess, why?"

"Well, I was wonderin'. Them clothes of his'n ain't much, but they'd just about fit my nigger, Bert. Cato don't need 'em no more, no ways."

"You can have them, Adam. They'll be at th' jail." Mistuh Jack turned away in disgust.

Cato was gone, but his ragged garments would keep his memory alive until a few more patches were sewed on them. Then, the last remembrance of the first Negro at the Falls would slowly fade from the minds of men.

Another had heard the cries of the multitude for his life. Another's garments had been coveted as he hung upon a cross, one thousand, seven hundred and fifty years before.

*

"What about th' rope, Jack?" It was the deputy, Martin. "Want to keep it like it is or cut the knot off when we take him down?"

"Cut it off and burn it," the jailer said crisply. "And I hope we can use the rest of it for more pleasant purposes."

The crowd was gone now, the old settlers along with the newcomers. Freddy, Robby and Danny were at Freddy's house, playing with his puppy.

*

"Wal, hit wuz shore some show," said Jim Trench to Humble as they walked back to the latter's shop, "Oney thing, it took 'em too damn long! Bet th' boys is wonderin' whure in th' hell I be."

Humble did not reply. The affair had sickened his soul. If Cato hadn't really meant to kill John Donne Sr.

They walked in silence, and but for Humble's last words, they almost parted the same way. He handed the rifle to his customer. "I hope you never fire it, save for a righteous purpose."

Trench, puzzled by this odd farewell, said goodbye and walked away. As far as he was concerned, they had just killed a brown bear. He mused, does a son-uv-a-bitch go straight tuh hell when he dies, er does he wait til Jedgment Day? Shrugging his shoulders, and with it, any further reflection, he grasped his new rifle at its balance and took off in an easy lope for the place of departure.

CHAPTER 33

Jim Trench could see them clearly from the top of the bank, and he noted with relief that there were two boats moored alongside each other. But his pleasure at finding the men all there and waiting for him caused him to regret the anxiety that almost caused him to miss the hanging. Mought have knowed it, he thought, them sons-uv-bitches ain' liken tuh ever be in no hurry.

Drawing closer, he discerned that all appeared to be engaged in something that held their rapt attention. Just as he believed his approach had been ignored, one of them hollered, "Whure th' hell yuh bin? Hit's a damn good thing yuh finely got here. These here two damn Frenchies has jest 'bout got us broke. Never seed sech damn luck! Le's get th' hell away from here, 'fore they starts another game."

The Frenchmen had proven vastly more adept at cards than this crew of saltmakers turned sailors.

Tardiveau, a mischievous twinkle in his eyes, exclaimed, "C'est l'étranger! Je suis content de vous voir!" He grabbed Trench's hand and shook it excitedly.

Honore, though his expression was pleasant, merely said, "Il est très tard."

Perplexed, Jim called to Jack Santoire, who was of French extraction, "Whut's they talkin' 'bout?" He pointed to Tardiveau and Honore.

Santoire replied, "One said, 'It's the stranger! I'm glad to see you!' and the other said, 'It's very late.'"

The translation eased his dubious mind and he smiled. "That all they said?"

Santoire nodded in affirmation.

Back came queries from the others as to his whereabouts for the past two hours. He told them of the hanging, but made it appear that he would not have delayed there had it not been that the gunsmith was also there, and that he was forced to wait until it was over before he could obtain the rifle. This explanation focused everyone's attention upon his newest possession. They all inspected and handled it, taking turns in raising and sighting the weapon.

Tardiveau was curious about the hanging, however, and, with the aid of Santoire, Trench patiently described the affair to him. He shook his head in bewilderment, commenting to himself, but audible, "C'est sauvage, c'est sauvage." "It's wild, it's wild." He could not understand why the punishment had not been more swiftly executed.

Honore, who had but one thing on his mind, getting their furs on to New Orleans as quickly as possible, urged his companion on to departure. They had been delayed long enough. The two boarded their boat and prepared to cast off as soon as the Americans' craft was in the current.

Trench found everything in order. The kettles, in rows of five, were snug against the planking on each side. Inside of them was stored most of the cargo. Wooden blocks at the end of the rows prevented their slipping or shifting.

Goodbyes were exchanged and the two boats swung out into the stream with the one carrying Trench and his men in the lead. Glancing toward the stern, he watched the man handling the sweep oar. As the latter's face turned in his direction, he realized he wasn't a member of the party that had come from the licks. "Whose thet handlin' th' oar?" he asked of no one in particular.

"Thet's Billy Baxter. He's a new 'un. They's three more 'sides 'im," Tom Graham answered.

"Whut's he know 'bout pilotin'?"

"Him? He knows more'n we does, claims he's been down th' Ohio a good piece past Salt River. Says he's made th' trip before. Ain't none uv us handled a flatboat much, so we'uns figgered it couldn't hurt none fer him tuh try his hand at it some."

"Guess yore right on thet. Whure's th' others?"

Graham called them by names. "Thet han'some feller with th' red hair is Nate Galpin, he's from Culpepper, an' thet short li'l feller is Ike Cason. They's both from Virginny—he comes from Orange County. Th' one standin' next tuh him is Monk Damron. Ain't no use askin' why they calls 'im Monk, is they?"

Trench smiled, saying, "Hit shore ain't, if'n looks hed enything tuh do with his bein' on this here boat, he'd done been in th' river."

Monk smiled sheepishly, but laughed with the others. "Where yuh from, Damron?" Jim crammed a handful of tobacco in his mouth as he asked the question.

"Me an' Baxter come down from Fort Pitt yesterday."

"I means, where yuh hail from?"

"We both was raised in Berks County."

"Where be thet?"

"Pennsylvania. You has heared of Daniel Boone, ain't you?"

Trench nodded his head.

"Well, that's where he was borned."

Jim spit with the wind, readjusted the wad in his mouth and said, "Too damn bad y'all didn't make up yore mines tuh go with us until after we'uns hed done built this here boat."

"Be that as it may," said Baxter from the stern, "you built a good one. She handles right handsome."

Trench's prideful smile evinced his accord with this assertion. "Whut makes yuh all think yuh wants tuh go tuh Bullitt's Lick?"

The answer was the same. They had heard there was money to be made there.

"Hit ain't easy money; yuh'd best know thet. Then, gittin' an' keepin' ain't th' same thing, if'n y' know whut I means. Yore gonna fine hit's th' roughest place this side uv hell. We'uns whut works fer Tom Chism gits 'long all right, an' long as yuh stays put with us, yuh'll git by fair tuh middlin."

"They knows all thet," said Tom Graham. "We done tole 'em whut tuh 'spect down there."

"Well, so long as they knows whut's comin, reckin they knows they own mines." Trench's tone became a little sharper as he said to Santoire, "Git back there with Baxter an' see if'n we cain't get goin' a li'l faster. Like tuh git as fur up Salt River as we kin, 'fore night fall."

They were careful to keep the craft away from the shore, but yet well without the swirling, main body of the current that churned so angrily to their right, carrying in its center all manner of debris, chiefly, immense logs and trees, and which would, of themselves, imperil, if not doom, any craft in their close vicinity. The crew kept up a running conversation with the Frenchmen behind them, whenever they were close enough to be heard.

Fortunately for their excursion, there wasn't the slightest hint of rain. Rather, the sun's rays were warm to the point of inconvenience, and the men stripped to their waists.

On the shore as they passed, there was evidence everywhere of a most prolific spring. All was verdant and new. Warm weather had brought forth such an extravagant profusion of blooms and blossoms as to incite in one the desire for luscious, colored sweets. Kentucky certainly appeared anything but foreboding on this bright day. They had been lulled almost into a feeling of complete security as to the course and termination of the voyage, when whisps of smoke rose from inland. Instantly, they began to scan the river's bank, peering intently, hands cupped over their eyes.

"How long yuh reckin' we bin movin'?" asked Trench, and then suggested his own answer. "'Bout two hours?"

"Jedgin' from th' sun, mebbe half hour more'n 'at," said Graham.

At this moment, their sharp eyes caught fleeting sight of darting figures on shore and of canoes partly exposed by the lapping water from their places of intended concealment.

All hands were alerted to the possibility that the Indians might attempt to pursue them. The next two miles their craft covered were as ten. At length, they began to breathe more easily.

"Reckin we got nuthin' tuh consarn ourselfs 'bout them Injuns back there enyways," Trench said thankfully. "Funny thing, though, they wuz all painted up. Looked like Shawanese some."

When Graham finished speaking, Jim thought a while, then said, "Mought be they wuz goin' after some other Redskins. They does thet, y'know."

"Shore hopes thet's whut it be, an' not some pore settlers."

"I shore hopes so too, Tom."

But savage eyes had seen them and had ended the vigil they had begun four days earlier. Feet trained in racing the trails of the wilderness would now wing their way to where the renegade Vehrmon and his band were encamped, taking the information that the quarry had at last been sighted.

The afternoon was all but gone. Across the Ohio, the sun was half hidden by an expanse of uneven hills. Soon, there would be only the reflected light from its rays. Vast numbers of pigeons, their total so large as to stagger the imagination, sped overhead to their chosen roost, a spread of tall trees on the Kentucky side, some distance beyond the men in the boats. The feathered caravan seemed endless, and this was just one species of bird life.

"There's many a pie up there. Never saw so many in my life before!" exclaimed the red-headed Galpin.

"They's lots uv 'em a'right! But thet ain't nuthin' ornusal. I seed a bunch uv 'em one day whut hid th' sun."

Trench's assertion was too much to be swallowed whole by the new men, and their smiles were disbelieving.

He caught their doubt and sought to convince them. "Ask eny uv th' boys, if'n whut I jest sad ain't th' truth, an' with no trimmins'."

Affirmative rejoinders forced the doubters to accept this incredible statement as one of fact and not of fancy.

An alarm from Graham, stationed at the front of the boat, brought their eyes from the heavens back to the water. "Looks kinda hazy up ahead, there at th' left!" he hollered.

Simultaneously, Tardiveau and Honore were closing in on their right. The former was shouting to them, mostly in French.

Santoire interpreted quickly. "He sez tuh watch out er th' whirlpool near where th' Salt hits th' Ohio. Sez, if'n we gits caught in it, it'll suck us under, fer shore!"

Baxter nodded as he heard this. "Tell them we'll watch out for th' pool. We'll try to move just past it on th' right and swing around it. Then we'll work our way on up into Salt River."

Santoire relayed the message and then came back immediately with further word from Tardiveau. "He sez they'll try tuh hole their boat back, as best they kin, so's in case we'uns needs their help."

The helmsman acknowledged their auxiliary intent with a wave of his hand. Then, as if he were the master of his own craft, rapidly issued orders to the rest of those aboard.

Trench, at first moved to protest this clear usurpation of his authority, held his tongue when reflection made him admit that his leadership was best exercised on land, not on such unfamiliar surroundings as water. As he listened to the sharp and succinct directions Baxter gave the crew, admiration for the curly-haired, well-muscled, young man caused him to say, "Yuh'll do moughty fine at th' licks, young feller." Baxter nodded his head in appreciation.

The mouth of Salt River was clearly visible now, less than a half mile in front of them. Each man understood his duties, and each was tense in the anticipation of their performance. Three men were on the sweep oar, ready to pull or to hold, as the situation might demand.

Tom Graham called attention to a large log well ahead of them and slightly to their right. The timbered derelict swung over, so that it lay directly in their path, then rolled in a slow, curving course to the left. Suddenly, it appeared to be traversing the circumference of a huge circle whose center was some hundred yards from the river's mouth. Now, the maelstrom had full power over the huge piece of wood. First beyond vision, then briefly returning to view, it seemed as something animate, trying frantically to escape the unyielding clutch of the vortex. Now it spun with such velocity that the eye could not follow it. At length, it reached the center. Like a salmon attempting to hurdle a perpendicular obstruction, it appeared to be trying to leap straight upward, only to be pulled down and out of sight.

All the while, the boatload of kettles and men was coming closer to the moment of trial.

Jim Trench expressed the sentiments of the saltmakers and the three recruits when he said, fervently, "Damn glad they's somebuddy whut knows he's a-doing on thet there oar back there."

As they moved onward, however, the certainty of their belief in Billy Baxter began to fade. It appeared that the flatboat was following the exact course of the ill-fated log. Nearer and nearer they came. Tom Graham yelled in a voice colored with fright, "Whut in th' hell yuh tryin' tuh do? See how clos't yuh kin come to it? Swing 'er out some!"

Baxter appeared not to have been affected by his words, but the sweat on his own shoulders and upon those of the other two men at the sweep was cold as ice.

Jim Trench said impassively, "Don't reckin eny uv yuh all hankers tuh do eny swimmin', does yuh? Jist s'posen yuh keeps yore heads an' lets Baxter alone." Jim made a mental note that it might be a good idea for him to learn to swim if he ever got back to Bullitt's Lick.

The wild fury of the whirlpool was just minutes away and the eyes of the maiden voyagers were drawn irresistibly toward its gyrations. Their hearts thumped madly against their ribs. At this point, they had very little confidence in one Billy Baxter. The slightest increase in their proximity to the awesome eddy resulted in just that much less faith in their young helmsman.

Lurching violently, the craft swung to its right. This, plus the added impetus received from the extreme fringe of the vortex, served to snap the boat around and away from the latter's swirling path. Skillful maneuvering of the sweep oar kept them from going on over into the dangerous main current and guided them safely beyond the perilous, conical pool. Now would commence the struggle to propel the flatboat against the Ohio's fast-moving, though lesser, current.

The faces of the company, so taut moments before, were now completely relaxed. New hands were upon the oar, replacing those that had steered the party to its present safe position.

Baxter's breathing was still uneven as he talked with Jim Trench. "You know, if we hadn't kept fairly close to the pool and had gone over into the main stream, we'd have been five miles downriver by now. If we had been lucky enough to have stayed afloat, instead of having to work upriver a quarter of a mile, we'd have had about six or seven, maybe more than that."

"I knowed yuh knowed whut yuh wuz doin'. Yuh done a damn fine job uv hit." Jim meant every word.

"To tell you the truth, I wasn't so tarnal sure I could handle it. I knew that eddy was there, but it never was no damn whirlpool like it is now. You think maybe all that water that's backed up Salt River could be trying to come out, an' th' two currents kinda gets themselves twisted together?" Baxter's forefinger flung the perspiration from his brow.

"Sounds reason-like, when yuh looks at it thet way, but I shore don't know a damn thing about it. Tom Chism didn't say nuthin' 'bout it, neither. Th' way he tole it, seemed all we'uns hed tuh do, wuz tuh git on th' boat an' float down th' river. Well, demme, I plumb fergot 'bout them!" Trench pointed to the Frenchmen, laboring to hold their craft within shouting distance.

"Whut they sayin', Santoire?"

"They sez, if'n we thinks we kin make it from here on, they'll git on their way!"

"Tell 'em we'uns thanks 'em fer they help' an' thet we'll do all right." He waved to them as Santoire relayed his message and was immediately joined by the others in so doing.

The farewells ended when the French boat headed down the stream they so affectionately called la belle riviere, the beautiful river.

"Thet shore shows how damn selfish a feller gits when his own hide be in danger. Bet they ain't a damn one uv yuh whut thought 'bout them Frenchies til now. They hed tuh come past thet circlin' son-uv-a-bitch back there, same's we done." He smiled guiltily and added, "I gotta tell th' truth, I wuz consarned 'bout Jim Trench, an' nobuddy els't." Eyeing the group, he asked, in mock seriousness, "Eny uv yuh fellers think 'bout me, yuh dirty liars?"

Everyone laughed uproariously. When they stopped, he said, still in jocularity, "Y' knows whut? I shore am sad thet I hed tuh git back tuh th' licks. Bin moughty nice tuh hev took a nice boat ride tuh New Orleans." He slapped his thigh, then ceased laughing as he said, "Damn if'n I hain't fergot all 'bout m' hevin tuh let water. Back yonder, I thought I wuz gonna bust open. I hed tuh do it so damn bad. Wudda done hit then, 'cept I wuz a-feared thet one more drop uv water in thet damn river wud send us all straight tuh hell. Thet's 'bout all hit wud hev took."

The laughter rang out as he walked to the rear and relieved himself. When he finished this requirement of nature, he asked them, "How comes nobuddy els't hez tuh do it? Er did yuh scummy fellers do it in yore britches?"

The merriment was a fitting aftermath to their hazardous experience.

Slow and tedious as the task was, the flatboat finally reached the river's mouth. Once it gained entrance upon the tributary, the sweep oar moved much easier. The absolute absence of current accounted for this facility of propulsion.

Salt River was approximately two hundred feet in width at this point, narrowing gradually as one progressed up its course. Miniature in comparison with the Ohio, it nevertheless held a position of respect among the inland streams of Kentucky.

The shadows thickened after they had proceeded about two miles, and Jim Trench ordered a welcomed halt for the night. A heavy chain, whose free end was linked to a big hook was secured to the roots of a large tree on the north shore and the boat made fast. Trench and two other marksmen disembarked and climbed up the bank. Shortly, shots were heard, marking the last roost of the unlucky fowls chosen as targets. Soon a fire was blazing away and whetted appetites were satisfied. Six men were selected to serve as sentries, two for each of the three-hour watches until daylight. The first pair of sentinels assumed their duties and the rest of the party returned to the craft, their path lighted by the flames on the shore. The first act of the sentinels was to douse the fire. Presently, the quiet of the wilderness would be broken only by the cries of the night birds and the varied snores of the exhausted travelers.

CHAPTER 34

The three—Tom Chism, Abe Foster and Mercer—trudged along together, in the van of their hastily organized force. Tom had been able to muster but eighteen, instead of the twenty-five that he had estimated originally. Thus, with the twenty-two whom Barth had assembled, they were forty strong, or weak, depending on the number or the enemy they would have to face.

Though they moved side by side, the three were not together in their thinking. Abe was strong for getting as far downriver as possible before the darkness fell. The other two were just as adamant in their opinion that they should make camp while it was yet light. Abe was reluctant to yield to their decision, saying, "Hit's boun' ter make sense. The fu'ther we gits ternight, th' quicker we meets 'em in th' mornin', if'n we ever does meet 'em." There was always the possibility that the craft might have floundered and been lost.

There was logic in his reasoning, but it could not overcome the belief shared by Barth and Tom that the boat might not have even started upriver, or if it had, it hadn't gotten very far, and that the crew might be even now putting to shore for the night. If, in fact, something had happened, if they had met with misfortune, then that made their argument the more sound. Again, there was no way of ascertaining where the Indians might be up ahead of them and proceeding in the half-light was tantamount to inviting disaster. Moreover, a good rest would benefit the men and assure an early start in the morning.

They had reached the approach to a big curve in the river when Abe at last gave in to their desire. A watch was established on all sides, and the men bedded down under strict instructions to not fire their rifles for any cause unless one of the three leaders gave his approval. Tom was to check the first watch, Barth the second and Abe the third and last.

Barth might just as well have taken Tom's place, or made the rounds or the sentries with him, for he could not sleep. The impending clash with the savages was on his mind, of course, but not as much as were Dracie and Johnny. His concern for the former had led him to pen a letter to her and to write a hastily executed will that he had left in the keeping of Rosie Tindall, then safely inside Brashear's Station. He had informed Rosie as to the testamentary character of the writing, and she had promised its delivery to Dracie, should anything happen to him. He had also left Sagitta with Rosie, as the horse, far from being useful on this expedition, would be a decided hindrance. The enemy could not be stalked on horseback. Johnny's whereabouts were not known to him. When he had returned briefly to the cabin, neither the little follow nor his mule, Wallingford, were anywhere to be seen. He had asked Rosie about him, and her answer, "I haven't seen him, an' I don't never want to see him again," had just added another twist to the puzzle of Johnny's unexplained absence. Barth felt certain he hadn't gone to George May's without advising him of his intention to do so. Besides, Johnny knew he would have to take along the plat of the land to be claimed. He finally dismissed Johnny from his mind, but he continued to think of Dracie Claycomb, and the moments he had spent with her in what seemed ages ago. When he found himself dwelling on the passionate event of their last night together, he got up and walked until he found Tom Chism and engaged him in conversation for a long time before he came back to his earthen bed and once more sought his rest.

*

Vehrmon sat with his left leg bent and crossed, its foot resting just above his right knee, which was drawn up so as to furnish the necessary support for the weight thus placed upon it. He grunted as he bent forward, grasping the underside of his left foot in his left hand while he carefully pared the calloused sole with the knife in his right. The end of a roasting stick, some smoking meat still impaled upon it, had been stuck into the ground within his easy reach. This accessibility was no accident. In between his parings, he sliced off bits of the venison and stuffed them into his mouth.

As he chewed his food, he reviewed his plans for the morrow. He knew the flatboat hadn't been able to make more than a few miles up Salt River, at the most, before the night had halted it. Information he had received from his Shawnee scouts about an hour ago convinced him he was correct in this assumption. The same source numbered the boat's crew at ten. He was uncertain, however, as to the other boat his Indians had sighted and which they said had two men aboard. Skinner had not said anything to him about another craft being involved. Perhaps, it was going on farther down the Ohio. In any event, its presence wouldn't matter, especially since it carried only two adventurers. Twelve men couldn't cause too much trouble for his band of fifty-four. The odds were just about right for the Indians. Unless they had the preponderance of numbers, they hesitated, even sometimes refused, to enter into warfare with the White men.

This brought to mind the intelligence he had received just a few moments earlier as to the position of the party from the licks. He knew when and where they had stopped, and he had been advised of their approximate strength, about fifty-five men. From his experience in Indian campaigns, he had learned long ago that the savages were prone to overestimate the number of their antagonists. This was done purposely, so as to require more offensive strengths to be obtained by adding proportionately more warriors to their own war party. Hence, he figured the true number of the Whites to be about forty to forty-five. In either event, right or wrong, he and his band had no intention nor desire to engage so large a force. The plan was only to wipe out those who were coming upriver, and to take what plunder they could conveniently carry away. The kettles were to be submerged in the stream, with a view to their later recovery by Skinner and his friends.

The attack would have to be executed quickly, otherwise they would have the larger group to contend with. The latter he figured to be about seven or eight miles east of the boat, or five or six miles farther away than were himself and his Indians, who were camped to its north.

Once the mission had been accomplished, he planned to retrace his path, cutting around to the north of the settlement at Bullitt's Lick, sending only a small raiding party of ten savages through the settlement itself. In turn, this smaller band would rejoin the main body at a prearranged point north of the knobs. From there, they would proceed to their meeting place with the British major who had ordered this present foray.

These were his plans, but he was not unmindful of what might happen to alter them. Once savages were turned loose to kill and plunder, it was frequently difficult to keep them under any semblance or control or authority. Like a pack of dogs, unleashed after long confinement, they would not always follow commands. However, the isolated location of the proposed attack would seem to negate the probability of any such trouble on this occasion.

As he pulled his boot on his foot, the thought which had baffled him ever since his first meeting with Ben Skinner returned. What was the reason that would cause the diversion of himself and his band to such a small, unimportant undertaking as this one? He knew Skinner and Mace Hardin were in sympathy with the Crown, but that couldn't be a satisfactory answer to his perplexity. Nor could Hardin's position at the licks. Salt was available there to anyone, British or American, for its price. Now, if the licks were to be the object of a large-scale assault, like those being planned against the settlements bordering on and east of the Kentucky River, it would be a different proposition. Whatever the reason, there could be no doubt that Skinner must have influential friends somewhere up the line. The major had as much as told him so when he sent him on this mission. "Those are my orders," he had said.

Vehrmon got to his feet, stretching himself as he did so. There was no use thinking any more about the matter. Maybe, some day, he might find the explanation. If not, well, it wouldn't make too much difference. It was just that he knew, instinctively, that there was something much more important in this affair than the mere massacre of the men now sleeping on Salt River and the taking of the cargo.

He made the rounds through the camp, conferring briefly with the leaders of the three tribes that composed his murderous band. Although the plan for the attack had been explained repeatedly to them, he nevertheless reviewed each detail, knowing that in all probability his orders would not be fully executed. Always, in every raid or battle in which Indians of more than one tribe were engaged, he had found that commands were disregarded in some particulars, usually resulting from a suddenly conceived decision on the part of one of the chiefs. After the purpose of the deviation had been secured or finally lost, the deviating complement would return to the original design. All that he could do in advance was to be sure they understood what he desired to be done and how he wanted them to do it. If they secretly disagreed, or carried out the plan otherwise than directed, he could only try to persuade them to conform to its main objectives. Because of this, he had determined not to break camp until it was fully light. He reasoned that the adventurers would shoot game and then breakfast before renewing the journey upriver. All of them would be on shore for this purpose, and if they were allowed to begin the meal, their vigilance might be lessened and they would present themselves as easy targets for his braves. Thus, the mission would be thoroughly and speedily executed, and he and his men would be on their way, far from the scene, before the blood stopped dripping from the scalps hanging from some of their waists. When those coming down from the licks reached the spot, they would find an empty raft—two empty rafts—if both had in fact come up stream, and ten or twelve dead men with bloody heads. So complete would have been the surprise of the attack, no shots would have been fired at him or his red-skinned cohorts.

This was the manner in which Vehrmon hoped his plan would be accomplished. This was the reason he now, for the last time, so patiently strove to impress the minds of his savage subalterns with its essential features.

*

Mace Hardin waited only until after Mercer and his volunteers had moved off to join Tom Chism's force, before he, himself, departed.

As he rode homeward, his spirit was high. If everything went according to plan, the troublesome Captain Mercer would not return alive from this venture. His instructions to Gibbs and Mallory had been simple. If contact with the Indians was made, and the battle joined, Gibbs was to position himself so as to be behind Mercer. Then one, well-directed shot would be sufficient.

Not being familiar with what Blackie Vehrmon might decide to do, he had set up an alternate procedure, in the event the latter had already concluded his attack and had withdrawn in advance of Mercer's arrival. Should this occur, Gibbs or Mallory, according to which one had the best opportunity, was to kill Mercer "by accident." The expected resulting furor would have to be calmed, but he could take care of that situation, if and when it arose. Whether by declaring open warfare on Chism and his workers, or through the simple expediency of letting Chism take care of whomever did the killing, he had not determined. However, Gibbs or Mallory, or both of them, was expendable at any time, and certainly they would be the more so if either died as a consequence of Mercer's demise. Th' high an' mighty 'son-uv-a-bitch' wouldn't call him Mister Hardin no more, and things would take up as they were before Mercer had come to the licks. Best of all, it would be difficult to lay the blame for the killing at his doorstep. Patrick Henry, nor anyone else, couldn't do anything more than to make a formal investigation as to what had happened.

He had yet another snare to set, and that was the occasion for his riding to his home. He was looking for Jeddy-Boy. If Mercer evaded the other traps, which he had laid for his life, Jeddy-Boy would finish him off for sure. Cautiously, he alighted and looked about. If Massalene's temper had not cooled, a direct approach might be hazardous. Satisfying himself that she must be somewhere inside the cabin, he called to her, "Ole womern, yer seed enything uv Jed?"

If she was there, she did not answer. He entered, calling for his son, on the off chance he was asleep in the loft.

"Him no here." The quiet utterance spun him around. She sat in the farthest corner.

"Why th' hell dintcher answer me when I called yer?"

"No hear you." The words issued through lips that parted just enough to emit their sound.

"Wal, hear me now, damn yer! Whar's Jed?"

"No see, long time."

"Thet damn boy!" Jeddy-Boy had failed his pap again. Now, one of his other plans would have to bear the murderous fruit.

"Wal, jest don't set thar! Git me some vittles."

Massalene arose in mechanical fashion and set about her ordered task.

After he had eaten, he asked, "Whar's Nancy?"

The laconic reply was barely audible. "Her no here, no be here no more."

"Whut th' hell, yer means, her no here? Whar in hell ez she?"

"Her with preacher feller."

"Yer means she's at thet damn Flinden's?"

Massalene nodded solemnly.

"Thet hain't gonner be fer long. Soon's I gits m' bizness tended tar, I'll whup her dirty lil ass all the way back here."

"Her no come back. You no make." It was a simple but positive statement.

"Wal, I aims ter see ter thet. Yer unnerstan' me, ole womern? Whar ez thet idjit Hawkstraw?"

"James no here. Him not come back no more too."

Mace roared, "Whut th' hell yer means by thet? Whut th' hell's hepp'nin' 'round here?"

Again came the quiet answer. "They no come back, no more."

He controlled himself, saying only, "Wal, I'll take keer ov 'em proper, when I gits th' time fer it."

Massalene tersely reiterated, "They no come back, no more."

He ended the redundancy. "Ole womern, I be a mought tarrer, an' I aims ter sleep a spell, jest long 'nough fer thet grease yer fed me ter settle down some. See thet I don't sleep fer long, yer unnerstan'?"

"Me wake you, time come."

Thus assured, he lay down on Nancy's pallet, reclining on his back, his forearm flat against his forehead.

When his snoring found its pattern, she unsheathed her knife and moved stealthily toward where he lay.

From the outside, there came a cry. "Boss, y' in there?" Mace heard the call, subconsciously, and slowly opened his eyes. He saw the knife in Massalene's hand and leaped to his feet. Sidestepping her lunge, he quickly disarmed her. Puffing from the sudden exertion, he warned, "If'n yore here when I kums back, I'm gonner kill yer, damn yore treacherous hide to hell!"

She glared at him defiantly as he went out the door.

Unwittingly, Jack Doniger had done the one thing he would never have done intentionally. He had saved Mace Hardin's life.

Without divulging the underlying cause of his gratitude, Mace greeted him. "Much 'bliged ter yer, Doniger. Yer shore kum at th' right time fer me. Whut y' want?"

"Yuh told me to get word to yuh, if I seen or heared of Jed, 'member?"

"Thet's right, a'right. Whar is th' no good bastard?" Mace mounted as he asked this.

"When I left to come here, he was over at Mud Garrison, drunk as hell. Had hisself a ruckus over there, an' Hilda Tressel come lookin' for yuh to take care of 'im. I comes after yuh, right away."

As they galloped toward the place where he hoped to find his son, Mace gave forth with some advice. "Doniger, don't never hev nuthin' ter do with no female whut's got Injun blood in 'er. They's right purt when they's young, an' yer kin lay with 'em without no worryin' 'bout catchin' th' pox, but if'n yer marries 'em, they gits fat an' greasy, an' hit don't matter a damn how long yer lives with 'em, they still thinks an' stinks liken a damn Injun."

Doniger listened, blankly, and when he had finished said, "I'll 'member that, boss," wondering what was responsible for this unusual advice.

They might have saved themselves the ride. Jeddy-Boy was gone, and the best they could learn was that he had ridden off in the direction of Dowdall's, beating his horse unmercifully as he raced away.

Night had descended when they returned to the licks. After posting his guards, Hardin rode off toward Ben Skinner's.

*

Mercer's sleep had been spasmodic, and with the advent of the false dawn, the bedlam created by the roosting birds ended whatever chance there might have been for further rest. He went to the river's edge and cupping water in his hands, splashed it upon his face. Now thoroughly awakened, he walked carefully among the sleeping company whose sleep-borne noises seemed to protest the coming of the day.

He called softly to Abe Foster, who upon recognizing him inquired, "Whut yer doin' up so early?"

"Couldn't sleep, Abe, so I just as well be up and about."

"Worried about whut's ahead uv we'uns?"

"Some, I'll admit. But mostly I'm concerned for the safety of the men on the boat. They'd be mighty easy game if the Indians were to come upon them."

"Well, Cap'n, hit ain't gonner be too long 'fore we knows suthin', one way er t'other. Liken yer, I'm hankerin' ter git ter it. My druthers is ter git goin' soon as hit's light 'nough ter move."

Mercer was in complete accord. "Let's go see what Chism has to say about it."

Tom Chism needed no encouragement. He too was restless to press on. It took scant time to arouse the men and advise them of their decision.

Breakfast was foregone, but numerous ones chewed on pieces or the ever-present jerked venison as the party moved forward.

The half-light swelled to visibility, threatened no little by the full mist that enshrouded Salt River on their left.

By arrangement, the force had been divided into three groups, each responsible to, and controlled by, Mercer, Abe Foster and Tom Chism, respectively. Mercer, with thirteen men, covered from the river's bank roughly 100 yards to the flank of Foster's patrol, which in turn extended a like distance to where it joined that of Tom Chism. Foster's group numbered the same as Mercer's. Chism had fourteen.

The leaders moved in front of their men who advanced in a skirmish line, each man being within easy contact of those on each side of him. It was not open going, however, as the way ahead of them was forested and heavy with underbrush. So covered was the terrain in some stretches of their progress that a companion a scant twenty feet away was unable to be seen. Mercer and Abe Foster alternated in ranging well in advance of the others for the purpose of scouting the route of march.

The adventure continued without incident. Speculation was rife with expressed opinions that they might have to proceed all the way to the Ohio, for it seemed to all that the flatboat would have made its appearance had it been on Salt River since the evening before.

CHAPTER 35

Jim Trench woke up coughing. The mist was so heavy, he was unable to distinguish the forms of the still slumbering men at the other end of the boat. Rising to his feet, he began awakening those who still clung tenaciously to their rest. "Git up, boys, yore dreamin' is done finished."

Wearily they stretched themselves to alertness. "Hit'll be a wonder if'n we all don't git th' sickness, breathin' all thet there steamin' stuff." Swinging into the day's action, he called to Tom Graham. "Tom, git thet hook off'n them roots an' let's git movin'. Quicker we starts, th' quicker we gits tuh th' licks."

"Ain't we gonna eat fust?" Graham's question found many prepared to give an affirmative vote, but Jim Trench was not one ot them. "We kin eat enytime. I want tuh git on hup there some." So saying, he told Baxter, "Boy, yuh got sharp eyes. Yuh set yoreself up there in front at th' left an' keep us goin' straight. This fog won't slow us none too much, an' yuh knows damn well if'n we cain't see up yonder on th' bank, nobuddy up there kin see us. Don't 'spect no Injuns, but if'n they's eny aroun' they hain't gonna see we'uns less' they looks powerful clos't."

With two men on the sweep, the craft moved easily up the currentless stream.

*

The day had not fully dawned before Blackie Vehrmon was forced to make a change in his well-laid plan of attack. A breathless Delaware scout brought the disconcerting information to him before the renegade was fully awake. Gesturing, the savage exclaimed, "Bad see. Smoke from the river big like snow. White man no cook on ground. Boat gone."

Boat gone. That was the message in itself. No other words were necessary. Black Lester's mind had not envisioned the thick morning vapors arising from the waterway.

His thoughts now concentrated on a new mode for the destruction of his prey. But scarcely had he formulated the rough outlines of the new assault before another panting courier made his appearance.

The men from the licks were already on the march!

The possibility of a pitched battle was now fast becoming a probability and he had no heart for such a happening. Had his orders been at all flexible, he would have, at this point, abandoned the attack, but such choice had been denied him when the major had given him his instructions. The bedeviling thoughts came again. Why was this mission so important to his superiors? What influence could Skinner possibly have with them, and what was its source?

Brushing these annoying queries from his mind, he summoned the leaders of his confederates for a hasty conference.

Precious minutes rolled away before he was satisfied that everyone understood his part in the latest battle design. Twenty-four of his band were to be sent to intercept the oncoming adventurers, staggering their numbers so that four would make the first contact, eight at a point roughly a half mile distant, and the remaining twelve, a like distance from the latter. Theirs was to be strictly an attempt to delay the advance of the White men. Survivors of each group were to fall back slowly, but consistently. If successful in withstanding their foes until the attack on the flatboat had been accomplished, they were to rejoin the main body of warriors at a rendezvous on the other side of the knobs to the north. In the other extreme, that of a fray still being in progress, they were to reinforce the assault upon those on the river.

Vehrmon gave the signal and the camp was broken. The attack had at last been launched.[22]

*

"Hear thet, Jim?"

"Hear whut? Yuh means, them birds?" As he answered, Trench looked at Tom Graham, who had asked the question.

"Naw, not them. I been hearin' them too an' they 'pears a mought disturbed. But thet ain't whut I means. Seems liken I hears a pack-train bell."

The two moved to the front of the boat.

Billy Baxter attempted conversation with them, but they quickly silenced him. "We're listenin' fer suthin'," Trench explained sternly. Their ears didn't pick up anything, and after a bit, Jim Trench relaxed the rule and said to Baxter, "Whut wuz yuh goin' tuh say a while back?"

"Just that the fog is getting thinner."

"Been noticin' thet m'self. I wuz jest—'"

Tom Graham interrupted hastily, "There it is agin!"

"What you listenin' for?" Baxter asked before Graham's raised hand had conveyed its meaning.

"Fer a bell ringin'," Trench whispered. "Th' pack trains at th' licks has 'em on th' oxen so's tuh let folks know its them animules, an' not Injuns, a-comin' through th' brush, Tom thinks he's hearin' one on shore."

At that moment, the sound came unmistakably. Broad smiles relieved the concentration of the earlier moment. "They's come lookin' fer tuh meet us," Graham exclaimed joyfully.

"Mebbe so, mebbe not," Trench said. "Head into th' bank an' ketch thet chain on them roots yonder. Tom, yuh an' Santoire scramble on up there an' scout aroun' some—keep yore rifles ready. Jest mought be a trick, though I doubts it."

The two explorers quickly made the ascent and were soon out of sight amid the trees that crowded almost to the waterline. Graham was in the lead with Santoire close behind. The bell sounded from a little farther inland. Increasing his pace, Graham stopped suddenly in his tracks. A Shawnee brave had stepped from the covering of a small cedar, directly in front of him.

"It's a trap! A ambush!" Graham prayed his cries of danger, instantly relayed by Santoire, could be heard by those off shore.

There was the crack of a rifle shot, and Tom Graham fell to the earth.

The vocal warnings had not been strong enough to carry to Trench and the others, but the report of gunfire threw the party into immediate alarm. Volunteers were out of the boat and on top of the bank before Jim Trench could counsel caution. The first moving object that met their eyes was the dodging figure of Santoire, the wounded Graham upon his back.

Jim Trench thundered, "Git tuh th' boat! Back tuh th' boat, ever' one uv yuh! I'll take keer uv them two a-comin'!"

He ran forward, darting from tree to tree, until he neared Santoire and his bleeding burden. It was then he saw the savage raise his rifle and aim it at those fleeing his pursuit. At that moment, the ruler of life decreed that Santoire should stumble and fall. The lead passed over the prostrate men. The warrior vainly tried to obtain cover as the powder flashed in the pan of Trench's new weapon. A red spot appeared beneath the Indian's breast. His arms lifted as he flung his gun, rolled backward and collapsed. The stolen bell tied to his waist tinkled once and was still.

Santoire was again supporting Graham when their rescuer reached them.

"I'll tote him th' rest uv th' way. Yuh go on ahead." This direction by Trench met with stubborn refusal, ending in the two of them carrying the disabled one to the temporary haven of the craft and their comrades. Despite their dire apprehension, no other Indians made their appearance.

"Whut part uv yuh got hit?" Trench's tone was solicitous.

Graham, barely conscious, answered weakly. "High up inside my leg."

Trench's inquiry was occasioned by the fact that the blood had so covered the lower half of the body that its source might have been from anywhere up under Tom's jacket. Quickly his britches were cut away, exposing clearly the gaping hole from which the red stream spurted. Frantic fingers tried to stem the bleeding, but the wound was on the middle inside of the limb, almost to the crotch, and it was apparent to all that nothing could be done to save his life. Graham had lost consciousness. It was just a matter of time.

Jim Trench knew it was just a matter of time also before there would be more bloodshed. Leaving Santoire to look after the dying man, he began his preparation for the expected attack.

"Kin yuh swim, Baxter?"

The latter acknowledged this ability by a nod of his head. The chain had been pulled loose from the anchoring base of the sycamore, allowing the boat to swing out into the river, its head perpendicular to the shore and some ten feet away. The hook, however, had become firmly caught on a submerged root, and all efforts to dislodge it had been fruitless. Hence, the need for someone who could work in, and under, the water.

Baxter was overboard the next instant.

*

"Once a thing starts bad, it's hell ter keep it from endin' th' same way." Vehrmon said these words to a Wyandot who nodded his head sagely, as though he understood their meaning.

The renegade had heard the exchange of rifle fire a short time before. With the first echo, he knew that his task had been made the more difficult.

The Shawanese whose blood was even now drying upon his bare torso had been sent on ahead of the war party with instructions to lure the voyagers into the forest by the use of the bell. He had been forbidden to fire his weapon, but the desire to take a scalp had proven too strong for him to resist.

Black Lester had experienced disobedience of his commands before, and would do so many times in the future, but the failure of the savage scout to perform his duty this day had increased the danger of having to reckon seriously with those coming from the saltlicks. He grimaced in anger and motioned his warriors forward.

*

Billy Baxter ducked under once more. He opened his eyes, but it was too dark to make out the hook even when he pulled it nearer the surface. His lungs screamed for relief and he came to the top for a few breaths before another submersion. For a second, the noises he heard were bewildering, then he knew them! The boat was under attack! A ringing fire and wild, frenzied shouts filled the air. One look at the boat and its perilous position was evident. The Indians were pouring raking volleys down the open way from stem to stern. The kettles offered but little protection to the crew. The craft must be freed from its enforced anchorage quickly or all onboard were doomed. He found the chain and traced its length until he reached the ensnarled catch at its end. Grasping it firmly with both hands, he braced his feet against the tangled mass in which it was enmeshed. Summoning every ounce of strength he possessed, he pushed himself violently backward. The hook came free, bearing with it the offending piece of water-soaked root that had blocked the previous attempts to disengage it. Surfacing, he came up at the head of the boat and pulled himself high enough out of the water to fling the chain onboard. Instantly, lead began to whiz and wing about him.

Jim Trench's warning, pleading in tone, reached his ears despite the battle sounds. "Git down' boy! Fer God's sake, git down! Come aboard at th' back end."

Before Billy Baxter could submerge, the rustling movement of a weighty tree branch that extended well out over the water arrested Trench's attention. His sharp vision saw the warrior, rifle in hand, balancing himself to a standing position, and then bracing himself by resting his back against a higher, parallel limb. Hugging a sheltering kettle, Trench laid his rifle barrel against the rim of the huge pot and pulled the trigger. The report of his shot rang out in unison with that of the foe above him. There was an innocuous water splash a foot past Billy Baxter's shoulders. The Indian hurtled from his perch, his shaven head striking the rounded belly of the kettle with a sullen thud. The cranium broke under the impact and gelatinous blobs of brain splattered upon Jim Trench's face and upon the still form of Tom Graham. The ailing body, slowed momentarily by the striking, sank slowly in melting fashion between the boat and the shore, imparting a vermillion swirl to the engulfing water as it disappeared.

On shore, while the discharge of weapons was more rapid than those from the river, the fire was not as accurate. Whether this was due to the still slightly obscuring mist or the inability of the attackers to attain proficiency in the use of firearms was a matter of purest conjecture. Whichever was responsible, Vehrmon counted seven of his band dead and four badly wounded out of the original thirty who had begun the attack. He had no way of knowing how many of his enemies were out of action. If th' damn Injuns would jest take a little more aim before they shoot, he thought. But it was too late to preach deliberation now. They were on their own. Their firing continued as before: heavy at times, intermittent when the ramrods were being employed to ready the guns for their next use.

Jim Trench wiped the red smudge from his cheek and took stock of the situation during the lull that now ensued. Of his ten men, including himself, only six remained alive and two of this number were seriously hurt, although they courageously continued to fight. As he looked to the rear, he saw Baxter's head coming up through one of the few remaining puffs of fog. "Pull on thet oar, if'n yuh kin, but keep down while yuh does it!"

Baxter heard him and attempted to slide his body over the end and into the boat. He lost his grip when his hands slipped, and he started to fall back into the stream. Monk Damron, his shoulder bleeding from a deep wound, sprang to the aid of his friend. His left hand caught hold of the black hair and the other clutched tightly a gathering in Baxter's jacket as he pulled him over the edge.

"Git, down, yuh damn fool!" Jim Trench's voice was lost in the fury of the fusillade that began as he shouted the first word of his admonition. Blood gushed forth from a hole at the base of Damron's head. As he pitched forward, he fell upon Billy Baxter stretched on the floor beneath him. Countless missiles tore at Damron's inert form, causing it to jump each time it was hit, but he did not feel them. The first bullet had done its work. Monk Damron, born in Berks County, Pennsylvania, now lay dead on Salt River, a small tributary of the mighty Ohio, which, as his course had been charted, starts from Pennsylvania and never returns.

Ike Cason and Nate Galpin had been killed with the first volley. Cason's corpse was on its back, a yawning cavity where his nose had been. Galpin had wallowed and writhed in his own blood until it stopped flowing from the severed artery in his neck. Of the four recruits, Billy Baxter alone was now numbered among the living.

With the advent of the clearer atmosphere, Vehrmon quickly ascertained the diminished strength of his adversaries. Only Baxter, hidden and protected by the fallen Damron, escaped his swift appraisal. Orders rolled from his lips in

Shawanese and in the tongues of the Wyandot and the Delaware. Four warriors leaped from their places of concealment and rushed down the bank.

Jim Trench hastily withdrew the ramrod from the rifle barrel, aimed and fired. The foremost of the savages rolled down the slope like a rounded object. The others, close on his heels, tumbled over him and into the water. By the time the assaulters had recovered their bearings and their weapons, the White men were ready for them, shooting down two of the trio as their hands reached for the wood planking on the front of the boat. The third had carefully aimed at Trench's head, catching him in an exposed position from the outer corner of the craft. When the trigger was pulled, there was no report. The Indian had forgotten his weapon had been in the water. He made a miraculous escape, lead from four guns narrowly missing him in his zig-zagging sprint to cover.

Meanwhile, Billy Baxter, working under the impediment of Monk Damron's dead weight, maneuvered to get his hands on the sweep oar, a feat he had nearly accomplished before the bobbing of the lifeless head and shoulders drew the marksmanship of the bloodthirsty ones above the river and the ire of Blackie Vehrmon at what appeared to be an indestructible foe. The concentration of bullets literally plowed the back of the shirt from their target, but still it kept on moving. Baxter gave a tremendous push on the oar and the boat, at last, paralleled the shore and moved toward the far bank. Another mighty exertion and the craft floated farther away from the Redskins whose wild cries bespoke their rage at this threat to the commanding advantage they had enjoyed thus far in the battle. Vehrmon's arm lifted and swept forward. Eight Indians made for the stream, entering it some seventy-five feet in front of the flatboat, and began the crossing in single file. Each held his weapon aloft and free of contact with the water. Three shots rang from the boat and three savages went under.

In the rear, Billy Baxter grew careless, raising himself to half-height. The riddled but still sheltering carcass of Damron slumped and dropped to one side. Instantly, there was a lone, quick report and Baxter swayed. Before another rifle could be aimed at him, he had fallen.

CHAPTER 36

As he looked back at those in his charge, Abe Foster didn't like what he saw. "Scetter out, thar! Whut th' hell yers think yers ez doin'? Jest 'cause we comes ter a openin' don't mean yer kin git so damn sociuble! Thar yer be, all bunched up tergether, jest like a bull's ass in fly-time. Thet's jest th' way Blackie Vermin wants yers ter git, so jest yers keep a-doin' whut he wants, 'n' mebbe they won't none uv yers hev ter walk back ter th' licks—ever damn one uv yer bastards'll git hisse'f kilt."

Abe made his impression. The men assumed less vulnerable positions upon the flat stretch of open land, which was clear of any cover save for a patch of cornstalks still standing from the previous season and which lay some distance ahead to their left, bordering the river.

Well out in front of his group, Mercer cautiously entered the thicket at the same time Abe was making his pointed analogy to the beleaguered bull. He moved cautiously through the old cane, placing his feet in near silent sequence. In the manner of the woodsman, he divided the sector ahead of him into three portions, staring intently, first at the right, then at the middle, and lastly at the part that ended on the far shore of Salt River. A few steps more and he would be in a clearing. He hesitated before leaving the cane. There were two beech trees in the foreground, perhaps a hundred and fifty feet away. Their trunks appeared to be on a line and about five feet from each other. Except for the beeches, there were no obstructions between himself and the renewed forest several hundred yards ahead. He gave thought to the near bank of the stream. Perhaps he had better check that portion of its course that was hidden from view. As the idea moved from perception to acceptance, his eyes remained focused upon the two trees. His nerves tightened. Was it a trick of his vision, or had an object crossed the light between them? He soon had his answer. An Indian darted to the bank and dropped from sight. Mercer raised his rifle and prepared to break for the river. Suddenly, he saw the top of a man's head appear above the edge of the bank, midway between himself and the point where the savage had just disappeared. The head momentarily went below the line of vision, but he lined his rifle and awaited its reappearance. There it was! His finger tightened on the trigger, but he did not complete its pressure. A White man had come up over the bank! It was Hawkstraw!

Mercer had not remembered him as being a member of the party when it left the licks. What was his purpose? Was he here to aid settlers, or did he come as an expectant scavenger? Whatever the reason, he was moving alone and independent of the other White men. Fascinated, and ignoring his duty to warn his comrades of the presence of the Indian, Barth followed the route's movements as the latter appeared to be heading for the trees. It was then that Mercer, from his place of concealment, saw the savage, a Delaware, come up over the bank. As he crouched, he drew his tomahawk. Barth fired as the war axe left the Indian's hand, the successful shot causing the tomahawk to wobble in its flight so that its handle bounced harmlessly off Hawkstraw's shoulder. Though stunned, the dumb one realized his narrow escape and as Mercer, who was responsible for saving his life, came clearly into his view, he ran to him and grasped his hand. While no sound came from his lips, Hawkstraw's eyes met his savior's, and the gratitude Barth found in them satiated his heart.

Tom Chism and Abe Foster restrained their men with difficulty. Mercer's shot had alerted the entire company. When he and Hawkstraw returned to the line of advance and the rest of his men, Tom and Abe were waiting.

"Why didn't you let us know what was happenin' before actin' like a hero? You might have been a dead one, you know." Tom Chism wasn't too pleased and showed it. But after Barth's explanation, he was satisfied.

"Whut yer gonner do with thet dumb son-uv-a-bitch?" asked Abe, pointing to Hawkstraw with his free hand, as he picked his nose with a finger of the other.

This was no time for niceties, but Barth wished Abe hadn't used such language in referring to the young unfortunate. Turning toward Hawkstraw, Mercer asked, "You want to stay and help us fight the Indians?"

Hawkstraw nodded his head up and down.

"Good. I can use you. You stay with me, you understand?"

Again came the affirmative movement of the head.

The three leaders now bent their joint minds to an analysis of the situation.

"If'n Vermin's hup ter his usual tricks, thet thar dead Injun's got some friends uv his'n in thet woods hup yonder. Most liken, they ain't more'n eight er ten uv 'em, but thar'll be some more on behine them a-ways. Them whut we fust meets'll be jest ter kinder slow us down some."

Mercer and Chism agreed with Abe's shrewd reasoning. "They surely picked a good spot to delay us," said Barth.

"There isn't a bit of cover but those two beech trees from here to the forest."

"Yup," drawled Abe. "They's some uv us is shore ter git hit 'fore we gits in thar, less'n we be moughty lucky."

Their deliberation was brief. The conclusions reached were simply that all must keep as close as possible to the ground in the advance. None were to become separated from the main body of men. Thus, there would be less likelihood of an ambush or of capture by the Indians.

When the discussion had ended, Abe made his way to where the dead savage had fallen. Although the Indian's head was fully shaven, he nevertheless scalped him, hanging the hairless trophy from his waistband.

From the distance, rolling to them on a westerly breeze, came the sound of a solitary rifle shot—the one that was to shortly result in the death of Tom Graham. A few minutes later, they heard the echo of Jim Trench's avenging weapon.

"How far away do you think those shots were?"

Tom Chism studied Barth's query, then gave his opinion. "I'd say around two miles. What you think, Abe?"

"'Bout th' same, mebbe not thet far. One thing sartin—we'uns hed better git goin'. Hain't no one shootin' at no game this time uv day. Hit's trubble, an' nuthin' els't."

The three Indians in the woods ahead fired sparsely at them and then made for the eight comrades supporting their not-too-immediate rear.

The men from the licks pressed forward relentlessly, spurred on by the increased volume of musketry coming from the west, now being heard as frequent ragged salvos.

The retreating three met the eight who awaited them, and the eleven savages began to carry out Vehrmon's orders to delay the White men's progress.

Virgil Mallory and Justin Gibbs remembered their orders too—those of Mace Hardin. The first contact had been made. From opposite ends of Mercer's skirmish line, they waited for him to move into their proximities.

Mallory's opportunity was not long in coming. He saw the savage as he stroked the rod in the barrel of his rifle. Mercer was between the two and directly in the line of fire. Mallory called craftily to the men nearest him. "See thet Injun there behine th' fork uv thet poplar yonder? Watch me git him."

The stage was set. The killing of Captain Mercer would be a tragic but excusable mistake. The assassin drew as careful a bead as he had ever drawn on any target. The powder flashed in the pan of his gun, but the fire in that of Hawkstraw's gun came first. Mallory keeled over, a crimson blotch behind his left ear.

Mercer felt the hot, stabbing sensation along the side of his jaw and the warm blood flowing as he went down. When he came to, Hawkstraw's face was above his as he knelt beside him.

Mallory's intended alibi was there too. "Cap'n, it 'pears yore real lucky. Mallory wuz aimin' at thet Injun behine thet poplar tree. He called his shot 'fore he fired. He musta turn his head, 'cause he got it in th' back uv his noggin."

"He hurt bad?" Mercer asked dazedly.

"Bad as he kin be—he's dead."

Hawkstraw shook his head violently as he listened to them talk, but Barth was still too addled for his mind to attach any significance to the wild gesture. Although there was intense pain in the lower side of his jaw, the wound proved to be superficial. When he had recovered from the shock of the leaden trauma, he attempted to arise. All except Hawkstraw had moved on in pursuit of the withdrawing enemy. The mute one helped him to his feet and, grasping his hand, led him back to the body of Virgil Mallory. He pulled so strongly Mercer had to look at the fatal injury while Hawkstraw placed his own palm upon his chest, tapping it rapidly. He pointed his rifle at the spot where the ball had entered the head. With his hand, he motioned from Mallory to Mercer. Pointing toward the poplar, he shook his head as he had done earlier, and followed this movement by the repetition of the touching first of the sprawled form on the ground and then on the one whom he had saved. His eyes looked to the other for understanding.

Still incredulous, Mercer asked, "You are sure he meant to kill me?"

Hawkstraw tapped his head with his forefinger in knowing fashion.

"How did you know it?"

Again, the finger of wisdom conveyed its answer.

"I hope you did right, but I'd be awfully sorry if you were wrong."

The mute slowly shook his head.

"Right or wrong, I thank you for your kind intention."

Hawkstraw smiled and by pantomime endeavored to tell him that he had only repaid him for the previous saving of his own life. The two shook hands. The heart of the one knew that of the other.

Ahead of them, the rifle reports were becoming more pronounced, and Barth sent his silent companion to join the rest of the adventurers. He determined to permit himself to become more settled before he reentered the engagement.

The sun was well on its journey to its zenith. Its hot rays helped cake the blood on his wound, and he believed himself to be sufficiently revived to return to the fray. Reaching the trees, he found that the fighting had moved to a more distant battleground. He eased between two thorn bushes, toward a path made by those who had preceded him. The sling on his powderhorn snagged on the thorns as he reached the way and he turned to disengage it. He had little trouble freeing the strap, but before he could turn around, the muzzle of a rifle was thrust squarely between his shoulder blades. He had no time to weigh his captor's identity, but only to await the expected, momentary discharge of the weapon. He was surprised, therefore, when he heard the voice of a White man.

"Mallory didn't do so good, did he? But yer done fer, now, my fine bucko. Yer has done caused all th' trouble thet yers will—"

The voice gurgled and the gun left its snug emplacement. Whirling around, Barth saw the man lying face down in a small pool of blood that had been created instantly. Behind him stood Hawkstraw, a smile playing upon his lips as he noted the evident astonishment on Mercer's features. He ran the knife's blade between his thumb and forefinger, forcing the blood from the metal. Then, as Barth struggled to speak, he wiped it clean on the sleeve of his jacket.

Barth knew the knife. He had seen many of its duplicates from the first day he had ventured into Bullitt's Lick. He reached down and turned the victim upon his back. The head rolled crazily, exposing a bit of the pale-colored neck bone. Hawkstraw had almost decapitated him. Although Barth had not recognized the threatening voice, the face of the dead man was most familiar. It was Justin Gibbs.

Mercer's eyes told the dumb one he had been right in the first killing and now the second. There flashed through his returning senses the recollection of his wonderment when the two of them had so readily volunteered to serve with him on this dangerous mission. There came to him also the name of the one who had ordered his execution—Mace Hardin!

Fast upon this realization came another dawn of understanding. Mace must have known of his coming to the licks originally. But was it like him not to have finished the attack that he had made that morning if he had done so? Big and powerful, he would not have run away, leaving his task uncompleted. It couldn't have been him that time. Maybe the silent one who walked patiently beside him could supply the answer to that too. However, he would not risk the question. Whatever Hawkstraw may have been, or may have done before, each breath he would take for the rest of his life, he would owe to him.

The directed course of his thinking stopped abruptly. He had not thanked Hawkstraw! Turning his head, he said earnestly, "I am doubly in your debt. I can never repay you for what you did."

His companion smiled appreciatively and laid his hand on Mercer's arm, an act that carried with it his full acknowledgment of the expressed gratitude.

How the forces of the White man had fared elsewhere along the lines, Barth could not, at this moment, know. But he counted four dead Indians, all scalped, before he and Hawkstraw caught up with his own volunteers. Other than Gibbs and Mallory, they had not seen one adventurer wounded or dead.

As the word was passed that he had rejoined the group, Barth wondered if there were any others who had designs upon his life. He pondered also what action he would take were he to be fortunate enough to return unscathed to the licks. The matter was out in the open now. It had to be either him or Mace Hardin. There could be no pitched battle—Hardin's brawlers were too numerous. What could he do? The two unsuccessful attacks would not be the last to be tried, that much was certain in his mind. How far could he trust Hawkstraw? After all, he was Mace Hardin's son. This reasoning brought on confusion. Maybe Hardin hadn't ordered his death—it was still his son who had saved him. If not Hardin, who else would want him out of the way?

A heavy whisper that seemed to come from a nearby tree startled him. "I reckined yer wuz a dead son-uv-a-bitch th' last time I seed yer."

It was Abe Foster. Barth grinned as he said, "I wasn't one of those lucky ones you talked about back in that clearing. In fact, from what I've seen, I think I was the only unlucky one in our party."

"Thet's just about hit—hain't none uv we'uns bin more'n scratched. I bin takin' good keer uv yore an' my boys tergether. Th' Injuns hain't doin' so good, tho'." His white teeth loomed as lights against the darkness of his whiskers as he pointed to the string of scalps around his waist.

"How about Tom and his men?"

"Don't b'leeve he's lost more'n one, mebbe two, an' they hain't kilt dead. He's movin' on aroun' from th' right—we'uns ez tryin' ter squiz them Injuns inter th' river."

Pieces of oak bark sprayed on Mercer's head and shoulders.

"Better git yer some kiver. Yer jest mought not be so lucky agin, yer know."

With that, Abe was gone.

Barth could hear firing on beyond the immediate front at what seemed to be fairly close range. If it was those coming up the stream, and if they could just hold out a little longer.

"Thar goes th' sons-uv-bitches! They's fallin' back again! Keep a-pushin' 'em!" Abe's roar was a tremendous asset in fighting such as this. When not bellowing orders, he alternately hummed and sang his favorite refrain, as he was doing now. "Jes' scratch yore ear, an' scratch yore ass." He was humming the rest of it as he disappeared behind a large oak.

*

Black Lester cursed as he witnessed the telling effect of the fire from the boat. When he saw the three savages attempting to cross the river succumb to the defender's rifles, he called the others back to shore immediately. He now had eleven warriors—enough to successfully conclude the attack—if he had the time in which to do it. But the sands of time were running fast and all against him. He could tell by the sound of rifle fire coming from the east that the enemy was not more than a mile away. Only prompt action and new strategy could prevent what would surely be considered by his superiors as an inexcusable failure to accomplish his mission. He would not permit his reasoning to weigh the consequences of the defeat of his objective. He summoned the foremost of those emerging from the water. In native tongue, he told him, "Git ter them," pointing eastwardly, "an' tell 'em I said for 'em ter all come back here fast. Then I wants eight uv 'em ter cross th' river 'jest a little out uv th' range of them bastards in th' boat. Th' rest I wants on shore here with me."

Drops of river water still glistening upon his bronze-colored shoulders and back, the Wyandot started on his way the moment Vehrmon had finished.

The renegade Vehrmon cupped his hands over his eyes, shielding them from the infiltering sun as he searched for the Delaware he had ordered to the treetop. How in the hell kin them damn saltmakers see 'em ter shoot 'em like they does, if'n I kin't fine 'em, an' me knowin' whar they's s'posed ter be, he thought in nervous aggravation. Then he said to himself, with deep satisfaction as the breeze played upon the leaves of the lofty maple the savage had scaled, "I sees him now, th' red-bellied bastard." He stared steadfastly, then came the information he wanted. The lookout held up three fingers. Translated, this meant there were only three men alive on the flatboat. Blackie Vehrmon continued to look upward, hopeful for the sake of certainty that the signal would be repeated. Instead, he saw the Delaware take aim and fire. Seconds later, the Indian solemnly turned and raised his palm. Two fingers were upright.

On the stream below, Santoire scanned the tree for the telltale trace of smoke, but the mild wind had already dissipated it. He knew only the general direction of the shot that had just gone through Jim Trench's shoulder muscle. Chancing it, he fired into the tallest part of the maple. A flurry in the foliage gave the answer of success as the Redman's precipitous descent began. The yielding branches dropped him in a delayed series of falls, until his lifeless body thumped to the earth some thirty to forty feet from where Vehrmon was standing.

"Two uv them an' ten uv us—nine," he corrected, as he remembered the dispatched courier. At last, the victory was in his hands. He would order all the men into the river. Coming onto the boat from front and rear, the two survivors would be quickly overcome.

Santoire had slithered himself to the extreme rear of the craft, easing over the bodies of his fallen comrades whose riddled corpses imparted to the underside of his garments sticky stains from their congealing blood. His right hand found the oar, and he drew himself up and rested on his left elbow. Wedging his foot against the ribs of a red-headed cadaver, he dipped the oar handle and pulled it toward him. He was able to complete two strenuous sweeps before the Indians peppered the spot with lead. He felt the oar jerk as their shots struck it and chewed away at the wood. There followed a pause, and he thought it safe to make another attempt at moving the boat nearer the south shore while the enemy was reloading. He lifted his hand upward and his fingers grasped the rounded end of the sweep. Suddenly, his forearm burned like fire as he heard a rifle bark. Before he could lower the injured limb, the hot blood had run down into the hollow of his armpit.

Blackie Vehrmon chuckled as he sank the ramrod into the barrel of his gun. "Thet's one son-uv-a-bitch thet hain't gonner do much with thet arm fer a spell. If'n them Red sons-uv-bitches could shoot like me, I wouldn't have no damn worries."

But before the arm had been rendered useless, its efforts had not been without effect. The boat moved cross-stream until it was only a short distance from the opposite bank. Acutely aware of this, Vehrmon rushed the remaining savages into the river.

*

Tom Chism had at last encircled the Indians' flank on the north. Through a running contact with Mercer and Abe Foster, the latter knew of his determination to crowd the savages into a pocket bordering Salt River. The movement, properly executed, would result in an ambuscade and the annihilation of the enemy. He could not know that at this precise moment, the breathless Wyandot was expelling his message to the Shawnee sub-chieftain, Yellow Hawk, and that Vehrmon's orders to return were being carried out. When he gave the signal to open fire, he soon discovered the prize was lost. Recovering from this disappointment, the three White leaders led their men in what proved to be a full, unrestrained pursuit of the fleeing warriors. From a slight rise in the terrain, Mercer and Abe surveyed the straight stretch of the river before them. There was no activity to be seen. They swept forward like a furious wave, but the savages, aided by their head start, were far in front of them and out of range of accurate fire. They had reached a minor bend in the shoreline before the panorama of the flatboat and its attackers unfolded itself. They made out the motionless craft, apparently devoid of any life, and the Indians swimming toward it. Then, nearer to him, Barth saw Yellow Hawk and his band coming out of the water on the far shore and passed the word to the right for a volley on his signal. The thunder of the guns filled the air as he gave the sign. If any were yet alive on the boat, they would take heart. The Indians would take heed and might desist from continuing the assault.

Blackie Vehrmon heard the fire of the oncoming riflemen and was impressed. He commanded the withdrawal of those in the water and all but one obeyed immediately. That one had reached the front of the boat and would not permit himself to be denied the taking of the White men's scalps. His eyes beheld the immobilized bodies as he began lifting himself from the stream. That was all he saw. Jim Trench still had one good arm, and with all its power swung the butt of his gun against the invader's head. The unconscious savage hung over the planking and Trench kicked his painted face, dislodging the inert body and causing it to fall back into the river. Multiple bubbles rose to the surface. His strength thoroughly spent, Trench dropped to the floor of the boat. From the rear, Santoire, weakened by loss of blood, had watched helplessly. He heard the salvo ordered by Mercer but his fainting mind believed it came from the Indian on shore and that this was the end. Had he been able to see his enemies, he would have seen the returning Wyandot and four other braves as they ran to where Vehrmon had assembled the remnant of his forces.

Black Lester raged in wrathful disgust. He had failed miserably. His men were a pack of disgruntled dissidents. Not one bloody trophy hung from any of their waists and they blamed Vehrmon for the absence. They mocked him openly, taunting that he was fit to wage war only against squaws and children. It took the appearance of their first pursuers to stop their recriminating bickering and to send them not in retreat but in headlong flight into the deep forest. They carried their wounded with them, but should the White men press too closely, these would be instantly abandoned.

From his concealment on the south shore, Yellow Hawk saw the wild departure of Vehrmon and the others. He had planned to board the boat, now so conveniently located for his purpose. He and his men would take the scalps and carry away the plunder. He would run the renegade chieftain, Vehrmon, to everlasting shame when he proudly displayed the evidence of the success of his leadership and his men gave forth with scalp halloos upon their return to the rendezvous. Great would be his stature among the Redmen, when the word spread far and wide that he had accomplished that which the famed Vehrmon had been unable to do—the same Vehrmon upon whom his Red brothers heaped such lavish praise around their council fires.

His moments of envisioned glory were short lived. The White men, in great numbers, came into full view on the north shore. He ordered a few scattered shots, none of which hit their marks. When the enemy retaliated in kind, and then sent men into the river above and below his position, he reluctantly made the decision to move eastward and lead his braves as a raiding party against such hapless settlers as might be found outside the sanctuary of the garrisons near Bullitt's Lick. He would circle around and move from the east toward the rendezvous on the other side of the knobs. His band would yet have some scalps to show for their efforts when this day ended.

CHAPTER 37

Across the river, Chism, Foster and Mercer took hurried counsel. As a result, Abe chose twenty men and set out after Vehrmon's fleeing rabble. This action was not intended as a full-fledged pursuit but only to reconnoiter. If the Indians had, in fact, finally withdrawn and no ruse was involved, Foster's detail was to return upon the completion of the reconnaissance. If their investigation of the situation revealed the possibility of continuing peril, a courier would carry that information back to those remaining at the shore and all then would move immediately to reinforce the exploring party.

Meanwhile, it being evident that Yellow Hawk and his band had definitely left the scene, Mercer recalled the men from the stream. He disrobed and dove headfirst into the river. The water was cold but invigorating. Using long, powerful strokes he quickly reached the flatboat and hoisted himself onboard.

His first look sickened him. This was Charon's ferryboat, all its passengers were dead. All but him. A sense of shame at his own nakedness came over him in the presence of this dire carnage. Had it not been for their sides—blood-smeared and pitted by countless, wild-flying ricochets—the kettles would have readily lent themselves to the imagination as being large funeral urns. These things Mercer thought as he stepped carefully among the fallen. He recognized the still form of Jim Trench and, from a distance, that of Jack Santoire—the gold ring in his pierced right ear proclaiming his identity. The footing was inclined to be slippery, the wet soles of his feet tending to liquify the blood on the deck beneath them. He raised his leg to step over one who was bare from the waist down, his thighs colored a dull red. A sickly red too was the man's limp, uncircumcised penis. He watched as a green fly nimbly ran its length. Vanity of vanities, saith the preacher. The life-producing organ whose like had been the source of birth of all these cold bodies around him inspired this recollection of the words of the son of David, the king of Jerusalem. He turned the man's head, and he knew him. It was Tom Graham. At last, he reached the end of this macabre row. But before he could lay hold of the sweep oar, he had to lift a corpse whose jacket had been rented from its back, exposing a mass of bullet holes. As he moved the body and piled it on top of another, he felt as though he were handling a heavy rag doll. The arms flayed aimlessly and the head rolled loosely. He swung the boat about and pulled for the north shore. During the brief crossing, he resurveyed the grisly scene. There had been no previous opportunity to know any of the men except the three whom he had recognized, but his lack of familiarity with the others did not lessen either his feeling of shock or of sympathy. His mind wandered from the set, agonized features of the faces of the dead and their mutilated bodies to the two poles of all human existence, time and chance. Whose lights and shadows determine destiny, either by commission or omission, the insoluble mystery of the realm of "ifs." If the men from the licks had started earlier; if the boat had come yesterday or even tomorrow; if instead of coming by water they had come overland and if they had done so, if the Indians might not yet have attacked them and with the same result. If . . . if . . . if . . .

"What th' hell's th' matter with you, are you deaf?" Chism's voice was part vexation.

Barth looked up as sturdy hands pulled the flatboat onto the bank. "I'm sorry, but I didn't hear you," he replied.

Deep indeed had been his engrossment. Not only Tom Chism but also most of those on shore had called to him, anxiously inquiring whether any of those on the raft were yet alive. When Tom again asked this of him, he answered, "I'm afraid they are all dead."

While Mercer donned his clothing, Chism took his place. He affectionately patted the head of his trusted friend, Jim Trench, and was about to pass him by when he noticed the trembling of what he had supposed was Trench's lifeless hand. Quickly and joyfully, he called for help in removing him to land. Glad cries rang out when Trench opened his eyes. They did not attempt to question him, but instead, Tom Chism procured a piece of linen from the contents of one of the kettles and, dampening it with river water, used it to cool the brow of the stricken man. As he ministered to Trench, he asked Mercer, "Think we ought to go after Abe Foster? They been gone quite a spell now."

"Let's wait a little longer. Abe's too smart to be trapped. And even if he did find trouble, he'd get word to us somehow."

Chism nodded his intention to abide by Mercer's counsel. Wisely he did so, for it was only a matter of minutes before the exploring party came from the dense woodland. Abe was in the lead, a string of scalps in his hand.

"We runned them Red bastards but we never kotched hup with 'em. But we made hit so damn hot fer 'em they hed ter drap three uv they wounded." He held up his bloody trophies and picked among them. "Thar they be, them three right thar. I sculped ever dead, Red son-uv-a-bitch whut we found. Them sculps," he continued, pointing to the flatboat, "is fer them thar pore bastards whut never hed no chanc't ter take 'em."

Chism wanted to know more about the enemy. "Where'd you last see th' Injuns?"

"A-headin' north, an' fast. They cain't be more'n twelve or fourteen uv 'em, at th' most. They whar movin' too fast ter be many more'n thet. Take m' word fer hits, they's done fightin' fer terday, an' mebbe a lotsa more days then this'n." He had given his report. Now he changed the subject. "Who's thet pore feller a-lying thar?" He walked over to see for himself. "Why hit's Jim Trench! Git hup, ya ole fakin' son-uv-a-bitch! Yer hain't hurt none, yer jest makin' a axcuse ter take hit easy."

Uncertain as to Foster's intentions, both Mercer and Tom Chism stepped between him and the injured man.

"Ain't you got no sense a-tall? Jim's got it bad in th' shoulder and Lord knows where else," Tom said angrily.

Jim Trench opened his eyes and smiled. "'Lo, Abe. Hep . . . me . . . up."

Abe looked pityingly at the two men restraining him and let out one of his monstrous guffaws. "Why, yer fellers jest don't know Jim Trench. I does. Why, I saw him a-fightin' a b'ar one time when th' furry son-uv-a-bitch knocked Jim thirty foot away. Ole Jim got hisse'f hup an' cut th' insides outer thet critter. Whut's more, him an' me et them raw stuffin's. They wuz real good, wuzzn't they, Jim?"

Trench smiled feebly and nodded his head. Perhaps the memory of consuming the uncooked entrails was responsible, but whatever it was, it induced the necessary strength in him to stand unsteadily upon his feet while Abe fashioned a sling to support the injured shoulder.

"Too bad," said Abe, "thet they hain't no deer handy. I'd cut his throat an' let Ole Jim swaller th' blood. He'd be strong liken an ox in a minute, if'n they wuz eny blood fer 'im." Condescending to permit Trench to sit on the ground, Abe propped Jim's back against the base of a walnut tree. "Is he th' onliest one whut's livin'?" Abe asked, as he straightened up.

"Don't know for shore," said Tom, "but it 'pears that might be th' facts. We just started lookin' at 'em a little 'fore you come back."

"Wal, let's git th' hell on with th' lookin'!" Abe roared. "Lemme on thet boat!"

"Hold your horses, Abe. Your feet are too big to move among the bodies," Mercer admonished.

"I reckin yores is liken a dancer's, huh?"

Abe's sarcastic comment made Barth laugh. "I don't know about that, but if anyone else is alive on there, all you'd have to do is to step on him and he'd be deader than any Indian could ever kill him."

"Mebbe, yer mought jest be right on thet." His raucous laughter rang to the treetops.

Chism came upon the semi-nude Graham and he cursed the savages with every oath at his command. He controlled his emotions until he reached the prostrate Santoire, and he repeated his tears and maledictions. Then, surprise stopped both abruptly as he called out to those congregated at the front ends "Here's four I ain't never saw before!"

Abe Foster spoke his immediate thought. "Mebbe they's renegades!" He brandished his knife as he continued. "Th' least we'uns kin do ez ter sculp th' dirty bastards an' heave 'em in th' river! Hain't fitten thet them scum lies 'longside our boys!"

"Hold your tongue, Abe," Chism ordered. "Let's be sure of what we're doin'. We can ask Jim Trench about them when he's feelin' better. Then, if they turn out to be renegades, you can do what you want with 'em."

Acting prematurely upon Tom's suggestion, Abe was kneeling by Jim Trench's side in a matter of seconds. "Whut 'bout them four strangers on th' boat, Jim? They he'p th' Injuns?"

Trench shook his head weakly, then answered. "Naw. Them wuz all good boys. Wuz comin' tuh work with we'uns. Jined up with us at th' Falls. Good boys, special thet black-headed one. Is eny others livin'?"

"We hain't finished lookin' at em," Abe answered. "Yer jest set whar yer be a spell. Soon's I fines out, I'll let yer know." Abe raised himself and relayed the information.

"I'll need some help here, two will be enough. Any more, an' it'll be too crowed to move around." Answering Chism's call, Mercer and Ed Jenks climbed quickly aboard. On shore, Barth saw Hawkstraw pointing to where Yellow Hawk and his warriors had been. He rolled his arm eastward, took his knife and put its edge to his scalp, then sheathed his blade, and raised his rifle as though aiming at a target. Mercer caught the significance instantly. "Tom, we're overlooking something. Someone ought to get to the settlement and warn the people that there are Indians heading that way."

Chism showed his concurrence by designating two men to spread the alarm. As they were being named, Hawkstraw pointed hopefully to himself and was quite crestfallen when he was not chosen. Barth nodded his disappointment and said to Tom. "I wish you would send another man along—the mute over there."

"You mean Hawkstraw? I didn't even know he was with us. Since I wasn't countin' on him anyways, can't be no loss if he left too."

Hawkstraw was overjoyed. Ever since Yellow Hawk and his party had headed eastward, he had been most concerned. Aaron Flinden's cabin was on the south side of the river and would most certainly be in danger if the Indians stayed on the same side of the stream. While he wished no harm to the Flindens, his consuming fear was for Nancy. As the three raced from sight, it was Hawkstraw who led in the race to the garrisons and their immediate environs.

It was not a pleasant task. Starting at the front, Barth and Tom Chism began moving the dead men. Ed Jenks was to lift the corpses, aided by either Mercer or Chism, as the position of the dead bodies dictated, and the latter two would then place the cadavers in a straight row, two bodies deep, alongside one of the lines of kettles. This arrangement would give clear passage the length of the boat and would provide free space at each end.

Jenks gave a terrified yell. So unexpected was the outburst that Chism and Mercer dropped the body they were then handling. Excited inquiries came from those on shore. Jenks did not leave them long in doubt as to what had occasioned his piercing scream. "They's suthin' kotched holt uv my ankle!"

It was true, a blood-streaked hand still retained its unyielding hold, though the frightened Jenks had kicked vigorously in an effort to free himself from its clutch. The encircling fingers belonged to Jack Santoire. As they sought to loose Santoire's grip, Barth heard a whispered moan. Tom Chism quickly found its source. It came from the lips of a curly black-haired young man upon whose face rivulets of blood had coursed and dried. Their source lay somewhere beneath the spot where the hair had become matted on his head. Abe again roused Jim Trench from his stupor. "Yer shore muster bin hup moughty late las' night, bein' so damn sleepy-headed terday." As Trench opened his eyes, Abe asked him, "Whut th' hell is th' name uv th' young feller with th' black ha'r?"

The reply was slow in coming. When it finally came, it was in strained, faltering speech. "Bax . . . Baxter. Billy Bax . . . Billy Baxter."

"Wal, yer ole faker, he's still livin', him an' Jack Santoire."

Trench's eyes drooped shut as he acknowledged Abe's words. "Thet's good. Real g-good." The effort had taken its taxing toll and his head dropped forward.

After the two recently discovered wounded had been made as comfortable as possible, Abe left them and climbed into the flatboat.

"Now, what in th hell do you think you're a-doin', Abe?"

"Don't go tryin' ter git me off'n this here boat, Tom Chism. No tellin' how many more uv them pore bastards ez still breathin'. An' stackin' 'em hup liken yore a-doin', yer prob'ly makin' some pore wimmens widders whut don't hev ter be none sech. Bet thet thar son-uv-a-bitch whut yer an' Mercer's a-holdin' now hain't nowhars near dead."

Barth and Tom looked at the shattered body of Monk Damron, which they were preparing to place in line with the others. Tom turned his eyes upon the giant lumbering toward them, then said to him, "Abe, you damn idiot, this here boy's got so damn much lead in 'im he's heavier than any two we has lifted!"

"Never mine 'bout th' lead. Lemme hev a look at 'im. Thet lead don't mean nuthin' a-tall. Why, onc't I knowed a feller name uv Stubbs, Charlie Stubbs, over in Virginny. Wal, I seed thet son-uv-a-bitch git hisse'f shot ten times. We guv 'im some water ter drink, an' demme if'n th' damn stuff dint run right outer his belly frum three diffrunt places. Thet's how damn bad he whar hit."

Barth interrupted. "This fellow here must have been hit at least twenty-five times!"

"Don't make no diffrunce. Stubbs wuz prob'ly hit more'n this pore bastard. We'uns dint hev no time fer ter be a-countin' no bullet holes. We wuz interested in savin' his life, not in seein' how much lead wuz in 'im. Lemme look at thet pore feller!"

Abe not only examined Damron's corpse but also those of the others as well. He took longer with the one that had a hole where the nose had formerly been. At length, he gave forth with a solemn observation. "Bet this here son-uv-a-bitch could've breathed real good, if'n he'd a-lived."

"Are you satisfied that they are all dead?"

"They's dead a'right. I admits ter thet."

Tom wasn't one to let Abe off so easily. "What about that fellow, Stubbs, you were talkin' about; he die too?"

"Hell no, he dint die! Why th' las' time I seed 'im, he hed done wore out three wives."

"How did he wear 'em out?" Before Abe could reply, Tom continued. "Oh, I know. I reckon he had a wife for each one of them three holes you was sayin' was in his belly. Must've been powerful tirin' on 'em, keepin' what he et an' drunk inside of 'im. No wonder they was wore out. He was lucky at that, th' law might've got 'im for havin' three wives at th' same time."

In spite of the grim surroundings, Barth was unable to control his laughter. Abe gave the two of them a look so sour it could be tasted and commented, "Some bastards jest hain't got no respeck fer th' dead."

Tom had his fun, now he was serious. "Let's count heads an' see how many able-bodied men we got left."

A quick but accurate roll call disclosed that out of the original forty men on the expedition, forty-one including Hawkstraw, five had been killed and six had been wounded, none seriously. Counting the three who had been sent to warn the settlement, there were thus twenty-seven of them fit for full duty. The remaining six, of which Mercer himself was one, had only minor disabilities and would be available in case of emergency. A breakdown of the casualties among the three leaders disclosed that Mercer had lost two men—Gibbs and Mallory—and had no wounded. Abe Foster had lost none and only one wounded. Chism, whose flanking maneuver had drawn concentrated enemy fire, had three dead and five disabled.

Tom called to Ed Jenks. "Ed, I want you to take th' boat to th' licks. You'll have two men with you and there'll be ten more on shore, moving along with the boat. That way, there'll be protection for you, an' you can have th' men change positions from time to time so that you can have fresh men on the sweep oar. You ought to be able to make it to the licks before nightfall. Th' rest of us is goin' to carry Jim Trench an' Santoire an' that other wounded fellow along with us."

Jim Trench got to his feet shakily. "I brung thet damn there boat this far. I-I-I'll take her th' rest uv th' way." He took a step and collapsed.

"I reckon that ends that idea of his'n. Now, fix up somethin' to tote them three hurt boys on. Be sure there ain't nothin' hard for 'em to lay on. Get somethin' like pine boughs, somethin' that'll give a little."

The makeshift litters were quickly constructed according to Chism's directions. As the last one was finished, and after he had selected the men to accompany the boat, he said to them, "On th' way back, we're goin' to pick up them five dead men of our'n, an' after we get 'em, we're goin' to bring 'em over to th' riverbank. You put 'em on th' boat with them others. I sure hope we can get back to makin' salt when we get home an' that there ain't been no trouble there."

The party moved off. Chism and Mercer walked alongside each other. Barth could see Tom's mind had new worries, and it wasn't long before he knew their cause. "I'm wonderin' if that damn Mace Hardin ain't done somethin' to my works."

No amount of assurance by Barth could ease Chism's fears. He would not rest until he had seen the safe condition with his own eyes.

The party returned by the same route it had followed earlier, but somehow the distances between recognized points seemed much closer together than they had appeared before. When they reached the general locality where their comrades had been killed, Chism detailed five of those who had been under his command during the fighting to secure their bodies. At his own insistence, Abe went along with the detail. A halt was declared, and the stretcher bearers lowered their burdens gently to the ground. Jaws strained at tearing mouthfuls of dried deer meat, and tired bodies rested themselves, some against trees, and others upon the dank earth of the forest.

The three slain partisans were quickly located along with two dead, unscalped savages, a condition Abe quickly remedied, adding their number to the circle of those he had previously strung. Unexpected prizes were found in the form of two British rifles, causing Abe to remark, "Them Injuns muster bin in one helluva big hurry ter git away frum hyar." His contagious laugh drew reciprocal mirth from the others. Although he was a self-appointed member of the group, Abe assumed its leadership. One, he directed to carry the weapons recovered, those of the fallen adventurers and the two Indians. The remaining four were assigned to bear two of the victims, two live men to each of the two dead, on their trek to the Salt River's shore. Abe himself carried the third corpse, which was heavier than either of the others, lugging it effortlessly on his right hip, leaving his left arm free to carry his own rifle and those of the four men who bore the other bodies.

They were approaching the glade where their waiting companions rested when Abe's vigilant eyes spotted a moccasined foot high in the foliage of a tree to his left. A playing breeze had first covered, then uncovered it, exposing it to the view of any whose vision was sharp enough to detect its presence. Abe growled his words of warning and unceremoniously dropped the corpse and rifles. He moved catlike around the trunk of the tree, peering upward. He found that for which he was searching. The Indian was sprawled on the branches above, his legs and arms dangling. A little farther down, his rifle balanced itself upon a number of small crossing limbs. "Hit's a-right now, yers kin move on. I'll be hup with yers soon's I sculps thet damn bastard hup yonder."

If Abe's lust for scalps appeared fanatical, it was with good reason. As a boy of eight, he had watched, terror-stricken, from his place of hiding while a raiding party of Shawnees had tomahawked and scalped his mother and father. He heard the savages' devilish glee as they mutilated and tortured them, the pitiful moans of his parents that almost tore the heart from his young body. His mind still held the picture of a warrior astride a spotted horse, holding this mother's scalp in his upstretched hand, and how her beautiful golden tresses streamed in the breeze as the Indians rode away, their fierce halloos echoing through the little valley where his father had toiled so hard to make a home for him and his mother. He remembered his vain attempts to find some spark of life in their warm bodies and how he had cried himself to sleep by them. And how he was awakened the following morning by a drenching rain whose force was strong enough to wash away some of the blood, but was unable to force their eyelids over their eyes, eyes that always had held nothing but love for him in their glowing raptures, eyes dull and listless, seeing nothing. He could not forget his digging of the graves, and how he had struggled to ease the bodies ever so gently down inside them, how he had hated to cover with dirt those whom he loved so dearly. All these things had seared his youthful brain. As the young twig had been bent, so the giant tree had inclined. The anguish of that early experience was many years old but yet ever new. It was fresh now as he climbed from limb to limb until he reached the dead Indian and viciously cut away his scalp.

Those on the ground had marveled at Abe's agility despite his enormous size as he went up the tree. One remarked that he "clumb like he lived there." Then they had gone on ahead.

Needing the use of a free hand in his descent, Abe held the scalp between his teeth. One hand held the rifle of the fallen brave and, between the use of his forearm and the other hand, he made his way to the bottom. If there had been amazement at his swift ascent, it would have been replaced by incredulity at the manner in which he had descended. He did not bother to string his latest trophy. Still holding it in his mouth, he gathered the firearms and the dead adventurer under his arms and strode toward the river.

Tom Chism was about to inquire as to Abe's absence when the big woodsman made his fright-inspiring entrance. "Like some wild animal, carrying its kill in its mouth," was the way Mercer was later to describe it.

"You oughtn't to do that, Abe," Chism chided. "Someways, you're as bad as them savages."

Abe removed the offending portion of the Indian's topknot from his mouth after depositing his burdens in a convenient spot next to where Herman Tressel was sitting. As he bent down, he inhaled the strong fumes comin from Tressel's pipe. "Demme!" he exclaimed. He spit tobacco juice with his exclamation, producing a yellowish-brown overlay on the bloody traces of the scalp that had stained his black whiskers. Tressel continued his methodical puffing. Abe pointed a massive forefinger at the German and said, "Herman, I wuddn't wantcher ter never let them Injuns git a-halt uv yer, but I shore as hell wisht them red sons-uv-bitches wud git holt uv thet damn pipe!"

Tressel puffed all the harder and replied, "On der vad uf terbacker mitt der troat you schudt, schoke, yet!" Pensive, he added dryly, pointing to the nearby corpse, "Dot feller dedt?"

A voice from the gathering amplified Tressel's banter. "Ain't none uv 'em dead til they begins tuh stink. Ain't thet right, Abe?"

Abe glowered, then laughed in company with the good-natured fun at his expense.

CHAPTER 38

The homeward journey was resumed and continued without incident save for the momentary returning to consciousness of Santoire and Baxter. Jim Trench's condition was unchanged. Loss of blood and complete nervous exhaustion served to keep him mercifully oblivious to the often violent bumps and jolts of the passage over the rough ground. As they neared the clearing where they had been pinned down by the first of Vehrmon's band, there was a moment of surprise and of awe upon the discovery of the body of Justin Gibbs. Speculation ensued, chiefly over the fact that neither his scalp nor his rifle had been taken but after deliberation, it was the consensus that the Indian who killed him was either wounded simultaneously with the act or was being so sorely rushed he had no time for the further use of his knife. Abe Foster was not convinced, however, giving as his opinion that the killer would not have foregone his trophy under any circumstances. Mercer listened guiltily, but said nothing. He would reveal the cause of the deaths of both Gibbs and Mallory to Chism and Foster after his return to the licks. To make any open admission now might invite additional danger to himself.

They crossed the great open space separating the forest, and Mercer saw the cane stalks through which he had so carefully threaded his way. And the sober thought came upon him that but for the seemingly chance appearance of Hawkstraw, the sun above would have been beating down upon his remains, and the insects milling over his body. The mute one had prevented this. But what if he had been late, the slightest instant, with his shot? Or if he had missed? What if Hawkstraw had not disobeyed his orders to join those up ahead, instead of hovering near the thorn bushes? His would have been the corpse the adventurers found, and Gibbs would have been shrewd enough to have lifted his scalp. There would have been no wonderment as to the agent of his death. Suddenly the scene seemed old, as though, rather than having happened only this morning, the events were aged. His thinking became random until the party reached the spot where it had camped the previous evening. As he passed through, the apprehensions he had felt at that time were vivid once again. How futile had been his fears! His direst misgivings had never entertained the attempts upon his life by those of his own followers. *How much of life is spent in the dread of those things that never come to pass, and how little of it is given to realities*, he thought. There was justification, though, for certainly three of the dead consigned for shipment back to the licks must have had their individual doubts and fears. The shadow of "if" had fallen upon them, its light had shone upon him.

Reason seldom sleeps, even in the dullest brain, and never in an alert mind. It called to Barth that if he placed his foot in the line of its apparent trajectory, he would step squarely in a pile of fecal matter, deposited there early this morning by one of the men. A swarm of voracious flies buzzed from beneath his boot as it barely missed the offensive heap. The flies were green and their color brought back the sight of Tom Graham's body and the mood that had prevailed at that time, that of absolute futility. Since all were destined to dust, since sooner or later every pitcher would be broken at the fountain and every wheel at the cistern, and since man's steps inevitably take him to his long home, why does the spirit of man so move him that he should seek gain beyond his needs? Searching himself, Barth acknowledged the personal application of those thoughts. The ownership of the saltlicks was the least among the items of his inheritance. When he had determined to ascertain the cause for their being unprofitable, and had come to Kentucky on that account, he had thought such action to be in keeping with good stewardship, the fulfillment of an implied obligation he felt he owed his dead father for having left the properties to him. But now, he wondered if that had been entirely true. Had not the knowledge of the lucrative feature, the enormous profits to be realized, been fully, perhaps overpoweringly, present? Whatever may have been his past reasons for being here, the resolution now came upon him that he had seen all he wanted of raw death on this or any other wild frontier. That whatever motives might activate other men, his course would be to marry Dracie Claycomb at Harrodstown, if Reverend Wyeth or any other minister was there at that same time. And if not, to return to Williamsburg for the ceremony. He had only two desires: to marry Dracie and for them to live out the remainder of their lives together in the quiet, familiar surroundings of his father's beloved homeplace.

Even as he adopted this master plan for his future years, he knew that there was much to be done before he could ever take his leave of Bullitt's Lick. Mace Hardin would have to be discharged, and the services of a new overseer obtained. This, he admitted, could not be done right away, but he would get to work on the idea. Perhaps he would be able to find someone at Harrods, or at some of the other stations on the way. He had determined earlier that he would put off his visit to Dracie no longer. The first thing he intended doing when he got back to the licks was to write, telling her he was safe and that he was leaving for Harrodstown the day after tomorrow. With good luck, his letter would reach her almost a day in advance of his arrival. His thoughts drifted back to the cabin at Bairdstown and thence to those erotic excursions upon which only a lover's mind may embark.

How long he had been thus preoccupied, he did not know, when his ecstasy was shattered by a coarse-toned voice, even as an undue vibration is wont to shatter a goblet of finest glass, "Hear thet bell off yonder?"

Barth heard the tinkling nearby, and its sound was one of welcome to his ears. It meant they could not be too far from the settlement and the end of this harrowing experience.

Deep within the well of his unconsciousness, seeping ever deeper, the ringing clatter began to register in the brain of Jim Trench. Each succeeding metallic peal grew in intensity until combined with the others they burst open the door of rationality, and understanding rushed forth. He came to in frenzied fashion, waving his arms wildly and shouting, "It's a trap! It's a trap!" Before his surprised attendants could marshal their wits, he was on his feet, shouting his warning again and again. Then he crumpled in a heap.

"Look after him, boys," Chism said quietly. Then in a loud voice, he called to all, "Could be a trap, like Jim said. Abe, scout out a piece. Th' rest of you take to cover."

It was only a matter of minutes, but many breaths were checked as minds conjured up all manner of fearful imaginings. Had Vehrmon obtained reinforcements? Maybe the Indians had surrounded them! Again, maybe the settlement had been wiped out! So close to the licks, and this had to happen! Thus ran their misgivings. But sense of time and of safety returned together when they heard the booming bass of Abe Foster proclaim mockingly, "Take keer uv yoreseffs! They's a ox out here whut's got a bad look in 'is eye!"

The animal turned its head and appraised them carefully as they came out of the forest and onto the cleared land, then bent its neck and resumed its interrupted grazing upon deer grass.

Spirits soared once more when their eyes beheld the smoke of the salt furnaces rising above the trees in the distance. Tom Chism looked eagerly to the northeast. And the taut muscles in his jaws relaxed. The usual spirals were visible. By his side, Mercer discerned the pleasing change of his friend's countenance and silently shared his relief. As he noted the altered expression, he remembered Tom's pledge of abstinence and observed to himself that the probationary period was almost at its end, and he wondered if marriage to Abby would solve his problems. Certainly it should banish his loneliness, but whether or not his love for his young bride-to-be would be strong enough to overcome his tendency toward drink, he would not attempt to say. As he mused, he glanced at his companion's easy, ground-covering stride. Discounting his drinking, here was his overseer, a trustworthy man of courage, industry and ability. And, most important of all, a natural leader of men. If Chism would take the job, it would be his. He would make the offer to him tomorrow, or perhaps tonight.

Into Barth's mind came the picture of the other one in whom he had confidence—Little Johnny, his deputy. Just thinking of him and his impish characteristics made him smile outwardly and inwardly. If only Johnny would rid himself of his habit of sulking. "Hope the little fellow is on hand to meet us." He spoke without realizing he had done so.

Tom Chism, presuming the words were for him, asked, "Who you mean, Mercer?"

Barth confessed to thinking out loud and Tom affected a quizzical air, saying, "I know this business has been rough. But was it that bad?" Both men laughed.

They came to the place where the company would split up—those who worked for Chism and those who labored for Mace Hardin. Before their leaders exchanged farewells, Abe Foster made a terse comment. "Thet war party wuzzn't no ord'nary bunch uv Injuns. Ever damn one uv 'em hed him a rifle. They wuzzn't nary a arrer shot in all thet shootin'."

Barth and Tom acknowledged the correctness of this observance, with Tom saying, "I hadn't thought of it, Abe, but you're dead right. Somebody sure didn't want me to have them kettles."

"They's more'n th' kittles, ter my way uv thinkin', but I admits ter not knowin' whut hit mought be."

As they parted, Abe walked a little way with Mercer. After a short period of silence, he half-whispered to him, "Cap'n, I'm a mought curious 'bout whut feller cut Gibbs's throat—mought be th' same one whut kilt Mallory. 'Pears yer wuzzn't s'posed ter kum back livin', don't hit?"

Barth was taken completely by surprise, but he managed to reply. "You're right, Abe. I'll tell you and Tom all about it tomorrow."

Abe laughed. "Hain't no damn hurry 'bout it, Cap'n. I jest thought I'd letcher know I knowed whut happened." With that, he slapped Mercer's back and moved off after Tom Chism.

So Abe knew. But how could he? Then Barth remembered the search for Bad-Eye Smith. Abe had gotten the full story from the footprints by the thorn bushes.

The licks were in the immediate foreground. Suddenly, Barth was aware he had given no thought as to what he might say when he met Mace Hardin. What would he answer when questioned as to the deaths of Mallory and Gibbs? What report could he make? Report—the word irritated him. This was his saltworks. He owed responsibility to no one! But only he and Hardin and Tom Chism knew of his ownership. He would have to report. He did not attempt to plan his words in advance. He would meet the situation when it confronted him. That being determined, he thought of the families of the dead men coming up Salt River and he wondered whether the two men who had tried to kill him were married and had families who would mourn them. He felt no remorse over their just demise, but only sympathy for their survivors, if any there proved to be. His mind regressed to the bodies on the flatboat. There would be weeping of widows and the wailing of children, when it was secured to the shore. Sadness and sorrow in many families whose men had worked for Tom Chism. It was an unfathomable working of Providence. They had been, for the most part, perhaps their entire number, good men. Much better than those who worked for Mace Hardin, yet Hardin would have lost no workers had not the two assassins made the attempt upon his life. Maybe that was not so. They might have been slain by the Indians as were the other three who had died. He caught himself wandering into the land of possibilities again and, recognizing the fact, he channeled his thoughts to the four newcomers, three of whom had given their lives in the adventure. There would be no tears for them. No one would even be interested in their burial, other than to avoid the stench certain to come from their decaying bodies. That was wrong. There might be one mourner, if he lived. The youth on the stretcher behind him. Mercer resolved that he would attend to their proper interment. As to the one yet living, he would have him taken, along with Jim Trench and Jack Santoire, to Doctor Grainger's. Or, thinking better of it, he would take them to Rosie Tindall's. Grainger could treat them there, and Abby and Rosie could look after them under his direction. The only other wounded member of his party had served under Abe Foster in the engagement and had an injury of no consequence. Frontier remedies and nature would be sufficient for his recovery.

Hardin would think it strange he returned with three of Chism's wounded. Chism had requested this, as his headquarters was a greater distance from the settlement than was Hardin's. But Mace could think as he wished, damn him! His curse was intended.

The damned one was waiting and came forward from the small group that had assembled, awaiting their return. "Cap'n, hit's moughty glad I be thet yer ez back, all safe an' sound. How many uv our boys did we lose?" Then Mace noticed the dried blood on Mercer's jaw. "Yer did git yerse'f scratched, dintcher?"

Barth did not answer him. Instead, he directed his words to the men bearing the wounded. "Take those men to Rosie Tindall's. Four of you will be enough for that. The rest of you, go find Doctor Grainger and get him over to Rosie's as quick as you can."

Now, he turned and faced Mace Hardin. "What were you saying, Mr. Hardin?"

Mace accepted the affront without any display or its effect. "I jest wuz sayin' how glad I wuz thet yer wuzzn't hurt none ter much an' I wuz wonderin' how many uv our boys wuz kilt er wounded. One of thet damn Tom Chism's bunch come through here 'while ago with some damn story thet th' Injuns wuz on t'other side uv th' river, but all uv Chism's bunch is damn liars liken he is. We hain't saw th' first Injun yet. Enyways, he sed Mallory wuz kilt, thet right?"

Barth had controlled himself when Mace had slurred Tom Chism, but his jaws were tightly set as he snapped, "That's right, he's dead."

Hardin tried to be casual as he glanced among the other returnees, but he fumbled as he asked, "I-I-don't see Justin Gibbs. Whar's he at?"

"Coming up Salt River on Chism's boat. Mallory's on there too."

Mace feigned irritation. "Them damn fellers jest won't do whut they's tole! I tole 'em ter take special keer uv yer! Now I fines one uv 'em dead an' t'other takin' a damn boat ride!"

"Gibbs isn't enjoying the ride, Mr. Hardin. He's dead also." Barth noted Mace's lower lip as it dropped and quivered.

Regaining his composure, Mace said strongly, "Wal, guess we best be thankful they's th' onliest ones we lost. How many wuz wounded?"

"Just that one there." Barth designated the injured man and then added, "I'm going to Mrs. Tindall's. I'll see you early in the morning." He did not mention his own wound.

"As yer sez, Cap'n."

Mace started to move away when a sudden query from Mercer halted him. "Mr. Hardin, did either Gibbs or Mallory have families; were they married?"

"They bin married—lotsa times—an' they's got children. But they hain't got no wives here, an' they wuddn't know they chil'rens, an' th' chil'rens wuddn't know them, if'n yer knows whut I means. Ain't nobuddy goner miss 'em 'round here, so don't worry yerse'f none on thet account." Mace corrected himself. "I take thet back some. Thet damn yaller dog whut's a-smellin' yer boots mought miss Gibbs." He swung his foot and the animal yelped and fled. "Mought uv knowed Gibbs wuz dead, thet son-uv-a-bitch dog's bin howlin' his damn fool head off sence late this mornin'." Emphasizing his earlier assertion, he said, "Jest don't consarn yerseff 'bout them two. They jest never did a job right, liken they wuz tole. I'm plumb sorry they din't take keer uv yer, an' I 'pologizes ter yer."

"No need for that, Mr, Hardin. They both tried to do what you told them to do. They were just prevented from doing their job by being killed, that's all."

Confusion stood out vividly on Mace's puzzled features. All he could bring himself to say was, "As yer says, Cap'n, as yer says." Then, belatedly, he called to one of his men. "Git up off'n yer damn ass an' ride th' cap'n ter whar he's goin'."

Barth thought of two things during the short trip to Rosie Tindall's. He wondered at Johnny's absence and whether or not it was purely his imagination. He believed he had detected a pervading spirit of open resentment toward him among those workers who had remained at the licks while he and the others had gone after the Indians. He knew the latter feeling had existed previously, but it had been more concealed. Was this more of Mace Hardin's doing? Had he instructed them to finish that which Gibbs and Mallory had tried to do?

"We're here, Cap'n." Only when he heard the driver's words did he realize the wagon had been stopped for some time before they had been spoken. He hastily conveyed his thanks and alighted.

CHAPTER 39

From the moment of the departure of the three messengers dispatched by Tom Chism to forewarn the settlers, Hawkstraw had run in the trio's van. His intimate knowledge of the maze of trails and paths that wound around and through the dense growths and his extraordinary fleetness of foot resulted in leaving his companions far behind. At first, they had called to him, advising it would be much safer were they to be not too far apart from one another, but when he did not slacken his pace, they then sought vainly to follow his course. They abandoned their attempt when they discovered they were traveling in circles. Half-heartedly, one of them had expressed the thought that Hawkstraw would not be able to run very far at his present rate of speed, and they would thus catch up with him after a bit. However, they both knew they were thinking wishfully that the mute one could run much farther than this present errand would require him to do. And they admitted also there would be no appreciable diminution of his swiftness. He had the gift, common to all creatures of the wilderness, of being able to take some indefinable measure of rest as his body expended its energy. He would reach his destination tired, but in no manner exhausted. His sense of direction was unerring and this peculiar ability, combined with his familiarity with the region to be traveled, would result in his having to cover about a third less than the distance the other two couriers would have to travel to reach the licks. Once he was there, he would obtain a mount and ride on to Dowdall's and Brashear's garrisons. There he hoped to enlist the aid of some of the male residents in forming a party to ride to Aaron Flinden's cabin and, if all were safe, then to scour the surrounding territory.

Hawkstraw had no hope that the Flindens and Nancy might have taken refuge at either Dowdall's or Brashear's. He knew only too well the Quaker's complete belief that the savages would not harm him nor any of his household. Nor did Flinden's conviction seem strange to him. But Hawkstraw reasoned that while Brother Flinden's faith might protect himself, it could safeguard no one else; otherwise why couldn't Nancy's believing affect the miracle of granting him the power of speech. No, he thought, Flinden's trust could not save Nancy from the Indians, should they decide to attack his house. Had not the good man admitted this to be true when he had answered her question regarding the delay in his being able to talk? Hadn't Flinden said that perfect faith would be necessary before words could come from his lips? Nancy both hated and feared the Indians. She harbored not the faintest belief that they would spare her were she ever to be exposed to them. Therefore, Hawkstraw concluded, she would be in grave danger should they choose to attack Brother Flinden's place.

Hawkstraw weighed the possibility that she had heeded the previous warning and had gone to the haven or the stations, but decided in the negative, knowing she would not leave Ursula and Aaron. The three would be there at the cabin, come savage or White man.

He quickened his pace as he came out of the forest. Ahead lay only cleared land—no more trees. He could see Mud Garrison, his first objective. There he would borrow the horse and give the inhabitants notice of the roving band of Indians.

He found the gate to Mud Garrison loosely barred. Tiring of trying to get someone to open it from within, he searched until he found a length of hickory that he inserted through the gap between the two sections of the barrier and pressed upward against the bar. Stern effort raised it from one of its holders and thus freed, one end rocked as it hit the ground. Seconds later, the other end slid from its confinement and thumped on the packed earth inside the entrance.

Nothing met his eyes that even remotely suggested any state of alarm on the part of the inhabitants—residents or those who had sought temporary protection inside the stockade. The scene might have been that to be witnessed there on any evening. The cattle and horses in the center of the enclosure, old manure piles evincing that to be their accustomed place. Children ran aimlessly about, voices were high and loud, and many men and women showed signs of the unsteadying influence of corn squeezin's.

Hawkstraw sought to impress the more sober residents with the seriousness of his information. Some could not, or would not, concentrate on what he strove so earnestly to tell them. Even the word INDIANS, which he etched in the hard ground, and his gestures indicating the Indians were on the south side of the river and the sweep of his arm designed to show that the savages were moving toward the settlement, failed to arouse anything more than a passive acknowledgment. Despairing of his fruitless inculcations, he asked for the loan of a horse on which to continue his mission. He scratched the letters HORS and pointed to one of the animals. He whom he asked took the stock from his hand and printed the word COW and then demonstrated his knowledge by weaving his way to the side of a scrawny member of the bovine species and slapping its boney rump. Hawkstraw did no further asking but hastily selected a mount tethered alongside an old gray mule. He did not bother with a saddle. Throwing the reins over the horse's head, he leaped upon its back. As he passed through the still open gate, he hoped someone would have sufficient presence of mind to close and bar it behind him.

He could not know that as he had vaulted onto his mount, a certain John Littelby was lying on the other side of the gray mule. Neither could he see Johnny raise his drunken head nor hear him mutter with a thick tongue, "Thet son-uv-a-bitch, Hawkstraw. He stole hisself a horse." It mattered not, for Mr. Littelby's head fell again, and he reentered his intoxicated stupor. When he sobered, he would have no recollection of time or any of its embraced happenings. He would condemn himself and opine in characteristic disgust, "A man shore must be a damn fool er damn drunk er both whut sleeps 'longside a jackass an' uses a pile uv ole cow droppin's fer a piller."

It was about a mile to the east of Mud Garrison that Hawkstraw saw the three horses, their flanks flashing wet in the sunlight. They were grazing on the deer grass and wild pea vines that covered the flat land almost to Dowdall's Station. This meant but one thing. The animals had crossed the river from the south. Infrequently, one animal might escape his owner's control, but three of them were not apt to do so at the same time. He looked across the stream. There was no sign of smoke. If the Indians were moving eastward, it was unusual that they had not fired the dwellings in their path. Maybe, instead of continuing in the direction they had taken earlier, they had doubled back and crossed Salt River far to the west or where the flatboat had run into disaster. He tried to coax his way near the liberated steeds, but they were not taking any chances of losing their newfound freedom and shied quickly away. If the Indian scare proved false, their owners would reclaim them after they had tired of their wanderings. If the savages had set them free, and their masters had not gone to the garrisons when warned to do so, the horses would most likely have new owners after the Redskins had moved on. Right now, he was not concerned with lost or strayed animals. Nor was he weighing the case. His thoughts were solely those of possible effect.

As he approached Dowdall's, the lookout at its northwest corner called down for the gate to be opened, and Hawkstraw rode inside the fort without slackening his horse's speed. Fortune was indeed with him. The first man at his side was Ethan Belden who, from the many hours spent with him in the surveying party, was able almost instantly to understand the grave tidings he brought and immediately impart them to the others. Paradoxical smiles appeared on their faces as Hawkstraw imitated Brother Flinden's mannerisms to perfection while endeavoring to identify his cabin as being the primary object of concern. ·

Belden himself carried the warning to Brashear's and alerted that station. He returned speedily and reported ten volunteers were prepared to join whatever number might be raised from Dowdall's. After carefully considering the garrison's requirements for its own safety, it was determined that fifteen men, including Belden, could be spared for service in the planned foray. All the while the discussion had continued, Hawkstraw paced back and forth. And when the decision had been made, he continued his nervous walking as he awaited the arrival of the volunteers from the neighboring fort.

*

Drusilla Grainger felt most inconvenienced. Out of deference to her husband's position as the only doctor in this wilderness, other than at the Falls, they had been accorded the best cabin that Dowdall's boasted. If appreciation of this special consideration had been expected by any of the station's residents, particularly those who had surrendered their homes, there was none forthcoming on her part, although the doctor himself had expressed his gratitude for this respect of the comfort of his wife. Relations had become a bit strained when Drusilla had requested, demandingly, that Chate, Callie and Jason also be quartered nearby. She added to the already burdened atmosphere by holding herself aloof from everyone, ignoring whom she wished and speaking only to such persons as might be necessary to fill some real or imagined personal need.

Just now, she was strolling about, apparently for the pure exercise and diversion of walking. Callie trailed her mistress in proper fashion. Little Jason was aside his mother.

Pretending not to notice a handsome, well-dressed man as she passed him, she nevertheless had observed his animated conversation with two comely young girls, and she recognized the character of his laughter after he had whispered in their ears. Though she saw and heard that which she wanted to, her manner betrayed nothing. She walked in formal fashion, her eyes seemingly focused on nothing in particular. To the casual observer, she appeared to be completely impervious to the many glances her striking beauty drew to her person. But it was not so. She was knowingly receiving the homage she claimed as owing her. Callie knew this and basked in her lady's reflected glory. Dem fo'ks orter see her lak ah sees her fust thing in th' mawnin' when she gits outer dat bed. Dey eyes would really do some poppin', she thought.

Drusilla's path, for all its apparent chance, had been deliberately chosen. She had seen the good-looking fellow from across the enclosure. As she walked by, she had seen his head turn so that his eyes might follow her as she receded from his presence. A glance from the corner of her eye had told her this. She reached for her lace kerchief, and it fluttered earthward in a perfect execution of a seemingly uncalculated act. Before Jason's little legs could cover the distance to retrieve his mistress's property, long limbs had carried another to the place where the exquisite bit of lace now lay. The would-be gallant had to force himself in front of her to attract her attention. He bowed and raising himself said in an intriguing voice, "Your kerchief, my lady."

Drusilla favored him with a condescending smile. Gazing in this proximity upon such loveliness, he was thoroughly entranced, so much so, he found himself awkwardly impeding her way. He apologized and began, "May I introduce myself? My name is—"

He got no further as she interrupted. "I have no desire to know you. Now, if you please."

He stepped aside clumsily and stared fixedly after her as the little procession moved on. When he recovered, he would be momentarily embarrassed by the realization of how completely she had deflated his poise and of how deeply she had wounded his pride.

Callie had difficulty in keeping her giggling inaudible. She had been her mistress's confidante too long not to know the incident was one of design. She had witnessed its enactment on many previous occasions, though seldom with one of such apparent inferior social caste. Always, after such an occurrence, there would be a time when she and her lady would be together, secure from the doctor's sight or hearing. It was then the scene would be replayed, and they would indulge themselves in unrestrained mirth at the hapless victim's discomfiture. Callie was fully cognizant of Drusilla's motives in staging these meetings. They fed her vanity and they maintained her confidence in the power of her charms. Equally important, she knew, was the feeling of satisfaction that came over her mistress when she was successful in destroying her prey's self-control and in effecting his total embarrassment. No man whom she had wanted had ever resisted her attractiveness. Those to whom she gave herself and her devotion would never again be content with anyone but her. To those, like the young man in today's episode, whom she but teased, such a meeting was an unforgettable event whose memory would be fresh for many a future year. A naughty chuckle escaped Callie's lips, followed by a faint word stream. "Bet wuz dat to be Cap'n Mercer, 'stead-a bein' dat young fella, dey'd be moughty li'1 teasin'. Lawdy! Comes de day dem two gits wif each udder, dey'll burn de house down, sho' 'nuff!"

Jason looked strangely at his mother as she talked to herself. Noting this, she became silent. Just as they reached their quarters, the garrison gate opened and ten mounted men came inside. They conferred briefly with a large group at the far end of the station where the horses were stabled, and shortly thereafter the whole party rode out of the fort.

"'Whuffo all dem men goes out lak dat, Miz Drusilla?" Callie asked curiously.

"I don't know, and I care less, Callie."

*

Aaron Flinden was tired. He had spent the greater part of the day in his cornfield, which ran the length of the level land in front of his cabin. He sat facing the open doorway, watching the sunrays as their castings gradually disappeared from the door itself. Soon they would all be gone and the sun would be at its setting. He had accomplished much this day. The corn was now free of suckers and a good rain would send the stalks skyward. Such labor as he had done was sweet to him. Nowhere, he thought, is there a more perfect communion between God and man than in an open field with heaven furnishing its own canopy. Small wonder the early Christians worshipped out of doors, for it is the gathering together, and not the edifice, which determines the church.

Ursula blasted his reverie! "Aaron Flinden, close that door! Thee makes me think thee would welcome a visit from the bloodthirsty savages. Thou knows that we have been strongly warned of their coming. If thee think lightly of thy own safety, have some care for the protection of Nancy and me."

Flinden moved in response to his wife's directive but not fast enough to please her mood. "Bar the door instantly, Aaron Flinden! Like as not, the heathens will rush inside our home before thee can bring thyself to move!"

How much alike, he observed silently, are an annoying rain and a contentious woman. Resignedly, he secured the door.

"Don't sit thyself to dreaming again, Aaron Flinden! Thy meal is just about ready!" She mellowed as she said to Nancy, "Thee will like what I have cooked this evening."

Once they were seated, they bowed their heads and Flinden embarked upon the saying of his customarily prolonged grace. As he gave his abundance of thanks, Nancy thought of the difference between the eating manners of this household and those of the Hardins. How much better the food tasted here! Not only because of Ursula's ability as a cook alone but also the atmosphere in which it was prepared and eaten. True, she disliked the Flinden's rigid rule of silence while she ate, but she gladly restrained herself, considering her obedience to the strict table discipline as being her own rendition of thanks to God for bringing her here. She tried to concentrate her thoughts on Flinden's words, but as they rolled on and on, her attention strayed and she found herself thinking anew of material things. If the Indians should come here, what would they do to protect themselves? Flinden surely must have a weapon somewhere around the cabin. She would ask him about this when he finished grace. She looked at her folded hands. That was one thing she liked better at the Hardins. Every time she ate here, she had to wash her hands before she came to the table. Lost in thought, she didn't realize the prayer had ended.

"Nancy Landers, be thou asleep? I have finished grace."

She unclasped her hands and opened her eyes. Dutifully, she asked, "May I speak?"

Permission being granted readily, she inquired, "Where does—I mean do—you keep yer rifle?"

Flinden looked at his wife before answering. "We have no rifle or any other weapon in this abode." Having made his reply, he began to eat.

Not so with Nancy. She studied a moment then blurted out, "Seems like yer givin' th' Lord a helluva lot uv extry work. Looks like thet's whut guns wuz made fer—ter pertect yerse'f with."

Shocked, he didn't know which of her transgressions to correct first. Then the order suggested itself. "Nancy Landers, thee did not ask permission to speak again. If that were not fault enough, thee used a wrongful word. Thy language was that of the Hardins."

She used her apology to express a partial justification. "I am sorry for what I done—did thet is—but hit looks like th' Lord wud never hev let them—th' guns—ter be made, if'n he didn't expect 'em ter be used."

Flinden spoke his firm conviction. "'Tis not for us to answer. The Lord made man good, but he nevertheless became evil. Man made the weapons out of things that are of themselves good and peaceful. That will be all that we shall say about the matter."

Ursula made no comment on her husband's pronouncement, but she raised her eyebrows and shook her head in hopeless abjuration.

The meal finished, he complimented her, saying, "'Twas indeed good food thou served this evening."

A full stomach has a way of influencing one's outlook on life, particularly is this true if one was blest with as good digestion as was Aaron Flinden. Gone, for the present at least, was his always controlled irritation at Ursula's constant nagging. He excused himself as he arose, the indication to the others that the meal was formally completed. A short nap, and he would study the Holy Script. Then he would be ready for his full night's rest.

Nancy and Ursula set about the task of cleaning the table. Everything would be washed; the scraps carefully emptied in a wooden pail, not thrown out the door as at the Hardins.

CHAPTER 40

Due to their inclination to indulge their overwhelming curiosity, Yellow Hawk had to constantly urge his warriors on. Thus far, they had found no settlers at home. The presence of untethered horses in the vicinity of the various cabins suggested their owners had left hurriedly as if in response to a warning. One by one his warriors had secured these mounts for themselves. There had been an opportunity to capture three more steeds, but these had frightened easily and broke away, swimming the river to the other side, and scampering off in the direction of the garrisons. Some of the warriors wanted to give chase and capture them, but their leader forbade any pursuit. His plan was to stay south of the stream as they had done since leaving the scene of carnage at the flatboat. By so doing, the possibility of arousing large numbers of the settlers would most likely be avoided. His men were too few to risk any combat involving more than three or four White men at any one time. For this reason, he had not permitted fires to be set to any of the dwellings they had come across, for to have done so would surely have drawn the attention of the settlement to their presence. He had allowed the first few cabins to be broken into and ransacked but the innate tendency of his braves to explore the interiors and the difficulty he had experienced in getting them to leave one place and go on to another had resulted in his stopping this practice. No scalps could be taken from settlers who were absent from their homes, and it was scalps he wanted to wave in the face of Vehrmon this night, as he sat before the fire at the rendezvous. Somewhere ahead, there would be people in their cabins. To waste time, as his men were so prone to do, might cause the loss of the trophies he coveted so greatly. Hence, his zeal in driving them forward.

For some time now they had seen no habitations. Their progress was necessarily slow due to moving through covered ground, the trees furnishing a natural impediment to any speed on horseback. At length, they left the forest and were once more on cleared land. A cornfield was in front of them and behind it a cabin from whose chimney smoke curled lazily upward. There were his scalps!

The band moved cautiously as it approached the dwelling place. At Yellow Hawk's signal, his men deployed around it. Yellow Hawk himself walked to the entrance.

Inside the cabin, Flinden slept contentedly. There was a loud knock on the door, but the sound did not awaken him. Nancy and Ursula heard it, however, and looked anxiously toward its source. There was a pausing silence, then the knocking was resumed, heavier than before. Ursula sprang to her husband's side and shook him unmercifully, yelling in her harshest tones for him to wake up. Strangely, Nancy was quietly looking through the few belongings she had brought from her former home.

A man's voice called from the outside as Flinden opened his eyes. His brain still befogged with sleep, he did not comprehend the words that had forced their way inside his mind. Ursula's hands remained upon his shoulders but she did not shake him further. Instead, she said in a lowered voice, an uncommon doing on her part, "There's someone outside who just called to us. I truly fear 'tis a savage."

He looked severely at her, before he answered. "Ursula Flinden, I can abide thy baseless fears when I am awake, but why must thou disturb my rest to tell them to me?"

Just then, the voice came again. "Who keeps house?" The words were spoken clearly and evenly.

Without replying, Flinden started toward the door. His wife, sensing he was about to admit whoever was there, rushed in front of him and spread herself so that her back was against the bar. Then she implored him. "Aaron Flinden, don't let him inside. I feel to my soul that it is an Indian!"

For a moment, he said nothing. Then he spoke to her. "Thee heard how he talked. 'Twas not the voice of a savage."

"Thou knows their trickery! Tell him that we are abed and that we wish no visitors." Her tones were recapturing their accustomed sharpness.

"Thee surely knows that I will not tell an untruth, and were I to so sin at thy behest 'twould not be believed; 'tis yet daylight outside."

While they talked, Nancy found that which she sought. She put her other things away, holding the knife in her hand as she did so.

Outside, Yellow Hawk was becoming impatient. He had used his position as chieftain to gain the right to take the first scalp. He had memorized only a few words of the White man's language, but those he knew, he spoke perfectly. He determined he would speak once more in the foreign tongue. If the ruse did not then work, he would employ force. Two braves were at each of the front corners of the cabin. Powder had been poured on a portion of one of the logs and their rifles were being held in an inverted position so that when the flint sparked, the powder would blaze.

"Hello, inside."

To pacify his wife, Flinden answered the greeting. "Hello. Who is there?"

The smooth reply came through the closed portal. "Friend—a friend."

Ursula knew the door would now be opened. Before he directed that she step aside, she did so, but she did not act submissively. "Aaron Flinden, 'tis a good wife I have been to thee! I followed thee when I did not have to follow. I endured the shame and humiliation when thee chose to leave Pennsylvania. I have worked the skin from my fingers for thee. I suffered the privations that came to us in Virginia. I followed thee to this awful wilderness. I did all of these things because

I was a faithful wife. How doth thee now repay me? By opening that door so that I may be slaughtered before thy very eyes!"

When Ursula paused to wipe her tears and her nose, Nancy spoke to him. "That feller don't sound none too much like no White man or like anybody from 'round here. He said th' words all right, but if'n he was frum th' licks, he would hev tole yer his name."

"The word is told, not tole, Nancy. I doubt that whoever is awaiting entrance to this house would make that mistake in his speech."

Yellow Hawk was making his last effort, as he intoned, "Open the door." He could hear the bar then being lifted and he smiled broadly. He readied himself to take advantage of the slightest inward movement of the door within its frame.

Nancy moved closely behind Flinden as he started to pull the door toward him. To his complete surprise, she reached past him and suddenly jerked it open. Expectant as Yellow Hawk had been, he was yet caught off guard. For the slightest fraction of time, the two men stared at each other. Flinden, refusing to believe that an Indian confronted him. Yellow Hawk, wondering why he had not moved with the swing of the door.

The reflexes of young people were swift as the wind. Nancy pushed Flinden violently forward, causing him to bowl the savage from his feet as he himself tripped to the earth.

Yellow Hawk had been given the opportunity to lift the White man's scalp and he had failed. A tomahawk in one hand, another brave now rushed forward and dug the fingers of his other hand deep into Flinden's heavy hair. On his hands and knees, the intended victim pulled violently away, but the Indian's grip was unrelenting. When Flinden attempted to arise, the savage struck at him with his weapon, missing his head, but striking his shoulder.

The remainder of the raiding party, except for their chief, now poured into the cabin, brushing past Nancy who had withdrawn from the entrance and had flattened herself against the wall, hoping that she might shut the door and thus possibly save Ursula and herself. There was no time to reason whether or not she had done the right thing in precipitating the collision of Flinden and the savage. She moved with the present, not with the immediate past. When she saw that Ursula too was beyond her aid, she edged her way to the door, reaching there just in time to see Flinden and his Redskin antagonist grappling with each other. Behind the combatants, she saw the Indian whose face had first met her eyes a moment before. His eyes glued on the struggle, he missed her presence. He could not help the warrior, unless it would be to save his life. Otherwise he dared not interfere.

Flinden's efforts were all defensive. He had no wish to hurt his opponent, only to keep the Indian from killing or inflicting further injury upon him. His shoulder ached where the war axe had struck, and the arm was almost useless. Despite this disability, however, he had managed to straighten himself up to his full height, making him tower above his clay-colored adversary who yet held tightly to the shock of hair. Fortunately, Flinden's good arm, his left, was in opposition to that of the savage's right, whose hand wielded the tomahawk. Blows from that source had been stayed by taking a firm hold upon the threatening wrist, forcing it away from him by the superior strength in his vein-swollen forearm.

Nancy maneuvered herself so that she was behind Yellow Hawk, whose attention remained fixed upon the wrestling pair. Tightening her grip on the knife, she crept stealthily upon him, not daring to breathe, in mortal fear of being discovered. There was a shriek from within the cabin. They have killed Ursula, she thought. The Indian in front of her turned his head at the sound. As though deliberating whether to stay where he was or go inside, he looked back at his warrior and the White man. Then he hurried toward the house. When he moved, Nancy's chance to kill him ended. She watched him until he disappeared from view, then she ran to where Flinden was waging his desperate, uneven attempt to survive. He had stretched his head backward and away from the Indian's hand in a frantic endeavor to free his hair from the Redman's clutch. The muscles strained in his neck, but the savage held on. The pain was maddening.

Worse than the excruciating feeling in his scalp or the anguish he suffered from his bleeding shoulder was the confusion in his mind. Hadn't his faith been strong enough? Was this the reason the Lord had permitted the Indians to attack his home? Was he to die as a penalty to the weakness of his belief? He had believed fully! There was no such frailty! Was this visitation or evil due to some transgression of his—of Nancy's—of Ursula's? No, that could not be. The Lord's will be done? What of his wife and the young girl? Would they be killed or had they already died? Had his faith been really strong enough? What of the mute, James? Was his faith no stronger than that of the afflicted one? The dumb one had not spoken, though he too professed a deep conviction that his lips would utter words. Ursula—Nancy—the Lord's will—the Indian means to kill me—I harbor no ill will toward him, yet he wants my life . . . why?

The savage crossed his leg around and behind the White man's ankle. Now thoroughly off balance, Flinden fell, his opponent on top of him. The imprisoned tomahawk was set free. The sinewed hand which held it high began its swinging descent.

Nancy had watched helplessly as the scales began to weigh against Aaron Flinden. The two figures had whirled about so fast she had feared to strike, lest she stab her benefactor. When the two crashed to the ground, her dilemma vanished. As the war axe began to fall, she drove the knife, which Massalene Hardin had given her when she had told her goodbye, deep into the Indian's back, the blade touching the spine in its inward plunge. The flat of the axe yet reached its mark, catching Flinden a little above his left ear and rendering him senseless, but it was the weakly executed act of a dying Shawanese warrior. The tomahawk slipped from the savage's fingers as they slowly opened. It was as though the knife had been a key that had unlocked the iron grasp.

Nancy seized the weapon as it fell and with it rained blow after blow on the savage's head and body. The dry, thirsty clay exchanged its hue for that of the warm, red liquid draining into it.

A series of shrill shrieks streamed through the opened cabin door and bombarded the air outside. They were Ursula's, and Nancy's heart beat faster with the revelation she still lived. Her pulse slowed instantly, however, as she acknowledged her hopeless plight. Brother Flinden could be saved, though, if she could but lift him onto one of the horses tethered beyond the cabin. She tested her strength before going after the mount. It was impossible. She could barely lift Flinden's head and shoulders; he was all dead weight. She did manage to tug at his unconscious body until she had moved it round the side of the cabin where it could not be seen by the riding party when it came out. This having been accomplished, she returned to the spot where Flinden had lain to retrieve the knife and the axe she had been forced to leave behind. She was in the act of picking them up when she saw Yellow Hawk emerging, dragging the still screaming Ursula by the braids of her hair.

The chieftain saw the dead brave and the young White girl at the same instant. Hurling an order to his subordinates, he released the yowling woman. The girl holding a knife and a tomahawk in her hands had turned in flight at the first moment he had seen her and had thus gained a good head start. Yellow Hawk ran toward the horses a short distance away. The chase would be brief.

Ursula's terror-filled eyes took in the scene slowly. Gradually, her mind received the images of the prostrate savage and of Nancy's fleeing form. That which she saw induced a wild deduction and she gave voice to its formation, yelling hysterically. "The everlasting shame is upon thee, Aaron Flinden! Thee has murdered they fellow man! All thy teaching and preaching have been a mockery! Thou art confounded and thou hast confounded me with thee! Oh, thou baseless creature, to save thyself and leave a faithful wife and an innocent girl to the mercy of the savage heathens! Thou vile deserter of thy faith and family! I told thee and told thee. I begged thee not to open that door! What will I say to our good friends, should I be spared? How will I tell them that my husband abandoned me? They know my untold sacrifices. They shall think me a fool that I followed thee so blindly! And it was thee I obeyed all of my long-suffering years with thee. Think not that it was the teachings of George Fox or the example of William Penn! It was my love for thee, Aaron Flinden. And how hast thou rewarded my devotion? By cowardly desertion!"

She dabbed at her tears with the hem of her dress. Before she could launch a new series of denunciations, a hand, its palm wet with sweat, clamped over her mouth. "White squaw make bad noise. Me stop," one of her captors said in a guttural monotone.

Yellow Hawk's heels dug into his pony's flanks, and he was in full pursuit. In a matter of seconds he would be alongside the little White squaw and sweep her from the ground. She was heading for the woods that lay to the north, but she would never be able to reach there before he would overtake her.

At this moment, the rescue party from the garrison broke cover directly in the line of the chase. Hawkstraw was foremost among them as they came into view. Nancy saw him and tried to run even faster than she had been doing. The added speed was costly. The strain was too much for her and she fainted.

Yellow Hawk pulled his steed and turned in retreat when he saw White men ride out of the forest. Now, it was himself and his band who must save themselves. Reaching the cabin, he jerked the convulsive Ursula from the custody of the one who held her. Throwing one arm around her middle, he raised her from the ground. Hastily counting his numbers, Yellow Hawk thundered for the immediate presence of two of his men who were still rooting around inside the dwelling. They came out quickly, carrying various articles that had appealed to their fancies. They vaulted onto their horses, and the raiding party was in flight. The body of their slain comrade lay across his stolen steed, rising and falling with each galloping stride. Trailing in the rear was Flinden's gentle mare, vainly pulling back her head in protest of this unaccustomed rough treatment of her tender mouth.

The Indian leader reviewed the situation in his mind as he rode furiously toward the distant trees. His female captive was of slight frame, yet her weight was beginning to prove a burden to the supporting arm. He had not scalped her, for if hers was the only one he was to take, it would certainly draw jeers from those whom he wanted to impress most. On the other hand, to return with a White squaw would be a praiseworthy accomplishment. Especially would this be true if she came, as she would, with eleven stolen horses. He pictured himself at the campfire later tonight. He would approach the renegade Vehrmon with the failure that had cost the lives of so many of his Red brothers. Pointing his finger in scorn, he would say in the tongue of his fathers, "Through your bad leadership, many braves have been lost. What has the great Vehrmon to offer in place of the departed ones—the empty places around the council fires? Many scalps? A few scalps? Even one scalp? What plunder did the great fighter of squaws and children secure for us?" He would wait for effect and then continue. "Perhaps he has captured many prisoners or even one prisoner? Surely, such a great warrior as the White chief brags himself to be has brought us many fine horses, at least one horse. Arise, oh renowned one, and tell us of your deeds and prizes!" Then he would scowl at the White usurper and would prod him on. He visualized the knowing nodding of heads in the great circle, and he could see the reflection of the firelight in their eyes and on their cheekbones as they looked at Vehrmon and then at himself. When the White man failed to defend himself or when he had finished making his unacceptable excuses, he, Yellow Hawk, would recount his own exploits. "Where that one," designating Vehrmon with great disdain, "has returned without many of our brothers or their bodies, has come to this campfire like a beaten dog with its tail between its shaking legs, has brought us no prisoners or prizes, see that which I, Yellow Hawk, have done with but ten warriors!" The flashing approval on their countenances would match the flames in brightness when he paraded before them the White squaw, the many articles of loot and the eleven horses. "Yellow Hawk and his small band went forth on foot, but lo they returned on horseback! While Vehrmon left the many bodies of our dead brothers to be desecrated by the White man and to be fed upon by the creatures of the wilderness, leaving only their whitened bones to bear evidence that once they too were men, Yellow Hawk has borne to this meeting place the one dead brave who was lost by him! Have we not had enough of this so-called leader?" After the ensuing vote had been taken, he, himself, would drive Vehrmon into the darkness. Then the British major would have to deal with Yellow Hawk. No more would he be given orders! He would issue them!

The terrified Ursula, sickened by the motion of the horse and her bumping against her captor, screamed through her vomit-stained lips, "I told thee, Aaron Flinden! I told thee! I told thee!"

Yellow Hawk, spared the obnoxious stench occasioned by her sickness through the rapid speed of his mount, nevertheless tired of hearing the same shrill words. He inclined his mouth to her ear and growled, "You stop noise. No do . . . me drop!" He loosened his hold slightly and her body sagged, her feet skimming the young growth of broomsedge beneath them. Had her mind dared to defy his brusque ultimatum, her heart would not have permitted its defiance. It pounded so heavily she could not utter a sound.

Ursula's certain inclusion in Yellow Hawk's dream of triumph was dependent upon one vital factor. If the White pursuers followed too closely, she would be tomahawked and flung to the ground. If the White men stopped at the cabin or paused in the chase, her life would be spared. If they came on without pausing, she would be killed, a fate she momentarily feared but only because of her precarious suspended position.

Yellow Hawk glanced behind him. The White riders were passing the dwelling without stopping. He freed his hand of the reins, dropping them loosely upon the neck of his mount and causing the horse to break forward in a new burst of speed. His hand felt for the war axe at his side. Fortunately for his captive, he continued to look back as he did so. The White men were now wheeling around and returning to the cabin where something had evidently drawn their attention. He recovered the drooping reins. Thus, by a decision of chance, Ursula lived. Given this advantage, the Indians would not now be overtaken.

A wide path between the trees ahead beckoned him on. Barely had his horse's hooves cleared the dividing line of meadow and forest, when Yellow Hawk took one last reassuring look toward the Flinden home. Satisfied, he straightened his vision. Too late, he saw the narrow, low-hanging fork of the tree branch. It grazed past his animal's head.

*

When Ursula recovered consciousness, she found herself astride her husband's mare, her hands bound tightly behind her. Instead of riding at the head of the party, she was now in the rear, traveling between two horses, each one bearing the body of a dead Indian, that of her former captor being on her right. The reins of all three mounts were held by the savage directly in front of her. She had no memory of what had happened, or of how the chieftain had come to his death, but she reasoned they both must have fallen or have been thrown to the ground.

Other than a severe headache, she had suffered no injury of any significance. Whatever fate lay ahead of her, she determined to meet it in Christian fashion. Like the martyrs of the church's early history, she was in the hands of unbelievers. The gait slowed to a trot and, its jolting characteristics notwithstanding, she fell asleep as the evening shadows merged. The rhythmic rolling of Yellow Hawk's head on its broken neck would continue until the rendezvous was reached.

*

When Hawkstraw drew near where Nancy had swooned, he leaped from his horse and ran the few remaining yards to her. Cradling her in his arms, he kissed her again and again, the tears streaming over his cheeks. Opening her eyes, she cried joyfully, "James!" He responded by renewing his kissing of her face and lips. Through his anxiety sprang the realization that he loved her, not as he had cared for the one whom he had called Little Legs, but as a man loves a woman.

Nancy sensed this change in the complexion of his affection for her. It was what she had prayed for so earnestly—that and the ever-offered prayer that he be able to speak. As he kissed her, she gave her thanks to God. This supplication had been answered, if only the other might also be granted. As she related to him all the details of the attack, he listened to her words for the first time as those of an adult and not of a child.

*

It had been Ethan Belden who had spied the unconscious Flinden and who had called ahead to the other riders. He would never know that had he been less observant, the captive Ursula would have forfeited her life. Her absence was not discovered until the men had returned and searched the cabin. They had found its interior to be entirely one of havoc. Even the wooden receptacle that had contained the refuse had shattered. They noted, however, that its former contents had been first spilled upon the floor, then scattered, evidently in the mistaken belief that something of value had been concealed within them. When their search inside had ended, they looked around the dwelling. Failing to find any trace of Mrs. Flinden, they knew that she had been carried away.

Belden and another of the party stayed with Brother Flinden. The rest rode off in an effort to rescue his wife.

The Quaker revived a little but was still in a comatose condition. He rambled unintelligibly. The only word he said distinctly enough to be understood by Belden and his other comforter was, "Why?" The two lifted the wounded man gently upon one of their horses and while one kept him upright, the other mounted behind him, encircling Flinden's chest with his arm. They paused briefly as they met Nancy and Hawkstraw, informing them of their intention to seek medical aid from Doctor Grainger at Dowdall's Station.

Their words stirred the mute's memory. He had forgotten to tell the doctor that there would be those needing his skill among the returning adventurers. He described his omission to Nancy and they got hastily upon his horse. The young girl, if her nervousness remained under its present control, would convey the message.

CHAPTER 41

Rosie's sympathetic nature overcame her, and she cried openly at her first sight of her old friend, Jim Trench, and his wounded companions. She had cried earlier this afternoon, when the news came to her that Willie Roller had passed on. Everyone had thought he would recover. His arm stump had responded to treatment and there appeared no reason why he should not get well. Then today his heart had suddenly stopped.

The sight of blood appalled Abby. Consequently, the unpleasant task of cleansing the faces and persons of the three men devolved upon her mother. Reluctantly, Abby had consented to rinse and wring out the saturated cloths.

Rosie began with Jim Trench. Dust kicked up by the feet of the litter bearers and the other adventurers had settled on his face and in his hair, weakening the dried color of the gory stains and blotches. Though she tried to make her touch as light as possible until she had ascertained where he had been hurt, she was not always able to do so. Particularly was this true in the bathing of his hair and beard, which had become clogged with blood. As a result, numerous washings were required. The frequent application of the wet cloth, rinsed gingerly by Abby in the cold spring water, served to revive him. He blinked his eyes and a twinkle came into them as he said, "'Lo, Rosie."

She smiled, and asked, "How do you feel now?"

"Purty good, I reckon. 'Cept'n this damn shoulder uv mine."

"Were you shot anywhere else?"

"Hell, Rosie, I don't know. I mought be but it's the shoulder whut's givin' me hell."

She did not rebuke him for his language. For certainly, she thought, allowances should be made for his condition and for the experience he had survived.

"How many's here whut's still ahead uv th' devil?" He winced as he attempted to turn on his side and see for himself.

"Jack Santoire's next to you. Next to him is the young stranger they brought here with you and him. You know who he is, anything about him?"

"Billy Baxter. Rosie, I'm gittin' fearful, fearful weak, agin." His slight strength had ebbed from the mere speaking of the few short sentences.

"Of course you are. I declare, I'll never have any sense makin' you talk like that. Now, you just don't try to say nothin' more." She called to her daughter as though she were in the next room, rather than at her side. "Get some of that broth I made this noon!"

"Mamma, I'm right here. You needn't yell at a body like that."

"I know, honey. I just forgot. Now fetch it for me, like a good girl."

Trench swallowed the nourishment with apparent gratification. Then he bore the pressure of Rosie's ministering hand with stoic fortitude as it weighed a bit too heavily on his wound. A little later she had finished with him, but not before he had lapsed again into unconsciousness.

"Th' upper half of him is as clean as it ever was," she remarked as she arose from her knees and stretched her limbs. "Now for Jack."

"Must we wash him, Mamma? You know it won't make no difference to him. I don't never remember ever seein' him look clean."

"Sh-sh-sh, Abby, he'll hear you. He gets washed just th' same." She knelt by his side. A gasp escaped her, as she saw that his eyes were open—fixedly. In a whispered voice, she said, "I'm afraid he won't need no washin'—not right now anyhow."

Abby bent over and looked at him, then drew back in awe. "Honest, Mamma. I'm sorry I just said that. I didn't mean it really." Her words were spoken in reverence.

"'Course you didn't. Don't worry about it. He must have died while I was tendin' to Jim! I saw him breathin' when Jim tried to see who else was here. Don't guess the doctor could have saved him, but I sure wish he'd get here soon."

"Mamma, you're not goin' to wash th' other one, are you? I mean, not with him in here, are you?" She pointed faintly at Santoire's body. "Maybe we could just wait outside, or some other place, til Doctor Grainger comes. Couldn't we, Mamma?"

The resolute tightening of her mother's lips was answer enough for Abby. She gave a wide berth to the dead man as she carried the pail to where the stranger lay. It was her first intimate contact with death. And young as she was, the realization that the cold, reaping wind would someday pass over her numbed her senses so that she moved as an automaton.

The first cold trickle of water to reach Baxter's eyes stirred him, and when the cooling liquid had cleansed his face, he had a brief moment of consciousness. His head was so inclined that Abby's image was that which he saw hazily, then clearly. "'Tis beautiful you are." As his sight once more became cloudy, he said softly, "Don't go away." His eyes closed easily.

"Oh, Mamma, you don't think he'll die too?"

"Not this young man. He received a bad wound in his head, but unless he's hurt worse than that, there isn't much danger of him dyin'. Here, let's look at th' rest of him." She raised his jacket and peered within. "Can't see nothin' on his chest or belly. Let's turn him over. Careful now, just in case he's got a bullet in his back."

The two found no indication of any other wound, but his back was soaked with sweat, prompting Abby to suggest they remove the buckskin shirt.

"'Fore we do, look and see if there's any blood on the lower part of his legs. That way, if there ain't none, we'll know it's just his head that's hurt."

"How would you know that, Mamma?"

"Because if he was shot below th waist, th' blood would have run down his leg. Sakes alive, Abby, can't you even figure out somethin' that easy?" Her look as she said this was not one of any maternal pride.

Abby pulled up the trouser legs, then reported, "There ain't no blood on either of 'em, Mamma. Don't 'pear to be any hair on his legs neither. He's got real nice-lookin' legs, Mamma."

"Trust you to notice such things as that. Remember, you'll soon be a married woman."

"Well, I ain't married yet."

"No, but you're goin' to be, an' you just as well get used to havin' eyes for only one man the rest of your life. Get me one of those shirts of your papa's that's put away. No, wait; I'd best get it myself. I know exactly where to find it." Rosie had kept some of her late husband's clothes in the hope her next man could wear them.

While she was out ot the room, Abby studied the young stranger's features. "Billy—Billy Baxter. That's a nice-soundin' name. You know, you're downright handsome lookin'." She said the words to herself but so taken was she with him, she might have said them audibly had there been others present and capable of hearing them.

Rosie soon returned with the shirt, talking as she entered. "Let's try this one. It ought to be just about right for him. You know, he's got shoulders like your papa had. They was real nice lookin', they was. An' he was a good-lookin' man too." She sighed and her brief reverie was over. She cautioned her daughter, "Take it real easy-like, now. We don't want to bother him no more'n we have to."

The damp jacket was slipped over his head. It was Abby who had her arm behind him, bracing his back and shoulders, as her mother eased his arms from the sleeves one at a time til they were free.

"Oh, Mamma, look at his muscles! An' his neck and shoulders! An' look! There ain't no hair on his chest at all." She lowered him gently, then stood up and admired him. "Oh, Mamma, ain't he purty—the purtiest thing you ever saw?"

"No purtier than your papa."

"Yes, even purtier than him."

"Abby, must I remind you again that you're supposed to be in love with Tom Chism? Now, you just stop acting like that. 'Tain't a bit decent."

"Oh, Mamma. Now I know how Dolly Dusenberry felt when she first looked at Bobby Williams!"

"Dolly Dusenberry looked at whom? Whatever are you talkin' about, child?" Rosie was both confused and suspicious.

Abby thought fast. "Oh, he was just a nice-lookin' boy that she knowed when she was livin' in Pennsylvania—before she got to doin' things she oughtn't."

"Hmm, is that so? And, pray tell me, when and where did you hear that from Dolly?"

Abby veered sharply from answering. "Mamma, be truthful, ain't he purty?" She stepped back, the better to view him. She felt the calf of her leg touch the corpse behind her. She screamed and ran outside.

Unmindful of what had caused her daughter's exclamation and her hurried exit, Rosie observed casually, "He ain't all that good lookin'; but he is real purty. I'll have to admit to that." She turned and walked toward the door, almost bumping into a perspiring Doctor Grainger.

Before she could greet him, he spoke snappily, "Where are they? Your daughter said that they were in here and that one of them was dead. Might have saved him if I had known earlier. That idiotic mute and that young girl told me that there were some wounded and that the others were bringing them back with them, but they didn't know where they were to be taken. It was just a little while ago that one of the party brought the information that they were at your place. Then, that Quaker, Flinden, had a bad nose bleed, and I had to stay until I had checked it." He talked as he walked to where the men lay.

As he bent to examine Jim Trench, Rosie asked, "You think Brother Flinden'll be all right? Did he fall or something?"

"Indian hit him on the side of his head." He pushed Trench's eyelid open with his thumb, then ordered, "Here, I'll need some more light. Get me a candle."

His manner, repelling any further inquiry as to Flinden's condition, she complied quickly with his demand.

"See you've washed him; that's good."

"It's his shoulder, Doctor," she advised.

He looked at her coldly. "Are you a doctor?"

"Well, no, sir, but . . ." She didn't finish the sentence.

It appeared to her that he was a bit rough in his handling of the injured man, but she held her tongue. His examination was thorough, however, and drew her respect.

He moved to Santoire. Apologetically, she said, "Didn't seem none too much use in washin' him, leastways not right away."

He made no reply but examined the body as exhaustively as he had Jim Trench's. Then he said, "Couldn't have helped him much, even if I had seen him three hours ago."

He stepped over the dead man and knelt beside Billy Baxter. Tilting the candle in order to better view the wound, he negligently allowed a few drops of the melting tallow to fall upon the youth's forehead, where they hardened instantly. If he was sensitive to their hot impact, the injured one did not show it. As Grainger arose, he asked, "Did you find anything else—any other wounds?"

Restraining a sarcastic impulse to reply, "I'm not a doctor," she answered in the negative.

He might have spared himself the possible risk of her sarcasm, for he bent over and resumed his probing of Baxter's person.

Before, when he had removed Trench's buckskins, she had stood behind him and had turned her head, thus avoiding the resultant exposure. This time, however, he was prescribing as he examined, telling her what he wanted done for Trench as well as for the young man. His voice was methodically low, and his words sing-song in their delivery, requiring her to stand close to him in order that she might understand him. Though she tried to avert her gaze as the youth's trousers receded from his waist, she found difficulty in so doing. Grainger noticed the turning of her head, and his tone was blunt. "You act like a schoolgirl—ridiculous!" As though enjoying her discomfiture, he ordered, "Take this candle and hold it closer while I look at him."

From above her reddened cheeks, she saw by degrees all of Baxter's nakedness, as the doctor slowly pulled the britches away from the waist. First, the abdomen and the hips, then the bare expanse to the knees. With the barring of each part, Grainger would make his examination and then expose more of his patient's anatomy. She tried to concentrate her eyes on the youthful thighs—"pillars of marble," Solomon had called them in his song in the Bible. As her memory served her more fully, she recalled portions of the verses. "Belly is as bright ivory—legs are as pillars of marble—His mouth is most sweet: yea, he is altogether lovely. This is my beloved—white and ruddy—his locks are bushy, and black as a raven. His eyes are as the eyes of doves … fitly set—his cheeks … as sweet flowers—his lips …"

"Here, woman, watch what you are doing! You're spilling tallow all over him! You let one of those drops land on a more tender spot and this young fellow is liable to jump right through your roof." Rosie quickly alerted herself, straightening the position of the candleholder.

Grainger smiled as the incident swept a like happening of the past clearly into his mind, then he gave voice to his memory. "That makes me think of old Dr. Patterson. It seems, one day before I had begun my own practice that was, well, one day, I was present when the old gentleman was about to perform a circumcision upon a boy, twelve or fourteen years old, somewhere around those ages anyhow. The doctor smoked a pipe incessantly, and this day was no exception! As he leaned over to examine the subject of the operation, some of the burning tobacco spilled from his pipe. You don't have to guess as to where the lighted fragments lit! That's pretty well put, isn't it? Well, anyway that boy let out a yell that could have been heard all over Boston. He ran out of Patterson's place as though the devil himself had stuck him with his burning pitchfork!" He laughed fully, then concluded. "Ever after that, until the day he died, the poor old fellow was referred to jokingly as having been the discoverer of a new method of removing the foreskin and as being the only doctor ever to have used it." His appreciation of the recollection eased off in a series of intermittent chuckles. Then he recovered Baxter's nudity. This done, he moved toward the door with Rosie still blushing vibrantly following him.

His foot was on the first step as he said to her, "Just follow my orders, and they ought to be all right. I'll be back in a few days to look at them again. Meanwhile, if any changes occur, let me know immediately."

"Doctor," she called after him. "What about the dead man? Hadn't you better get him out of there?"

He had made the transition from a jovial mood to another less cordial. "Bury him! I'm not a grave digger!"

CHAPTER 42

She again had wanted to ask him about Brother Flinden, but he had given her no opportunity to do so. She was certain he must have been hurt rather badly if it had taken Doctor Grainger as long as it apparently had to treat him. Ethan Belden had come to Brashear's Station, where she and Abby had sought sanctuary, with the glad tidings that the Indians had been routed and that those who wished to could return to their homes. While they were thankful for their shelter at the station, practically all of the refugees had welcomed the release from their close confinement and had started eagerly for their own abodes. On her way home, she had met with the last of those leaving Dowdall's Station, and that had been some time ago. "Yes," she concluded. "Aaron Flinden must've been hurt right bad."

From the direction he took when he had left Rosie's, Grainger and his family must also have moved back, for his steps headed homeward.

"I bet Mrs. Grainger really suffered, being made to live close to them settlers as she had to, even though she didn't have to stay non' too long," Rosie remarked.

Standing nearby, Abby echoed her mother's sentiment. They neither one cared for the doctor's wife, a feeling common to every woman in Bullitt's Lick.

Now that things were settling themselves toward normalcy, Rosie knew that more than likely a few of those who had vowed to ever after spend their nights at home with their wives and families would shortly recognize that the cause for their pledges had now disappeared, and they would soon be drifting inside her place. She still had some things to take care of before she would be ready for them. Foremost among them was the removal of Jack Santoire's body. Then the two wounded would have to be bedded down some place other than in the main room. The latter she could arrange for immediately but the former posed a problem—a difficulty whose solution presented itself with the arrival of two thirsty saltmakers. She promised each of them a drink in return for removing the corpse.

As they lugged the remains through the doorway, one of them laughingly said to her, "Hell, Rosie. I could've carried Ole Jack by m'self. I oughter thought of that. I'd a-had m'se'f two drinks, 'stead uv jest one."

They covered the body with a piece of old canvas, wrapping it thoroughly. Then they placed it snugly against the wall of the house.

"Anybody as is out thievin' tonight and takes this here booty is in fer a helluva big surprise when he finds out whut's inside," said one of them, nudging the corpse closer to the wall with the side of his boot.

His companion laughed with him and said, "Well, thet's enough fer th' dead. Let's go in an' take keer uv th' livin'.'"

Trench and Baxter had been made comfortable, and Rosie had succeeded in getting Abby away from them. Closing the door, she said, "I declare. I never thought I'd live to see th' day you would be so willing to take care of a sick person. Wonder was it just Jim Trench, if you'd be so anxious."

"Oh, Mamma, you know I would."

"I don't know about that, but I do know that if I had been as all fired crazy as you've been to marry Tom Chism, I'd have gone to see 'im soon's I heard he was back."

"That works both ways, Mamma. He should've come here right away. I bet I know what he was a-thinking most about—them old salt workin's of his'n."

"Well, it's good an' proper for a man to think of his work. That's what he oughta do."

"Mamma, it 'pears to me you've kinda changed your thinkin'. Before, you didn't want me to get married to Tom; now you're strong for it. How did that happen?"

"I gave my word that you two could be married, if Tom didn't drink for a month. He's keepin' his part of th' 'greement, an' I'm keepin' mine. Right now, I ain't so sure 'bout how well you're doin'.'"

A retort was on the tip of Abby's tongue when Mercer entered. Their discussion was abandoned and they greeted him effusively. A welcome so sincere, it made him feel he had returned to his own home rather than to the house of friends. Following their gratified expressions for his safety, his first question of them was, "How are the men? I would have been here sooner, but l stopped by my place first, and I stayed longer than I meant to."

"Oh, Captain Mercer! What's happened to your face? You was wounded too! Does it hurt bad? Here, let me look at it."

He resigned himself to her consideration. "It's not bad, Rosie—just a glancing lick. Outside of my jaw being a little sore, there isn't much to it. In a couple of days, I will have forgotten all about it."

"Oh, ain't that turrible!" Abby said, crowding upon her mother to make a closer inspection, an act that caused Rosie to say, "If you want to help, go get somethin' to wash his face with." When Abby hesitated, Rosie exclaimed, "Did you hear me? Go on an' do like I told you!"

His jaw stung when Rosie cleansed it. But with the application of some sort of aromatic salve, the burning sensation eased. "There, it'll be all right now," Rosie apprised him. "It ain't as bad as it 'peared first off. Just a nick but it is all swole up. How'd you get it?"

He avoided her question, asking, "What about Jim Trench and the others? How are they making out?"

She respected his concern, not repeating her own unanswered question.

Her voice broke when she related Santoire's passing but revived quickly as she described the condition of the other two. "Doctor Grainger says they'll be all right, given a little time. They ain't come to their full senses yet, though they has come to for just a spell." Adding to her assurance of their recovery, she said, "They'll do all right here. Jim Trench for sure. The young one will too, if Abby don't nurse 'im to his death."

Barth smiled as he saw the crimson's instant appearance on Abby's cheeks. He did not add to her self-consciousness, however, but asked, "Has Tom been here?"

"Not yet. He oughta be along soon, if there's nothin' wrong at his works," Rosie answered.

"That was all he thought about on our way back to the licks—whether the Indians or someone else had done any harm to his operations."

"See, Mamma. What did I tell you?"

The puzzled Mercer said nothing, but her mother spoke sharply. "Hush, Abby. Captain Mercer isn't interested in our personal affairs."

"Just th' same, I was right, wasn't I?"

"Abby Tindall! Now you get yourself busy. Folks'll be comin' around here in a little while!"

When Abby left, Barth made a request. "I'd like to write a letter to someone, Rosie. Do you have anything to write with?"

She laughed as she nodded her head. "Seems you are always wantin' to either read a letter or write one. Who's it goin' to—your young lady?"

It was Barth's turn to blush, and she was a bit shamed by his embarrassment. Easing it, she said, "I'll get you a quill and a piece of paper, an' I'm sure there's some berry juice somewhere 'round here, if I don't have no ox gall juice. Th' gall juice is better, but the other will do, unless she wants to save th' writin' for her children to read."

"Just so it will stay on the paper long enough for her to read it," he said amusedly.

"When you're done writin' it, Captain, I'll see that it gets over to Brashear's right away. There's some friends of mine leavin' th' first thing in th' mornin' for Harrodstown."

"By a strange coincidence, that's exactly where this letter is going. I feel real fortunate and grateful to you, Rosie."

He penned his message and had just sealed it, when she called to him. "Captain, when you're through, come and set down with us. Th' food's mighty good, if I do say it myself."

The thought of Rosie's cooking was delectable in itself. In assumed seriousness, he said to her as he handed her the letter, "It's only because you are going to see that my letter gets to Harrodstown that I'm consenting to eat with you." They both laughed as he was seated.

When his appetite yielded, he asked her, "Rosie, what's the matter with Johnny? I stopped by our cabin on the way over here, as I told you earlier, and he wasn't there. All of his things are gone, though nothing of mine had been touched. He's had spells before, as you know, but I really expected him to be waiting for me when I came back. He wasn't at the licks, so I decided maybe he was over at our place. I can't figure out what could be the matter."

She delayed in answering, and when she did so, it was apparent to him she was speaking with some difficulty. "Captain, I'd best not say anything. I know you think kindly of him, and what I might say might be th' wrong thing."

"Why Rosie, I thought you felt more than kindly toward him. I thought you—"

"Loved him?" she interposed.

"Well, yes. I did think that and I could understand your affection for him."

"I guess I did kinda love him. But I can see now, it wasn't th' kinda love a woman oughta have for a man. It was more like a mother lovin' a growed-up son—though I didn't realize it 'til that day he beat up that poor, humpbacked little peddlar. After that, it was all clear to me."

At Barth's confession of his ignorance concerning the incident, she recounted the affair fully. When her narration was complete, she said, "Oh, I had noticed a few changes in 'im before that, like his bein' more self-confident an' such, but I figured that was the result of your influence on him, an' I felt real good about that. But after this other happened, I got to studyin' 'bout 'im, an' I saw him just like he was, an' he is."

"How is that?" he asked. "Go ahead and tell me. Don't worry about what I might think."

"Well, when I saw what he'd done to someone just like himself—poor, I mean—it just brought the words of the Good Book right into my head. You know that proverb where it says, 'A poor man that oppresseth th' poor is like a sweeping rain which leaveth no food'? Well, that's what come to my mind. Then I could see how selfish he always had been, how conceited he was without no good grounds for him bein' so, and how he never spoke no good of nobody he didn't like an' of so many other things that I can't put into words. But I know what they are an' they ain't good things, I can tell you that. I don't think he's honest, not 'cause he don't mean to be exactly but still he knows if he's got a advantage of someone an' he don't have no feelin's 'bout usin' it if he can get what he wants. Why, there's talk now that he's struttin' around like a rooster. He's supposed to be goin' into some business, though I don't know what it could be, but its' s'posed to be here at Bullitt's Lick. Oh, my! I plumb forgot that was told me in secret, an' here I've just told it to you! You won't tell anybody, will you, Captain?"

Pledging his secrecy, he added, "I'm glad you told me what you have, Rosie. You know, sometimes we make friends too quickly and allow friendships to deepen much more than we should. I might have made that mistake with Johnny, as you did. But I hated to hear of his viciousness from you. It may seem strange, but I had never thought of him as ever being an aggressor. It was always just the opposite in my mind. To me, he was always the one in need of protection."

"Just like me, Captain Mercer, that's what you was."

Other words would have come from her but for the entrance of Tom Chism who sat down unceremoniously beside Abby as though he had just left the table for a moment and was now resuming his seat.

Abby reached over and kissed his cheek as a greeting. He did not appear to have noticed its lack of warmth, the perfunctory manner in which it had been bestowed. Whether this lack of perception was due to his extreme fatigue or the savory aroma and sight of the food or all three, Rosie and Barth could not guess, but the incident did not escape either of them.

Near the end of the meal, Abby startled her mother by asking Tom if he cared for something to drink.

"Why, Abby Tindall. What in the wide world are you thinking of? You surely don't mean brandy or whiskey, do you?"

"Yes, I do, Mamma. He's so tuckered out, I think a drink would do him good."

"Do you realize what you are sayin'—what you might be a-doin'?" Rosie asked incredulously.

"Oh, Mamma. When Tom made that promise, nobody knew he'd have to go through anything like what's happened to him today. Just one little drink ain't like he was to get drunk, is it?"

Rosie would liked to have told her, "You little vixen, haven't you any sense in your head? Don't you know that one drink is all it takes to get him started?" Instead, she said crisply, "I agreed to your marriage on one condition. You both know what that condition was."

Tom Chism showed his first interest in what they had been talking about by saying, "Abby means well, Rosie, but I ain't wantin' no drink an' I ain't takin' none, so you can just rest your mind on that." He reached for a piece of cornbread and covered it with gravy.

The mother was pleased with his assertion, but to Barth's eyes, it seemed that the daughter was piqued no little by her intended's statement. Whatever the cause, it was clear to him that Abby had changed. Whether this was but a mood of the moment or whether it was grounded more deeply, only time could tell.

The men said little to each other as the women cleared the table. Both were well within their own thoughts. Chism's mind being on his business, and Mercer's contemplating the prospect of Chism entering his employ. Several times Barth was on the verge of speaking to him about the matter, but in each instance he decided against doing so. He would talk with him on the morrow, as he had determined previously.

Contrary to her expectations, Rosie had entertained few customers this night. As the hours aged, she decided to close her door. Not wishing to offend either of them, she suggested they sleep at her place, and she was genuinely pleased when the weary men accepted her invitation. Soon, thereafter, the candles were snuffed and the place was quiet.

CHAPTER 43

He who had been the object of such serious consideration at Rosie Tindall's, Mr. John Littelby was continuing to enjoy his newly acquired position of eminence in the community—more properly among the saltmakers who labored for Mace Hardin and Mercer and among certain of the independents. His first move had been to persuade Mitch Strickler, his former tormentor, to be the overseer for his new saltworks. Entirely dubious at the inception of Johnny's persuasion, Strickler had become convinced when he had gone to the stretch of land claimed by his would-be employer and had seen the ringed tress, the token improvements and the letters J.L. carved so profusely throughout the length and breadth of the area.

To Strickler, Johnny had divulged that Mercer was the real owner of the licks Mace Hardin ran and the further information that Mercer planned to fire Hardin and all of the men working under him. Part of his statements Johnny knew to be true. The balance he added as a sure source of discontent, once the men had learned of it. Mitch had wasted no time in spreading what had been imparted to him through the ranks of Mace's workers. And he saw to it also that those who worked on shares, the independents, heard of Mercer's scheme to terminate the arrangement with them. "He's gonna run th' lot uv ya away frum th' licks," he had told them. The antagonism Mercer thought he recognized upon his return had not been any fancied resentment. The impression he had gathered was more accurate than even he had supposed at that time.

Strickler had his own plans. Once the new licks were in production, he intended to take over as Mace Hardin had done at the other place. He alone had, and would have, the close contact and control of the men. Mr. Littelby would be a figurehead. He had also considered the effect of the withdrawal of such a large number of men from Mercer's licks upon the operation. A way might develop whereby he could gain the same power over them also. Through his well-sowed discord, the intention of the dissidents was uniform. "We'll quit 'fore thet son-uv-a-bitch gits th' chance tuh run us off."

Until such time as this channeled undercurrent came out into the open, and for a brief interlude thereafter, he would continue to furnish Mr. Littelby with shelter, food and drink. He would keep up his flattering of him. But once the snare had been sprung, that would be the end of his wearisome pretense.

*

Long before dawn of the following day, while the moon appeared to be cutting through the racing clouds as though it feared the advent of the sun, Abe Foster arose and set out to perform the obligations of his employment—that of chief hunter for Tom Chism and the voracious appetites of his men. Yesterday and its Indian fighting were gone. Gnawing bellies would care naught for the triumph of that departed day.

As Bullitt's Lick continued to grow in population and the more hardy of the pioneers dared the wilderness, building their cabins ever more remotely from the settlement proper, there was a consequent diminishing of ready game. It seemed to Abe that just within the last year he had to travel lots farther in his search for provisions than had been the case formerly. The constant scent of humans, borne steadily downwind to the nostrils of the fractious wildlife, was the cause.

The section in which Abe had determined to hunt this morning lay to the west and south of the licks, on the other side of Salt River, the route skirting the land on which Mace Hardin's cabin stood. As he reached that particular point, he would have passed on by but for his ears picking up the sound of a horse neighing. At first he saw nothing when he looked toward the dwelling. Then the clouds shifted and the moonlight revealed a very stout woman in the act of mounting. While he was fairly close, he yet was too far away to obtain even a semblance of her features, but he knew from the fat, bear-shaped silhouette it could be only one person—Massalene Hardin—who by now was cutting across his path, just a little ahead of him. What looked like the shadowy outline of a large bundle, or bag, was resting on the pommel in front of her. He would take back to Tom Chism more than the fruits of this day's hunting. Mace's wife had run away from him, most probably to join the tribe of her dead father.

Had Mace Hardin known of his abandonment by Massalene, he would have been greatly angered and upset. Not because of her leaving him, but due solely to her riding out of his life on his best horse. The same beam of the moon, which had enabled Abe Foster to see her, was at that exact time skirting on the roof and coating the side of Ben Skinner's store. Since evening, as soon as Skinner had closed his place for the night, he and Hardin had been closeted inside.

On the shadowed side of Skinner's store, his ear pressed closely to the wall, a most patient Jack Doniger strained to hear their conversation. He had followed Mace from the licks earlier, as he had done a number of times before. On each previous occasion, he had learned nothing that would help his cause—freedom from bondage for Dolly and her sister and himself. Before, Mace and Skinner had talked in low tones and their conferences had been of short duration. Their meeting tonight already had proven to be different in one respect. They had been talking for a long, long time. However, he had been able to hear only a little of what they said, none of which had been of any importance. Now, though, their voices were beginning to rise and he set himself the more firmly to his eavesdropping.

Jack Doniger was approaching the point of desperation. He had heard of Little Johnny's scheme to alienate the workers from Mace Hardin, and he knew that he must act fast or there would be no opportunity for him to incite the men to open rebellion against Mace. If this were accomplished, it would not then matter to him who the men worked for. Just so Mace Hardin was taken out of the picture. But if this did not happen soon, Johnny and Mitch Strickler would make it impossible for it ever to come to pass.

"Mr. Ballister ain't goin' to like it a damn bit!" It was Skinner speaking— rather yelling. Doniger's sweat ran cold.

"Ter hell with thet son-uv-a-bitch! Yer don't think I keers whut he thinks, does yer? He's yer worry—not none uv mine!" Mace's voice was as loud as Skinner's.

"You've had too much to drink already. Don't drink no more!"

"Yer listen to me, Ben Skinner. I ain't drunk an' if'n I wuz, hit wuddn't be none uv yer damn business! Yer hain't near big 'nough, ner man 'nough, ter order me 'round, damn yer!"

A lengthy silence ensued, which before it was broken made Doniger fearful his hopes had risen too quickly. *Maybe Mace has had too much whiskey and has dozed off!* The thought swept him with consternation. Then he heard unintelligible words. They had lowered their speech again.

"I sez, damn Harry Ballister! Th' son-uv-a-bitch kin holler all he wants ter, up thar whar he ez. He don't bother me none." Mace's voice was as clear as though he had spoken through an open window.

"Yuh might change your tune, if he sends his men down here."

"Whutcher mean, Ben Skinner? Let 'im send 'em, an' 'is black soul be damned! He hain't gittin' none uv thet salt, an' that's yer damn bit uv hit! He'll send men, yer sez! If'n they ain't no bettern thet Blackie Vehrmon and his Injuns, they ain't gonner consarn nobuddy. More'n fifty Injuns, an' they cuddn't even whup ten men on a damn flatboat! Vehrmon'll take keer uv 'em, yer sez. He shore played blue hell a 'doin' hit."

Skinner's voice broke in. "Yuh ain't done so good, yorese'f. First, ya lets Mercer come here. Then yuh says you'll have Gibbs an' Mallory take care of him. Whut happens? I goes over tuh hear about how Mercer wuz kilt and 'steada seein' his body bein' hauled in, or hearin' where they buried 'im, there he comes, bigger'n life! 'Steads him bein' dead, I finds out thet them two, whut you said wuz sure tuh get 'im, is dead theirse'fs!"

Mace did not reply immediately. Doniger considered that Mace was unable to answer the truth of the assertion.

It was Skinner speaking once more. "Y' know, Mr. Ballister has been purty free with his money. Wonder whut yore men would do if they knowed ya had kept it all yorese'f."

There was a thunderous smash of fist upon wood, unmistakable to Jack Doniger's ears. He could hear the table as it rocked on its legs.

"Threatenin' me, are yer, yer bastard! I wunner whut yer wud say if'n I wuz ter git yer damn neck in m' hands an' guv it a damn good squeezin'. Holler fer

Mister Harry, I reckin. Yer gonna be a dead son-uv-a-bitch, if'n yer ain't moughty keerful."

The other's voice was lower and anxious. "Now, Mace, yuh knows I wouldn't do nuthin' like thet. I was jest a little mad when I said it. As fur as the money, there'll be more—lots more, if we can get thet salt tuh Mr. Ballinger. Yuh oughta know thet yorese'f."

There followed another extended pause. Mace too dropped the pitch of his words, but they were still loud. "They's jest this damn much to hit. I'm th' oney son-uv-a-bitch livin' whut knows whar thet salt ez hid. Them two dead bastards, Mallory an' Gibbs, wuz th' oney others whut knowed whar it ez, 'cause they moved it thar. An' they ain't gonner tell nobuddy th' hidin' place, less'n it's th' devil."

No sound came for a while, then Hardin resumed. "Reckin' I hain't done so bad at thet. With them two outer th' way, Ballister's got ter meet my price fer it, an' hit ain't gonner be no low figger. Hit's all thar too 'cept'n th' little I brung out fer Mercer thet time he wuz so damn set on shippin' it. Whut I guv 'im never 'mounter ter nuthin' compared ter whut's left."

"Yuh're overlookin' one thing, Mace. Can't nobuddy do nothin' with it, long as Mercer's alive, an' he ain't nobody's fool."

"Yer right on thet—fur as yer goes. He's a smart 'un, all right, cl'ar down ter his damn bowels. But he ain't gonner last much longer. He's leavin' fer Harrodstown soon, an' he hain't never gonner reach thar. Then, th' rest uv whut I jest tole yer holds good. An' thet Tory son-uv-a-bitch Ballister ain't gonner do nuthin' but pay whut I wants fer it. I hain't a-keerin' whut side wins—th' Tories er th' damn Continentals—I'm jest a-lookin' out fer Mace Hardin. If'n Ballister wuz so big, whut did he run away from Virginia fer, when it got a li'l hot thar fer 'im? Yes, sir, Ben Skinner, I kin take keer uv m'se'f. I hain't a-thinkin' er a-fearin' whut yer damn Mr. Ballister wants er does, an' I don't rightly git why yer so damn worked up 'bout 'im fer. Yer claims ter be a-doin' whutcher doin' fer England an' King George. Fer England, yer skinny ass! Whutcher hez got out uv it wud prob'ly make my share look like nuthin'! Th' British needs th' salt, ye sez. Til they gits it, don't let none uv it git ter th' Colonials. Wal, hits damn little they got frum me, an' they wuddn't hev got a grain uv it, if'n Jeddy-Boy hed done liken I tole him, damn his drinkin' soul ter hell!"

"Yuh're makin' a big mistake, Mace. Better be satisfied with less, an' livin' to spend it, than all of it fer a while an' then a knife in yore back. Wait. 'Fore yuh gets mad agin, I'm jest tellin' yuh th' truth." Skinner spoke excitedly, but his words were straightforward.

Back came Hardin's answer. "I hain't gonner be happy with a damn bushel less'n all uv it. I hain't even gonner guv them damn furnace bosses uv mine a peck uv it, er a peek at hit. They knows it's hid somewhars an' I kept 'em with me by promisin' each uv 'em a share—a equal share." He laughed heartily before continuing. "An' th' dumb sons-uv-bitches b'leeved whut I sed!"

Mace was still talking, but Jack Doniger had heard enough. He now held higher cards than Little Johnny and Mitch Strickler could ever hope to draw.

Overhead, heavy clouds had replaced those of an hour before and had blackened the moon. Doniger slipped quietly from his listening post and into the blackness beyond.

CHAPTER 44

When a man's feet are firmly implanted on fortune's threshold, it is only natural that such a one should have some justified feeling of importance. Likewise, it is to be considered consistent that one indulge oneself, somewhat, in practices and enjoyments previously denied in a former and lower estate.

Viewed in this understanding light, it was not unusual, therefore, that Mr. John Littelby was now deporting himself in a manner far different from that which he had done when he was Captain Mercer's deputy. While he had not been exactly impecunious before the present promise of sudden affluence, it was true he seldom had been able to permit himself to purchase more than one drink on any occasion. To have done so would have been the highest order of extravagance. Formerly, his opinions, whenever he dared express them in gatherings, were either laughed at or just ignored. His presence had been tolerated as a necessary nuisance. The articles that he carried in his pack had far greater influence than did the one who toted them. Now, all was changed. Though, to be sure, his purse had never been more empty, it mattered not. For there was always that ever-present friend who was most anxious to give him a generous draught from his jug or to buy him one, if he happened to be where liquor was being sold. His food and lodging were eagerly furnished him, likewise without charge. His words and his ideas were accorded the fullest attention. In short, the change in Little Johnny had been most complete. His appearance alone remained as before.

To every man, in the course of his lifetime, there comes at least one dream. Johnny was now having his, and he was not wasting a second of its duration. At first, he had been suspicious of those who flattered him and were so considerate of his desires. Gradually, however, he had come to walk the halls of his dream castle as one who rightly lived within its rose-colored walls. He accepted the favors shown him almost condescendingly. At the inception of his state of hopeful fancy, he had been aware of the fact that it was inevitable that some day there had to be an accounting with Mercer. He did not then see, nor did he now see, any reason to hurry that day. Consequently, he made sure that their paths did not cross unnecessarily. He had, however, given thought to their eventual meeting. Whenever it did happen, it would be his word against the other. Mercer, being a gentleman, would not resort to violence but should he be wrong in that conclusion, Strickler and his men would afford ample protection of his person. However, if gentlemanly Captain Mercer adhered to his usual pattern of behavior, he would go to law over the ownership of the property. Win or lose, it would be years before a decision would be reached. By that time, or probably well ahead of any judgment in the matter, he would have accumulated enough money to allow him to leave Bullitt's Lick and to spend the rest of his life elsewhere in comparative luxury—ease of living that he had thoroughly envisioned. He would move in high circles of society and it would not be an uncommon accomplishment. He knew of quite a few men who had pulled their feet from heavy boots and pushed them into shiny slippers. He had seen many a pair of bony knees encased in buckled satin knee britches, their legs still itching from the nettle lint of the linsey-woolsey trousers that had formerly covered them. More than once, he had witnessed the rising puff from a powdered wig, whose owner clawed it frantically, trying to get at the frontier louse, which yet lived in his hair. What others had done, Johnny felt he could do also.

Johnny was most cognizant of the fact that any dream, if it is to be realized, must be anchored, else it floats away. That any vision must be sharply focused and kept so, lest it dissolve itself, as a cloud in the sky changes from distinct form into some meaningless shape and is quickly dissipated. It was because of this cognizance on his part that Strickler had moved fast among the saltmakers, enlisting them in Johnny's employ. Only the furnace bosses and a handful of the other workers had refused to leave Mace Hardin, but these few would not matter. Final preparations for the exodus were now being made. Within another week, Hardin would suddenly find himself without any working force, and Mercer would discover that he owned a lot of salt wells, which had overnight become nonproducing water-filled holes in the ground. Then the new licks would begin their operations. By the time Mercer and Hardin had recruited the necessary manpower to once more put their works into production, the Littelby Lick, as he was already designating his holdings, would be well established. Being situated in a much better location—nearer to Dowdall's and Brashear's Stations than the other salt works, it was to be logically assumed that an advantage would be gained thereby, which would never be surrendered or overcome. Impatience is full brother to error. Johnny had not acted rashly. He had planned carefully and moved ahead surely toward the execution of his scheme.

CHAPTER 45

It was shortly after Doniger had left that Hardin and Skinner ended their violent session. As Mace felt his way along the path to where he had tied his horse, he paused and listened intently. The sounds of the restless movements of two animals came to his ears, as certainly as if they had been the separate voices of men. He left the familiar passageway and walked in an arc to the hitching post.

"Pap, Pap! It's me—Jed!"

The whispered words startled him for an instant, then he answered caustically. "Thet shore makes m' heart feel good ter hear yer voice. Whar th' hell yer bin? An' whut th' hell yer doin' here? Mebbe, yer scairt ter go home by yerseff."

"Pap, I needs yer hep—real bad—I needs yer ter hep me." Jeddy-Boy's words were near pleading.

"If'n it's money yer wants, yer jest as well not ask fer it—fer I hain't got none fer yer."

"Hit hain't money this time, Pap. I'm in bad trouble."

"Why th' hell dintcher wait fer me at home, 'stead a comin' up on me like this?"

"I wuz feared ter, Pap. Th' ole womern wud uv heerd us talkin', shore. An' yer knows she hain't bin feelin' none ter kinely lately." Again his tone was entreating. "I'm in bad trubble, Pap. Real bad, Pap, real bad."

"Aw right. Whutcher did now?"

"I kilt someun this evenin' an' I didn't mean ter really do it."

"Fust time thet I ever knowed thet yer consarned yerse'f 'bout a killin'—who wuz it?" As he spoke, the net of hopeful surmise tightened around his next thought as he asked, "Wuz it Mercer?"

Jed's negation was unnecessary. Mace knew that his own anticipation was pure vagary—that his son would not now be the least disturbed by his act had Mercer been his victim. The exhilarating effect of the whiskey he had consumed earlier had worn away, and this, plus the tedium induced by the long, heated discussion with Ben Skinner, had so sapped his verve that he merely asked wearily, "Who th' hell did yer kill—George Washington?"

Back came Jed's amused, thoroughly frightened reply. "Dolly Dusenberry."

Despite his extreme fatigue, Mace's first impulse was toward mirth and an attendant belittling of his son for his foolish tears. Then the serious aspects of the deed made their appearance. True, the woman and her sister had no standing in the settlement, and there was only a few men among the nicer people who had come in contact with her, but those who lived in Mud Garrison and the riotous, lusting saltmakers looked upon her in an entirely different and favorable light. To them, she was ample reason that they worked all day so that they might spend the night, or at least a part of it, with her. Molly's illness had made Dolly in even greater demand than formerly and her company the more requisite. Even before Molly had become sick, Dolly had been the first choice of most of the inclined men. She was the more spirited, the more fun-loving and uninhibited of the two. Every army has its camp followers, and the laborers in this salt encampment were but adhering to an age-old practice. In a place such as Saltsburg, or anywhere along the frontier, men always far outnumbered the women, and the sex urge, the strongest human instinct, had to have its natural outlet. Because of this need, girls just entering puberty had been raped or seduced, and the alarmed authorities had invoked drastic penalties for such acts, but the violations yet continued. All these things Mace knew only too well, and he readily acknowledged the useful purpose the Dusenberrys served. Nor was he unmindful that there was a degree of genuine affection that his men held for their partners in sin. Dolly would be missed by these workers of his, and the one who had murdered her had good cause to be worried were his identity to be discovered. It was also certain that her death would induce dissension and its aftereffect—discontent. These must be prevented.

Jed was jabbering. "I'm yer son, Pap. I got yer blood in me. Yer gotter hep me!"

Mace slapped his son's cheek with his open hand. "Yer hez thinned thet blood a hell uv a lot. Yer hez strained it moughty thin! Now, git on yer damn horse ant le's git goin'!"

For sometime thereafter, only the clatter of hooves broke the night-ladened quiet. One rider's senses were benumbed; the other's were sharpened, striving diligently to find a remedy for the difficulty that confronted them. It was not until they were approaching his cabin that Mace spoke. "Whar didjer do hit?"

A meek and submissive voice answered. "I don't rightly know, Pap. It wuz somewhars along thet level stretch uv ground over by th' river. I s'prized her as she kum out of th' garrison an' kerried her thar on m' horse. I wuz drunk, Pap, er I wuddn't did hit."

"Somewhars along thet level stretch! Hell, thet runs fer a couple uv miles. Is thet th' best yer kin remember?"

"I know 'bout whar it heppened, Pap, but I kain't tell yer th' 'act place. I cud fine hit in no time, wuz we ter go thar."

"Why in th' hell din'tcher burry her? Thet way, nobuddy wud uv throwed they finger at yer."

"Pap, I didn't mean ter kill her. I jest got ter drinkin' too much. As fer coverin' 'er with dirt, I cuddn't do hit, Pap. I couldn't do hit!"

Mace couldn't see Jeddy-Boy, but he knew he was trembling. "Yer want me ter guv it ter yer good?"

"Naw, Pap. Don' do hit ter me, Pap! I needs hep, not a beatin'! Kain't yer see thet?"

"If yer wants me ter hep yer, yer gotter git a-holt uv yerse'f, yer unnerstand?"

"I'll try m' best, Pap, but yer hez gotter hep me!"

"Le's start talkin' some sence. I knowed yer wuz drunk. I wuz over ter Mud Garrison lookin' fer yer."

"I wish't yer hed foun' me, Pap. I wish yer hed foun' me. Then this wuddn't uv heppened."

Mace leaned from his saddle and struck him again and Jed whimpered.

"Stop it, yer dumb bastard! Now, whutcher means, yer cuddn't burry thet damn dead slut?"

Jeddy-Boy stifled a sob. "I jest cuddn't, Pap. I loved her—I din't want ter kill her!"

"Why th' hell didjer do hit fer then?"

"I wuz jest crazy drunk, an' I got ter thinkin' 'bout whut she called me th' las' time I wuz with her."

"Whut wuz thet?"

Jed didn't answer immediately, and Mace became more irritated. "Whut th' hell did she call yer, damn yer?!"

Jed had to force the words from his mouth. "A half-breed son-uv-a-bitch." The pitch of his voice trailed to a whisper.

"Wal, yer ez one, hain't yer?"

"I reckin I ez, Pap. But it cut me ter hev her say it."

"Yer will be damn lucky if'n yer don't really git cut—by thet damn rope thet them fellers'll tie aroun' yer neck if'n they fines out yer kilt her."

"Whut kin we do, Pap? How we gonner work hit?"

"Git off 'n yer damn horse. We're home. I'll tell yer whut we're gonner do after we gits inside."

"Whut 'bout th' ole womern?"

"She best not bother me none. If'n she does, they's gonner be more'n one dead bitch ter be buried." He unfastened the bellyband and lifted the saddle with its wet blanket from his sweating mount. As he placed them on the rail to his right, he became aware that the next stall was empty. His lips poured a stream of blasting blasphemous oaths.

"Whut's wrong, Pap? Didjer hurt yerse'f someways?"

"Shut yer damn mouth. Now we got two jobs ter do, kum daylight. Thet damn Massalene hez let thet good horse git loose whut we got off'n that feller up th' crick. Le's git in th' house. Yer goin' ter see th' ole wom'n git th' whuppin' uv her life—th' damn greasy bitch!"

"Pap, we done thet real good—I mean th' way we took keer uv thet feller whut use't ter own thet horse. 'Member, I done jest liken yer tole me ter? Bet he's done floated clear to New Orleans by now."

"I tole yer ter shet yer damn mouth!"

As they reached the door, they found it open. "Whut th' hell's th' matter with her? She lets th' damn horse run away an' she don't even close th' damn door after her! Git a candle lit!"

In a few minutes, Mace knew the answers to both of his perplexities. Massalene was gone. There was nothing of hers left in the cabin. He stormed through the place, strewing its contents in his path.

Jed cried nervously. And strangely, it was the sound of his anguish that settled his father's wrath. Mace put his hand on his boy's shoulder and said to him, "Wal, thet's done, Jeddy-Boy. Now, hit's jest yer an' me whut's left. Set thet table back on its legs an' le's talk 'bout fixin' yer trubble." When Jed had done this and had placed the bottom of the candle in some of its melted wax, Mace continued. "Soon's they's daylight nuff ter see by, we rides over an' fines th' body. Then we burrys th' son-uv-a-bitch so's nobuddy kin ever fine hit. An' if'n yer feels yer kain't hep me do th' burryin', I'll do hit m'se'f an' I won't hold hit agin yer none. We'uns hez got ter stan' by each other frum here on! Now, we'll jest set a spell—no sleepin', mine yer, 'fore we starts."

The dawn was slow in breaking, but they departed with its first mist-filled haze. As they reached Mud Garrison, they saw the vague shapes of four or five men huddled outside the gate, and father and son experienced a kindred feeling of disaster. Something was amiss!

One of the group called to them as they rode up. "Ya hear th' news? Dolly Dusenberry has been killed!"

Jeddy-Boy's face was as chalk. Mace saw him blanch and sought to prevent anyone else from noticing his son's condition by directing the attention of the others to himself. "Whar 'bouts didjer fine th' body?"

The original informant answered him." None of us found her. It were one of them fellers what had his horse driv' away by th' Injuns yestiday. He was a-sneakin' up on it when he stumbled over her."

"Thet's shore too bad," Mace said solemnly. "Whar'd it happen?"

"Up yonder a piece, in th' flat land near th' river."

"She still a-layin' up thar?"

"Last thing I knowed she were. They's quite a few gone tuh look at 'er."

"Think we'll go hup ourse'fs. C'mon, Jed. Le's go see whut a dead whore looks like." His words were in character, but they were sheer bravado.

They had barely ridden out of the sight of those behind them when Mace pulled his reins. As they stopped, Jeddy-Boy retched strenuously, spewing the nauseating matter upon the side of his mount's neck and its shoulder and foreleg.

Mace did not allow any pause for his son's recuperation, rather he called to him to follow as he spurred his horse. This Jeddy-Boy did, though he rode with his head bent down with both hands gripping the head of his saddle. Mace doubled back and around Mud Garrison. Shortly, they were home again.

Mace helped Jed dismount and lent his support to him as he walked to the cabin. Inside, Jeddy-Boy stretched out upon the floor, a very sick man. Mace spoke to him reassuringly. "Jest 'cause they fines her dead, don't mean thet yer done hit. Why, lotsa people cud uv kilt her."

Jed shook his head weakly, then said faintly, "They'll know it wuz me, Pap. I carved 'er up some."

"Thet damn knife uv yer'n!" Mace exploded, then calmed. "Aw right, so they knows—er thinks—yer done hit. Thet still don't mean they kin fine yer. Yer goin' ter stay in this hyar house, an' any son-uv-a-bitch whut comes noseyin' aroun' will wish he damn well hed stayed cl'ar uv here! I'll tell th' men I hain't seed yer, thet I wuz lookin' fer yer over ter Mud Garrison m'se'f. Thet wuz yestiddy, an' Herman Tressel's wife seed me thar. So they haz ter b'leeve me when I tells 'em I hain't seed yer sence I wuz over thar." He thought a bit. "Jest keep yerse'f inside. If'n it gits ter hot fer yer, I'll gitcher out uv here an' ter some safe place. Jest remember now, bar thet damn door when I leave an' don't let no son-uv-a-bitch see yer. Yer unnerstan'?"

Jeddy-Boy nodded his assent. Mace helped him to his feet, then said, "I'm a-goin' ter th' licks. I'll be back about noon, er some'eres 'roun' then." After the door had shut behind him, Mace waited until he heard the bar drop into place, then strode to his horse. Before he got in the saddle, he gathered the reins of Jed's steed. He rode off briskly, the other horse loping easily by the side of his own mount. His course was southeast until he reached Salt River. Once there, he led his son's animal to the water's edge and whacked its flanks with a willow switch, driving it into the stream. He watched it make the crossing and climb the bank on the other side. Then he turned and headed for the licks.

CHAPTER 46

Jack Doniger's eyelids weighed heavily upon his eyes. The natural consequence of two successive sleepless nights—the one just ending and the prior one when Dolly and he had talked about their hopes and plans until early morning. As they had prepared to go to bed, Molly had suffered a coughing spell, and in comforting her they had lost any chance they might have had to rest. Along with Molly's children, they had taken refuge at Mud Garrison, and it was there that he was to meet them and see them safely home later on this morning. He had one more furnace boss to see and then he would be free to go back for them.

When he had divulged to the others that which he had heard Mace tell Skinner, quoting the former's words in their full substance, if not verbatim, they had all agreed to band together and force a showdown with their treacherous overlord. He would either disclose the location of the salt deposit and share it with them then and there, or they would drive him from the licks. If he refused their demands and would not leave the settlement, they had resolved to kill him. Eight of them had so determined. Caleb Bucher, the ninth and last, Doniger was sure would fall into the same line.

There had formerly been ten furnace bosses, until Mitch Strickler had lost his place, the day he and Mace had fought and he had been so badly beaten by him. Knowing that this had engendered an animosity, which was nourished bitterly by Strickler, Doniger reasoned that all that would be necessary in order to enlist him in this cause would be to inform him of the group's purpose. One of his friends would see to that.

With these converts already assured and joined, he walked to where Caleb Bucher was standing. Calling him aside, he recited Mace's perfidy and related what the others proposed to do about it. Though it was barely light, Doniger caught the angry look that enveloped Bucher's features. Through grim lips, Bucher said, "I'm with yuh, if'n whut yuh says is th' truth. How can yuh prove it tuh me? I ain't one fer gittin' m'se'f out on no limb, yuh know."

"We're meetin' this evenin' just 'fore dark at th' foot of Kahaz Knob. You can come an' see fer yourself."

"I'll be there," Bucher said resolutely.

Before Doniger could leave, one of the kettle tenders rushed up to them.

"Didya hear 'bout 'em findin' Dolly's body? Somebody kilt her over to th' river!"

Good God! It couldn't be his Dolly! Doniger rammed the disavowing thought into his brain. The man talked on, but he didn't hear what he was saying. It couldn't be his Dolly! Bit by bit the barrier he had raised began to crumble. He turned away, shaking with involuntary sobs.

It was Dolly's body, but it wasn't her face, not that pretty face and lips he had kissed just yesterday evening. The cheeks on each side had been cut from the corners of the mouth to the lobes of the ears. The blood had not yet dried, giving a red mask effect to the lower portion of the face. The neck was carmine streaked from another wound that a continuous slash, across the width of the throat, had produced. The breasts were bare, the right one gleaming in its contrasting whiteness to the raw, scarlet mass that was the left, whose nipple remained in its center. But, encircling it, the skin had been peeled out and away, so that it was ringed by a number of irregular curlicues. By his side, a horrified voice said, "It's th' work of a devil!"

Jack Doniger knew the devil's name, but had he not known, the sadistic appearance of the body would have told him. Whatever fate might befall Mace, Jeddy-Boy was going to die.

The eyes of even the curious were moist, and frequent curses came from the mouths of those in the crowd who had known her well. As Mace Hardin had conjectured, the life of her murderer would be forfeited, were he to be found.

Grieving men bore Dolly's body back to Mud Garrison. In their wake, Jack Doniger stumbled along, the life gone from his legs. How would he tell Molly? How would he tell her that Dolly was dead? The unanswerable questions tore at his soul.

CHAPTER 47

Barth arose minutes ahead of Rosie, but early though it was, they found that Tom Chism was already up and gone. They breakfasted lightly and when they had finished, he said to her, "I don't want it generally known until after I have left." He was still mindful of yesterday's attempts on his life. "I'm leaving for Harrodstown in the morning. I have some clothes that need a little attention, which I wish to take with me. I was wondering if you might be able to find the time to tend to them for me. I'll pay you well for your trouble."

"It will be no trouble, Captain. And as for me taking anything for doing a little something for you, I just won't do it. How long do you expect to be gone?"

"A week, possibly ten days, maybe a little longer than that. It all depends."

"Going to see your lady, aren't you?"

He laughed. "What other reason could there be that I would leave someone as sweet and kind as you are to me?"

She blushed, then flayed her hand toward him. "Ain't you somethin' now? You just fetch them things of your'n over here an' I'll make 'em look real nice."

"That I will do, as soon as I come back from Dowdall's Station. My horse is still over there."

"You're not figurin' on walkin' all that way, are you?" she asked solicitously.

"How else? Besides, the walk will be good for me." He had to laugh at his own remark, remembering the exhaustive adventure of the day before. Actually, he had had enough walking to last him for a long, long time to come. He still felt the effects of it.

Whether the recent hardship was in her mind and prompted her or whether it was only her customary concern, she nevertheless said to him, "Jim Trench's mare is back there just waitin' for someone to ride her. She ain't had no exercise since Jim went to the Falls an' you know he ain't a-goin' to be ridin' her for some time. Really, you'd be doin' him a favor and th' animal too. Go on an' get it." He did not wait to be urged further. Thanking her, he went around to the rear, pausing as he passed Jack Santoire's shrouded body.

The mount bridled and saddled, he stepped in the stirrup and raised himself onto its back. Seconds later, he was on his way. When he had left the cabins behind him and had entered upon the edge of the forested stretch between them and Dowdall's, he noted a strong breeze had come up. The leaves of the maple trees ahead were showing white to the wind—a fairly accurate indication of coming rain. The sun was shining, but its rays were weak, much as a wan smile on the face of a hopeless invalid. *That sun won't be out too long. Wouldn't be surprised if it was raining before I get back*, he thought, squinting as he looked skyward.

With Mercer's departure, Rosie began the day's chores. Busily devoted to them, she raised herself sharply at the calling of her name.

"Rosie! Have you heard about it? Ain't it terrible?"

It was a neighbor of hers from down the way a piece—Sarah Jenks, an excited Sarah Jenks. Before Rosie could make any inquiry, Sarah blurted out, "Dolly Dusenberry's been killed! Poor Dolly, to have to die like that! Maybe it was God's punishment on her for th' life she lived."

Rosie blazed. "What do you mean by sayin' such a awful thing? You'd best be careful or God will give you some of that punishment you're so quick to say has come to Dolly Dusenberry. Dolly was a good girl. She had her one fault, and I admit it was a bad one, but th' rest of her was good. She was kind and thoughtful and she forgave all of us what looked down on her. Some women I know was just envious that they couldn't be as attractive to th' men in this here place as she was. Not that they wanted to be like her all th' way, you understand."

"Are you meanin' that I was jealous of her?"

"No, no, Sarah. I wasn't thinkin' of you when I said that. But why do you ask?"

"Well, I didn't know who you was aimin' at. To tell you th' truth, I'm kinda sorry I rushed here, like a good neighbor, to tell you about it. Maybe next time I'll know better."

"Now, now, Sarah. Just calm yourself. I didn't mean to offend you, and I do thank you that you thought first of me when you heard about it."

Her feeling soothed, the good neighbor said guiltily, "To be truthful, Rosie, you ain't th' first that I told about it, but I did think of tellin' you right away. I knowed how nice you been to them two, poor bad women."

"Sarah, let's have no more talk of bad women or you'll get me started all over again."

"I'm sorry, Rosie. I won't say it no more."

"That's as it should be. Now, when did it happen? Do they know who done it?"

Sarah Jenks gave her the full story, adding, as is always the case with bandied sensationalism, a few extra touches of her own. When she had concluded her distressing narration, Rosie commented sadly, "Th' poor, long-sufferin' soul. I pray th' Lord in heaven has her with him at this moment."

Sarah's surprised look brought Rosie's observation. "You ain't forgettin' Mary Magdalene, are you, Sarah?"

From Sarah's drooped lips came the succinct admission. "No."

"Now, Sarah, there ain't nothin' we can do for poor Dolly, 'cept to bury her and pray for her soul. But there's others I'm a-thinkin' needs our help. That poor, sick Molly an' them two sweet little children. Wait here, while I get my bonnet. We're goin' over to their house this instant."

"They ain't at their place, Rosie. They're over to Mud Garrison."

"Then we'll get over there." As she adjusted her poke bonnet, she called to her daughter, "Abby, we're not openin' up til I come back. Somethin' important has come up an' I have to go over to Mud Garrison for a spell. Don't let nobody in, less'n it's someone you know real well. Better bar th' door after me."

No answer being immediately forthcoming, she called in a stronger voice, "Abigail Tindall! You hear me?"

As always, the formal use of her name resulted in Abby's prompt acknowledgment. "I heard you, Mamma. I won't let nobody in til you come back."

"If'n we was to hurry, we might get a ride over to th' garrison. It's a fur piece over there, you know," Sarah informed her. "They was a waggin from over there at Ben Skinner's just a bit ago. If'n it ain't gone 'fore we gets there, we can most likely go back with whoever owns it."

Rosie's fingers deftly manipulated the strings of her bonnet, tying them securely under her chin. They were ready to leave. As they hurried away, their broad rear expanses shifted from side to side with each hastening step.

Seated at Baxter's bedside, Abby inserted a finger in one of the curls in his hair, accentuating its spiral by gently rolling it. In deference to the hot weather, his jacket had been removed when he had been placed in the bed and it was on this exposed portion of his torso that her eyes rested. She had seen the bare-waisted men of the licks and she detested the hair that seemed to abound on every chest, and even on some of their backs. To her, such appearances were suggestive of animals, not of human beings. She had wondered whether or not Tom Chism had such growths of hair on his body and if their wedding night disclosed their presence whether she would be able to reconcile herself. She had never seen Tom without his shirt on, and once or twice she had been tempted to ask him to take it off. Fearing that further garments might be removed, and doubting her self-control if they were, she had refrained from doing so. Now, she gazed upon the well-developed shoulders and chest of Billy Baxter. Not a trace of hair did she see.

She leaned over his sleeping features, admiring his long eyelashes, the sweet, relaxed formation of his lips and the clean, wholesome cut of his jaw and the way his ears sloped along the sides of his head. Since he slept, she spoke freely to him. "Billy Baxter, I've said it before, and I'll say it again, You're th' purtiest man I have ever saw in my whole life!" Closing her eyes, she lowered her lips to his and kissed them. To her shocked astonishment, his mouth responded to hers. Her opened eyes found themselves looking straight into his, and she was conscious of their color, a velvety brown. She held the kiss, unbelievingly.

Behind her, the door was ajar. She had failed to close it when she had replied to her mother. A man's face was at the opening—Tom Chism's. The eyes watched silently for a moment, then the face withdrew.

Finally she rallied her senses and raised her head. Always quick to show embarrassment by the easy flushing of her features, Abby blushed her supreme blush as she heard Billy Baxter say to her, "The first time I saw your face, I thought I was dreaming. Now I know you're real. No dream kisses could ever be that good."

She was so choked with surprise, no words could be formed. Recognizing her confusion, he waited patiently for her to say something.

When her mind and her throat muscles had relaxed, she spoke rapidly and tartly. "You can't be no gentleman—to let me talk like that—to say the things I did to you—and to let me even kiss you while you pretended you were asleep! You ought to be ashamed of yourself! One thing certain, I'll never talk like that or kiss you again!" She paused and, as if to emphasize her seriousness, added, "An' that's for sure."

At this show of indignation, Billy Baxter smiled ever so slightly. She was quick to observe this. "That's right. Go ahead an' laugh at me! I reckon I deserve it!"

"You deserve nothing of the kind, except more kisses like the one you just gave to me. Honestly, I had been asleep, and when I heard your voice I thought I really was dreaming. Then when I felt your lips on mine, I opened my eyes and it was real! That's th' way it happened. Honest it did! You believe me, don't you?"

For her affirmation, she bent over him, then moved her cheek against his. The roughness of his young beard lent a peculiar thrill, much like the plucking of a rose from a thorn-infested bower. Turning her head slowly, her lips once again found his, and when they did so, there they remained. She permitted her body to ease downward until her breasts and her thumping heart were upon his chest. There was an unconscious movement of their arms, as they locked themselves together.

*

Just when Barth believed he would make it back to Rosie's before the heavy clouds unloosed their burdens, the drops began to fall, and it was a wet horse and rider that pulled into the stall behind her house. Before attending Sagitta, he unsaddled the borrowed mare that had trailed with him from Dowdall's and saw that she was bedded down properly After he had hung his own steed's dripping bridle on a peg, he ran along the side of Rosie's place toward its entrance, seeking to avoid as much exposure as he could. The filled canvas that had been Santoire was directly in his path and he skipped around it, observing as he did so the little sagging places in the covering that had filled with water. As he reached the door, it was opening, seemingly by itself. Then he found himself face to face with Tom Chism, with whom he narrowly averted colliding. Tom stepped back, allowing him to enter.

"It's really coming down out there," Barth said. "You just get here?"

"I was just leaving. I was waiting for some of my men to come and help me with Jack's body. Figured on buryin' him today, but with all this," he indicated the rain, "I reckon we'll have to do it tomorrow." Opening the door a little, he looked out. "Here come my men now." He made as if to move outside.

"Tom, before you leave, I want to ask you something that I've given a lot of thought to. But before we start talking, let's sit down over there and have Rosie bring us something—I'm sorry, I forgot you're not drinking these days." As he said this, Barth was puzzled by the look that came over Tom's face.

"I haven't been drinking, Mercer, that's true. But this might just be the very day I start again. Much as I'd like to, I can't sit down with you at this time. Some other time maybe." Barth nodded his assent, and Tom continued. "Days like this here one plays hell with th' wells. Got to be real careful that th' rainwater don't get in 'em. But you know that, I'm certain. Say, how comes you're not over at your own place?"

"I'm goin' to Harrodstown for a few days. Got things to do before I leave. I had wanted to discuss an important matter with you before I left. Guess it can wait until I get back."

"I sure hope so. You understand about today, though, don't you?" Tom was earnest.

"Surely—sure I do. It'll wait. By the way, I wonder what's a-keeping Rosie?"

"I looked for her, but she 'ain't here. She's probably down th' way an' got helt in by th' rain. She'll be 'long in a minute most likely. Here, let's see if we can raise anybody around this place." He began beating loudly on the door.

Barth was surprised, but he made no comment.

In the room in the rear of the house, the devouring embrace had been broken by the sounds coming from out front. Abby literally forced herself from Baxter's encircling arms. She did not notice the door to the room had not been closed. Her first thought was to stop the commotion so she might return to Billy Baxter. Other things ran through her mind too. Dolly had seen all of Bobby Williams before falling in love with him. She had seen only half of Billy and she already loved him. Mamma seen all of him. Wonder would she tell me about th' rest of him if I was to ask her? One thing I know. Tom Chism can't hold no candle with him, not if kissin's got anything to do with it. I'm gonna tell Tom th' next—' Her thoughts jumped. That is Tom and Captain Mercer standing right in front of me!

She managed to greet them. Then, speaking directly to Chism, she said, "Tom, there's somethin' I been meanin' to say to you an' now's the time to say it. I—"

He broke in upon her words. "Looks like that's what rainy days is for—for people to speak to each other about somethin'. First, Mercer here says that to me, an' now you say th' same thing. Only I believe I know what you've been meanin' to say. You left th' door open, Abby. I saw you back there, just a minute ago."

Her mouth flew open. Then she tried to talk. "Tom, I'm ... I'm awful sorry. I ... I ... just don't know what to say to you."

""That was what you was goin' to tell me, wasn't it?"

"Yes, Tom, that's what it was. I'm sorry as I can be. I didn't aim to hurt you none."

"It's done, Abby. Maybe it's for th' best. Maybe I would've been too old for you. Guess Rosie was right in th' first place." He seemed to be pondering something. "Well, at least I kept my part of th' bargain. Now it's done with." Addressing Mercer, he said, "Next time we meet, I'll take that drink—th' biggest one you want to buy me."

He did not bid them goodbye, but turned on his heel and pulled the door open. They saw him speak to his men, while standing there in the muddy street as if impervious to the drenching rain. They watched until Santoire's body had been placed in the wagon and the horses turned in the other direction. Then they closed the door.

Aware that silence was best observed in situations such as this one, Barth made no inquiry. "I'll wait til your mother returns. You just go on with what you were doing when I came in," he said. She nodded her head and walked away.

In one way, she was sorry she had forgotten to bar the front door. Had she done so, she could have told Tom herself instead of him having to learn of her change of heart in a manner that must have not only hurt him but also which must have been totally embarrassing. Yet, harsh as the way had been, there was no denying its effectiveness. He now knew, beyond any question, that she loved someone else. Her steps quickened at the thought of one who was waiting for her.

This time the door was closed tightly.

CHAPTER 48

Sitting there, waiting for the downpour to abate, Barth reflected upon the scene he had just witnessed. He had been correct in his belief that Abby had changed. He now realized the change was no mood but was permanent. He propped his feet on the bench in front of him and closed his eyes, intending further contemplation of the situation between Abby and Tom. He nodded a few times and his chin dropped. He was fast asleep.

When he awoke, he noted the door was open and that the sunlight streaming through it almost reached his elevated boots. He lowered his feet and placed the palm of one hand on the back of his neck, stretching his head backward in an effort to relieve the slight cramp he had sustained by reason of his strained sleeping position.

Rosie came up to him and said, "Had yourself a good nap, didn't you? I declare, you looked so peaceful there, I didn't have no heart to wake you."

His expression bordered on sheepishness. "Bet I snored like all get-out, didn't I?"

She was diplomatic in her reply. "You was sawin' away, all right. But I ain't never saw no man worth his salt wha' didn't do it soon's he closed his eyes. My man used to claim that th' reason he made such a racket when he snored was because he was a-forcin' th' tiredness out of his body so that when he woke up, he would feel real fresh." Her eyes twinkled. "You know, Captain. I used to tell him that if what he said was true, he was th' tiredest man I ever heert of." She laughed and gathered her lips mischievously. "An' you know somethin', Captain Mercer. I reckon you must've been a right smart tired yourself."

He rallied his wit. "And do you know something, Rosie? It's been a female trick, ever since Eve first used it, for a woman to allay criticism of herself by pointing out a man's fault to him before he can get started on hers. Now that you've been caught red-handed, what time is it? And just where have you been all this time?"

She laughed and the ripples of her infectious mirth seemed to roll down to her toes. "It's right at dinner time. I just got back from bein' over to Mud Garrison."

Her brow wrinkled instantly, and all the lightness left her countenance. "Oh, Captain, it was turrible! That poor thing!" She appeared on the very brink of crying as she went on. "I always have believed that vengeance is for th' Lord to handle, but for this once I hope they find out who done it and that they make 'im suffer for it 'fore he dies."

When she found he had heard nothing of the tragedy, she cried as she told him the lurid story, stopping frequently as she used her forefinger to carry away the constant tears. Foolishly, she angrily related, those who had brought the body to the garrison had let Molly see the mutilated corpse, and this imprudent act had caused her to fall into a state of shock so severe, she appeared to have lost her mind. They had buried Dolly during the heaviest part of the rainstorm, and Rosie herself had said the only prayer over her soggy grave.

Barth's first question was, "Who did it?"

Now the heels of her hands wiped her damp eyes, whose pupils functioned in seas of fiery red. She sneezed, placing her hand on his arm to steady herself during the involuntary spasm. "I hope I don't come down with nothin'. I was wet to th' bone when I come back here. I got out of my things as fast as I could." Her mind moved back to his inquiry as she said, "I'm sorry, Captain." With his reassuring nod, she answered him. "They don't know for sure, but most of them seems to think it was that Jed Hardin. You 'member Jack Doniger? 'Member Mace Hardin sent him here once't with a warnin'?"

"I remember, Rosie."

"Well, you'd have thought he was kin to Dolly, th' way he cried an' carried on. He swore Jed had done it, that Dolly had told him he had threatened to kill her not so long ago. There was one or two fellers there that claimed they saw Mace at Mud Garrison early this mornin', an' that one of them told Mace about them just hearin' that she had been killed. Another feller said that some man was with 'em, an' he thinks it was Jed. They said, though, that it wasn't real light and they couldn't tell it was him for sure."

"Which direction were they headed?"

"To'ards where it happened. Someone is s'posed to have asked Mace Hardin whether Jed was with him, and they said he claimed that he wasn't, that he hadn't seen him for th' last day or so. Hilda Tressel told me herself that Mace was there yesterday afternoon lookin' for 'im."

"What do you think, Rosie? You think he might be the one?"

"I don't know, Captain. Jed's got a bad name from usin' his knife. Ain't so much his usin' it, as how he uses it. Guess I'm gettin' you all mixed up, ain't I?"

"I know what you mean."

"Well, I ain't sure in my mind about him. He might've been th' one. But if he was with Mace, like that man said he was, most likely Mace would say Jed had been with 'im when Dolly was killed. That way, Jed couldn't have did it."

"Do they know when it happened?"

"Some says they saw her leavin' th' garrison 'fore dark last night."

"But, Rosie, didn't you say that Mace claimed that he hadn't seen Jed for some time?"

"I know I did, Captain. But that might be just talk. Th' way they is all a-feared of Mace, I can't see any of them askin' 'im somethin' like that."

Her reasoning was sound, Barth thought, as he said to her, "If Jeddy-Boy is th' one, you can bet that Mace will swear that he found him long before Dolly was supposed to have left Mud Garrison, and that he spent th' night with him. If he does that, they'd never be able to convict him."

"Captain, it ain 't no question 'bout no convictin'. Them men is all stirred up. You're thinkin' like the lawyers think. If them men decides he's th' one, that's all th' convictin' they'll need. I tell you, they wasn't but one feller I saw over there, what wasn't upset about this' an' it was Johnny—I mean—Mister Littelby," she emphasized his name.

"Did you talk with him? How is he?"

She drew herself up. "Captain Mercer, I told you I'm done with 'im. Besides, he acted like he didn't see me. But I know he did all right. 'Stead of being concerned about th' killin', he really 'peared to be worried cause all th' men was payin' more attention to th' murder than they was to him. Even that Strickler feller', what I hear he's been so thick with, wasn't payin' 'im no mind."

The mention of Little Johnny caused Barth to digress. "Rosie, when I get back, I'm goin' to corner Johnny and find out why he walked out on me."

"Better leave 'im alone, Captain. It ain't a very nice thing for me to say, but when you come across manure in your path, you walk around it, not through it." She blushed as she spoke the words.

"I'll give it some thought, Rosie."

It was she who abandoned the previous discussion. "Did you bring them things you was talkin' about?"

"I haven't been to my place, Rosie. I stopped here on my way back for a drink, and I fell asleep, like you found me. Tom Chism was leaving as I came in."

"Him and Abby together, was they?"

He evaded the literal for the figurative. "Yes, they were together just before he left." Her relieved expression made it clear she had been misled by his answer and he quickly decided it was not his place to tell her about that which had actually taken place.

Once again, she was her attentive self. "You still want somethin' to drink?"

"Well," he drawled the word, "I was interested in one, but didn't I hear you say it was around dinner time?"

"If you ain't th' one!"

Her smile did wonders for her face. He marveled at the maneuverability of her emotions. Just a little while ago, she had been in the depths of grief over Dolly's dire destruction.

"You just set right there. You an' me will eat to—"

A cry of panic came to them, followed by a tearful Abby. "Mamma, come quick! I'm a-feared Billy—I mean Mr. Baxter—has got some bad sickness!"

Barth was a poor third in the race to the wounded man. Incongruously, he found Baxter sitting up, smiling broadly.

One quick glance at his radiant face was enough to dispute the dread her daughter had instilled in Rosie's breast. "Abby Tindall, I declare. What in the world has got into you? I've told you, over and over, Doctor Grainger says he will be all right. How many times do I have to tell you that before you'll believe me?"

"Oh, I know, Mamma, but look at his forehead. Looks like he's caught somethin' bad!"

"I told her there wasn't nothin' wrong, ma'am, but she insists there is." Baxter put his fingers upon his brow. "This here's what's worryin' her."

Rosie tilted his head to one side, to better view the source of Abby's alarm. There, plainly visible, were two slick, hard welts. Maybe they were a sign of some approaching malady, she thought, A sudden enlightenment came upon her. Catching her fingernail on the edge of one of the spots, she peeled off a piece of the hardened tallow she had so carelessly permitted to drop there the evening before and held it between her thumb and forefinger for her daughter's inspection. "See, Abby, it's just some candlewax that I spilled on him yesterday. You should have heard Doctor Grainger fuss at me when I did it!" She didn't tell them what the doctor had said to her.

"Oh, Mamma, you don't know how good you have made me feel!" Abby crossed her hands on her breast.

The others laughed at her needless anguish, causing Rosie to admonish them. "Mr. Baxter's about ready to get up from there, but Jim Trench, over yonder, is in for a rougher time of it. How's he been doin', Abby?"

"Oh, Mamma, he's been sleepin' ever since 'fore you left this mornin'."

"That's good. There's been enough excitement around here for a while. Now you," she addressed Baxter, "get some sleep, if you can. The rest of you get out of here." She nudged Abby gently on her way.

Abby thought Jim Trench had been sleeping. She would never have recovered from her embarrassment had she known that, while his eyes had been closed, he had been fully awake.

It would be Jim who would tactfully tell Rosie a few days later that he thought Abby and Billy were interested in each other.

The meal Rosie had suggested they eat together bore out once again Barth's contention that she was the best cook on the frontier. The two had asked Abby to join them, but she had professed she was not hungry. To him, this was the surest sign of all that she was truly in love. When a girl possessed of an appetite such as Abby had declined to eat, she was either ill or her mind was too busy concentrating on the man of her choice to permit her to think of food.

While Barth was eating, he watched her hovering outside the closed door as she made unnecessary trips in its direction. Love is the tenderest and yet the harshest of human emotions, he thought, as he visualized Abby's concern for Billy Baxter, and then, her honorable, but nevertheless brutally frank, admission to Tom Chism that she no longer cared for him.

He swallowed the last sip of his brandy before saying to Rosie, "Have you told Abby about what happened to Dolly?"

"Not yet," she replied. "I know how it's goin' to upset her, and I just ain't been able to bring myself to doin' it."

"They'll be talking about it in here, soon as they start coming in. She'll hear it then and it might shock her more than if you told her beforehand."

"All right, Captain. If you think it's best, I'll do it now. I won't be gone no longer'n I have to be."

"Don't worry about that. I've got some matters to attend to myself. I have to be leaving anyway."

"You're not going to get mixed up in th' business of tryin' to find Dolly's killer, are you? You'd best stay out of it, if you'll excuse me for sayin' so."

"I intend staying out of it, though I confess there is a temptation to do what I could to bring the murderer to justice."

She appeared relieved. "I hope you keep on thinkin' that way. Them others will find th' one who done it, if he can be foun'."

He excused himself as he arose. She sighed and started toward where Abby sat dreamily, her head resting against the wall that separated her from the young man on its other side.

Mercer was halfway out the door, when he heard Rosie call to him. "Captain, don't forget to bring them things you want done up!"

"I won't, Rosie. I'll be back here by suppertime." With that, he bade her goodbye again and went to the stall for Sagitta.

CHAPTER 49

At the licks, this afternoon seemed as any other. And if Hardin was troubled by the morning's discovery and its repercussions, there was no outward evidence of the fact in either his speech or his actions. Barth conversed briefly with him, telling him, as he prepared to leave, of his intended departure sometime on the morrow. He did not disclose his destination or how long he would be gone. By keeping Mace ignorant as to the time when he would be back, Barth felt he would have less reason to worry while he was away. After the first four or five days, Mace would see to it that everything was as it should be, as a precaution against his returning unexpectedly.

Barth had promised Abe Foster he would give Tom Chism and him an explanation of the deaths of Mallory and Gibbs. For this purpose, he now rode to find them. Had Mercer taken the time to inspect his own operations, he would have seen the little groups of men huddled together as they talked of the meeting to be held later on in the day. Only when Mace Hardin was in their vicinity did they disperse themselves.

*

It was a shaken Doniger who answered Mace's summons. All the way to the storehouse, his overburdened brain dwelt on the cause of his sending for him. Had Mace heard of the meeting? Did Mace know of his leading part in arranging it? He had talked to a large number of the saltworkers. Had one or more of them pretended to be in sympathy with his cause—and then gone to Mace and informed on him? Or could the purpose of this call have anything to do with Jeddy-Boy? Would Mace ask him to help perfect an alibi for his son?

Despite the fear these thoughts instilled in him, Doniger's determination did not falter. But he silently prayed that he not betray himself by any showing of his consternation. He did not know what he would do if Mace questioned him as to the conspiracy or accused him of having a part in it. Nor did he know what his answer would be if he were asked to aid Jeddy-Boy in any way.

There was Mace Hardin, standing by the storehouse entrance. Doniger summoned all of his self-control. Am I climbing to th' end of that limb Caleb Bucher wuz worried about, he wondered.

"Yuh sent for me, Mace?"

"Yer knows damn well I did! Whar th' hell yuh bin hidin' all day?"

Doniger was certain the limb was being cut behind him. "Nowheres in particklar, boss." He hated to call Mace boss. "I come soon's I heard yuh wanted me." The words had taken some of the stiffening from his already weak spine. Now I'm in fer it, he thought. This'll be m' finish. He glanced about him, wondering if anyone would come to his aid, but no one was near—just Mace Hardin. Soon he felt there would be just Mace.

"Doniger, ain't I allus trusted yer? An' ain't I allus took keer uv yer fer doin' whut I tole yer ter?"

Weakly, he gulped, "Thet's right, boss."

"Wal, I heerd suthin' ter day thet I figgers yer kin hep me with."

Here it comes, Doniger thought.

"Howjer like ter do a special job fer me—one thet'd pay yer extry good?"

At least Mace ain't connectin' me with whut I bin doin'. The thought brought immense comfort to him. The limb wasn't shaking as much as it had before. He had a firm backbone again.

"Whut yuh want me tuh do?"

"Lissen clos't now. Mercer's leavin' termorry. Th' son-uv-a-bitch ain't tole me, but I know he's goin' ter Harrodstown ter see thet womern uv his'n. But I ain't got no idear whut time he's figgerin' on goin'. Now, whut I wants yer ter do ez ter foller th' bastard until yer sees 'im start out frum here. Then yer kums quick as hell ter me an' let's me know. Yer got it now? Yer does it good an' I sees yer gits took keer uv real proper."

It was easier for Doniger to talk now—the weighty dread had cleared from his mind and his legs were strengthened. He was no longer up a tree. His feet were firmly on safe earth. "I'll 'tend tuh it, boss." Never had he taken greater pleasure in lying.

"See thet yer does. Th' son-uv-a-bitch jest took off in th' direction uv Chism's. Yer picks 'im up on his way back an' keeps a-follerin' 'im 'til he leaves. Y' unnerstan?"

"Boss, yuh gotta remember, I ain't got no horse. It'd be hard as hell tuh foller 'im on foot."

"Now ain't thet suthin'! Borry a horse, yer dumb bastard! Now, git ter it!"

Jack Doniger's reprieve was now complete. He was leaving unscathed. He laughed to himself. By the time Mace learned of Mercer's departure, the captain would be miles away from Bullitt's Lick. That is, assuming Mace would be alive to hear of it.

*

When Barth reached the other saltworks, he was glad Tom Chism had not given him a chance to talk to him. Abe Foster had just conducted him to where Tom lay in a drunken sleep.

"Ole Tom's makin' up fer lost time, Cap'n. He whar awright til after we burried Jack Santoire, then he got hisse'f a jug. He drunk damn nigh all uv it." Abe picked up the opened container and raising it to his ear shook it violently.

"They ain't much left in thar," he said appraisingly. "But they ain't no use lettin' th' air git ter hit—takes th' stren'th frum it—yer know." He laughed as he said this. "An' seein' as how Tom ain't gonner drink it, why, they's no use uv lettin' it go ter waste, ez thar, Cap'n?" He put his finger through the hole in the handle and turned it away from him, so that the jug rested on his forearm. Then he tilted it to his mouth. From the number of swallows he took before he had drained it, it was clear there had been more whiskey in it than he had thought there was.

Abe flipped the empty jug to one side and watched it bump along over the uneven ground until it spun slowly around to a halt. "As yer kin plainly see, Cap'n, Tom ain't in no shape ter do no talkin'. Ez they enything whut I kin do fer yer, til he gits able?"

"Thanks, Abe. What I have to say I was going to say to both of you. Since Tom is like he is, you can tell him for me." He then gave his account of how Hawkstraw had saved his life.

"Cap'n, yer didn't need to splain ter me about them two dead sons-uv-bitches. I knowed whut heppened 'fore yer tole me—knowed 'bout it yestiday. Cain't figger thet Hawkstraw out though. Wunner why he done hit fer? Mace wud kill 'im' if'n he knowed he cros't 'im hup thet a-way."

Barth told how he had saved the mute's life, and Abe acknowledged perhaps that might be the answer, but he added, "Hit still ain't like 'im none. He hain't never been one ter 'preciate enything whut nobuddy done fer 'im—strengest feller yer ever knowed."

They talked at length until the sun had moved toward its setting. It was then Barth mentioned his forthcoming journey, and Abe wished him Godspeed. The last Mercer saw of him, Abe had picked up the discarded jug and was holding it to his nostrils, sniffing deeply.

Barth's stay at his cabin was brief—just the time required to gather his possessions. This done, he rode toward the settlement and Rosie Tindall's, where he planned to sup and spend the night.

*

Thirty-seven men were assembled at the base of Kahaz Knob as the purple shadows ushered in the dusk. Included were all of the furnace bosses. Many more of the saltmakers had expressed a desire to be present. But, fearing that was too large a number to absent themselves, Mace might be tipped off as to the meeting and probably as to its purpose, Doniger had asked them not to come.

Jack Doniger was heartened by the full turnout. The furnace bosses were there solely for selfish reasons; the others had come because of Dolly. One who had been among the first to arrive was present out of deadly hatred—Mitch Strickler.

At first, there was much confusion, as the dead prostitute and the name of her suspected slayer were foremost in the discussion. However, order was achieved with the designation of Caleb Bucher to preside over the vengeful assemblage—an appointment Bucher clearly did not relish and one he accepted with the greatest reluctance.

They concluded the meeting around an immense fire, after having fully mapped their strategy. At midmorning of the next day, when Mace could be expected to make his customary appearance at the storehouse, they were to leave their tasks and gather there. First, the furnace bosses would have their say, and expose his intended treachery. They would then make their demands of him. Upon his submission to their wishes, or after he had defied them, whichever occurred, he would then be questioned as to the whereabouts of Jeddy-Boy, and if he claimed he had no knowledge as to Jed, the man who had talked with him at Mud Garrison this morning, Luke McCready, was to come forward and establish that he had seen Jed with him on that occasion. If Mace denied this was true, as he had done earlier, or if he refused to talk, he was to be dealt with according to how he had reacted to the previous propositions, which the furnace bosses were to have made to him. His life would be spared if he would disclose where he had stored the salt, but he would have to leave Bullitt's Lick immediately. If he refused to comply with the latter demand in either of its particulars, he was to be put to death forthwith by hanging. Then they were all to go after Jeddy-Boy. They would hang him also, if and when they found him.

To ensure that these plans would be carried through to their complete execution, each man present had been pledged to secrecy and had been required to allow another to puncture one of his fingers with a thorn. Their confederation was thus sealed in their own blood. Had any been uncertain as to whether or not he wished to be finally bound by the night's proceedings, or had there been the slightest indecision as to his participation in the anticipated showdown with Mace, that man would not have undergone this final test of allegiance.

For it is a common incidence among men—the bravest and strongest included—that they are most loathe that their blood be let, save in case of a sickness whose exigency necessitates that it be done or where they enter into combat, knowing it to be unlikely that it would not be shed. So, the voluntary spilling of blood was an act of deep significance. At this time tomorrow, Saltsburg would be without Mace Hardin, or Mace Hardin would be without this world.

Significant also was the part Jack Doniger was playing and the courageous manner in which he was acting his role. His primary purpose in arranging this insurrection as an avenue of escape for Dolly had failed. Jed had already prevented that with his knife. The present end toward which he was now striving had been born with her death. When it had been achieved, he would take Molly and her two children and leave for the long dreamed of gap in eastern Pennsylvania.

CHAPTER 50

It had been Barth's intention to sleep late this morning, then to eat a full breakfast. Late, to his reckoning, was about two hours after dawn, and it was at that approximate time he felt his shoulder being gently tugged. He opened his eyes slowly, then rolled them upward where they rested upon Rosie Tindall. He smiled his appreciation, and it also served as his greeting to her.

"Captain, it's a good rest that you've had, and I'm callin' you like you asked me to. Besides that, you've got a visitor who's waitin' to see you."

He got hastily to his feet. Maybe Dracie had tired of waiting for him and had come here. "How long has she been here?" he asked.

"Calm down, Captain Mercer, it's not a she. It's a young man who has a message for you, which he refused to give to anyone but yourself." Her eyes held a certain roguish sparkle.

He slipped his jacket over his head and adjusted it to his body and went to meet his early caller. His face lit up in a humorous warmth, which he sent toward Rosie, as he looked back at her after discovering the identity of the one who wished to speak to him. It was Jason from Doctor Grainger's.

"Good mawnin', Cap'n Mercer." Without waiting for a response, Jason delivered his message. "Yoah presents ez respeckably rec-recwested at Doctuh Grainguh's home, suh, an' yo' ez s'posed ter tell me if yo' ez comin', an' how soon yo' ez ter be spected." There was no denying the relief Jason experienced when he had finished delivering the carefully memorized invitation.

Barth placed his hand on the little messenger's head and lightly swished it over his kinky hair. "You delivered the message just fine, Jason." His hands yet clasped behind his back as they were when he had spoken by rote, Jason dropped his head to hide his bashfulness.

"Do you know what I'm going to do?" Mercer asked.

Jason did not look up, but shook his head from side to side, its range being just full enough to permit Mercer and Rosie, who had meanwhile drawn near, to catch at its one extreme, a glimpse of an eye opening wide and the accompanying rising smile on his lips. A shy, low-spoken, "No, suh," was whispered to the floor.

Barth did not keep him long in doubt as to his intention. "I'm going to give you another coin and this time, I am going to tell your father that I will not let you return it."

It was as though the top of Jason's head was, in some mysterious way, connected to the money piece in Mercer's pouch, for as it was withdrawn, the' little black head was raised, exposing the happy face of a boy who was on the verge of regaining that which he had believed to have been lost forever.

"Thank yo' kinely, suh." Jason had to restrain himself, lest he grab the bit of shining silver from the captain's hand. The second it touched his palm, however, he closed his small fist around it and ran out the door, only to return immediately to ask breathlessly, "Ez yo' comin', suh, an' when ez yo'—if yo' ez?"

"Yes, Jason. I'm coming." He stopped briefly to let his welling mirth escape, before adding, "Just as soon as I have eaten and tended to a few things here. You may say that I'll be over shortly."

"Yassuh, Cap'n." He called the words over his shoulder as he raced away.

Rosie covered the table with food, then seated herself opposite him. The two conversed as they ate. The recollection of the cherubic, little, chocolate-colored lad lingered in Mercer's mind as he said to her, "Rosie, if the good Lord has made anything cuter than a little Negro boy, he has not yet revealed it to mortal eyes."

"Th' little girls is cute too, Captain, White an' colored."

"Of course, they are, Rosie, but the little boys are cuter," he said in a teasing manner.

"Now, ain't that just like a man to say that! It's a pity th' men don't think like that when th' girls is growed up. They'd be a lot less of trouble in this world, if they did."

"A lot less trouble but a lot less fun also, wouldn't you say?"

Both laughed at his truism. They ate silently for a few moments before renewing their conversation. At its conclusion, as they prepared to arise, she said, "Captain, I have your things all nice an' ready for you to take with you. Let me get them, an' see how you like them." He tried to tell her that there was no immediate hurry, but she would not be stayed, saying, "Now it won't take me a minute to fetch them."

When she had returned and had spread the garments on a table, he inspected them. "They are done up beautifully, Rosie. Your husband really had a good wife."

A bit embarrassed by his praise, she said, "Oh, Captain, you're flatterin' me!"

"No, I'm not, and I am going to insist that you let me pay you."

"Really, Captain Mercer. I don't want—"

He did not let her finish. "I'd feel greatly offended were you to refuse to let me do so."

Recognizing his seriousness about the matter, she accepted first the payment for his night's lodging and meals, and then the money he gave her for her work. Her eyes widened when she realized how much he was paying her. She checked a sincere desire to protest the amount as being too much for what little she had done. It would truly displease him, she admitted to herself.

After she had cleared the table, and he had finished his packing, she asked, "Are you coming back here before you go?"

"I don't think so. I'll probably leave from Grainger's."

In a matter of minutes thereafter, he was ready to leave. She wished him a safe and pleasant journey, adding to her goodbye, "You just tell your lady some of them things you tell to me. All women loves to hear 'em. Course, I 'magines you'll be tellin' her a whole lot more, an' more personal, if you know whut I mean. Prob'ly be more kissin' than talkin' though, I expect. Been so long since I was kissed by a man, I done forgot what it's like."

Taking her by complete surprise, he lifted her from her feet and kissed her lips. She was so stunned, she could say nothing as he lowered her to the floor and began gathering his possessions. Waving to her as he turned to go for Sagitta, he said laughingly, "That will have to last until the next lucky man comes along."

Her natural color returned gradually, and with it a thought that had entered her mind as she had listened to Jason reciting the invitation. When he had dropped in to see Jim Trench and Billy Baxter yesterday, Doctor Grainger had mentioned he was leaving for Falls of the Ohio at dawn today to aid the doctors there in their attempts to combat a threatened epidemic, which had risen, and to help treat its victims, whom he understood to be quite numerous. Thinking back upon the doctor's transient moods, she considered he must have changed his mind, or else he too had slept late this morning. She stood in her doorway until Mercer, astride his horse, rode past. She watched after him briefly, thinking enviously, If I was ten years younger and had been born into his world.

Abby and Billy Baxter, ambulatory on Doctor Grainger's specific order, startled her as they approached from the rear.

"Land sakes, Abby. You like to scairt me to death!"

"Honest, Mamma, we didn't mean to. We was just walkin' natcheral like."

Addressing Baxter, Rosie said sternly, "Now, young man, just cause th' doctor said you can get up, don't mean you're to overdo it, you understand?"

"Yes, ma'am," he replied with a pretense of servility. "With your permission, Abby would like to show me around Bullitt's Lick."

"All right, but mind you don't do too much walkin'." Her gaze followed them, as they artfully dodged the many mired places in the street, Abby tittering at each narrow evasion.

As Rosie turned to her work, she said to herself, "There wasn't nothin' of Tom Chism in that girl's eyes. Somethin' must be wrong between them. Come to think of it, Abe Foster acted a little queer when he was here yesterday evenin' to see Jim Trench. I 'member now, when I asked him was Tom comin' later, he just said Tom couldn't come. Didn't give no reason. Tom must've been drunk—that's about th' trouble."

CHAPTER 51

There was something fascinating about the manner in which the door was opening in response to his light tapping of its rough surface, not unlike the heightened suspense engendered by a slowly parting curtain at the unveiling of a new painting by some renowned artist. Indeed, there was a suggestion of the mysterious, as the floor beyond the sill was revealed in smoothly motioned degrees. With each fraction of movement, a fragrance from within, faint at its onset, grew tantalizingly stronger.

The portal now had completed its inward circuit, but Mercer's feet were still on the outer side of the threshold. He waited, expectantly, for the precise attendance of Chate, but he did not appear. Barth was beginning to experience a feeling of conspicuous isolation, when a dulcet voice entreated him, "Please, come inside, Captain Mercer." The words were Drusilla Grainger's.

He entered, stepping obliquely so that the door might be closed freely behind him, then turned around to present himself to the doctor's wife. Instead of finding her directly in front of him, his eyes discovered her in the act of dropping a miniature latch, sufficient to bar the door in accomplishment of its peaceful, daytime purpose, the ensuring of the privacy of the household. His eyes discovered her, and astonishment prised their lids in amazement at her flimsy attire, whose transparency solved the enigma of his delayed admission. Propriety overcame his confusion, permitting him to say, "Doctor Grainger requested that I come over." Then the thought of what would happen, were the jealous doctor to find him with his wife in her present state of dishabille, provided the necessary words for an excuse to avoid such an occurrence. "I see that you were not expecting me this early. Please tell the doctor that I will wait for him outside."

She stood between him and the door, and she made no effort to remove herself from his way. For a moment, there was an awkward silence. Then she spoke. "The doctor didn't send for you. I did. Ever since the night you visited with us, I have waited for you to come to me, but you did not come. I have made my pride yield to my desire for you, and now that you are here with me, I am glad that I have done so. It is a small sacrifice compared with its reward. For the first time in my life I am going to say the words that a man has always said to me, before I addressed them to him. "I love you, Barth Mercer. I have loved you from the moment I first laid my eyes upon you."

Drusilla was saying these things—was openly professing her love for him. She was standing there in all of her passion-inspired, thinly veiled nakedness. He was in this room—within an arm's length of her—yet it could not be true. This is the sort of situation in which one finds oneself only in baseless dreams. He tried, desperately, to reason against reality.

She misconstrued his silent incredulity. "You need not worry about Richard. At this moment, he is well on his way to Louisville. Some person named Wilkins brought him a message a few days ago from the doctors there. He would have left before today, but the Indian scare discouraged him from leaving any sooner. He will, in all likelihood, stay at the Falls for at least two weeks—possibly three. And all the time he is gone, we can be together." She put her arms around his body and raised her face hungrily.

Again, she misinterpreted his failure to speak. "I have given strict orders to Callie and Chate. They will not disturb us or permit anyone else to do so."

Her words alone could not have ensnared him. But the carefully prepared ingredients she had blended so finely—the intoxicating intimacy of heavy perfume, her own suggestive nudity, the privacy offered, her evident desire for his body, the element of devastating surprise—coordinated themselves to produce the planned effect. The throbbing within his temples, pounding away as though trying to force an exit through the very skin that restrained it and the ever-increasing flow of hot blood roaring into his brain fashioned their own thoughts. Discretion is a mockery to be exercised by fools who have never had this flaming opportunity thrust upon them—who never had the chance to taste the sweetness of stolen waters or to partake of the satisfying bread eaten in secret.

He wrapped his arms about her, pressing her to him. So tightly did he hold her, her panting breath came in jerky, intermittent gusts. The thickness of his buckskin clothing could not keep out the heat searing from her limbs to his nor could his jacket prevent the feeling of the firm impressions of her breasts.

Their faces were afire as his lips came to hers. He saw the magnificence that bathes the features of a woman in her passion, when her beauty achieves absolute perfection. Her lips parted, and she ran the tip of her tongue lightly around the contour of his mouth, another faggot to further feed the flame. He slid his lips free of this exciting sensation, across her cheek and to her delicately framed ear, kissing it deeply. Her lips roamed about his neck, the underpart of his clearly defined jaw.

She read his intention and relaxed her arms at the first lessening of the pressure upon her person. Grasping the edges of his sleeves, she held them high as he lowered his head and moved backward to aid in the removal of the impeding leather shirt. As she pulled it from him, he bumped the table behind him, causing the raised lid of the dueling case to fall shut—a sound that did not register upon ears whose acuteness had been smothered from within.

It had long been claimed by many that, of the two sexes, the female mind adapts itself more readily to undue stress and excitement than does the male. If this contention has any merit, its correctness must find its basis in the fundamental difference existing between the two, namely that woman is an emotional creature by her very nature and man's emotions are inherently few, though many are after acquired.

However opinionated the learned may be on this subject, there was no denying that Drusilla's reasoning powers were well balanced, even when interwoven with the coarse strands of lust. She pursued her objective, and she knew the means of its attainment.

Mercer, the amateur, was being ruled solely by desire. To be sure, he had engaged in previous affairs with women, though notably few. But whatever experience he may have gleaned was of small aid to him now. Drusilla led and he followed without recognizing her dominance.

He took the sweaty jacket from her hands and cast it aside, not caring where it dropped. Before he could take a forward step, she said to him, "Just stand there a moment. I want to feast my eyes upon you." She was satisfying one element of her passion in viewing the bared portion of his body. When she was ready to enter upon the final phase—the actual union of her body with his—this image would persist and would add to the part her imagination would play in its enjoyment. Thus, the picture would be complete. She meant to have full nudity through a later sequence in their lovemaking.

As a trembling hound, anxious to continue the chase, he stood as he had been bidden, his powerful chest muscles expanding and contracting with each nervous breath.

She lowered herself gracefully to the richly carpeted floor and was fully reclined. Then she beckoned him, and he came, standing over her as she had meant for him to do. Her eyes had feasted upon him. His eyes now devoured the shapely whiteness of her nakedness.

To her, this was the penultimate moment—the adoration of her physical perfectness by the one she had chosen to be her lover. So highly intensified were her sensations, she drank of such admiration as fully as if it were rare liqueur from a glass.

He was beside her. The back of her shoulders, resting upon his arm, pinioned beneath them. Then he drew her to him, so that she reposed on her side, her face looking into his.

The inherent masculine instinct of masterfulness was beginning to assert itself. Having set him fully upon the course of her desire, she would now be content to share its direction with him.

Their progress thus far had overruled the use of words. Rather, they had communicated through their racing senses, by their heartbeats and their kisses, by their responsive embracing. Then she spoke. "You are the one for whom I have been searching, even before I met Richard. It was you whom my heart loved at the inception of its feeling. Though I moved among hundreds of other men, yours was the face, yours was the body, yours was the charm, which I was ever seeking. And at last, I have found you. When it seemed that you were nowhere to be found, it was on the edge of this nowhere that you appeared. Now that you are mine, I shall never let you go."

She spoke, and yet her throaty words were not wholly for him, and he sensed their division. The sensual haze that had blinded his reason was becoming less dense. Thoughts began to form through the medium of solitary words, then through their coupling.

Though as yet unbroken, the spell she had woven had been weakened. The depths of his enslaved concentration had been penetrated.

She perceived the declination in the degree of his ardor, though its variance was shadow thin. His lips were upon hers, but the level of their intensity had lowered. She sped her tongue over them to revive his passions as one attempts to fan a flame back to its former brilliance. But the fire grew weaker, not stronger. Her mouth was about his ear, exploring the open fibrous channels of its outer structure, then the entrance to the organ. Though he responded, it was not with full zeal.

She spread her tapered fingers upon his cheek and brought them lightly down its side, dipping them around his jaw and the length of the neck beneath, thence over and under his breast and the underlying firmness of the flesh upon his ribs, taking leave of the skin above his hips as she reached the leather, which yet covered the rest of his person. Her thumb and forefinger gathered a tuck between them and tightened upon it. Then she exercised the slightest downward pull. This was to be the moment, predetermined by her, when she would relinquish the initiative unto him. But he failed to assume it. He made no move to shed his covering. She worked her fingers around his waist, between the band of his britches and his abdomen, in a vain effort to direct his straying attention to that which she wished him to do. Though he kissed her neck and shoulder, he did not move his hands, nor did he change his position. She knew then his hypnosis was no longer complete.

When prudence would have dictated an obedient silence in the garden, Eve had uttered the words that cost her true desire. Drusilla had employed words when none were needed, and she was in grave danger of losing that for which her entire being throbbed so desperately. The useless word, the needless word, the trademarks of woman.

She beseeched him pointedly. "Barth, dearest, don't you want to now?"

He did not answer her. Someone else, somewhere in his befuddled memory had called him "Barth, dearest." Then it came clearly to him, squeezing through the oppressive bulwarks barricading his mind against the entry of anything other than passion. Those words—Barth, dearest—had been written and whispered to him by Dracie—Dracie Claycomb.

Drusilla was being beset by the early stages of frustration, and she recognized their appearance. She availed herself of every artifice of enticement she had ever known in an effort to restore his former tumescence. His kisses and the strength of his arms attested that she was succeeding. Then, once again, she unwittingly ruptured the web she was striving so furiously to weave. "Just think, darling, this is only the beginning of our enjoyment of each other! Richard will be away for a long time, and we can be together every night. Oh, I'm so happy! And I'm so wondrously glad I waited for you." She released herself from his hold upon her and kissed his face, arms, chest and stomach in rapid, violent succession, returning her reaching lips to his when she had finished, only to find his interest again ebbing away.

Malcolm Mercer had well instructed his only son. He had conveyed to him the lessons learned through his own experience. All through Barth's childhood and into his youth, he had imparted the observations of other relative human conduct. And he had seen to it that Barth became well acquainted with the basic rules of life. The Bible had been the backbone of his instructions, the most accurate measure of truth or falsity, of that which was right, of that which was wrong.

Malcolm Mercer's teachings were, at this moment, bearing their fullest fruit. Drusilla's words had brought back to his mind his earlier speech and together they suggested, and became in his mind, the picture of the biblical harlots he recalled from Proverbs. "So she caught him, and kissed him, and with an impudent face said unto him . . . Therefore came I forth to meet thee, diligently to seek thy face, and I have found thee. I have decked my bed . . . I have perfumed my bed . . . Come, let us take our fill of love . . . let us solace ourselves with loves. For the goodman is not at home, he is gone a long journey . . . and will come home at the day appointed."

He had come to his senses. Stability had returned. As he freed himself from her arms, the nails of her fingers dug into his flesh and marked it with long, bleeding stripes.

He did not answer her fury. The remembered words from Proverbs kept coming. "With her much fair speech she caused him to yield, with the flattering of her lips she forced him. He goeth after her straightway, as an ox goeth to the slaughter, or as a fool to the correction of the stocks." He heard the conclusion of the passage in his father's voice. "Her house is the way to hell, going down to the chambers of death."

From the recent past, there came to him Doctor Grainger's quotation from Rochefoucauld. "In her first passion, a woman loves her lover; in all the rest, she loves only love." He picked up his jacket and worked his head through its opening, the wet leather sticking to him as it passed over his shoulders and about his body. All the while, she beat upon him with her fists, convulsive sobs interspersing themselves among the flailing blows. She continued her treatment of him until he opened the door. Then her arms dropped loosely to her sides, and she stood there as one afflicted. The sunlight enveloped the entrance for an instant. In the ensuing second, she was alone in the subdued light of the room she had sought to make her bedchamber.

Outside, he mounted Sagitta and reined away from the dwelling. The temptation to return assailed him briefly, but like one other in the Holy Writ, he did not look back. The literal significance of the pillar of salt was now made clear to him.

He had not noticed the little colored boy peeking around the corner of the house when he had come out. Nor did he hear the boy calling, respectfully, as the lad tried to tell him his father had agreed that he could keep the coin. His forward-looking eyes could not see the stranger, who walked brusquely past Jason and knocked on the door.

This time, Drusilla's shaking hands opened it quickly, and her heart sang. "He has come back to me!"

There was nothing of disappointment within her as her emotion-controlled brain recognized the man she had humiliated at Dowdall's Station. She saw in his face his purpose, and it was the same as hers. She closed her eyes. In her pulsating prurience, she needed him. Immediately they were together, then upon the floor.

The scene that Abby Tindall had visualized, but found wanting at Dolly Dusenberry's, was here, and its lustful actors were playing their parts.

CHAPTER 52

The hour was at hand. Mace dismounted and looped the reins around the hickory hitching bar in front of the storehouse As he went inside, they began to assemble without. Soon, they numbered more than a hundred. Then commenced the period of nervous anticipation until he would appear. A few lost heart in the mere waiting and drifted away. None of these who remained made any conversation. What few words were spoken were passed in terse, low voices.

The tension enlarged with each pressing minute. Caleb Bucher perspired freely. The palms of his hands were moist, and he rubbed them dry on the sides of his britches. Then the huge frame of Mace Hardin filled the open doorway.

At first, he appeared taken aback at the size of the throng before him. He seemingly was scanning every face, as though committing each one to indelible memory. A fear, instilled by his silent peering, moved numerous ones to ease themselves away and return to their work. But the majority stood firm.

When he spoke, the sound of his deep tones struck them as a mental sledge. "Whut th' hell is th' meanin' uv this? Hez all yer sons-uv-bitches lost yer brains?" He looked at the furnace bosses, as he continued. "Whut's th' matter with yer bastards—a-standin' 'round here, this time uv day?"

The subleaders stared at their spokesman, Caleb Bucher, but his dry tongue refused to function.

For a moment, it appeared the cause would be lost. Jack Doniger, who had fomented this insurrection, knew that his fate would be sealed if Bucher, or someone else, did not speak quickly.

Caleb Bucher was thinking too. If he did not say anything, and the crowd dispersed without any action on its part, Mace would soon know of what he had come there to do. Silence would condemn him more surely than would the performance of the duty assigned him. His lips opened and the words slowly formed. "We'uns is here tuh talk with yuh." Not questioning the faithfulness of those aligned with him to their pledges, he nevertheless made sure that Mace be informed of their membership in the confederation. "All us here wuz at a meetin' last night. Th' rest ot the boys," he indicated his fellow furnace bosses, "an' most of them whut's standin' here—"

Mace interrupted him. "I know 'bout yer meetin'. I knowed it when yers wuz hevin' it."

Bucher glanced around apprehensively, expecting to see some Judas come forward and doom them all. The tightness in his chest made it difficult for him to breathe. He waited for Mace to relate the discovery of the plot against him.

"Yers hed yer damn meetin'. Now s'pose yer tells me whut it wuz fer." He saw Doniger and, believing he was there to tell him of Mercer's departure, he said irritatedly, "Now, do yer damn talkin' fast! I wants ter talk some with Jack Doniger. I bin 'spectin' 'im." Then, without making any reference to Mercer by name, he asked, "Thet feller left yet, Jack?"

All eyes shot to Doniger. Doubts ran rampant as the conspirators wondered at the import of Mace's question. Had Doniger led them on? Was this whole thing the planned trickery of Mace Hardin to either test their loyalty or to provide him an excuse for ridding himself of them? Jack Doniger had always been a damned coward, protected only because Mace, for reasons known only to himself, had seen fit to use him. Had everyone been betrayed by this weakling?

Had Doniger known their thoughts, he could not have uttered his next words, but in his fortunate ignorance, he made his bold reply. "If'n yuh means Cap'n Mercer, he might be halfway tuh where he's goin' fer all I knows, an' I hopes he is. Somebuddy might kill 'im someday, but it ain't a-gonna be you what does it or has it done. I ain't saw 'im an' I didn't try tuh see 'im. I wuz at that meetin' yuh said ya heared about."

The effect was electrifying upon both the assemblage and upon Mace Hardin. The spirit and intent of the former was completely revitalized, and its unity of purpose thoroughly welded. The latter refused to believe his ears. "Thet spineless li'l bastard—that skinny-assed son-uv-a-bitch a-talkin' to me liken thet!" The thought captured his tongue and held it prisoner.

Caleb Bucher was now sure of his support. "Mace, I'm speakin' fer th' bosses. We wants our part of that salt what yuh got hid an' we wants it now! We found out about how yuh was plannin' tuh trick us, an' we ain't aimin' tuh give yuh the chanc't tuh do it!"

Mace eyed him bitterly and coldly. Crises, major and minor, were common occurrences. He had lived with them all his life. Without a second's hesitancy, he said, "Now, yer look at me, Caleb Bucher, an' lissen damn good ter whut I hez ter say. They ain't no son uv-a-bitch, yer er anyone els't, gonner tell me whut I hev ter do. An' as fer th' salt I got saved, if'n yer dumb bastards dint hev no more sense then ter think I wuz goin' ter guv yers some uv it, then yers wuddn't have th' sense ter know whut ter do with hit enyways. Now, all yer scummy bastards git yer asses back ter work, an' I wants ever one uv yer ter keep in yer mines thet I'm gonner take keer uv ever damn one uv yers, soon's I gits th' time ter do hit!"

He meant what he said, and the conspirators knew that he did. Individually, they feared him as much as they ever had, but as a unified body, they knew he could not prevail against them.

It was Caleb Bucher again. "Yuh has had yore say, Mace, an' yuh ain't a-scarin' nobuddy. We're givin' yuh one last chanc't tuh save yore life. If'n yuh shares th' salt, yuh kin leave th' licks with what all yuh kin take with yuh. If'n yuh don't give us our fair share or tell us where y' got it stowed, then we're goin' tuh kill yuh." He pointed to the many weapons in evidence. "Them boys'll use 'em on yuh, sure as hell's fire is hot. Now, what's it goin' tuh be? Yuh want tuh live or yuh want tuh die?"

"Yer kint be meanin' whut yer sez. Yer must be daft er jest plumb crazy. Not thet I'm worried none about whut yer sez, y' unnerstan. But, jest s'posin' yer wuz ter hev 'nough nerve ter try it, don'tcher know yer kint jest kill no one fer whutcher claims I aims ter do? Who in th' hell ever heered uv sech goin's on—killin' a man 'cause he won't guv yer his own propity?" He shook his head and laughed.

"Yuh has done it fer less'n that—lotsa times."

Mace snapped his attention to his accuser. "Look at th' son-uv-a-bitch whut sed that—Ab Washley! Seems ter me, I 'member th' reason he kum here wuz 'cause he kilt a feller whut caught 'im with his wife. An' th' rest uv yers," he swept his hand inclusively, "they ain't but damn few uv yers whut ain't kilt someun er stole frum 'em."

Washley fired back at him. "Most of 'em whut has done them things, yuh wuz behind th' doin' of 'em!"

Hardin evaded the truth. "Thet's whut yer sez! Th' rest uv yers knows better'n thet. Yer knows how I hez allus looked out fer yers."

Washley kept after him. "They knows a damn lot more'n yuh thinks they does. They knows about whut good care yuh took of Bad-Eye Smith. Good care, yuh says? They knows how yuh had Jeddy-Boy foller 'im an' sculp 'im. Ain't a damn man here whut trusts yuh!"

"Yer a lyin' son-uv-a-bitch, Ab Washley! I kin prove by Ben Skinner thet I tole 'im ter git some money ter the Falls fer Bad-Eye, soon's he got hisse'f thar!"

"Yuh shore picked a good-un tuh back yuh up. Yuh knows Ben Skinner left th' licks early this mornin' with Doctor Grainger an' some others. Yuh know he ain't comin' back—that he's sellin' his store."

"Th' sneakin', dirty bastard!" The exclamation sprung from Mace's lips before he could close them. "So, it got too hot fer 'im—the dirty, scheming, son-uv-a-bitch Tory! Prob'ly runnin' ter Harry Ballister." Mace's features depicted his thoughts, furrowed brows above a murderous scowl and the crescent scar producing a satanic picture of evil.

"Yuh means yuh ain't heared of his leavin'?" The skeptical Washley asked, then said, before Mace could reply, "Like hell, yuh ain't!"

"I shore ez hell ain't knowed nuthin' uv it afore this!" he retorted hotly.

"Don't make no damn bit of diffrunce, if'n yuh knowed it or not—ain't none of us b'leeves yuh nohow." Washley turned himself so that he faced toward Caleb Bucher and said to him, "Bucher, yore s'posed tuh be th' leader of this here bunch. Ain't yuh heared enough from 'im tuh know he ain't gonna give us none of th' salt an' that he ain't gonna tell where he's got it hid? Whut yuh waitin' fer?"

Mace did not let Bucher answer. A plan had come to him, while Washley was talking. "Now yer knows these damn fellers is done at these hyar licks." He was ignoring the furnace bosses and addressing the others. "An' yer knows thet them bastards'll wish they never heered uv me 'fore I'm done with 'em. Now, I figgers thet they made yer pore sons-uv-bitches kum here with 'em." His eyes rested on Jack Doniger. "All uv yers, 'cept'n Doniger thet is, an' thet cowardly bastard'll git tooken keer uv proper. Now, yers all knows them damn fellers ez got good jobs an' they hez ter be filled. An' hit jest mought be thet some uv yers cud git them jobs if'n yers wuz ter walk on off frum here an' git back ter work. Now, if'n yers moves right quick, I promises ter fergit yers wuz in sech bad comp'ny liken yer hez been this mornin'."

There was a shifting of feet, but no one accepted his offer. He waited, then thundered at them. "By God, thet does it! They ain't more'n sixty uv yers, all tole, an' whut ain't here is lots more'n thet. I kin count on them others ter hep me run yer dirty, back-stabbin' asses cl'ar outer Saltsburg!"

"Yuh can't count on any uv 'em. Most uv 'em wuz leavin yuh 'fore this come up. They is all gonna work fer me at th' new licks whut Mr. Littelby owns south uv th' river. Yuh an' Mercer wuz gonna have these here workin's all tuh yoreselfs, oney yuh didn't know it. Now, it looks liken it's jest gonna be Mercer, if'n this here bunch means whut they says they does." It was Strickler intervening.

"Mitch Strickler, yer a bigger damn fool than I reckined yer fer bein'. Mister Littelby yer calls 'im, does yer?" Mace's laughter was genuine, and it caused Strickler's face to color.

But before Strickler could take up the issue, Doniger was speaking. "Them fellers," his forefinger was directed toward Bucher and the other bosses, "is here fer one thing, an' yuh knows by now whut that is. Th' rest uv us come here tuh find out where Jed is at. We thinks yuh knows th' answer tuh that an' we aims tuh hear yuh tell us."

Mace was glad Doniger had interrupted. It would give him a chance to think as he answered him and would stay any overt move against him. He began by posing a question. "Whut makes yer b'leeve thet I knows whar he mought be? Yer knows Jed. He's liable ter be in Bairdstown or mebbe over ter Severn's Valley. Yer knows how he goes. Besides, whut's so damn important 'bout knowin' whar he be?"

Doniger's voice was firm. "He killed Dolly Dusenberry an' we're goin' tuh find him an' hang 'im. Yuh wuz with 'im early yesterday mornin'. Him an' yuh stopped at th' gate over at Mud Garrison. Luke McCready wuz there, an' he says he thinks he heared yuh talkin tuh 'im."

"Thinks he heered me, yer sez! Yer damn polecat, yer orter be more sartin 'fore yer goes accusin' people! Whar's thet McCready, er whutever his name ez?"

"Right back there." Doniger called to him. "Come up here, Luke, an' tell 'im whut yuh seen an' heared!"

A visibly shaken young man came forward. Mace glowered his fiercest, as he said to him, "Young feller, yer best be damn shore uv whutcher doin. Yer ain't bin 'round hyar long, hez yer?" The youth acknowledged by a negative movement of his head, and Mace asked loudly, "How long yer bin here?"

"Four months."

"Four months, he sez! Did yers hear 'im? An' yers ez gonner take 'is word on suthin' liken this? I tole thet son-uv-a-bitch whut asked me 'bout it yestiday thet I hedn't saw Jeddy-Boy fer a couple uv days. Why, damn yer, Doniger, yer wuz with me yerse'f when I wuz a-lookin' fer 'im!"

Doniger passed over the assertion, asking McCready, "Like, yuh ain't been here long, but yuh knows Jed Hardin when yuh sees 'im, don't yuh?"

McCready gave his confirmation. "I seen 'im lots of times over to th' garrison."

"An' yuh are shore ya heered Mace say somethin' tuh 'im an' call his name?"

"It sounded like he did to me."

Mace could not contain himself. "Look here, boy, it wuz damn nigh dark when I wuz thar! How th' hell cud yer be so damn shore thet Jed wuz th' one with me?"

McCready was hesitant, and Mace seized upon this. "See thar? Th' boy kint say it wuzzn't dark. He knows damn well he kint be shore who wuz thar with me!" He shot another leading question at the youth. "Boy, yer ain't ter damn sartin thet yer heered Jed's name liken Doniger claims, are yer?"

"It sounded a lot like it, best I can recollect it."

"Yer ain't shore, though, are yer?"

"No, I ain't real certain about it."

The realization had come to Mace that he had made a mistake in not claiming Jed had been with him at that time and the entire night before. An ironclad alibi had offered itself, and he had overlooked it for a more involved defense.

He asked the witness another question. "Boy, yer knows it's bad ter say suthin' thet mought git someun in bad trouble, dontcher?"

"Yes, I do," came the honest reply.

"Now, boy, cud yer swear ter God thet yer seen Jed an' me tergether? Wud yer be willin' ter do thet?"

"I don't reckon as how I could swear it was him, but I think it was all right."

"Yer thinks it wuz him!" He spoke to the throng. "Damn sech evidunce ez thet! Why, yers all knows if'n I wanted ter lie ter yers, I cud say I wuz with Jed all th' night 'fore thet pore girl got kilt." He strayed, to emphasize his regard for the dead woman. "Why, I hez spent some time with 'er, liken th' rest uv yers, an' I wuddn't uv wanted nuthin' ter heppen ter her liken whut did. She wuz all right, she wuz. Course, thar wuz them whut dint think so, but not me. An' I wuz damn bad sorry ter heer 'bout her bein' done in. I feels liken yer does. Th' son-uv-a-bitch whut done hit orter be strung hup by 'is damn balls!" He now returned to his defense. "So, yers kin plainly see, I hain't got no reason fer ter lie ter yers, an' yers ain't got no reason ter 'cuse me uv pertectin' Jed. Jeddy-Boy dunt need no pertectin'. He hain't th' one whut done hit. Now, I thinks yers all 'grees with me on thet, so, whyn't yers all git on 'bout yer bizness an' lemme take keer uv them greedy bastards yonder?" He motioned his head toward the furnace bosses.

Ab Washley didn't intend to let the attempted diversionary move get started. "If'n whut yuh says, 'bout Jed not bein' with yuh is th' truth, then who wuz with yuh at Mud Garrison, yestiday mornin'?"

Mace stalled for time to think. "I thought yer wuz interusted in salt not in th' whore." Immediately, the expressions on the faces of those before him told him that he had erred gravely in his reference to the one now dead. He realized the folly in trying to soften his careless allusion and continued. "Mebbe hit ain't th' salt or th' pore, dead critter's killer yer wants a-tall. Mebbe hit's jest thet yer wants a excuse ter git rid uv me!"

Washley would not be sidetracked. "Whut wuz th' feller's name?"

He knew he had to answer. "It wuz jest some feller whut drapped by ter 'range fer buyin' some salt."

"Whut wuz his name?" Washley kept boring.

Mace's face lit up. "Now whyn't I think uv thet afore this? His name wuz Ned—Ned—lessee, damn if'n I kin bring ter m' mine his las' name. So, thet's whut thet young feller, McCready, heered! I kin see plain, how he cud get hisse'f mixed up." He looked at the crowd. Disbelief stared back at him.

Doniger broke in with interrogation. "Are yuh willin' tuh help us fine Jed? An' if'n we does, are yuh willin' tuh help string 'im up?"

Mace had moved so that he was near the unsuspecting Caleb Bucher. Any answer Mace would make to the question would bind him, except one made in defiance of the mob. He caught the group's surging temper and determined upon escape. Grabbing Bucher, he swung him quickly around. In the same action, he pressed his left forearm against the latter's windpipe and held him securely against his chest. Then he began backing toward the hitching rack. "Go ahead an' shoot, yer scummy bastards. Hit wont hurt Bucher none too much."

Bucher's heels were dragging, and he clutched Mace's arm in a vain effort to loosen the suffocating hold. His eyes pleaded with the others not to endanger his life by trying to fire at his captor, who hurled these words at them. "Yers thinks yers ez purty damn smart, dontchers? Yers wants ter kill a innercent man, an' yers wuz tryin' ter force me ter 'gree ter hep yers. Jed hain't done hit but if'n he had, thar ain't no father, less'n he's outer his mine, whut wud jine a pack uv dirty dogs liken yers an' hep 'em ter fine his own damn son an' hang 'im!"

Only a man as powerful as Mace Hardin could have accomplished his next feat. Jerking the reins free of the post with his right hand, he shifted his hostage so that Bucher remained a shield from their guns, then he flung the leather bridle straps over the head of his mount and grasped them firmly against the saddle's pummel. His left foot found the stirrup unerringly and with a tremendous show of strength, he seated himself, turning sideways as he did so. All the while, the struggling prisoner continued to pull at the bar of muscle that was slowly choking him into unconsciousness. As Hardin rode away, Bucher's body was still too much a part of the target for any to chance a shot at the fleeing horseman.

They had not counted on this. The nearest horses, what few were there, were hundreds of yards away. Mace had made good his escape, momentarily at least.

Nor had they contemplated the schism that now threatened to divide their unity of purpose. Everyone was attempting to speak his mind as to their next move. Those who were members of the faction bent on avenging Dolly's death felt that their part in the union had ended, and that it was up to the furnace bosses to pursue Mace Hardin. They would go after Jeddy-Boy. As many as had, or could obtain, horses would ride together. The others would go on foot. Each of the groups, the mounted and those unmounted, would search a definite portion of the surrounding land.

Ab Washley finally succeeded in making himself heard. "Yuh fellers is all fergettin' suthin'. Yuh agreed, in yore own blood, tuh stick together on this. An' if'n any buddy is bein' fergetful, we all agreed tuh either let Mace leave free, if'n he come up with th' salt that he owes me an' them." He designated his fellow furnace bosses. "An' if'n he didn't, we wuz tuh hang 'im." He paused for their reflection. "Then we wuz all tuh take out after Jed an' do th' same tuh him, when he wuz kotched. Ain't that right now?"

The twenty-nine remembered the bloody prick of the thorn. The reminder of the would-be avengers, who had not attended the meeting of last night, consented to honor the agreement made by those who had done so. Thus, with the nine whose purpose had been primarily mercenary, their numbers totaled sixty-two. Mace's earlier approximation of their strength had failed by the slim margin of two men, including the kidnapped spokesman.

If Ab Washley were to have his way, there would be at least two more in the hunt for Mace and Jeddy-Boy: Abe Foster and Davey Middleton. When questioned as to what interest they might have that would be such as to cause them to leave their work, Washley answered, "Abe Foster is the best tracker at these here licks, an' he knows ever' damn foot of th' land 'round here. An' he's a man, ain't he? Yuh knows he didn't spend all his time huntin' an' drinkin'. He wuz at Dolly's lotsa times an' he liked 'er more'n th' doin' of it too."

Jack Doniger hung his head and tears came to his eyes. Dolly had liked Abe, for she had told him so. "Big an' rough like he is, he's real gentle with me. I don't mind pleasurin' 'im too much." Her words had knifed his heart when she had said them to him. He had wanted, so deeply, to take her away from here and to have her all to himself. Now she was buried in the sodden earth. He walked away from the gathering to conceal his display of grief.

"All right fer Abe j'inin'," one said. "But whut reason would Davey have?"

Washley's answer came speedily. "Mebbe none right now, but when I tells 'im 'bout Mace puttin' Bad-Eye up tuh hittin' Willie Roller with that kittle bar, an' ta cuttin' Davey himself, I reckin they wont be no doubts as tuh his comin' with we'uns. Willie's dead, yuh know, an' y'all 'members what good friends they wuz. He'll come, an' he'll come a-runnin'. Yuh jest see if'n I ain't right."

They had experienced no difficulty in drawing their plans for the manhunt. Those on horses would ride directly to Mace's cabin to see if he was there or had been there recently. The prints of his horse's hooves would tell them this. If neither proved true, they would widen the search, with two of the mounted men serving as liaisons with those on foot.

True to his prediction, Ab Washley had returned promptly, accompanied by Abe Foster and Davey Middleton on horseback even though the still drunken Tom Chism had not known of their leaving. At that, it had taken a half hour for all of them to reassemble. A half hour that might just be the difference in the apprehension or loss of their quarry.

The hunt was on.

CHAPTER 53

Annoyed by the imbalance on its left side, the animal was becoming more and more fractious, twisting its head in an effort to wrest control of the bit from the rider. And while Mace yet continued to dominate the creature, the thickness of its throttle, with its strong muscles, required the exercise of the fullest strength of his hand and arm. Had his left hand—the one which normally handled the reins—been free, there would have been no such trouble.

Bucher had surrendered to the vise that held his neck and instinctively sought to give some measure of support to the rest of his body by pulling himself up as best he was able. One second, his mind was colored with a blackish-yellow; the next, when the horse's movement caused the slightest relief from the pressure, a wave of light would rise from within the dull orange and red that filled his forehead. All the while, there was the racking pain of his arched back as it hit and recoiled upon contact with the animal's lathering side. Now, all became black. He had reached the limit of physical opposition. His hands released themselves and the weight of his arms carried them to their extreme positions where they jumped and jiggled, as though performing some Aboriginal ritual.

Mace estimated he had put about a mile and a half between himself and those at the storehouse. He reckoned on certain pursuit, but he decided that the unconscious Bucher could be of no further use to him. Sliding his foot from the wooden stirrup, he raised his knee and then forced it out and back at the same time, allowing his forearm to fall away to the rear. Thus, the prisoner was hurtled to freedom. He would be severely injured, when he struck the yielding, still rain-soaked clay, but he would be alive. The impact would restore his circulation and his breathing. Approximately an hour later, he would be discovered and administered to, but his part in the blood-bound confederacy would be ended.

Mace cut to his right and toward his cabin. He kicked his heels into the flanks of his mount. Freed of its cumbersome burden, the horse responded to this cruel urging with tempestuous celerity. Clumps of mud sprayed the air behind flying feet.

It took both of Mace's hands to pull back the horse's head as it stopped right at the door of the dwelling. The animal reared at the halt, its froth-covered tongue writhing from between its still straining jaws.

Within the house, Jeddy-Boy's anxiety was overpowering, his mind obsessed by the fear of discovery. The idea of leaving before his father's return had come to him repeatedly but what little sanity he retained vetoed the thought as being foolhardy. No compassion for the one whom he had murdered troubled him, only the haunting, selfish dread of retribution. The confining logs of the walls contributed to his feelings of entrapment. From without, came the fear-pregnant sound of an approaching horseman. In his imaginative brain, the one became many, and he ran his fingers through his long, thick hair with alternating hands.

"Jed! Open up. Boy, its yer pap!"

He heard his father's voice, but he doubted his hearing. He did not dare to reply.

"Jed! Damn it, boy! Lemme inside—quick! We hain't got too much time, boy!"

He made himself obey the desperately spoken demand.

Mace burst in before the door was fully open and headed straight for the fireplace and knelt there, his hands working furiously. He lifted the box from its hiding place and set it upon the table. Stretching a piece of cloth, he began taking coins from the receptacle, scattering them in a narrow line the length of the linen. He rolled them compactly within, leaving an unfilled space at each end, which he grasped and flipped over his head. Twisting his arms behind his back, he brought his hands forward so that his gripping fists were at his hips, the improvised money belt looped around his waist. He worked it up under his jacket and knotted the loose ends securely.

Jeddy-Boy watched dazedly. Mace recognized his condition and did not waste further words upon him, shoving him through the doorway ahead of him. He mounted his horse and pulled his benumbed son up behind him. It was not until the double burdened animal had circled the cabin three times that Jed spoke. "Pap, we hain't gittin' nowhere."

"A-course we hain't, boy. I'm doin' this here so's ter slow 'em up some when they gits here." He rode out from the circle and then back again. This maneuver was repeated a number of times before he finally reined his mount away from the cabin and to the northwest. As he did so, Jed asked, "We meetin' Ben Skinner?"

"Hell, no! Th' son-uv-a-bitch hez runned out on us! I better never meet up with 'im! Th' damn stinkin' Tory bastard!"

"Pap, I hain't got no gun an' neither hez yer. Dontcher reckon we orter hev 'em? Whut'll we do if'n they ketches up with us?"

Mace turned his head and spoke from the corner of his mouth. "Boy, if'n they ketches us, guns ain't gonner hep us none. I got m' pistol stuck here in m' britches." He patted the weapon as he continued. "I don't aim ter git kotched, but if'n I does, them whut tries it is gonner hev ter git past some lead fer they gits me."

"Whar we headin', Pap?" Jed spoke the words more to take his mind from his nervousness than for a desire to know their destination.

"We follers th' knobs an' then crosses th' trace. Then we goes straight to th' north. Somewhars up thar, we orter be runnin' inter Blackie Vehrmon er some uv his Injuns. Then we be safe. We rests a spell, n' figgers whut ter do next."

He admonished Jeddy-Boy. "Holt onter th' saddle—yer pullin' me back'ards."

*

Abe had encountered no difficulty in picking up the hoofmarks of Mace's horse. Bucher's unconscious form had been found, and the injured man taken back to the licks.

"Ole Mace set hisse'f ter flyin', after he drapped Bucher. See how fur apart them marks is? If'n he kep' goin thet fast, th' son-uv-a-bitch cud be ten mile away by now."

Davey Middleton nodded, sharing Abe's opinion. "That he could be, if he didn't stop nowheres."

The cabin was in sight. Abe cautioned the other riders, "When we gits thar, keep a tight holt uv yore horses an' don't move 'round none. I hain't 'spectin' ter fine nobuddy thar, but if'n yer rides over th' ground, it'll jest make it harder fer me ter pick up 'is tracks."

The rest of the group did not know what to make of Abe as he rode around the cabin once, twice and then for the third time. They watched him ride off and then return time and again. The thought in their minds was common. What's Abe up to now?

He soon gave them their answer. "Over thar is whar he left frum. He done all them," indicating the labyrinth of tracks, "ter git us mixed up. Done a purty damn good job uv it, at thet. An' he's gittin' farther away frum us all th' time whut we bin stopped." His index finger was digging the spent tobacco from between the lip and gum of his upper lip, forcing a cessation of his words. He crooked the digit and hooked a small, black lump from behind his jaw tooth, spitting out the tiny remnants in a succession of yellowish spume.

Then he refilled his mouth immediately with such a quantity as to induce the impression that he was eating the fresh tobacco, rather than stowing it for use. The loading operation ended just when it seemed his mouth could hold no more. He chewed heavily, then sent a full-colored stream of expectoration groundward.

One of the party, now freed from the momentary enchantment of watching the stuffing process, quipped smilingly, "Mace has done gained another mile on us while you wuz puttin' all that terbaccy in yore mouth."

The contagion of mirth spread among the group, Abe himself being the first to pick it up. He continued laughing as he walked to a string of hoofprints and pointed to them. "Them's th' one's whut leads outer here." The fringe of deep grass was unfathomable to the other viewers but not to him. He selected a young redhaw bush and released a mouthful of saliva upon it. Instantly, the greenery had a premature coloring of fall, but not from autumn's brush.

The true guide instructs his charges as much by question as by his own answer to their queries. Spotting an isolated hoofmark, Abe asked, "See thet one? See how fur down hit's sunk? Thet's cause th' horse wut Mace is ridin' is a-kerryin' double. An' if'n yer wants m' mine on it, thet other rider ez Jeddy-Boy."

One of the more impetuous listeners spurred his mount and sped away, calling to the others to join him. Abe bellowed loud enough to have been heard atop Kahaz Knob. "Kum back here, yer crazy son-uv-a-bitch!"

When the overzealous one returned, he was met by a barrage of words from Abe. "Who in th' hell does yer think yer is chasin', a big-bellied ox? Jest 'cause them tracks leads outer here, don't mean they cain't change they course, yer damn, thick-headed fool! Now, all yer lissen ter me. We is gonner split ourse'fs hup inter three bunches. I an' Davey Middleton, an' a few mores, is gonner foller this hyar trail whut we know he took outer here on. Ab Washley, yer takes some men an' heads off yonder." He sliced the air with his arm as he demonstrated the direction in which he wished them to ride, roughly a forty-five degree angle to the northeast. "Th' rest uv yers, I wants ter kiver th' land frum here past Brashear's, then kum on aroun' in a circle til yer hits th' trace ter th' Falls uv th' Ohio."

Using his fingers, he quickly counted the company's number. "They's twenny-five uv us, an' we splits hup three ways. How many be thet fer each bunch?"

Davey Middleton corrected his arithmetic. "It's a damn good thing you makes your livin' by huntin'—there's twenty-eight all told. If you wants to divide us three ways, it won't come out even, there'll be one man left ever."

"Thet don't make no bother. Jest cut th' extry feller inter three parts an' don't han' me th' part whut'll hev th' ass on it. Yore's ez big 'nuff fer th' whole damn bunch uv them whut'll be with me."

Despite the fact that he had inspired the side-splitting laughter that followed, Abe broke it up with a stern reminder of their objective. When he was certain of their absolute attention, he said, "Strickler, I points yer ter be th' leader uv th' bunch goin' upriver. Th' fust thing I wants yer ter do right off is ter send some-un ter tell them fellers whut ez comin' on their feet ter split theyse'fs up, liken we is doin'. One part uv them, I wants ter foller th' way Washley's goin'. One part behind yore bunch, an' t'other I wants ter split th' distance betwixt th' two uv yers. Keep yorese'fs in tetch with them whut's walkin' by sendin' a rider back ter 'em ever' onc't in a whiles. Spread yorese'fs out good, so's ter kiver as much as yers kin'. Now, enybuddy want ter ask enything?"

Ab Washley was the first to pose a question. "What makes yuh so shore Mace is goin' tuh be over in th' part we aims tuh search?" He moved his arm in an arc from due north to Salt River. "Then it mought be that Mace has done turned an' headed fer th' river. If'n he done that, he's clear 'crost it by now. An' mebbe he ain't gone none of them ways. He mought have taken off west tuh th' Ohio."

Abe scratched his chin whiskers with the top of his right hand, spit and then drawled, "Yore jest plumb full uv questions, ain'tcher? An' yer is better at askin' than answerin', ain'tcher?" Washley matched Abe's joshing grin with one of his own, as Abe continued. "Ab, yer knows thet th' Salt River is swole liken a bitch full uv twins jest 'fore she drap 'em. An' yer knows th' ford is way upstream." He paused for Washley's prompt acknowledgment. "Whut chanc't does yer think a horse kerryin' two riders—two big uns—wud hev ter git acrost without droundin' theyse'fs? Yer knows damn well thet they'd sink liken lead an' yer orter be smart enough ter know thet Mace'd be too sharp ter try eny sech damn fool trick. An' it ort not take too much thinkin' ter see thet Mace cuddn't go very fast, wuz he ter go ter th' west. Them trees ain't gonner move outer his way, yer knows, So, if'n enybuddy wud want ter git away frum hyar in a hell uv a hurry, an' he cuddn't cut acrost th' licks, whut th' hell d'rection wud he ride?"

"Tuh th' north an' long th' foot of th' knobs," Washley concluded logically.

"Thet's right. Mebbe my bunch kin kotch 'im 'fore he turns north er south. If'n we cain't, an' he does go t'ard th' river, yer er Strickler orter run acrost 'im. If'n he heads north, I hain't gonner foller 'im none too fur. Liken Davey jest sez, I makes m' livin by huntin', not by chasin' Mace Hardin. 'Sides, it wud be 'nuff fer me, wuz we ter jest be shed uv 'im." He punctuated the end of his discourse by once more emptying his mouth of its hoard of juice, then asked finally, "Is they eny more questions?"

"Jest one more," someone said. "S'posin them whut's walkin' don't come out even when they is divided up?"

Abe's eyes twinkled sharply. "Jest cut whut's extry up liken I sed before. Oney yer had best guv th' part with th' brains ter Ab Washley. He kin shore use some."

The rollicking guffaws born of Abe's witticism ended the planning. Thus it was, that three groups of laughing men resumed the chase. A chase that if successful would bring death to two men.

CHAPTER 54

The fugitives did not attempt to exchange words. Each was beset by vexing thoughts. Jeddy-Boy, blindly hoping for escape, reviewing his last conversation with Ben Skinner. Ben had apprised him last night that the men were having a meeting, and they had both speculated as to its purpose. Evidently, Skinner had found out later on the significance of the gathering. Or perhaps he knew it when he had talked with him. "Th' damn, desartin' skunk!" His utterance carried past Jed's ears.

"Whut's thet yer jest sed, Pap?"

No reply being made, Jed did not press his father to make one, but gave himself back to his fears, his perspiring hands shifting their grip upon the saddle, timing their movement to coincide with the upward rise of Mace's buttocks from the seat.

Kahaz Knob was before them, and Mace slowed the horse's gait as he swung his course to the west. To round the hill on the east would be to invite recognition and discovery. The licks were less than a mile away at some points along the base of the knob. He threaded his way until he had reached an open space between Kahaz and the chain of hills running to the northeast, when he spurred his mount into a full gallop once more. The rocking chair motion of the riders came as a distinct relief after the rough up-and-down jogging of the slower pace. They covered the three miles to Blue Lick Gap without incident, save for an occasional reduction of speed whenever their animal crossed marshy ground. As they reached the opening between the hills, Mace was undecided as to whether he should go north through the gap or ride on a mile or two farther to the east where he would hit the trace running between the last two knobs in the chain. He stopped briefly and loosed the reins, permitting his blowing horse to graze while he made his decision. Jeddy-Boy took the halt to be of some weighty import, asking his father, "Pap, whut's th' trubble?"

"Hain't no trubble. I'm jest figgerin' th' best way fer us ter take. Through here," he pointed to Blue Lick Gap, "ez th' quickest, but we mought run on ter some uv them fellers from Cl'ar's Station." The avoidance of these settlers determined his choices. "Hain't no damn use chancin' it. We'll go on ter th' fur gap, then on 'crost th' crick whut's up a piece frum thar."

The animal snatched one last mouthful of grass before yielding to the violent jerk of the bit.

Mace approached the trace cautiously. No travelers were to be seen. He dismounted and placed his ear to the ground. There were no vibrations, and he remounted.

They sped up the trace for a quarter of a mile, then headed northeast. Suddenly, there was a sharp, cracking report, as from a rifle, and immediately the horse and its riders spilled to the earth. Mace was on his feet quickly, but Jed did not arise.

"Kum on, boy! We kain't 'ford ter git slowed up by no damn scratches." He walked to where his son lay groaning and twisting, the trunk of his body moving from side to side.

"Pap, I kain't git hup! Hit's m' damn left leg! Hit's busted bad."

Mace examined the injury hurriedly. "Yer right, Jed. Hit's broke all ter hell, jest 'bove th' ankle."

"Whut'll we do now, Pap? They'll ketch me, shore." His attendant moans were a combination of fear and of excruciating pain. The bone had splintered— the razor-sharp edge of one portion having cut through, so that it was clearly exposed. Jed looked at it and fainted.

When he regained consciousness, Mace was knotting the last leather thong around a makeshift splint embracing the leg from the knee to the foot.

"Yer bleedin' kinder bad. If'n hit don't stop none, we'll hev ter shet it off some, but we hain't got th' time ter fool with it now." He bent down and put his arm around the back of his injured son. "Now, putcher left arm 'roun m' neck an' hole on tight so's we kin git yer onter yer right leg."

Jeddy-Boy maneuvered himself painfully until he stood erect, supported by his father.

"Now kums th' hard part—gittin' yer back on thet horse." Father and son turned awkwardly toward the animal, which still lay where it had fallen, though it was making an effort to regain its feet. Mace put his arms under Jed's armpits and carried him the remaining distance. When he reached the prostrate mount, he gave its rump a vicious boot. There was a piercing whinny—unmistakably pain-laden—as the creature raised its shoulder and vainly sought to lift itself up on its right leg. The left foreleg dangled from its knee. For an entranced moment, Jeddy-Boy forgot his own misery as he watched the futile struggling of the lamed animal, its head moving up and down, then sideways, as its wild eyes implored assistance in its frantic efforts to right itself.

Jed's thoughts resumed their selfish vein. "Whut'll we do now, Pap? They'll git me shore now!" He broke into tears.

Mace ignored his son's breakdown. "If'n thet damn Massalene heddn't a-stole thet other horse, this here wuddn't heve happened. Damn her no good, ornery soul ter hell enyhow! He lowered Jeddy-Boy none too easily to the rough terrain, then moved to the horse. He shouldered the animal over and then pushed it to a standing position, exclaiming as he did so between the breaths of his herculean exertion, "Yer dumb, no good son-uv-a-bitch, yer gonner kerry us, if'n yer hez ter do it on three legs!"

The tortured animal wobbled shakily forward, then collapsed. Mace kicked at its flanks, but it did not even move its head.

*

Abe's raised hand signaled those riding behind him of his intention to stop. As they drew even with him, he said, "Don't nobuddy git off'n they horse. 'Pears liken Ab Washley don't need thet extry head—hit's me whut orter hev it. See them bushes over thar—them by th' hackberry trees? See how they's spread out? Mace hez took out fer th' west after all. I'd a guv 'im credick fer more sense than thet. Wal, if'n he hez gone thetaway, he hain't gonner git fur, 'fore we ketches up with 'im. Le's git movin'."

The trail did in fact lead westward—but for less than a mile, then it veered to the north and to the northeast, and at length seemed to straighten itself eastward. When Abe was sure of its fixed direction, he called to his followers, each of whom relayed his words. "I take back whut I sed awhiles back, they kin still give th' head ter Ab."

It was difficult for the grimness of the mission to take its proper place in the perspective of the manhunt when its leader's serious words were couched in levity. A leader who seemed to know but the one song, whose theme had become his philosophy of living.

Nearing Blue Lick Gap, the pursuers paused as the fleeing ones had done earlier. Abe dismounted and looked around, then gave his findings. "The animule hain't gonner last none too much longer. See thet hoofmark? Hit's th' left front foot—see how it's shaller-like? That's cause hit's faverin' thet leg. Mace's bin pushin' it too hard, a-kerryin' sech a load. Him an' Jeddy-Boy's too heavy fer a long gallopin'." As he swung his giant boots over the dip in the saddle, he directed, "McGruen, git ter them whut's walkin' this way an' tell 'em I sez fer 'em ter kum ter this here gap an' then ter foller our tracks. Mace's gonner hev ter rest thet horse uv hiss'n afore long an' thet's damn sartain. Tell 'em ter git a move on theyse'fs, if'n they wants ter be 'roun when we ketches them fellers." The dispatched McGruen wheeled away to the southwest as the remaining seven riders followed Abe to the east.

*

Jeddy-Boy's nervous spasm had grown steadily worse, despite the efforts of his father to break its tension through first, calm words, then appeals to his son's deeply buried reason. When these had failed, Mace had employed threats and finally force. And though Jed's cheeks colored from the open-handed blows, he was too far under the spell of terror to feel them. All the while, the blood from his wound kept draining from his leg.

Realizing further slapping was useless, Mace straightened himself and walked over to the horse, cursing and kicking it again and again—the only outlets for his exasperation. Then he returned to his son, saying, "Jed, thar be jest one thing whut I kin see ter do. I'll hev ter kerry yer ter some place an' hide yer n' then kum back fer yer later on."

These were words that a wild mind could digest, anxiety-inspiring words upon which an excited brain could feed, and they made Jed's lips move in a torrent of speech. "Pap, ye kain't do thet ter me, Pap! They'll fine me, shore! They'll kill me, Pap! They means ter kill me! I dunt want ter die, Pap! Yer kain't leave me fer them sons-uv-bitches ter fine! I dunt want ter die, Pap! I'm skeered uv dyin'—dunt leave me, you hear! I'm yer son, Pap, yer own flesh an' blood, Pap! Yer kain't leave me fer them bastards, Pap! Yer kain't do hit, Pap! I dunt want ter die. I dunt want ter die." His voice trailed off into an irrational mumbling. But in between its vacant ravings were interspersed the repeated words of his dread. "I dunt want ter die—I dunt want ter die!"

Mace ignored the frenzied appeals and lifted him roughly to a standing position. Then he told him sternly, "I'm gonner kerry yer. Ketch yer arms 'roun' m' neck when I moves in frunt uv yer."

Jed's arms locked just under his father's chin, reaching backward. Mace's hands hoisted him upon his back, the legs astride his hips in the same manner he had done so often when Jed was a little boy. The terribly active pain gave violent outcry through Jeddy-Boy's lips. The injured leg jolted with each forward step Mace took. The one who had delighted in the infliction of pain upon others, whose mind had been magnetized by the sight of suffering, was now being agonized by the object of his worship. He cried out but even as had the cries of those others, his own entreaties fell upon deaf ears.

Mace had borne Jed about a half mile, patiently enduring the crazed pleas and protests of pain. His eyes constantly searched ahead of him, seeking a place of concealment. A small knoll in the immediate foreground, forested on its sides and its top, caught and held his attention. When he reached its base, he had great difficulty in persuading Jeddy-Boy to release his arms from his neck. This accomplished, he placed him in a slanting position on the hillside and then knelt on his hands and knees, his ear firmly against the earth. He listened, but Jed's screaming prevented him from hearing anything. He got up and walked to where his son lay, shouting at him, "Damn yer, Jed. If'n yer don't stop thet damn yellin', I'm gonner leave yer right whar ya be!" The threat produced the desired effect. Though he continued crying, Jeddy-Boy uttered no other sound.

Again, Mace's ear was to the ground. He arose quickly. "They's some-un comin' this way. Thar's more'n one uv 'em, an' they ez a-comin' fast."

He leaned back in a half-crouch and Jed put his arms around his neck. Mace raised himself up and grasped his son's legs. The soil had eroded from the slope up ahead of him, creating step-like edges of rock, which extended almost to the trees beyond. Using this natural stair, he soon gained the thicket. Continuing on for perhaps fifty yards, he discovered a small clearing near the crest on the far side and prepared to relieve himself of the weighty one whom he carried.

This time, Jeddy-Boy would not release his hold. Instead, he drew his arms tighter against his father's throat.

"Jed, damn yer ter hell. Yer chokin' me! Leggo uv me, damn yer!"

Insanely, Jed further strengthened the strangulation. So overwhelmed was he by the prospect of being abandoned, he ceased his crying and clung to the one refuge he had known in his life. Acutely aware of the oncoming pursuers, Mace did not attempt to reason with him. "I hates ter do this, Jeddy-Boy, but hit's gotter be did." Dropping Jed's right leg, he used the hand thus freed to find his knife. Then he cut through the gripping fingers that locked the forearm against his windpipe. The arms loosed, and he grabbed one of them to prevent his son from falling. He eased himself around as gently as he could and laid Jed on the ground. As he hurried away, his boot kicked one of the severed fingers in its path. Jeddy-Boy made no sound. Mace ran to the edge of the thicket and then carefully retraced his steps, backing into each footprint. Thus he preserved his son's hiding place. This done, he raced ahead, seeking his own safety.

CHAPTER 55

Abe spotted the object when he was still more than two hundred yards away. Shortly thereafter he called to his men. "Di'n't I tell yers, thet horse wuz 'bout done? See 'im up yonder, this side uv thet hill?" By the time the others reached the stricken creature, he was examining its injury. He arose, shaking his head. "Hit's a dirty, damn shame, thet's whut it is—leavin' a pore dumb animule ter suffer liken thet." He methodically roughed two lines across the hair of the horse's forehead with his fingernail and marked the point of their intersection with a speck of clay. Drawing his pistol, he carefully loaded and cocked it. Placing the muzzle squarely upon the mark, he pulled the trigger. There was a quivering of equine flesh and muscle, and a swarm of gnats, driven from their tormenting by the smoke and percussion, returned to the animal's expressionless eyes.

"Thet pore, dumb animule." Abe shook his head compassionately, as he blew the clinging wisps from the mouth of the barrel.

It was easy to follow the large footprints. Leading his mount by its reins, Abe strode briskly to the foot of the knoll. The others kept to their horses, awaiting his further instruction.

"See right hyar?" He ran his hand over the bent grass on the hillside. "Thar's whar somebuddy was a-lyin'. A-lyin' sideways, he wuz. An' he wuz a-bleedin', he wuz. I thought that was blood, back thar by th' horse. Wunner which one hit be, Mace or Jed? One uv 'em ez hurt, thet's fer shore."

He moved along until he came to the rocks jutting out of the hillside like immense teeth. "They stopped here a spell, prob'ly restin'. One's kerryin' th' other. Cain't tell which—they's both big men." He called the rest of the group to him as he resumed his tracking. Mounting, he said to them, "Looks like them tracks be lighter frum here on, as fur as I kin see. Mought be th' ground is harder. One thing is shore sartin, which ever one is bein' kerried di'n't git off'n t' other's back, not less'n he hed hisse'f a pa'r uv wings." He raised in the saddle as he turned and looked up the hill. He scanned the landscape, then settled down in his seat. "They is up ahead uv us somewhars. Now's th' time fer we'uns ta sketter ourse'fs out. Be keerful, less'n yers kin see ever'thing in frunt uv yers. T'ain't liken they hez got rifles—not with one uv 'em kerryin' th' other. But they's prob'ly got pistols. If'n eny uv yers spots 'em, fire yore rifle, an' th' rest uv us'll kum fast as we kin. Best hev th' rope handy-like. Which uv yers hez got hit?"

A hasty inspection disclosed the fact that it had been forgotten completely. So intent had they all been on entering upon the chase, no one had thought to bring along the means of the proposed execution.

"Whut'll we do when we catches 'em?" one of them asked Abe.

"We jest keeps a-holt uv 'em 'til some uv them others kums up."

"S'posin' they ain't got none neither?"

"Then we sends some-un ter git one."

"I don't see no need fer that. I says we oughter jest shoot 'em."

Abe glared at his erstwhile questioner. "I sez! Who th' hell be you, Will Luckett, ter try an' change th' way them sons-uv-bitches ez gonner git kilt? Th' 'greement wuz thet they wuz ter be hanged." He looked at him disdainfully. "Hain'tcher got no respeck fer th' law? Don'tcher know it hain't lawful ter 'gree ter kill a feller one way an' then do hit diffrunt frum thet?"

Luckett was unabashed. "They ain't no jedge er jury said Jed an' Mace has got tuh die. That 'greement don't mean it's no law. Besides, yuh is jest s'posed tuh be doin' th' trackin, not th' bossin'."

Abe was riled. "While yer ez s'posin' 'bout me, s'posin' I heddn't bin along with yer? Yer wud still be runnin 'aroun' Mace's cabin, follerin' them circlin' tracks, yer dumb-ass bastard!"

Davey Middleton stopped the incipient argument. "Ain't no sense a-arguin' betwixt ourselfs. You is jest givin' Mace an' Jed more time to get away. Abe ain't a-tryin to boss none of us. Some feller has got to be th' leader of this bunch, an' Abe is as good as any."

Luckett still held to his own opinion. "He kin be th' damn leader, if'n he wants tuh, but if'n I sees Mace or Jed, I ain't a-goin' tuh wait fer no rope. If'n yuh hears a shot, an' I done th' firin uv it, it won't be no signal. It'll be me a-shootin' at 'em!" He whipped his horse and sped away. The last they saw of him, he was cutting up the hillside at a spot where the trees appeared to be thinning out.

As Luckett disappeared from view, Abe remarked wryly, "One thing he dint say. If'n we hears two shots, it mought be them a-shootin' at him. Th' damn fool will jest bout git hisse'f kilt."

Will Luckett's impulsive dash rekindled the lure of the hunt in those he left behind, and they now followed his lead. All except Abe, whose forward progress was more sauntering as he still looked for the footprints. Always the tracker, he wanted to make sure of where he was going. He yelled vain curses at two thoughtless riders whose forward paths were marring the important marks in the ground, observing to himself, "When they gits through rushin' aroun' liken chickens with they heads off, they won' be no way ter fine out whar them Hardins hez gone."

*

Mace had heard the merciful shot fired by Abe, and its echoing determined the change of course he was now making. Instead of continuing on, and crossing Blue Lick Run before it was joined by Clear's Run, he had chosen to move southwardly and ford the stream at a more accessible place, where he would be less likely to encounter anyone. The trunk of a storm-felled pine served admirably as a walkway and would leave no clue as to the point of his departure from his former route. When he had traversed the slanting length of the dead tree, there was but a short open distance before he would reach the protective covering of a grove in what was otherwise a sparsely timbered stretch of the knoll. He solved the problem of an undetectable crossing by hacking off a number of branches from an evergreen that the tree upon which he now stood had brushed past in its fall. Casting one of the bushy limbs on the ground before him, he slid from his perch onto it. Alternately placing and retrieving the boughs after he had stepped upon them, he thus completed an unmarked passage to the woods. Once inside the little forest, he inserted the now unnecessary branches among those of a plump cedar and plodded on. The uphill climb, coming after his earlier running, had winded him and he looked about for a resting place. On the downward slope, he found what was, or had been, the entrance to a den—wolf or fox he did not know. In front of the hole, there was a large apron that furry feet had dug out of the hill so that it was partially covered from above by overhanging earth. He sat down and stretched his legs as his mind now entertained the thought suggested by the shot he had heard on the other side of the hills. Did it mean that they had found Jed? And, had they wounded or killed him? To go back and try to find out now would accomplish nothing except his own death. But the fate of him who had been the crown prince of his empire of salt worried him as nothing had ever done before. He minimized and excused his son's shortcomings, all except one: the inability to control the fear that had lately beset him. This defect too he almost sanded smooth. This was the first time Jeddy-Boy had ever lost his nerve. Mebbe, Mace thought, th' pore bastard really loved thet damn whore.

Will Luckett was riding furiously. As he swept along the hillside, birds left their nests and young trees were trampled. Mace heard his approach and, though on his feet, held to his shelter. The horseman checked his wild pace as he began skirting the grove.

The hunter and the hunted spied each other at the same instant. Both fired simultaneously. Each one hit the target at which he had aimed.

Mace had been spun halfway around by a ball that entered his right upper chest, causing him to drop his pistol. When he tried to pick it up, his right arm would not obey his will, and he snatched the weapon hastily with his left hand. Luckett's left arm had been hit and he had fallen from his mount, but his fist still clutched the reins, resisting the animal's efforts to pull them from his grasp. Half-stunned, he lay in this same indefensible position as Mace came up to him, pistol in hand. Luckett did not note that Mace held the gun in his left hand. All his dazed mind could register was Mace Hardin towering over him, pointing the muzzle of the weapon straight at his head. His own firearm had disappeared. How, he did not know, but his right hand was empty.

"Leggo them damn reins er I'll blow yer damn brains outer yer heard." He heard Mace's threat and would have obeyed its demand, but he couldn't marshal his senses to comply.

Strangely, Mace didn't shoot him but kicked him in his ribs and jerked at the leather straps, which he held so unwillingly. At last, Luckett's hand opened and fell to the ground. Will's confused brain could not understand why Mace had not killed him or why Mace had experienced so much difficulty in mounting his horse. And when what seemed a long time later, Davey Middleton and the others had found him, he was unable to tell them in what direction Mace had ridden away. All that came clearly to him was the miracle of being alive. Had Mace Hardin had the slightest use of his right hand, the miracle never would have happened.

Luckett's faculties had revived somewhat by the time Abe and the rest of the men rode up. Abe looked at him and then said, "Wal, whutcher think uv thet? Fer a secunt, I wuz thinkin' it wuz Mace Hardin a-layin' thar, all shot up in his arm! But 'tain't Mace a-tall! Hit's thet smart feller, Will Luckett!"

Abe's sarcasm hurt more than the wound Will Luckett had suffered. He would like to have answered Abe in kind, but there was no answer. Abe had been right, and he had been wrong.

Abe did not rub any more verbal salt into his comrade's wounded pride. His manner was now that of consideration. "Will, how's yer arm? Better lemme hev a look at hit." After a careful inspection, he continued. "Looks purty good. Yer feel liken yer cud do suthin' purty important fer me right now?"

Abe's frontier psychology never worked better. Luckett perked up. "I shore do—shore kin! Whut yuh want me tuh do, Abe?"

"I wants yer ter ride back an' see if'n yer kin fine them whut's comin' on their foots, an' tell 'em ter hurry theyse'fs some. Think yer feels good 'nough fer thet?"

"Hell, yes, Abe! Ain't nuthin but a scratch."

"Aw right, then. You take Lot Mifflin's horse." He directed Mifflin. "Lot, yer ride with Sim Hester. Th' both uv yers hain't heavy nuff ter bend a straw bridge."

He turned, facing Luckett once more. "Will, yer hez done all yer kin here, with thet arm hurt an' all. After yer takes th' word ter them fellers, git on home."

Luckett protested futilely but agreed to do as he was ordered. Abe was the leader.

"The spirit of a man will sustain his infirmity," so the great book says, and the saying was never more exemplified than in the case of William Luckett. The wound he described as a scratch was both deep and painful but at this moment his exuberant spirit had smothered his anguish.

"Demme!" Abe exclaimed to the others, as Luckett rode away. "I meant ter tell 'im ter tell them others ter be on th' watch for Jed. We knows now thet he wuz th' one whut wuz hurt back yonder. An' if'n Mace rode away on Will's horse, Jeddy-Boy musta bin left somewhars there 'bouts."

Middleton asked, "You plannin' on tryin' to find him first?"

Abe shook his head. "Jed ain't gonna git very fur, if'n he gits enywhars. If'n he heddn't uv bin bad hurt, Mace wuddn't uv bin kerryin' 'im. I figgers we'd best ketch the old man, if'n we kin. If'n he jest hedn't uv got Will Luckett's horse, we wud uv hed 'im, shore as hell." He scratched his whiskers with the end of his pistol before he continued. "We goes after ole Mace! Le's git movin."

They rode down the hill, then broke into a gallop, as Abe signaled he had picked up the trail again. It led toward the creek.

At this time, Ab Washley and his party were riding hard from the south, approaching the same general vicinity.

CHAPTER 56

Jack Doniger, for all his important role in fomenting and organizing the uprising against Mace and Jeddy-Boy had been relegated by circumstance to being one of the nine men who were now traveling on foot toward Blue Lick Gap. He had been unable to borrow a mount, and his failure to ride with the others had distressed him sorely. At length, however, he accepted his disappointment, exchanging it for the determination to be one of those whose hands would pull the knotted rope that would swing Dolly's murderer into hell. And when the body would be cut down, he had some designs of his own as to what would happen to it before it was buried. Before the rider had brought Abe Foster's word for them to head for Blue Lick Gap, he had no certain knowledge that the group he was with was headed in the direction Mace had gone. With the positive intelligence that the quarry's trail had been found, he knew that, while he might miss the capture and possibly the hanging, he yet would be there before Jed's corpse would be disposed of. He would not be entirely cheated of his deep-seated desire for vengeance upon him who had desecrated his loved one. He labored over these ideas as one turns the various intricacies of a planned business venture through the myriad channels of one's mind, matching anticipation with sure-footed promise. He was so doing, when Will Luckett, riding from the east, hailed him and his cohorts and told them the details of the chase and of his brush with death at Mace's hands. Then he gave Abe's request that they speed themselves as much as possible. Doniger inquired as to Jeddy-Boy but the courier only had knowledge of the one who had been flushed from his hiding place. The message delivered, the rider headed for the licks.

All except Jack Doniger intended to follow Abe's directive that they search for Mace, but they could not influence Doniger to go along with them. He added to his refusal. "When we gets tuh th' hill, I'm goin' over there. If Jed ain't there, I'm goin' tuh look all aroun' it. If I don't find 'im, I'll come on an' try an' catch up with yuh."

They could not dissuade him from his resolve, though they talked of nothing else all the way until they reached the knoll. They still called after him as the heavy foliage closed behind him. Farther on, they found the bold trail Abe and his party had taken. They went its way. A few looked back to the hill, then turned their heads and trudged along with the others.

Doniger's eyes had become thoroughly acclimated to the shade within the woods and he walked surely, though slowly, in a snake-like course from the base of one side to the base on the other. He had reached the midpoint of the length of the elevation when he saw it. Not until he picked it up, did he believe his sight. It was a finger, severed at the knuckle joint. The dirt under the nail, black as pitch. The blood had not fully dried upon its raw end. The hand that it had formerly belonged to must be nearby. He sought some evidence of artificiality in the area about him. There was none.

Jeddy-Boy roused from the coma into which he had sunk when his father had laid him in the little obscured clearing. His right hand throbbed unmercifully at his side, the violated nerves shooting their molten charges to his brain, where they became entangled with those that had dredged their way upward from the splintered leg. In the resultant state of dementation, his eyeballs rolled back and his teeth bit through his lip. The panic, which had been forced into the subconscious by these unrelenting onslaughts upon his conscious mind, battled to regain its former domination of his senses. And the red streams continued to flow.

Doniger parted the brush and looked upon the murderer. He lowered his rifle and rested its barrel in the fork of a convenient chinquapin tree. The leg and the hand told him it would not be needed.

Now that he had found him whom his heart had cursed so unceasingly, he wept. Here was the one who had stopped, forever, the gay tossing of her head; who had disfigured her appealing features; who had stilled her voice, so that he never again would hear her say, "Jack Doniger, yuh pleasures me—yuh pleasures me so." He did not say any of the many things he had stored in his mind for their use at this moment. There was no time for them. The bloody rivulets, worming their escape over and around the dead leaves, so informed him. Jed was near his last unconsciousness. Before that insensibility ended in death, he must be made rational long enough for him to understand that Dolly's murder was being avenged. He must know the vengeance that was going to be wreaked upon him.

Doniger knelt on one knee and spoke into Jeddy-Boy's ear. His voice was steady and its tone, clear. "It's me, Jed. Jack Doniger! I'm goin' tuh kill yuh, for whut yuh done tuh Dolly! Yuh hear me, Jed? Jack Doniger, an' I'm goin' tuh kill yuh!"

Panic wrestled free of the chains of pain, and the white rolled down, and the eyes returned to their normal position. The pupils received the message and the lips gave answer. "No, Jack! Fer God's sake, no!" In all his weakness, Jeddy-Boy yet mustered strength enough to raise himself on his left elbow, attempting to twist away. The movement involved his broken leg, and panic again retreated before anguish. But before its final surrender, it held on til Doniger could say, "I'm goin' tuh cut yore head off'n yuh, for Dolly!" Jed heard and understood. This would be his final reasoning thought. He had roused for the last time.

Doniger drew his knife and sat down behind Jeddy-Boy's head, one foot braced against each shoulder, his knees bent with the head between them. He clutched the shaggy hair just above the forehead with his left hand and jerked it back, exposing the neck below the chin. Then he began cutting and sawin', finishing the decapitation in a rushing, gurgling torrent of blood. He plunged the blade into Jed's heart and left it there.

He came out into the sunlight and wended his way through the tall grass and down the hillside. Following the trail of his comrades, he walked along, the severed head, hanging by the hair clutched in his right hand, swinging back and forth like the ball of a pendulum.

CHAPTER 57

A small stand of young oaks lay between Mace and the swollen waters of the creek. He damned all who had played a part in bringing about his present predicament. Dolly for dying. Jed for having killed her and for slowing his flight. Doniger for inciting them whore-lovin' sons-uv-bitches: the mutinying furnace bosses, Mitch Stricker and Ben Skinner, th' desertin' bastard. Had he known that Abe Foster and Davey Middleton were participants, they would have also been remembered in his violent condemnations. Oddly, Mercer escaped his invectives, and those who had charge of the furnaces were less roundly cursed than the others who he felt contributed to his plight. "I cud uv handled Bucher an' them others," he reasoned aloud. "But not th' whole damn works." But the one who was the most soundly denounced by him was he who had fled without letting him know what was in the wind—Ben Skinner, th' Tory-lovin' son-uv-a-bitch.

What little reconciliation that was required as to Jed's fate had come easily. "He asked fer it, an' he got it," had been his unmoved summation.

The loss of the use of his right arm worried him, less because of the possibility of his being intercepted by the settlers, for he now felt that there was little likelihood of that happening, but largely as to whether or not the condition would be a lasting one. A man of his disposition and habits needed two good arms—one might not even be sufficient for survival—let alone to accomplish the shaded aims he would pursue.

The normally shallow crossing of the stream was now level with his horse's belly. The animal drifted sideways, and he had to wrap the reins about his wrist, using the might of his forearm to straighten its direction. He still held the butt of the unloaded pistol in his hand, which had begun to cramp from the tightness of his grip upon the weapon. Once he had topped the little rise, which now served as a bank of the flooded stream, he would swing around and follow the creek for about a mile. Then he would ride north until he made his hoped-for contact with Vehrmon and his British allies. He was not guessing as to their presence in Kentucky. Skinner had told him of the plans to lay siege to the larger settlements near and east of the Kentucky River and of the preparations then being made for these large attacks. He remembered Bryan Station as being one of the coming objectives and he recalled also that it was because of the demands of these future major operations that Vehrmon had been unable to lead a larger band in the recently concluded unsuccessful assault on the flatboat on Salt River.

His mount reached the top of the embankment and its feet slipped slightly as he spurred it downhill. However, it soon regained its footing. Rounding the base, the unexpected suddenly confronted him. Two riders were bearing down upon him. They seemed to have come from out of nowhere but one of them who had so appeared was Ab Washley!

If Washley and the other man were riding as detached searchers, he was confident of his ability to elude them. His horse was possessed of good speed and was apparently a sound animal. But should this supposition prove false and were more men to be close on the heels of these two, then he might be in serious trouble. The constriction in the muscles of his hand was now acute, and the aching spread above his wrist as he whipped his steed back up the incline he had just descended. His horse bobbed its head as it tried to obey the sharpness of the bit-directed order for more speed in traversing the flooded waterway. Emerging on the other side, it sought to dig its hind hooves into the muddy earth so that it could do what the sharp heels in its flanks were insisting upon. The feet slithered sideways, and the animal's haunch smacked the earth resoundingly. For an instant, it appeared as though its head and tail were trying to meet, as it rolled over struggling to right itself. Then it recaptured its equilibrium and dashed away.

Mace had been thrown to the offside. He had landed with his right arm underneath his body, but he felt no hurt. He wished that he had done so, for the limb was as before, devoid of any sensation. Miraculously, his left hand, though the reins had been torn from its fingers, still clutched the rounded handle of the pistol. He scrambled to his feet and quickly sought cover in a coppice of young oaks. Ab Washley's head came into view at the second Mace reached the woods.

At first, it seemed they would ride on, deceived by the clear hoofmarks in the soft ground. Then Washley took a closer look, and they both dismounted and tied their mounts.

Mace damned his luck, as he heard Washley exclaim, "His horse spilled itself all tuh hell jest after it got out of th' crick! Let's have a look around, jest tuh be shore it didn't run off an' leave 'im hereabouts." They soon discovered the deep imprints of his boots and began tracking them to the thicket.

Mace hastily stuck his pistol inside his waistband, flexing his fingers and thumb vigorously. He searched his mind as to his next move. If he remained where he was, they would surely find him. He looked about him as he thought, his shifting gaze turning toward the stream where a good-sized sycamore was rooted. The thought came suddenly. He ran to the tree. The limb was low enough for him to hook his elbow around it. Hoisting himself upon it, he scaled to the fork above and straddled it, so that his left hand and arm were free on the side from which his pursuers must approach.

He did not have to wait long for their coming. As they reached the trail's end beneath the sycamore bough, he saw Washley remove his cap and scratch his head. He heard his words as they floated up to him. "Demme, if'n it don't 'pear liken he jest mixed hisself into th' damn air."

Washley walked to the water's edge, his companion following closely. "Mace couldn't've jumped that far, but he shore as hell must've did it—they ain't no other tracks."

They came back to where the footprints had stopped. Ab's fingers again scuffed his scalp. This time, he craned his neck as he did so and looked up. His companion followed suit. There, in the path of their eyes, was Mace Hardin. So startled were they by this seemingly impossible vision, they shook visibly. So shocked were they, indeed, they did not see the pistol lined directly at them until their minds had taken in what he said to them in an easy, matter-of-fact voice. "Yer boys lookin' fer some-un? Mebbe me?"

Fear and astonishment bound their tongues. He did not wait unduly for them to answer. "Damn yer lucky hides thet I don't kill th' both uv yers. Now yers pay sharp mine ter whut I'm gonner say. Fust, drap yer guns. Washley, yer pistol, an' you other son-uv-a-bitch, thet rifle uv yer'n."

The weapons fell instantly from their hands. Then he continued. "Now, I wants ter see how damn fast two jug-assed bastards kin fly theyse'fs acros't thet damn crick, an' over thet damn li'l hill! An' remember, this here seat I'm a-settin' in looks both ways. Yers try eny tricks, an' one uv yers is a dead son-uv-a-bitch! Th' other, I'll tend ter, soon's I scrambles down frum this here perch! Now, git movin'."

The two men needed no urging. With incredible swiftness, they tore through the water and up the incline. Neither one breathed securely until they were on the other side. Mace yelled after them as they fled. "Dunt worry none 'bout them horses uv yer'n. I'll take real good keer uv 'em!" He again inserted his pistol in his shirt and, for the first time since he had tied the money-filled roll around his midriff, he was conscious of it being there. As he climbed down, he debated whether he should hide it, to forestall its seizure were he to be captured, or to take it with him whatever the consequences. He spoke his decision. "I've hed it with me this fur. Reckin I mought jest as well take hit th' rest uv th' way—wharever it goes."

He picked up the rifle from the ground and strode over and threw it in the water. After examining Washley's pistol and finding it ready for firing, he shoved it between the money belt and his abdomen, at the same time withdrawing his own empty weapon. He sat down and, holding it between his knees, he managed to load it. Then he crossed it with Washley's inside his jacket. He walked to where the horses were tied and loosed their reins. Mounting the nearest one, he booted the other, sending it wildly away. He did not recross the creek but chose instead to ride upstream through the water, a few feet from the flood-made shore line.

CHAPTER 58

"Look at that horse up ahead of us! See 'im yonder by them bushes?"

Abe did not need Davey Middleton to direct his attention to the grazing steed. He had seen the animal before Davey had spotted it. "Mought be a good ideer, wuz yer ter git over thar an' see whut he's a-doin' thar all by hisse'f." He twisted himself about in the saddle. "A few uv yers hed best ride 'long with Davey."

When more than a few of the riders started to break from the group, he shouted, "Three ez a-plenty. Hain't no use fer all uv yers goin' over thar. We-uns'll wait here fer yers!"

He watched as the trio, after a little chase, corralled the riderless mount. In a few minutes they returned, Middleton leading it by its reins.

"This here is Will Luckett's horse. Wonder how it got shed of Mace."

Abe scratched his whiskers. "Thet's a good question. Turn th' son-uv-a-bitch aroun' some, so's I kin git a good look at 'im." He scrutinized the creature as though he were its prospective buyer, then asked, "Davey, yer damn shore that's Will's horse? How yer know it be his'n?"

"'Cause of that white markin' on th' one front leg—runs most all th' way up. I noticed it before."

"Wal," Abe drawled, "if'n thet's Will's animule, liken yer claims, 'tain't hard ter tell why Mace hain't a-ridin' 'im. See thet hindquarter how th' mud's all cakin' on it? He hed hisse'f a fall, prob'ly on th' bank uv th' crick. Musta throwed Mace off'n 'im an' runned away before he cud ketch 'im agin."

He looked at the two men who were riding double. "Lot, yer kin take this horse uv Will's', seein' as how he's got yor'n."

Before they resumed the hunt, Abe had another word for them. "We sticks tergether til we gits ter th' crick. Then we spreads out some, not too fur, mine yers! Mace mought jest shoot a li'l more straight then he shot at Will Luckett."

As they rode on, the trees bordering the stream came clearly into view. And even as they saw them, another horse, also without a rider, raced out into the open. Abe didn't turn his head as he said, "Davey, sence yer th' horse ketcher uv this hyar bunch, take them other two an' git this one."

Again, there was a delay until the runaway was captured. When the animal was led back to the group, its identification came quickly, Lot Mifflin shouting,

"That's Ab Washley's mare. I've rid her many a-time. I'd know 'er anywheres."

Abe answered the information with a bellow. "Le's git ter th' crick! Ab's bunch musta met up with Mace!"

Hooves churned the stretch to the stream. From the prints in the soft earth, man and animal, Abe soon reconstructed what had happened, missing only Mace's descent from the sycamore and the part the tree had played. After he had traced the fleeing footmarks to the water's edge and had discerned that the pair of bootprints ended where the two horses had been tied, he noted the hoofmarks leading into the creek.

"Looks liken Mace hez either went acros't or els't he's ridin' up th' crick. Davey, yer take three men an' scout roun' some on th' other side uv thet fur bank. Don't piddle 'roun' none if'n they ain't no sign uv nobuddy. Circle wide an' then kum back an' ride up 'longsides th' crick. I'll take these here other three fellers an' ride hup this hyar side. If'n yer spies Mace, fire yore damn pistol fer a sign, liken we-uns agreed ter do. Le's git th' hell a-goin'. He hain't gonna ride no fu'ther in th' water then he hez to ter throw us off'n his trail."

Abe started up the dry land on his side paralleling the waterway, followed by three cautious riders, the last one leading Washley's mare. Middleton led the rest across the creek and over the hill.

On the other side, Middleton's party found an open expanse, almost free of any vegetation. Innumerable crayfish mounds were everywhere, jutting up like so many miniature volcanoes. The party began the ordered swing around the terrain, covering to the tip of a forested area, which extended, peninsula-like out on the cleared ground. As if by prearrangement, as they rounded their side of the wooded strip and passed its end, another band of riders cleared the other border and the two groups suddenly fused before their surprised leader could halt the union.

In the brief parley that followed, Ab Washley and Tom Ferrence recounted how Mace had outwitted them, the subsequent loss of their weapons and horses and how they had hastened back to where the rest of their party was waiting for them, while they were presumably scouting the land up ahead.

"Ab, why didn't you fire yore pistol when you found them footprints of Mace's?" Middleton asked.

"I figgered we could ketch 'im by ourselves," Washley replied sheepishly.

"That's what Will Luckett thought too an' he damn near got hisself kilt." He then described the events experienced by Abe's contingent and the recovery of the two animals.

As he heard the latter, Washley exclaimed, "I shore am damn glad tuh hear that. I wouldn't take nuthin' fer that mare. She's a real good-un. Where's she now—who's got her?"

"She's with Abe. But that's enough talkin', let's git goin' like Abe wants us to."

*

Mace continued along his watery course, pushing his mount ahead despite the often uncertain footing beneath the surface. In front of him, the stream was curving and he realized he was entering the lower part of its bend—the same bend he had intended to cross originally before necessity had altered his planned route of escape. He drew his reins and let his thirsty mount suck from the creek while he tried to determine the best fording place. The pause brought an immediate sound of alarm. Faint hoofbeats warned him that his pursuers had not been deceived by the ruse he had employed to lose them. He pulled heavily on the reins and the steed reared up on its hind legs, its forefeet pawing the air. He loosed the lines a fraction as he booted the animal's flanks, driving it into deeper water. It swam briefly, then splashed its way to the other shore. There was no cover beyond the bank for about a quarter of a mile in either direction. Genuinely confused by the absence of any protective element, he deliberated for a split second, then determined to reverse his way. He would go downstream on this side, utilizing the thick growth of trees along its shore, while those chasing him would be riding to the opposite north. When he reached the strip of forest in the distance, he would cut to the east and then back on around as he had previously wished to do.

He heard the searching party as it thundered past on the other side. Expecting their coming, he had stationed himself in a cluster of willows in such a position as to be able to see them as they traveled by. As best he could make out, there were but four of them, none of whose faces were clearly seen. Certain there must be others following them, he waited patiently for their passing but they did not come. When he could detect no further oncoming sounds, he concluded that if there were any more, they must be farther up the creek. He congratulated himself upon his decision to come down the east side of the tributary. Boldness returned to him and he rode out into the open.

No sooner had he emerged than he was discovered. Davey Middleton's pistol boomed. Some distance beyond, Abe Foster and his men, still looking for tracks leading from the creek, heard the report and instantly wheeled around and headed back from whence they had come.

Mace was now as a rabbit flushed from cover. He raised the reins to his mouth and bit hard on the leather. His clenched teeth were not so firmly shut that vile blasting at his limp arm could not pour forth from his mouth. He drew one of the guns from his waist and tilting his palm, while his thumb held the upper part of the pistol against the line of his index finger, he lifted his hand above the reins, then lowered it so the lines ran through his fingers and between the pistol butt and the inside of his hand. He clamped his fist, locking them within his grip. As he eased the pull on the bit, his mount streaked forward, its tail feathered with the wind and its mane flying. Behind him, the manhunters whipped their steeds over the fissured clay. He bent his wrist, tearing his horse's head to the left and toward what appeared to be a likely crossing place, only to find that a large, uprooted elm blocked his way to the water. He threw his left arm away from him, drawing the reins flat past his animal's neck, jerking the creature into the desired bearing to the right. He straightened his course, then suddenly obliqued into the stream and on across.

As his horse's feet struck firm ground, the first impression upon his mind was the sight of four horsemen sweeping toward him. The trap was beginning to fall about him and his impulses tripped over one another as they formed in his brain. Blindly, he rushed back across the creek, hastily reckoning that the pursuers on that side would be farther away than those he had just avoided. But as he cleared the mucky bank, he was dismayed to discover he had erred in his frantic calculation. The hunters over here were equally as close as had been those on the far side, and they were in greater numbers. He saw that one of them was within firing distance and had leveled his pistol. Mace struggled to cock his own rein-wrapped weapon and to retain the dominance of his mount. His effort was the essence of awkwardness. His left hand, ill accustomed to handling firearms, fumbled the butt as the racing animal stretched its neck, and the weapon wobbled as he snapped the trigger. The shot went wild. The startled horse bolted back toward the waterway, exposing its rider's broad, unprotected back to Davey Middleton's aim, not sixty feet to the rear. The powder flashed, and the ball sped toward its mark. Mace slumped and swayed in the saddle. Before another shot could be fired, he had recovered his seat and regained control of the reins. The horse sensed some loss of mastery on the part of its rider, but the pressure of the bit was still strong enough to induce obedience and the horse headed upstream.

All at once the creek was filled with shouting horsemen. Some were in the water up ahead; others were on opposite shores. Rearward, Mace could hear the sloshing progress of still more. He was completely encircled.

"Use yer other pistol!" one part of his brain ordered. He slipped his hand to the weapon and cocked it inside his jacket. He withdrew it, and the ball of his thumb brought with it the wetness of his belly. He fired at no one in particular. Anyone he chanced to hit would be as good as another. He had just one charge, and he must make it count. His finger pulled hard on the trigger. Instead of a flash, there was only a dull hiss. The sweat of his body had seeped into the powder. The one at whom he had attempted to fire grabbed hold of his right arm, seeking to unseat him. Mace wrenched his shoulder away and hammered at an unprotected jaw with the rounded end of his weapon. The man rolled head first into the creek. He swung at his attacker, striking their arms, hands, and heads. His bewildered mount, its reins dangling, wildly sought some opening in the close-knit circle of men and horses, threshing the muddy water into a topping of white foam as it reared and whirled about, started forward, reversed and stepped sideways, bumping the unyielding obstructions to its escape. A hand reached from the side and almost secured the bridle. The sudden action increased the animal's frenzy, and it stood erect upon its hind legs. Mace fell over backward and somersaulted into the stream. Abe Foster and Davey Middleton were two of the four men who seized him and bore him to the west shore, Abe holding his legs, despite their violent attempts to kick their way free. As they reached dry land, Tom Ferrence jerked a rifle from another's grasp and aimed at close range. Abe dropped Mace's struggling limbs and knocked the barrel upward as it discharged.

"Whut th' hell's th' matter with yer, Tom? Yer knows damn well he's gotta be hung." Abe drew his pistol and pointed it at Ferrence. "Now, drap thet damn gun, er I'll shoot yer right through yore damn belly!"

For the second time within an hour, Ferrence discarded a rifle, but not without protesting. "I shore never thought yuh would be protectin' Mace Hardin. What th' hell differunce does it make whether we hangs 'im or shoots th' dirty, murderin' bastard?"

"Hit jest so heppens, it wuddn't be accordin' to th' law, thet's all!" Abe glanced around at the rest of the men. "An' if'n eny uv yers shoots 'im, I'll shoot 'im whut does it m'se'f! Yers unnerstan' me?"

There was no reply. They understood.

Davey Middleton had noticed the limpness of the arm he was holding, but he did not lessen his hold or his vigilance, notwithstanding the fact that Mace had relaxed somewhat and seemed resigned to being captured. However, as Abe Foster moved a step farther from him, the captive jumped to his feet and turned slightly to his right, bringing the one who held his left arm tripping over his left leg. And with the same lightning movement, causing him who stood guard behind to be knocked from his footing by Middleton, who yet retained his hold upon the useless limb. In a second, Mace kicked and beat himself free of Middleton's grip and ran toward a thickness of trees near the water's edge. The odd taste of blood surged in his mouth, and he felt the trickle at the corners of his lightly pressed lips. A wave of sickness came over him, and he knew that he could not run much farther. The trunk of a big chestnut loomed hazily before his eyes, and he made for it. Reaching the tree, he settled his back firmly against it, bracing himself that he might continue to stand on his feet.

Ferrence was loud in his denunciation of Abe Foster's restraint as the party came up, lashing at him with his tongue. "Yuh damn nigh let th' son-of-a-bitch git away!"

A scowl from Abe silenced him, as he asked, "Whar's th' rope?"

"Hell, we ain't got none," exclaimed Ab Washley. "We thought yore bunch had it!"

Immediately, there was a turmoil of words, most of which demanded that Mace be shot and the hunt concluded. Abe was the lone dissenter. "He hain't dyin' less'n he's hung!"

"Let's take another vote on that," someone shouted, and there was a chorus of assenting voices.

Abe's finger was at work on the lump of tobacco in his jaw. When he had expunged it, he said, "We-uns ain't th' majority. We gotta wait til th' rest uv the fellers gits here. They prob'ly hez a rope, enyways." No manner of talking could dissuade him from his determination that Mace Hardin had to meet his death in the agreed way. He did accept the suggestion that riders be dispatched to locate the missing members of the conspiracy, those who walked and those who rode, and hasten them to this place where the creek made its meandering way in a big bend.

CHAPTER 59

Mace's mind and sight began to clear and with their lucidity came the irrefutable conclusion that further flight would be not only futile but also impossible. There remained but the slightest chance that he could avoid the noose about his neck—the fragile possibility of oral persuasion. He turned his head slowly about him, noting the surrounding faces carefully. When the riders whom Abe had sent after the others had departed, Mace directed his speech to him, being acutely aware of his leadership and of his apparent reluctance to alter from that which he believed to be the law. Mace's beginning was interrupted by a siege of coughing, during which he spat red blotches upon the ground. The cloth around his girth had become saturated from the wound in his back, and its coins were being washed by his blood as it ran its many ways down his limbs. He steadied himself by shifting his feet to a wider stance and spoke slowly. "Abe Foster, yer knows th' law, and I b'leeves yer respecks it. I heered yer a while ago when yer sed I hed ter be handled liken whut wuz 'greed ter."

Davey Middleton's voice was loudest in the furor, which ensued as Mace began talking. "Abe, you ain't a-goin' to lissen none to 'im, are you?"

Abe looked at his bruised companion as he answered him. "Cain't be no harm in lettin' th' son-uv-a-bitch talk. Yer knows damn well thet 'fore they hangs enyone, they hez got th' right ter speak they piece. Let's jest liken th' law does it, an' seein' as how Mace is gonna git hisse'f hung, I sez he kin talk some, leastways til them other fellers kums with th' damn rope." He glared about as he added, "Enybuddy got eny objeckshuns?"

Mace timed his resuming with the silence that followed. "Yer shore are right about thet, Abe. Now, I 'preciates yer obeyin' th' law. I knows I mought hev did some things whut ain't bin right straight 'longsides whut th' law sez. An' I'm shore sorry fer m' bad doin's, but jest 'cause them fellers claims I promised 'em some uv my own salt ain't no reason ter hang me 'cause I won't guv 'em whut they claims. Thet's fer the law ter decide. If'n th' law wuz ter say it wuz they propity, why uv course I'd hev ter guv it ter 'em but not til th' law sez so. Now, ain't thet right, Abe?"

"Hell, naw, it ain't right! Fust place, it ain't yore salt—hit's Cap'n Mercer's. An' we done 'greed thet yer ez gonna be hung—thet's th' law."

"Wal, I thinks yer be wrong on thet, Abe. Yer knows thet even a damn nigger hez ter be tried 'fore a jedge. Why jest th' other day, up at th' Falls, they hanged a nigger, but they guv 'im a fair trial 'fore they done hit. Yer knows th' law sez yer kain't hang no White man, less'n he's tried in Virginny fust." He looked hopefully for what impression his argument might be making.

Abe battered down his expectancy, saying, "We-uns be too damn fur frum Richmond ter foller them rules uv th law. We follers th' rule whut sez we kin perteck ourse'fs, an' we 'greed that th' perteckin' means yer gits hung. So yer hed jest best fergit thet part uv th' law yer ez talkin' 'bout."

Mace was temporarily stymied. He didn't dare risk pressing his argument—a perfectly valid one and correctly stated. If he persisted, he might so set Abe's mind that all avenues leading to a source creating a doubt as to the legality of the proceeding would be finally barred. Harboring this thought, he turned to another approach. "Yer knows Cap'n Mercer wuddn't hold ter yer doin' nuthin' whut wuzzn't lawful, yer knows thet. An' I heppens ter know thet he be a extry good friend uv Patrick Henry. I seed a parchmint onc't, whut th' Cap'n hed, whut wuz signed by 'im, I did. Now, whyn'tcher jest wait til Cap'n Mercer kums back an' let 'im take proper keer uv me?"

For a moment, Mace thought his effort might have weight, as Abe appeared to be studying what he had said to him. His own intrepid gaze searched Abe's eyes for some indication of acknowledgment. Then Abe spoke.

"Yer hed damn well fergit 'bout Cap'n Mercer. Fer th' one thing, he hain't gonna be here fer a good whiles yet. But if'n he wuz here, right now, it wuddn't do ya no good. He knows 'bout how ya tried ter hev 'im kilt by Virgil Mallory an' thet other cutthroat uv yor'n, Justin Gibbs."

Mace's composure slipped when he heard this, but he instantly regained it. "Why, thet's plumb foolish talk. Mebbe, if'n I wuz ter tell yers thet Cap'n Mercer owns th' licks whut I'm a-runnin', yer mought cud see thet whutever son-uv-a-bitch tole yer thet 'bout me is a damn liar."

"Thet'd be th' cap'n, hisse'f, 'cause he's th' one whut tole it ter me." Abe's tone was sharp-edged.

"Then somebuddy must hev lied ter 'im. I wuddn't harm a hair on thet head uv hiss'n, not fer all th' salt in them damn licks. 'Fore God, I wuddn't."

"'Pears ter me, Mace," Abe observed sagely, "yer hed best call on some-un whut yer knows a mought better. Now, yer wud be wise wuz yer ter wait til them other fellers gits here. If yer keeps on a-talkin', one uv them whut's standin' 'roun' yer mought shoot 'fore I cud stop 'im."

"Mebbe, yer are right 'bout thet, Abe, but less'n yer wants ter hang a dead man, yer hed better see if'n yer kin stop th' bleedin' frum th' hole in m' back."

Abe and Davey Middleton inspected the wound. The ball had entered just below the right shoulder blade. At length, they succeeded in stanching the flow but not without observing the bulk around Mace's abdomen. Their sense of touch told them what it was. Prudently, they made no disclosure to the rest of the company. They lowered his shirt, and Mace seated himself so that the tree again supported his back.

The afternoon was well on its waning way when the last of the three divisions of men reached the site. Only one member was absent—Jack Doniger. No one had remembered the necessity of the rope. A debate immediately ensued—a one-sided discussion—with only Abe Foster favoring adherence to the original agreement as to the method of execution. He did not tell his opponents he had never witnessed a hanging.

The inevitable vote was taken, much to the chagrin of Mace Hardin who had hoped for a violent disagreement leading to a common brawl. A show of hands—Abe's powerful lungs might have induced an aura of doubt had it been by voice—disclosed that all but him were in favor of death by pistol shot. Abe made a last-ditch attempt to change their minds, saying, "Now, I 'grees ter be bound by thet thar vote whut wuz jest took, but yer hed orter wait fer Jack Doniger ter git here. After all whut he's did, he's got th' right ter be here at th' finish. An' he oughter hev a piece of rope with 'im. If'n he hain't, we cud git one, real quick-like, frum th' licks."

A volley of down-shouting voices shattered this indirect plea for reconsideration of the previous decision.

As he had listened to Abe, Mace had been struck by the irony of his undoing at the hands of Jack Doniger. A jackal had trapped a lion. A living coward's love for a dead prostitute had numbered his days.

It appeared each member of the throng now coming at him had designated himself to be the executioner. Mace was relieved when Abe Foster intervened, bellowing, "Jest 'cause I 'greed ter shootin', 'stead uv hangin', don't mean I hain't th' leader uv this here bizness! Now, ever' damn one uv yers back up an' stay back!" When his command had been obeyed, he added, "Davey Middleton'll do th' killin'. Hit wuz him whut shot 'im an' kept 'im frum gittin' away."

Protests were loud, but ineffectual, and Middleton began the readying of the weapon. Mace's eyes followed each movement of the preparation. When it had been completed, and as the pistol was cocked, he inched his way up until he was erect. Then he began speaking, looking directly at Abe Foster. "Abe, yer sed I cud talk some more when th' rest uv 'em got here, hain't thet right?"

Abe nodded his head, and Mace continued. "Wal, yer fellers hez kotched me, an' yers hez 'greed ter kill me. But I'm a-tellin' yers, yers are a-fixin' ter git yerse'fs in a heap uv trubble. Yer knows liken I done tole Abe Foster thet they hain't nobuddy but a nigger, or a Injun, whut kin be kilt legal, less'n it's done by th' law in Richmond, Virginny. Yer kills me, an' yers will all hev te answer ter th' law for th' doin' uv it. Remember thet, 'fore yers lets it heppen."

His words were seriously taken in by his listeners. He had correctly stated the law, and most of them were familiar with it. He sensed the first signs of wavering on the part of the confederates.

It was Abe who dispelled their fears of punishment. He thundered, "Aw right, s'posin we be wrong if'n we kills 'im, which I doubts, y' unnerstan. But, jest s'posin' whut th' son-uv-a-bitch says ez th' truth, which I also doubts kumin frum him. Does yers think thet th' law ez goin ter consarn hitse'f eny about it?

Yer knows damn well hit won't. Speshul after we tells 'bout all th' laws this son-uv-a-bitch hez broke: murderin', robbin', an' workin' fer th' damn British! How does yers think th' Injuns kum ter attack Tom Chism's flatboat? I'll tell yer how! I seed Blackie Vermin an' Ben Skinner a-talkin' tergether, early one mornin' not too fur back. Yers knows how clos't Skinner an' Mace hez allus bin, don't yers? Wal, thar ez yore answer!"

Before Abe had finished, the group had become a mob. The only determent, the only factor which effectively prevents the formation of a lawless body's fear of individual safety, had been banished.

But Mace was not through. He shouted at Abe. "Yer promised me th' right ter make m' speech, yer son-uv-a-bitch, an' I'm a-makin hit!"

Caught by his own understanding and interpretation of the law, Abe held both his temper and his tongue except to say to the men, "Let 'im hev his say. He hain't gonna hep hisse'f none."

Ignoring Abe's remarks, Mace began anew. "Now, yers all hed better lissen real good ter whut I'm gonner say ter yers. Yers hez refused ter guv me a trial liken I tole yers I wuz 'titled ter hev at Richmond. Yers hez took th' damn law inter yer own han's. Wal, here is suthin' yers kain't git aroun'! I claims th' benefit!"[23]

Abe was confounded by the mysterious and important sound of that last word. "Whut th' hell does yer mean, yer claims th' benefit?"

"Th' benefit uv th' clergy, thet's whut I means!"

"Whut th' hell good ez a preacher gonna do fer yer, yer dumb son-uv-a-bitch? 'Fore th' next one comes 'roun' these parts, yore gonna be so damn deep in hell, th' devil, hisse'f won't even be able ter fine yer!"

"Yer are th' dumb son-uv-a-bitch, yer ownse'f, Abe Foster. If'n enybuddy kin read, they kin claim th' benefit jest liken preachers an' priests kin do, when they ez charged with doin' enything wrong, even killin' some-un. Thet's th' strongest law, an' hit don't make a damn bit uv diffrunce whut I hez did er ain't did. Th' most whut kin be did ter me is ter burn m' hand so's ter show I hez claimed th' benefit. Yer kin oney claim it once't." He stretched out his left hand for all to inspect and then took hold of his useless right arm and held up its hand. "Yers don't see no scars on 'em, does yer? I claims th' benefit, an' I dares yer not ter guv it ter me!"

The magic propensities of the short sentence, with its intimation of ecclesiastical sanction, combined to induce a profound doubt in the minds of most of those present. Only a few among them could write their names or read the simplest words. The awe and respect that the illiterate had for learning and for the church might now save Mace Hardin's life. Even Abe Foster had been influenced. If Mace was right and there was such a law, Abe knew he would have to answer to the authorities if he ordered his death.

But Davey Middleton had no such doubts or apprehensions. Speaking to his confused companions in a crisp voice, he said, "What Mace jest said about claimin' th' benefit is right. I have heard of it before."

The condemned one's lips worked into a smile, only to have the corners of his mouth droop, as Middleton spoke on.

"That wuz th' law back in England, an' mebbe some of th' colonies pays attention to it, but I ain't heard of it in Virginny, an' if'n it ain't th' law in Virginny, it ain't no good here."

There was a rising murmuring, as Mace strove to hold his advantage. "Hit's th' law in North Car'lina, an' thet's whar I'm frum. An' jest 'cause thet son-uv-a-bitch thar," he pointed at Middleton, "says he hain't heered uv it bein' th' law, don' mean thet it hain't! Whut th' hell does he know 'bout th' damn law enyways?"

Middleton's answer was decisive. "I know as much about it as you does an' mebbe lots more. One thing is certain, I ain't no damn liar, like ever'body here knows you are. An' I think them what's here will take my word 'fore they believes yores."

The effect was spontaneous. They had been listening to, and had almost believed, one whom they knew to be entirely untruthful. Now, their eyes had been fully opened again. They would be fooled no more.

Abe Foster was the first to recover from his entrancement. "Ya hez sed yore last, Mace Hardin. If'n yer knows eny prayers, yer hed best say 'em quick."

A Black bear at Falls of the Ohio or a White man near Bullitt's Lick. When sentence has been pronounced, no words can long stay its execution.

But Mace Hardin, unlike Cato Watts, was not held by rope or bondage. He rolled around the broad trunk of the tree and started running. A rifle fired and he fell. The lead stopped in his backbone. When they came to him, they found he was paralyzed from his neck down. He could move his head and that was all.

Abe Foster's fist knocked Tom Ferrence to the ground, ten feet from where the blow had landed. "Damn yer, Tom Ferrence," he said angrily. "If'n he dies 'fore we kin shoot 'im, I'm gonna kill yer, shore as hell's hoppin' red!"

But Mace lived on. Davey Middleton stood over him, pistol in hand, in the clearing near the big bend of the stream. He bent down and tried to place the muzzle between Mace's eyes, before pulling the trigger, but Mace turned his face from side to side. Middleton straddled his head and drew his feet close upon it, preventing any movement. He leaned down, the weapon in the hand of a scarred forearm, and as his finger tightened upon the trigger, he said, "This here's fer Willie Roller!" Mace's eyes widened in recognition. There was a blast. When the powder smoke cleared and Middleton had stepped away, Mace lay on his left cheek, as though looking out upon those who had watched him die.

Jack Doniger had heard the shot and quickened his steps. He imagined its significance, but he did not care, for he held by its hair the head of the one who had murdered his Dolly. The others would see it and know that her death had been fully avenged.

He walked into their midst unnoticed, until someone tired of looking at the motionless body of Mace. There was an involuntary recoiling from the gruesome spectacle, then everyone became aware of Jeddy-Boy's head at the same moment. The boiling lust for blood, which had begun to cool, now rose to its former pitch. Mitch Strickler helped its rise. "Mace hain't no better'n Jedd-Boy. Let's cut his head off'n 'im too!" He took his hand axe from his belt and walked back to where Mace lay. Pressing the heel of one hand upon the forehead above the bullet hole, he forced it back and held it there while the other hand wielded the axe. Two chopping strokes, and the head rolled free. The pent-up blood gushed from the opening and over the jagged edges of the neck. He picked up the head and carried it to where Doniger had laid that of Jeddy-Boy. Father and son were together again.

"Let's make it three!" incited Strickler. "Let's go git Hawkstraw, an' wipe all uv th' damn Hardins out while we're a-doin' it! Jist as well do it up proper!"

Abe stamped the fire from the sanguine fuse before it could spread. "They ain't gonna be no more killin'. We hez did whut we 'greed ter do. Thet's all whut we kin do, 'cordin' ter th' law! They hain't nuthin left ter do 'cept ter burry them two sons-uv-bitches! Let's do hit an' git away frum hyar. Them pore fellers whut walked here hez theyse'fs a long ways ter go back, an' they hain't gonna make it 'fore dark if'n we don't hurry some."

"Burry them bastards?" It was Mitch Strickler again. "Why they ain't fitten tuh be burried. I sez stick they damn heads on some poles, so's tuh be a warnin' tuh other sons-uv-bitches liken them."

Abe made no effort to countermand the suggestions, rather he thought it a good idea. And after a moment of indecision, while it waited for any forthcoming objection on his part, the mob voiced its accord.

Three horses accompanied Jack Doniger, on a borrowed mount, back to where the rest of Jed Hardin lay on the hill. The riderless horse in their company would be burdened on the return trip.

During the interim, eager hands began to disrobe Mace Hardin's decapitated body. When the red-colored money belt was uncovered, the greedy discord that erupted quickly assumed the proportions that the dead Mace had hoped for earlier in avoidance of his fate. Had he thought to use the money as a bargaining agent, perhaps his head, instead of being a hundred feet away, would now repose upon his thick, muscled neck, and his sly brain would still be planning his salvation. If he had only remembered that most of the mob was as avaricious as himself.

It took all of Abe's persuasive powers, oral and those of physical force, to bar them from their coveted plunder. Branding it as stolen property, he claimed the money on behalf of him whom he declared to be its true owner—Captain Mercer. And had not Jack Doniger and the others returned with Jeddy-Boy's headless corpse, the reclamation might have been challenged further and with increased contention. But the timely arrival of Jed's remains diverted their attention. Doniger was plied with questions, and the admiration of him by his questioners was most evident. He had become a man in their eyes.

When all the details had been revealed, the men began to grow restless. They had accomplished that which they had set out to do. As a cat tiring of playing with a dead mouse, their inner urgings were to move on to other interests. But there yet remained something to be done before their mission would be completed.

Two locust saplings growing side by side were quickly topped and trimmed. Their ends were sharpened, so that they became living pikes as tall as a six-foot man. Because it had been first severed, the head of Jeddy-Boy, its features caught and held in all their terror of death, was the first to be impaled. Jack Doniger lifted it from where it lay, the glazed eyes seemingly following his opened fingers as they reached down to grasp the jet-black mop of hair. He stretched as he raised the fearful object, his palms on either side of its temples, and centered the pointed end of the shaft beneath the bloody orifice. Then, shifting his hands to the top, he bore down with great exertion. Crunching sounds, those of barriers being broken, attended the downward course until the unyielding inner wall of the skull prevented more descent. Pockets of captive blood, opened by the intruding pike, oozed slowly groundward.

Perfunctorily, Mitch Strickler took hold of Mace's full-lobed ears and hoisted the head into position. For a languid instant, an inquiring sunbeam glistened upon the scar on the face. Then the pike's entrance reproduced the crackling noises heard before. As the point scraped at its stopping point, Mace's eyelids relaxed unaccountably and dropped, covering his defiant eyes. Death itself had been unable to conquer that defiance. Perhaps their lowering was a peculiar testimonial to a lifetime of bold, unflinching courage, wrongfully employed though it had been.[24]

In the place of the Great Reckoning, Willie Roller would know that Mace's head, like his own, had been separated by the sharpened edge from his body. And Dolly Dusenberry and Cuthbert Smith would recognize the awesome horror that had borne down upon Jeddy-Boy with its clammy talons.

The naked bodies were placed against the barked locust, their hacked necks touching them. Then the murdering band took its untroubled leave, straggling from the scene. As its last member became lost to view, the inharmonious bass of Abe Foster, voicing his song of vulgar indifference, labored back to the creek and lingered there.

The carnivorous creatures of darkness would strip the prostrate bones, and the carrion fowl of the day would tear away the flesh from the faces. When morbid curiosity had been satisfied, one would intentionally visit this site of sadistic interment, until long after the grinning skulls and the skeletal remnants beneath them had disappeared.

The elbow curve in the creek's course would be given a name. Acknowledging the order of precedence, it would first be called Jed and Mace Bend, then corruptly Jedmace Bend. As the memory of the wicked is wont to rot, so the name would die in the minds of men. And when, in later years not too distant from the scene, plows turned the fertile earth, bringing up sections of gum and sassafras pipes, there would be none who remembered the hideous happening in the clearing that bordered the big bend in the stream. Young lovers would blissfully recline in the shade of a friendly elm, near where two young locusts once grew.

CHAPTER 60

The spirited Sagitta, reveling in the long awaited exercise, tried to break from a gentle lope into a full gallop, only to feel the bit deny that desire as Mercer drew firmly on the reins. The sun was warm, and he was perspiring freely, particularly so about his neck. He became aware it was just the one side that seemed to be so affected, and he crossed his right hand above his left as he wiped the outer side of his throat. It was not sweat that answered his touch, and he looked at his palm, thinly coated with blood. Strangely, he had forgotten Mallory's near miss and the lancing wound it had inflicted upon his lower jaw. Until now he had not noticed the dull aching of his hurt. He thought back, wondering when it might have been reopened. Perhaps, Drusilla Grainger had broken the scab in the last moment of her frustration. Odd, that it had not occurred during all the preceding love play in which they had indulged so unrestrainedly. His pulse quickened at this vivid memory and the passionate recollection made him waver from his determined way. Only after he had ridden a quarter of a mile back toward the settlement did his will reassert itself. And when it did so, it was regained more by rote than through self-control. "He goeth after her straightway, As an ox goeth to the slaughter, or as a fool to the correction of the stocks; Till a dart strike through his liver; As a bird hasteth to the snare, And knoweth not that it is for his life … Her house is the way to hell, Going down to the chambers of death." These thoughts from Proverbs wheeled Sagitta away from Saltsburg.

Had he continued in the changed direction, he would have arrived at the Grainger home in time to see the stranger, his face still flushed, close the door behind him and mount his horse and ride away. Had he looked closely, he would have seen a curious little Jason run from around the far side of the house in mock pursuit of the departing horseman.

In the interest of time, Barth had chosen to follow the main, or town, fork of Salt River after he crossed to its south bank. By roughly paralleling the upward course of the stream, he would be able to save better than twenty miles in his journey to Harrodstown. Had he elected to follow the accustomed route, he would have gone from the ferry at Dowdall's to Bairdstown, or Bardstown as it was fast becoming known, thence crossing Chaplin Fork to Harrodstown, bypassing the station that lay some nine miles southeast of the town. This itinerary he knew to be about fifty-five miles in length. By his best estimation, his present route would cover a little more than thirty miles, from Dowdall's to his destination just east of the upper reaches of Salt River and not far from its rise. If his progress was without incident the rest of the day, he would have traversed the greater portion of his journey by nightfall, without unduly extending Sagitta. Tomorrow morning, he would have but a short, easy ride to Harrodstown.

Traveling as he was, off the beaten path, his eyes found many diversionary objects to keep his mind occupied. There were the birds—gaily colored paroquets in great flocks of small bodies, blackbirds, yellow-breasted warblers, redbirds, an occasional hawk and many species of owl for which he knew no name.

He identified the different trees that he passed: pawpaws, cucumbers, buckeyes, the tulip laurel and the coffee tree, which resembled the black oak and whose pods contained the beans that the settlers crush to make a substitute for coffee, a hard-to-get commodity since the blockade. He saw the sugar tree, and he filled himself with the fruit of the black mulberry. There was the honey locust, whose thorny spikes called for careful picking of its long pods, which yielded the ingredients from which an excellent tasting beer could be made. The large green burs of the chestnut and the smaller ones of the beeches aroused within him a trace of nostalgia as he thought upon the huge hearth at Williamsburg, the pig on the turning spit and the nuts roasting to their most delicious taste. But the homesickness withdrew with the flight of an ivory-billed woodpecker from a balled walnut in front of him. Many a frontiersman, believing the oft-repeated story that the bird's bill was pure ivory, had caused a fatal flurry of snowy feathers, only to find that the beak was without pecuniary worth. But the fallacious idea to the contrary continued to exist. Man's ageless desire for easy treasure overleads him to hopefully bask in the reflection of anything that glitters, whether above him, below him or on the earth he trods with expectant step.

He wound his way through wonderful stretches of cane—the attraction for so many of those coming to Kentucky. "Fine cane land" had been among the magic words he had heard when this country first had been described to him.

Now he rode through as expanse of broomsedge, resembling from a distance a field of grain, but being next to useless. Stock and wildlife would eat of it but sparingly. On one side, he observed a row of redhaw bushes, which had been trimmed to a convenient height by the feeding of the deer and elk that had just been distributed into precipitous flight by the scent of his approach. He reasoned these animals must be numerous in this region. Otherwise, the redhaw would not be so leveled by their appetites. Left alone, he knew these bushes would grow upward to twenty feet above the ground.

Gray squirrels chattered wickedly in a hickory grove to his right, as the broomsedge thinned and wild flowers took over. Two of the delights of the senses were now being served—the vision of the beauty of color and the enchantment of delicate fragrance.

Sagitta's stride had been easy. Barth had made sure that it had been kept so, and the animal appeared untired. Yet when he came to a shaded spot, he dismounted and gave the horse a rest. Finding a spring nearby, the thirsts of man and beast were leisurely satisfied.

Resuming his journey, he continued to hold to an eastwardly course by frequent reference to the position of the sun and the shadows of the trees. He had a definite guide on the north by reason of Town Fork itself, which he knew to run generally east for approximately twenty miles, whence it dropped to the south though still veering eastwardly. As it narrowed, he would then know he was nearing Harrodstown.

He avoided the tree-covered hills and their ridges by keeping to the bottoms and following buffalo paths, though the latter practice necessitated numerous crossings and recrossings of the river. Though this way was easier to travel, he recognized reluctantly it was also longer than the route he had planned originally. He realized also it was time-consuming, and the realization brought with it a measure of impatience, a dissatisfaction that grew when the sun began to sink in the west. As he rode from the stream to its south shore, he came upon a fine stand of young cane. He dropped the reins that his mount might feed briefly upon this delicacy, so favored by it and others of its kind.

While Sagitta was eating, Barth reached down and opened his saddlebag. Expecting to find only the dried meat he had placed there, he was amazed to discover it contained the legs and a generous portion of the breast of a turkey as well as some corncakes. Somehow, Rosie had managed to put the food in there without his knowledge. A glowing feeling of appreciation for her thoughtfulness encompassed him, enhancing each mouthful he consumed. Sweet, lovable Rosie. Amid all the vulgar, profane, violent and greedy characteristics of Bullitt's Lick, how could such principled kindness and unselfishness, as was hers, endure? He found himself wondering at the inconsistency, again conjecturing as to what her life might have been if fate had permitted her to have been born of higher antecedents. The first haze of twilight stayed both his reflections and his appetite. He must move on.

The buffalo path was now running to the south, farther and farther away from the river, and he decided he would have to leave it and rely upon his own sense of direction. In front of him, the land appeared as a continuous succession of broken hills. Undesirable as it seemed, this would have to be the way he would travel.

He rode from half-light into near darkness, guiding Sagitta in a winding path until he reached the ridge. There he noted with satisfaction another buffalo trail, and he stayed upon it until the fast dropping night made further progress untenable. He left the trace and dismounted. Leading his horse, he carefully felt his way until he found an oak of great circumference. Unsaddling his mount, he tethered it and seated himself crossways in the saddle, his back reclining against the tree, his rifle across his knees. For a while, the night sounds alerted him. Then, as he became accustomed to their variation, he nodded.

How long he had slept, he did not know, but he roused when Sagitta began to move nervously about. A piercing scream awoke him thoroughly. It seemed to have come from very close in the blackness beyond. He sprang to his feet, his weapon in readiness. Again came the shrill cry—a penetrating wail, like the anguished lamentation of a woman in travail. Shortly he heard a movement, seemingly from above Sagitta to his left. He fired as the peril flashed upon his senses. Another weird outcry matched the report of his rifle and he heard the creature's body as it struck the ground. There was a scurrying and a moment of intense concentration until it could be determined whether the animal, wounded or frightened, was moving toward or away from him. While he waited, he worked to reload his weapon. His hands shook appreciably, increasing the difficulty of this effort. As the silence lengthened, he concluded, hopefully, that the beast had fled the scene or had withdrawn to nurse its wound.

Now the startling effect upon his brain had been largely erased, and he confessed he had been completely deceived by the near-human quality of the panther's cry. Painters, the frontiersmen called them, and they all dreaded its voice, no matter from what far distance it reached their ears. Of all the unnerving tones that ringed the wilderness night, the torture-ladened screams of this big prowling cat alone sapped the blood of adventurers and undermined their courage. So weird and deep-reaching is the fearful impression, the memory is indelibly stained, as though tinged by the supernatural. And long after the waking hours have passed, the chilled, nervous feeling persists. Once a man had heard the nerve-shattering wail, he never forgets it nor no matter how many times he may hear it thereafter can he be reconciled to its repetition as commonplace.

Barth patted Sagitta's neck, speaking calmly to the animal as he did so. And though he eased its fears, his own uneasiness mounted. Unfamiliar with the hunting methods of the panther, he knew not whether it moved with its mate or alone, whether the one he had fired at had actually gone away or was but waiting somewhere out there in the unfathomable depths of black. Each later noise that broke the stillness was cloaked in premonitory supposition. Thus he waited out the night until it began its transition into shade. When it was light enough, he cautiously searched for traces of the panther but found none.

Even with the full dawn, it remained semilight within the forest. The thickness of their growth kept the trunks of the trees free of lower limbs, and a matting of vines gave the appearance of a canopy of green above him. He saddled Sagitta and led him to the trace from which he had departed the evening before. As he rode the path made so long ago by the hooves of countless thousands of buffalo, he first realized that the ridge upon which he was traveling was a watershed, dividing Chaplin Fork to the south and Town Fork to the north.

The route he was following was not entirely original with him. He had heard that Colonel William Fleming[25] had journeyed this same way, generally, three years earlier. Although, instead of going to Harrodstown, or Harrodsburg as Fleming wrote it in his journal, he traveled from that place to Bullitt's Lick and thence to Falls of the Ohio.

With the sun came anticipatory thoughts of Dracie Claycomb, and had the terrain permitted it Barth would have increased the gait of his mount. But there were often abrupt changes of direction, dips and rocky rises, which could have made more speed dangerous in the extreme.

At length, the trace took a definite pattern to the north and he left it, riding into the sun. A little while, and he was on open ground—earth denuded by man not by nature. He looked eagerly for a cabin and spied one in the immediate foreground. Though he had left Bullitt's Lick less than a full day before, his solitary journey had weighted the relativity of time, and he hungered for the sight of human beings and the sound of their voices.

He found the cabin door open and the place deserted. Riding on, he came upon the remains of another dwelling, its roof caved in and its timbers charred with old ashes. Just beyond the ruins of the house was a row of six graves, their mounds not yet settled to the evenness of the earth about them. Tragedy had feasted here and moved on. What hardships had been endured in vain by those who had perished here with their hopes? What laughter of children had been stilled by savage hands? What memory was there of these who had ventured here? What destiny could be so cruel to lead them on to die in the void of this wilderness? Why had it happened to these particular ones? Had those in the first cabin escaped or had they fled their home only to be caught and slaughtered with their neighbors? What moved men so strongly, that they would desert safety, family and friends, and enter into such an uneven struggle? What right did they have to sacrifice the lives of the young ones who trusted them so lovingly and so blindly? How could these sacrificial offerings have any influence in the settling of this land? What reward could there be for these untimely dead?

He knew not the answer by any human reasoning. But one explanation presented itself. Somehow, for some purpose, it was the will of God. He forced himself into an obedient acceptance of the thought, but as he rode from the disconsolate setting, the finite continued its perplexing conflict with the infinite.

He crossed the thinning river and reined up, undecided in what direction Harrodstown might lie, then chanced it northwardly. Patches of cleared ground increasing in the frequency of their occurrence inspired confidence in his decision and, for the first time since the previous afternoon, he allowed Sagitta to accelerate the pace they had been traveling. He came over an immediate slope and there before him he saw three men on horseback, riding slowly ahead. An uncommon thrill came over him, and he hailed the travelers, who turned in unison at his call. A brief gallop and he was with them. There was a warming exchange of identities and of destinations. They were from Harrodstown and the settlement was just a few miles away in the direction they were headed. Conversation flowed rapidly and most pleasantly until one of them asked where he had come from. With his utterance of Bullitt's Lick, their talking slowed and their words came guardedly and with a suspicious overcast. He sought to offset their hidden doubts, telling them he was from Williamsburg, that business interest alone accounted for him being at the licks. But Saltsburg's contaminating reputation prevailed in their minds. The four rode in near silence until the stockade came into view. His heart leaped at its sight and the thought of the one waiting for him there. He bade his companions goodbye. Then he spurred Sagitta toward the open gate.

CHAPTER 61

No sooner had he ridden into the stockade than he realized the error of his rapid entrance. Alarmed by his sudden coming, the residents gathered hastily around him. To them, such breakneck speed could have only one logical inspiration—Indians!

He introduced himself and offered the aroused settlers his apology—an open admission of his absolute thoughtlessness. He dared not tell them the whole truth, that his heedless approach had been caused by his desire to find his sweetheart as quickly as possible.

That his excuse fell short of making full amends was apparent from the frowns that still remained on several faces. This is not Bullitt's Lick, he reminded himself. This is Harrodstown, the oldest settlement in Kentucky. And its people, by and large, represent the highest type to be found anywhere on the frontier.

Though his own words had failed to gain their complete pardon, the handsome Sagitta, displaying his best manners, had thoroughly captivated them. Each gentle tossing of the animal's head necessarily involved its finely shaped neck. And, as if by some reverse process of alchemy, the golden streams of the sun became transmuted into filaments of purest silver the instant they touched the glorious flowing mane.

Mercer allowed ample time for their admiration of his steed before he ventured to ask concerning the Harmon family. When he did so, one of those who had impressed him as having been most critical of his rash entrance gave a smiling response to his inquiry. "You mean Carter Harmon and his wife, Martha? Or maybe you're looking for their daughter, Lucy?" The man winked at the others before adding, "If it's her you was in such a all-fired hurry to find, I can't say as how I blames you for rushing in here like you did. She's a right pert young woman." His elbow nudged the ribs of a companion whose sense of humor needed no prodding; he had been laughing before the priming jolt was delivered.

Politeness decreed a short duration of their mirth. One of the women ensured its observance by offering directions as to the location of the Harmon cabin. "It's about fourth cabin on the left as you ride out of the fort. No, let's see . . . It's th' third place—that's right. It's the third cabin on your left. You passed it on your way in. It's not very far, just a little ways down the road."

Barth thanked her and apologized once more for the abrupt manner of his arrival. After excusing himself from their company, he remounted and proceeded slowly until he reached the gate. Behind him, his informant was saying, "He's a handsome man, he is. If he is Lucy Harmon's, she'd best be careful when he meets that friend who is a-visitin' her." The poke bonnets of the other women bobbed up and down with her observation. They had all met Lucy's guest.

He was experiencing a let-down feeling. Though he knew he could not have reasonably expected to find her the moment he entered the garrison, such had been his hope. Suppose she wasn't at the Harmon's cabin and it was somewhere else and he would have to go searching for it? He drew his reins as he neared the third cabin.

The door was open. Rather than risk another impetuous error, he rapped loudly, then stepped back. He nervously bided the next few seconds. Surely, someone must be home. He imagined a movement inside the dwelling. All at once a feminine figure emerged from the indistinct interior and the sunlight became a fiery burst as it struck her auburn tresses. It was Dracie! She was here!

There was an infinitesimal interval of shocked surprise. Then their lips met in the purpose of their creation—the expression of their love for each other. Like stems of roses entwined by the wind, their arms held their bodies in a swaying embrace. Not until their ardor had lost some of its intensity did either break the amorous silence. Only then did she speak. "Barth, dearest, I thought I was dreaming when I saw you. I couldn't believe my sight. I'm not certain, even now."

Her words stopped in midsentence. "Oh, Barth! What is the matter with the side of your face? It's bleeding!"

He fussed good-naturedly at her ministering efforts with her kerchief, insisting the healing wound had been the merest sort of accident. When she sought to learn how he had received it, he put her off, promising to tell her later. He kissed her cheek, only to have her push away from him. Before he could seek an explanation, she whispered, "Not anymore, dearest. Someone has been watching us."

He looked, in time to see the halted traveler move on his way.

"We must have made an interesting picture, framed in this doorway," she laughed mischievously. "Let's go inside. We'll have some privacy there."

They crossed the threshold and after she had closed the door, she fell in his arms. In the lone second of their freedom, her lips sighed, "I've wanted you so, dearest! There were times when I thought I must go to you, if you did not come to me."

His eyes faced a little room whose curtain was open, an alcove off the main room of the cabin. There was just space enough for the bed and the small chest it contained. Saliva lodged in his throat and he had difficulty swallowing.

She sensed his intention. "Not now, dearest. Lucy and her mother are visiting a neighbor down the road a little ways. They are liable to come back at any time. And I have no idea where Mr. Harmon is." The cautioning words were spoken thickly and her backward steps were not truly reluctant.

The bed . . . his face above hers . . . "I have wanted you for so long," she murmured.

He shut his eyes and reopened them. For a confused instant, he had imagined the passionate features were Drusilla Grainger's.

When the door opened, everything was circumspect. Dracie sought to hide the nervous traces of her passion by rising from her chair to greet Mrs. Harmon and Lucy as they entered. "You have another visitor," she exclaimed. "Barth arrived shortly after you all had left." Her enthusiasm was artful as she drew them to him. "Mrs. Harmon, may I present Captain Barth Mercer?" She dropped her formality, as she added, "And, dearest, I know that you and Lucy have met before."

He acknowledged the introductions in pleasant fashion. "I'm most pleased to make your acquaintance, ma'am. And I certainly am happy to see Lucy again. Though I must confess she has caused me to change my memory of her. I had always pictured her as being a little girl. Now I find that she has become a charming lady."

"And I remember you as a handsome, gallant gentleman. And your picture has not changed one whit." To the equal astonishment of her mother, Dracie and the unsuspecting Barth, she raised on tiptoe and placed her palms against his cheeks. Then she kissed his lips. "That," she said, "is for your continued gallantry."

Dracie now strove to control a more violent emotion—the biting jealousy that followed the uncalled-for kiss and the attendant blush upon Barth's face. But her power of concealment was not to be tried further. Carter Harmon returned and she introduced Barth to him. By the time the mutual expressions of the pleasure of their meeting had been exchanged, the vehement flame of her irritation had cooled, and she had forgiven her friend her offense.

Mr. Harmon had moved to the fireplace. As he was in the act of dipping a ladle into one of the cooking pots, his wife said, "Carter Harmon, what are you doing? Haven't you had any dinner? When you left, you—" She suddenly thought of the newly arrived guest. "Bless my soul, Captain Mercer! I'm so sorry. I'll bet you haven't had any dinner either. You gentlemen sit yourselves down and I'll fix you all something right away."

With the eager assistance of the younger women, the meal was quickly readied and served.

Although he appeased his appetite, he did not fully enjoy the food. The fork that rested between his thumb and fingers was of silver. Only once since his coming to Kentucky had he eaten with a like implement, that night at the Graingers. Why, of all times, when he was with the one he loved, did he think of Drusilla? Was it because she had aroused him and he had lusted for her? Had this unpremeditated desire provided an underlying conviction that he had been false to Dracie—that he had betrayed her trust and her love?

"Barth, dearest, you're not eating. Is anything wrong? Are you ill?" Dracie asked concernedly.

At her words, his hosts also became solicitous. He quickly arrested their apprehension, blaming his absentmindedness and asked their pardon for his unintentional transgression.

Dracie smiled sweetly. "Barth, dearest, you live so much of your life in reflection. Why must you miss so much of the present by thinking upon the past? The past is dead, and it should be buried. It will bury itself, if you will but let it do so."

He chided her indirectly for her gentle rebuke. "Mr. Harmon, what is your opinion of a woman who talks like that to a man before she is married to him? Is she likely to become a shrew after their marriage?"

Mr. Harmon had finished eating and was lighting his pipe when the question had been put to him. "That is the risk that any man takes when he marries. Of course," he hastened to interject, "in my case, there was no such risk at all. Further than that, I will not say. If there is one lesson a married man should learn, and learn quickly, it is to keep his opinions to himself. If there be another with which he should be most familiar, it would be to learn how to execute an orderly retreat when the shooting begins." His eyes twinkled. "And it appears to me that this might be a good time for you to start practicing. And I will help you. Let's ride to the fort. Colonel Harrod[26] is there and some others whom I would like for you to meet, among them Mr. Edmund Lyne and Colonel Stephen Trigg. They are all land commissioners for Kentucky. Two other members of the commission left yesterday for Falls of the Ohio—it's called Louisville now, as you probably know. You'd like them too—James Barbour and Colonel Fleming. All appointed by the governor and—"[27]

"Carter Harmon! What in the world are you trying to do? Captain Mercer comes all the way from Bullitt's Lick to see Dracie and here you want to take him away before he's hardly had a chance to talk with her. While you're so busy telling him things to remember, you'd best tell him that when a man gets married, he should never forget that an unmarried man likes to be with his sweetheart. Besides, Captain Mercer can meet Colonel Harrod and the rest this evening after supper. We'll go with you." She turned to the young women. "Won't we, girls?"

Harmon assumed a browbeaten air as he said, "You see what I mean by making a retreat? One thing I forgot to say. It had better be done quickly, or you'll find your retreat has been cut off and you will be surrounded, like we are now."

Everyone laughed. But when Harmon left for the fort, he went alone.

Dracie insisted that she help with the clearing of the table and the cleansing of the utensils. Barth too would have lent his hand to the after-dinner obligations had she not refused his aid and said, laughingly, "Dearest, there is another bit of advice that Mr. Harmon might have given you. Preparing meals and cleaning up afterward are women's work. Men only get in the way and hinder what's to be done. It will only take us a minute anyway."

When Lucy and her mother added their support to Dracie's words, he made a despairing gesture and said, "What is it the good book says? 'And if one prevail against him, two shall withstand him; and a threefold cord is not quickly broken.' I believe that's the gist of it. Anyhow, I'm no dullard. I have sense enough to know when I'm not wanted. I'll just go outside until you all are through."

Inside, Mrs. Harmon remarked to Dracie, "He has a fine sense of humor. That's good."

Another horse was tied alongside Sagitta. A bay mare. Must be Mr. Harmon's, he thought. Probably walked to the fort. He looked up the road toward the stockade. The garrison seemed out of place in its peaceful setting.

As he waited, he cast frequent, unobtrusive glances into the cabin. It sounded like carefree work, with all three of the women chattering at the same time. The side of his jaw itched and he scratched it, realizing too late it was a healing symptom. Had Mallory been a better shot, he thought, instead of scratching myself, the wild fowl would have been scratching the dirt on my grave. The thought produced a chuckling observance. That is, if anyone would have taken the time to bury me. His lightheartedness left him as Drusilla reentered his thoughts. There was just one thing to do. He would confess everything to Dracie. Then his mind would be free. But if he did, how would Dracie feel toward him? And if he didn't tell her? What then? Would it grow old on his conscience and be forgotten in time? Or would its weight increase?

Lucy and Dracie came through the doorway and found him in his engrossed state. "He's back in Bullitt's Lick, Lucy." He stirred at the sound of her voice. "No, Dracie, you're wrong about that. I was just wondering how such little work could take three women so long to do it."

"Dearest, Lucy's father might also have told you that when three women get together, they do a lot of talking."

"Dracie, please," he beseeched. "Let's have no more of Mr. Harmon's advice. After all, I didn't ask him for it, you know."

"Yes, you did too," she said laughingly. "You started it by asking him if I would make you a shrewish wife."

"Well, I only asked him that one question." The corners of his mouth were fully raised, as he added, "And I wouldn't have asked even that, had I known of the consequences. Let's declare a truce. How about it?"

"All right, dearest. Peace is declared. Now, why don't we talk somewhere before the afternoon is gone?"

Lucy atoned, at least partially, for her earlier audacity by declining to accompany them, and by suggesting that since her father's horse was saddled and waiting, Dracie and Barth might go for a ride. As if to encourage their adopting the suggestion, she added, "The mare is gentle as can be. And Dracie's almost as tall as Papa. The stirrup straps won't hardly have to be adjusted at all."

After they had mounted and as they turned from the dwelling, Lucy waved to them and then reentered the house. Well, at least I have been unselfish, she thought. But I have talked myself out of something I would have enjoyed doing. Her mother broke in at this moment to ask where Dracie and Barth had gone, and she told her.

"Captain Mercer is certainly a handsome man. And he's so gentle and refined. Dracie is a lucky young woman," Mrs. Harmon observed.

Lucy did not comment on her mother's observation. But she thought, I wish it could have been me. She fluffed the pillow and lay down on her bed. As she reclined, she fancied she detected a male scent within the room. But she quickly dismissed the idea, rebuking herself. Besides having a selfish disposition, I also have a wicked imagination. It was probably Papa. He takes a nap in here once in a while. But the thought was rooted and disturbed her rest. She arose and went to the doorway and looked longingly in the direction they had gone.

They were barely beyond Lucy's hearing, when Dracie said to him. "Dearest, isn't Lucy sweet? She's the most precious and unselfish friend I have. But you know, I have a confession to make to you. When she kissed you, a horrible jealous feeling swept over me. It made me mad enough to have killed her. I was actually ashamed of myself afterward."

The word confession set his mind on his own absolution and he groped for the best manner in which to bare his conscience to her. But she knew only that he had remained silent following the admission of her guilt. "Barth, dearest," she said. "I believe you to be the most noble person I have ever known. But there is one thing which you do that gives me great concern. You have developed a habit of becoming so lost in your own thoughts that I feel terribly shut off from you. I know how greatly troubled you must be by the many problems you have at the saltworks. And I can understand your worrying about them. However, what worries me most, is that I seem to sense in your thoughts something that goes deeper than those matters. I don't know what it is that I feel, but it is as though you are wrestling with life itself. As if you are constantly trying to adjust the balance of your conscience so that they weigh perfectly. I think you must realize that this can never be accomplished. In fact, I have heard you comment on man's imperfections. Yet you refuse to tolerate them in yourself, and you continue to pore over them as though by so doing you are performing penance. You have overlooked the fact that if you sharpen the point of conscience too fine, it will prick you at your every turning. If you must insist upon perfect balance, let natural imperfection to be the counterweight that you use on your scales. Don't try to balance the spiritual and the material. That's for God to do."

Her next words were those of an offender expecting immediate punishment. "There now, I have said it. I don't know whether to feel sorry or glad. I know only that I want you to be happy and that I don't think you are when your mind is so weighted down." She paused. "Have I been too frank? Are you provoked with me?"

He had been fascinated by her dissertation and though it was directed at himself, he yet felt pride and admiration for the depth of her analysis. He answered quickly, lest she think him displeased. "Darling, I have no cause to be angry. Perhaps you are right. But I, of course, have never seen myself in that light. I admit to a practice of meditation. And it could be that it has become an excessive habit with me." He smiled and said, "But I promise you that I shall try to be the husband you want me to be."

"Is it any wonder," she said, "that I love you more than life itself?" She pulled her mount close to his and reaching over squeezed his hand. "You know what I wish, dearest? That we were back in Lucy's bedroom, this very moment."

"What if someone were to come in?" he asked facetiously.

"Then they would just have to come."

CHAPTER 62

She pointed to a hill in the immediate foreground. "See those bushes on that slope up ahead of us? We'll have to dismount when we get there."

"Darcie, when you were talking a minute ago, you were talking of a room in a house. It would be bad enough to be discovered by your friends. I could stand that, I guess. But out here, it might be Indians who would do the intruding."

She blushed furiously. "Barth, you dickens, you! I had no such idea, and you know it. I want to show you the most peaceful scene I have ever looked upon. It's up over that little hill, and we'll have to lead our horses. There's a path that runs between some blackberry bushes and it's too narrow to ride on." The thought came belatedly, but she decided to say it anyhow. "So you wouldn't want to be with me if there were any Indians nearby. That wouldn't have stopped me some of the times when I have wanted you so desperately."

They still were laughing when he helped her from her horse.

As they made their way up the trail, they soon discovered that there were others on the hillside. The bushes were loaded to the ground with the largest, blackest and juiciest berries he had ever seen or tasted. And scattered throughout the extensive patch were at least twenty settlers, including their children. All were busily filling their pails, like so many bees gathering nectar. The briars bordering the path had long been cleaned of their pulpy fruit. As a consequence, there were no pickers to further congest the passageway. As it was, Barth had to exercise care in leading Sagitta between the prickly borders.

Dracie called to him, but he didn't hear her and he continued on, passing an intersecting footway that wound off to the right. She called again, and this time he looked around. "We turn off here," he heard her say, as she entered the opening. Before he could follow, it was necessary that he back Sagitta down below the entrance, and she was well ahead of him on the curving course and soon disappeared from view. But he did not become alarmed for her safety. There were berry pickers here also. When he finally emerged into the open, he found himself on the other side of the same hill they had started to ascend. She had already dismounted and was waiting for him.

"Why did you turn off, Dracie? I thought we were to ride to the top. What made you change your mind?"

"That spring over yonder," she answered. "I became thirsty and decided to come here first. The water tastes as good as that at the fort. You knew there was a spring inside the stockade, didn't you?"

"No, I didn't. Actually. I just rode in and rode out again. I was looking for you, if you will remember."

She was in the act of drinking and did not immediately answer. But as she arose from her kneeling position, she said, "You found me too, didn't you, dearest?" He knew her reference and met her ready embrace.

"Your lips are hot as fire, dearest."

"So are yours, Dracie."

"We'd better get control of ourselves. Don't forget about those Indians," she teased.

"They don't worry me. It's those settlers in the berry patch," he answered humorously.

As they calmed themselves, she said, "This is my valley, my Valley of Eden. The first time Lucy and I came here, I gave it that name. It must be the same as when God first created it. Don't you agree, dearest?"

He gazed upon the gently receding slope a few moments before replying. "It is one of the prettiest places I have ever seen."

"Let's go up to the top of the hill, dearest. We can see it better from up there, and you can tell me what it is that's troubling you."

"Troubling me? What do you mean?"

My face must surely be a poor mask, he thought.

They did not remount, but led their horses leisurely upward. When they reached the brow of the hill, she said, "All right, dearest. Now you can tell me. I've become quite curious."

He tied the animals to a sapling and then sat beside her in the cool shade of a leafy maple. "Dracie, before you and Lucy came out of her house, this was on my mind. I don't know whether I had fully decided to tell you then. But later, when you made your confession about having been jealous, I knew that I must make a confession of my own. I pray to God that it will not change things between us. For what I did, I had no intention nor desire to do beforehand. I was caught in a web of circumstance, and it was almost too late when I came to my senses and struggled free of its entanglement."

"What on earth did you do, dearest? Tell what happened, before you try to absolve yourself."

He made a full disclosure. From the time he first met Drusilla until he shut the door of her home. Nor did he omit his turning around and starting back to her door. When he had finished, he bowed his head as he asked, "Do you understand, darling? Does it make any difference? Can you ever forgive me?"

She threw her arms about his neck and kissed him. "That is my answer, dearest. Everything is the same between us as it has always been and always will be. Don't blame yourself. It was not your fault. I believe that and so must you. Free your mind, dearest. Let's both forget it ever happened."

He kissed her hand, then her lips.

There was no doubting the fullness of her forgiveness, and he marveled at this display of ability to channel her thoughts so that they completely bypassed her emotions. He joined in her enthusiasm over the tranquility of the little valley. It was as she described it—as it must have appeared at the end of the sixth day of creation.

Instead of returning by the way they had come, she guided him through what appeared to be a natural archway, whose straight course ended in a clearing at the top of the patch through the blackberry patch. On their descent, they noticed a few of the settlers were still there. But they were all men. The women and children were gone. When they reached the bottom, and as he assisted her to her sideways position in the saddle, she said, "Dearest, tell me. What does Drusilla Grainger look like? Is she pretty?"

"She is a most beautiful woman," he answered truthfully.

"Then I am the more proud of you and love you all the more. Had you gone further with her, I still would not have blamed you."

This time, it was he who leaned from the saddle and did the kissing.

As they rode along, he told her of the happenings at the lick, ever minimizing the dangerous propensities that existed there. He interspersed Johnny's antics and she expressed an amused interest in him. His narration was general, but she learned of one of his problems, the need of an overseer to replace Mace Hardin. Her heart prayed for a speedy solution when she heard him declare his intent to leave Bullitt's Lick as soon as a suitable replacement could be found. Tears of happiness filled her eyes when he told of his plans for their marriage upon his return to Harrodstown after this had been accomplished.

Before they reached the Harmon home, Dracie called his attention to the two figures standing near the door. When they were close enough for them to see more clearly, she said to him, "Dearest, it's Lucy and her father. Do you suppose he might have wanted to use his horse this afternoon?"

"I hope not. I should hate to think we have caused him any inconvenience."

He lifted her from her mount and they learned immediately that their supposition was baseless.

"Captain Mercer, do you know a man named Mace Hardin at the saltworks? Or his son—the one called Jed?"

"Yes, indeed I do. Hardin is my overseer. I've never met Jed, but I do know of him. Why do you ask?"

Mr. Harmon's visage became serious and he held his answer a moment. "I didn't know either one was connected with you. I'm afraid I've some bad news. They're both dead. There was a sort of rebellion at the licks and the ones who killed them cut off their heads and stuck them on pikes."

"Oh, no!" Dracie exclaimed.

Barth asked further, but Mr. Harmon had related all he knew. Some travelers on their way to McAfee Station had brought a fragmentary report of the terrible occurrence.

When they had eaten supper and the things had been put away, Mr. Harmon lit his pipe. He sat idly, watching the smoke as it first massed, then broke into gracefully rising swirls, which curled and uncurled as they met the infiltrating air from the door. A dream, he thought, that's what the smoke reminds me of. At first it appears to have such substance a man could grasp it in his hand. Then it swirls away, leaving flimsy streams to mark its transition to nothingness.

That was the way it had been with his dream. A friend of his boyhood, Colonel Richard Henderson,[28] had returned to Virginia from North Carolina with a glowing account of a new land venture he had been chosen to head. To Harmon, this appeared as the opportunity of his lifetime to build his small estate into a great fortune, and he invested heavily. He knew Henderson to be able and trustworthy and he was most confident of the success of the vast undertaking, which was to involve the purchase of some twenty million acres of land from the Cherokee nation.

For a time, it appeared that his had been a most prudent investment. In March of 1775, an agreement was reached with the Cherokees whereby they sold the land to the Henderson company for ten thousand pounds of sterling, paid in trade goods such as guns, blankets and ammunition. The proprietors had promptly named the new territory Transylvania and had entered upon the business of the company, that of selling land to persons desiring to make their homes in the Virgina region.[29] In May of the same year, a legislative assembly had been held in Kentucky, at Boonesborough, and laws had been passed for the government of the colony. Then the assembly had adjourned to meet again in the autumn.

But it never again convened. The dream, like the smoke from his pipe, began to disintegrate, spurred on to its oblivion by the Declaration of Independence adopted in 1776 by the Continental Congress. In 1778, the Virginia legislature annulled the purchase of the Transylvania lands. The total of 200,000 acres awarded the nine proprietors as compensation for their loss was an insignificant return on investments that had originally promised gigantic dividends.

So, Carter Harmon had followed the fading traces of his dream to Kentucky, where he hoped to salvage something from his overwhelming loss. Thus it was that he now found himself sitting alongside the troubled Captain Mercer. He knew only too well the heart-dropping effect of sudden misfortune. And it had been painful for him to look upon the captain's face, as the latter had strained his conversation in a futile attempt to hide the shocking impact of his overseer's death.

Off in another corner of the room, Mrs. Harmon was whispering to Dracie and Lucy. "Carter really should go to the fort this evening. Colonel Harrod and the other two commissioners are supposed to leave early in the morning, and Carter has something very important that he must discuss with them. Something that cannot wait. But," she motioned toward her husband, "he'll just sit there feeling sorry for Captain Mercer unless we make him go." She directed her next words to Dracie. "Honey, would you think me inconsiderate of Captain Mercer's feelings, if I suggested to Carter that we all go up to the stockade?"

"I think you would be doing the best thing you could do for both of them," Dracie answered. "It will furnish a most necessary diversion for Barth. Poor dear, it must have been a tremendous shock. Maybe," she paused before expressing herself further. "Maybe it might help were I to make the suggestion. That is, if you won't mind."

Mrs. Harmon nodded her consent.

Dracie walked naturally to where Barth was seated. Approaching him from behind, she casually draped her arms about his neck, her palms resting upon his chest. "Dearest, don't you think it would be nice for us to go to the fort with Lucy and her mother and father? Mr. Harmon has an important matter to take up with Colonel Harrod and the other land commissioners. And I would like you to meet some of the people there. They have been most gracious to me during my visit here."

He patted her hand and tilted his head so that he might see her. She daintily kissed his upraised brow before repeating, "Wouldn't you like to do that, dearest?"

His answer was not a truthful one, but he affected sincerity by borrowing on humor. "Darling, ever since Mr. Harmon so kindly offered to help extricate me from female domination, I have had a compelling desire to seek the companionship of the men at the garrison." The puckish upturn of his lips straightened as he said, "Seriously, I would like to go there, if for no other reason than to thank each person who might be present for the slightest consideration shown you. You cannot begin to appreciate my mind's ease when I was at the lick, knowing you to be safe among friends here at Harrodstown."

His kiss brought a throbbing doubt as to the wisdom of her artifice. Why had she not suggested the Harmons go on to the fort by themselves? That way, she and Barth could have been alone and without fear of surprise. Her face felt suddenly warm and she turned her head, so that the others might not view the tint she imagined to be upon her cheeks.

The bed loomed directly before her eyes.

CHAPTER 63

Twilight was settling as they strolled through the still-opened gate at Fort Harrod. The Harmons were well-thought-of by the residents and for a while Barth was so occupied with introductions, he feared he might later remember but few of those whom he now was meeting. "Ann Pogue." Mrs. Harmon corrected herself. "I'm sorry, I mean Ann Lindsay. She was married to Will Pogue. He got killed by th' Indians. He surely was a person who could do anything. Made everything from shoes to plows. Of course," she added quickly, "Ann's present husband, Joseph Lindsay, is a mighty fine man too. Did you know that Ann was one of the first to introduce pigs, chickens and ducks to Kentucky?[30] Well, she was. And here's someone who's just visitin' here like you. Mrs. McKee from Logan's Station. Her husband was with Washington at the Battle of Brandywine."[31] She remarked to Mrs. McKee, "Captain Mercer's from Williamsburg. He served under General Washington too."

When she had run out of available adults, Mrs. Harmon introduced as many of the children whose names she could recall. As she talked, Barth sensed the softness of the eventide, the tranquility within the garrison and its friendliness. How long will it be, he thought, before Dracie and I will share evenings like this one? There is something akin to the sweetness of the Sabbath, he mused, which seems to impart itself to the fading hours of the day, nursing them into the night with a joyful tenderness.

He chatted with his new acquaintances until Carter Harmon broke into the conversation, saying, "I hope you folks won't mind me taking Captain Mercer away from you all. I would like for him to meet Colonel Harrod."

They walked diagonally to a blockhouse at the southwest corner of the fort. "This is what you might call the headquarters," Harmon explained. "That tall, black-headed man is Colonel Harrod."

As he shook Harrod's hand, Barth felt an awe that brought back the memory of his first meeting with Patrick Henry. And when he had met the other commissioners, Edmund Lyne and Stephen Trigg, their mere presence told him they were no mean men but were persons of importance. Mr. Harmon did not slight others in the group, presenting him to all. But their identification became quickly fogged in his memory, obscured by his concentration upon the illustrious trio that had preceded them.

The conversation that his introduction had interrupted was resumed and he listened attentively. Suddenly, from somewhere behind him, he heard the strong-striding man but a second before he exclaimed, "It's George May!"

They gripped hands with a zeal that belied their young friendship but which expressed perfectly their mutual pleasure at this unexpected meeting.

"What are you doing here?" Barth asked.

"I might ask you the same question, Captain Mercer, but I won't. I'm with the land commissioners." As he answered, he motioned his head toward them.

"You mean Colonel Harrod and the others? You know them?" Mercer's incredulity was clearly apparent.

"Of course I know them. How else do you think that such a dolt like me could have been appointed land surveyor for Jefferson County? I know them," he added joshingly, "but they don't know me. Leastwise, not as well as they think they do. If they did, they'd know about the mistake I made in copying that survey over near Bullitt's Lick. Say!" he yelled the word. "So that's why you are here! You want to get back the money you paid me on that wager I thought I had won from you!"

"The wager you thought you won from me? I don't understand." Barth's brows puckered for a second, then he suddenly remembered. "You mean—"

"Yes, that bet. I only discovered the omission a few days ago. I believe you knew it all the time. Come now, admit it."

"But, George, honestly, I still don't understand what you mean. Isn't the copy I have accurate?"

May was still joshing. "Don't try to act so innocent. You can only fool me once, my friend. I'll have to say this for you though. You sure are Johnny-on-the-spot when it comes to collecting." He laughed at his own words. There was a bit of serious reflection, however, as he continued. "I don't know why I'm so happy. Good whiskey costs twenty-four shillings a gallon these days." He brightened with a compensating thought. "At that, it'll be cheaper than what I had to pay at Bullitt's Lick—" The smile left his lips. "I'm sorry, Captain Mercer. I forgot. I just heard about it this afternoon. The news must've raced through the settlements to get here so fast. When did you find out about it?"

May had digressed so completely, Barth's reply was retarded. When the reference became clear, he said, " I only heard a few hours ago." He thought a moment before confiding. "Mr. Hardin's death has added to my problem. I had intended to discharge him after I found someone to handle his duties. Until the news came, I had hoped I might find someone here who would be interested in the position. Now, I'd hesitate to even mention it to anyone. Meanwhile, I don't know what is happening at my saltworks. One thing about Mr. Hardin, he could handle the men. They're a rough lot, as I'm sure you know."

"The roughest and wildest I've seen anywhere," May agreed. "I can appreciate your difficulty. I suppose you'll be going right back there, won't you?"

"I don't know. I ought to, but I just got here. I had intended staying a few weeks before going back."

Must be awful important business he has here, May thought. But he kept his impression to himself. Instead, he said, "You know that fellow standing over yonder? Looks like he's waiting for someone and I know it ain't me. I never saw him before. Been standing there for some time now."

Barth looked around to where Carter Harmon was standing patiently. He beckoned him over and introduced him. As he did so, he became aware that it was nearly dark and that Colonel Harrod and the rest of the group had disappeared. "I guess I forgot the time," he remarked. "Where are the womenfolk, Mr. Harmon?"

The older gentleman laughed. "I doubt that they have missed us. Women forget about time too when they get to talking. But we'd better find them and start for home before it gets any later."

May interrupted to excuse himself from their company. As he was leaving, Barth asked, "I'll see you tomorrow?"

"Not unless you get up before sunup. I'm leaving for Lexington with Colonel Harrod and the others. Tom Marshall's the surveyor for Fayette County, but he's been sick and they want me to help out. Hope you're still here when I get back, but I doubt you will be. I'll be gone a couple of weeks. Anyhow, if I don't get to see you, I sure hope everything works out all right."

"I hope so too, George. Goodbye and good luck."

With May's departure, Mr. Harmon said, "We'll probably find them at Widdicombe's. Martha and Mrs. Widdicombe have common ailments or think they have anyway."

"Oh, my land sakes alive!" Mrs. Harmon exclaimed, when her husband called her attention to the darkness. "I've most a mind to just spend the night here."

"Why don't you, Martha?" Mrs. Widdicombe asked sincerely. "It'd be no bother. We could put you and the girls up with us. And the men could sleep upstairs at one of the blockhouses. There's always room for one of them."

"I don't know. I kinda worry about being away from my house, with nobody in it I mean. Besides, I don't know how good I'll rest. My back, you know."

Her pained expression found kinship in Pearl Widdicombe's features. "I have the same trouble, Martha, but I'm sure you'll be comfortable here. Why don't you do it?"

Mr. Harmon recognized the onset of a prolonged discussion of aches and pains and he moved to avoid it. "Martha, I believe Pearl is right. Captain Mercer and I will find us a place somewheres."

"Well, Carter, if you think it best, we'll stay."

She had no idea to do otherwise, but it didn't hurt to let him think he had made the decision.

During the conversation, Dracie and Barth had eased themselves from the cabin. Their quiet withdrawal and the stillness of the night made the kisses they shared seem clandestine and the more enjoyable. They heard Mrs. Harmon's decision and as a consequence they were not caught unawares when Mr. Harmon appeared in the doorway, saying, "Captain Mercer, we're spending the night here at the fort. The womenfolk are going to stay with the—" He stopped short and directed his voice inside, "Where's Jim Widdicombe? I just thought about him. He'll be sleeping with the rest of us bachelors, won't he?" He chuckled at the designation.

"I plumb forgot to tell you about Jim," Mrs. Widdicombe said. "He's down at Logan's Station. Be back tomorrow some time. I told Martha, but I guess I just forgot to mention it to you. Didn't really have time to," she added.

"We'll try the big blockhouse first," Mr. Harmon said, then explained. "That's the headquarters I told you about, sort of a meeting house. Funerals, weddings—all public business is conducted there. Sort of a town hall. Ought to be room for us. If there isn't, we'll have to try the other houses. The single men do most of the sentinel duty here at the fort. Leaves the married men free to be with their families."

There proved ample room at the main blockhouse and they located some feather ticks, which they spread upon the floor. Their light was a feeble candle and as Barth prepared to remove his jacket, he noted a shadowed figure nearby. It moved into the dim light and the faint rays brought instant recognition of George May.

"Looks like I'll see you in the morning after all," Barth said lightly.

May laughed softly. "You won't even hear me leave. When you awake, I'll be ten miles from here."

After he and Mr. Harmon had readied themselves, Barth blew out the light. He had almost fallen asleep when he heard Geore May's voice. "Cap'n Mercer? You still awake? There's something I think you ought to know. Meant to tell you before. That little fellow you had with you back at the lick . . . Littelby, I believe his name was. Well, he filed a claim with me for the land that was left off the map we had the bet on. I tried to tell him it had already been claimed. In fact, two men filed separate claims covering it. Briscoe and Broughton . . . I think they are the ones. Yep, I'm sure they are. At first, I thought you were behind it. But when he said he wanted it in his own name, I knew I was wrong. I tried to tell him he couldn't get title by settlement or preemption anymore.[32] That he'd either have to have a military grant or a warrant, but I couldn't convince him. I let him file his claim. Of course, it isn't any good. Preemption and settlement rights to land in Kentucky ended more than two years ago—two years ago last March to be exact. But he accused me of trying to cheat him. Raised such a ruckus, I took his claim just to quiet him. But it's a good thing he did it. If he hadn't, no tellin' when I'd have caught the mistake I made. You still listenin', Captain?"

"I heard everything you said, George. What were the names of the men who had filed claims on the land Johnny was after?"

"Briscoe and Broughton. Parmenas Briscoe and Charles Broughton. Can't see how Littelby could've missed seein' some of the trees with their initials and dates carved on them. They's all around there."

I can, Barth thought. I missed them myself. But he said nothing, as May continued. "I know Littelby stays with you at the lick, and I thought maybe you might get him straightened out on this. Make him understand that just because I took the claim from him doesn't make it any good. And if the others find out about it—Briscoe and Broughton, I mean—it might be too bad for him."

"Don't worry, George. I'll straighten Johnny out all right. I promise you that."

"That's fine, Cap'n. Thanks a lot. And Captain, about that whiskey. I'll see that we are all squared up the next time I come to the lick."

"Don't bother about it, George. I conceded the wager. Remember?"

May yawned as he answered. "If that's th' way you want it, I sure ain't going to complain none. Well, good night to you."

"Good night, George."

Carter Harmon's snores were near melody, so gentle was their tone. But Barth's turbulent thoughts were much more suited to violent accompaniment, and the rhythmic snoring was productive only of discord. The first blush of his anger at Johnny's act faded, and he tried to reconcile the deed and the man. The Johnny he knew wouldn't have done such a thing. However, he admitted Johnny had acted queerly at times. But he considered such conduct just a quirk of his nature. Johnny had always seemed too open-faced to harbor guile. Still he had evidently done so, or he would not have attempted to file the claim. He was the one man at Bullitt's Lick whom I trusted above all others, Barth thought. The one in whom I felt I could safely confide, Now, he has proven unfaithful. What could have been his purpose? He surely knew that what he did could not be kept secret. Barth recalled the man who had bought the mule from Johnny and who had come to Bullitt's Lick to get his money back. The man had been right in his estimation of the little peddler. But selling a half-blind, crippled animal was a lot different than betraying a friend, or had he only imagined Johnny's friendship?

He dozed briefly, awaking to find his thoughts on the saltworks. If he was ever to leave Bullitt's Lick, he must get an overseer. Or was that true? Couldn't he and Dracie go on back to Virginia? Couldn't he find someone there who would take the job? And have him be killed like Gabe Claycomb had been? A defensive thought suggested, Mace Hardin is dead. Maybe it wouldn't happen to the next man I send to Kentucky. But he then acknowledged there would always be men like Mace Hardin at the licks. Hardin had been only a type. They would just bear different names. If he could only get back there, maybe he could do something about the situation. But he had promised Dracie he would stay here awhile. He couldn't go back on his word.

The next time he awoke, Johnny held the stage of his mind. Another napping, and it was the saltworks. He awakened again, and it was daylight, and he felt more tired than when he had gone to sleep. As he opened his eyes, he saw that the floor nearest him, where Mr. Harmon had been, was bare. He looked about. He was the only one in the room. He arose quickly and donned his jacket, then rolled his bedding and placed it atop the other rolls that had been piled in a corner.

CHAPTER 64

Before he had reached the Widdicombe cabin, he was sweating heavily. This day, he guessed, would be a hot one before it was over. He felt grimy, and he wished for a razor that he might remove the stubble from his face. He saw Dracie and Lucy disappear inside the dwelling and he wondered that neither answered his greeting. But the moment he entered the cabin, he knew the cause of their apparent indifference. A hot meal was on the table. As she kissed him, Dracie said, "We thought you were never going to get up. My but you really slept late this morning." She kissed him again, to show she wasn't being critical. "Your whiskers tickle my face," she giggled. But it was a contented complaint she uttered. It reminded him, however, that he had not washed his hands or face since arising, and Lucy quickly answered his inquiry as to the location of the water pail by fetching it for him. "We just filled it at the spring," she explained. "We hurried back here with it for fear you might come in our absence. We wanted so much to surprise you." As he started toward the door, she said hastily, "Wait. Here's a cloth you can use to wash your face with."

Green had seeped into the red in Dracie's veins. She felt piqued that Lucy had usurped that which she considered her prerogative. Is Lucy doing that designedly? she asked herself. Or am I being oversensitive about her attention to him? Well, she resolved, I'm not going to take any chances. Catching the cloth as it was passing from Lucy's hands, she smiled and said disarmingly, "Let me wash your face for you. I'm afraid you might forget about your wound and start it bleeding again." She noted Lucy standing in the doorway while the washing was taking place, and a triumphant feeling came over her. After she had rinsed the washcloth, she linked her arm with his, and Lucy was forced to give way that they might pass through the dwelling's entrance. However, as Barth seated himself and began eating, she did not mind Lucy's sharing the enjoyment that comes to women when they watch a man of hearty appetite devour what they have prepared for him. As he ate, Dracie analyzed her feeling. It was a slight cousin to sexual satisfaction, she concluded, but a cousin, nevertheless.

He had almost finished his breakfast before he remarked on the absence of Mrs. Widdicombe and Lucy's father and mother.

"Mother wanted to get home before it rains," Lucy said simply.

"Before it rains?" he asked incredulously. "Why, Lucy, the sun's beating down, and there's no sign of a cloud."

"I know that, Barth. But mother said her foot was cramping. That always means rain. And the worse the cramp, the harder it pours."

He smiled as he commented. "All I can say is it's a good thing your mother wasn't alive at the time of the flood."

"If she had been, she would have been the first one aboard the ark." Lucy's repartee drew its praise in immediate laughter.

Once again he was ushered outside while the women tidied the cabin. Three horsemen had ridden into the compound and he noted one of their mounts was a gray. Instantly, he thought of Sagitta, but the rushing concern ended quickly. Mr. Harmon had undoubtedly attended the horses upon his return home. The perplexing problem at the lick came to the fore again, and the dead weight of insatiable worry was once more upon him.

"Whew! I'm glad we're through." Dracie ran the back of her wrist across her brow. "There's something worrying Barth, Lucy, and I've got to find out what it is."

"Why, Dracie, honey, you know what it is." Lucy's shoulders shrugged involuntarily. "It's that horrible business at Bullitt's Lick. Just think! What kind of barbarians are they anyhow? I mean the people who live at the saltworks. Cutting off men's heads and sticking them on poles. And when one of the men was someone you knew, why it's no wonder that he's worried to death."

"I know. It is terrible to think about, Lucy. But there's something else on his mind, something new that's happened to further upset him."

"How can you tell?"

"Lucy, if you loved a person as I love Barth, you'd know. Poor thing. Did you notice the lines in his face? He probably didn't sleep a wink last night."

Lucy did not answer. She was thinking, *if you loved a person.*

Dracie walked across the room and picked up an empty bucket. "This needs filling," she said. "It will give me an excuse to have him walk with me to the spring. By the time we come back, I'll know what new worry is on his mind."

Again, Lucy looked upon the receding figures of her friend and her lover. She stared after them until Mrs. Widdicombe's return ended her gazing.

Dracie strolled easily at his side. His steps were slow and shortened, matching the tempo of his thoughts. She did not intrude upon them until the pail had been filled and they had started back. "Dearest, tell me what happened last night. Did that stranger you were talking with bring more bad news?"

He grasped her hand and squeezed it. "Nothing I do escapes your eyes, does it?"

It was her turn to squeeze his hand. "What new worry do you have, dearest? Tell me all about it."

They had nearly reached the cabin before he concluded his narration of Johnny's treachery. They walked a moment in silence before she said, "Barth, dearest, I want you to promise me one thing. When you do go back to Bullitt's

Lick, promise me that you won't harm him. In your anger you might kill him, and I don't want the blood of any man upon your hands. I know that you were not overly disappointed when you learned the land belonged to someone else. But I am sure you must be terribly wrought up over what Johnny tried to do. Will you promise me you won't harm him?"

Vengeance was in his heart and he did not wish its surrender. His promise came slowly. "I won't harm him."

She took the pail from his hand and carried it into the cabin while he waited outside.

"Did you find out anything?" Lucy whispered her curiosity.

Dracie nodded her head as she lowered the water bucket to the floor.

"What is it?"

"I'll tell you all about it, afterwhile," Dracie spoke briefly with Mrs. Widdicombe before again going outside.

When she came from the cabin, Barth was looking intently at the sky. "You certainly have a faraway look in your eyes," she teased.

He lowered his head, unmindful of her wit. "You know, Dracie, it is going to rain, and soon. And it may be a storm." He studied a second, before adding, "Maybe Mrs. Harmon would have been the first one on Noah's Ark at that." There was a delightful moment of mirth. Then, as though emphasizing the accuracy of his forecast, large, scattered drops began falling. They retreated hastily inside the dwelling.

The rain came in a sheeting rage. In seemingly unbroken streams, like the snapping tails of a million beating whips. Each drop, the tip of a vicious lash, stinging and scattering the overlying dust, as it bit deep into the hard ground beneath.

He stood in the doorway with his arm around Dracie, looking out upon the driving deluge. The horses tethered to the hitching post in the center of the enclosure shifted their positions repeatedly, vainly attempting escape from the castigating darts striking so ferociously at their bodies. Where the earth had been hollowed by their pawing hooves, puddles formed and quickly overflowed, the water running away in some of the instantly created gullies that now covered the sloping terrain of the fort.

Recognizing his prepossessed state, Dracie remained silent, waiting until such time as his eyes might be uncovered from their mental blanket and her conversation invited.

He had fallen back into his reviewing of Johnny's treacherous folly. He recalled Rosie Tindall's denunciation and disavowal of Johnny as though she, rather than Dracie, were at his side and was first telling him of her discovery of Johnny's true character. He vaguely noted a figure racing toward him through the rain, and he stepped aside out of habit to avoid the wet garments as the man ducked inside.

Dracie plucked gently at his arm, repeating words that had been unheard by him at their first utterance. "Barth, dearest. Mr. Morey brought you this letter. Wasn't it kind and thoughtful of him to come through all that rain?" She hesitated for his answer. Then fearing unintentional discourtesy, she essayed to convey his appreciation for him. But the words, "brought you this letter," had recalled him from his preoccupation.

"Thank you for your consideration of me, Mr. Morey. I'm sorry you had to get yourself so wet, just to bring this to me. It could have waited until it had stopped raining, but it was most thoughtful of you to do so."

Moving to where the fire was blazing for the noon meal, Morey lied graciously. "'Twasn't nothing. I had to come over here anyway. But seein' as how I did fetch it for you, you ought to go ahead and read it."

Til now, the letter had been slanted downward between Barth's thumb and forefinger. He broke the crude beeswax seal and stepped more squarely into the light from the outside. The first few lines of the initial page had been dampened by the rain, and the blueberry juice with which they had been penned had been weakened, causing some of the words to blur. He studied the first sentence until he had deciphered its meaning, then glanced through the pages, seeking the author. In firm, open script he read, "Y'r ob'd't servant, Rosie Tindall." He had the presence of mind to excuse himself for his intended silent reading of the letter, which Dracie acknowledged by kissing his cheek. Then he started back at the beginning of the writing. Once past the faded lines, he read swiftly.

> I reckon you have already heard about how Mace Hardin and Jeddy Boy was killed and their heads stuck on poles. Wasn't that awful? Makes my flesh quiver just to be thinking about it. There are all kinds of stories going around and you are in some of them. Some says you own the lick that Mace ran. Heard too that he meant to kill you or have you killed the day you left Bullitt's Lick. That sneaking Jack Doniger was supposed to let Mace know when you was leaving, and then Mace was going to go after you or have someone else do it, I don't know which.
>
> You didn't know Molly Dusenberry, did you? Well, she was Dolly's sister, the one that Jed Hardin killed or everyone thinks he did anyway. Well, her and Jack Doniger has left here. Left yesterday morning. They took them sweet little children with them. I heard they was going to Virginia and then to someplace way over in Pennsylvania. It don't seem right to me. Poor Molly sick like she is, and them children going away with the likes of that Jack Doniger.
>
> That Mr. Littelby is a dirty low-down polecat, Captain Mercer. Him and that Mitch Strickler got most all of the ones what worked for Mace, or for you (if what they says is true), and has them working for them over at some new licks over near where Brother Flinden's cabin is. That's on south of the river. I ain't intending to worry you none about this but I think you

ought to know about it for sure if someone hasn't already told
you about it.

"Worry me?" Barth's mind was whirling, but he continued reading.

Tom Chism is supposed to have sent Abe Foster and
Davey Middleton over to your lick (if you own it) and they are
supposed to (pardon this writing, but this quill is awful bad but
it's the only one I can find), anyway them two is trying to take
care of things for you until you come back. But I wouldn't hurry
none if you will forgive me for suggesting what you should do.
Abe and Davey has got quite a few men working and at least,
Captain, if they don't get much done, it ain't likely that anybody could do no damage to your place (if it is yours) while you
are gone. I heared that you paid Davey Middleton and Willie
Roller (fore he died) wages when they was laid up. If that is
so, I think it was mighty nice of you in the doing of that. Tom
Chism is supposed to have told Davey Middleton about what
you done for him. You know if that is true, Davey ain't going
to let nothing happen to your property. Or Abe Foster, neither
will he.

Everything will be all right, Captain Mercer. Just don't you
worry none. Maybe I ought not have told you about this and I
hope I haven't done the wrong thing, but it seems like you ought
to know (if it is your property). I could find out for sure from
Tom Chism but he don't come to my place much no more. You
see Abby and Billy Baxter is going to get married. Reverend
Rice passed through here on his way to Falls of the Ohio. He's
coming back soon and when he does, Abby and Billy will get
married then. Reverend Rice is from over to Harrodstown, did
you know that? Abby is about to drive me wild. I declare she is
so impatient. Maybe it ain't nice for me to say it but I believe I
am going to have a lot of grandchildren.

Brother Flinden is figuring on going back to Pennsylvania. He
is getting better. His wound that is. But he seems like his mind ain't
clear like it was. He keeps blaming himself for the Indians coming
and for Ursula being taken away by them. He . . .

Barth didn't finish the letter. It would be tomorrow before he reread it and
learned, as anew, about the new lick, of Abby and Billy Baxter, of Aaron Flinden's
condition and the incidental trivia that preceded Rosie's signature. The pages
slipped from his fingers and Dracie hastily retrieved them before their legibility
could be further endangered by the rain, still coming down only a few feet from
where the missive's pages had fluttered to the puncheon floor. She refolded it and

asked, solicitously, "Is it bad news, dearest?"

He nodded his head.

"Do you want to tell me about it?"

"Not just now, Dracie. I hope you understand. Later, when I've collected my thoughts, I'd like to tell you."

"I understand, dearest, but I do hope it is not too bad, or if it is, that there is something I can do to help you with it."

He did not reply but stared once again at the out of doors. He did not note the rain had suddenly ceased and that the sun was back in all its brilliance. He looked at, but did not see, the horses, still switching about, their tails vainly flailing the flies and sweat bees, which now pestered their drying hindquarters.

He continued his pointless staring until he heard Dracie say, "Barth, dearest. Mrs. Widdicombe wants you and Lucy and me to have dinner with her. Morey is going to eat with us also."

"Isn't that rather an imposition upon her, Dracie?" he suggested.

"That's exactly what Lucy and I both told her but she wouldn't hear of us not staying. We helped her get things ready, as much as she would let us that is. Just one bit of caution, dearest. She's about out of salt. So use it sparingly."

Her remark caused him to observe that it is good to think of salt as a seasoning for food rather than for men's greed. However, his reply abandoned his observation. "I'll be careful. But isn't it ironical? All the salt I own, and I do not have enough to sprinkle on my food."

They laughed briefly before turning from the doorway.

Neither appetite nor conversation lagged during the course of the dinner. Tom Morey was a likeable, interesting person and one whose genuine character was as easily read as simple language on an open page. He had come to Harrodstown from the general locality where Colonel Harrod had formerly lived—Ten Mile Creek in Pennsylvania. As Morey had related this, Barth's recollection had stirred. One of the young men who was with Jim Trench on the bloody flatboat had come from Pennsylvania. He thought it was Billy Baxter, but he was not certain. Dracie had then sensed his wandering look and had purposely led his thoughts back to his present company.

The guests thought the meal finished and were about to congratulate Mrs. Widdicombe on its excellence when she served a baked apple to each of them, saying, "They're from the McAfee's orchard. I hope you like them."

The dessert proved a most enjoyable surprise and swelled the praise they now heaped upon a delighted Pearl Widdicombe. Her face was still wreathed in smiles when they said goodbye.

Morey walked as far as the gate, where he parted from them. Before he did so, he said, "Cap'n Mercer, when are you figuring on going back to Bullitt's Lick? I'm going to Louisville—Falls of the Ohio—next week sometime. Maybe we could ride together as far as the licks. Think you'll be leaving by then?"

Barth cast a hasty glance at Dracie. "That would be fine, Mr. Morey. But I'll be staying a little longer than that. Many thanks, though, for thinking of me."

Dracie noted he had not said he was sorry he couldn't go with him, but she knew that to be his feeling. It was not that he was inconsiderate of her, but only the uncertainty regarding affairs at the lick that had brought regret to his face. He would leave with Tom Morey. She would see to that. But she would not tell him of her decision beforehand.

She never could have conceived, during all the lonely weeks of longing for him, that she could have ever parted from him so quickly once he had come to her. Nor would she have believed their hours together would pass as drops of water, falling slowly from the lip of a vial. But so, time crawled on to the week's fulfillment. What moments they spent alone were few. And there had been no other opportunity such as had presented itself the day of his arrival. There were embraces and kisses, but always some circumstance arose to prevent the complete sharing of their love, and to further the frustration she first had sensed when Mr. Harmon had relayed the news of Mace Hardin's death. She tried to be with Barth as frequently as possible. But there were too many occasions when decorous conduct decreed that he be with the men or that she should not absent herself from the company of Lucy and her mother or that of either woman. And so Dracie sadly viewed the dawn of the day before Tom Morey was to set out for Louisville—the day she had determined to tell Barth of her decision that he should leave with him.

The chance to talk with him came unexpectedly. Shortly after breakfast, one of Lucy's friends had dropped in and had persuaded Lucy to accompany her to the fort, and Mrs. Harmon had decided to go with them. Then the ever-considerate Carter Harmon had suddenly thought of something requiring his immediate attention. Their passion was fresh as the morning itself, and they were in each other's arms the instant they were certain of his departure.

Much as she thrilled at the touch of his lips upon her neck and the tight enfolding of her body with his, she yet mastered her emotion. "Barth, dearest," she said softly. "I've something I must tell you."

"Not now, darling. Later. Mr. Harmon won't be gone for long. He left his pipe on the table. He's sure to be back soon."

"I know, dearest, but it's most important I talk with you while I have a chance."

"More important than this?" He set his lips firmly upon hers.

She turned her head slightly, so that she might speak. "Yes, dearest, more important than your kiss. But only at this moment." Before his lack of understanding could settle fully upon his face, she said, "Dearest, I want you to go back to Bullitt's Lick. I want you to leave with Tom Morey in the morning."

"But why? I don't understand."

"I think deep down in your heart, you do. I know how you have been fretting about the saltworks. Not that you haven't managed to conceal it from Lucy and her mother and father, nor that you haven't tried to fool me into thinking you weren't anxious to return. But you can't hide your thoughts from me, dearest. Last week, when Mr. Morey asked as to when you intended leaving here, I knew then you should leave with him. And if I had any doubt as to the wisdom of my decision, it was dissolved by the expression on your face when you read Rosie Tindall's letter to me. Heaven only knows how hard it is for me to suggest your leaving. But I do not want to hold you here, knowing your mind is constantly struggling with the uncertainty as to what is happening at Bullitt's Lick." She did not continue immediately, pausing to link the relevancy of her thoughts. "All women are selfish, Barth, dearest. And I, perhaps, am one of the most selfish. I want you to go with Tom Morey, because I know things must be settled at the lick before we can ever be happy. And the sooner you leave, the quicker my desire will be fulfilled." Again, she hesitated. "There is one other reason that I want you to straighten things at the saltworks. Something I have never mentioned, for fear of your misunderstanding. I cared deeply for Gabe Claycomb. He was a good husband. He lost his life before he could accomplish that which you had sent him to Kentucky to do. I think I owe it to his memory to see that his death was not in vain."

She caught the hurt look in his eyes when she confessed her regard for her dead husband and she hastened to ease his anguish. "I cared for Gabe, dearest, but I love you. Yours was my first love and the only love I'll ever have. Had it not seemed so certain that you and Neicia Warren would be married, I would never have consented to become Gabe's wife. When she broke off your marriage, it was then too late. I had already married Gabe."

He raised her hand to his lips and kissed it in humble adoration. His tenderness moistened her eyes and she looked to the sky beyond the open door. As though by so doing, strength might be summoned to contain the sad happiness, the simple token of his devotion had brought to her being. Almost subconsciously, she saw Carter Harmon approaching. "Barth, dearest, kiss me, and hold me close. Quickly, dearest, Mr. Harmon is coming."

As their lips lifted, she whispered, "Oh, dearest, take care of yourself. If anything were to happen to you, I don't know what I would do."

Hardly had Mr. Harmon returned than they had excused themselves and started for the fort. Their sudden exit caused him to observe, thoughtfully, Maybe I came back too soon. I thought I had allowed them sufficient time.

When they reached the garrison, Dracie stayed with Barth until they found Tom Morey. Then she left and went in search of Lucy and her mother.

It was an hour later before he had taken his leave of Morey and had come upon Dracie and Lucy in front of the Widdicombe cabin. Dracie had not informed anyone of Barth's impending departure and her greeting of him carefully avoided its reference. When he started to mention it, she made certain he followed the apprising roll of her eyes toward Lucy, and he skillfully guided his words to a comment upon the accuracy of Mrs. Harmon's aching foot as a weather prophet.

Lucy tossed her head and laughed. "Oh, her foot's all right. The cramp left when the rain came. Now she has a pain in her head. That's what's keeping her so long. She's trying to convince Mrs. Widdicombe that her head hurts worse than hers does. They're always comparing their aches and pains."

"After that storm came from out of nowhere, I'm thoroughly convinced that when your mother's foot cramps, it means rain. What I'd like to know now is, what does a pain in her head indicate?" Barth glanced hurriedly at the sun. "If it means snow, I'm going inside Mrs. Widdicombe's before I freeze to death."

The dimples came to Lucy's cheeks. "A pain in mother's head usually means a headache for father."

"Where is your father?" It was Mrs. Harmon. She had come outside as Lucy finished speaking.

"Father did not come with us this morning. Don't you remember? He stayed home," Lucy reminded her.

"Oh, my land sakes alive! How forgetful can a body get? We'd best get a move on ourselves. It's nigh on to dinnertime, and he'll be getting hungry. Then the first thing you know, he'll be getting into everything. The place will be a mess. Let's see . . . What would be nice to have?" Martha Harmon smoothed her hair along the side of her head as she answered herself. "I guess we'll just have to see what he's done, before we decide."

Only his sharp hearing kept Carter Harmon from being surprised in the act of ransacking the little cabinet he had constructed for his wife and in which she kept such foodstuffs as were not likely to spoil. Fortunately, he had heard her voice and had moved to the doorway as she approached. When she saw him, Mrs. Harmon turned to the others. "Thank heaven, we are in time. I don't suppose he's done anything yet."

He did not comprehend her meaning, but to be on the safe side, he practiced one of his marriage rules that was as simple as its proven effectiveness: When in doubt, kiss her.

This time, his strategy backfired. "Carter Harmon," she said, "you've been at the stew! Land sakes! Can't a body turn her back without you gettin' into things? I declare, you are just like a little boy! What else you been into?"

He had forgotten that the grease from the stew remained on his lips and it never occurred to him that his kiss had betrayed him. So he merely credited her detection to the remarkable faculty of discernment he had come to know so well. He answered her accusing question fully and truthfully. "I got hungry, Martha. And when you all didn't come, I figured you had stopped by Mrs. Widdicombe's, so I took a little taste of the stew and was going to get some honey from the cabinet when I heard you coming."

"Stew and honey? Is it any wonder you are always complaining about the misery in your stomach!" She addressed Dracie and Barth. "Did you all ever, in all your born days, hear of anything like that?"

Mr. Harmon saved their comment. "Martha, let's eat. I told you I'm hungry."

Following dinner, the afternoon seemed endless. Dracie and Barth were unable to have a moment alone. As though fearful of being remiss in the entertainment of their guest, Mr. and Mrs. Harmon vied with each other in showing them attention. And when their endeavors would abate, Lucy was always there to lend her best efforts to the cause. Once, Dracie suggested to Barth they take a stroll, and they did. But Lucy had foiled their purpose and walked with them.

At supper's conclusion. Dracie told of Barth's forthcoming departure and she made his excuses that he might get to the fort before darkness fell. He was spending the night with Mr. Morey, she explained, so there would not be any delay in setting out together in the morning.

Had she been looking toward her, Dracie could not have missed the momentary trace of shock on Lucy's face.

They did manage to kiss each other when Dracie accompanied him to get Sagitta. Even so, their embrace was almost interrupted by Lucy's unexpected appearance.

He kissed Dracie again, before setting his foot in the stirrup. As he mounted, Mrs. Harmon admonished him, "Be sure and leave your saddlebags empty. Stop by in the morning and I'll have some things for you to get that you can carry with you."

Though he waved at them all, his goodbye was intended only for Dracie.

Dracie slept in the bed in the little room that Lucy and she had shared during Barth's visit. Tonight, in deference to company, Lucy had insisted upon sleeping on a pallet on the cabin floor. Perhaps the thoughts that had preceded Dracie's slumber were responsible for her awakening in the quiet night. Her desire was upon her and she yearned for him. Her heart pounded, as fear came with the contemplation of his leaving. Suppose he should be killed or grievously hurt? "Dear God," she hastened to pray, "please return him safely to me."

Barth's meditation came before sleep. Longing was in his breast also, and he too wondered at the goodbye he must say in the early light of dawn, His words too were beseeching. "Oh, God, please keep her from harm."

As it developed, six men rode through the lifting shadows of the garrison's gate. However, only Barth and Morey would fork to the right when the little group reached the Dutch settlement. The others were bound for the Crab Orchard.

Dracie saw the riders as they began to take shape in the shrouded road and spoke excitedly to Lucy and her parents. "Here they come! I don't see him … Yes! There he is! See him? He's on our side of the road."

The rest of the party did not stop, as Barth cantered to the Harmon cabin. He dismounted and embraced the tearful Dracie. Recognizing the need for haste if Captain Mercer were to rejoin his companions before they rode from sight, Mrs. Harmon quickly placed the promised provisions in the saddlebags. When she secured their straps, she moved to where her husband and daughter were standing, waiting for the lovers to part so that they might extend their own farewells. They heard Barth as he half-whispered, "Nothing will happen to me, honey. Just take care of yourself. I promise I won't be gone long. If I can't work things out in a few days, I'm coming on back here. I made my mind up sometime ago that our life together was far more important to me than any saltworks could ever be, no matter how lucrative it might be."

She was weeping softly. "Oh, Barth, am I making a mistake? I know it should be done, that you should go. But I'm so afraid of what might happen to you. And if anything does happen, I will feel responsible for it the rest of my life. Oh, please, dearest, be careful. Don't take any chances." She placed her head upon his chest and sobbed. "I just couldn't bear it."

He stroked her hair and then gently patted her cheek. "I'll be all right, dear. I'll be all right." He raised her chin, lowering his face to hers. Courage came to her, and she said, "I'm sorry to have made our parting so difficult. I hadn't intended to. I just lost all control of myself. I love you so, dearest, that's my only excuse."

"I know, Dracie. I hated leaving so much, I almost changed my mind this morning. But it won't be for long, and when I do come back, we'll never part again. There will be no more goodbyes. Just remember that, and that I love you with all my heart. Pray for me, as I'll pray for you." His tone lightened. "You must admit, God has done a pretty good job of watching over us. Suppose we let him continue?"

She smiled, but her lips were trembling. When they broke their embrace, Lucy put her arm around Dracie's shoulder, hugging her close, and added her own wish for his safety. He acknowledged her concern by kissing her lightly upon her forehead. He clasped the hands of the sympathetic Carter and Martha Harmon, thanking them for their hospitality and begging their continued watch-fulness over Dracie.

Tears blurred Dracie's vision as he mounted, and when he rode from her, her heart dragged after him.

As Lucy waved to him, she muttered absentmindedly, "Dracie Claycomb, I don't know how you could have ever let him go back to that awful place." She did not realize her voice had accomplished her thought until she heard Dracie acknowledge sadly, "I don't either, Lucy. I don't either."

CHAPTER 65

Strangely, the impatience that had gripped him all the while he had been at Harrodstown began to lose its vigor the moment he caught up with Tom Morey and the others. Freed from the fetters of restraint, the urgency of his return to his saltworks lost some of its former driving force and he was actually beginning to enjoy the journey. Travelers were being met constantly and their numbers grew once he and Morey had left Low Dutch Station. When hailed, some of the passersby said they had come from Bairdstown. Quite a few had come all the way from Falls of the Ohio. Significantly, they had used the names Bardstown and Louisville in referring to their points of origin.

"In a few more years," Barth opined thoughtfully, "Bairdstown and Falls of Ohio will have been discarded entirely. Tom, how many settlers would you say there are in Kentucky?"

"I heard Colonel Fleming and Jim Harrod discussing that the other day," Morey answered. "They figured there must be close on to thirty thousand."

"And more coming every day," Barth added. "When the war is finally over, why there'll be a hundred thousand, before you know it."

They passed Harlan's Station, riding on to Potts before they rested. Barth would have preferred pausing a little southeast of Potts, but Morey had expressed a desire to seek out a friend of his at the latter place and Barth had readily deferred to his companion's wishes.

It developed that the one whom Morey sought was absent at the time, but they replenished themselves from the contents of Barth's saddlebags as they had planned earlier. As he ate, Barth's thoughts were of Dracie, and he continued under their spell long after the journey had been resumed.

Morey and Barth debated whether to try to reach Bairdstown before dark or to ride in the slower company of the party they had just overtaken and, when night fell, camp with them on the trail. After determining there yet remained approximately six hours of daylight and that their horses were in shape, they decided to push on. If they found they couldn't beat the darkness to Bairdstown, they could always ride back to where the party was encamped. At the time of their decision, they had covered more than twenty miles, just about half the estimated distance to this day's goal. It would be a most exacting trip and they reflected ruefully upon the much shorter route they might have taken. One that would have enabled them to have reached Bullitt's Lick in a long, but single day. They could have followed the east fork of Coxs Creek and forded it at the mouth of Rocky Run, where they would have picked up a buffalo path running down the south side of Salt River and thence to Dowdall's Station. But because it was less widely traveled, the shorter way was more dangerous. For this reason, it had been rejected.

The afternoon eased away. They crossed Pleasant Run and moved north-wardly, splashing across Doctor's Run and on up Cartwright Creek. The sun was down when they passed Parker, and the banks of Chaplin Fork were in shadows as they forded its darkened stream. Two more miles that seemed to stretch themselves endlessly, and the drooping riders pulled the reins of their exhausted mounts. They had reached their objective. They were in Bairdstown, its cabins huddled in the darkness. No feeling of elation came to either of them. Only a sense of wearied thankfulness. They knocked on the doors of three dwellings before gaining even a cautious inquiry from within. And when the third door was finally opened, one of the occupants held a lighted taper and another clutched a pointed rifle. Long minutes later, the distrust had been overcome and they had secured shelter for their animals and lodging for themselves. They fell asleep as though the same breath had extinguished both candle and consciousness.

Morning came as an unwelcome guest that would not be denied. With the daylight, Barth remembered his host's face from the previous stay at Bairdstown, when Dracie and he had lived briefly together prior to his leaving for Bullitt's Lick. Barth had not known the settler's name then nor did he recall it now. Though it had been given him again last night, his fatigued mind had refused its memory. He tactfully confessed his remission and became reacquainted with the man and his young wife, thanking them for the refuge afforded Morey and himself.

When they had breakfasted, they saw to their horses before settling them-selves to await the coming of the party they had passed yesterday afternoon.

To their pleasant astonishment, a little more than an hour later, the travelers made their appearance. They had spent the night on Cartwright Creek and had broken camp at daybreak. Tom Morey was pleased to learn most of them were going on to Louisville after a night's stopover at Brashear's Station. A few had boldly declared Bullitt's Lick as their destination and Barth wondered at their purpose. If to procure salt, it was understandable. If for any other reason, he pitied them.

He chafed at the slow pace they were pursuing, and had it not been for his promise to Dracie and his consideration of Morey, he would have left the party and gone on by himself. But he knew the party's speed was governed by the distance to be covered, and he curbed his restlessness by deliberate conversation with this companion. However, the discourse waned with the miles and they fell to their thoughts.

Barth was reliving the days he had spent with Dracie. His mind kept returning to the little room in the Harmon cabin and he became conscious of the natural, recurrent rolling of his buttocks in the saddle. He shamed himself for his thought and again sought diversion in speech with Morey. The effort accomplished its desired end. But, as before, their words gradually became fewer and fewer until they again rode in silence and he returned to his musing. How understanding Dracie had been, when he had told her about Drusilla. As he reflected upon the incident he realized, for the first time, the affair might have other consequences. Suppose Doctor Grainger were to learn of it? If that were to happen, would Drusilla try to shield herself by blaming him? What could he say to her jealous husband? "Enough of that," he said to himself. He recalled Drusilla's mentioning the precautions she had taken to ensure their privacy. She certainly wouldn't tell her husband he had been there. And since the Graingers did not associate with the people of Bullitt's Lick, how could Doctor Grainger ever find out about it? He turned his thoughts, saying to Morey, "Can't be too much farther. I remember that big oak we just passed."

CHAPTER 66

"Wake up, Miz Drusilla, de doctah has done kum home. He's down dere, right now, a-askin' for yo'!" Callie opened the drapes to their fullest and then turned back to her mistress, who had covered her head to avoid the dazzling brightness coming through the window. "C'mon, Miz Drusilla. Ain' no use hidin' yoah sef. Yo' has got tuh git up and git yo-se'f dressed. De doctah will be a-wantin' tuh see yo', honey. It's late, honey, late in de mawnin'."

From under the comforter came muffled, unintelligible expressions. Though their sound was confused, Callie recognized them as being peevish utterings, protesting the disturbance of her rest. "C'mon, Miz Drusilla. 'Tain't gwineter do no good tuh fuss at me. Yo' want de doctah tuh come up heah an' get yo' up hiss'f?"

The possibility of this undesirable happening penetrated the satin barricade of wakefulness and Drusilla twisted herself about in the bed so her position was reversed and she now lay upon her back. There was a momentary hiatus before a white elbow made its appearance. Again, all movement ceased, and the ensuing pause lengthened.

"C'mon, honey, yo' has got tuh git yo-se'f dressed."

"Damn the doctor! And you too, Callie! Now go on away and let me sleep a little longer!"

"Now, Miz Drusilla. Yo' knows yo' has tuh git up. C'mon now, honey. Callie'll hep yo' git de sleep out ob yo' eyes. C'mon, honey."

"I said go away and let me sleep! You bother me one more time, and I swear I'll have you sold at the block like the damned no' account nigger you are!"

"Now, now, Miz Drusilla. Yo' wouldn't do dat ter poah Callie, would yo'? Yo' ez jes' a li'l out ob so'ts dis mawnin'. Mebbe it's dat ole libber ob yoahs whut am causin' de trubble." Callie repelled an attacking giggle. She had gone through her mistress's hard-to-wake spells many times before. As in all the other successful waking campaigns, Callie stepped quickly to the edge of the bed and bent over the outline of the lethargic body.

Suddenly she dug her fingers into the smooth covering until they made contact with Drusilla's ribs and tickled her sides. Immediately Callie ducked, and the pillow passed harmlessly above her kerchiefed head.

In the wake of the flying cushion, Drusilla poured her vituperation upon her tormentor. "Callie, I'm not fooling! I'll have you stripped to the waist and flogged across your breasts until they are cut to ribbons! Leave me alone, you black pest!" In mock fear, Callie assumed dire abjection. "Miz Drusilla, yo' wouldn't do dat tuh poah Callie, would yo'? Yo' knows Callie lubbs yo', but yo' has ter git up, honey. Yo' knows dat's de truf." She retrieved the pillow and came to the head of the bed. "Now, honey, lemme put dis back wha' it b'longs. Yo' will hab tuh rise yo' haid fo' me tuh do it, honey."

"Oh, all right, Callie, I'll get up. But why must Richard come home so early? It's just like him to be so inconsiderate. I expected him to be at the Falls at least another week."

"Honey, yo' knows dat's th' difference twist de man an' de wimmen. De men is always a-wantin' de wimmen when de wimmen ain't a-wantin' dem." Callie's mischievous smile translated her general statement

"Callie, I do believe you are thoroughly bad!" Drusilla was in good humor now, laughing at her servant's sly reference to the desires of men.

Callie answered her mirth with a series of unrestrained giggles. "Yo' know, Miz Drusilla, whut ah said ain't always de truf. Dey's some men whut de wimmen am always ready fo'." Callie continued her tittering, but the merriment faded from the eyes of her mistress. The memory of the man whom she had wanted and who had refused her clawed within her breast. Her words came sharply. "Help me into my things, Callie!"

Callie's mood sobered with that of her mistress. She assisted her to full dress—the outer garment, a red velvet polonaise.

"Go down and tell Doctor Grainger I will be with him in just a moment, Callie. I'll tend to my hair myself."

Her husband had finished breakfast and was leaving the table when she made her appearance. He kissed her dutifully upon her forehead, glancing at his watch as he did so, and then said, "Made excellent time coming down here from the Falls. Started at daybreak. There was a Presbyterian preacher in our party, quite a learned man. His name is Rice, and he's from Harrodstown. He's a good listener, unusual for a minister to have that attribute. Seemed to have a very good understanding of basic medicine—agreed with all of my theories."

Most ministers have one common characteristic, Drusilla thought. They are patient men. She could visualize Mr. Rice's inner boredom with his traveling companion's opinionated conversation. She smiled pleasantly at her husband, however, and asked, "Is everything all right at Louisville now? I mean, has the epidemic been halted?"

Instead of a simple reply to what was intended only as a polite inquiry, she realized too late she had opened the floodgate, which had imprisoned the full waters of medical dissertation. He escorted her to the living room and casually motioned her to be seated. He remained standing.

"Yes, my dear, the epidemic has been checked. Rather, if you will remember my modesty, I checked it. Until I got there, the other physicians were at a loss as to what should be done. They are good doctors, within their limitations, of course, but utterly lacking in experience with matters of this sort. You will recall the threat of the plague when we were in Boston, I am sure. And then, there was that outbreak of sickness in Philadelphia. Textbooks will help a doctor, but to be effective, he has to have hand-to-hand experience. Frankly, those at Louisville were totally lacking in even the rudiments of what was necessary to be done. They were just a little more help to me than some of the nurses who have assisted me in times past. I would hate to find myself ill and dependent upon any of them for medical aid." He filled his pipe and accepted its lighting by Chate, who withdrew respectfully with the first puff of smoke. "Imagine, seventy people—men, women and children—taken with the sickness in a settlement of possibly two hundred and fifty persons! The whole town could have been wiped out! And, consider those countless hundreds who passed through the town and who might have carried the disease to the entire frontiers or, returning to the east kindled its spread along the way to their homes. So, you see, my services actually benefited the whole country." He puffed stoutly as he contemplated this mass salvation and the room began slowly filling with a blue haze. "It was an ordeal for me, make no mistake about that. It wasn't done by uttering any Latin formulae. Suffering people, demanding unreasonable attention, as the afflicted always do. Fever so hot, it almost scorched my hands. And the vomiting! The bile they spat was as green as verdigris! I deduced that this common disorder with which they were taken was occasioned by a relaxation of the solids—from bilious complaints—which bring on such a corruption of the fluids with a viscidness of the juices that it degenerates and breaks out in cancerous-eating sores. It was not uncommon to find the maxillary and the glands about the tongue and throat entirely destroyed. This was true in young and old. Then, there was the added complication of lung congestion and the attendant coughing seizures. I pointed out to the other doctors that the innumerable swamps around Louisville were the cause for that prevalent sickness. I am afraid Louisville will never be much of a city. Indeed, the settlement may have to be abandoned. The place is just too unhealthy for any lengthy duration." He tamped his pipe and Drusilla squirmed uncomfortably. Before he could continue, she arose and moved to the window nearest the door.

"I'm not finished, Drusilla. Please be seated while I tell you more of what I've been doing."

She faced about sharply. "Richard, you have been gone two weeks. You were talking medicine when you kissed me goodbye. You have scarcely returned, and you are again talking of it. Can't you understand that I would much rather hear about the people you met in Louisville—the news you've heard? What people, healthy people, were doing there; what social life, if there is any, exists at the Falls? Don't you realize that I am weary of constantly hearing you talk about your profession? I have been penned up in this desolate place so long, I would have welcomed the exposure to any disease, if I could but have gone with you to Louisville and mingled with the people there. Can't you see I am starved for companionship and the feeling of satisfaction that accompanies pleasant association with others? There is absolutely no one in this Godforsaken place whom I can even talk to, outside of those in this house! I might just as well be dead! Indeed, I have been dead these past few years!" Her eyes were watering, and she knew she must cry. She started to walk past him, intent on reaching the haven of the dining room before the tears came.

He intercepted her, taking hold of her arms just below her shoulders and bringing her around so that she faced him. "Drusilla, you must either be ill or about to become so. Let me feel your forehead." Placing his palm upon her brow, he waited a few seconds before pronouncing, "You've no fever. Perhaps you are just upset." His gaze settled on her features, then coursed the graceful exposure of her bosom. Suddenly, his casual examination was arrested, followed by his exclamation. "You have a rash there! Maybe you are coming down with a sickness! Here—" He pulled her forcibly back to the window she had just left. "Let me take a closer look!"

Startled, she stood passively while he studied the faint red marks that had seized his attention. Minutes passed, but he continued to stare at the pink blotches. Her surprise had given way to a growing feeling of irritation. At length, it reached its apex and she raised her arms from their motionless position at her sides, fending him from her. "Richard, must you find something wrong with me? You are overdoing it! Must you always persist in exhibiting your thoroughness?"

He caught her savagely and whirled her to her former position, his fingers pressing the soft flesh of her arms against their bones.

"Now, Richard," she began irately, twisting her limbs in an endeavor to free them.

But before she could say anything further, an incredulous, "Impossible!" came from his lips.

Astonishment quelled her struggles and she quickly asked, "What do you mean impossible? What is it you see?"

"This rash you have on your breasts and chest. How long has it been there?"

His concern over this apparent insignificance reinduced exasperation. "Oh, Richard! You almost had me frightened for a moment. Now, release my arms! What in the world has come over you?" When he failed to accede to her demand, she yelled at him, "Let go of me this instant!" She renewed her ineffectual squirming. Tiring of her fruitless efforts, she kicked viciously at his legs and ankles.

Her cheek stung. He had slapped her soundly. The flushed skin had begun to lose its exaggerated tint before the full realization of his act came to her. "Richard, you . . . you struck me!" Awed and confused by this unprecedented occurrence, she ceased her resistance.

He gave no answer, but carefully avoiding any contact with the rash, he tore open her waist garment and stripped it from her body, so that she was bare to her hips. The field of red patches was now fully exposed to his view. Both breasts were encompassed, and stray blotches were present upon her upper abdomen. "There can be no further doubt," he muttered to himself.

All the while her husband was thus preoccupied, the feeling of indignation had been seething within her. Now her ire was again at its crest. "There can be no further doubt you are a pompous fool! For a brief moment, I thought you meant to have me forcibly. I should have known better. Please permit me to leave this room!" She gathered what shreds of her rent garment she could in an attempt to shield her nakedness.

He stepped aside, saying as he did so, "You can leave not only this room but also this house. You called me a fool, and you were right. Not only have I been most foolish but also I must have been quite insane. Otherwise, I would have told you to leave years ago, when I discovered your first infidelity. But there is now, as then, the matter of the offense to my honor. Who was the man? Was it Mercer? Was he here in my absence?"

Her eyes snapped with her words. "You are a long time deciding that I could leave! Why couldn't you have said that before you killed two men? Why didn't you grant my entreaties for my freedom before you murdered the first one? Now you say I can go. But no! You must prate about your honor! You admit to having been a fool—but not to the whole of it. I called you not only a fool but also a pompous fool! Your honor. You mean your damnable conceit. I have lived in hell from our first night together! I knew you were not what I wanted that first wedding sleep we shared. I was awake long before you were that next morning. I knew then that I had made a grievous mistake, but fear of the insidious reprisals of society forced me to accept the consequences of my assent before the altar. I have the courage not to deny my past errors—sins if you will. I am sorry that I did not have the courage to admit my first mistake—that of marrying you. For it was a greater fault than any I committed thereafter! I learned too late, and to my irredeemable sorrow, that the individual is not patterned after the word but only after him who gave it. I was born rejected and no matter how hard I might have tried to join the elect, it could never have been accomplished. I have one complete satisfaction. I at least know my state. You cannot see yours for the fog of self-indulgence which envelopes you."

He again barred her way. "I have but one interest in anything you may say. Was Mercer here while I was gone? Was he the man?"

Instead of answering, she retorted hotly, "Well, Doctor Grainger, you have examined me thoroughly—so finely—that at last you have decided you no longer want me! I wish I could have known long ago that there was something about my body that was so repugnant to you that it would have caused you to disavow me as your wife! What is it that you have discovered today that you could not have known the very first day of our marriage or certainly within our first year together? Come now, the patient is always entitled to know the result of the doctor's examination!" Her manner was that of satiric coyness. "What did you find, doctor?"

He spoke grimly. "I found that I had been most fortunate in that you had refused yourself to me in the past. It has been said that man cannot through his finite character recognize his blessing beyond each day's end. Until today, I never realized the full measure of truth that those words embody—"

She interrupted. "I did not ask for a treatise, Doctor Grainger. Merely, what did you find that is so abhorrent to you?" Her emphasis of his name gave biting effect to her chiding.

He was bristling, but he repeated his former question. "Was Mercer here?"

From within her subconscious, her pierced pride answered for her. "Of course, he came to see me at my invitation. Are you surprised that he did? Now, answer me! What was it you found?"

"I knew he was the one, but I wanted you to admit it. I shall see him and demand satisfaction of him." His glance was toward the pistol case near the door. "However, you have asked me to tell you what I have discovered, and I will take the greatest pleasure in telling you. I found that you have contracted a disease which is as incurable as the lust that lines your whorish heart."

She laughed in his face. "Really, Richard, if you think to frighten me, you are wasting your time. Now at least be sensible. You know there is nothing the matter with me. The little breaking out on my breasts is purely heat rash, and I was aware of it yesterday. It has been quite warm, and I had too much bedcovering."

"You had too much bedcovering perhaps, but not the kind that you imply. Correctly expressed shall we say, you had the wrong covering—the wrong man. One who was infected with the disease and passed it on to you. One thing puzzles me, however, the premature appearance of the rash."

"So, jealousy will not permit you to tell me the truth, is that it?" she asked angrily.

"I am telling you truly," he said. "You how have, and will have until the day you die, what was first called the Neapolitan disease, the one evil that man can inflict upon no creature except his own kind. The original name came from the location whereat the disease first attracted widespread attention—Naples, where it broke out among the French soldiers engaged in the siege of that city. That was late in the fifteenth century."

Noticing her growing impatience, he admonished her. "You had better listen to me. Right now, there is nothing more important for you to hear than what I am going to tell you. Do you remember that beautiful woman in Boston? Rather, the woman who had once been beautiful and who became ill and whose sickness had persisted for some time before her physicians asked me to look at her? That was right after our marriage. Do you recall her?"

Drusilla remembered the woman. Her beauty had been widely renowned. And only the fact she was ten years older than herself had kept Drusilla's envy from becoming outright hatred. With the remembrance, she nodded her head affirmatively and her husband continued. "Do you remember our seeing her together that time we passed her on the street—the afternoon we were going to pay a social call on Dr. Gipperich and his wife? That woman had the disease, far advanced."

She nodded again, though she had forgotten all else connected with the happening except the incident itself. The woman's face, then devoid of any pleasing feature, her pitiful efforts in walking, endured clearly in her memory. But most vivid of all was the ugly open sore, which ate at the lower lip. The recollection was too real! Drusilla shuddered.

Grainger observed her involuntary reaction, commenting, "I thought you would remember her. I remember the woman also but only because of the flattered feeling I experienced when those learned physicians, who were much older in years and practice than I was at the time, asked me—a young surgeon—to give them my opinion as to her condition. Not that this recognition was not due me—I had studied the disease for a year—in London, Paris and Vienna before I made my final decision to concentrate on surgery exclusively. I have never regretted that decision, I might add." He was now walking along the medicinal path. The fact that his wife was the subject had been relegated to unimportance. This was a medical case, and the years of his impersonal practice asserted themselves. "During my research, I saw hundreds of victims of this disease—mild infections and the gravest there were. As a result of my studies, I reached the stage of expertness in recognizing it. That is why I am now so certain that you are now suffering from it in its incipient period."

Drusilla aroused her courage. "I still think you are trying to frighten me. You yourself admitted that this rash would appear so quickly, if it was this disease—whatever name you said it had."

"Originally, it was Neapolitan disease but that name gave way to French Pox or Great Pox. However, it is also called lues disease and syphilis—the latter from the name of a character in a Latin poem composed by a physician poet named Fracastoro in the early sixteenth century."

The dread words, French Pox, paradoxically, gave her a feeling of deliverance. "I recall you once pointing out a young girl to me whom you said had the French Pox, and I distinctly remember that the breaking out was at the base of her neck—not where it is on me."

"That is perfectly true," he admitted. "Though I don't recall ever showing you such a person." Rapid cogitation produced a theory. "Is it possible—would it be possible—that if you once contracted the disease in its weakest form that it might have remained quiescent and only reawakened recently when you were reinfected by Mercer?"

"You are assuming something that is not true!" she exclaimed hotly. "I didn't say that I had anything to do with Captain Mercer, or any other man, while you were away!"

"Come now, Drusilla. You admitted Mercer came to see you at your invitation. I confessed to being a fool but not to being that big of one!"

"You are a bigger fool if you really believe that!"

"Of course, I believe it! What else can I believe?"

"Then believe what you like! I've heard enough of you trying to build a simple case of heat rash into a fatal disease! There's one other thing you can believe. I'm leaving, and I'm taking Callie with me! Jason can stay here with Chate. I hope, with all your wondrous powers of memory, that you will recall that Callie belongs to me!"

"The law might hold differently, but I won't object to you taking her with you. When are you leaving?"

"As soon as I can conveniently do so. After I have packed my things and can find a respectable group of travelers to accompany."

"That could be a long time—if you are going to insist on the respectability of your fellow travelers." A false smile was on his features. "But, since you do plan to leave, you might want to know some of the common symptoms of your disease just so you may recognize the progress of your heat rash. There may be, and may already have been, a small chancre, which may have escaped your notice. There will be a swelling of the lymphatic glands. Oh, yes. The small sore I mentioned might be within your body rather than on the outside. It may or may not heal, depending on the severity of infection. But if it does, rest assured it will be but temporarily inactive. It may be dormant for a spell—sometimes for years—but sooner or later it will either reopen or new sores appear elsewhere.

"Perhaps, the chancre may heal unbeknownst to you. The first stage of the disease will pass away and you will think it is over—that you are well. But after a variable period, generally about two months, the secondary symptoms will make their appearance. The rash upon the chest, fever, loss of appetite, vague pains all over your body, possibly sores in your mouth and throat, head-aches, swelling in the bones—quite painful—and a general enlargement of the lymphatic glands. Untreated, or improperly treated, the second stage will move quickly into the tertiary or third phase, characterized by the growth, indiscriminately throughout the body, of masses of granulation tissue—hard nodules in the skin—or tumor-like lumps in the muscles. Should this diseased tissue affect the marrow of the bones, the latter will thicken. However, should you be so unfortunate as to have such a development in the brain or spinal cord, you will indeed be in greatest distress. The woman you saw that afternoon in Boston had suffered that misfortune. Her nervous system was so affected that she experienced difficulty in walking. There were deep ulcers on her limbs and breasts, much like the smaller one on her mouth. Eventually, her senses left her entirely."

His dire prognosis had its effect. She seated herself, her throbbing brain still dwelling upon the hideous picture of the afflicted woman. She remembered, now, how it happened that she had observed her closely. The poor unfortunate had lost her balance when her troubled limbs had failed her, and she would have fallen in front of Richard and herself had he not caught the derelict's arm and righted her. She recalled also the smug feeling that came to her upon discovering that the woman, that pitiful wreck, was the one whom she once envied so greatly. Now, she too might lose her beauty. What her husband had said about the disease must be true. Whatever his faults might be, he was a good doctor. He was most learned in his profession. Sometimes, he might exaggerate things somewhat, and he was often loquacious. That was it! He had said all those dreadful things just to alarm her! He didn't really want her to leave him! This was just his way of trying to ensure that she would remain with him!

She smiled as she arose. "Richard, your little scheme won't work. You thought to frighten me so thoroughly that I would stay here with you, but my decision is unchanged! I am leaving you!" She studied his face for the effect of her words.

The tightness of his lips did not ease nor did the bent brow relax. Instead, he said to her, "Drusilla, you had better believe what I have tried to tell you. It is the truth. But headstrong as you are, I doubt that you will. Having no concept of honor, it is understandable that you cannot comprehend its observance by others. If you are really leaving, I must warn you that is how this disease is spread. When you die, I doubt that hell itself will have you." He went to the fireplace and knocked the dead ashes from his pipe. Returning, he continued. "You know, Drusilla, you too have a strained sense of honor—pride, if you will—in that you never gave your favors to anyone whom you considered beneath your station. I believe, however, that you may have stretched the point with Mercer. I admit I misjudged the man but I intend to rectify that error in judgment. You cannot do so. I shall not talk further with you. You may go when you are ready to wherever your lusting heart and mind may take you. After you have gone, I intend to leave here also. But my journey will be back to all that is respectable. Quite a contrast, won't you agree?" Quickly, he added, "No, of course, you won't. I sacrificed everything for you because I loved you. It is too bad you couldn't have rewarded my sacrifice with faithfulness at least."

Her mien was serious also as she spoke. "Richard, you are a most peculiar person. You profess to love me but when you think that I have been violated, your voice remains as matter-of-fact as ever. Love requires emotion. You are emotionless! If you made any sacrifice, as you claim, in your self-indulgent fashion, it was for yourself alone. You loved me? How self-deceiving can you be? What you did, you did not for me or because of me—it was to shield your own bigoted self! Honor! If the word means jealous selfishness, then you do indeed have honor and in the greatest proportion ever known to the world." She moved to the dining room entrance. Turning, she said, "I am certain of leaving; you are not." Explaining, before he could ask her meaning, she told him, "You are going to challenge Captain Mercer to a duel. Did it ever occur to you that perhaps you will die? That when the smoke of the pistols has cleared, it will be your body upon the ground? It matters not to me what happens to either of you. But this time, you'll not be facing at close range one who has had no experience with a firearm, as was the case with each of the others whom you murdered. When you meet Mercer, you had better look well upon him. He might be the last man you will ever see. And if there could be anything to the foolish faith that some adhere to, that the dead return in spirit to avenge or help as the case may be—and I don't believe such foolishness—yet, if it could be true, then surely the hands of the two whom you killed in cold blood will be as one upon Mercer's weapon when it fires, that the course of the bullet may be straight to your self-righteous heart!"

Taken aback by her words, he would have replied, but she was gone.

CHAPTER 67

From the kitchen, Callie's wail emerged to fill the entire dwelling. The soul in desolation has but one supreme mode of expression—the indescribable cry of excruciating anguish. It screamed forth upon the infant world from the breast of Eve, standing forlornly outside the gates of the garden. Thus was alpha, and thus will be omega. Callie had learned of Drusilla's determination to take her from her child.

The doctor and his wife did not eat the noon meal in each other's company. Grainger, adhering rigidly to his daily schedule, ate and then went to inspect the large field of corn where Chate was laboring. Drusilla kept to her room, abstaining from eating, as Callie and she packed her belongings.

Callie's eyes were still wet and her heart heavy. But the thought of rebellion never entered her mind. She was a slave and, after her first outburst, she had accepted, though without reconciliation, her mistress's right to her decision. It was not a totally new experience for her. When she was a young girl, Drusilla's father had purchased her from her mother's master. At least Jason would still have the comfort of one of his parents. Callie never saw, and never knew, her father. And all the strings that would have led from him to her heart were entwined the more strongly with those of her mother. And though the sadness of their enforced separation had been dulled by the passing years, it had been resharpened by the prospect of her impending division from her only child and its own finality. The pangs of parting would be softened, as before, but there would ever be the insatiable longing for that which had been, but would never be again. She would wonder every day where he was, what he was doing and whether or not he remained the same, lovable boy whom she had so often held so close.

She mourned leaving her husband who, beneath his mask of austerity, was as gentle as the wisdom that was so innately his. But he was a strong person. He would endure this bitter lot. Jason was such a little fellow and he needed her so. Maybe Chate would find someone after she had gone. But where would the woman come from? Not from Bullitt's Lick. Perhaps Doctor Grainger would buy a woman for him at the Falls. Would she be kind to Jason and good to Chate? Or would she be just an ornery nigger? Her mistress's voice broke her gloomy speculation.

"Callie, I've worn myself out. Draw the curtains. I want to rest a while. And, Callie . . ."

"Yes, ma'am. Miz Drusilla?"

"See if you can't be a little more cheerful. I feel downhearted enough without you adding to it by walking around on the verge of tears. This isn't the end of the world, you know. When we get back to Boston, you'll be glad you left here."

Some White fo'ks jes' ain't got no feelin's, Callie thought, as she put the room in shade.

"Callie."

"Yas, ma'am?"

"I won't be downstairs this evening. If I become hungry later on, I'll call you."

"Yas, ma'am', Miz Drusilla." Thus freed of any immediate duty, Callie went in search of Jason. She knew where she would find him. If Chate were still in the field, Jason would be with his father. She dreaded revealing the woeful thing that was to happen to them.

*

Grainger wiped the pistol with a soft cloth, before restoring it to its place in the chest. Without giving his reason therefore, he had inquired of Mrs. Tindall as to the whereabouts of Mercer and had been disappointed to learn of the latter's temporary absence from Bullitt's Lick and that the affair of honor would have to await his return. He had questioned her closely as to whether or not Mercer, in truth, intended to come back, and her reply had inspired confidence he would do so. It was just a matter of waiting until such time as he reappeared. Grainger reflected that this interval would afford him ample opportunity to practice his own marksmanship in preparation for the encounter. Not that he felt the need of any refreshing of his skill with the firearm, for he prided himself as being an expert shot, but such procedure would guarantee the keenness of his aim on the day of accounting. Drusilla's admonition, as to the possibility of him being the loser, crept into his thinking. How did she know Mercer was proficient with the pistol? No doubt, he had boasted of his ability. Well, he would have his chance to prove it. The man had no character, that was proven thoroughly by his adultery with Drusilla. But he did appear to be a cool, self-controlled person. He might lose some of his sureness, however, when he turned about and faced another's fire! Of course, Drusilla had spoken more in the hope that Mercer would kill him, rather than in any sincere belief that this would ever happen. She probably would go away with him if this improbable result were to occur. That must have been the reason she had so quickly embraced his decision that she leave. Of course! Foolish as always in her reasoning, she really believed that Mercer might win! Well, if that happened, the two diseased lovers deserved each other! "If that happened!" He spoke the words slowly, and at once became aware the possibility was rooting itself in his mind. He picked up the pistol he had so lately polished. He would practice its use now. Mercer would be the loser. He resolved to aim at his opponent's bowels. Such a wound would be fatal, but only after an indeterminate period of deepest suffering. Perhaps a matter of hours, perhaps after a number of days—all depending upon how well placed the bullet was when it entered the abdomen and upon the constitution of the victim! "If that happened!" He uttered the words and continued to a conclusion. "It would be because I had suddenly lost my vision completely!" Mercer would be the one lying on the ground, and he would kneel beside him and tell him of the nature of his wound and the hopelessness of recovering. True to the requirements of his oath, he would administer to Mercer to the best of his professional skill. Medical attention would be fruitless, but he would relish observing the ensuing complications as they set in. He would make sure Mercer was informed, at frequent intervals, of the changes as they evidenced themselves and of his progress toward death. He would remind him of his act with Drusilla, pointing out this was his punishment. And he would ask him if the fleeting sexual satisfaction he had experienced was worth the dear price he was now paying for it. He would repeat these statements as long as Mercer's mind was impressionable. When it ceased to be so, he would continue to watch him until he died. "If that happened!" The persistence of the annoying implication provoked him to shout angrily, "That will NOT happen!"

CHAPTER 68

Additional landmarks confirmed Barth's previous observation as to the party's progress, but he did not comment on them. Though first denied and passed over, the possibility of Grainger discovering that he had been with Drusilla continued to suggest itself until he now believed that sooner or later Doctor Grainger would confront him concerning his visit and its obvious inference. He recognized that the doctor would never believe him were he to relate that which had actually occurred—the seemingly innocent invitation and his ignorance of Grainger's absence. His quandary mounted. The doubt was absolute that the truth would not dispel the husband's jealous conviction as to his purpose. What then should be his course? He could not deny he had been there nor the hair's breadth by which he had escaped the union of his flesh with Drusilla's. He doubted that his own father, were he now living, would have believed him in this instance.

There came to him the realization that lack of trust is the characteristic fault of man—the difference between that which is mortal and immortal, that the degree of doubt in each man's mind determines his nearness to heaven or his proximity to hell; that doubt is twin to worry, whose maculate conception stems directly from the violation of God's commandment above all other commandments, belief in him and in his divine love and care. Yet acknowledging this, he could not reconcile his mind that Grainger would accept the truth. He made an approach to faith. He would admit he had seen Drusilla, but deny he had entertained any wrongful intention when he entered the house. To add anything, particularly the fact that his actions with Drusilla had ended short of consummation solely through his own resistance, would be to tax Grainger's credulity to the extreme.

So, man's faith, if not in God, cannot be in himself or in his own doings. Worry continued as Mercer's demanding companion, as Sagitta's every step hastened the moment of the meeting with Richard Grainger. But for all his lack of faith, the words from the Gospel of Luke yet would not be beaten away. "Settle it therefore in your hearts, not to meditate before what ye shall answer: for I will give you a mouth and wisdom, which all your adversaries shall not be able to gainsay nor resist."

The name Littelby, uttered by a member of the party, drew his attention.

He turned his head and noted the speaker pointing to the smoke rising above the treetops to the east of them and he listened intently as the words continued. "He was just a pedlar. They say he just had his sack and his wares when he come to Bullitt's Lick. Now, look at 'im! Owns that whole works! He'll be rich in no time! I tell you, there's fortunes to be made at th' licks, and I aim to make mine! Course, everybody can't expect to be as lucky as he was. A fellow told me the other day that Littelby was checking over some maps when he found that acres and acres, including the ground where the new lick is, were missing on one of them. The settlers and land locators had just overlooked it somehow. Anyways, he filed his claim and got it for himself. I never knowed him, but I seen him one time, over to Logan's Station. I never thought he'd ever be a big man. But look at him now! I tell you, this here place is the place to make it! It's the busiest place on the whole frontier."

Morey nudged Barth. "That fellow best be careful when he gets to Bullitt's Lick. He might find himself tripping over some of those chunks of gold he thinks arc waiting to be picked up!"

Mercer smiled at his companion's remark. "Poor fellow, he's due for an unpleasant surprise when he gets there. More than likely for a lot of surprises."

It was Morey's turn to smile before his lips straightened and he said, "I reckon he ain't heard about those two heads stuck on those poles."

Morey's observation flashed through Barth's mind—the grim retribution that had come to Mace and Jeddy-Boy. Its gruesome barbarity could never be justified or understood by anyone who had not lived close to the brawling, sweating men who labored at the saltworks. For a satisfying moment, he reflected upon that which he would like to do to the parvenu, John Littelby. He felt the urge to leave the others and to collar Johnny without further delay and serve him his just deserts. With the punitive imaginings, the adrenal juices began their flow, gearing him as a man about to enter combat, but he abruptly stemmed their current by reminding himself of his predetermined plan for dealing with the little pedlar.

They were at the head of the slope to Salt River and its crossing place. How different the approach this time! Barth struggled to make himself admit the previous existence of the prior happening when he had first traveled this way a few months before. A few months? It seemed much, much longer than that. It seemed months since he had left Bullitt's Lick, yet it had been less than two weeks. All at once he felt a strangeness, as though he had never been here. Rosie Tindall, Mace Hardin, Tom Chism, Abe Foster, the Graingers—they were all people of his imagination—as persons met in dreams, recognized for the moment, then dissolved in consciousness. His confusion ended when one more character entered the cast—Little Johnny.

The party mounted the steep bank and followed the path to Dowdall's Station. The travelers entered the open gate and were at once met by the warm welcoming of the residents, who hailed them as visiting kinsmen. Though few days passed but what similar parties made their like appearances, the heralding of each new group was ever sincere. Such was the thirsting fellowship of the frontier.

After Mercer had dismounted, he tied Sagitta nearby and moved among the settlers, never talking very long with any of them. His companion, Morey, seemed to be thoroughly enjoying his conversation with some of the residents. Noticing this, Barth extricated himself from the gathering, intent only upon finding a place where he might rest an impatient while before resuming his way to the licks. It was then he spied Aaron Flinden, Nancy at his side, walking slowly in his direction.

He noted that Flinden's recognition of him was the least bit slow. The Quaker had removed the broad-brimmed hat he habitually wore and was mopping his forehead. His drawn, almost haggard, features bespoke the inner conflict they mirrored. The erstwhile gleam of enthusiasm had disappeared from his eyes and their color had lost its vividness. The firmness of the mouth had been upset by its sagging corners, and the resolute jaws had slacked. His erect bearing was now marred by a slight slumping of his narrowed shoulders. Only the head of beautiful wavy hair remained to recall the physical glory, which had once been so completely Aaron Flinden's. The vision of Apollo was no more.

Mercer's reaction to Nancy was astonishment. The grimy little girl in the cabin with the knife in her hand had vanished. Here before him was a young woman whose countenance, if not pretty, possessed a vestige of beauty with the definite promise that its pleasant, even features would be further enhanced as she moved toward maturity. Looking at her and then Flinden, he saw, on the same stem, the withering rose and the bud bursting into radiant bloom.

At first, their conversation was jagged, but it gradually smoothed and Barth began to doubt Rosie's written reference to Flinden's mental condition. Their talk had been of generalities with little mention of local happenings. Nancy kept a discreet silence, appearing to be genuinely interested in her elders' discourse. Almost casually, Flinden related his intention to return to his former home in Pennsylvania. He had entreated Nancy that she leave with him, but she had refused his pleas. She was bent on marrying the mute, James, and while Flinden thought her too young for marriage, he had not attempted to obstruct the union. Nancy hung her head in youthful embarrassment as he talked. He had promised his land to them as his wedding present and would have to see to the completion of the transfer before he departed from Kentucky. Mercer volunteered his aid in this regard, if needed, but the offer was politely declined by Flinden with the assurance that he possessed the necessary knowledge to perfect the passage of title.

It was at this point that Barth thought the Quaker's manner underwent a definite change. He seemed tense, as though striving for self-mastery. He spoke tersely to Nancy, asking that she excuse herself from their company, a request with which she promptly complied. When she had gone, his voice trembled. "Friend Mercer, I feel the weakness coming upon me. Let us be seated on that bench." He indicated its location in front of a nearby cabin and walked unsteadily toward it. Mercer steadied him and saw him seated before sitting beside him. They sat silently for some minutes until Flinden had become somewhat composed. Then he said slowly, "Friend Mercer, the book of Proverbs says, 'The spirit of a man will sustain his infirmity; but a wounded spirit who can bear?'" Barth nodded his remembrance of the passage and Flinden continued. "The spirit has failed me, friend Mercer, as I have failed the spirit. My imperfect faith has cost me my wife, Ursula, and has resulted in her death or imprisonment, I know not which. All because of my own weakness. The infidels . . . She was there . . . The savage is trying to take my life . . . Ursula, where are thee? I did not fail thee . . . I was senseless . . . Oh, God, return thy spirit to thy servant . . . to Pennsylvania . . . I see the savages all about." He rambled on in trance-like fashion. Barth did not disturb him, waiting for the spell to run its course. The transition was not long in its coming. Flinden's eyes showed amination as he said, "My frailty overcomes me frequently, friend Mercer. 'Tis my punishment for not believing fully. I hope to overcome it when I return home and have the comfort and assistance of the Friends with whom I formerly worshipped. One cannot touch the fires of hell and not be burned. I have moved among the ungodly at Bullitt's Lick and I have been contaminated by them." His speech had taken on firmness and its former incoherence had vanished.

Observing this, Barth determined to risk an appeal to his reason. "Mr. Flinden, you are blaming yourself for something in which you had no fault. The same Bible which you quote tells you that the rain falls upon the just and the unjust. God knows that you are imperfect and he does not expect perfection—only its sincere pursuit. That is the difference between the dust that scatters with the wind and the indissoluble spirit. All that is mortal is prey to the things that are mortal. God, who notes the death of a sparrow, certainly has seen what has happened to you and your wife. Does it mean nothing to you that he spared you? And, since the Indians did not kill Mrs. Flinden immediately, it is most likely that she still lives. Undoubtedly, in some future prisoner exchange she will be released from her captivity. That is something for you to work on when you get back to Pennsylvania." His words were being intelligently received, and he spoke further. "What you have been doing, in effect, has been to question the will of the Lord. You have asked that which was and is forbidden you to ask: Why hath thou made me thus? What you view now as tragedy is the working of the Lord. You do acknowledge that his will be done, don't you?"

Flinden nodded affirmatively as he said, "That I do, friend Mercer. That I do."

"Then practice your belief. When you feel the weakness, as you call it, coming on you, force your attention on these words: 'I believe. It is God's will.' Do this long enough, and your fear—for that is really what you think is the weakness—will disappear. I do agree with you that this can best be done away from here. Then, if you so desire, after you have recovered your strength, you can return to Nancy and James."

"I shall not ever return to this seat of the ungodly, friend Mercer, but thy words have given me hope, and for that I am most grateful to thee. Yet, there is something else that deeply troubles my soul. I promised James that were he to believe, the power of speech would be given him. I think he has the faith, sincerely, but he is yet mute. I feel that through my own lack of faith, he shall be deprived of that gift. How can I reconcile my failure and my promise to him?" Flinden's eyes were alert as he looked at Mercer.

"You promised something unwisely—something beyond your right and power to promise. James's condition is the work of the Lord. If it is his will that James talk, he will do so, if and when he so decrees. As before, the Lord's will be done."

Flinden's lips echoed the words. "The Lord's will be done."

Barth waited a tolerant second, then asked, "You surely recall the Lord's admonition as to offensive members of the body, don't you?"

Flinden showed his knowledge. "If thine eye offend thee, pluck it out."

"Well, I would say that of all the trouble-making human capabilities the tongue, or voice, is the most evil. Perhaps, and I do not say that it is so in James's instance, perhaps his lack of speech is a gift to him from God to ensure the goodness of his soul. Whatever the reason, God created him as he is. I think that I know James quite well. I do not believe his faith will waver if it is not rewarded. You know, Mr. Flinden, perhaps you have given him the power of speech and have not recognized your own gift."

Flinden was agog. "What do thee mean? I do not understand thee."

"I have heard that you taught him his letters. But for you, he might never have learned them. Can't you see that you have given him the power of written speech? If he applies what you have taught him—maybe, are still teaching him—"

"I am," the Quaker interjected.

"Then he surely will be able to express himself, and you alone, with God's permission, will have done that for him."

"I never considered that thinking, friend Mercer." His features glowed at this revelation. "'Having eyes they see not.' I have been blind! I have been truly blind!"

"I don't think that, Mr. Flinden. You have just said to God, 'I want this man to talk with his mouth,' and perhaps God wanted him to talk in another fashion. I have made the same mistake, many times. I have prayed to him for aid, knowing full well that which I wanted to accomplish required heaven's doing. But yet, I found myself persisting in telling him how I wished it to be done or to come about. I am sure God must have smiled at my unintended directions to him."

"Thy fault has been mine also. I shall guard that it be not repeated by me."

Barth regarded him attentively. For the past few minutes, he was certain Flinden had been completely rational. He wondered how long this lucidity would continue, whether another breaking wave of emotional instability might not wash away the direction of the steps the Quaker had taken toward recovery. The seed had been implanted. If only it were to take firm root! His pensive mood was interrupted. Flinden was speaking to him.

"Wonderful. It has been wonderful talking with thee. I feel much better. I shall try to remember the things thou has told me. Thee has the faith, friend Mercer, and it is most sustaining."

Barth was spiritually uncomfortable. Had he presumed upon the inviolate authority of God by counseling Flinden according to his own theories and practices? After all, a man's faith is most singularly his own concept of what he has felt, seen, heard and read. Had his well-meant efforts to soothe and reassure a troubled spirit actually been an unwarranted invasion of a defenseless mind?

Flinden beckoned Nancy, who had waited respectfully out of their immediate hearing. As she approached, he explained to Mercer. "I always asked Nancy to leave when I felt the weakness—fear, as thee rightly called it—coming over me. I pray I have done so for the last time."

They conversed a while longer. At length, Barth's thoughts reverted to the urgency of his presence at Bullitt's Lick and he made known to Flinden that he must leave. When they parted, the two shook hands warmly. It might be the last time they would ever see one another.

As if by arrangement, Morey was waiting for him where Sagitta was tied. They bade each other farewell, promising to meet again at Harrodstown.

Riding from the garrison, Mercer was about to speed his mount when he heard his name being called. It was Nancy. He dismounted and walked to where she was standing. Before he could seek her reason for hailing him, she said nervously, "They's suthin'," she stammered and flushed as she corrected herself. "There is something," she emphasized the words, "that I want ter tell you." Now she waited for him to speak, as though his consent were required.

"Yes, Nancy? What is it?"

His soft tone reassured her, easing her speech. "James—you call him Hawkstraw—but thet ain't—I mean isn't—his name—has told me about how yer saved his life, and I want tar thank yer for th' doing uv hit."

"Did he tell you that he saved mine, not once, but a second time?"

"No, he dint, I mean didn't."

"Let me tell you about what he did."

A bit of her former self was in her sharpened brows as she replied, "If'n James wants me ter know, he'll tell me. But that ain't—isn't—whut I want to talk about. James and me thinks yer ought to know suthin'. Mace Hardin stole a lot of salt whut James sez is really yer'n an' he sez—we both sez—you ought to have it, seein' as how hits yer proppity." This had been difficult for her to say. She spoke rapidly, and her grammatical errors escaped her detection. He would have interrupted, but her anxious lips were forming new words. "Mace an' them other two whut got kilt—Mallory an' Gibbs—they kerried it all ter a cave an' stowed it. Mace never knowed thet we knowed about it, but we seen 'em goin' inter th' cave one day, a-kerryin' th' baskets an' kegs. After they wuz gone, we looked inside. They's a arful lot uv salt in thar an' James sez that it be all yers."

Her revelation staggered him. The past became immediate, as he reviewed the morning of the salt shipments—the broken keg, the dry salt and his belief it had come from some secret storage. A cave! Its even temperature had accounted for the dryness of the crystals. From his meditation came the question, "Where is this cave, Nancy? How will I find it?"

"About a mile below Mud Garrison. Me an' James'll show yer whar, when yer wants him ter do hit." She was conscious now of her misuse of language, and she blushed.

"I can't begin to tell you how much I thank you and James for telling me about this. I had always suspicioned that Mace had salt hidden somewhere, but until now I had no inkling of proof that he had done so. Now, I know. You tell James I am going to give you all a reward for doing this for me."

Again, the wrinkles came upon her forehead, dipping downward as she said, "Me and James don't want nuthin' for tellin' you about hit. James sez it be th' right thing ter do."

Honesty's parents are spiritual, not physical. Of this, Barth was certain. The union of Mace Hardin and the Indian, Massalene, could never have produced this quality in their mute son. Observing the persistence of Nancy's facial disturbance, he said, "Nancy, I understand what you mean, and you are right. James is a man of character."

She wasn't at all sure what the word character implied, but there was something in the way in which Mercer had said it that made character mean it was good on James's part that he possessed it. Her features evened, and she smiled, stressing her own comeliness. With the favorable change in her expression, came studied, certain words. "You know, I never cared none fer—too much fer you. When Mr. Flinden told me it wuz bad tar hate some-un, I kept on a'hatin' you. I couldn't fergit you wuz th' one whut cut Massalene's face, th' first mornin' yer kum ter Bullitt's Lick. I loved Massalene. Her an' James wuz the only two whut wuz good ter me 'fore I met Mr. Flinden an' Ursula. Massalene dint—I mean didn't—tell me you done hit. But I asked about ever-body whut kum ter th' licks early on thet mornin', an' you was th' only one what I heerd—heard—of I mean. So I knowed it hed ter be you whut done it. Massalene kum home thet mornin' 'fore daylight, and I woke up when she kum in. They—there—was blood a-runnin' down the side uv her face an' I asked her who done it, an' she tole— told—me a man cut her. When I know it wuz you, I would kilt yer, if'n I had got th' chance. Like thet—that—day I had th' knife behine yer back. When James told me 'bout you savin' him, I got sorry about ever'thing, an' I didn't hate yer no mores."

She had spoken the words, but he refused to believe his ears. It was incredible that the fat squaw had been the one who had tried to kill and rob him at the ford! The slashing of her check had occasioned that wild cry in the darkness! So she had been the one who fled across the river and rode away. He could see Massalene now, facing him in the dimly lighted, squalid room of her cabin, the freshness of her wound so clearly evident. But who would have ever thought it had been she who had dropped down upon him? He remembered the rumor that Mace had cut her. Even had he not heard it, he would never have suspected her. Now he was anxious to ask Nancy more about the happening. A desire that was disappointing as she said, "I got ter be goin' back to Mr. Flinden. He ain't real well." With this, she ran gracefully toward the gate.

He continued to stare in the direction she had gone even after she disappeared from view. As he mounted his horse, he shook his head in bewilderment. This passive young girl had unlocked the enigmas that had stumped his every guess at their solution. She had known the answers all the while. Sagitta's flying hooves were matched by his master's rapid thoughts. If he had not seen the Indian intent on Hawkstraw's life; if he had missed; if Mr. Flinden had not brought faith into the lives of Nancy and the mute who claimed her complete affection . . . How much salt was in the cave? How much was it worth? One thing, any loss he may have suffered, or might suffer in the future through losing his workers, would be amply compensated for by the discovery of his stolen fortune—and it must amount to that. It had been a long time that he had not received any return from the lick, before he had come here to ascertain the reason for the nonpaying operation. Mace Hardin's thievery had turned out to be but a saving for the one from whom he had stolen. He stopped short in his thinking as a reproaching realization came upon him. The pound and the dollar rule the human mind. And even the shilling, pence and cent are lesser nobles of that kingdom, who command and receive this fealty.

"Be that as it may," he said to himself. "It will make my leaving here a lot easier and sooner than I had hoped for." There, to his right, was Rosie Tindall's. He would stop for a few minutes, say hello to her and have himself something to eat and drink. Then he would ride directly to the lick.

As he finished tethering Sagitta, he glanced down the street. He was again looking into the heart of Bullitt's Lick, and his first impression returned in a reinforced state. The place was evil. The removal of Mace and Jeddy-Boy, or for that matter all those like them, could not change its character. He brushed past a solitary individual leaning against the side of the house near the doorway. A surly look of appraisal resulted from the unintended contact, but there was no voiced complaint.

CHAPTER 69

Rosie's greeting was elation itself. "Captain Mercer! You gave me a start, comin' in the' door like that! It's glad I am to see you. Now, you just set yourself down an' let me fix you somethin'. I'll bet you haven't eaten anything since mornin'."

Barth wondered as to the absence of her usual helper, Abby. But her mother, after she had piled the table with food, gave a ready explanation. "I'm sorry that Abby isn't here to greet you . . . Oh! I don't guess you know! Her an Billy Baxter was married by Reverend Rice four days back. Ever since then, they ain't hardly left their room, an' when they does, they don't stay out none too long—just for time enough to eat something." The little puffs that were her cheeks became full-hued, as she instantly recognized the implication her gushing words had created.

He circumvented her predicament. "I hope they will be very happy together. Tell me about the wedding."

He had guided her away from the embarrassment of her effusive words and she embraced the new topic delightedly, recounting every detail as though the wedding had not taken place but was yet in immediate expectancy. The pinpoints of light in her eyes were magnified into twin stars, as she relived the joyous event, dimming only at its conclusion. "The only bad thing that happened, was when they had th' shivaree,[33] an' Tom Chism got drunk an' got in Abby's bed. She didn't think of it bein' him that was under th' covers. She thought it was Billy. But everything turned out just fine, though Tom ain't been back since then. I sure am glad that Abby didn't marry him. He's married to his jugs an' ain't got no business havin' another wife!"

Again, Barth steered her course. "What are Abby's and Baxter's plans? Have they told you?"

"Oh, Captain Mercer. I plumb forgot th' best part! They're goin' to Pittsburgh to live, an' I'm goin' with 'em! Ain't that just grand?"

He joined in her happy anticipation. "That's what you have always wanted, isn't it? When are you leaving?"

"Soon's we can get things ready."

"What about your place here? Have you sold it?"

"Not yet, but I hope to, if I can find someone who wants to buy it real quick. If I can't, I'm just goin' to walk off an' leave it."

He cautioned her against such hasty action, but she disregarded his concern. "Like you remembered, th' main thing I want, now that Abby an' Billy is married, is to get away from here." She winked wisely at him. "I got 'nough saved up to see us settled in Pittsburgh, an' when we gets to there, I'll find myself something to do."

Barth did not deny her convincing assertion. Anyone as industrious as Rosie would be able to get along anywhere. She would take care of herself.

He thoughtfully suggested that others were waiting for her services. While she protested that they could wait a little longer and made inquiry as to his lady, he did not accept her unselfish offer of her company. Instead, he arose, saying, "Rosie, I'll not take up any more of your time. Truthfully, I have a lot of things to see after. I haven't been to the licks yet."

"You do own th' saltworks what Mace Hardin run, don't you?"

"Yes, Rosie, I do. There was a reason before for me to keep that fact secret. And thanks for writing me."

She did not comment on the contents of her letter nor attempt to draw from him the purpose of his secrecy. "Well, Captain, like I told you, I'm leavin' 'fore too long. I hope to see you some more before I go."

"You will, Rosie. In fact, I might be sleeping on your floor tonight like I did the first night I spent in Bullitt's Lick. Remember?"

"That I dos an' you're welcome to do it again." Her lips pursed for a moment. "It would have to be the floor again though. Abby an' Billy has got th' room that Johnny—I mean Mr. Littelby slept in." For just a tracing interval, she was in reverie. Whether it was regret or bitterness that he saw in her features, Barth could not determine before she said with an air of farewell, "You be sure an' come back." He nodded his goodbye. As he passed through the door, the spread fingers of his hands were resting contentedly upon his stomach in the appreciative manner of one most pleased with a hearty repast. Indeed, that was the trend of his thoughts. Bullitt's Lick would never again see the equal of Rosie Tindall as a cook. Nor, for that matter, he reflected soberly, as just a plain, good woman.

He satisfied Sagitta's plea for attention by stroking the animal's mane. As his hand moved to the pommel of the saddle, he found himself facing the oncoming figures of Doctor Grainger and, close behind him, the man who had been loitering outside. Sudden confusion, stirred by Mercer's guilty conscience, threatened to overpower him, but Grainger's call broke its paralyzing hold.

"Mercer, I want to see you!" In a matter of five or six puffing strides, the doctor was in front of him. There was another step and the momentary recognition of the flesh-colored course of Grainger's open palm. Then came the rocking slap to the side of his face—the same side whose jaw had been creased by Mallory's bullet. Grainger's livid face was matched by the trace of blood he saw on his hand. Mystified as to its presence, Grainger was silent a brief instant, then his pent-up rage found its outlet as he loudly denounced the angered man he had slapped. "You violated my wife in my own home! I lowered myself by associating with you. I trusted you, and you repaid my trust by sneaking into my home the moment

I had left it! I demand satisfaction of my honor! I believe you know enough of the ways of gentlemen to understand what that means! That is, if the pox has not already done its work upon your brain! I challenge you to a duel to the death!"

Mercer's first impulse had been to grasp the vicious doctor's throat between his hands and squeeze it until the red face turned white. The suddenness of Grainger's attack had produced this insane urge and yet had served to stay its physical expression. He found himself wondering strangely within his wraths. What does he mean by inferring that I have the pox? Or is it just his purpose to insult me, to make certain that I will accept the challenge? His thoughts settled and he mastered some self-direction. If he struck Grainger, or laid hands upon him in any way, the doctor would prove his superiority of station. A gentleman would settle the affair in the manner of a gentleman. But even as he so thought, his memory recited the words of scripture. "Can a man go upon hot coals and his feet not be burned? . . . so he that goeth into his neighbor's wife; whosoever toucheth her shall not be innocent." While there had not been complete misdoing with Drusilla, he yet had done that which his accuser had generally charged. He had violated his home. Grainger was entitled to satisfaction. With this self-confession, there came speech. "Doctor, I accept your challenge. It would be futile for me to attempt to explain to you that which happened in your absence. Though you will not believe me, I can only state that I was deceived into coming to your house. I thought you were there." Grainger's lips had set his features in disbelief before the explanation had ended—a facial expression that was paired with the scoffing smile of the informer who had lingered to watch the result of his informing of Mercer's return. Barth abandoned further explanation. "You have challenged me and I have accepted. If I remember the ways of gentlemen, as you have credited me, I believe it is my privilege to have the choice of weapons. Am I not correct?"

"You are correct," Grainger answered contemptuously.

"Then I shall make my selection from among one of the following: knives to be used Indian fashion, your right wrist strapped to mine; rifles at twenty paces; adzes at five paces; tomahawks at ten or pistols at twenty. I do not believe that I must determine my choice at this moment, must I?"

Angry surprise enveloped the doctor's countenance at this unorthodox turn of events. He replied sneeringly, "Gentleman usually convey their decisions through their seconds. I trust only one man in this settlement, my manservant Chate. He will be mine. You will have yours meet with him and make the necessary arrangements. Good day, sir!" He turned abruptly and strode rapidly away, the informer breaking into a half-trot to keep up with him.

Mercer's eyes followed the pair until they halted on the other side of the street. There was a heated discussion between them, which ended with the doctor extracting something from his purse and pitching it to the other man, who immediately placed the object between his teeth and bit upon it before he pocketed it and moved leisurely away as the fuming Grainger headed for his home.

Barth knew he had taken the doctor by surprise by indicating the possible use of one of the primitive methods for settling their dispute. This would give the challenger something to worry about. But, actually he had made his choice. It would be pistols, even though his adversary had thought to heighten his insulting treatment of him by designating a Negro as his second. Second! The realization suddenly came to him that Grainger's wrathful departure had happened without his ascertaining who would serve as the other second in the affray. Had Barth been asked the name, he could not have furnished it. The lowest character at the licks, if he were White, would not meet with a Negro. Tom Chism certainly would refuse. Maybe, Abe Foster would understand and would help him—though this hope too was faint. Maybe, some traveler to Falls of the Ohio might have a slave with him. This appeared the only solution. If not, what then? He reined Sagitta around and rode toward the saltworks.

Grainger had scarcely dismissed Chate before the full import of Mercer's answer to his challenge began filling his mind. Suppose Mercer were to choose one of the savage weapons he had named. The doctor never had even touched an adze or a tomahawk. The knife, he had used only in prescribed surgical fashion. Nor had he any experience, other than a few firings, with a rifle. Perhaps Mercer might decide on pistols. This saving possibility fell with his next thought: a pox-infected adventurer like Mercer would not likely make such a civilized decision. "If that happened!" The words no longer expressed a remote probability. Their portent now might well prove a dire probability, and the nightmare, an omen, erroneous in but one respect. There would be no smoking pistol, but his body would be the one upon the ground, a tomahawk lodged firmly in his skull. What Grainger now took to be justifiable anxiety on his part would shortly assume its true proportions—fear, cloaked in the clinging, soiled robe of cowardice.

CHAPTER 70

Barth knew not the inclination that impelled him to stop in front of Ben Skinner's store, but he found himself tying the reins to the rack outside. He wondered at the magnetic attraction that brought him to the door of this place. Inside all seemed as he had remembered it to have been. Then he saw Little Johnny. Not the buck-skinned little peddler whom he had helped that early morning on the rutted pathway to Bullitt's Lick, but a small man, fashionably dressed, whose actions, until his eyes recognized the one who had just entered, had proclaimed him to be the proprietor of the establishment. As the enraged Mercer advanced upon him, Johnny's voice came in high-pitched, frantic warnings against each oncoming step. "Yew git on out of here! This here's my place—yew git on out of it! Yew lay a hand on me, an' Mitch Strickler an' my boys'll take keer of yew! Stop, I say!" Mercer drew even nearer. "Mace Hardin's dead an' most of them what worked fer him works for me now!" He began backing away from the man he had once called kepteen, his retreat ending only when he reached an empty corner of the room. There were few persons there, other than the two principals, but they, battle-wise, had taken themselves to the walls, out of the path of what appeared certain violence.

Mercer had not as yet spoken a single word. His mind held the picture of Mace Hardin coming out of this very room, holding Johnny by his collar and pummeling him with each stride. The recollection fathered a regret that he had stopped Mace from beating him.

Johnny cringed, half-stooped, as Barth's hands took hold of his coat and lifted him free of the floor. His frenzied words protested once again. "Yew leggo of me! Mitch Strickler'll pay yew back fer doin' this tew me! Don't yew hit me! Yew'll be damn sorry yew ever tetched me—yew hear?" When these threats of reprisal failed to penetrate the armor of Mercer's anger, he switched his defensive pleadings. "I told yew, th' first time I knowed yew to watch out fer me, if they was a dollar to be made!" His next words were jumbled. Barth was shaking him unmercifully, and Johnny's wobbling jaws bit involuntarily, catching his tongue between his teeth. By timing himself, he managed to squeeze out his speech. "Yew—are—jest mad—be-be-cause—I-I—outsmarted yew!" This utterance proved most disastrous. Mercer shook him until his eyeballs rattled, before dropping him to the hard floor.

As Johnny lay there, Mercer's words rolled out in a blazing stream. "You damned, worthless skunk! I'm sorry I didn't let Mace Hardin kill you! And to think I had even remembered you in the will I made the night before we had that trouble with the Indians! Outsmarted me, did you say? Why, you damn little thief. What would you say if I told you that you have stolen nothing from me—that it already belonged to someone else? In fact, that at least two other men each claimed, and are still claiming, ownership of the ground on which your new lick is located?" He paused to let what he had said sink into Johnny's mind. "What would you say to that?"

Johnny gave a timid answer. "Yew are jest makin' that up. Hit's jest sour grapes!"

"You are not that lucky, damn your little rotten hide! You want to know the names of the owners? No, you wouldn't like that, but I'm going to tell you anyway. That land, at least the part with the lick on it, belongs to either Parmenas Briscoe or Charles Broughton. I know that's the truth because George May told me all about them. The plat that you and I saw, and from which I made the map you stole from me, wasn't a true copy. Whoever copied it had made a mistake and omitted the part that had the salt lick on it. So it appears that you have outsmarted yourself, not me!" He turned and pointed to those who yet remained inside the room. "You see these men? They have heard every word I have just said! How long do you think it will be before Mitch Strickler—the same Mitch Strickler who had your buttocks boiled that time—how long do you think it will be before he hears about what I have told you? And what do you think will happen to you when he does? And how long do you think it will take for someone to tell him? I'll tell you, he'll know all about it by the time you get back to the new lick. By tonight, you will be dead and floating down Salt River! You remember the gorge that the river runs through, over near Mud Garrison? Well, your body will sweep through it, and by tomorrow evening the fish in the Ohio will be nibbling on your carcass! Now, how smart do you think you have been?" Without waitin' for Johnny's answer, he walked briskly from the room. Buzzing voices quickly rose, trailing his exit.

He mounted Sagitta and rode toward his saltworks. It had been difficult, but he had kept his promise to Dracie. He had not harmed Johnny physically. His pledge had not been intended to cover what others might do to him.

As his hips moved with the even progress of his mount, the duel with Grainger became his thinking. The unexpected encountering of Johnny had swept it momentarily from his mind. Barth was resigned to its happening. And though he was no coward, he was not so foolhardy that he was not gravely concerned as to its outcome. He had his future life with Dracie waiting only upon his return to Harrodstown. Would it be a trick of fate that he would never have that happiness, now so close to his grasp? And what of Dracie? Would he be the second man she would lose? Could the estate she would receive under his will compensate her for that? And it was all so foolish—this crazy business of the duel. All inspired by a fool—a damned fool—Doctor Grainger and his vain pride. It just didn't make sense. He didn't want to hurt Grainger, much less kill him. If he emerged unscathed, he had no intention of taking his adversary's life, but if the doctor wounded him, he knew that the latter would load and fire again. The damn blind fool. Since the engagement had to be kept, further worrying should be avoided as much as possible. He could not forget that he must risk his life, but he could, and would, prevent its becoming a devastating obsession. He looked at the sky and saw the ascending smoky columns. His mind was free of the future's fortunes. There was activity at his lick. He knew now how Tom Chism had felt that evening when they had returned from the battle with the savages.

Long before he reached the storehouse, he had made out the huge figure of Abe Foster, and almost immediately he heard a corresponding recognition of himself by Abe. He had just dismounted when Davey Middleton joined them.

"Wal, Cap'n, we hez did th' best we cud fer ya. Davey here hez did more'n I hez, but we hez both bin bizzier than bees 'round a bear's paw. Davey hez bin here all uv th' time, but I hez ter feed them bastards whut works fer Tom Chism, an' that's one helluva job—what with Jim Trench not quite ter hisse'f yet."

Barth interrupted to inquire as to both men. Abe spat some of the juice from his flooded mouth. "Tom ain't did nuthin' but hole thet jug ter his mouth sence Abby got married ter Baxter, but Jim's a-doin' right fair-like. Ya know," Abe winked his eye and smiled mischievously. "I'll b'leeve thet ole son-uv-a-bitch is jest a-fakin', so's he don't hev ter work none."

Barth chuckled with Abe and Davey, but then became serious. "How much salt have you been able to make?"

Abe passed the inquiry to Middleton. "Yer hed best tell 'im, Davey."

Middleton responded, "About half of what we should. We just ain't got th' men. A few of them what left to work at th' new lick has come back but not enough to count for much."

"Demme! I most fergot! Davey, go git that money we took off'n Mace Hardin!" Middleton bent inside the storehouse and Abe continued. "We saved suthin' fer yer, anyhow. We ain't never counted it, but they's considuble."

Here were two honest men, Barth thought. Two good men. If he could only keep them working for him. He knew Abe would never leave Tom Chism. But what about Davey Middleton? His decision was half-formed when he asked Abe, "What do you think about Middleton? Think he would be a good overseer for me, if he would take the job?"

Abe dug into his whiskers and scratched away. "He be a damn good man— one uv th' best. S'posin' yer asks 'im."

Middleton panted as he raised himself after placing the coin-filled roll of linen in front of Mercer. The rust-colored stains made by Mace's blood had faded out a little. "There it is, Cap'n. Just like we got it. It's all yo'rn—every damn bit of it."

"Not mine," Barth corrected him. "Some of it is yours and Abe's and the rest of the men who stayed on here. The balance can be used to pay everyone who left and who will agree to come back to work for me. I think there'll be quite a few who'll be glad to come back 'fore too long." He hastened to point out a distinction between those who had stayed and those who might return. "Of course, the men who never left will each get more than those who did."

Abe shook his head in amazed fashion. "Cap'n, yo're putty sharp. But how does yer figger them fellers over ter th' new lick will be wantin' ter kum back?"

"You just wait and see if I'm not right." He spoke directly to Middleton. "Davey, I'd like for you to take Mace Hardin's place. I'll pay you well if you'll take the job."

Middleton did not answer immediately. It was evident he had been surprised. At length, he said, "Cap'n, if you want me, I'll take it. You can pay me what you think is fair. I'm beholden to you for what you done for me when I got cut an' I ain't forgot it. As for your givin' me any of th' money me an' Abe has been watchin' for you, I ain't goin' to refuse it, but I don't expect you to give me none. 'Sides, it was Abe what really saved it for you from all them what was there when Mace was killed. When they found out about it, they all raised hell an' tried to make Abe divvy it up right there, but he stopped 'em."

Abe speedily renounced his own interest. "I hain't 'spectin' none neither. I knowed hit wuz yo'rn an' them others sons-uv-bitches dint hev no rights ter it."

"We'll settle that right now." Barth was in mock severity. "You're working for me, aren't you, Davey?" Middleton nodded his head. "Then, you'll have to obey my orders. You and Abe take a fair share for yourselves. Handle the rest of the money like I have told you."

Abe laughed. "Yer fergits. I hain't workin' fer yer."

It was Barth's turn to laugh. "Doesn't make any difference. You two take the money, and my thanks go with it." He was about to add to his expression of gratitude when the duel and its possible consequence jumped into his thoughts. "One thing I want to ask you to remember, Davey. If anything should happen to me, I am going to give you the name and address of the person who will inherit this property. You will continue to oversee things here unless she should decide to sell the saltworks. This is the most important thing that I will ever tell you. Please do not forget it or fail to do as I am asking you."

"I'll remember, Cap'n. You can stake your life on me. I won't fail you." Middleton spoke the words as though he were taking a formal oath.

"Good! Now let's go inside the storehouse and get you all straight on what your duties will be and agree on what you will receive for your services."

Abe declined the invitation to accompany them, saying, "I'll jest set m'self here fer a spell."

Barth found Middleton to be most intelligent and he had little difficulty in instructing him as to his requirements. He told him of the salt in the cave and of his plans to ship it as soon as it was recovered. They finished their discussion and came outside just in time to hear Abe bellow, "Buck, yer Black-assed son-uv-a-bitch, kum back hyar!" And then to witness the meek approach of the blackest slave Mercer had ever seen. A Negro! Here was his second! The duel was rimming his thoughts, closing in on them at every opportunity. Abe was talking to the Black. "Buck, hain't I tole yer, yer don't hev ter work yorese'f ter death? Hit's gettin' on ter sundown. Yo're done fer th' day. Y' understan'?"

The Negro nodded. "Yassa, Massa Abe."

"Don't massa me, yer Black bastard. Jest do liken I tole yer."

"Wait a minute," Barth said. "I want to talk to that boy."

"Ya heerd th' cap'n! Waddle yore Black ass over here!" As though the slave were tied by a cord, Abe's strong tones pulled him back to stand nervously before Mercer. Abe noticed his shaking and tried to calm him. "Now, Buck, they hain't nuthin' ter be a-feered uv. This here's Cap'n Mercer whut owns this here salt-works. He hain't a-looking fer yer fer no trubble."

The change in the Black's composure was complete. His terror had been replaced by a side, red-lipped grin before Barth told him, "Buck, I want to see you in the morning, first thing, you understand? If I don't call you, you come to me anyway. Is that clear?"

"Yassa."

"Now, get on with you." The soles of Buck's bare feet flashed as he ran from their presence.

"Where did he come from, Abe? Who does he belong to?"

"Don't nobuddy know. Some feller brung 'im ter Skinner's place th' day Mace an' Jeddy-Boy got whut wuz a-kumin' ter 'em. 'Pears he wuz s'posed ter be Ben Skinner's boy, but Ben hed done tooken off. Th' feller whut brung 'im, jest left 'im. Claimed thet his orders wuz jest ter bring 'im ter Skinner. Wal, seein' as how I doubts then, es I does now, thet Ben will ever kum back here, I jest kinda took charge uv 'im. When me an' Davey took holt uv yore saltworks, why, he wuz jest another feller whut we cud use, so we put 'im ter work. Trubble is, th' pore Black son-uv-a-bitch works his ass off. He's scairt he mought git runned off. Near's I kin make out, th' pore bastard thinks someun is lookin' fer 'im. Whoever owned 'im before must uv bin rough as hell on 'im." As though he hadn't changed his trend of thought, Abe continued. "Wal, hit's a-gittin' on ter dark. I'll see yers tomorry. Night, Cap'n. Night, Davey." With that, he got on his horse and rode away.

Looking after him, Barth observed to Middleton, "He doesn't waste words, does he?"

"That's Abe, Cap'n."

"I know. You need any help tonight, Davey? I'll be glad to stay."

"Won't be no need for that, Cap'n. I got guards an' all. Everything's tended to."

"Well, if you are sure about it, I expect I'll leave. If you should want me before morning, I'll be at Rosie Tindall's. Good night, Davey, and I'm glad you're going to take charge of the lick for me."

"I'm real pleased, myself, Cap'n. See you in th' mornin'."

Barth gave Sagitta a loose rein. Thus given its head, the gray streaked into the twilight. A little later, they were at Rosie's. After seeing his mount bedded down, he went inside. He ate a light meal and, despite the fact the place was quite crowded and voices high, secured a pallet from Rosie and lay down in the farthermost corner of the room. It had been a strenuous, eventful day. His repose was immediate and complete.

*

As soon as he was certain Mercer had gone, Johnny scrambled to his feet and yelled to the open door, "Yew are a damn, sneakin', lyin' son-of-a-bitch! Wait til I tell Mitch Strickler whut yer said! Him an' my boys'll take good keer of yew, damn yer to hell! I'm a-closin' this here place an' goin' over to see Mitch right now! I'll show yew who owns thet there proppity!" He took in the faces of those about him in one, all-inclusive glance and he thought he saw the impression he had hoped to create by his denunciation of the departed Mercer.

He did not allow them any present opportunity to dispel their perplexity. "Yew fellers'll have to git out. I'm a-closin' up. Got to go see Mitch Strickler right away!" The store was quickly emptied, but he did not follow the last one to leave. Instead, he barred the door and then went to the row of shelves on the back wall. He threw things right and left until he found that for which he searched. Folded in a square, was his old peddler's pack. No touch of sentiment had been involved in its retention. It had been kept for the day of its possible sale. No one who had spent the years, as had Johnny, in peddling wares would discard anything, no matter how small its worth. Johnny knew Mercer spoke the truth. The curse of character upon a roguish mind is the infallible attribute of being able to distinguish between truth and falsity. He would bemoan the untimely loss of the quick wealth, which only this morning seemed surely to soon be his. But such commiseration would be postponed until he had reached a place of safety, far from Bullitt's Lick. He knew, as Mercer had said, it would be but a short while before Strickler would be fully informed. Johnny was making sure he wouldn't be around when that occurred. The men who watched the store that night for him would find the door unbarred and no one inside.

Out front, he hastily mounted Strickler's horse and kicked its sides until it sped like a runaway. The early haze of evening had already begun to gather. He must reach Mud Garrison before the gate was closed for the night. If he failed, there would be the lengthy delay before his admittance. Time was most precious—it was his very life.

His objective at the garrison was Wallingford, even now munching contentedly upon his nightly provender. Never before had the mule enjoyed more to eat and less exercise than he had since the day his master began the operation of the new lick. It could not know it owed its well-filled flanks to Johnny's desire and intention to sell it and to the lack of an interested purchaser. Wallingford's life of ease ended suddenly with the hitching of a full-lathered horse to the rack next to where he was then tethered. Moments later he fought the bit that Little Johnny finally forced into his mouth. He attempted to kick when the saddle was slung across his rounded back, but fat had robbed his leg of its old-time zip. An overly perspiring Johnny just managed to buckle the well-worn bellyband in its last notch. Then Johnny unfolded his old pack and shook it to make it lose its adhering creases, preparatory to filling it with a few things he might be able to sell later on. As he did, a Jew's harp, snagged by its tongue in the raveling of an inside corner seam, sailed forth and fell unnoticed a few feet away. Willie Roller had wanted it. He had no use for it now.

Johnny reined up the blowing Wallingford at the gate and spoke briefly to one of the residents who was waiting to bar the portal after his departure. "I got to go back to Saltsburg an' I'll stay there fer th' night. Ain't no use of me comin' back fer m' horse til mornin'. Mought be Mitch Strickler mought want it fer I gits back—it's really his'n. So, if he comes a-lookin' fer it, why jest let 'im have it. If I don' t get over this way in th' mornin', yer mought send word over to th' lick that it is here. Thet a-ways I kin go on up to Clear's Station without comin' back to Mud Garrison. Save me a lotta time, thet a-ways." The residenter waved as Johnny rode out and bade him good night. Johnny waved back. It was not goodbye. It was farewell.

Johnny rode eastwardly, hoping fervently he would meet no one, or if he should do so, it would be in darkness. If Strickler and the rest of the duped men should try and follow him, they would ride a long piece out of the way, if they took the bait he had dropped at Mud Garrison and looked for him at Clear's. If they did so, they would probably give up any further chase when they realized he had tricked them and that with his head start he would then be many miles away. Of course, honesty had absolutely nothing to do with Johnny's leaving Strickler's horse. It was just that Mitch would never have stopped searching for him had Johnny ridden away on his animal.

Mitch Strickler had given Johnny plenty of rope—attention, money, whiskey and authority, as well as giving him the use of the horse. He had given him plenty of rope, but Johnny had not hanged himself. He had slipped its noose.

CHAPTER 71

Wearied from her unaccustomed physical exertion of the afternoon, sleep came upon Drusilla as a leveling wind. But, though her body rested, there moved through the off channels of her mind, the fearful doubt her husband had instilled earlier. Like some veiled specter, roaming endlessly through the darkened, deserted chambers of a many-roomed mansion, ever fleeing something feared in a prior existence, her indecision raced the avenues, calling vainly upon logic to strike down the terror that clung to it. But logic slept, and reason was drugged.

She awoke in the darkness unstartled but yet afraid. For though her eyes were open, she remained in the limbo of insensibleness. Only her conscience was truly alerted, unhampered, but by the same token unaided by the forces of evasion and of perspective. Confession, with no hint of avoidance, brought regret, remorse and repentance in factual sequence to prostrate themselves before the bar of self-incrimination where conscience sat as judge and jury. Merciless punishment—the thought of the dreaded infectious disease—weighted down one pan of the scale of decision.

Slowly, her torpid faculties revived. And with their return came self-addressed reasoning. Richard must have meant to frighten me . . . I couldn't have the disease—I have not been ill . . . The man I gave myself to, could he have been infected? There was nothing to indicate there was anything wrong with him . . . The rash—did I have a fever yesterday? I seem to recall having had a headache then . . . Suppose I do have the pox, will I really come to look like that woman? Oh! God, merciful God, that couldn't be! Her pulse was a trip hammer, driving the fiery blood through her every vein. She flung the cover from her perspiring body, her naked body welcoming the caresses of the cool night breeze of the Salt River Valley, which gently swayed the drapes. She lay at ease for a few precious moments. Then back stormed the ravaging forces of trepidation. A flash of fire began at her feet and swept through her, settling in her brain. She imagined the rash upon her breast to have enveloped her neck, yet she feared to touch her throat or its base or to light a taper lest her suspicions be confirmed. The pounding within her mind matched the fluttering of her heart and she surrendered to the besieging misgivings. This frightening warmth, was it the fever Richard spoke of? The pains in my mind—are they the headache of the pox? Are the glands under my arms swelling? Doubt had subjugated memory and was searching its minute possessions. Two years ago, in Pittsburgh, I was ill for a few weeks, though I concealed it from Richard. I had headaches then and there was fever! I had a little breaking out then too! And it was between my breasts and my throat! Oh, God! Have I had the disease all this time and not known of it? That friend of Richard's—Ledinger! Had he been infected? It happened about three weeks . . . or was it a month or more after that I became ill? That man who came in after Captain Mercer left—damn them both—I did not even ask his name! Oh, my God, how foolish have I been? "Dear God, may this not be so! May I not have this disease I pray you. Oh God, spare me! I would not choose to live another day, if I do have the pox." If die I must it will not be after I have lost my beauty! It will not be after I have suffered the tortures of hell! If hell it must be for me, I will seek it! I shall not wait for it!

She turned upon her side, then upon her stomach. But the engendered warmth angered the rash and she rolled hastily upon her back. She lifted the pillow from beneath her head and wrapped it around her face. Breathing was difficult and she removed it almost immediately. She tossed about all over her bed, but the terrifying thoughts relentlessly followed her every move. At long length, exhaustion became the master and she slept.

Downstairs, rest did not come easily to another. Grainger's improvised bed was comfortable, but its unfamiliar setting hindered the closing of the door of consciousness. When he did fall asleep, it was but for a brief interval. In his drowsiness, the words "If that happened" repeated themselves endlessly. Then he dreamed. He was looking at his own body, lying on the dew-covered grass. Blood trickled from a hole in his forehead—in its exact center. Drusilla was standing there with Mercer. They both were laughing as Mercer blew the smoke from the barrel of his pistol and then tossed it at the feet of the inert figure. The vividness of the vision awakened him, and so lasting was its effect, it was some minutes before reality rejected the fancied picture. His disciplined mind recalled further invasion, but the sleep he entered upon was yet a disturbed one, even though the irksome suppositional phrase had been silenced.

*

The Grainger home had become a house of dread, dark as the night. Not soft, enveloping darkness, but the blackness that feeds the destructive mouth of fear until it becomes raging terror. Each soul within the dwelling hid its own hemming shadow. For Callie, Jason and Chate, it was separation. For Drusilla, each second and its smallest fraction increased the certainty of the pox. For Richard Grainger, it was gory death on a wilderness greensward. If there were any honorable means, however slight the pretense, by which he could retract the challenge, he would readily—eagerly—do so. But there was none. The die had been cast irrevocably. He no longer hid from himself the fact that he was afraid to die. Earlier, he had disguised his consternation with excuses. It was not Mercer he feared, but the weapon Mercer might choose. He was not familiar with its use, whether it be knife, adze, tomahawk or rifle. He knew the knife, but only the direction of its blade through flesh and bone. Gradually at first, then in a rush that singed his brow and cheek, he acknowledged the weapon held no danger for him unless it be in the hand of one more skilled than he in its handling. This admission gave transparency to its only conclusion. He feared the user. He was afraid of Mercer. He offered the truth as a sacrifice, as though by his confession the plaguing fear might be satisfied. He saw himself a coward and did not shrink from the stigma. Better a coward and alive, than courageous and dead and unknowing. The brand need only be temporary. He could quickly wash away its stain, once he returned to Boston, where no one but he would know of its purposeful sufferance.

Many times since his palm had drawn the heat to Mercer's cheek, he had considered sending Chate to his adversary with an apology. He was sure Mercer had no desire to duel with him, and if given the opportunity to gracefully evade the combat, the captain would do so. The duel had been forced upon him.

Flight had repeatedly urged itself upon Grainger and he had thought heavily about it. The attendant implication of cowardice meant nothing to him. But the one unyielding facet of his character was pride. Though thrown into the disdainful company of fear and made its subject, his arrogance would not acknowledge it as master. It would not permit him to apoligize, nor would it let him leave.

As if the sand was mired at the opening within the hourglass, the night moved slowly on until the wayward hours before dawn. The slaves slept in a threefold embrace. Grainger sprawled in his favorite chair. An empty decanter, the source of his sleep, still held by his dangling hand, though its bottom rested upon floor. Occasioned by the bent head upon his chest, his labored breathing broke frequently into alarming, gasping snorts, as though each exhalation would not be relieved by a responding inhalation.

The taper's light shrouded Drusilla's face as she came silently down the stairs. Through previous nighttime descents, her determined feet knew their way. She paused briefly as she passed the drunken figure of her husband. Satisfying herself he would remain impervious to her presence, she walked toward the door. She set the candleholder on the nearby table and the rays illumined the dueling chest and, reflected by the highly polished wood, the carved serpent coiled around the stem of the holder, its uplifted mouth holding the candle itself. Unhesitatingly, her slender hand raised the lid and lifted one of the pistols from its concave encasement of green upholstery. I am separating it from its mate, she thought abstractly.

As the unlocked chest suggested, the weapon was ready for immediate use. Flint, powder and ball awaited the action of thumb and finger. Holding the candle so that its rays directed the pistol in her right hand, she slanted the muzzle firmly beneath her breast, making sure the barrel was level—that there would be no unnecessary disfigurement of her body. She held the strained grip only an instant, but yet the muzzle slipped. There was a flash and a loud discharge. The powder seared her flesh even as her flimsy night attire became inflamed. In her mad planning, it had never occurred to her she could not be touched by fire and not be burned. The lighted taper fell from the serpent's jaws as her hand struck the floor and its flame feasted on the rich carpeting, rolling away from the moaning Drusilla, whose fingers yet held to the serpentine carving.

As in the beginning, the serpent and the woman . . .

*

The three Negroes awoke with the explosive sound from within the house. A faint glowing, enlarging as they watched, guided them to its origin. Thoughtlessly, Callie failed to close the door behind their entrance. The draft rushed past them and the flames swirled toward Grainger's intoxicated form. Chate pulled his master from the chair just ahead of the reaching fire, shielding the doctor by exposing his own back to the young inferno. At the same time, he moved sideways to the temporary haven of the dining room. Once away from the flames' dance, Chate shouldered his senseless owner, whose limp arms beat upon the slave's badly scorched back as he hurried through the house and out its rear. He stretched his master upon the ground just as the light of the spreading conflagration revealed Callie running toward the rear door with a pail of rainwater from the cask at the far outside edge of the house. He called to her, shouting the futility of her action and she ran to him. The pail was emptied on Grainger's face. He stirred with the cold dousing and roused slowly. As the significance of the billowing flames became clearer, he sobered. Meanwhile, Callie picked up Jason and ran around to the front to look to the safety of her mistress. She called loudly to ensure her voice above the roaring din of the holocaust. Though she pleaded repeatedly, "Miz Drusilla, whar ez yo at? Doan tease poah Callie," there was no reply. She placed Jason well away from the burning residence, commanding that he not move. Then, in desperation, she ran to the front door and pushed it ajar. Again the draft followed her action. The interior was dazzling in its brilliance. Drusilla lay as though on an island in a sea of fire. Oddly, until Callie had opened the front door, the draft from the rear opening had caused the flames to eat at the back of the room and to work forward along its walls. Now, the new flow of air appeared to be forcing the flames away from the inert body—all but the sheet of fire moving toward it from the front entrance. Suddenly, Callie's eyes saw her mistress through the fiery barrier. Whether or not it was a trick of the blazing atmosphere, she thought Drusilla's arm had moved, and she ran for help. Soon, Doctor Grainger and Chate were peering at the spot where Callie said she had seen her mistress. The intensity of the heat precluded any sustained study and they took turns trying to look within. Chate volunteered to soak his clothing and attempt an entrance, but his master would not give his consent for the effort. He added to his refusal, saying, "You cannot help her. Better she dies quickly in this fire, than in the slow, torturing way in which she would have later on."

"But, Massa Richard. Ah seed her ahm a-movin' in dere! Hones' ter de Lawd. Ah seed it! Miz Drusilla ain' daid! She 'live in dere! Git 'er out, Massa Richard. Please git 'er out ob dere!"

Grainger was unmoved by her tearful entreaties, shaking his head with finality as he said to Chate, "There's nothing we can do. I can't let you risk your life. Let's hurry to the other side and see if there's any chance to save some of my books." When he had been first awakened, he had sent Chate into his study for his moneybag and the satchel containing his surgical instruments. His manservant had saved both, but when he came out, he brought with him the odor of burnt hair. Chate knew the books would perish with his mistress, but he did not voice the certainty. Instead, he followed his master to the far backside of the flaming structure.

Callie clutched Jason to her bosom, alternately crying and sobbing. The little boy had lived the day in a vale of his mother's tears. She had never cried before. She was always laughing. He held out his most prized possession—the coin Captain Mercer had given him. The firelight brightened it as he tried to hand it to her. "Mammy, yo' kin hab dis—its lots ob money, Mammy. Please doan cry." But she only shook her head and, hugging him closer, cried all the harder. "Dat poah Miz Drusilla . . . Dat poah dahlin . . . Dat beau'ful body ob her'n a-buhnin' in dere, lak it wuz a pig a-roastin' . . . Dat poah baby . . ." Jason shared her tears.

She gave no thought that only through the death of her mistress could she have regained her son. She loved and wanted them both.

*

Rosie was awakened by the smell of smoke. She jumped from her bed and opened the door to the big room. There was no sign of fire, but the fumes were heavier in there. She dressed hastily and ran to the front. The only window was, as always, tightly closed, so that it admitted neither light nor air. The only entrance was on the right side, near the corner of the house. She unbarred the door and as it swung open, the smoke irritated her nostrils. The outside was lit by an artificial glow, clear enough that she could see the wooden steps. She looked to the other side of the street. Doctor Grainger's house was a mass of fire! She hastened to awaken her household.

Barth led the others in their excited dash to the flames. Even as he approached, it was apparent there could be no survival for anyone so luckless as to be trapped inside. He moved around the perimeter of the blaze. As the fire roared into new timbers, there were loud, popping noises, and sparks shot spectacularly upward into the darkness. A faint breeze drove the flames in a rolling swell. Faces and hurrying figures were revealed for an instant in the background, only to disappear as the breeze shifted. Voices came in muffled snatches. "Th' high an' mighty Graingers . . . They wanted to be alone . . . Good thing for us, he built his damn house way back from the rest of us." There was not a single expression of sympathy. Envy's fruit had ripened.

Fortunate for the neighbors, it was indeed, that the desire for privacy had influenced Doctor Grainger and his wife. Though the cabins on either side would feel the warmth of the flames, the fire itself could not bridge the intervening open spaces. Pride had unintentionally become a neighborly benefactor.

The flames died with the night, and the day began to break. Of all those who had been drawn to witness the spectacular destruction of the Grainger home, only Rosie and Barth remained. They watched silently, but their thoughts were the same. Had the doctor and his wife escaped, or were their cremated bodies somewhere within the smoldering ruin? Rosie could not withhold the question. "Do you think they all got out?"

He answered, "That is what has been on my mind. I haven't seen the servants either."

"Do you really think . . ."

"I'm afraid to, Rosie. Let's walk around to the back."

Sparks shot out at them from a charring log that had rolled free of the parent blaze. Like an animal that had separated from the pack to devour its share of the kill, the selfish fire chewed upon the dry timber. As Barth pulled Rosie from the path of the spraying, burning particles, he saw shadowy shapes. His eyes adjusted themselves and the forms became more distinct. There were the three slaves and the doctor! Where was Drusilla? Perhaps, she was reclining beyond them. He said to Rosie, "Here they are! See them!" When she had difficulty in their discovery, he turned her so she faced in their direction.

She moved toward them as she exclaimed, "I don't see Mrs. Grainger!"

He answered quietly, "I don' t either." Then he followed her anxious steps.

Grainger's arms were folded, his hands gripping his elbows, as he stared at the seething debris. Callie and Chate, with Jason between them, were, as always, a subservient distance behind their master.

"Oh, Doctor Grainger! I'm so glad you all are safe!"

Grainger looked at Rosie, then back to the glowing embers. "Why should you be? What interest is it of yours?"

But for Rosie, Barth would have turned on his heel. Grainger's misfortune hasn't changed his attitude toward others, he thought. Don't suppose anything, however bad, could do that, though.

Rosie bit her lip, but the words would not be contained. "Is Mrs. Grainger safe? I don't see her anywheres."

The doctor's gaze did not leave the smoking plat. He did not answer and his rude indifference raised her ire. "Doctor Grainger, where is your wife?" she said heatedly.

"It is none of your business!" he snapped. "You are on my property. Just because my house has been destroyed gives you no license to come here without invitation."

Callie's pent-up tears broke the dam that restrained them. "She daid in de fiah! She daid in dere!" Her wail changed to moaning before she cried, "Dat beau'ful body! Ah tole Massa Richard ah seed her a-movin' in dere! Ah tole 'im, but he doan do nuthin' ter save 'er! Ah tole 'im! Ah—"

"Stop that damn foolish talk, Callie! You want me to sell you?" Grainger's threat reduced her grief to stifled sobs. Chate's jaw muscles knotted.

Barth noted the convulsive movements of Rosie's fingers as they interlaced, freed themselves, then relocked, only to repeat the frenzied cycle. He knew the turmoil of her sympathetic soul but he felt powerless to solve the conflict of her emotions, and he despised himself for his utter uselessness.

"If there's anything a body can do . . ." Rosie began.

The doctor moved toward her wrathfully. "I said, get off my property!" As he neared her, he suddenly recognized, for the first time, the identity of her companion. His face slipped, and the former terror, forgotten in the wake of the fire, returned upon him. The duel! Was that why Mercer was here? Had his second already seen Chate and made the arrangements? What was the choice of weapons? Had the fire prevented Chate telling him these things? He looked at his servant, the inquiry upon his tongue but he said nothing.

In the unfathomable mode of mental communication, whether through signals of the eyes from deep within the tiniest centers of the pupils or by direct transmission from one brain to the other, Barth's mind also reverted to the coming affray. Now that the one who had caused the challenge had been consumed by the flames, was there any sensible reason why the affair itself should die? Or was the doctor's abrupt manner a manifestation of grief for his wife? If so, there would be no gainsaying his desire for the life of the one whom he believed had violated her before the tragedy of her death. And the happiness or despair of Dracie Claycomb hung in the erratic balance. But, if the duel was unavoidable, would it not be a humane consideration, in view of the night's destruction, to propose a delay? Or would Grainger seize upon the wrong interpretation of such a suggestion?

Had Barth known the doctor's reasoning at this instant, he would have made his proposal. For Richard Grainger was also studying the possibility of averting that which he had once considered to be an affair of honor but which, almost from the moment of his challenge, had promised nothing except his own death or grievous dishonor. Drusilla, the cause of it all, lies dead in those ashes, he thought. Certainly, I could lose no face were I to point out that fact to Mercer and tell him that her death rendered the duel unnecessary. No, that would not do. His thinking was faulty, he admitted. But I could advise him that I was so overcome with grief and was so unnerved by it, that, reluctant as I was to do so, I wished a postponement of the affair. But that would be no solution; it could not be postponed forever. His pride became vicious at the contemplation of seeking any boon from such a lowborn person as Mercer. "No, by God!" he exclaimed under his breath. "I'll meet the damned bastard!"

Barth also had determined the futility of broaching his thoughts to the seemingly resolute doctor. Quietly counseling Rosie, he took her arm and the two walked silently away. Richard Grainger returned to his steadfast gazing. As the day continued to lighten, its departing gray would color the ruins in the foreground. Charred bones would have to be buried.

Forgotten during the course of the fire, time and its divided urgencies recovered their mastery of Mercer's thinking. There was much to be done this day. The arrangements for the duel, however, had unquestioned priority. When he had seen Rosie home, he would head immediately for the lick.

Rosie's mind was likewise occupied with the many things that would require her attention. She hoped Abby had not gone back to bed, but had taken care of some of this morning's tasks for her. Abby had not been too much help lately. But, was I any different? Rosie thought, recalling the wonderful new physical delights she had experienced following her own marriage. "He was a good man; he knew how to make a woman happy." She sighed. Blissful connubial memories, freshened by the retained images of herself and her husband, came over her. Her features softened, and her lips, so firmly set by the tragic scene she just viewed, relaxed themselves. Oh, it was good in those days! The hour or the place had never mattered to them. That certain cast of the eyes of either of them had been both invitation and acceptance. Whether he had just finished hewing timber, or she had spent long hours upon her feet, it mattered not. They were always ready—eager—when the desire came. And it seldom was far from them. Perspiration dropping from his chest upon her breasts, the first cold shock when his chilled body touched hers when she would be abed before him—the rapidity with which he warmed once he embraced her. It had never been too hot nor too cold for them. Fears, worries, sometimes sickness and ailments, had disappeared, if only momentarily under its magic spell. It was surely the nearest earthly thing to a cure-all a man or woman could obtain. So what if Abby was in bed with Billy Baxter? She wondered if Abby enjoyed herself as she had. Her thoughts went further. Did he get the same pleasure that her husband experienced? Her eyes closed as she tried to visualize her daughter and son-in-law together. The vision thrilled her, in a gentle fashion, and she softly voiced her feelings. "I hope she's with him right now!" She stumbled and Barth caught her arm. She opened her eyes, deeply embarrassed as she became acutely cognizant of her companion, whose presence had faded during her dreaming.

He asked, "What did you say, Rosie?"

She recovered quickly. "Nothing. I was just mumbling to myself about Abby. Must be getting old, I guess." She added, under her breath, "But not too old to remember!"

He had been daydreaming also. Otherwise, he would have heard her errant words. Strangely, his senses, so confused that day when he had unwittingly called upon Drusilla Grainger, had stored the picture of her lustful loveliness. And as his thoughts dwelled on her fate, he remembered clearly her physical perfection. A vagary embraced the breeze and Drusilla's ashes. Suppose their specks were wafted away as seeds are carried, to be breathed by other women. Would their inhalation affect their passions? He was at the point of denouncing this freakish thought when Rosie made her misstep and ended his meandering.

They had reached her home. He bade her goodbye and went to saddle Sagitta.

Even as Rosie and Barth moved out of hearing, Grainger was asking Chate concerning the duel. When he had ascertained that its terms had not been set, he told the Negro, "As soon as you hear, let me know immediately. You understand?"

It was then that Callie decided to make her shameful revelation. She liked Captain Mercer. She was loyal to her master.

One small coin, given to her son, had paid for her regard for the captain. Many coins had purchased her loyalty. She did now as Chate had ever counseled her. "Always repay kindness with kindness." Her husband would not like what he would hear her say in her obedience. Speaking loudly at first, to gain attention, her voice dropped to faintness as she told of Drusilla's using the innocent Jason as an agent for her trickery, and she stopped for an awkward while before she admitted that she had spied upon her mistress and the captain. She spared no details. Her account was as vivid as had been the situation itself. She described Drusilla's enacted displeasure when Mercer repulsed her desires.

There was another hiatus until she told of hearing the knock upon the door, and how she, like her mistress, had mistaken its sound for Mercer's return, only to find it was the man with whom Drusilla had engaged in flirtation when they were over at the garrison.

"Tell me his name!" Grainger demanded. When she told him she did not know, he was not easily convinced of her ignorance as to the man's identity nor of his wife's lack of that knowledge. After much questioning, he permitted her to finish her narration.

To give unquestioned integrity to her story, Callie pictured even the sexual act and how, at its conclusion, her mistress lay upon the floor, her eyes closed, her forearm on her brow, her breasts still heaving. The man had dressed and left without saying a word. Drusilla did not look after him as he departed. Callie had barely made it to the rear door before Jason was there, telling her of the strange White man who had just come out of the house and ridden away.

Having finished, she awaited the lash of her master's tongue, before she would feel the whip upon her back. Instead, after an agonizing silence, he thanked her for telling him, though he admonished her that she should have done so sooner. He did not tell her of the fear her words had driven from his mind with the speed of light, or that possibly she might have saved his life. It was logical then that when he said, "So she lowered herself with a nameless adventurer," and laughed, Callie reiterated her most common observation. "Jes' ain' no figgerin' how de White fo'ks thinks."

Callie and her master would never have believed, even had they known of it, that Drusilla had forced her imagination so that it denied her sight. She had accepted the stranger as the one for whom she had longed so far beyond the limits of her passion. The stranger, gambling at cards in Carolina, could never be convinced that his intercourse with that beautiful, proud woman in Bullitt's Lick had been possible only because she had forced herself to believe he was another for whom she had lusted so long and so fruitlessly.

The sun was reflected in the doctor's countenance. The certainty of his own safety had overwhelmed the loss of his possessions. His only regret, and it was slightly measurable, was that he had lost his medical books and treatises. But they could be replaced by the same wealth, safely held for him in Boston, which would minimize the lost furniture and furnishings. He had not lost Drusilla—she had been given up before her death. Indeed, he reasoned, I gained when she died. She intended taking Callie with her. The full legal import of Drusilla's demise dawned upon him. She had a large estate, left her by her dead parents. "For her separate use, free of any control of her husband, the same to be held by her as a femme sole."[34] He remembered the wording as though he had written it. And for good reason. It had occasioned his suggestion, later reluctantly agreed to by Drusilla, that they write mutual wills, naming the other as beneficiary. And so, he concluded, *I shall be well paid for the shame she has caused me.*

Callie and Chate waited patiently for their master's instructions. Stirred to activity by the nervous energy of childhood, Jason was striking a stick against a smoking log. Each blow produced a small flurry of sparks. Ordinarily, the doctor would have reprimanded him severely for distracting his thoughts, but this time, Jason's noisy activity was ignored. At length, Grainger spoke, but it was to Chate, not Jason. "Chate, when Captain Mercer's second calls upon you, tell him there will be no duel, that the fire settled the affair. After he leaves, you can take what few things we have saved over to Dowdall's. We'll be staying there for a few days before we leave for Boston. Don't bother about anything else. What tools or implements there are, leave here. We won't need them anymore. However, if you learn of anyone who wants to purchase them, tell whoever it is to see me. I'll be at Dowdall's." Strictly in a vein of afterthought, he added, "I expect you had better see if you can find any of Mrs. Grainger's remains. Bury what you find and make a mound or something." Thus he told them of their intended departure and the preparations to be made.

Tears spilled from Callie's eyes. Her loving hands would bury her mistress. Her voice would rise in prayer above the heaped soil that would mark her resting place.

CHAPTER 72

Buck was waiting for him when Barth reached the storehouse. "I'se heah, Massa Cap'n. Jes' lak yo' tole me." A wide grin filled the Negro's face.

Barth looked at him kindly as he said, "Take my horse, Buck. I'm going in the storehouse and write a note, which I want you to deliver for me."

"Yassa, Massa Cap'n."

Inside, Barth wrote the conditions for the duel, being careful to achieve clarity in his description. He had chosen a site near where the Dusenberry woman had been killed. The ground was level there and complete privacy could be anticipated at the hour he was setting—sunrise the next day. The weapon would be pistols at twenty paces. The duel to continue until blood was fatally shed. He had just finished when Davey Middleton entered. After greeting him, Middleton said, "I heared about you an' Doc Grainger. He's just a plain damn fool, jealous as all hell about that wife of his'n. Heared she got burned up in th' fire."

"That's right."

"Won't be no use of you all fightin' now, will they?"

"I've been thinking about that. But, as you say, the doctor is a plain damn fool. I don't think Mrs. Grainger's death will change his mind."

"You need any help? Want me to be . . . What do they call it . . ."

"Second? No, I thought of you, but Chate—that's Grainger's Negro—is acting for him, so you see—"

"Th' son-of-a-bitch! That wouldn't have bothered me none. That's what you want with Buck, ain't it?"

Barth nodded. "I've written it all down for him."

"When's it goin' to be? I'll be there."

"I'm sorry, Davey. I can't tell you that. This is a private matter."

"Just you an' Grainger an' th' two niggers?"

"That's all."

"Cap'n, there ought to be something I can do for you."

"There is, Davey. Remember me telling you about the woman who will own this property if I die?" He waited for Middleton's assurance, then continued. "Well, sometime today, I'll get a letter that I have written and give it to you. If anything happens to me, I want you to go to Harrodstown and tell her what happened. Do it right away, you understand?"

"I give you my word on it."

"That's fine. Now I want you to get someone to take Buck over to Grainger's."

"But, th' place burned down, Cap'n. There won't be nobody there."

""There's a cabin where the servants live that's still standing. Chate will be there or near-about."

Barth followed Middleton from the room. Buck was like a dog who had waited for his master. "Ez yo' a-wantin' me now, Cap'n?"

"Buck, I want you to listen closely to what I want you to do for me." He handed the Negro the folded writing. "One of the men here will ride you over to where you are to go. You'll know it's the right place by the ashes of a big fire that you will see there—"

"Ah bin heahin' de mens talkin' 'bout dat," Buck interrupted.

"Well, that's the place. Now, I want you to give this," he indicated the paper, "to a Negro named Chate. Is that clear?"

"Chay-ate," Buck repeated.

""Then, the man will bring you back here."

"Yassa. Dis hab ter do wit de due-ell, Massa Cap'n?"

"That's right. Here comes the man who will take you now."

"Yassa, Massa Cap'n. De niggah's name is Chay-ate, ah 'membahs dat." Buck's grin was prideful as he climbed on the wagon. The driver's face looked faintly familiar. It was not until the dust had swirled and settled that Barth remembered. The driver was the same man who had told Grainger of his return the day of the challenge! So that was how the news had reached the lick. He had wondered as to the source of Middleton's knowledge. To the best of his recollection, he could not remember having seen anyone but Grainger and the informer. He felt certain Rosie knew nothing of the incident, or else, being fearful for him, she would have said something about it. Just as she had, following the killing of Dolly Dusenberry, when she begged him not to take part in the search for the killer. He knew she would hear of the duel, but he hoped it would not be until after it was all over. The message would be delivered within the next half hour. As a result, before the next day's sun would be fully risen, death would be dared to return to the oft-visited confines of Saltsburg. So ran Mercer's thoughts until Davey Middleton said, "Worryin' 'bout it ain't goin' to do much good, Cap'n."

Barth shrugged off the observance, asking, "Who's the driver—new man?"

"Says his name is McClason. Why?"

Barth quickly related the previous day's encounter. Middleton's immediate response was heated. "I'll fire that bastard out of here th' second he gets back! It was him what told me 'bout your trouble with Grainger, but he didn't say nothin' 'bout him playin' no part in it!"

Barth calmed Davey's exertion. "I don't want you to get rid of him, Davey." Before the puzzled Middleton could speak, he continued. "I remember something Mace Hardin told me shortly after I came here. That he couldn't be too 'choicey,' I think that was the word, as to the men he employed. No, we'll keep him on, that is, if he does his work properly."

"If that's what you want. But I'd sure like to run 'im out of here. One thing is sure certain, he'd better do his job good. I'll be watchin' that feller, you can bet on that!"

Barth smiled at Davey's vehemence. "We've got more important matters to think about."

"The furnace bosses might cause you some trouble, Cap'n. They was right mad about Mace not givin' them their share of the salt what was hid, you know. That's why they was in th' bunch what killed him."

"I'll take care of that, Davey. Our first problem is to get the salt back here. I'll see if I can't get hold of Nancy and Hawkstraw this afternoon and get them to show us the location of the cave. Then—"

Middleton found the cause of the captain's abrupt curtailment of his conversation as he turned and his gaze joined Mercer's. Buck was driving the wagon and McClason was not to be seen. Their thoughts, like their eyes, were in unison, but it was Davey who shouted to the Negro. "Where's McClason? Anything happen to 'im? "

"Nassa, Massa Mid'ton. He jes' ax me ez de cap'n de ownah ob de licks, an' when ah says dat's de truf, why he jes' say dey ain' no use foah 'im ter come back, cayse he hab ter git out when he do. He say, 'Yo jes' drive dat damn waggin back, yo-se'f,' an' den he walk off an' lebe me." Buck's feet puffed the dust as he jumped from the driver's seat to the ground.

"Well, that takes care of McClason, doesn't it, Davey?"

"Reckon so, Cap'n. But I'd still like to have told 'im to get."

Barth's thinking passed over the remark. "Buck, did you deliver my message to Chate?"

"Yassa, Massa Cap'n. Ah seed dat fella Chay-ate. He wuz a-brushin' some horses. He say dey gonna lebe dis place. Massa Cap'n, dat fella doan talk lak no niggah ah done ebber hud. He speech jes' lak de White fo'ks. He say de fiah—it wuz all black dere whar de fiah it—"

"Damn the fire!" Mercer's voice scaled with his impatience. "Was his owner there? Did he say anything about the message you gave him? You did give it to him, didn't you?" As he asked, his eyes spotted part of the paper sticking out of the waist line of the Negro's britches. "Buck, haven't you any sense in that kinky head of yours? Why didn't you do as I told you?"

The sharpened words had a devastating effect. Buck cringed in expectation of the usual punishment that had always followed the wrath of his former master. Mercer caught the fright in the Black's eyes and his irritation lessened. He asked gently, "What happened, Buck?"

There was a pause, before the nervous answer. "Massa Cap'n, ah seed dat Chay-ate, an' ah say ter 'im, 'Yo' name Chay-ate?' Den he say, 'Wuffo,' only he doan say, 'whuffo,' ah dis'membahs 'zactly. But he ax whut does ah want, an' ah say, 'Massa Cap'n he tole me ter han' yo' dis.' And ah han's 'im de writin' lak yo' done tole me. Dat niggah doan hardly squench his eyes at it, fo' he say, 'Dey ain' gwine be no due-ell, cayse he ain' gwine ter be dere.' Den he han' de writin' ter me n' he say, 'Take dis back ter de cap'n.' Only, he say yo' name, which ah dis'membahs."

"The high and mighty insultin' bastard!" Davey's appraisal of Grainger was misinterpreted by Buck, who imagined his own actions to have drawn the angry exclamation. The rosy grin of accomplishment quickly disappeared from his face. What had he done wrong? he pondered.

His chagrin was short-lived and his mouth stretched happily as Barth commended him. "You did fine, Buck." Then, addressing the fuming Middleton, Barth's voice evidenced his own feeling of relief. "Davey, it looks like our damn fool has finally gotten some sense. I don't mind telling you that I'm glad he did."

Davey scratched his armpit. "All I can say, if he's whut they calls a gentleman, I sure as hell hope I never get to be one!" He would have enlarged the discussion but for Nancy's unheralded appearance. Her bare feet moved in a direct line to Mercer. Behind her came the smiling Hawkstraw. Without waiting for any greeting, she launched into the reason for her presence. "Me an' James has come ter . . . to . . . show you th' cave. So yer don't fergit, me an' James specks ter be paid fer he'ppin' you move it out uv there."

Amused by her forthright declaration, he yet refused to give license to his mirth. It might be ill-taken by the determined girl. "I haven't forgotten. I'll be happy to pay you for your help. But just show me where the cave is. The salt doesn't have to be moved this afternoon. We can do that tomorrow."

She shook her head seriously. "Me an' James is gittin' married this evenin'. If'n yer wants us to he'p, it's got ter be did now." Hawkstraw's features were in jubilant agreement.

Barth did not voice his thought that he had plenty of men to transport the salt from the cave to the storehouses. The expected earnings were too important to her. Instead, he said, "We'll do it right now. Does Mr. Flinden know about the wedding?"

"Me an' James has tole 'im. He's figgerin' on leavin' here tomorrer. Me an' James is goin' ter live at Mr. Flinden's place til he comes back, if'n he ever does. If'n he don't, he says we-uns kin—can—have th' place. He sez he'll make hit 'cordin' to th' law, when he knows fer shore he ain't a-comin' back here."

Flinden must be better, Barth thought. At least his sense of frugality has been restored. The ever imperfect acknowledgment of both God and mammon, that is never absent but only varied in degree, lives in the heart of Aaron Flinden, just as it exists in the hearts of all men. His meditation came to its answer. Is it because it is the most prevalent human weakness? It lives because Flinden lives. Again, is not vanity its root? Flinden wrested his land from the forest. His hands built his cabin and its furnishings. His back strained in the toil of tilling the reclaimed earth and in the harvesting of its yield. His mind had planned these things and their orderly accomplishment. His human frailty rendered this homage to himself and his own labors. When Gabriel sounds the last blast, both the quick and the dead will try to hold to something mortal, whether it be a possession of the flesh or of the spirit.

How long he had mused, he did not know. It was Nancy's impatient "Right now means quick-like. Don't take all that thinkin' to get movin'," which drew him from within himself and caused him to say, "Davey, you'd better get a pack-train ready—say six horses. Pick out about ten of the best men you have. Oh, yes! Be sure Herman Tressel is one of them and that Willerhorst isn't." When Middleton's brows lifted at the ordered exclusion, Barth laughed and explained. "He's got bad feet, remember?" Davey laughed too as he and Buck walked toward the wagon.

Nancy's anger reddened her forehead. "Them others ain't needed. We-uns kin do hit ourse'fs!"

Mercer angled into her irritation. "Why, Nancy. I'm just thinking about you and Hawkstraw." She glared at the use of the nickname and he hastily corrected himself. "About you and James, I mean." Her brow loosened and he continued. "You want to get married this evening you said, didn't you? Suppose it takes us longer than you expect it will. Maybe the preacher might think you have changed your minds. He might go on to Bairdstown or Harrodstown. Then you'd have to wait until he came back or until another one came through here. Might be some time, you know, before that happens."

She could not deny his logic. The preacher might go off somewhere, as Mercer had said. "Them damn preachers ez jest borned go-ers," she said to herself.

Ethan Belden appeared in the storehouse doorway. "You want me to go along, Cap'n?"

"You stay here and look after things while we're gone, Ethan. You'll have plenty to do before we get back." Barth turned to Hawkstraw. "Why don't you go inside and see Ethan til we're ready to leave?"

Hawkstraw looked at Nancy. She overcame his hesitancy, saying, "Why don't you do hit, James? Mine yer don't stay too long." He needed no further persuasion. The talk inside would not be of salt but of surveying.

"How far is it from here, Nancy?" Barth asked.

"'Bout a mile, mebbe a little mores, on th' fur side of th' river."

He was considering her recurrent lapses into what Flinden had termed the language of the Hardins, and her reference to the river almost escaped him. "River? You mean, the cave is across the river?"

"Thet's whar it be."

"Then we'll need a raft or a flatboat, won't we?"

"Less'n yer aims ter swim it acrost," she said laconically.

Poor Hawkstraw, he thought. Once a woman gets a man, she changes, as she tries to change him. Wonder if she's sarcastic with her James? They are an odd pair, all right. He recalled Johnny's words concerning love. "See thet butterfly . . ." Before the rest came to his mind, he winced. He had been truly fond of the little cheat.

Nancy had her thoughts too. Thet Cap'n Mercer's a strange-un. Allus fig-gerin' suthin' in his mine. He kin talk, but he don't. Why, James talks better'n him, an' he hain't got no voice.

Davey Middleton was back with the men and the packhorses. Barth quickly told him of the cave's approximate location. "That means we has to have a boat, don't it?" Davey weighed his own question. "'Course, that flatboat of Tom Chism's is still over by Mud Garrison. Remember it?"

Remember it! Barth mused, could he ever—would he ever—forget it and its cargo of carnage? "I doubt if we could use it, Davey. The river is down now, you know. The boat would barely clear the banks on each side. Besides, it would take some time to get it downstream. It would take more men too."

"It'll take a lot of time to build a raft. Have you thought of that?"

"I've considered that, Davey, I—"

"If'n yers had any brains, yers wud know they wuz a boat already there," Nancy broke in abruptly. "Don't you think Mace Hardin had ter git acros't, hisse'f? It's hid on this side uv th' river. I know th' place. Le's git movin' 'stead uv yers standin' thar a-jawin' 'twixt yerse'fs."

Damn you, thought Barth. You stayed too long with the Hardins to ever overcome it. Mr. Flinden just wasted his time. But his words to Davey were different. "She's right, Davey. We should have realized that Mace had to have a way to get the salt back and forth. Let's go."

"A little mores" proved nearer two miles than one. When they had finally halted at Nancy's curt direction, they found the boat—a sturdily constructed raft—in its ingenious hiding place, concealed by a mass of vines. As the men strained at moving it, Davey remarked, "Mace did ship th' salt down th' river, didn't he? I always wondered, though, how it was that Gibbs an' Mallory managed to get back so soon after they left. They claimed they met someone who took it from them, on to where it was supposed to go."

If the raft had been artfully camouflaged, the cave's entrance was a masterpiece of visual deception. Just when it seemed the trail upon which Nancy was leading them would end face on with a barrier of rugged stone, she turned sharply to the left, and there it was! Faggots of dried pine disbursed the darkness, revealing an immense room, jammed full of baskets and kegs. Salt—Salt—Salt! Had he been penniless before he entered the cavern, Barth would have become instantly wealthy the second he stepped inside the arid chamber. But the salt was not all he saw by the light of the flames. In a corner was an aged skull, the lower jaw missing. His foot rolled, as he stepped on an obscured thigh bone. Long before Mace Hardin had discovered it, others had known of this secret place.

As he watched the unceasing loading and reloading of the raft, he fitted the last piece into the enigmatic picture of his experiences at Bullitt's Lick. Mace's purpose had been to create a monopoly. The attempts on his life, the battle with the Indians, the feuding with Tom Chism and all the other lesser happenings, stemmed from this desire to preserve and add to this hoard of salt. Beyond a doubt, the killing of Gabe Claycomb had been an executed part of Mace's plan ... Gabe and Dracie, he thought. If I had not sent him to Kentucky, they would still be together. But would I change it if I had the power to do so? Would I give up Dracie? It was a thought he could not master. Its sequel proved to be just as unfathomable. Am I less free of guilt than David was? Does circumstance, without intent, make evil men of all? He was certain he would not have sent Gabe could he have foreseen his path. But with its occurrence, he could not bring himself to say he would have changed its resulting effect upon his own life. A near mishap with the raft demanded his instant attention and when it had been avoided, he feared to let himself wrestle further with his thoughts.

Though he had only overseen the work, Barth was exhausted as the day began to fade, and the last of the salt had been loaded and the packtrain started on its final return to the lick. Leaving Davey Middleton to follow the plodding line of weary packhorses, he sped on ahead to the storehouse.

Ethan Belden had earned this day's pay. Every available spot in the storehouse had been utilized, leaving only bare passage between the door and the counter that served as a desktop, and still the kegs and cane baskets had kept coming. One by one the outbuildings had been filled. Even the anvil in Herman Tressel's shed had been inched outside to make more room. Motty Willerhorst had protested vainly. "Dot Herman vill raise der hell blenty ven vunce he comes!" Now there remained only the sheds where the animals were stalled. "Won't be much more comin'," Belden had been promised, two packtrains before. There had better not be, he thought, or else it would have to be stored under the cover of the furnace shelters themselves. There would be no other place to stack it.

Were the problem of storage not enough to harass him, Belden had to contend with the constantly appearing workers from "that son-of-a-bitch Littelby's lick" as they invariably put it. Invariable too was their first inquiry. "Who pays th' money fer we-uns a-comin' back?" A source of mystification to him, neither Mercer nor Middleton had informed him of the reemployment bonus to be paid them. Such immediate results of the offer had not been anticipated. At the moment of Barth's welcome return, Belden was surrounded by these returnees whose impatience had been to kick the suspicion of trickery into their reasoning. Ethan's eyes had never beheld a more timely threat of distrust, promising, "You men go home tonight, and report to Davey Middleton the first thing in the morning. Those of you he rehires will get your money then. Unless you aren't good workers, I feel sure he'll take you all back." As the group began to file away, he cautioned, "Don't any of you come back drunk or drinking. You'll just be wasting your time." With their departure, he inspected the storage work and approved its placing.

Barth barely had seated himself and leaned his back against the storehouse wall, when Nancy and Hawkstraw were after him. Rather, it was Nancy who was demanding the day's wages for the two of them. The last of the payment in her hand, she reached inside the loose top of her linsey and withdrew a leather pouch. She recounted the coins, placed them in the bag, and restored it to its former repository between her filling breasts. Addressing both of them, Barth asked if James would care to work alongside of Ethan Belden. Hawkstraw's eyes lit up at the suggestion, but Nancy's brow lowered. "He kain't do hit. Me an' him is gonner work fer ourse'fs. We aims ter work Mr. Flinden's land. They's plenty ter be did thar." So saying, she said goodbye and, with James following closely, walked away, but not before Hawkstraw had given Mercer a smile of appreciation. The mute's eyes still shone, though the glint occasioned Barth's offer had disappeared. As they were leaving, Mercer called hastily, "I hope you all find the preacher! Good luck to both of you!" She acknowledged his good wishes with a succinct "Thank yer."

Poor fellow, Barth mused. She'll run his life, and he'll love her the more for it. It's plain to see he worships her. That Nancy, she's different than she was just a few days ago. Flinden hasn't left yet, and she already discarded most of his teachings, if her language is any indication. His mind reverted to Hawkstraw. She's got him wrapped around her little finger. Had he known that last night flesh had met flesh, he would have understood Hawkstraw's submissive adoration.

The last packhorse had been unloaded and led away to its provender. True to Motty's prophesy, Tressel was not happy about the appropriation of his workshop. "Mit der saldt, I shoe der foots?" he both asked and stated. Mercer eyed him humorously before replying, "Remember, Herman. Vrum der boss, der money comes." Tressel studied a second, then shrugged his broad shoulders. "Ya, vrum der boss, der money comes." With Motty Willerhorst as his companion, he walked toward Mud Garrison. A little of what he called beer and his weariness would be eased. The glockenspiel would ring out over the Salt River flats tonight.

The night was upon them by the time the last guard had been posted. Barth had given up the idea of returning to Rosie's. Delectable as was her cooking, he was too exhausted to eat, and since the floor at her place was no softer than that of the storehouse, there was no reason to ride over there just to sleep. He would spend the night here. He called to the Negro. "Buck, I'm giving you a special job tonight!" Take my horse and tie him up behind the storehouse. Then you stay with him. I'll tell one of the guards to keep an eye on the two of you, in case you should fall asleep." From out of the darkness, Buck's voice responded, "Yassa, Massa Cap'n. Ah takes good kah ob 'im."

For a while, Barth sensed the restrictive walls of salt that lined each side of his resting place. No sooner had he become accustomed to them, however, than he became fretfully aware of the sonorous snores of Davey Middleton, sleeping just beyond him. But he was not disturbed for long, for his mind was at ease. There was no dread of tomorrow. There would be no feverish waking from a terrifying dream of a duel at dawn. No distressed guessing as to whether it would be Dracie and himself or Dracie alone. Her face came to him in a half-dream. Another moment and his weariness dropped him gently into peaceful oblivion.

CHAPTER 73

"Cap'n...Mercer...Cap'n Mercer." Barth opened his eyes. For a few confused seconds, he struggled to orient himself. Then he recognized Ethan Belden. "Hate to make you get up, Cap'n. You was sure sleepin' like a log. But I can't go 'round you, an' I can't jump over you—you're too long."

"That's all right, Ethan. Where's Davey?" He was on his feet, now stretching himself as much as the narrow aisle would permit.

"The last I seen him, he was around back," answered Belden, as he squeezed past his still drowsy employer. "You'll prob'ly find 'im stuffin' his jaws. Th' hunters was comin' up, just 'fore I came in here. Looked like they had done real good. I know they had at least two turkeys. One was a big-un."

The dry taste in Mercer's mouth was not conducive to appetite. He raised the lid from a keg filled with spring water and filled the hollowed gourd that served as a cup. He went to the doorway and rinsing his mouth, spat outside. The air was redolent with roasting fowl, and his stomach stirred. He refilled the gourd and spilled the water upon his face. Making no attempt to dry himself, he proceeded to the rear of the storehouse where he came upon Davey Middleton, cuffing his mouth with his sleeve. Instead of greeting him, Davey said, "Cap'n, we-uns'll need more vittles than what we got. I sent the hunters out for more. Yore idea 'bout them fellers comin' back for their jobs is sure workin' out like you claimed it would—too good, if we're goin' to feed 'em all. I got some of 'em busy makin' another place to store th' salt." Switching to the obvious, Davey asked, "You ain't et yet, has you?" Before Barth could answer, he directed one of those at the fire. "Give th' cap'n a good slice of that bird." A generous carving was thrust toward him and Barth grasped it, full handed, only to drop it immediately. He had not reckoned on its burning warmth. As he bent to retrieve it from the ashes, Middleton joshed him, "Reckon that's just part of that peck of dirt what you'll have to eat before you die."[35]

The meat was savory, and he would have taken another helping, except that he reminded himself of the breakfast Rosie would cook for him a little later. He did not want to fill himself beforehand. Davey misunderstood his refusal, commenting, "For a big man you sure ain't got much appetite." Barth laughed off the remark, and directed him to come with him to the storehouse. They found Belden thumbing through a ledger, and they waited until he had found that for which he was searching. When this had been accomplished, Barth explained to Davey and Ethan his plans for the future operation of the lick. The salt on hand, despite its enormous accumulation, would be speedily disposed of, he assured them, largely through the demands of the Continental Army and by shipments to Carolina and Virginia. He made certain they understood the character of negotiable receipts and prepared a facsimile of the receipt he intended to give to buyers in order that they would have knowledge of the genuineness of any paper they might later receive purporting to bear his signature. He concluded his instructions by expressing his desire that the operation of the saltworks be ultimately changed so that it be converted entirely to a share basis, explaining that in this way, the labor and production of the salt by others would result in their efforts being confined to the storing and sale of the salt received by them. There would then be no problem of, or responsibility for, the actions of the shareworkers with anyone else. Then he told them of his determination to leave Bullitt's Lick immediately and of his intention never to return. They could not credit their hearing nor comprehend the finality of an absolute farewell. He laughed at their disbelief, saying, "You all had better take a good look at me, so you will remember what I looked like."

Outside, he found Buck, waiting with his charge, Sagitta. "Massa Cap'n, heah he ez. Ah slept wif me eyes plumb open. He de puttiest hoss ah ebber done see, an' he smaht az a man." Buck softly stroked the appreciative animal's bobbing head.

The idea came unexpectedly. "Buck, how would you like to go back to Virginia with me? You could take care of Sagitta all of the time then. How would you like that?"

"Massa Cap'n, yo' ain' funnin' wif Buck, am yo'?"

"Honest, I mean it."

The Black's features fell from their heights of hope. "How ah gits ter Vahginny? Does ah walk?"

"No, you won't have to do that. I'll get you a horse." Barth's smile brought the glow back to Buck's countenance.

Davey Middleton, standing by the door, broke into the conversation. "Cap'n, I know a horse you can have for him an' it won' cost you a penny. In fact, he's tied up near Herman Tressel's shed right now."

Uncertainty hung in Barth's mind as he asked, "Who owns him?"

Uncertainty, which first became confusion, when the answer came, "No one," but which changed to understanding with the words, "He was Willie Roller's." Moments later, unrestrained joy, in the person of an ebullient Negro, came around the corner of the storehouse, seated on a chestnut roan with a blaze face. Though it had been a long time, Barth knew the animal. It was the horse he had ridden the night he and Tom Chism had gone to see Aaron Flinden. An afterthought struck him. "You can ride, can't you, Buck?"

"Ah rides lak one ob dem Injerns. Ah doan eben hab ter hab dis heah saddle."

Barth laughed and said to Middleton, "I'm going to try and find Abe. I'd like to see him before I go. If I shouldn't catch him, tell him goodbye for me. I want to see Tom Chism too. He's pretty sure to be over at his works. But Abe might not happen to be around when I'm over there." Another exchange of farewells followed, and the master and his new servant rode off together.

As Barth had surmised, Abe was absent. Tom Chism was there, however, but Barth's greeting and goodbye were said to a stupefied drunk, whose red-glazed eyes were unable to recognize a friend and whose dull ears failed to comprehend his intended departure. They did not tarry longer, but set out for Rosie's. As Barth passed Ben Skinner's, he caught a glimpse of the figure in the doorway. It was Mitch Strickler.

Billy Baxter waved his arms as Barth started to ride around to the rear. "There's nobody here, Cap'n. They're all over at Brashear's. Rosie was worried when you didn't come over last night, and she had me stay here, in case you came over this mornin'."

"When is she coming back? I'll wait for her."

"'Fraid you'd have a long wait, Cap'n. We're all goin' to Louisville—goin' to stay there a spell. Then we're goin' on to Pittsburgh.'"

He had not imagined she would leave so soon. He could not account for the saddened feeling that came over him.

"Did she get a price for her place?"

"Didn't sell it, Cap'n. Turned it over to Jim Trench to look after. If he sells it, he's to send her th' money. But I reckon she knows that ain't much likely. Prob'ly be just a case of walkin' away an' leavin' it, like she says. Didn't seem to bother her none, though. She makes up her mind an' that's it. You know Rosie."

They talked a bit longer before Barth recalled that the last time he had seen Baxter, the youth was being carried away unconscious. He quickly asked as to his recovery and being assured by him that "It wasn't nothin'," Barth offered his belated congratulations on his marriage. "Abby's a fine girl, Billy. You're a lucky man. I would have congratulated you before this, but you and Abby were too busy for company when I was last here."

Baxter caught the import and blushed. "I understand, Cap'n. We was, what you might call busy." He laughed, but embarrassment clung to his features and to his words, as he said, "Rosie would like to see you 'fore she leaves. Can you spare th' time?"

"I surely can and will. How'd you get over here—on foot?"

"No, sir. Jim Trench give me th' loan of his horse. He's waiting for me over at Brashear's."

They rode at a canter, their words jostling with the gait. "I was glad to hear there wasn't going to be any duel." As he said this, Baxter looked at Mercer, as if expecting him to divulge the details. When Barth merely said, "So was I," and made no further comment, he pursued the matter. "What was ailin' Grainger? They tell me he slapped your face. I'd have given it to him right then. What was he so all-firin' riled up about? Some says his wife was th' cause of it, that right?"

The queries born of innocent curiosity nevertheless produced an irritating effect in Barth's breast. A curt reply formed in his mind, only to be checked by the understanding that Baxter meant no offense and was only asking that which most of Bullitt's Lick would like to know. When he next spoke, his words were uttered civilly. "Mrs. Grainger sent for me in her husband's absence. I thought him to be home. He attached an improper purpose to my visit, though there was none." He delayed, admitting he could not risk the truth of a full explanation even with this young man, and so passed over the unbelievable details of his entrapment. "Grainger fancies himself a gentleman, and he followed the custom of that class by challenging me to a duel. The slap on my face followed his accusation of me and completed the challenge."

"He sure must've thought you done somethin' bad to his wife. What did he claim you done?" Billy caught the bluntness of his words and attempted exoneration by continuing immediately. "Nothin' a'tall, prob'ly. I reckon he was just jealous—blinded. Why do you think he called it off? Reckon he was a'feard of you?"

"I don't think he was afraid. Maybe Mrs. Grainger's death in the fire changed his mind."

"Looks like that would have made him madder'n ever. If it was me, an' Abby had got burned up, I sure never would've quit until I had killed that feller or he killed me." Mercer's tightening facial muscles flashed their warning and he mitigated his intimation. "You understand, Cap'n, that's what I'd a done, if she had been wronged. Not that I thinks you wronged Mrs. Grainger."

The tone of his voice sought pardon for his impropriety and Barth accepted the inferred apology. "I know what you mean, Billy, but I expect we had best talk about something else. I don't know why Doctor Grainger didn't go through with it. Perhaps he discovered he had been wrong in his thinking. Whatever the reason, as I said before, I'm glad that he did so."

Baxter completed the transition of subject. "Anyway, Cap'n, he won't cause you no more bother. Him an' his niggers left with a party for Louisville this mornin'. We passed right by 'em, and seen 'em as they was leavin'." He had one last inquiry of the captain and he gave out with it. "Cap'n, I been meanin' to ask you somethin' ever since you rode up to Rosie's. Who's th' nigger who came up with you?"

"You really are asking questions this morning, aren't you?" The youth's head dropped in abashment as Mercer turned and glanced toward the Negro in the rear. Buck's face was cleft by a monstrous grin that subsided to normal proportions only when Barth faced about. "That's Buck. I'm taking him with me. I had forgotten he was with us."

Brashear's gate was ahead. Otherwise, Baxter would have liked to ascertain how the captain had come by the slave. *Rosie will find out,* he consoled himself. *I'll ask her.*

Buck took their horses and went to tie them up. Midway of the garrison's enclosure, Baxter pointed, saying, "There's Rosie now. Talkin' to them women over there. See her?"

Cautioning Baxter to move quietly, Barth sneaked up behind her and twirled her around. Before her astonishment vanished, he said, "I passed up some good roast turkey this morning just to eat with you. And when I got to your place, what did I find? The fireplace cold and that you had run off somewhere." Caught in the following web of merriment, the two women with whom Rosie had been conversing added their laughter. The engulfing gaiety had almost died when Rosie revived it. "Captain, if you're certain it's just eatin' you were interested in, you ain't missed anything. Mrs. Gilper and Mrs. Banford here are two of th' best cooks a body can find anywhere." Her unstinted praise of their particular ability involved a display of modest protest, which she bridged neatly. "Course they won't admit it, but it's th' truth!" A devilish spark darted into her already animated face as she said coyly, "But if you have anything else in your mind concernin' me, then you just forget about them two beauties and see me by m'self." Mrs. Banford threw up her hands and brought them quickly down. Her shrill, "He-he-he-he," spaced and repeated, caused nearby residenters to stop what they were doing and stare in her direction. Mrs. Gilper's laugh was more modulated but no less restrained. The others, Rosie abreast of their voicings, contributed their masculine appreciation. Though Mrs. Banford's tones yet soared, Mrs. Gilper's voice approached normalcy as she said, "Rosie, you shorely are th' one. Whutever gits into you to make you say sech things?"

Rosie's only answer was a continuance of the smile that still tarried from her previous laughter. As the smile eased slowly into mere pleasantness, she said to Barth, "Seriously if you're hungry, Mrs. Banford's man went out real early this mornin' an' aint' back yet. She was just sayin' 'fore you got here that she'd have to busy herself fixin' his breakfast." This was a hint that Mrs. Banford accepted readily. "Why, sure, Captain . . . uh . . ." She suddenly realized she was fumbling for a name she had never heard. "Rosie, I do declare! Here you got me askin' a man to eat my cookin' an' you ain't even told me who he is!"

Prefaced by Rosie's prompt apology, introductions were quickly accomplished. At their conclusion, Mrs. Banford and Mrs. Gilper excused themselves and went, as Mrs. Banford had said they must, about their business. But not before she had completed the invitation to Barth to eat with her husband as soon as he returned. Courtesy, rather than appetite, impelled Barth's thanks and acceptance. When they had gone, Rosie said, "I'm awful glad to see you, Captain. You'll never know how worried I was about you. Lucky for me it wasn't too long after I heard there was goin' to be a duel that Billy found out from Chate that Doctor Grainger had sent you word that it was off. Why in the world didn't you tell me about it? What was th' cause of it all?"

Barth looked at Billy Baxter and smiled. "Billy and I have been all through that on our way over here. He asked me enough questions to have kept me busy all morning answering them. Finally, I had to stop him, but I think he'd still like to ask some more." Baxter's expression did not traverse the assumption.

"Well, you might have at least told me there was goin' to be a duel," she said, feigning umbrage, which elicited a considerate, "I didn't want to upset you."

"Well, Captain Mercer, I do declare!" Abby had joined them, seemingly from out of nowhere. "I really should be peeved that you didn't come to my wedding. I thought you surely would be there and would kiss me." Jealously plowed Billy Baxter's forehead at her affected coquetry but he held his tongue. Rosie, however, took her daughter sharply to task. "Abigail Tindall Baxter! Aren't you ashamed of yourself? Talkin' like a brazen hussy! An' right in front of your husband too! It's a good thing it's Captain Mercer. He knows how addle-headed you can act!"

"Oh, Mamma, you all know I was just a-foolin'! Ain't no use of you a-makin' a big fuss over it."

"Abigail . . ." Rosie began, but she did not have to continue as Abby said contritely, "I'm sorry."

"There. That's better," her mother approved soothingly. But Abby wasn't ready to relinquish the position of attention she had achieved. Her lips opened ahead of Rosie's as she asked, "Captain Mercer, you will tell us all about the duel that nasty Doctor Grainger challenged you to, won't you? I declare, I'll just bust wide open if you don't." She casually avoided her mother's rebuking eyes.

"Oh, Abby, not you too!" Barth exclaimed in near genuine despair.

Before the puzzled Abby could say more, Rosie half-ordered her son-in-law, "Billy, you'd best get Abby inside. I'm beginning to think th' sun's getting' th' best of her." As her husband tugged her away, Abby continued to look back at them until her legs became crossed and she almost fell. Only then, did she turn her head.

"Looks like Billy Baxter will have to get Abby some blinders to keep her walking straight," Barth remarked.

"Ain't she turrible! Lord knows, I done my best with her." Rosie shook her head as she spoke.

"Oh. I wouldn't worry about her. She'll be all right, once she settles down."

"Ain't it about time she's doin' it? I thought when she got married, she'd get over some of them silly doin's of hers." Rosie's tone was despondent.

Barth chuckled. "She'll change. Just give her a little more time."

"I sure hope to th' Lord it's soon. Well, we might as well go see if Mr. Banford's got back. I know you must be starved." As they walked along, she told him of her intention to leave for Falls of the Ohio at Louisville the next day, if it could be arranged. Once again, he heard of her turning her place over to Jim Trench, and he asked as to the latter's whereabouts, learning that Jim had gone over to Dowdall's earlier. It was then he told her he was leaving Bullitt's Lick within the next hour. Her eyes followed the path of her feet for a few steps before she spoke again. "You know, Captain Mercer, it's strange but I didn't think about you going away. I knew that you would sometime, but, well it's hard for me to say what I'm thinkin'. When a body leaves a place, even if she knows she ain't never comin' back to it, she kinda feels like she's got ties there, if there's somebody still there that she liked real well." He reflected upon her words, believing he understood until she said, "I wonder, if things had been different, if I had been borned closer to your time, an' we had knowed each other . . ." She cut the birth cord of her fantasy. "Ain't that silly to be a-thinkin such as that? Still, it does put a body to wonderin'. You ever think about what it'd be like, if you wasn't to be you?" Her incongruity made her smile. "I mean, if you hadn't been borned in Virginia, but somewheres else, an' if your folks had been sorta poor like?" She became self-conscious. "Now you see where Abby gets her crazy doin's." They had reached the Banford's quarters, the boundary of Rosie's realm of ifs—but not of his. Time and chance, he thought, are the guideposts of life.

Mr. Banford was not there, and his wife worried. "I'm a-gettin' kinda con-sarned about 'im. But it might be he dropped over to Dowdall's 'fore comin' home. Still, I can't figger John a-doin' that 'fore he et." She shook her head. "Well, everything's ready, Cap'n Mercer. You just as well eat it, while it's warm."

The food, well-prepared though it was, didn't have that extra something that Rosie was able to impart to anything she cooked. However, he did relish, exceedingly, the cornbread and wild honey and would have eaten more of it had he been unmindful of the absent John Banford, who would undoubtedly be fam-ished whenever he did return. He arose, thanking Mrs. Banford and praising the meal. He winked slyly at Rosie, as he said, "Rosie told the truth when she said you were a good cook. It was the best breakfast I have ever eaten." After this, it was but a matter of minutes until he and Rosie had bidden her goodbye. They had proceeded only a few feet from her cabin, when he stopped short. "Rosie, I forgot all about him!" Noting her curious look, he told her about the Negro and then said, "I'll bet he didn't have a bite to eat before we left the storehouse." Moments later, Buck's grinning red lips advised him his solicitude had been needless. Abby and Billy joined them, and a short while later formal goodbyes had been exchanged. Goodbyes, whose continuity would not be broken until he rode out of the garrison gate. He expressed his intention to stop at Dowdall's and say farewell to Aaron Flinden.

"Brother Flinden's done left," said Rosie. "He was with Doctor Grainger an' them what we saw as we come here." In response to Barth's inquiry as to his well-being, she replied, "His body's all right but they says sometimes he just sets around like a bump on a log an' don' t say nothin'."

"It surely was too bad it had to happen to him," he observed. "Maybe he'll be better after he gets home." Secretly, Barth felt a sense of relief that Flinden had gone. His departure had spared him from what could have been somewhat of an ordeal. The last time they had seen each other, a few days ago, they had said good-bye, though they had both entertained the possibility of their meeting again before their final parting. "Life's permanent separations are akin to death itself. Those who part are but memories in one another's minds." Though he spoke the words, he had intended them for himself alone. Rosie's eyes moistened. Suddenly, she kissed him. "That will have to last you until you see your lady!" she said, and the tears that had threatened her were quickly dried by the humor of her words—words that reminded him of the time he had kissed her and expressed a similar thought.

"One thing, Captain. Be sure an' trim your whiskers 'fore you kisses her. They're like pine needles." Billy and Abby, not knowing what to make of Rosie's impulsive act, now ceased their wondering and shared fully in its mirthful aftermath.

As he laughed, Barth told Rosie, "You had better not charge Abby too severely. After all, she didn't ask me to kiss her." His own words suggested his ensuing observation. "Abby's just like you must have been when you were younger. She'll turn out to be just like you are now. You can be mighty proud of her."

This time, the tears could not be stopped. Rosie watched silently as he mounted his horse and leaned from the saddle to shake hands with Billy Baxter. The three waved at the departing horseman and the Negro who rode behind him until both had ridden out of the station.

CHAPTER 74

He stopped at Dowdall's just long enough to ascertain if there was a party planning to leave soon. There was none, though he learned that a group of some fifteen travelers had crossed on the ferry, headed for Bairdstown (Bards Town, the fellow had called it) about an hour before. With this information, he knew that unless the travelers were moving unusually fast, he and Buck would be able to catch up with them and would thus have company for a good portion of this day's ride. Leaving the station, they crossed the ford and were soon on the trace. As though the simple traversing of the stream accounted for the change, Barth imagined the air purer. As though the river divided the atmosphere itself, barring the evil from the good, vile feculence from that which was refined or which sought refinement. Bullitt's Lick was behind him forever. He gave his silent prayer of thanks to his Maker, that he had kept him safe, not forgetting to include the exercise of divine grace, which had decreed there would be no duel—a prayer he had made many times since Buck had brought Chate's message.

As for Buck, his god was his new master, at whose side he now rode. A master who had no bullwhip, who seldom raised his voice. There were but two threats to his serenity, two possible catastrophes that disturbed him. The first, fear that someone who knew him, or his former master, would see him and thus cause his return. The second, that they might be attacked by Indians. It was the latter apprehension that was foremost in his mind at this moment. The trace was narrowing up ahead where it cut through a particularly heavy forest growth. He edged his glance toward his master several times, before asking diffidently, "Massa Cap'n, yo' doan reckin' dey's none ob dem Injerns a-hidin' in dem trees up yondah—yo' doan, does yo'?"

Barth's immediate reaction was to have sport with him, only to have reconsideration reject the idea as involving a degree of cruelty. "I don't think so, Buck. However, you never can tell about Indians." Noting the concern his words implanted on the Black's features, he added, "I haven't heard of any being around here recently, but I'll keep a good, sharp eye out for them, just in case." He patted his rifle and his smile was a protective one. Buck's spirits buoyed with this reassurance.

Massa Cap'n ain' a-skeered, he take keer ob me. Bet dem Injerns ud be sahry dey bodder us, does dey try to, he thought. Still, there were but two of them, and there might be many Indians. And even now the trace was being shaded by the dense foliage above it. It gave him some comfort when he said, "Buck, let's gallop through here." But Buck's tight chest did not relax until daylight showed between the trees bordering the buffalo path. There would be many more scary places like the one they had just passed through. "Massa Cap'n, how long yo' figguh, 'foah us kotches up wi' dem udder fo'kses?"

"Not too long, I'd say."

"'Fo' de night kums, yo' reckin'?"

"Long before that."

"Dat's good." As he said the words, Buck began wondering if it was good after all. Suppose one of the travelers recognized him? Maybe the captain would not ride with them but would only trail the party. In any case, he decided that the Injerns held the most terror for him. At least the White folks wouldn't scalp him. He rubbed his free hand over his thick, kinky hair. "Whut dem Red devils wan' dis ole hahr fo'?" he said to himself, and then asked, "Massa Cap'n, how fah 'way is we fum dat place wha' yo' libs at?"

Barth studied briefly. "Somewhere around sixty miles from where we are now. What's the matter? You're not getting tired already, are you?"

"Uh-uh. Not dis niggah. I'se jes' axin'."

Barth's smile settled as the realization came to him that Buck was woefully in need of clothing. The hand-me-down linsey shirt and britches he was wearing were both dirty and torn. The folks at Harrodstown would wonder what kind of a person he was not to provide his slave decent raiment. He spoke to the Negro. "Buck, I'm going to have to find you some better clothes. I left some things over at Harrodstown, but they wouldn't fit you anyway. We'll have to see if we can't get you some before we get there. I can't have Mrs. Claycomb seeing you looking like this." He reinspected the apparel. "Buck, you haven't got any lice . . ." Buck's brows contorted at the word, causing Mercer to explain. "I mean, do you have any bugs? Do you ever itch?"

The Negro's face unlined. "Massa Cap'n, de onliest itchin' whut Ah does, is when Ah gits in de pizen iv'ry." They both laughed before Barth asked, "Think you could wear boots, if I can find a pair to fit those big feet of yours?"

"Does Ah hab ter, Massa Cap'n? Dey huhts ma foots. Ah doan hab ter, does Ah? Yo' ez jes' a-foolin' wif me, ain't yo'?"

"I'm not fooling, Buck. I can't have you going around barefooted."

Secretly, Buck was pleased. He belonged to real White folks now. But having shoes was one thing, wearing them was something else.

If master and slave had exchanged thoughts, both would have admitted to a few hunger pangs. Barth recalled the last time he had reached into his saddlebag and discovered the surprise that Rosie had put there. This time he was certain it was empty. He hadn't figured on eating until they reached Bairdstown. He reached down to search the inside of the bag. There might just happen to be some venison scrap in the corners. The second his fingers were inside, he knew. "Rosie, again!" he exclaimed, quickly adding, "But how? When?"

"Whut yo' means, Massa Cap'n?"

"Did you see anyone put this food in my saddlebag?"

"Dat lady whut giv yo' dat big kiss, she do it. She say, 'Doan tell de cap'n. Ah wants ter s'prize 'im'." Buck's complete observance brought a touch of warmth to Barth's cheeks.

"But, Buck, when did she put it there? She was with me all of the time I was at Brashear's."

"Not all ob de time, Massa Cap'n. She come out ob dat cabbin whar at dat lady feed yo'."

Now he remembered. Rosie had excused herself, while he was talking with Mrs. Banford.

"Dat lady sho' am nice. She sho' mak' a man a good womern, Massa Cap'n." Buck hadn't met Dracie. He had seen Rosie.

"She surely would, Buck." His thoughts were her words. "If I had been borned closer . . . If . . ." He repeated himself. "She surely would, Buck. She surely would."

They slowed their horses to a walk as they ate. After they had finished, Buck continued to suck on a wing bone until it lost its succulence. They rounded a bend in the trace. In the near distance were the bobbing figures of five travelers, riding on either side of a small, covered wagon.

It seemed to Buck he and his master would never overtake those up ahead. He wished devoutly they would never do so. In his imagination, he saw one of the party nudging another and whispering, "Ain't that Brent Fields's nigger? Looks just like 'im." And he could see the confirming nod of the listener's head as he too recognized him. The gap continued to narrow. Now they had caught up with the party. He hung his head in avoidance. He heard Mercer's greeting and he listened acutely for its acknowledgment. Actually, it was promptly rendered. But to his fearing ears, the sound seemed delayed in its coming. When he did receive it, his tenseness abated. The voice he heard, and the voices which quickly followed with their strange inflections, could not have come from the throats of anyone whom he knew or who might know him.

There were, as Barth had been correctly informed, fifteen persons in the group: five men, three women—one of whom held the reins with the other two seated alongside her—and seven children who were inside the wagon. The men, as earlier pictured, flanked the vehicle when the trace was wide enough for them to do so. When it was not, two rode in front and three in the rear. All were Dutch, headed for the Low Dutch Station settlement on the other side of Harlan's Station but bent on spending this night at Bairdstown. Their language both fascinated and amused Mercer, who often found difficulty in restraining what he masked as a friendly smile from becoming too flexed. Buck at once gravitated to the rear of the wagon and talked with the children within. Strange-sounding words proved no barrier to either the man of color, or to "dose leedle vuns" as the leader of the party had referred to them. Open hearts have no difficulty in conversing or in understanding one another. Their language was that first given to man before his tongue mastered speech.

In this good-natured company, time and distance sped by. They passed Cox's Station, and now Bairdstown was before them, a mile away. Soon they were there. The children scrambled out of the wagon and began chasing one another around and under it, despite the frantic pleas of the women and the stern reminders from the men of punishment to come. When obedience had been obtained, warm handshakes were pressed and Barth rode away, Buck following in respectful proximity. From behind them, the Dutch vocalized their wish for Godspeed, combined with the suggestion that they not continue to ride "til der dey gone down." Barth looked at the sun. The afternoon was almost half spent. He and Buck could reach Harbison Station before dusk. They paused at Chaplin Fork and watered their horses before fording the stream. When they renewed their journey, it was at a much faster pace than they had traveled with the Dutch company. Two hours later, they were at their stopping point, a small stockade with a few scattered cabins—Harbison Station.

They found the residenters most friendly. Harbison himself insisted that Barth sup with him and his family, promising to see that when Buck returned from tending the horses, he too would be fed. Barth wondered what his reception would have been had he told them that he was from Bullitt's Lick rather than Williamsburg. Fortunately, they had not been over-inquisitive when he mentioned he had been to Bullitt's Lick on business and was now returning to Harrodstown. It developed that he and Buck were the only travelers at the fort, information welcomed by him since there could be no threat to the good reputation for integrity enjoyed by Harbison along this part of the frontier. Nor would there be any cause for concern as to their personal safety while they slept.

Mrs. Harbison appeared disturbed as she came from her cabin. Her apologies began before she reached him. "I'm sorry to have to tell you this, Cap'n Mercer. I was plannin' on surprisin' you—but th' beef an' th' flour is all bad. They was all right th' last time I looked at them. Maybe you won't like what else we're havin'." He quickly assured her he would be most grateful to share in anything she might have prepared for her family. Soon thereafter, she called that supper was ready. His assurance, so readily given her earlier, would not have been as effusive, had he now expressed it. They were having opossums. It was a favorite of her husband, she explained. Barth's distaste for the dirty animal could not be overcome, no matter how great his effort to conceal it. However, he ate all that was served him, but his heart was not in the thanks he extended at the meal's conclusion.

To Buck, the "leavin's" that were given him, constituted a true repast. "Dey ain' nuthin' lak de possum. Dat's de bes' eatin' dey is," he rapturously told his master. To which Barth silently opined, *The good Lord makes different men with different tastes and provides for the satisfaction of each. Thus, waste is avoided.*

The night was clear and fairly cool and after he had overcome the protestations of his host that he sleep in his cabin, rather than in the open, Mercer and

Buck bedded down near Sagitta and the roan. But he soon moved farther away from the colored man. Though the possum had been eaten, its odor lingered on from the grease about Buck's mouth and hands. And though he moved once more, the disturbing smell still faintly pursued him. Somehow, it was difficult to envision the morrow and Dracie in such a repulsively scented atmosphere. He looked at the stars, hanging just above him like countless brilliants suspended in elaborate profusion from a covering of blackest velvet. The peace of the night stole over him and weighed softly upon his eyelids. On his left, Buck was sleeping the sleep of the contented, a greasy smile upon his placid countenance.

They awoke with the first rays of the breaking day and found the residenters likewise rousing. Breakfast consisted of heaped helpings of hominy and little else, but it was tasty and satisfying. While Barth conversed with some of the settlers, Buck busied himself grooming the horses, carefully inspecting their hooves in the process. His master came up just as he finished the chore. Rubbing his cheeks as he walked toward him, he said, "Buck, I expect I'd better get rid of these whiskers." There was a reflective pause. "And you'd better do the same thing. We want to look our best when we get to Harrodstown." Barth ran his finger lightly over the edge of his knife. "It could be a little sharper," he observed.

"Doan yo' bodder yo'sef 'bout dat, Massa Cap'n. Ah does it fo' yo'. Den Ah takes keer ob m'sef." Buck's wish was near-insistence, inducing his master's complaisance. The Negro honed the blade of the knife on a leather saddlestrap. When he was satisfied as to its keenness, he procured a small lump of clay, mixing it with spring water until he achieved a thin, paste-like consistency. Catching Mercer's apprehensive glance, he grinned. "Massa Cap'n, dis heah'll warsh righ' off—doan trubble yo' haid 'bout dat."

It was the coolest shave Barth had ever experienced, and even the tough stubble on his chin had yielded easily to the blade. With the cold rinsing, there came an invigorating feeling that lasted until well after the last chilled drop had dried on his features.

While Buck had been shaving him, Barth was acutely reminded of the Negro's need for clothing. What was not tattered was almost skin-thin, and in what might prove to be the most embarrassing places. The garments reeked of stale sweat. No wonder, he thought, that stinking possum didn't bother him. He decided to do something about it immediately. He waited patiently while Buck cropped his own whiskers, marveling at the seemingly reckless abandon with which he successfully whisked the large cutting edge under his gaping nostrils and about the corners of his big lips. Then he directed him to come with him.

The search was a brief one. The hum of a spinning wheel across the compound focused his eyes upon the most likely place to make inquiry. Minutes later, he had purchased a good shirt and a well-woven pair of britches for five pounds, six shillings. Buck had protested. "Massa Cap'n, deys ter fine fo' dis niggah." However, it didn't take him long to find a place of concealment and make the change from the old to the new. But he didn't discard his former clothing. "I jes' save dese. I kin wah 'em when we gits ter yo' place, Massa Cap'n." Barth made him drop the things where he stood. Laughingly, he suggested to the woman from whom he had purchased the new articles, "Better put a log on them til you can arrange to burn them. They're strong enough to get up and walk around by themselves." As they left, Buck looked back at the heap of soiled rags. He had worn them a long time. It was like leaving a part of himself.

Barth had paid his respects to the Harbisons and a few of the others whom he had met and was now ready to resume his way. He judged the time to be about two hours past sunup. He should be in Harrodstown easily by noon. As he rode toward the gate, he pulled to one side to permit the passage of a party of newcomers. They were past him when he caught snatches of what one of them was saying. "Over near Brashear's Station, yesterday morning . . . Indians fired on three men . . . two wounded . . . one feller killed and scalped." He reined up, listening acutely. "Name was Banford—John Banford, I think it was. Any you all know 'im? There was s'posed to be about seven or eight Indians, from what I heard."

It would have been a long time, had he waited to meet John Banford. He pictured the sorrow that lived among the good people at Brashear's on the evil side of Salt River.

It had taken them no more than an hour and a half to cover the ten miles from Harbison to Harlan's Station. Another ten miles, perhaps a little less, and they would be there! The thought of Dracie—embracing and kissing her—spread throughout his entire being, stirring his latent desire for her, a desire which, though it rested, never fully slumbered.

But for the incident that now occurred, he would have ridden through the settlement without even stopping to exchange the customary pleasantries. The sight of two men in violent dispute would not have served to distract him. Such public quarrels were frequent on the frontier, and he was ever mindful of the wise man's admonition in the Bible. "He that passeth by, and meddleth with strife belonging not to him, is like one that taketh a dog by the ears." He had no intention of violating the judgment rule, and he would not have drawn on Sagitta's reins, had he not heard one of the adventurers hotly exclaim, "I tell you, this here rifle is mine! A little feller, on a ole gray mule 'bout th' color of that horse there—" He indicated Sagitta. "—sold it to me two days back! I paid 'im my good money for it and it's mine!"

An equally angry throat rasped the words, "You're a damned liar, that's what you are! I leaned that rifle against th' side of Matt Sissons's cabin, an' when I come out it was gone. Somebody took it and since you got it now, it musta been you what stole it—you damned thief, you!"

"Better be damn careful who you're callin' a thief, damn your soul to hell. There ain't no markin's on this here gun. How th' hell can you be so damn sure it's your'n?"

"I'd know that gun if I felt it with m' eyes shut plumb tight. I can tell you how it fires—you fired it yet?"

"Ain't had no need to 'fore now. But I'm aimin' to find out real quick!" He raised the rifle and cocked it. "Now, you git on away from here or I'll put a ball through your in'ards!"

Buck watched in tension-filled consternation as his master leaped from his horse and strode between the near combatants. *Whut in de worl' ez Massa Cap'n a-doin'? Dat ain' none ob his bizness! He git hisse'f kilt! Jes' soon's Ah gits me uh kine massa, Ah loses im!* The thoughts reeled through his distraught brain.

So surprised were the two men, they nearly forgot their argument. Barth used the disrupted interval to its best advantage, gaining their complete attention. However, he spoke only to the one who claimed to have purchased the weapon two days before. "I suggest that you fire the rifle, not at this man, who I think is its rightful owner, but at that knot in the trunk of that oak tree across the road there. I think you'll find that it does shoot high and to the right, like this fellow claims it does."

The man eyed him suspiciously. "This here ain't none of your consarn. What're you buttin' in it for?"

"Just because I happen to know something about the man I heard you say sold the rifle to you. He's a rogue and a rascal."

"Seemed like a right nice little feller to me. Said he was comin' from th' Tennessee country, down in Carolina."

"That sounds just like him," Barth said. "The truth is, he was running away from Bullitt's Lick. There's a man over there who would have killed him if he could have got his hands on him."

"That little feller?"

"He fooled me too. Now, to prove it's the same man, that mule of his was blind in one eye and always stood on three legs. You noticed that, didn't you?" There was a reluctant confirmation of his assertion and he continued. "So that there can be absolutely no doubt about the matter, his name is John Littelby, and when he says 'you,' he squinches up his nose. You remember him doing that?"

"That's him all right. But that don't prove he stole this here rifle."

"If you knew him, it would. But since you don't, why don't you see if you can fire it accurately? Then, let this other fellow, who claims it's his, shoot it."

"How 'bout him shootin' first?"

"I think that's fair enough." Barth turned to the claimant of the weapon. "Any objection to that?"

"None a-tall," came the ready response. The rifle immediately changed hands, still cocked, as anger had readied it. There was a precursory sighting before the trigger was pulled and the powder flashed. The lead hit the knot, chewin' a path as it angled free of the tree's hardened deformity. Barth had not waited for the claimant to fire but walked to his horse and remounted. As the now dubious purchaser stroked the ramrod in the barrel, Barth said to both men, "You'll find that I've told you the truth. That rifle belongs to the man who just shot it." He loosed the reins and Sagitta moved off. Buck followed his master but lagged behind, looking back to see the conclusion of the matter. Shortly, he heard the rifle fire and saw the one who fired it cross the road and finger the spot where the bullet had hit. It was high and on the right side of the tree. He could not see the man's puzzled expression, nor hear him exclaim bewilderedly before turning and shaking hands with the other. "Damned if that feller ain't right. I aimed at that knot, dead center. I couldn't have missed it, bein' that close."

So, Johnny had come this way. How many more disgruntled settlers would he leave in his wake, before reaching whatever destination he had determined upon? Barth's musing veered to the recondite. History would never record the doings of the countless Littelbys who moved in their devious ways among the frontier peoples. Nor would there be any mention of the seamy life at Bullitt's Lick. There would be no revealing picture of the lusts and crude passions of the brawling adventurers who settled the wildernesses of America and tamed its new boundaries. All would be portrayed as heroes, and their women heroines, all virtuous and courageous, God-fearing and devout, motivated by lofty ideals. So, they would be depicted for posterity. No base quality of the settlers would appear in print. He thought upon the contemporary histories he had read—the noble White man . . . the treacherous murdering savage. Nowhere was it mentioned that the settlers and adventurers merely followed the continuous cycle of man, wherein the rich strive to increase their riches and the poor man to better his lot, all without any conception as to the final total of their individual efforts. Patriotism, of which he had so widely heard, was but imaginative preaching. Men were deemed patriots if it so happened that they harbored the same desires or were possessed of kindred fears. And the consequent union of such persons, selfish in its origin and in its perpetuation, was but a natural, logical affinity. Still, he conceded, that is how nations are formed. Maybe the present confederation of the Colonies would endure as Ben Franklin and Thomas Jefferson and all the other leaders avowed it would. That is, Mercer thought soberly, if the selfishness involved does not become a crown of selfishness.

"Massa Cap'n, how fah ez we got ter go fo' we get dar?" Buck's upper lip was a cradle of sweaty droplets. He did not wait for an answer, but gave his reason for the question. "Dese heah new clo's ez pow'ful wahm. I wish't eh had dem whut we done lef' back yondah. Dem holes use ter 'low de aih ter git 'ter m' hide."

Barth's lips curled as his absorption eased. "You look a lot better, Buck, and I want you to make a good impression on Mrs. Claycomb. I'm only sorry I was not able to find any boots for you."

Buck resolved to keep his mouth shut. It could have been worse. His feet weren't meant to wear shoes. Even moccasins were uncomfortable. He accepted slavery as being his lot, but he wanted his feet to be free. *Ah wondah. Does we git ter Vaginny, does Ah hab ter kiver m' foots?* These thoughts kept him silent, as he and his master rode along.

They could not be more than a few miles from Harrodstown. Barth's greeting to those whom he met in passing became increasingly cordial. And when he glimpsed the first outlying cabin, an aesthetic tremor swirled through him, urged by the spontaneous alliance of impatience and exaltation. For an instant, the exhilarated sensation danced through his brain. Then his rein hand lifted and

Sagitta shot north, his hooves beating upon the well-traveled way, giving meter to his master's thoughts. *Dracie is waiting. Dracie is waiting. Waiting for me. Waiting for me!*

The roan would have moved with Sagitta, but Buck was taken by complete surprise at Mercer's unshared decision to increase the roan's flanks. His master was a hundred yards ahead of him—an interval that remained constant until the gray was pulled up in front of a cabin on the right side of the road.

Barth came out of the house just in time for Buck to hear him exclaim, "She's not here. She's over at the fort!" He wheeled the roan to coincide with Sagitta's movement, then trailed his prepossessed master toward the station. On the way, understanding seeped through his confusion. *He lookin' fo' dat womern! Dat why he ride so fas'!*

Their progress slowed to little more than a walk long before they neared the gate. It seemed that most everyone in the community was along the way. either coming from or going to the garrison. Barth managed to curb the reckless inclination to spur his mount through the slow-moving settlers, but his sharp words to the Negro clearly conveyed his rising impatience. At last, they were inside the stockade. He dismounted quickly and handed the reins to Buck, directing him to the place where the horses were to be hitched and where the Black was to wait for him.

CHAPTER 75

Though he must have searched twenty feminine forms and faces, he spied Lucy Harmon before he realized that the woman who stood beside her, with her head turned in conversation, was the one whom he sought so ardently. She turned her head and her eyes met his. Before her own eager feet had taken two steps, he had her in his arms, sweeping her from the ground so that their lips might meet the more easily. There was just the one kiss but its intensity and duration were such as to excite a tittering among the women in the impromptu audience—laughter that began to lose its restrained character as the lips prolonged their engagement. But the closed eyes of the lovers did not see the wagging mouths nor did their ears hear the buzzing sound of the swelling undertones of those who watched the amorous display.

It was Lucy who felt the embarrassment that should have been theirs and who tugged at his sleeve and called to them, as discreetly as was possible under the circumstances, all the while explaining in asides that they were to be married soon. Her persistent efforts finally succeeded, though Barth kissed the tip of Dracie's nose as he lowered her to earth. Then the laughter of the onlookers broke its bonds and made them acutely aware that their reunion had provided public entertainment. But the aftermath was merciful in its brevity. Other than one old settler's, "It sure make a feller wish he was young again," the episode was permitted to close without further emphasis. As though desiring to clear the scene of its principal actors, Lucy suggested tactfully to Dracie and Barth that the three seek a less crowded place for, as she put it, their conversation. The humor of the incident came upon them simultaneously, and they laughed as they moved away.

When they stopped, Dracie was not yet entirely free of her enthrallment at Barth's return, and her words, uttered seriously, reflected her abstraction. "Barth, you remember Lucy, don't you?"

"Come down from the clouds, Dracie. Of course he remembers me," Lucy said laughingly. "Anyway, it's a bit late for you to ask. You should have done that when he first came up to us."

Dracie's brows released the vertical crease between them, as the jest became apparent. "What would you have done, Lucy?" she asked mockingly.

"Just what you did, honey. But I doubt that I could have held my kiss as long as you did."

All three laughed for a moment, before Dracie said, "Oh, Barth! Let me look at your face!"

He was perplexed as to her purpose, until she said, "Why, it's all healed! And I do believe there won't be any scar, just a tiny one at most. Is it still sore, dearest?" Upon his assurance to the contrary, she changed her thought. "Dearest, it's wonderful that you came today. Reverend Wyeth told me this morning that he was going to leave Monday to visit the folks at Bryan Station and Lexington and all through there. He said he'd be gone a few weeks. Just think! If you hadn't gotten here before he left, we would have had to wait all that time until he returned! Isn't it wonderful? Now, we can be married tomorrow, on the Sabbath. Somehow, I don't know why, getting married on a Sunday would seem to make a marriage ceremony even holier than on a weekday. Don't you agree, dearest?"

He kissed her for his answer. As she talked, he had observed the vitality of her happiness. It was in her eyes, in her cheeks, in her lips, even in her expressive hands, whose supple fingers at times appeared to be waltzing figures.

Sudden inspiration rose to her lips. "Oh, Barth, dearest. Let's go see Reverend Wyeth right now!" A teasing smile engaged her mouth, as she said, "I want to prove to him that you really exist and are as wonderful as I have told him you are."

She caught his arm and they had taken a step before Lucy could exclaim, "Dracie, perhaps I better ask you what you asked Barth a moment ago—do you remember me?"

"Oh my goodness, Lucy! I forgot you were even here! I'm terribly sorry, and I hope you'll forgive me. You do understand, though, don't you?"

"Of course, I understand, honey. I was just trying to be witty. Actually, I should have left you two to yourselves, as soon as Barth met us."

"Don't say such a silly thing. You know I want you with us!" She added impishly, "Just now at least." They laughed as they went to find the minister.

Dracie had been under Buck's appraising eye from where he obediently waited near Sagitta and the roan. He was close enough that his perspective was not greatly affected, and he regarded her carefully before he formed his first opinion of his mistress-to-be. She putty—puttier dan dat Miz Rosie, but she skinnier. Wondah why Massa Cap'n he doan pick hisse'f a womern whut hab mo' on de bones. Dey wuks de bes', an' dey's mo' ob dem ter git hole ob. He shook his head with his thoughts, then said to himself, "Dat Massa Cap'n bizness. Ah reckin dat's jes' de diffrunce 'twixt de niggahs an' de White mens. But, Ah b'leeves we smahtah dan dem 'bout dat." His inquiring gaze continued until its objective became lost in the milling numbers across the way.

Barth found Reverend Wyeth to be a most engaging person, possessing a deft, dry wit. But the smiles that relayed themselves about the yielding points of the minister's countenance were scholarly, balanced by gray eyes that recognized laughter only for laughter's time. He was friendly in the correct fashion of his calling, as befitted one who wished to share with others his companionship with God. He admitted, quite frankly, his pleasure at the prospect of joining two members of his faith in holy wedlock and expressed his desire just as candidly that their union would be "fructiferous." As the meaning of the word became clear to her, Dracie's eyelids lowered, as though seeking to shade her burning cheeks. Her self-consciousness was but briefly endured, however, as Reverend Wyeth invited the conclusion of the informal audience saying, "I know you two must have much to tell each other. But before you go, I desire to remind you that it would be well that you prepare yourselves for Holy Communion in the morning before the ceremony." The reappearance of Lucy Harmon, who had thoughtfully absented herself earlier, terminated the discussion on that admonitory note. Lucy joined with Dracie and Barth in making a polite withdrawal from the minister's presence.

With Barth between them, his arms locked in theirs, the three proceeded toward the gate. Suddenly, he whisked them obliquely about, saying, "There's something I almost forgot. I have a surprise for Dracie." Despite their insistent demands, he refused to satisfy their curiosity until they approached Buck and the horses. The Negro's evident elation made his master's reference certain as he asked, "Well, how do you like him? And the roan. Isn't he a beauty?"

Dracie was overwhelmed. "Dearest, where in the world did you get them?" Before he could answer, she spoke to the Negro. "What is your name?"

"Dey calls me Buck, ma'am. I'se Massa Cap'n's niggah. He sho ez bin pow'ful good ter me."

"Your master is good to everyone, Buck," she said, conveying her sincerity to Barth by an adoring glance.

"Ah knows dat ter be de truf, ma'am. I'se uh lucky niggah. I sho ez."

She turned her attention to the roan, patting and stroking the animal's forehead. "He's a beautiful creature, isn't he, Lucy?"

Her friend ceased her own petting of Sagitta to agree. "As pretty as any I have ever seen." She moved to the roan and ran her fingers slightly through its silky mane.

Dracie and Barth were alongside her, indulging in silent admiration of the beautifully colored steed, when Dracie felt a gentle touching of her back. She turned to discover Sagitta in the act of nudging her. She embraced the horse's head, pressing her cheek to that of the animal, saying endearingly, "You didn't think I had forgotten you, did you, Sagitta? Why, you're still the prettiest, sweetest horse that ever lived." Her companions laughed at the confidential tone of her conversation and at the kiss she bestowed upon the side of the gray's face. She looked up to observe, "Dearest, I do believe he's jealous."

Buck thought happily, Eny womern whut lub hosses de way she do, she sart'in ter be kine ter Black fo'ks. Thus he sealed his wholehearted acceptance of his new mistress.

As if by some magical movement, the compound appeared almost bare. The cause of its apparent desertion did not become evident until their nostrils caught the heavy aroma of cooking. Lucy was the first to voice the significance. "Why, everyone has gone to dinner! No wonder there are so few people about. I never thought about it being noontime. You all must be' hungry, particularly Barth." She addressed him directly. "You must be famished."

He assured her, and truthfully so, that he had given no thought to food nor the hour. Shielding his eyes from the sun, he sought its position, then remarked, "Buck and I must have reached here earlier than I had calculated. It's just at noon now." The reference to the Negro brought him to mind, and Barth signaled him to follow them with the horses.

Mr. and Mrs. Harmon were waiting outside their door and greeted them most warmly. They expressed their pleasure at Barth's unexpected presence and ushered them inside. The table was already set for four, and Mrs. Harmon quickly added another place for Barth. Bidding them to be seated, she refused all offers of assistance from Lucy and Dracie and insisted on serving everyone before she herself would consent to take her seat.

The mealtime conversation pursued the usual pattern of mixed company. For a while, words were exchanged generally, but gradually the women gave their attention to one another's thoughts and the men to that which was of masculine interest. Mr. Harmon had heard the report of John Banford's death, though he did not call him by name, referring to him as "a man over near Brashear's Station." Barth started to relate his acquaintance with Mrs. Banford, but decided not to when he considered the fearful imaginings Dracie might entertain should she be listening. Before she would be through, she would picture him as having been with Banford and as having narrowly escaped his fate. He was doubly glad he had restrained himself when he noted that she was casting sly glances toward him before resuming her part in the feminine discourse. She had seemingly restored her full thought to something Lucy was then discussing. Mr. Harmon meanwhile had continued talking, unaware of his listener's digression. His face became deeply serious. "I tell you, Captain Mercer, I don't like it. Some of these settlers—not at Harrodstown you understand—Jim Harrod wouldn't stand for it one minute. But some of the others up from here are no better than the savages themselves. And it has happened more than once. I can tell you that too." Barth's straying attention returned as he pondered what Harmon was leading to. "Would you believe it were I to tell you, that just the other day, up beyond McAfee's, they killed a young Indian boy and then cut his body up and fed it to the hogs? Just think of that? Have you ever heard of anything so barbarous? I'm not forgetting how the savages torture their captives but they're uncivilized and that's more or less to be expected of them. But White men doing such a thing and to a young boy at that! It's no wonder that fellow was killed over at Brashear's. And it's my guess that he won't be the last either. You can bet the Indians know what happened to that boy. I'll tell you what I've about decided, though I've kept it to myself. I'm going to take Martha—" He nodded toward his wife. "—and Lucy, and we're headin' back to Virginia. We might be able to leave with you and Dracie, if you don't mind company. It's one thing to kill an Indian, but when he's dead, he's just like all dead people, Red or White, and his body is due the same respect that civilized people give to their dead."

Barth looked hastily toward Dracie. Apparently, she had not heard any of Harmon's words. The women had left the table and were looking at some newly made quilts. Dracie appeared to be in rapt concentration as she examined them. To forestall any further chance she might overhear them, he quietly indicated his concern to Mr. Harmon and the subject was discretely changed. However, his apprehension had made him restless, and he welcomed the lull in the ladies' conversation and Mrs. Harmon's sage observance. "I declare, we've been down right shameful, taking all of Dracie's attention." As if to remedy her unintentional oversight, she added, "Now, Dracie, you and Captain Mercer get off to yourselves." When Dracie made the customary gesture of offering to help clear the table, or to otherwise set the room in after-dinner order, she firmly refused. "You two run along! Lucy and I will tend to things."

Dracie's hand squeezed Barth's as they walked to the door. Reaching there, he paused. "Mrs. Harmon, I wonder if I might ask a favor of you."

"Why, of course, you may. What is it you want?"

"My boy, Buck, is probably a little hungry by now. Would you be able to scrape up something for him? I'll take it to him before Dracie and I go."

"Of course, of course. I'll be glad to feed him. I'm glad you remembered him. It had slipped my mind that he was outside. Otherwise, I would have fed him when the rest of us were eating."

"You sure you won't mind?" he asked.

"Not at all. Now you all just forget about things and have a good time." Her motherly instinct prompted her to add, "Stay close to the settlement, and don't stay away too long. It would worry me to death if anything happened to either of you."

"We won't be long, and thanks for everything." Though Barth said the words, Dracie's appreciative countenance made it clear he spoke for her also.

As they came outside, Barth experienced momentary concern. The horses were gone and Buck was nowhere to be seen. Bidding Dracie wait for him, he scanned the road in all directions. He was about to go back inside and ask Mr. Harmon for the use of his horse to search for the Negro when he heard his voice coming seemingly from behind the cabin. As he turned the corner of the dwelling, there was Buck, conversing with his equine charges. Barth assumed sternness. "Buck, you no 'count rascal. What are you doing back here, instead of out front where I left you?"

The Negro sensed his master's acting and grinned as he replied, "Massa Cap'n, dem horses wuz pow'ful hot in dat sun." He waited for the ensuing smile that drew Mercer out of his feigned character before adding, "An' ole Buck, he pow'ful hot wiv all dese heah new clo's on 'im. We's jes' 'laxin lak in de shade."

Barth's smile widened to fullness. "Buck, I'm afraid I'm spoiling you. You used to be a good, hard-working boy. I'm letting you get lazy. Now get up and bring the horses around front. Mrs. Harmon is going to give you something to eat. I think you'll like what she'll bring you."

Buck's eyes shone. "Yo' means mo' possum, Massa Cap'n'?"

Mercer's laugh was almost a roar. "Good heavens, no. It's not possum. Is that all you like to eat?"

"Nassa, Massa Cap'n. Ah laks ever kine ob eatin' whut dey is. But Ah laks possum de bes' ob all."

Barth was still chuckling when he returned to where Dracie stood talking with Lucy and Mrs. Harmon. When he had explained his amusement to them, their laughter recharged his own dying mirth, enlarging his former enjoyment of the Negro's humorous expression. Lingering smiles continued to bathe his listeners' features, as he lifted Dracie to Sagitta's saddle. He mounted the roan and after Mrs. Harmon had repeated her solicitous admonition, and he had responded with his assurance of intended care, he followed Dracie's lead, as she wheeled Sagitta about and rode leisurely away.

She did not wait long to increase the gait, but he sensed the coming change of pace, breaking the roan into a gentle lope the instant her hand eased on Sagitta's reins. The flowing motion of their mounts had its counterpart within the breasts of the riders—a resurgence that had found its start when his firm hands first raised her from the ground. A minute later, and they were nearing the entrance to the winding path between some berry bushes. Again, their hands moved almost simultaneously, as they drew sharply upon their reins. They prac-ticed the same procedure they had observed upon their last visit to their trysting place, dismounting and leading the horses through the closely bordering briars. His words were the first spoken. "Remember how full of berries these bushes were the last time?"

She nodded and added to his remembrance. "And how big they were! And so luscious! To look at these bushes now and the few scattered little berries, it's hard to believe we didn't just imagine it, isn't it? My, but what a lot of jelly and preserves they would have made!"

"And wine and brandy," he laughingly rejoined.

They had reached the clearing, and the path that ran to her Eden. As they neared the arbor, she exclaimed, gleefully, "Dearest, look at that! The trumpet vines are blooming! Look how the flowers are hanging, just like gaily colored bells, resting from their pealing. Oh, dearest, have you ever seen anything so beautiful? I know that people would think we are foolish, but wouldn't it be wonderful if we could be married here? The wedding party could form in the clearing and the procession would pass through this archway. Then the ceremony would be performed on the slope above the valley and . . ." She glanced at him and the slight deviation permitted reality, in the form of self-consciousness, to strain her cheeks and destroy her fanciful dreaming. "You must think me silly too, dearest, but it would be lovely, even though I know it could never happen." Her faint smile carried the suggestion of embarrassment.

He had dreamed with her, though all the while reason remained in the near background, slowly shaking her head forbiddingly, lest he himself be enticed into the ethereal flight. But his pragmatic bonds were not so tightly drawn that he could not understand and appreciate her wondrous sojourning in the land of make believe. And when he saw that her beautiful vision had flown and heard her justify its brief existence, when he read in her features the wistful look of the awakened dreamer, he drew her to him and pressed his mouth upon her ear, kissing it tenderly, as he whispered, "It would be wonderful, dear. It would be truly wonderful."

His warm breath bathing her ear, the softness of his voice, the delicate touch of his lips brought a racing thrill, merging her senses so that they cried to her passion that it satisfy itself and cease its dominion over them.

It was the roan's restlessness that broke their embrace. "Dearest, hurry and tether the horses." Her thickened words came as a deepened sigh. She gave no thought to the bower overhead as they walked the length of its cover. When they emerged, she sought the shade of the familiar maple and reclined herself. Not a word had been spoken.

When he returned, he lay down beside her, the weight of his chest and shoulders upon his elbows. his body at a slight angle to hers. Thus positioned, her face was beneath his own. A wisp of her auburn hair hung above her forehead and fluttered as he blew playfully upon it. She gazed up at him until his fascination with the reddish brown tendril had ended and he lowered his head. His eyes caressed her features, coming to rest upon her own eyes. How changeable is their color, he thought. Now it is a dark, silken green. Earlier, her eyes were almost a light blue.

"What are you thinking about, dearest?" she asked.

He smiled and, dropping his head, kissed the side of her neck, where it began its ascent from her shoulders. Instantly, her lips found his in savage fashion and they were one.

They rested contentedly now, her head upon his encircling arm, the pounding of their hearts gradually diminishing. The auburn tendril, thoroughly dampened, had lost its former mischievous sprightliness.

She turned her head. "Dearest, do you have the same contented feeling I have? Like you were gliding over the smoothest water with the most gentle of all breezes filling the sail? That's the way I feel at this moment." He was listening to her but did not answer, an omission she construed as evidencing his tacit agreement. Thus believing, she went on. "Honestly, the whole time we were at Lucy's, I was sneaking glances at you. I had the strongest desire to kiss you and have you hold me close."

He heard her as her pleasant voice continued, but it was the rhythmic tone, coming as soft strains of music, rather than her words, that his ears received. His afterthoughts were of a different nature, but none the less pleasing to his soul. For the first time in all their intimacies, there was no evil complex—the feeling he had sinned by having lain with her. How foolish I have been, he thought, to have let myself be plagued by a guilt that actually never had the right to assert itself! How could my mind have entertained such baseless misgivings? How could I have sought so unceasingly to imply fault where none existed? Tomorrow Dracie and I will satisfy the requirements of society and religion, but the ceremony will only be the sanctioning of a marriage that has already been consummated when we professed our love for each other, before our eager bodies had ever shared their first supreme delight. And to think I permitted that first sharing and all the rest to be marred by an inane searching for a wrong that wasn't there. What possible origin could there have been for such a feeling? Did it have its source in the pounded theory that evil is born with man and is ever hovering in his thoughts and deeds or in their formation? God does not countenance evil. How then could it be accorded this advantage over good? Some unbalanced zealot, some early actor in man's continuous presumptive interpretation of God's will and word had formulated this warped theory, and his successors had embraced it as genuine. Each passing year had added to its authority, each later century had strengthened its erroneous teaching until it had become firm doctrine. Why had men followed so blindly? Why did they continue to do so? Since it is written that good will ultimately triumph over evil, it must be that man is inherently good and that evil does not come from within the mind, but from without.

At long last, peace had come to his conscience. All of his self-induced tribulations were banished forever. No more would he wonder whether he wronged the memory of the dead Gabe Claycomb by his fleshly acts with his widow. More important, no more would he imagine the violation of the law of his God. The mind and the body are but the agents of the soul, he reasoned, and only the soul survives. If its earthly intentions and desires be righteous, how then can evil be imputed to that which it orders to be done? In the day of judgment, the soul, not the dust of the body, must answer to its Maker.

He became aware that Dracie was no longer talking, and he wondered how long she had been silent. Before he could offer an apology, she said softly, "Dearest, I don't believe I have seen your face so relaxed. Somehow, you seem different. It was probably just my imagination, but before today it always seemed that when it was over, you would drift far away from me, and I would lose the feeling of being close to you. But today I didn't feel that way at all. I can't explain the feeling, but it's there just the same. After our desire had been satisfied, you were always so quiet and I did all of the talking. But yet, you were quiet this time too. I talked but I didn't feel shut off as I did all those other times. Maybe it's just that I know that after tomorrow, we'll be together the rest of our lives. Maybe that's why I felt differently today."

He kissed her, marveling at the gift of intuition God bestows upon all women. She returned the kiss and it drew fire—fire that would have enveloped them had there not come to her mind the concern of Mrs. Harmon. She broke their embrace. "Dearest, we mustn't. Lucy's mother will be worried sick if we stay away much longer. Do you have any idea of what time it might be, of how long we've been gone?"

"Probably about an hour, not much longer than that at the most."

"Are you sure, dearest? It seems like we've been here a long time."

"That's because we were so thoroughly occupied." He smiled with his implication. "It always seems longer than it actually is."

Their lips met once more but the kiss was governed. He helped her to her feet and then went after the horses. Her eyes followed him as he secured the mounts and returned to her side. Before they turned to enter the arbored way, they took a last glimpse of the scene she loved so dearly. "Oh, Barth, dearest, isn't it beautiful? It's so peaceful here. We must come back before we leave Harrodstown. I want to carry this picture away with me to treasure always. Do you remember what I named it?"

"Your Valley of Eden." His words were pensive. "It is like Eden, before nakedness caused shame."

"How beautifully you define it, dearest! I have been trying to find words to describe it, but only one thought comes to me——undefiled."

"There could be no better description," he said seriously.

She kissed him and they turned their faces homeward.

CHAPTER 76

"Land sakes alive, but I'm glad to see you two back safe and sound. I was beginning to worry about you all." Mrs. Harmon smoothed her hair with her hand, her relieved smile impressing upon them the sincerity of her words.

"What the devil won't have, no man would surely want," Barth said impishly.

"Oh, Captain Mercer! Don't ever say such a thing!"

Lucy and Dracie laughed at the awed tone of the older woman's voice.

"Mother's a most superstitious person, Barth. She must have Irish blood in her somewhere."

Mrs. Harmon brushed aside her daughter's teasing.

"Just the same, I don't see any sense inviting trouble to come and sit on your doorstep."

Lucy laughed. "Well, at least you know that everyone is all right now and you can calm yourself. You've been fidgety ever since they left."

Dracie put her arms around Mrs. Harmon in genuine affection. "You shouldn't have worried so. You shouldn't have let yourself become upset over us."

"Don't you all pay no mind to what Lucy says." She glanced sideways at her daughter before adding, "You know how she exaggerates things—just like her father."

Her remark served to make Barth aware of Mr. Harmon's absence. He made his question pertinent by observing good-naturedly. "Now. Mrs. Harmon, you shouldn't say that about your husband with him not here to defend himself."

"Oh, my lands! I clean forgot! Tom Morey stopped by to see you, and he and Carter—that's Mr. Harmon—went to the fort." Her memory insisted upon her adding, "I forgot for a moment you knew my husband's first name from when you were here before. Anyway, Tom came just after you and Dracie had gone, said he'd see you later on. He asked for you in a queer way, though—wanted to know if the kissing man was here. What on earth could he have meant by that?"

The resultant gale of laughter reduced her to a state of hopeless perplexity. Before explanation could be given, Dracie suggested, "Barth, dearest, why don't you go on over to the garrison? Maybe Mr. Morey is still there. I know how much he thinks of you and I know you like him." Her consideration of him was not without restriction, however, as she added, "But don't stay too long, dearest."

He sought to be equally considerate, negating any urgency of seeing Morey immediately, but she would not hear of his staying. Bowing to her insistence, he asked Lucy, "Where's that rascal, Buck? He should be here now, taking care of the horses."

Mrs. Harmon answered him, rather than her daughter. "Captain, I imagine you'll find him out back somewhere. He really seemed to enjoy my cooking. Judging from his appetite, I'm afraid you're going to have to work him mighty hard to make any profit out of his keep."

Barth smiled and excused himself.

True to her prediction, he found the Negro stretched out upon the ground, a motionless figure, whose only movement was the twitching of a big, callused toe as it sought to avoid the persistent annoyance of a marauding bluefly.

"Buck, you worthless nigger. Don't you do anything but sleep when I'm not around?"

The sharply uttered words brought Buck scurrying to his feet. Surprise did not harness his grin, nor slow his ready excuse. "Massa Cap'n, Ah wuz jes' unlaxin' some til y'all kum back."

It was difficult for his master to keep a straight face as he instructed him, "Get on around front and look after the horses. I'm going to the fort for a spell. See that you stay awake while I am gone, you understand?"

"Yassa, Massa Cap'n. I'se done 'laxin'."

The Negro's feet were moving to comply with his orders when Barth stayed them. "And, Buck, you be sure and watch out for Miss Dracie now. You hear me?"

"Yassa, Massa Cap'n. Ole Buck gwine ter do jes' lak yo' tells 'im."

When Barth returned to the women before departing, Mrs. Harmon's eyes were moistened with laughter's dew. He knew the cause when she greeted him. "I declare, the kissin' man's back!" and her laughter pealed forth anew.

Her remark made the kiss he now bestowed on Dracie's cheek an embarrassed one and provided the setting for another swell of feminine mirth. They were still laughing when he paused to wave back to them. Women, he mused, can be counted on to wring the last drop from any humorous situation.

He found Carter Harmon without difficulty, but it developed that Morey had gone to the Dutch settlement to the south of Harrodstown and that the time of his return was indefinite. Harmon's manner was puzzling, holding an air of restraint that was neither offensive nor unfriendly but yet partaking of uncommon reserve. Barth's acquaintance with him had not been deep enough to learn whether or not he was a man susceptible to moods—spells, in the vernacular of the settlements. Ordinary propriety, therefore, discouraged any indirect inquiry that might possibly have disclosed some slight cause occasioning a condition of temporary reticence. It was but natural then that the older man's proposal that they return to his home met with favorable response.

They did not converse on their way to the gate. Barth's attention was focused upon a young matron in the immediate foreground, busily spinning by hand while her children romped noisily about. When he and his companion came even with her, he knew the reason she had compelled his intentness. She was holding the distaff in her right hand and the spindle in her left, reversing the usual functions of the hands in the spinning process. He gave momentary concern to the conventions of man that alerted the mind to recognize the slightest departure from that which his practices decreed normal. His reflection continued to the analogy between the weaving of cloth and the weaving of thought. Both must bow to the standard conformity and the least deflection therefrom is branded unorthodox.

The man at his side cleared his throat, causing Barth to give him an inadvertent glance. When the sound was repeated, he knew it was purposeful. Mr. Hamon was going to break his silence. Harmon's countenance had recovered its former open quality, the sternness had disappeared. As in water, face answereth face. Barth's features became entirely complacent.

Harmon cleared his throat, for the third time, before he spoke. "Captain Mercer, I must admit to having intentionally deceived you regarding Morey's absence and it has worried me. I did it out of consideration for you and Dracie, but since you'll find out sooner or later, I have decided it would be best were I to advise you myself in the fullness of truth. Tom Morey did go to the south of Harrodstown as I told you, but I withheld from you the purpose for which he went. A report came to the station that a small party of Indians, around six or eight as best could be estimated, had made a daring raid on the outskirts of the Dutch settlement, seizing a young boy whose screams brought instant rescue and pursuit. It seems five of the settlers had been out foraging and on their way back they had run upon the savages just as the boy had been captured by them. The Indians released the young lad and rode off. The settlers gave chase after the boy had been taken home. They lost the trail and came here to warn us. Tom and about ten of the residents, along with the five Dutchmen, left here to see if they could find any trace of the Indians. I should have told you when you first came. That was the reason I suggested we go home. I was afraid you might learn of it from some of the folks at the station." He paused. "I hope you'll forgive me for not telling you the truth and that you will believe my good intention in the matter."

"I understand, Mr. Harmon. Don't concern yourself any further about it. You know, we've often read of time and chance. Dracie and I were over in the same general direction earlier this afternoon. If the savages had spied us . . ." The dread implication choked his speech. He looked at the sun. It was about midafternoon.

"One thing, Captain Mercer. We know our womenfolk are all safe. There's little danger of those few Indians trying to raid a settlement as large as Harrodstown. By the way, there was something I honestly forgot to tell you." He smiled as he stressed the truth of his omission. "The Dutch claim the Indians were all painted up like a war party, few as they were."

Their steps quickened at Harmon's observation. Each man had the same fear. Suppose the small band was but a part of a much larger force encamped nearby.

Their anxiety mounted as they neared the cabin. From their approach they could see no sign of life from without and they broke into a run that ended only when they had reached the dwelling. Each noted with prayerful relief that the door was shut.

Mrs. Harmon answered her husband's anxious call, appearing immediately in the doorway. Her face revealed her bewilderment at the unknown cause of their agitation. "My stars! Is anything wrong?" she asked nervously, before adding, "Come on in. There's no sense standing out there."

Inside, Barth's eyes fought the lowered light, vainly searching for Dracie before he made his open inquiry. "Where's Dracie?" Before Mrs. Harmon could answer, he tacked another question to the first. "I don't see Lucy either. Where are they?"

Mr. Harmon's lips had moved silently with Barth's, his thought being identical to that expressed by the troubled tone. "Land sakes alive! What's got into you two? You all are panting like your lungs were fit to burst. Is anything the matter?" She eyed them with nervous suspicion, as though they might be partners to some concealment. Both men strained at her parrying of the inquiry, Carter Harmon breaking first. "Martha, please tell us where Lucy and Dracie have gone."

The urgent character of his voice brought not compliance with its demand but a singly worded question of her own. "Indians?"

Her husband nodded, saying, "Tom Morey and some others are trying to run them down. There was only a small band, a scouting party, probably. But where are the girls?"

Martha Harmon's mannerism of smoothing her hair betrayed her inner tension as she answered tremulously, "Lucy just went over to the Dowlings, down the way, a little while ago."

"What about Dracie?" Barth insisted. "Was she with her?" He watched for the first movement of her lips as though his attention might speed her reply.

"I don't think so—not unless she came back just as Lucy was leaving. I thought she had ridden to the fort to find you. You sure she wasn't there anywhere?"

He did not wait for her to finish speaking but rushed out the door and around to the back. Seeing no one, he yelled, "Buck! Where are you? Buck!"

The door of the shed swung open. The grin on the Negro's face fading with the recognition of his master's disturbed state.

"Where's your mistress? Why didn't you ride with her?"

The rapidity of the questions and their rapier-like propounding made the Negro's slow-thinking mind a mill that refused to grind his rushing thoughts, and the words that came were disconnected and inarticulate. "Miz Dracie . . . gone . . . Ah say to her . . . Massa Cap'n, he tole me . . ." The stone stopped its turning when Barth grabbed his shoulders and shook him. A look of utterly hopeless confusion came over him and his master, realizing the futility of further interrogation, shoved him roughly out of his way.

Mercer did not bother to saddle the roan but inserted the bit and pulled the animal from the shelter. Throwing the reins over the horse's head, he leaped upon the bare back and dug his heels into the steed's sides. The roan reared, its descending feet narrowly missing Carter Harmon as he came around the corner of the cabin. If Barth had seen him, he gave no recognition of his presence.

Harmon called after the wild rider but Mercer had sped away from the sound of his voice after shouting back, "I'll try and catch her. You stay with Mrs. Harmon!"

The bewildered Buck regained the use of his tongue as the millstone of him and began to slowly turn again. "Ah tole Miz Dracie. Ah say, 'Miz Dracie, Massa Cap'n, he say, Buck, yo' look atter Miz Dracie. Den she say, 'Buck, yo' stay whar yo' ez.'" The sigh of the approaching Mrs. Harmon, performing her nervous ritual of smoothing her hair, checked the useless flow of his speech. She spoke to him, and he followed her as she and her husband retraced their steps to the door of the dwelling.

CHAPTER 77

He knew now why he was riding to the south. Dracie might be anywhere. He recognized the vain course he was pursuing, but his compulsion would not allow him to abandon it. The unreasoning impulse that had caused him to gallop away so madly from the Harmon's concerned itself with its sole impression—the need of haste in finding Dracie. As he raced along, his eyes searching every moving object in the field of his vision, he fairly flew past a young woman walking in the opposite direction, vaguely noting the surprised look of recognition upon her face. He was a hundred yards beyond her before understanding made him draw hard on the reins and turn about. The woman was Lucy!

She had stared after him in unbelieving astonishment, gaping at the spectacle as the horse stood erect on its hind legs and pirouetted about. Her heart was pounding mercilessly within her when the roan's hooves dug into the earth almost at her feet and its forelegs braced themselves to a halt. Her discerning "What's wrong—what has happened?" and his frenzied asking, "Where's Dracie?" came simultaneously, provoking a pause that made both aware of its consumption of precious time. Though her own alarm had asserted itself, she yielded to his inquiry, answering, "I don't know, Barth. I thought she was with you." With her answer, his features fell in abject disappointment and she regretted she had made the first reply.

"Didn't she say anything at all about where she was going?" His imploring face stifled her voice. She could only shake her head. Summoning her self-control, she told him of her last conversation with Dracie. "I asked her where she was going, and I remember her saying that she felt so happy she wanted to get off somewhere by herself. 'Some place as lovely as my mood,' she said. Those were almost her exact words. I thought it was just an expression she was using, and that she really was going to find you. I . . ." She would have finished, but it was no use. He had bolted away, flailing the neck of his mount with the lapping end of the reins. Lucy ran without realizing her action. It had all happened so quickly. The wild light in his eyes. Had he lost his reason? A repeated "Thank God, you're safe!" made her own mind accept the visage of the dismounting man whose furious approach had made no impression upon her stunned senses.

"Father, it's you. What's wrong with Barth?" The question came as in her childhood when she had sought an answer for that which appeared unfathomable.

"He's looking for Dracie. Which way did he go? I'll take you home and then ride after him. Do you know where she might be—where she might have gone? Did she tell you?" His rushing inquiries only served to heighten fear's portion of her confusion

"Father, what's wrong?" The question came as a demand.

"We're worried about Dracie. She's nowhere to be found! There have been some Indians . . ." He caught her as she swooned. Minutes later, she was home, her mother bathing her forehead. He had ridden off toward the fort. Behind him, torn by inactivity when his every helpless thought dictated he should do something, Buck stood in front of the Harmon cabin, his head turning from one full side to the other as he scanned the horizon. Always, the White man had told him what to do. How, when his heart beseeched his troubled mind to guide him to his master's assistance, its servile character could only send from his lips in vain redundance, the words, "Whut muz' Ah do? Whut muz' Ah do?"

"Good God of all that is holy, spare her, I pray of thee! Great Lord of infinite mercy, let nothing happen to her! Help me to find her and may she be safe!" The prayers were the first use of reason since he had spoken to Lucy and had conceived the hope that Dracie might be in her Eden. Each time he switched the roan, the reins were smeared with a thick lathery foam. The little hill and its berry bushes lay in the foreground in seeming peaceful surroundings, bringing the supplication, "May all be as peaceful beyond." His entreaty had no opportunity for its repetition. Suddenly, Sagitta burst from the path's entrance—a riderless harbinger of the terror that lurked behind. The frightened steed did not recognize its oncoming master and abruptly changed course. As the animal swerved, Barth saw the vivid streak of crimson upon its gray haunch. He saw Sagitta, but his eyes were riveted upon the place from whence the horse had emerged. A man had appeared there, shouting and waving his arms in a frantic endeavor to halt him.

"Captain Mercer, pull your horse! For God's sake, stop! Don't go up there!"

Tom Morey might just as well have attempted to halt the tide rolling relentlessly to the shore. Sagitta's startling emergence—the blood—had converted the presentiments hovering in Mercer's brain into a blind conviction of disaster. He must find Dracie! He must get to her! Nothing—no one else mattered. The roan was near enough to Morey that he could see its reddened eyeballs, before he leaped aside. He recovered quickly and returned to the path in time to see the steed rear at its instantaneous braking and Mercer jump before the animal's forehooves began their descent.

A segment of the silent circle broke at Mercer's crazed approach. Those on the far side felt the flecks of foamy saliva that flew from the distended tongue of the gasping roan. All hearts strove to reach to Mercer. A vain effort, as each knew. But at this moment it was the only way possible. They had witnessed too many like tragedies, not to have learned the utter uselessness of words. To every rule there is an exception. One of the group began a movement toward the supine figure, saying, "We found her like—"

He finished the sentence from the ground, "—this." He had been knocked from his feet. His eyes caught the maniacal fury in Mercer's features and saw the clenched fist shaking, first at him and then at the others, as the words came to his ears. "Don't touch her! Don't any of you touch her! I'll kill the first bastard who does!" Then he saw the man-turned-demon kneel beside the still form in the center of the clearing.

With the utterance of his fulmine expression, he blotted out their existence about him. Dracie lay with her head back, her neck arched as though lifting her lips to him, just as she had done a little while before. A little while or was it ages back in time? He kissed her lips. They were warm! "Good God, be praised!" He called softly to her as his lips continued their gentle caress. "Dracie, it's me—Barth. Everything's all right now, Dracie. It's all right now. I'll take you to Harmon's. You'll get well. You'll be all right." He thought he sensed a gradual response of her lips to his, and he moved his left arm under her neck, unmindful of the blood that flattened the hair along her temples, staining the auburn strands to a richer shade as it ran slowly downward until it found his sleeve. Placing his other arm beneath her knees, he lifted her in a tender cradle til he stood erect.

Her eyes opening and a wonderful promise of hope encompassed him—a promise that seemed materialized, as she whispered, "Barth . . . Barth, dearest." He kissed her with all the pent-up fullness of his heart.

A fullness that made him pause to raise his face heavenward and exclaim, "Thank thee, oh God! Thank thee, most merciful Lord!" Still held in the fervor of his thankfulness, he bowed his head. His eyes closed by the intensity of his prayer. The moment of communion ended when he looked upon her again. The light of life in her eyes seemed to be rising and a slight semblance of its resurgence played about her mouth and cheeks. Then it began to fade. He lowered his head to kiss her, as though by touching his lips to hers, he might bring back the failing radiancy.

With a last summoning of reason, she recognized his intention, and the cords of her neck became markedly visible as they strained to lift her mouth to his. He felt her body tremble lightly in his arms. Her brows dropped, and her eyelids slowly covered her eyes. The lips, which only a second before had shaped themselves for his kiss, sagged and parted, leaving her mouth agape. In the wildness of his frenzy, he implored, "Dracie, come back! Don't leave me, Dracie! Come back to me! Come back, come back! Oh, darling, please don't leave me!" But he knew that he clutched only her body. He knew in his heart she had gone. He sought to draw her closer to him. At the movement of his arm, her head fell forward sharply and his eyes stared point blank at the raw, red swath cut by the savage blade.

The hideous sight made him turn his head from its gruesomeness. This could not be Dracie whom he held in his arms! This must be someone else. It could not have happened to her. His limbs grew weak and for an instant he feared he might drop his precious burden, light as it was in his arms. Dry sobs racked their tearing way through his chest. The tears that would have eased this moment of stress would not, could not, come. He cursed the discipline of his youth that had decreed them to be unmanly and the years that had dried their ducts. Too late, he had learned that tears were meant to bathe the searing of the soul.

He had been unaware of the arrival of others from the fort, Carter Harmon among their number. He did not hear the hushed voices of those who stood in respectful attendance at his hour of trial. He did not look at them nor did he look down at her whom he carried. Instead, he set his eyes upon the archway beyond.

Overhead, the trumpet flowers had begun their closing. The arbor had become a lychgate.

He placed her body where only a few hours before she had lain in glorious rapture. Kneeling beside her, he kissed her lifeless lips, lips that yet returned a deceptive warmth. How could she be gone? She could not be dead! This same warm mouth had spoken lovingly to him—had returned his kiss—just moments ago. Surely, there must be a greater distance between life and death than the mere span over which she had so quickly passed. He struggled to force the return of hope, but pitiless reason bound him to reality. He bowed his head in his hand. A blind desire for some mode of retaliation filled him and surged to his lips as he glowered at the sky beyond the rim of maple leaves. "Oh, God, why did you do this? Why did you give me hope and then take it from me? Why did you let this happen to this good woman? If she had to die, why did you let it be this way? Do you create beautiful things only that you may cause their destruction in ugliness? Why, oh, God? Why . . . Why . . . Why?"

The fingers so lightly laid upon his shoulders would have been ignored. The intruder who entered his Gethsemane would have remained unknown behind his back had the voice not said, "You do not inquire wisely concerning those matters, my son."

The hand so consolingly intended was swept violently away by his rise. He turned and faced Reverend Wyeth, his words coming with scornful coloring. "You preach of the mercy of God, of his love for those whom he has created . . ." He laid his open palm toward Dracie's body. "Is this . . . is this an example of his love—of his tender care? Is this the reward for her life's faith and trust in him—to be butchered like this, by some heathen savage who has never heard of him, much less acknowledged him? If there is a God . . ." Reverend Wyeth cringed at the blasphemy and would have stopped its continuance had he not been overwhelmed by the torrent of ensuing words, "If there is a God, as you claim, why would he let such a thing happen? Or, could it be that you are so afraid of death yourself, that you and others like you seek comfort for your fears by making yourselves pretend that there is a God who cares for sparrows and directs the falling of the stars from the night sky? Have you ever endured tragedy such as this? Don't babble to me of God with the woman whom you were to marry to me tomorrow—on the Sabbath—the Holy Day—lying there on the ground, her scalp torn from her head. The hair that you preach was given to her as her crowning glory, which is hanging even at this moment from the waist of the Red disciple of hell who slaughtered her! The book from which you preach also says, 'An eye for an eye and a tooth for a tooth.' Will you tell me that I am wrong if I tell you that I am going to find the devil that killed her and cut his scalp from his head while he yet lives? Will you tell me that? Can you tell me to forgive him?" His hands were upon the minister, shaking him vehemently.

It was Carter Harmon who stopped the insane display of force by appealing to the trend of Mercer's mind. "Captain Mercer, if you want to catch that Indian, you had best be getting about doing it. There can't be much more than three hours of light left. If you don't find him before nightfall, you may never find him. He has a good headstart on you as it is. If you wait much longer, he's certain to make his escape."

Mercer released the trembling minister as one drops a cloth once he has wiped his hands upon it. There was one overpowering thought in his mind—the exactment of vengeance. Harmon encouraged the diversion that he had brought into being. "You can take my rifle and powder horn and use my horse. It's much fresher than yours."

The light of acquiescence came over Mercer's features. Tom Morey caught its flash and kept it alive, interjecting, "We know the Indians came through here and went on down the valley." He bent to the ground. "See, here are the hoofprints of their horses. I know this country around here. There's nothing but heavy wood for a mile around this open land. Some of the men from the fort have already gone on to head them off. You see, there's a break in the forest on up ahead. The men will travel over the cleared ground beyond Harrodstown toward McAfee Station. When they hit that break, they'll cut on over and start moving back this way. The Indians will be caught in the middle, if we act quickly." He waited for Mercer's response, if one were to be forthcoming.

Instead of answering him, Barth spoke to Carter Harmon. "Mr. Harmon, I'm going after the savage. I do not want anyone to touch her while I'm gone. I will kill anyone who does. I mean exactly what I say. I'm grateful for the use of your horse and rifle but I must ask another favor of you. See that a grave is dug alongside of where she is lying. Dig it deep and large enough that she can be placed in it comfortably. I'll be back when I have done what I must do, whether it be before sundown or after darkness or in the light of tomorrow. Will you do this for me?" To add strength to his unusual request, he added, "You owe that much consideration of her surely." Harmon nodded his head, but before he could give voice to his assent, Mercer had turned to Reverend Wyeth. "You, man of God, might also show your concern for her by staying with him." Then he at last spoke to Morey. "Tom, I hope it works out like you have figured it will. But there's one thing I want to make clear. Unless the Indian who killed Dracie is already dead when we catch up with him, no one is to fire at him except me, unless it be necessary to prevent his killing one of us. If you and whoever is going after them don't agree to that, I'll go by myself." He did not allow for an answer. "How many will be in our party?"

Morey had been patient with his friend in his grief, but his words now carried an air of irritation. "Captain Mercer, there isn't a man here who doesn't grieve with you in your loss. Up to now, we have all made allowances for the way it has affected you. But you aren't the only one to whom such a terrible thing has happened. Practically every man here has lost some member of his family to the savages. So it is natural that we understand how you feel, but when you go so far as to forget that there are other lives to be protected, why we just can't go along with you. How do you know, or any of us know, but what the Indians haven't doubled back and are now behind us? And, if they are in fact moving ahead of us, can't you realize what might happen if one of them escapes us? Undoubtedly, they are but a part of a larger force camped somewhere farther up. For the past month, reports have been coming into Harrodstown that the Indians were planning something big. Maybe Harrodstown is to be the objective or the little settlements above and below it. So, you see, we can't let you do what you want to. We can't run the risk of you failing to get that one Indian, assuming that you could be lucky enough to run across his trail. If you were at your senses, you'd know that without me telling you. I hope you'll be reasonable about this, but if you're not, why we'll have to make you be." He turned to Harmon. "Mr. Harmon, since Captain Mercer is going to use your firearm, you won't be going with us. Will you take the body back to the fort?"

"I said I'd kill anyone who touched her! No one is going to lay a hand on her body, unless he kills me first!" Mercer had quickly positioned himself so that his legs straddled Dracie's body.

Morey made as though to advance on him, but found his way suddenly barred by Carter Harmon who oiled the seething waters. "Tom, you and the others go on ahead. Things will be all right here."

"But you might be in danger yourself—you and Mr. Wyeth." He looked sharply at Mercer. "Maybe Mercer don't give a damn what happens to himself, but you ought to be thinking about your wife and Lucy."

"Go on, Tom. I'll be all right, I tell you."

Morey glared at Mercer and found cold hatred in the answering look. A friendship was at its crisis.

Hardly had Morey and his party ridden off before more men had come from the station. Veiling his true purpose, Harmon adroitly suggested that it would be well for them to remain nearby, on the off chance that the Indians might still be somewhere in the vicinity, And after a short discussion, the group agreed to do so. This accomplished, he said, "Captain Mercer here has a special reason for wanting to go after the savage. He was to be married to this poor dead girl tomorrow. With all of you here, he won't need to stay any longer. We'll bury her when he gets back." He addressed Mercer. "Good luck to you, Captain. I'll see to it that everything remains as you want it while you are gone." The parting handshake he received was warm and firm.

CHAPTER 78

The Indians had moved northwardly through the forest. The light prints made in the earth by their unshod mounts established that certainty. Likewise, he was able to deduce the points at which the pursuing settlers had entered the woods. Part of them had followed their quarry directly. Others had proceeded above and below that place of entrance. He weighed their apparent strategy before determining his own plan of pursuit. When he had observed the wide setting of the trunks of the trees, he understood why the Indians and the adventurers alike had continued on horseback. But he still could not believe the White men would be so foolish as to attempt to hunt while mounted. Undoubtedly, if they became hard-pressed, the savages would abandon their horses, and if their pursuers did not do likewise, they would become easy targets for the concealed Redskins.

He reasoned that there was but one direction in which the Indians could flee, assuming that the advanced band of settlers had succeeded in heading them off on the north. They would have to move westwardly. Therefore, it appeared that the wisest course would be to go into the forest at a point well below that where the last settler had entered.

He rode perhaps a quarter of a mile beyond the last hoofmarks. A convenient opening presented itself, and he availed himself of its opportunity for ingress. Once inside the woods, he found cover for his horse and tethered it securely. As he went farther, the light lowered to an ever-deepening shade and visibility lessened accordingly. For the next hour or so it seemed to him he walked his way cautiously in what he believed to be a northeastward line. But the feeling came over him that he had lost his bearing and that the large oak to his right was the same tree he had marked as being on his left in his earlier progress. The sling of the powderhorn, which the slight Carter Harmon had loaned him, was uncomfortably tight about his chest, and he determined to carry it in his hand. He tried to orient himself, but each space between the big trees appeared the same. His concentration waned and his thoughts reverted mournfully to the still form lying on the gentle slope above the little valley. She couldn't be dead! She couldn't be! She couldn't be! He bent his head, shaking it from side to side, as though to expunge the memory and thus prove its falsity. Suddenly a wave of weakness struck him and he felt ill. I should be there with her, he acknowledged, instead of being on this hopeless chase. He admitted the great odds against encountering the Indian who had slaughtered her and thought to abandon his purpose. He had started back when a muffled rumble halted him. Like sounds followed in rapid succession. They were rifle reports! The savages had been intercepted! His lips began a prayer, "Oh, God, let me ..." but he aborted their effort. God had not answered the prayers that would have saved her. He would not now be here if there were truly a God who heard the pleas of men. A spirit of defiance stirred him and his resolve returned. The only trace of wavering was the realization that even if any of the Indians did cross his path, the one whom he sought might not be among them.

The firing became sporadic, but after each interval of silence the next shot seemed nearer. To his eager mind, this meant that the savages were fleeing in his direction. Straining to catch the fullness of the infrequent reports, he sought to move toward their source.

The air became less humid, and he thought at first he but imagined the forest less dark than formerly. And he attributed the greater depth of his vision to the fact his eyes had become more adjusted to the semidarkness. However, as he moved onward, definite ribbons of sunbeams began to slant through the foliage above him, til at last a burst of light made him shield his face and turn his back to its blinding brilliance. Retreating to shade, before he once again attempted to look forward, he saw a scene of destruction wrought by the wild-running forces of nature. A vast section of the forest had been leveled by a fire of comparatively recent occurrence—the blackened remnants of huge stumps and the stretches of charred limbs made that certain. But how had the fire been contained? What had kept it from spreading until this whole area of trees had been consumed? Undoubtedly, lightning had started it. Could it have been a violent rainstorm, following fast upon the fiery spree of the thunderbolt, had centered itself upon this part of the forest? However it happened, he concluded, it is to my advantage. The savages cannot cross this wide expanse without being seen and they must move into the sun.

But he had to correct his reasoning. Though the woods had been burned seemingly all the way to the open boundary on the north, there was a wide border of forest to the south. He scanned the uneven line of trees far across the way and deliberated whether he should hurry southwardly or gamble on the Indians attempting an open passage.

The first time, he ignored the brief, shining reflection. But its second appearance shot its significance to his brain. Someone was moving south along the distant edge of the divided forest. His thumping heart increased its furious beat with each flash of light, but whether it came from the metal of White man or savage, he could not tell. He kept a parallel course, however, as he watched the beacon's progress. Sometimes, minutes would pass without seeing it, then it would be suddenly visible. It was like the game he had played as a boy in the nighttime—chasing a firefly.

He had become so used to seeing the brilliant dot take its irregular appearances he was unprepared for the sight that next met his eyes. Across the blackened clearing was an Indian figure, naked above the waist. The shimmering gleam that had so thoroughly held his attention became a flashing sweep as the savage turned his body. When it had steadied, Barth was able to make out that the stream of brightness came not from the rifle in the brave's hand but from something around or on his right arm between the elbow and the shoulder. The warrior's turning movement had been purposeful, as was evident from the immediate emergence of a second brave. The two conferred briefly before breaking into an easy run, skirting the forest as they headed south.

He followed their progress, keeping his pace even with theirs but being ever careful his movement was covered by the trees. As he neared the southernmost end of the forest on his side, he wondered whether the Indians would continue in the direction they were traveling or if they would swing around bearing westwardly with the curving line of the protective foliage, in which event they would cross his path. The latter seemed the most likely to him, since if they continued on as they were headed they would have to leave cover once they reached the edge of the valley.

His surmise proved correct! They were tracing the dip of the fire-made clearing. He readied his weapon, slipping the sling of the powderhorn around his neck after he had finished loading. To be sure he would be free of its interference, he swung the horn itself behind his back. He felt instinctively for his knife and patted the sheath that held it on his hip, then found a place of full concealment from where he could watch the approach of his foes.

His watching was cold and calculated. No longer did anticipation swirl the blood through the submissive portals of his heart. The men who now loped toward him so unsuspectingly would be grist for the mill of his vengeance. As birds, hastening to the snare of the fowler, he thought. His lips tightened grimly at the simile.

They were near enough that he could discern the source of the reflection that had betrayed them—a metal band encircling the arm of the foremost one above its biceps. Now he could distinguish the colors of the warpaint upon their faces—lines of red, yellow and white—the feather in the leader's hair, the rifles being carried at their balance, the powderhorns and tomahawks at their sides.

"My God!" The exclamation escaped him before his throat closed, as though it had been gripped beneath his jaws by a hand of iron.

REDDISH BROWN TRESSES HUNG LOOSELY FROM THE LEADER'S WAIST, covering the savage thigh and reaching to the knee! THIS WAS THE ONE WHO HAD KILLED HER!

His blood turned to venom—venom that fed his brain but one thought. Now that he had found his prey, he must not allow him to escape. But with the insane reasoning came subtlety. The savage trailing the one who had taken her scalp would have to be killed first. To do this, he would have to follow them and wait for this opportunity. His own death did not matter but it must not happen until he had freed her scalp from the binding thong.

The Indians had reentered the forest, not a stone's throw from his hiding place. He watched them as they rested, the flesh thinning between their ribs and then refilling with each panting breath. He could hear their guttural discourse but its meaning was obscure.

He had determined upon his next move, and as they made as though to resume their flight, he sighted his rifle on the one he had marked as his first victim. The Indian seemed to be apprehensive, looking anxiously about, as if he sensed some impending danger and turned toward the other savage. When he did so, the back of his head became Mercer's target. The flash and explosion were concurrent. A dark hole opened instantly at the base of the shaved skull, and the dead warrior pitched forward upon his face. His companion took one compassionate step, then quickly reversed his way to the safety of the broad trunk of a hickory tree.

To Mercer, the ensuing seconds were as minutes, each one asking, "Has he stopped? Is he hiding? Or has he run away?" Unable to contain his suspense any longer, he darted to an oak, just to the side of the slain savage. Even as the tail of his jacket was whisked from view, there was another booming flashing and pieces of bark fell like hurried raindrops on the dry leaves beyond the oak's base. He stroked the ramrod furiously, then sought to pull the powderhorn to accessibility. Despairing of the slowness of this effort, he bent forward and pulled it over his head. The powder poured, he plugged the horn and dropped it at his feet, freeing his hands for their next action. Peering around his shelter, he caught a fleeting glimpse of an elbow jutting past the confines of the hickory. He noted the fast failing haze that was the dim light of the forest, and the fear of darkness covering his enemy urged him to boldness. He ran heedlessly to a tree set diagonally to his former position. When his reckless act drew no fire, he strained his eyes for some trace of his savage adversary. He moved away from his shelter, seeking clearer vision.

He saw the fire from the weapon just as he completed his move, and he ducked from the whistling drone of the lead as it passed between his head and the tree on his left. The advantage was now his—his rifle was ready for firing—the Indian would have to reload. He rushed toward the spot from which he had been fired upon, reaching it in time to catch sight of the retreating figure. Firing on impulse, he imagined the savage to have hesitated and swayed with the rifle's report. Following closely, he saw him disappear into a small ravine, in the fluttering wake of an owl that had been roused by the disturbing gunfire to set out upon its nightly meandering.

Within the darkened defile, the Shawnee half chief, Shawtowa, was beset by awe of the supernatural. Had not the white owl (the light underside of the laboring winds had deceived his hasty sight) flown across his path, right after the White man's bullet had torn through the shoulder muscle of his left arm? Was this not the omen of death, his own death? Is not the owl always the messenger of the Great Spirit? And what greater portent could there be than the appearance of the rare-colored bird?

Shawtowa acknowledged the summons stoically. He must soon go to the

Great Meadow. But before his departure, he could bring glory to his passing by bringing with him the spirit of the one who was ordained to kill him. This was why he had ceased his running and had sought the night that already inhabited the deepest part of the ravine. From there, he could see out. The White man could not see into its depths. Though his left hand, governed by the lower muscles, still clutched the rifle, it could not be used to load and fire. He propped the weapon up and casting away his powderhorn as being a useless impediment he awaited his pursuer's coming.

It did not affect his vigilance, that he now thought upon the years he had lived, as they neared their end. The days of his childhood, the precepts of his father, still living in the longhouse far across the Ohio, came to him in sad tenderness—the memory of the one called Little Brother, last son of his father, whom the settlers had killed and whose body they had cut in many pieces, feeding the dismembered portions to their hogs—even the sacred parts under the breechcloth. And they spoke among themselves of the Indian's irreverence and savagery! The desecration of Little Brother had caused the return of Shawtowa and his fellow braves in their warpaint. They had come, seeking a young White boy, to do to him that which had been done to Little Brother. But they had found the White man's children carefully watched, though they searched the settlements from the garrisons on the river near the salt lick, where game once was to be found in great numbers, on to where the settlers spoke in a strange tongue. There it was that they seized a boy of an age approximating Little Brother's, only to have to let him go in order to save themselves. Shawtowa stayed the procession of recent events through his mind. Why did the White man delay in his coming? Could it be that the omen had been misinterpreted? He recalled the tales of the old ones around the council fires—some had remembered a few times when the owl had not brought death or disaster. Was this to be another? Would the coming night shield him to escape? Had the Great Spirit decreed he should rejoin the large body of British and their warrior allies who were preparing to cross the Kentucky River on their way to the attack upon the stations to the east? Was it to be his will that he would be permitted to take the White major the intelligence as to the settlements as he had been ordered to do?

He became aware that the forest was filling with the voices of insects. Why didn't the White man come before their noise reached a crescendo, dulling the hearing?

Blood from his wound had dripped onto the hair of the woman he had scalped. Some of the strands had dried to his thigh and he pulled them loose. He had intended to avenge Little Brother with her body, but again, pursuit had denied the necessary time. And so he had only added her scalp to that of the man he had killed in the vicinity of the stations on Salt River.

He would not wait longer for his White pursuer. If the Great Spirit was going to call him, the demand would come when he willed, whether here or farther on. He had started up the sloping terrain, when his keen eyes were rewarded for their sharpness. A form had been silhouetted for a second before it vanished behind a tree to the left of the exit he was taking.

Prophecy or coincidence? The owl's significance would be known within the next few minutes. Shawtowa drew his tomahawk.

*

When the Indian had faded into the deep shade of the ravine, Mercer halted to reload his rifle. He felt about his neck for the thong, before he remembered he had failed to pick up the horn after dropping it. Were he to go back, the savage would get away. He sourly admitted the shifted fortune of the chase. The Redman had both rifle and powder. He kept his own gun only to bluff his quarry—it was too dark for the Indian to note the absence of the powderhorn. But he would once more have to expose himself to his aim. When the savage fired, and if he missed a vital spot, the issue would have to be settled quickly by hand-to-hand combat before the Indian's weapon could be again readied for use. For this reason, Mercer worked his way cautiously forward, fearing all the while the Indian had already left his place of concealment and escaped. So intent was he on discovering the presence of his foe, he did not realize his lips had responded to the imbedded habit of silent prayer. He thought he saw a movement as of someone coming slowly up the end of the ravine opposite him. This was no trick of the dropping darkness—it WAS the savage! It was then Mercer presented himself as a brief target. When nothing happened, he waited a few moments and repeated the maneuver. Still, there was no firing of the rifle! Surely, the other knew of his presence. But if he did, why had he not shot at him? There could be no more playing of cat and mouse. It was now or never, and he prepared to charge his armed adversary. If he could but get close enough to grapple with him.

*

Shawtowa saw the White man's repeated moves and the rifle in his hands. He has not seen me, or he would have fired his weapon. Perhaps, if I rush him suddenly, I will take him by surprise. These thoughts formed his strategy.

*

In the thickening haze of the forest, the mortal enemies made for each other. As the one swung his tomahawk, the other quickly swept the stock of his rifle upward, parrying the blow, the blade striking the seasoned hardwood and bouncing off it. Quickly, Mercer followed through, driving the rifle butt downward and into Shawtowa's mouth, knocking him upon his back. As he hurled his own gun away and dove upon his prostrate foe, he thought, What became of HIS rifle?

The savage fought only with his right arm, though Mercer could feel the fingers of the left hand digging into the flesh of his leg. They rolled sideways and the hand tried to tear at his privates before their positions shifted. Shawtowa felt the tomahawk being wrested from his grip and eased his resistance, holding lightly to its handle. The quick withdrawal of his strength fooled the White man, and the force he was exerting to obtain the weapon caused him to overbalance and fall to the side of the wriggling Indian, who bounded to his feet and recovered his war axe by grasping its head and jerking the shaft from the hands of his yet recumbent antagonist. But though he wielded blow after blow at his elusive rolling enemy, the tomahawk struck only the ground.

The tree, the objective toward which Mercer was propelling his body, was but a few feet away. He rolled in a curve and scurried to his hands and knees, crawling to the haven of the broad trunk as the Indian's axe sheared its bark in a futile striking. Not bothering to straighten himself, Barth did not hesitate, crouching as he ran on a tangent from the base of the tree, the savage close on his rear. Suddenly, he dropped to the earth, the line of his body across the direction of the chase. So unexpectedly had he done this, the fast pursuing Redman tripped and sailed over him. But before he could follow up his advantage, the Indian had gained his feet.

The winded opponents now faced each other, moving around in a wary circle, whose snail-like revolutions emphasized their fatigue. Even from the short distance that separated them, their features were barely discernible. As they shuffled their ways, each was concerned with the thickening gloom. Each strove to devise some plan of action that would end the struggle before all the aid of the dimming light would be lost.

It was Shawtowa who took the initiative. Trusting that its slow movement would escape the White man, he raised the tired right arm to a throwing position. He held it thus for a few steps, gauging the slight lead he must allow for to ensure accuracy. Down came the arm in a quick, snapping motion. The tomahawk sped from his hand.

The axe brushed the startled Mercer's shoulder and went on into the silent darkness before his mind reacted. He tightened his perspiring hand about the shaft of his knife and reversed his steps, then ran toward his foe.

Shawtowa could not believe he had missed his enemy, who now loomed out of the near night and was almost upon him. He drew his own blade from its sheath.

As they fell to the ground, the initial advantage belonged to the Indian. He had landed on top of his heavier adversary, and by a chance finding, the hand of the ineffectual left arm had closed upon the right wrist of the White man, holding it, and the knife in its hand, securely against his side.

For a time, the action was stalemated. Mercer's left hand checked the unending effort of the Indian to force his blade downward. The superior strength of Shawtowa's right arm over his opponent's left began gradually to assert itself, and the knife slowly inched its descent until its tip was at Mercer's chest.

On the murky battleground, the color of the combatants mattered not. It was man against man to the death. And death came quickly.

For one terrifying second, Barth thought he must let the Indian's thirsty knife do what it would. And his next move was not the result of any swift calculation but was inspired purely by instinct—the desire to live. He rolled on his left hip, raising his right knee and digging the edge of his heel into the soft earth. Thus he forced the arm and the threatening blade aside and away from his body. As he rolled, his right wrist brought the savage's gripping hand along in its turning. The shattered biceps of the Redman had no leverage and was powerless to stay the arched ascent of the White hand and the knife it still grasped. When the revolving bodies reached a half turn, the point of the blade was pointed toward the warrior's lower back.

Shawtowa's mouth opened grotesquely as his right wrist was pressed and firmly pinned to the ground. His face became an ancient mask of tragedy, its agonized lines accentuated by the bloody trickling that still flowed from the battered gums and lips down and around each side of the jutting chin.

Mercer's right hand tugged repeatedly to bring the knife from beneath the Indian's body. Then he realized what had taken place. He released his grip on the handle and slid his arm and hand from under the savage, immediately moving them to the aid of the left hand that had imprisoned the Indian's weapon. It was then he noticed that the Indian no longer struggled.

It took both of Mercer's hands to prise the warrior's tenacious fingers from the handle. He plunged the blade deep into the heart of his foe and left it there. As he did so, a curse ripped itself from his lips. "May God damn you to the lowest part of hell!"

But Shawtowa did not hear the fiercely uttered words. His moccasined feet were already in the grasses of the Great Meadow.

Mercer turned the dead savage and pulled the knife from its place of fatal penetration. He sliced the savage brow and sawed halfway over its head, scraping the skull, so deep was the incision. Like an animal, maddened by the smell of blood, he hacked and tore at the flesh until the scalp was free. As it parted from the Indian's head, a vision came back to him. A giant bewhiskered figure emerging from the trees into the clearing that bordered the north bank of Salt River—Abe Foster with the bloody scalp between his teeth.

When men thirst for blood, they understand others who do the same. He no longer wondered about Abe.

He severed the thong at the Indian's waist. And though it was now too dark to see them, his touch told him there were two—Dracie's and a man's. He stabbed a hole in the Indian's scalp and used the savage's own thong to string it.

Then he sheathed his knife and moved his exhausted limbs in the direction he hoped would lead him out of the forest.

Behind him, an owl flapped its wings as it left its perch.

CHAPTER 79

He based his bearing purely on its opposition to what he believed had been the way he had traveled earlier. He held to his course despite the trees he blindly encountered, sometimes striking one before immediately staggering into another. The buffeting did not end until the way lightened, shortly before he broke through a thicket at the valley's edge.

He was surprised to find it was still daylight, though the sky had become a deepening magenta. As chance would have it, he located the spot, without undue difficulty, where he had tied his horse and then rode up the valley.

Carter Harmon greeted him joyously. "Praise be to God, Captain Mercer, for bringing you back safely!" His voice fell as he said, "I'm sorry to have to tell you this—"

"You didn't move her?" He thundered the accusing question.

"No—No—No. It's not that at all. I kept my word to you. What I was going to tell you was the Indians killed Tom Morey."

The revelation fell on deaf ears. Dracie was dead. What did it matter if Tom Morey was dead too?

"They got all but two of the savages though. They got away." The older man shook his head. "It's a shame about Tom. He thought a lot of you, Captain."

Again, Barth ignored the passing of one who had been his friend. "Here is your knife, Mr. Harmon. I had to leave your rifle and powderhorn in the forest. I'll try to find them in the morning. If I don't, you can have mine in exchange." He looked toward Dracie's body before continuing grimly. "The two did not get away. I killed them both." Reaching as he spoke, he said, "Let me have your knife again for a moment."

He jerked the Indian's scalp from the severed thong and held it forward, the feather hanging limply from the little knot of hair that centered the raw perimeter. "Here's the scalp of the Red bastard who killed her." He turned and flung it far down the hillside.

When he had faced about, Reverend Wyeth was before him. "That was a brave, but foolhardy thing that you did, Captain Mercer. I—"

The fury glistened in Barth's eyes. "I did what I had to do," he snapped.

He walked slowly to where she lay. Before kneeling beside her, he said quietly to Mr. Harmon, "Here is another scalp—a White man's. The Indian must have killed him before he murdered her. Be good enough to bury it, if you will."

His heart within him cried anew, as he struggled to accept the fact that she must be put in the ground. From his sorrow-ladened soul, there seeped the anguished intoning, "Oh, Dracie. Dracie, my dearest Dracie. Why did you have to die? Why did you? Why did you? Why did you? I love you so. I love you so."

Tears spilled over the eyelids of Carter Harmon, waiting patiently for the terrible decision that would have to come as inevitably as the converging night.

Barth smoothed the hole within the auburn tresses and he choked as he remembered the wayward tendril. He lovingly fitted the scalp upon her head, striving to arrange the hair so that it concealed the disfigurement. When he deemed it satisfactory, he placed his lips against her cheek and whispered, "I wish that I were dead beside you, Dracie. I love you. I love you so."

His voice broke, as he asked, "Mr. Harmon, will you . . . will you help me, please?"

The time had come.

He knelt by the mound of fresh earth and began to cover her body, scooping the crumbling clay and letting it fall gently into the grave, first on her feet and legs, then onward until her face and neck alone were bare. He closed his eyes. "Oh, Dracie . . . my God . . . my God." He did not look again until the hole had been filled.

He heard Reverend Wyeth quote the Bible, as though from afar. "As for man, his days are as grass; as a flower of the field, so he flourisheth. For the wind passeth over it, and it is gone; and the place thereof shall know it no more."

What right had this meddler to invade this hour? His indignation fell with the realization that it was for Dracie and that she would have wanted it so.

It was more difficult for him to retain his composure, however, when the minister prayed, "Oh, heavenly Father, forgive this one who in his overwhelming grief hath lost sight of heaven and remembereth not the words, Thy will be done. It is the failure of the flesh, oh, Lord, not of the spirit. Forgive him, I pray thee, remembering that man is but dust. And grant his prayers, I beseech thee, when they shall later come for thy forgiveness."

They dragged the brush back and forth over the ground, leveling the grave and obliterating its outline. When the camouflaging was completed, he stood there with his head bowed until Carter Harmon patted his arm. "We must leave, Captain."

The simple, certain sentence with all its complex implication of finality moved his feet slowly away from her resting place.

The earth beneath the maple's spread was in darkness.

When they reached the clearing, the shadowy shapes of men and horses told him others besides Carter Harmon and Reverend Wyeth had waited upon him.

The last member of the waving line of silhouettes came from between the berry bushes and headed down the slope toward the settlement, joining the others as they formed themselves into companionate groups.

Only the two men who rode double and the one who moved at their side were silent—a quiet which remained inviolate until they reached the Harmon home. And it was Reverend Wyeth who spoke first. "Goodnight, Carter. I hope to see you at the service tomorrow. It will be my last at Harrodstown for a while, you know."

Harmon's reply was soft. "I know. I'll be there." He eased from his horse and waited for Mercer to dismount. But he did not do so, holding stolidly to the back of the saddle. Nor did his impassiveness yield when the minister said, "I know your grief, Captain, but God will comfort you, if you will but open your heart to him."

When the pause that followed his words lengthened, he said tactfully, "Good night, Carter. Good night, Captain Mercer."

There was another respectful interval before Mr. Harmon laid his hand on his companion's thigh. "Let's go inside, Barth." It was the first time he had ever addressed him so informally and the intimate use of the name seemed to stir Mercer, who now slowly alighted, slipping noiselessly to the ground.

Harmon had started to lead the horse around to the back, when he heard a low voice say, "Ah'll take 'im, Massa Hahmon. Yo' he'p po' Massa Cap'n. He need yo'."

When they entered, the door opened upon Lucy and her mother seated motionless beside a table whose set preparedness marked the time of the catastrophe as surely as the halted hands of a timepiece. Underlined by incessant weeping, their sorrowful eyes gave their features a look of extreme frailness.

For a stunned second, neither mother nor daughter moved. Then both rose at the same instant, rushing to Carter Harmon, alternately kissing and embracing him, their nervous tears inciting Barth to the desire that he too might have the gift of open sorrow.

No matter how firm the bond of friendship nor for how long it has endured, each first fears or rejoices only for his own. Minutes later, Lucy thought of Barth, and went to him, putting her arms around him and laying her cheek upon his chest, as she sobbed, "Oh, Barth, you poor dear."

His palm, gently patting her back, was not there out of compassion, but was simply an acknowledgment of her presence. He had no comfort for her. There was no comfort.

At Mrs. Harmon's kindly suggestion, he seated himself. But the sincere effort of his hosts to draw him from his somber shell was fruitless.

Thus the night crawled to lateness. Out of deference to him, they had joined him in his silence. And while he knew his thoughts, they could only sadly conjecture as to what phase of his sorrow was passing through his troubled mind. A twitching of his facial muscles, the setting and resetting of his lips, the lowering of his brow to his hand bespoke the shifting sands of his inner despair.

Each of his saddened friends yearned to lift the weight of his yoke, if only ever so slightly, but the way to his heart was closed. He was in his own impregnable fortress of grief. The gates were barred so that none might enter. And he alone could open them.

Only once had he spoken. "If I had not sent Gabe to Kentucky . . ." He did not elaborate upon the brief utterance. Whatever its meaning, it was expressed by the clenching and unclenching of his hands.

Just when they had begun to believe that this true wake would last the night, he arose abruptly, saying, "I am going to the garrison. I will see you in the morning before I leave."

Instantly, Mrs. Harmon was at his side. "Captain, you stay with your friends. You can have Lucy's bed. She can sleep with me. Carter will be comfortable on a pallet. He can sleep anywhere. You must get some rest."

As he looked toward the little room that served as Lucy's bedchamber, the memory engulfed him. On that bed, he had lain with her—held her close, kissed her and their flaming desires had been quenched. Lie there now, with her lifeless body in the cold ground? "No!" he thundered the word, and its volume caused Martha Harmon's knees to weaken as she exchanged anxious glances with her husband and daughter. The thought that rode their beams of sight was the same. Was his tortured brain at the point of breaking? A question he answered immediately by a terse apology. "I'm most sorry. Thanks for your consideration of me, but it would be better if I spent the night at the fort."

Only after Carter Harmon had pointed out that it was very late and that there might be difficulty in gaining admittance to the stockade, did he consent to stay. But he steadfastly declined to use the bed, insisting that since he would not sleep anyway the pallet would be adequate. Using the pretense he wanted a breath of fresh air, he discretely stepped outdoors while those inside the dwelling attired themselves for their rest. Pacing back and forth the length of the dwelling, he reentered just after Mrs. Harmon had whispered sadly to her husband, "That poor soul. What will he do? He loved her so much. And that poor, sweet girl— she lived a life of trouble. From the time her mother and father died, leaving her with nobody to look after her but that old mail aunt. Poor Dracie—it's hard to realize it really happened . . . that she's gone."

"Sh . . . sh." Harmon's warning ended as the door opened. Barth took a seat by the table, then leaned over and blew out the light of the lone candle that had been left burning for his guidance.

Outside, Buck's sad eyes had followed the pacing figure until the door closed behind it. The Negro suffered for his master with an aching that hollowed his devoted heart, creating a void he knew not how to fill. When the cabin was darkened, he returned to his bed of hay near Sagitta.

The night aged and died and was borne gently away by the gray messengers of the dawn, revealing the inconsolable one who still kept the seat of his lonely vigil. His eyes rebuked their weary lids for their tiredness and would not let them fall. When true light filled the room, he rose stiffly and moved quietly to the door. He eased it open and slipped outside, leaving the door slightly ajar to prevent any possible disturbance its closing might occasion of those resting inside—a precaution that was needless. Slumber had bowed to the sudden visitation of sorrow. No one had slept.

As he moved slowly along the side of the cabin, he saw Buck waiting in his path. Sharp words would have come, but the doleful countenance of the Negro dissuaded them. Instead, Barth ordered, "Saddle Sagitta and bring him around to the front."

Within the house, Martha Harmon whispered uneasily, "Carter . . . are you awake? Captain Mercer just went outside! You'd better get your clothes on and go after him. A body in his frame of mind is apt to do anything . . . no telling what. Be quiet, so that you don't wake Lucy, poor child. I'm glad she was able to sleep. I couldn't shut my eyes for thinking about what happened yesterday."

From across the room, Lucy's voice came drowsily. "I'm awake, Mother. I couldn't sleep either. I heard him get up too."

Her father's tired tones told his family he also had been denied his rest before he verified the fact while he hastily dressed. When he opened the door, Buck was in the act of handing Sagitta's reins to his master. Harmon gave his greeting from where he stood. "Good morning, Captain. You're up early."

Flat, expressionless words came from Mercer's lips. "I want to leave for Virginia as soon as possible."

"You surely weren't going without telling us goodbye, were you?"

The older man's evident concern enlivened Barth's reply. "No, sir. I had no intention of doing that. It's just that I will need my rifle and powderhorn, and I wanted to return to the forest and recover yours for you."

"You don't have to do that now, Captain. I'm sure you could describe the general locality, and I could get some of the men to go with me and get them later on today. It wouldn't even be necessary for you to go at all."

Barth's words were edged. "I won't be staying here, Mr. Harmon. I'm leaving as soon as I can do so. And I can't go until you either have your own rifle and horn or mine in their stead. If your weapon can't be found, I'll still have my pistol."

"But, Captain Mercer, we ought not go there by ourselves. And it's so very early. I doubt that anyone is awake other than the watch at the station. Couldn't we at least wait until sunup? Suppose there are savages about? You know they always try to recover their dead."

Mercer refused to be deterred. "Mr. Harmon, if what you told me yesterday is correct, all of the war party was killed. There wouldn't be any way for the other Indians to learn about their deaths, except accidental discovery of their bodies. I appreciate your offer to go with me, but I do not expect you to do so. If there are Indians, as you fear, one man would have a much better chance of escaping detection than would two."

Harmon would not hear of his companion setting out alone. As it developed, after some persuasion, Barth permitted Buck to be included in the party. A concession that made the Negro's saddling of Harmon's horse and the roan a positive pleasure. Nor did the fear of capture by the savages depress Buck's elation. Armed by his master with his pistol, he was ready for the "Injerns," should any be encountered.

As they headed northwardly, Carter Harmon did not question the longer route they were taking. The way would have been much shorter through the valley, but a young woman lay buried on the brow of one of its grassy slopes.

Harmon's tension had its beginning as they left Fort Harrod behind. A mile farther on, they deserted the traveled way for the open land that divided the forest. Approximately another mile and there appeared on their left a vast stretch of blackened ruin . . . an impressive sight in its early-dawn desolation. It was now that Mercer spoke the first words to be uttered since they had left the cabin. He pointed to the shadowy green border of the woods on the west side of the ravaged area. "We turn off there. I'll lead the way. Buck, you ride behind me." He handed his rifle to Harmon, saying, "Mr. Harmon, you'd better have this since you'll be bringing up the rear. Let me have your pistol." The exchange of weapons ended his speech.

They threaded their irregular course along the edge of the woodland until Mercer signaled his intention to enter the forest. Gray though the atmosphere had been before, it was as brightness compared to the depth of the shade into which they filed. Immediately thereafter, the party came upon a dead savage. As Harmon's vision settled to the change of light, he noted that the Indian's right buttock had been devoured and the flesh stripped from his right side, exposing the rib. He noticed the wide swing Buck made around the body, as the Negro followed his master who had not even paused at the sight.

To Barth, the partially eaten corpse had been only a marker along the route to the powderhorn that he had now returned to its owner. The horn, in turn, became a guidepost to the ravine, and the ravine to the body of Dracie's murderer and the rifle. The flesh-eating animals of the wilderness had been here also. The black hole below the still implanted knife attested their fondness for human entrails. The dark spots where the eyes had been, the pecked-away nostrils, the absence of the upper lip and the bared row of teeth. Beneath him feathered cannibals had partaken of their favorite delicacies.

The tender-hearted Carter Harmon experienced a touch of nausea that threatened retching until he turned his eyes elsewhere. But Buck watched his dismounted master steadfastly, marveling with bulging eyes and opened mouth, as he thought, Dat Injern ez sho' daid. Dat l'arn 'im ter fool wif Massa Cap'n. He saw something which had escaped him previously. De whole top ob de haid ez gone! When dat Massa Cap'n, he kill a Injern, he kill 'im good!

Mercer, looking upon the remains, relished what he saw. He considered the defilement that met his eyes to be entirely just, and the creatures that had brought it about were the after agents of his vengeance. His reflections ended, he picked up the rifle and handed it to his paling friend. He mounted Sagitta and the little group headed homeward the same way it had come.

Unnoticed had been the tomahawk, its axe end cleaving the forest earth. If it's aim had been true . . .

CHAPTER 80

The rising sun cleared the tree-lined horizon as they turned on to the way toward Harrodstown. And with its coming, the day became suddenly beautiful. But to the sorrowing Mercer, it was a day that might have been. And the soft rays brought only heartache and longing for the one who slept on the hilltop of her Eden. He looked forlornly toward the berry bushes in the distance, and his eyes moved imaginatively up the path and through the corridor of trumpet vines on to the maple and the plot of fresh earth its shade embraced. Biting his lip, he shut the scene from his mind and turned to his companion. "Mr. Harmon, after I've gone, will you put a small rock or stone—something that will be inconspicuous—so that her grave will be marked?" When Harmon nodded his head, he continued. "And when you come back to Virginia, if you meant what you said about coming back, will you bring her—her things with you? I know that I'm asking a lot of you, but will you do this for me?"

Compassion filled Carter Harmon's countenance. When the fullness within his throat had abated he said, "I will do that for you, Barth, when I leave here." Once more, the informal address had its effect and the stern mouth relaxed. They rode in silence for a few moments before he spoke again, "You know, Captain, when I do leave here, I will leave dead hopes behind also."

Barth thought, We have both lost our treasure. Harmon's was his fortune. Mine was far greater than riches, but he answered, "I realize that, sir, and I am truly sorry for you."

The first sight of the returning riders brought joyous relief to Lucy and her distraught mother. They had heard Carter Harmon's determination to accompany Mercer and feeling powerless to interfere had watched anxiously after him as he had ridden away from the safety of their cabin. Now, with his ever-nearing presence, their emotions overwhelmed them. And when he at last drew his reins and dismounted, they rushed to him, wildly embracing him and smothering his face with their tear-ladened kisses.

Comprehension dawned upon his astonishment and he said soothingly, "Now, now, Martha. It's all right now. You shouldn't let yourself imagine such frightening things. It's sinful, you know. You're not trusting in God when you do that." Though his words were to his wife, the gentleness of his voice reduced not only the fever of her nervous excitement but also that of their sobbing daughter as well.

Regaining a degree of self-possession, Martha Harmon said apologetically to the taciturn Mercer, "You must think we are just hysterical women. But we were so worried when you all left so quickly." She did not mention the now vanished resentment that had filled her breast for his having allowed her husband to accompany him on such a danger-fraught, utterly unnecessary mission. Nor did Lucy admit to the ensnarling conflict of sympathy, grief and dread, which had inspired her to say to her mother when she had seen her father's beloved figure fade in the distance, "Dracie's dead. Why should Papa risk his life? Barth has no right to let him go with him. We should have made him stay here." Her father's safe return had banished all thoughts of bitterness.

Buck had alighted before Mr. Harmon and had taken charge of the latter's horse, along with the roan, and awaited his master's dismounting that he might lead Sagitta with them to their stalls. But Mercer made no move to permit this action. Nor did he seem to hear Mrs. Harmon's voice. Warped by his affliction, he labored over the tearful reunion now being enacted. Why could not Dracie have been here? Why had it not been Lucy rather than she? Or why couldn't it have been any other woman? Why had chance settled upon Dracie? He was looking at the Harmons but he did not see then. His eyes were upon the shadow-filled pit and the little lumps of dirt that broke as they struck the hands he had crossed upon her breast. All was covered, except her face and shoulders.

"Barth . . . Barth . . . Barth!" Lucy's repetition of his name became increasingly louder as he continued to sit as a man asleep with his eyes fully opened. Her hands accomplished that which her voice could not. Pulling at the waist of his jacket, she forced his attention, before she again spoke to him. "Let's all go inside, Barth. I know you don't feel like it but you should eat something. We all should."

His words came in slow response. "I'm going back to Virginia, Lucy. There's no reason for me to stay here any longer."

"But, Barth, you don't mean you're just going to ride off from here, do you?" Her incredulity mounted as she continued. "What about your things and Dracie's?"

"Your father will take care of them. He'll bring them later on."

Lucy cast a puzzled glance at her father. "Papa, what does he mean?"

Carter Harmon's answer was not complete. "I've decided there's no use staying here any longer. What's lost is gone. It will be hard on all of us. But I'd rather be poor and safe in Virginia than to take a chance on our lives by trying to retrieve our fortune in this uncertain place. I told Captain Mercer of my intention, and he requested that I take his belongings with us when we leave here."

Lucy was still unbelieving. "Barth, you're not leaving right now. You surely could stay a few days—til you're—Well, til you've rested and then leave."

His reply was unequivocal. "I'm leaving now, Lucy."

Mrs. Harmon then exhausted her persuasive powers, only to admit finally, "There's no use, Lucy. He's bound and determined to go. If he must go, I reckon he must." With this acknowledgment, she turned and went inside the dwelling.

She reappeared quickly, her arms full of provisions, which she proceeded to pack in the saddlebags.

Her thoughtfulness was not immediately remarked upon by the object of her consideration. He was in the act of bidding them goodbye before he expressed his thanks for the hospitality that had been accorded him. His next words were for Mr. Harmon. "I'm leaving Buck with you. I had best tell you I have no title to him nor do I know who has. It was for the latter reason that I kept him, although had I known his owner's name I would have tried to buy him. He's a good boy, even if he is sometimes slow to understand things. I know you all will be patient with him." His speech was solemn, and he did not look to where the Negro was waiting submissively.

The bastardizing effect of what his master had said passed slowly through the Negro's brain, benumbing his senses when the import of the words fully pictured. He began to cry softly, moving Carter Harmon to his side to say to him, "We'll be nice to you, Buck. And when we go back to Virginia, we'll take you with us. Then you can be with Captain Mercer again."

His attempt at comforting the heartbroken slave was futile. "Ah be daid ef Massa Cap'n lebe me. I'se Massa Cap'n's niggah an' dat's all. He ongry cayse Ah doan watch atter Miz Dracie but Ah trys an' do lak he say, but Miz Dracie, she doan pay me no mine. She say, 'Buck, Ah—"

"That's enough, Buck!" his master exclaimed violently. "You are staying here. Do you understand? Get that into that thick Black head of yours! You hear me?"

The warm, salty tears ran into Buck's mouth as he sobbed. "Yassa, Massa Cap'n. Ah unnerstans yo'. Ah does whut yo' tells me." But when Mercer turned his attention from him, the Negro whispered to the sympathetic man at his side, "Massa Hahmon, he need yo' las' night. He need me now."

Harmon did that which the dejected Negro hoped of him, interrupting Lucy's conversation with Mercer, to say humbly, "Barth, you have asked me to do certain things that I will be most happy to do. Things I would have done without you having asked me." He paused, before continuing. "Now, I am asking you a favor, and I do not intend it in any bargaining manner. Will you change your mind and let Buck go with you? You'll have the roan with you, and he at least could take care of it and you—you wouldn't have to be bothered with the animal. It's a long way back to Virginia, you know, and he'd be company for you."

The unexpected request slowed Mercer's answer until he could settle its meaning. After a few seconds, he said earnestly, "Why, Mr. Harmon, I'm sorry. I intended for you to have both Buck and the horse. They are mighty little to give you in return for your kindness to me. They are both yours, though it is barely possible someone might claim Buck from you."

Now, it was Harmon's turn to think quickly. He forced his speech, trusting logic would come with it. "You misunderstand me. I appreciate your gratitude but I would not take any gifts for what little we have done for you." His line of thought wavered, but he straightened it instantly. "I really think that Buck should accompany you on your journey home. Besides, I'm sure she—" He carefully avoided the use of her name. "—would have wanted you to take him with you." He had said all he could in the Negro's behalf. The rest was up to Mercer.

A harsh reply coiled itself and made ready to strike. *If the damned nigger had obeyed me, she might still be here. The least the dull, Black bastard could have done would have been to have let me know she had ridden off by herself. And Harmon wants me to take him with me! Doesn't he have sense enough to know that his presence would be a constant reminder of what has happened? Good God! How could I ever find peace with him along?* But before the vehement thoughts could be lashed into words, there came to him the remembrance of her delight of yesterday—now receded in deepest time—when she had first viewed the roan and he had given Buck to her. *Harmon is right,* he reasoned, *far more right than he could ever know. Even though she is dead, they still are here, and she would expect me to keep them—not give them away. It is my duty to her—the only thing—the last thing—that I can do for her.*

Harmon had seen the sudden rise of blood to Mercer's face when he had made his appeal to him, and he was unprepared for the quiet utterance he now heard.

"I believe you are right, Mr. Harmon. I do need Buck and of course the roan. Thank you very much for making me realize that. He dismounted and shook the hand of the older man, repeating the gesture with Mrs. Harmon, reiterating as he did so his appreciation of their treatment of him.

But Lucy brushed past his extended palm and embracing him, kissed his lips. "You will be in our hearts, Barth, until we see you again. God willing, it will not be long until we do so."

For a fleeting moment, he was taken aback by her demonstrativeness, but he then reckoned it only a zealous expression of farewell.

Buck moved with alacrity to return Sagitta's reins to his master's hand from which he had taken them when Mercer had alighted a short while before. Though it was unnecessary, he held the horse's bridle until his master was seated and then went to untie the roan from the hitching rack. Much to the embarrassment of his benefactor, as he passed Carter Harmon, he knelt and kissed the hand of the one who had righted his topsy-turvy world. He would have returned Harmon's horse to its stall had not the elderly gentleman expressed a desire it remain where it was tethered.

Master and servant had waved their last goodbye and were not but diminishing figures in the distance. Carter and Martha Harmon had gone inside. Only Lucy still watched the disappearing rider. "If he had stayed a few days, perhaps I might have taken her place in his heart," she said softly. "If ever we should meet again . . ."

"Lucy, honey, come in and eat something. We'll have to hurry and get things done if we're going to the service." Her mother's voice turned her toward the door of the cabin. It did not matter. He was gone. All these years, she had loved him. But so had her dearest friend. Now she was dead.

"Lucy, honey, are you coming?"

Lucy quickened her steps. "Yes, Mama. I'm coming."

CHAPTER 81

They were at the Low Dutch Station, the convergence of the trails from Harlan's Station and Harrodstown. How different had been his spirit two days ago! If only it were today that he rode to get her! If only the magnet of fate had not drawn her to the valley. He reflected upon the perils he had escaped only to lose her forever. Aaron Flinden's description of life at Bullitt's Lick came to him. "Fair hell on earth!" He shifted in the saddle, looking back in the direction of Harrodstown. Not only at Bullitt's Lick but also anywhere on earth, life was fair hell.

As if trying to outdistance the bitter memories, he spurred Sagitta to a full gallop, riding recklessly through those about the station. Buck kept the roan on his master's pace but well off the traveled way, not returning to it until the settlement and the angered countenances of its settlers had been left far behind. By the time they reached Cowan, a mile farther on, the horses were at a walk. They galloped again briefly, then slowed as cabins began to cluster and they were in Danville. They did not tarry. Nor did Mercer return the many friendly salutations of the residenters, leaving them in wonderment at the manner of man he might be who disdained their neighborliness. Onward a half a mile, the horses were watered at Clark's Run Creek. Though Buck discovered a mint-draped spring, only he drank of its ice-cold flow.

They crossed a wide branch of Dix River at a point that brought them near Clark's Station. As before, there was no pausing and they headed for Logan's St. Asaph Station, about six miles away. Mercer was being more considerate of the animals, and it was more than an hour later that the first dwelling appeared.

The slave's powers of recollection stirred upon their arrival at Logan's. His memory was not so vacant that he did not recognize the fort as being the place his former owner had turned him over to the rogue who later took him to Bullitt's Lick. He urged the roan nearer his master's mount, a move compelled by the uneasiness now dominating his thinking. For Logan's Station was a focal point, the crossing site of the paths from the Cumberland settlement and the road running through the great wilderness and its branches, the one leading to Harrodstown and the other to Lexington. As in all places of confluence, there was a regular congregating of travelers, those departing or newly arriving and those who rested here before continuing their journey. For once, Buck was thankful for the introspection that so firmly held his master, causing him to ignore his surroundings and ride unhesitatingly ahead.

Ever since they had left the Low Dutch colony, the sun had borne down with all the strength of its late summer rage. But only the Negro seemed to feel its might—a discomfort he endured without protest, just as he refused to make a complaint of the aching that now wrung his belly. He remembered the cold draught at the spring and he was thirsty again. Thirst heightened not so much by its degree as by the thought he had not filled himself when he had the opportunity to do so.

Ahead of him, his master had left the trail and was angling toward a fern-covered slope that lay in the deep shade of a great oak. He saw him halt and wheel Sagitta about. His heart leapt when he realized the words were for him. "You can drink if you're thirsty. I remember it was here from when I passed here before."

"Massa Cap'n, ain' yo' gwine ter drink some yo'se'f? Yo' ain' had none all de day."

Mercer did not answer but the suggestion had borne fruit. Buck watched happily as he saw him swing from the saddle, the rifle crooked in his right elbow moving as a part of his body. The Negro waited for him to begin drinking before he got off the roan and knelt by the bubbling water at a point below where his master was cupping his hands. Buck had no intention of making the mistake he fancied he had made earlier. This time, he would drink to his capacity.

He had exceeded his thirst but would have yet continued had he not been cautioned sharply. "Do not drink too much. You'll get sick when you get back in the sun." When the Negro obeyed by instantly rising, Mercer said, "Reach in my saddlebag and get yourself something to eat if you're hungry."

Before Buck put his black hand into the bag, he asked, "Massa Cap'n, fo' Ah fetches it, doan yo' want ter eat some yo'se'f?" The respectful inference was clear. No White man would eat after a Negro.

A sharp retort—"Eat if you're hungry!"—was his answer. Perhaps the comfortable feeling that came with the satisfaction of his appetite was responsible, but it seemed no time at all before his master said, "This is Crab Orchard. We'll spend the night here."

Once again, Buck's qualms were upon him. There were numbers of persons about the station and the fear of recognition had reasserted itself. However, he noted, thankfully, there weren't nearly so many people as there had been at the other fort. He welcomed the night when it had fully descended. And his rest came easily, knowing his master was sleeping nearby between him and the tethered horses.

Buck rolled his head from the light of the morning but he did not long contest its summons. Opening his eyes, he looked to where he had last seen his master the evening before. He was gone! And so were the horses! Startled, the Negro scrabbled hastily to his feet, only to find immediate relief from his consternation in the sight of the approaching Mercer, leading Sagitta and the roan. He mustered his courage and asked, "Whuffo' yo' up so early, Massa Cap'n? Ah looks atter de hosses fo' yo', does yo' ax me."

"I didn't ask you. I found a farrier and had him look at the horses' feet. We've got a long, hard way ahead of us and I wanted to be sure they were ready for it." The explanation was given in cold condescension. The next words came as a command. "If you want to eat, get it out of the saddlebag, if you left anything the last time you ate. Be quick about it. I want to get on to English Station. There is a large party leaving for Virginia. If we don't hurry, they'll be gone before we can get there." Mercer's tone dispelled any hope the Negro cherished that his master's melancholy mood had changed. The White man rode with the living, but he lived with the dead.

They came into English Station and disappointment. The others had departed at dawn. Mercer's curt inquiry had drawn a brusque reply for which he expressed no thanks, leaving his informant cursing his rudeness—open expressions of contempt that fell on Buck's ears as he cantered after his master.

The fort they were now leaving would be the last outpost on the Wilderness Road in Kentucky.[36] Six miles beyond Cumberland Gap, they would come upon the small station at Big Spring. One hundred and twenty hostile, wilderness miles.

Though he could not remember the distance in miles, Buck would never forget the dragging terror he had known along this wilderness pathway the one time he had traveled its length. No matter how large the number of travelers, there would still be the constant fear of Indian attacks. Since he and his master would be the last to join the body, they would likely keep their rearmost position throughout the entire journey. And it was the tail of such caravans that the savages usually harassed. Let there be the least straggling and scalps would be missing and fierce halloos would sound. But the Red warriors whose throats sung the blood-noted score would be unseen. Even in closely knit units, there was always the danger of ambush.

He could not recall how long the passage had taken before, but he had no difficulty in bringing back to his mind the chilling nights and humid days he had endured in seeming endless succession. Nor was it difficult to summon the picture of back-breaking toil when a packhorse lamed and he had to tote its load. And every so often, there were trees to be felled to clear the trail.

Nearly two hours later, they caught up with the party after a sweltering ride over ragged terrain. Mercer satisfied the challenge of those guarding the rear and proceeded as directed to the head of the column where he reported to the leader of the expedition. He was questioned carefully as to his identity, where he was going and where he was from. There were brief inquiries concerning the Negro, who breathed a bit easier when his master's answers were accepted without undue explanation. However, Buck's concern rose upon the pronouncement that since he could not handle a firearm, he would have to travel in the middle of the party, when his services were not required for any of the varied tasks of labor he would be expected to perform. His anxiety calmed somewhat when he observed a young

Negress looking at him from the spot where he assumed he would be placed. She appeared to be well-developed and his imagination ran a pleasant course. It had been a long, long time since he had been with a woman. But he did not look at her again until he had first searched the countenances of the White folks he would accompany. When they all proved unfamiliar, his concern departed and he returned the girl's sly smile. It was not apprehension that caused his heart to resume its quickened beating.

Mercer learned what was expected of him—duties that were standard in all instances of common travel. As had been the case when he had come to Kentucky from Virginia, he would take a regular turn at guarding, scouting and hunting. Above all, he was obliged to obey orders, and he had to so agree before formal permission was granted him and his servant to join the group.

The halt occasioned by their arrival and integration had ended. The exodus resumed its former slow, but steadfast progression.

August blistered its way past its midpoint, Thus far there had been no sign of Indians. Nor had any serious mishap occurred to hinder the determined progress that now saw them passing peacefully through the awe-inspiring vista of Cumberland Gap into Virginia.

Somewhere in the land they were leaving, at a salting spot called Blue Lick, a tragic blunder had been made and White men were being slaughtered by Redmen. Stephen Trigg, whom Mercer had esteemed so highly, lay dead in a bloody arena. Fifty-nine valiant comrades would lie with him before the ambush had been concluded.[37] One of them, Israel Boone, had already given his life trying to protect his father during the unequal battle. Daniel Boone had snatched his fallen son from the hands of the victory-crazed savages and was, at this moment, placing the lifeless body across the back of his horse. Boone's tears broke their barriers as he recalled the memory of another son the Indians had killed when he was first bringing his family into Kentucky, approaching the great pass that divided the Cumberland mountains.[38] That day, Cumberland Gap had not been peaceful.

Though Mercer would be saddened when he learned later of the disaster, had he known it now, as it was occurring, his reaction would have been, "Was life any more precious to Trigg and to the others than it was to Dracie? Rather than diminishing, his despondency found new depths with the falling of each wilderness night and its ensuing lonely hours. And so deep had he dug the well of his mournful despair, the healing light of the day could not fathom its misery.

To Mercer's fellow travelers, he was a man apart. One who did not answer readily when spoken to nor speak to others unnecessarily. Nevertheless, he did all that was required of him and did it well, cheating the desire of those who would have welcomed an opportunity to rebuke him for his slightest failure.

He seldom had any word for Buck and scarcely noticed him when the Negro was in his presence—an aloofness that spawned fretful uncertainty in the slave's mind as to his lot, once this terrifying trek was ended by their arrival at what the White folks called the Blockhouse.[39]

The Blockhouse was a goal sought second only to home—the synonym of safety in the thoughts of all who traveled the danger-infested trail from Kentucky. The fact that this station had itself been subject to Indian incursions did not deter the hopeful reasoning. The Blockhouse was the symbol of the strength of civilization.

Buck accepted the Blockhouse as being the haven the White folks considered it, but to him it was a vague reference. Every station had a blockhouse. His utter inability to remember names obliterated its significance. And though he heard the name every day, it seemed to him the place itself would never be reached. However, one morning, the words were on everyone's lips. They had crossed another mountain, and the trail had wound itself to a river. It was after the stream had been forded, that he heard the talking about another gap. It had a snake's name. Everyone was in good spirits. Happiness that showed on the faces of the jubilant travelers and was evidenced by prevalent jocularity. There was only one person unaffected, whose features did not change their expression, who continued on his unemotional, solitary way.

A great shout rang out. "There it is—Moccasin Gap!" Though he did not know the cause of the celebrating, Buck put his arm around the young Negro girl at his side and squeezed her, just like the White men were hugging their women. The Negress—she had told him her name, but he couldn't recall it at the moment—made no protest, and he wished he had been bolder with her on previous opportunities. The fear of her complaining to her master had he attempted to fondle her during the darkened part of the trip had effectively restrained his sexual desires. Now that he knew her disposition, if he got another chance . . .

There was to be no further opportunity. The party cleared the gap and crossed the Holston River. With the excited cries of "There's th' Blockhouse," Buck now knew their meaning. He had been there before.

For a while, all seemed confusion as the newly arrived party was greeted by those at the fort. The welcoming subsided gradually. When it had ended, Mercer and the Negro found themselves alone. They had not shared in the common rejoicing. Indeed, few of the celebrants had approached them. And these had turned aside upon glimpsing Mercer's grimly set features. It had been as the north wind driving away a joyful rain.

Ordering Buck to remain where he was, Mercer entered the garrison. He returned shortly and had him follow to where some ten or twelve others of his color were quartered. He made no comment beyond saying, "This is where you'll stay." Then he left abruptly.

Just before darkness the slaves were fed. It was a good stout meal: beef, Irish potatoes, yams, cornbread and gravy. All dumped into two pot-bellied wooden bowls from which the hungry Negroes ravenously scooped the soggy mixture with their hands. Whatever was to be his fate, Buck too ate heartily. It was not until the night had fully closed that his worry for his future commenced its incessant jabbing, inducing varied waves of panic that would not let him sleep. Each attack left him the more certain that Massa Cap'n had determined to sell him. Perhaps he had already done so!

Near where the exhausted Mercer had bedded down for his first full sleep in weeks, men were talking. Had he been awake and listening, he would have heard this conversation. "We sure had a good trip. No rain to muddy the trail and slow us up. Seemed like it always rained behind us or way off to one side. It was hot as all hell, but we got used to it. And we never had no trouble of no kind, all the way here. We kept looking for Indians, but we never met no one on the whole trip! That kept me worried all the time. When we didn't run into anyone, I was sure that there had been Indian trouble on up ahead of us."

"You don't know how lucky you was," another voice commented. "About a week ago, we had th' biggest darn rain you ever seed. Looked like it was never gonna stop. And them Indians you was worryin' about was up ahead of you, all right. There was two different parties left here an' they all had to turn back. They're still here. None of them got much past th' mountains this side of Powell River 'fore they run onto th' damn Red bastards. An' ever' party had somebody killed or wounded. From what I heared, there must have been more'n forty Indians. A real war party, from what they all said."

Someone protested. "Talk somewheres else. These here fellers has got to git up early tomorry, and they needs all th' rest that they kin git." The conversation ceased.

CHAPTER 82

The Blockhouse was the common terminus of the traveled ways leading down the Shenandoah and Holston Valleys from the northeast, and from the southeast of those running through the valleys of the Yadkin and Watauga Rivers. These were the connecting routes adventurers followed to reach the Wilderness Road to Kentucky. And it was thus that settlers from Virginia and the Colonies beyond her boundaries met those coming from the Carolinas and the Tennessee country. Thus new friendships and families were formed. The new forces were joining in the continuous assault upon the wilderness.

Conversely, the Blockhouse showed the way home for the traveler who had wearied of adversity, and for those who, having found the new land to be to their liking, were returning for their kinfolk. Most rested the night before continuing on from this station, and the resultant integration produced a never-ending chain of news and views that encompassed the happenings in the old lands and the new.

But one of those who spent the night at this frontier haven—the Negro called Buck—had enjoyed no rest. And the other slaves who shared the pen into which they had been herded the evening before had not been communicative. Like himself, most of them were troubled in their thoughts of what the new day might hold in store. For the White man transacted business as he traveled, and slaves were sold and exchanged at the Blockhouse.

Buck worried to a certainty. Massa Cap'n had either sold or was going to sell him to some mean man who was on his way to Kentucky. If Massa Cap'n could only understand that he had tried to keep Miz Dracie from leaving, but that she wouldn't pay him no mind.

As the day broke, the gate of the little compound was opened by the same men who had brought them their supper. And the large wooden bowls filled with all manner of leftover food were the same unwashed receptacles they had fed from the night before. Buck ate solely because his new master, harsh as he was sure to be, probably wouldn't feed him again until nightfall. Other appetites were more active. In no time at all, the bowls had been emptied. Hands got in one another's way as their fingers methodically skimmed the inside of the containers, til only a thin coating of grease remained.

Someone was at the gate again. Buck did not look up until he heard his master call his name. He rose from his haunches and walked forlornly toward the new opened entrance. When the gate had been closed, his master spoke to him. But he couldn't believe his ears. Massa Cap'n had ordered, "Hurry along and get the horses saddled. We're leaving with some folks who are heading in the same direction we're going. Hustle it up now. I don't want to keep them waiting on us."

There was no need to tell him to hurry. What condemned soul would be laggard within sight of paradise?

There were no women in the small band with which they were now traveling. Nor were there any wagons. And their absence made for faster progress up the valley. It was not surprising, therefore, that the first day's end found them encamped nearly thirty miles from the Blockhouse. The miles had not been the lonely distances of the Wilderness Road. Their passage had been enlivened by frequent meeting with others who rode to the south. Only the grim Mercer had failed to wish them Godspeed on their way.

The next morning, the sky was overcast and rain seemed inevitable. But an hour later, the breeze had changed and the sun burned a bright path through the dirty sky. Before midmorning, the sea of gray was gone and a fiery ball rode the heavens, baking the traveler on the trail beneath. No longer did Buck actually have to see an oncoming party to know of its approach. Rolling clouds of dust in the road far ahead effectively served this premonitory purpose. And when parties passed, swirling eddies of powdered soil enveloped them, blinding them and rendering breathing difficult.

The Negro only could guess as to how far he had ridden at the close of the second day. But he knew they had covered almost as much ground as the day before. As he lay near the horses, he wondered how much farther he and his master would ride before they were home. And when they did finally reach there, would his master continue to treat him as indifferently as had been his recent practice? True, Massa Cap'n had seen that he was fed from the provisions purchased at the beginning of this trip and he had not suffered any abuse. But his master didn't talk to him like he used to. Now he just studied all the time. Buck had fought the suspicion his owner was, as the suggestion told him, "sick in de haid." But as the condition worsened, and though he still resisted the insidious implication, suspicion began to take factual root.

The next day's journey ended at Fort Chiswell, which they reached shortly before dusk. And it was here that their little band began to disassemble as six of its members bade their fellow adventurers farewell. The joinder of their lives with the twelve who would set out again tomorrow was severed forever.

Buck and his master consumed the last of their rations before joining the others in an early retirement.

With the sunrise, they were on their way. They followed rain clouds the greater part of the day. And though they frequently rode through water puddled in the road, they never caught up with its actual falling. The extreme humidity took its first toll, as two men were overcome and the group halted until the casualties had revived sufficiently to continue. They proceeded only a short distance before three of the travelers reached their destination and left the party. When the sky reddened that evening, nine men—half of the original number—halted at Ingles Ferry on New River. Four of these would not leave in the morning. They were home.

Ordinarily, they would have offered food and shelter to their erstwhile companions, but to do so on this occasion would mean they would have to include the strange man who was going to Williamsburg. Not wishing to offend him by excluding him from their invitation, they did not offer hospitality to any.

What was not offered him, Mercer purchased from another. He slept in a bed this night, and Buck rested on a pile of hay in the same stable that housed the horses.

When daylight came and the other travelers were not at the agreed meeting place, Mercer bought what he considered enough food to last himself and his servant until the next day, and they departed without waiting longer upon their supposedly tardy fellows.

It was well they did so. Those for whom the White man and his Negro had so briefly waited were not late. They were intentionally absent. After serious consideration, they had determined they did not desire to continue in the company of one whom they were now thoroughly convinced was most queer if not truly mentally disturbed.

Buck had not ridden far before he acknowledged the hope he had held when he and his master had ridden off by themselves was sterile. He had imagined wishfully that because they rode alone, Mercer would be more condescending toward him and might even revert to his former habit of pleasantness. When night came, and there had been no exchange of words between them, Buck regretted they had not waited for the others at the day's beginning.

Morning dawned on what proved to be another journey whose silence doubled the tedious miles of its duration. And at sunset, the dull-witted Negro knew a pattern had been set. It would be like this until they finished their traveling. And how much farther would that be? What would happen when they finally reached wherever they were going?

He lost track of the dawns that followed—all but the last one. It had been then that his master had failed to extract his pouch and purchase their food. A practice that had left a string of offended people, whose kindheartedness had been rebuffed by the surly insistence that they accept money for what they had wished to give freely.

The crows cawed their hoarse cries of rain long before the lightning flashed and the thunder rumbled through the clouds. Then it came. The heavens opened, and it was as if the rivers of water had been diverted from their earthly coursing. But they rode on. Where before they had pursued the rain, the tables were now reversed. Darkness was descending as they found shelter in a deserted windowless cabin by the wayside.

His master had spoken to him this day. But his words had been vitriolic upon each occasion, causing the Negro to weigh the desirability of such speech against silence. Strangely, however, there was no remonstrance when he asked permission to bring the horses in out of the weather. Nor was there any protests when he helped him find a dry spot on the cabin floor. He noted his master sank wearily as he lay down.

He unsaddled the drenched animals and slanted the equipment against the wall that the leather might be drained and given a chance to dry. Then he studied about for a dry place for himself and the horses. There was none to be found. The best he could do was to head the steeds into a corner. That way, only their hindquarters would be under the roof's leaking. He made his bed alongside, barely between them and his now sleeping master. He did not fare as well with the horses. Drops peltered down on him from his hips to his feet. But his weariness overcame their annoying constancy.

So thoroughly had sleep possessed him, he was perplexed by the light showing through the rotted portions of the roof. He lay there awhile, becoming gradually conscious of the uncomfortable sogginess of his britches from their all night dousing. It could not be daylight. He had fallen asleep only a moment ago. But the sounds he heard were those of the day: the birds and, when they were still, the identifying calm of morning. A sensed distinction between the tranquility of the waking and the resting hours was outside. He looked at the still-slumbering master. If it were day, why wasn't he up? He was always the first one to arise.

Buck got to his feet quietly, whispering gentle assurances to Sagitta nearest him. The door creaked as he pushed against it, and he cast a hasty glance toward his master. Satisfied there had been no disturbing of his rest, he crossed the threshold. As he did so, his bare feet were chilled by a pool of water that had filled the depression at the entrance, a sloping hole, worn by the untold comings and goings of those vanished ones who had lived and visited here in years gone by.

It was not raining at the moment, but the heavy sky seemed only to be biding its time before unleashing a torrential downpour. Though no human was in sight, habit directed him to the rear of the cabin where he removed his saturated clothing and then relieved himself. After wringing the water from his garments, he put them back on.

He reentered the dilapidated dwelling and eased Sagitta past the quiet figure of his owner and out the door. After tying the gray, he returned for the roan. He inspected the animals thoroughly and was distressed to find each had raw saddle sores in almost identical places. Another day's ride, with the saddles bearing down upon the wet blankets on their backs, and the sores would become inflamed and painful. Recalling Mercer's vile humor of yesterday, he hesitated to awaken him. He ran his hand over the roan's flanks, noting the prominence of the ribs. As he did so, he contrasted the excellent appearance of both horses at the start of the demanding journey and their present rundown condition. And he remembered that they, like himself, had eaten nothing since the night before last. Surely, Massa Cap'n would get food for them today. He led the animals down the road hoping to find some place they might graze, but what little vegetation he came upon was completely parched. The rain had come too late. He turned the horses about and as he neared the cabin, his master was coming outside. Even before he reached him, the Negro could see something was wrong. And when he came closer, he knew. Massa Cap'n was unsteady upon his feet. Buck spoke before he was spoken to. "Massa Cap'n, yo' 'peers a li'l tuckered. Whyn't yo' rest yo'se'f some more fo' us goes on?"

The ensuing reply was slow in its coming. But when it came, it was full of abuse. After he had finished berating him, Mercer ordered the horses saddled immediately. The severity of his voice lessened as he said, "Richmond can't be too much farther. We'll be all right, once we reach there."

Buck went inside and got the dampened saddles. He disliked the idea of using the wet leather and the soaked blankets. They should allowed to dry. But his master's last outburst had cowed him so, he dared not make complaint. Nor did he mention the sores on the animals. And he was careful to saddle Sagitta first, before he tightened the soddened leather bellyband on his own mount. They were about to leave when he realized he had forgotten the saddlebags. He slid hastily from his seat, wondering what his master's wrath would have been had they left without them. As he picked them up, he slipped his hand into first one and then the other, hopefully seeking some overlooked tidbit. But the bags were thoroughly empty.

They had ridden less than a mile, when it began to rain. Throughout the rest of the morning, their steeds sloshed through clinging mud, sometimes knee deep. And the steady downpour showed no sign of abating. Buck's spirits were at their lowest ebb. Try as he might, he could ignore no longer the esurient pains tearing so relentlessly at his insides. Suppose his master was wrong, and the town was lots farther away than he thought it was. Supposing they were lost. These thoughts conspired to aggravate his misery. He raised his head from the slumping position he had kept since the rain's beginning and looked toward the bent horseman in front of him. Seconds later, he realized his master was swaying in the saddle. He moved his horse close alongside Sagitta, just in time to keep Mercer from falling sideways to the ground. The white forehead rested on the black cheek. It was hot with fever.

"Massa Cap'n bad sick," he muttered. "Now whut does Ah do?" He managed to reach around the stricken man and catch his reins. Over to the left was a thick grove. He veered the horses toward it by pulling his mount hard against Sagitta in the desired direction. When they were beneath the boughs, he released his hold and quickly dismounted, turning to catch the unconscious form as it pitched from its seat. Then he retrieved the rifle from where the failing hands had dropped it.

He spread Mercer's bedroll on the least dampened spot he could find and stretched him upon it. He then unsaddled Sagitta and made a shield of the horse's dripping blanket, throwing it across the branches of a fork above his master's body. Then he sat down to try to think of a way out of their seemingly hopeless predicament. But the overwhelming feeling of helplessness kept suggesting itself, and all he did was sit and look at the feverish man at his side. As he watched, he saw the brows contort until they were joined, making the darkened depressions under his eyes appear the more sunken. The throbbing of the veins in the hollows of the temples was acutely visible and frightened him. He turned his head, only to look back again at the sharpened cheekbones and the matted beard covering the lower half of the face. The mouth opened and twisted fitfully. As it closed, the tongue renewed its coursing of the dry lips.

He was almost mesmerized through his steadfast gazing. Suddenly, his master began to shake violently. The exaggerated shivering brought on a fearful exclamation. "Massa Cap'n's got de ague! He gwine ter die, sho'!" Then came constructive thought. Mebbe, does Ah git a doctah, he kin sabe 'im."

His toe was in the roan's stirrup, before he realized that if he did find a doctor, he would need money. He did not weigh when or where that might be. But there was no use starting if he didn't have it. He bent over the trembling body and slipped his hand inside the neck of the jacket, extracting the pouch. There was a sense of guilt as he pulled it open. Suppose his master came to as he was handling the purse. Not knowing the value of the coins, he took a number of then, hoping they would be enough to satisfy the physician's charge.

As he rode off, he looked back with the thoughts as to what the sick man might think if he regained consciousness and discovered he was alone.

Ahead of him, the road curved sharply. As he rounded it, the rain commenced to slacken. A little farther, the sun came out. Another half mile, and he saw dwellings in the distance. This must be the place, whatever its name, his master had spoken of.

Sluggish as he was ordinarily in his thinking, he was smart enough to recognize it would not do for him to ride into the town on a steed of the roan's evident quality. At the next thicket he came to, he got off the horse and carefully concealed it. Then he struck out on foot.

There was no one about the street and he turned off onto a side way. Immediately, he saw two White men in apparent idle conversation, and he headed for them.

He lagged as he approached the men, speaking nervously. "Massas, kin Ah ax y'all somepin'?"

"What ya want, nigger?" one of them asked.

"I'se wantin' ter git a doctah fo' m' massa."

The same man asked, "What's your master's name?"

"He name ez Massa Cap'n."

"Kappen? How you spell it? That his last name?"

The unexpected questions became a snarl of words, and the Negro's wrestling features told the straining of his mind to produce the forgotten name. At last, there came a suggestion of its sound and he stammered, "M-m-ma-ma ... Mar ... Mar ... sar. Mar-sar! Dat's it!" His eyes shone with victorious light.

"You mean master? Don't you know his last name? You know, like John Smith? Now Smith would be the last name. What's your master's?"

"Massa Cap'n's name ain' Smith. He name ez Mar-sar."

The interrogator turned to his companion. "I seen a lot of dumb niggers in my time, but damn if this'n ain't got 'em all beat. If Marsar is th' name, it's a strange one. I sure ain't heard it before." He spoke again to the Negro. "You say you want a doctor? Ya could get Doc Braxton, he's a good one."

"Bracks-stum . . . Bracks—stum. Ah sho' gwine ter 'membah dat name. Thank yo' kinely fo' de tellin' me uv it, Massas. Wha' at does Ah fine 'im?"

"He lives in a big place out on th' edge of town. Now get about your business an' quite your botherin' me."

As Buck backed slowly away, he tried to ease in one last question. "Massa, please suh, kin yo' tell me whut d'rection he lib in?"

The White man considered the query presumptuous persistence and he lost his temper. "Damn you, nigger! Ain't you asked enough questions? I bet your damn master ain't even got no money to pay no damn doctor after you find 'im!"

The flustered Negro hastened to correct the insinuation. Extending the closed fist he had heretofore kept at his side, he opened it, disclosing the money it had concealed.

As the sunlight flashed on the coins, the two stared in wide-eyed amazement. One of them exclaimed, "I'll be damned! He's got a whole handful of silver!"

The other whispered through closed lips, "Get 'im to come closer."

"Come here, nigger!" When Buck hesitated, the command became harsher. "I said come here, damn you!"

Too late, Buck realized their intent and tried to run. But they were upon him before he could move. He shut his fist about the money. One of the men struggled desperately to force the hand open, while his companion restrained the slave's free arm. Maddened by his obstinance, the largest of the men cursed him profanely before saying heatedly, "I thought that damn name didn't sound right. Marsar, huh? Bet you aint' even got no damn master! An' if you do have one, you prob'ly stole this from 'im an' run away. Ain't no White man in his right mind what would give a damn nigger like you all this money. Damn your ornery Black hide, let go of it!"

Unable to make the terrified victim release his frenzied clutch, he attempted strategy. "We ain't goin' to keep th' money. We just want to see how much it is—to see if it's enough to pay th' doctor. Doctors charge high prices, you know. We'll even show you where he lives. Better'n that, we'll take you there if you let loose of it."

Buck shook his head stubbornly.

"Then we'll take you to th' law. How would you like that? The law would take th' money an' put ya in jail. Just give it to us an' we'll let you go free. How's that strike ya?"

When the Negro did not answer, the other man spoke up. "Look, Joe, this nigger's stubborn as a damn mule. Ain't no use tryin' to coax him no more. See that stone hitchin' post over yonder? Let's pull 'im over there and smash his damn fist open."

Though Buck balked every step of the way, they dragged him by his arms across the street. The man called Joe had both hands around the Negro's wrist and commenced beating the closed hand upon the obelisk-shaped stone. And though Buck was able to keep his hand from being hammered hard enough to break any bones, his knuckles were bruised and bleeding. The thought came to him that if his hand were to be injured severely he would be hindered in caring for his helpless master. He suddenly ceased his resistance.

The White men were after the coins as they spilled into the dust, unmindful the Negro was free. Buck had almost reached the main street before Joe missed him and started to give chase. His companion stayed the pursuit, shouting, "Let 'im go!"

"What do you mean let him go? There's probably a reward out for 'im."

The other merely smiled, "There's nearly four pounds here, if I've counted it right. That's enough to buy lots of that whiskey we was wishin' for when he come up to us. We could buy a damn barrel full an' still have money left to divide up." As he continued, he glanced knowingly at his confederate. "'Sides, if we was to catch 'im, there's some folks around here what might just believe what he says. You know, our word ain't none too damn good in Richmond."

Joe nodded his head in accord. "Never thought about it that a-way. He can run plumb to hell, for all I care."

CHAPTER 83

Buck fully expected to be caught. He knew his own slowness of foot from past efforts at escape. Each moment, he expected to feel the thumping impact of a hand upon his shoulder. But he ran as fast as he was able. Once, he narrowly averted colliding head-on with a fat colored woman who crossed nonchalantly in front of him. As it was, he brushed her shoulder and as he sped away, she yelled something at him. The muscles in his right thigh cramped, but he did not stop. He left the road and ran along its border. Then a minor calamity occurred. He stubbed one of his big toes on a protruding root. With an anguished cry of "Oh, Lawdy!" he sat down and rocked back and forth on his bottom, holding the foot with the bleeding digit in his hands. Suddenly, he realized he was looking up the road and that no one was coming. He forgot the hurting toe. "Dem White mens mus' have orful heavy feets," he mumbled wonderingly.

For a while, he favored the injured member by walking on the side of his foot. But he found this not only awkward but also tiring, and he soon reverted to his normal manner of travel. Every so often, he glanced over his shoulder, wondering what could have happened to his pursuers.

He had some misgivings when he mounted and rode from the little woods. What if Massa Cap'n had missed him? "Oh, Lawdy, Lawdy," he wailed.

He had a paradoxical feeling of relief when he came upon his still ailing master. But the sensation fled as he placed his palm upon the invalid's forehead. "He jes' bu'nin' up, he ez. Whut Ah gwine ter do? Does Ah tak him ter de doctah? Dem mens ez sho' ter be waitin' fo' me." He scratched his head in bewilderment. Subconsciously, he noted the descending sun. "Dat it!" he exclaimed, addressing the unconscious form. "Massa Cap'n, Ah waits til de night, den Ah gits yo' ter de doctah!"

By the time it was dusk, he was ready to leave. He tied Sagitta's reins to the roan's bellyband on the off side and, after great difficulty, succeeded in getting his master seated properly in the saddle. Then he climbed behind him and they began their ride into the falling darkness. He caught his breath. The rifle! Had he forgotten it? The lump left his throat when he remembered strapping it along with the bedroll on Sagitta's back. His master started shaking, and Buck tightened his arm about him. Then he kicked the roan into a gallop.

A strong, cooling breeze came up. They were nearing the town and he could see its scattered pinpoints of light. For the first time since he had conceived the night journey, he gave thought to finding the doctor's house. "Whut de mens say? Big place, dey say ... But wha' at ez de big place?" It was no use. He could remember no more. He felt a drop of water on his rein hand. There was a wild streak of lightning and a tremendous clap of thunder. It started to sprinkle. Then the rain came in earnest, whipped by violent gusts of wind. Recurrent flashes made the road light as day. The rain was cold, and he was shivering like the helpless one he held so tightly.

The next flare in the heavens showed a large house off to the left, and he made for it. There were lights in the downstairs rooms. A thunderbolt guided him to a tree-lined driveway and he pulled up the roan under the porch extending over the front entrance. There was a momentary consideration. "I'se s'posed ter go 'roun' ter de back, but Massa Cap'n, he pow'ful sick." He dismounted and slid his master from the saddle. He carried the limp body to the door. But he had to let Mercer's legs drop in order to reach the knocker. He rapped loudly and waited.

Inside the house, the sounds at the front door had rolled to the kitchen and the ears of an over-sized Negress who was grumbling to herself. "Dat Mah-cus! Ah declar'. Ebber day he git mo' no 'count." When the noise continued, she said, "Reckin' Ah hab ter do his wuk fo' 'im. Doan want de doctah should hab ter do it."

Buck had his hand on the knocker again but quickly released it as the door began to move. It did not open all the way. A colored woman, whose physical proportions nearly blocked the light from within, asked in a deep voice, "Who dat out dar? Whut y'all want?"

"Ah wants ter fine de doctah."

"Jes' a minute til Ah gits de light."

The door closed. Shortly after, she was back with a candle holder that held five lighted candles, which she pushed toward him. She scrutinized him carefully but did not see the face of the one whom he was supporting. When she had finished, she exclaimed, "Ah thought dat wuz a niggah out dar! Whut yo' mean comin' ter de front do'? Yo' git on 'roun' ter de back fo' de doctah, he set yo' stringin' 'way from heah wif dat pistol ob his'n."

Buck heard only the one word. "Yo' means de doctah lib heah?"

"Co'se he do, less'n yo' ez lookin' fo' some udder doctah. Now, yo' git on 'roun' wha' yo' b'longs."

She started to close the door, but Buck put the combined weight of himself and his master against it. He could not think of the doctor's name, but there was a way to remedy that and he pursued it. "Whut di head doctah's name?"

"Doctah Braxton. Now git yo'se'f 'way fum dat do'!"

He did not pause to secure the horses. Carrying his master in the same manner as before, he stepped from under the protective covering of the roof and into the rain. The storm had about run its course. And though the heavens were still illuminated intermittently, the rolling flashes were as the antics of playful cubs following the havoc-wreaked trail of parent bears. The downpour had slackened to a light shower.

She was waiting for them on the back porch, and she once again pushed the light into his face, commanding him, "Stay wha' you' ez! Whut yo' name? An' whut de name ob de sick niggah yo' ez kerryin'?"

He quickly corrected her affronting mistake. "He ain' no niggah, womern. Dis ez m' massa."

"Whut his name?"

He knew it this time. "Massa Cap'n Mar-sar," he said proudly. "Dey calls me Buck."

"Wha' y'all fum?"

The unconscious Mercer was spared the exposure of Buck's ignorance. In the first stage of delirium, he began gibbering and threshing his arms.

"Yo' sho' he sick? He act lak he drunk." She bent over him. "Doan smell no whiskey. Wait til Ah fetches de doctah. An' stay wha' yo' ez. Does Ah git back heah an' fine yo' in my kitchin, Ah fixes yo' good. Yo' hear me?" She did not wait for his answer.

He watched the light as it receded and was swallowed up in the darkness beyond the room. Moments later, the light reappeared and moved gradually toward the kitchen. As its full brilliance shone on him, he heard her say, "Heah he ez, Doctah. He kerryin' some White man. He say de man ez his massa."

The doctor spoke kindly to him. "What is your master's name, boy?"

"He name Cap'n Mar-sar."

"Marsar? That's a new name to me." He turned to his servant. "Arabella, go see if you can find Marcus. I'll have to take him upstairs, and there's no point in tracking water all over the house. They're both soaking wet."

After she had done, the doctor asked, "How did you all come here?"

"On de hosses. Dey's out in de front ob de house."

"I see. Where's your master's home? Where does he live?"

Buck made his honest confession. "Ah doan zackly know, Massa Doctah. Ah jes' dis'membahs."

Mercer's delirium evidenced its progress, as he lifted his head and his eyes opened wildly. Meaningless words came from his lips. Although he had not touched the patient, Doctor Braxton's diagnosis came quickly and he would have wagered on it accuracy. He observed calmly, "Boy, your master is a mighty sick man." He called into the house. "Arabella, you and Marcus hurry back here!"

As her master's voice reached her ears, Arabella had finally come upon the doctor's manservant, Marcus, soundly asleep in a comfortable chair in the study. "Yo mizzuble, no 'count, good-fo'-nuthin', shif'less niggah!" she exclaimed. "Heah, Ah been doin' yo' wuk an' yo' in heah a-sleepin'! Get outer dat chair fo' Ah knocks yo' clean outer it!"

Marcus had awakened at her first blast, but it had taken him a moment before he realized what was happening. At her threat of personal hurt, however, he organized his senses and raised his beanpole frame from the seat of easy repose to follow her to the kitchen.

Once they had returned, the doctor moved with dispatch. Marcus shouldered Mercer's dripping body. With Arabella lighting the way, the three filed through the doorway at the far end of the cooking room, leaving Buck anxiously peering after them from outside the rear door.

Was his master to die, maybe the doctor would let him stay here. He seemed like he would be a good master. But what if the doctor wouldn't want him? Maybe Massa Cap'n would get well.

Buck shook his head solemnly, practicing his habit of oral thinking. "He pow'ful sick, he ez. Dunno ef he kin git ober dis. He sho' ez pow'ful sick." Before he could envision further calamities, Arabella returned. He questioned her. "What de doctah say 'bout Massa Cap'n?"

"He ain' say nuthin' 'bout 'im. He say fo' me ter feed yo'. Den he say he gwine ter have Mah-cus fine yo' some place ter sleep atter he done helpin' 'im wif yo' massa." Her tone took on sharpness. "Yo' kin come on in. But does yo' mess up dis place, yo' cleans it up!"

He entered meekly and she ordered, "Yo' set yo' se'f down an' doan sashay 'roun'. Yo' heah me?"

"Yassam," he said submissively.

As she prepared his food, she kept glancing at him. All of a sudden, she came toward him, brandishing an enormous fork. "Ah knows who yo' ez! Ah reck-nizes yo'! Ah knowed Ah done see yo' befo'! Yo' dat Black trash whut 'bout runned ober me on de street dis atternoon! Yo' no 'count, wuthless scoun'rel!" The fork's forward progress stopped just short of him, but she continued shaking it in his face. "Ah feed yo' cayse do doctah, he done say fo' me to. But yo' gehd yo'se'f. Yo' watch yo' step else Ah fixes yo' good!"

"Yassam," he said, his eyes following the threatening movement of the culinary weapon in her hand.

"Yo' Black trash. When yo' 'dresses me. yo' says Miz Arabella, yo' heah me?"

"Yassam, Miz Arabella."

"Dat's better." Satisfied as to his complete subjugation, she busied herself at the hearth. Soon the room was filled with a soul-pleasing aroma and his distressed stomach growled demandingly.

To the hungry man, the food she placed before him was a feast straight from a banquet table. There were hog jowls, turnips, yams, cornbread and gravy. And something he had forgotten he had ever tasted—milk. Whatever her disposition, and no matter how her mean talk, this Arabella was a good cook. He reiterated the acknowledgment with each stuffing mouthful. So absorbed was he, he did not notice the well-filled, sloe-eyed brown girl who came in through the porch door. But Arabella saw her. "Whut yo' doin' up hear, Araminta? Ain' Ah tole yo' ter stay 'way fum dis house, 'cept'n when Ah says fo' yo' ter come?"

"Yas, ma'am."

"Den how come yo' dis'beys me?"

"Ah dunno, Mammy. Ah jes' thought mebbe Ah'd help yo' some."

"Ah doan need no helpin'!" Arabella retorted. "No yo' git on outer heah."

Innocent was Buck's inquiring look at the latest object of her wrath. Innocence departed and the look became a stare. Like a bee, darting at a tormentor, Arabella directed her irritation to him. "Ain' no use yo' lookin' at Araminta lik dat! Yo' goes messin' 'roun' wif her, an' Ah busts yo' haid open wif date skillet ober yondah! Ain' gwine ter heppen ter her, whut heppen ter me. Some high-yaller trash sweet-talked me one time. Jes' a-vis'tin', he wuz, jes' lak yo' ez. One day he lef', sudden lak, an' bime-by, 'long kums Araminta."

Her masculine voice scaled high as she concluded. "So, yo' stays 'way fum her whiles yo' ez heah! Yo' heah me? All de time, yo' keeps yo'se'f clean 'way fum her! Does ah fine yo' ain't, den dey kerries yo' 'way fum heah! Now yo' git on wif yo' eatin' so's Ah kin git dem dishes warshed whut yo' ez usin'."

Araminta dropped her head. She had heard her mother's threatening dissertation before. Every time a new man showed his face, Arabella repeated the story of her deception of sixteen years ago. Ah'll nebbah hab me a man, does Mammy keep dat up, Araminta thought soberly.

Her mood did not escape her mother. "Ain' no use drappin' yo' haid an' poutin' lak a chile. Git on back ter de cabin lak Ah told yo'! An yo' lissen good ter whut Ah says. Yo' stay 'way fum dis heah no 'count, mizzuble, good-fo'-nuthin', shif'less niggah, yo'se'f . . . Yo' heah whut Ah says?"

As Araminta went through the doorway she thought, Mammy allus 'scribes menfo'ks de same way. "No 'count, mizzuble, good-fo'-nuthin, shif'less." Or had she failed to include "good-fo'-nuthin'" this time?

Marcus returned just after her departure. Buck had finished and was sitting on the chair that had been moved back from the table and against the wall. Arabella had almost completed her tidying up.

"Doctah Braxton say fo' me ter help yo' wif de hosses an' den ter fine yo' a place ter sleep." Marcus tilted his head slightly and his raised eyebrows wrinkled the forehead above them as he made his solemn pronouncement to one whom by his manner and tone of address he wished to impress was beneath his station. He paused soberly, before adding, "Dat place wha' yo' sleeps ez in de bahn wif de hosses, does we fine 'em." He forced his lower lip over the upper, accentuating its protrusion. Then, with a grandiloquent gesture, he pointed to the door, saying, "Yo' leads de way." He found a lantern on the porch and, after lighting it, handed it to Buck.

The rain had stopped completely and the air was thoroughly humid. When they reached the front of the house, the horses were gone. Buck tried to search the darkness, but before he could enter upon his cycle of concern he heard them moving about off to his near right. The moment his feet left the carriageway and touched the wet grass, his fear vanished. Hungry as the animals were, he knew the meaning of the slow-moving sounds. They were grazing. When he had his hand upon the roan's bridle, he hated to lead it away from the long overdue feeding.

On the way back, the other Negro held the light and walked in front of him.

When Marcus had first returned to the kitchen from upstairs, Buck had wanted to ask him about his master. But he was a stranger in a strange land and he had held his tongue. And now, as he followed the austere servant, the inquiry filled his mouth. But he did not open his lips until after the horses had been fed and bedded down and his lordly guide was preparing to return to the house. As the boxed light swung away from him, he stopped its arc, asking, "Kin yo' kinely tell me 'bout m' massa? How he doin'? Ez he gwine ter die?"

For a suspense-filled second, he feared his question was going to be ignored. Then the light swung back as Marcus turned and said, "He doin' good as kin be 'spected. But de doctah say he bad off fum de chills an' de feber. An' he sez the wust thing 'bout 'im ez dat he ain' had no vittles in 'im fo' a long time." He digressed to satisfy a question of his own. "How come yo' massa ain' done spen' some ob dat big bag ob money whut he had 'roun' his neck an' buy his-se'f somepin' ter eat?"

"Cayse he bin pow'ful sick, dat's de reason," Buck answered tartly.

The light moved toward the house.

CHAPTER 84

Buck awoke at the touch of the small black hand upon his shoulder and was at once conscious of others moving about him in the barn. A timid voice said, "Wake yo-se'f. Miz Arabella want yo' up ter de house." He thanked the young boy for his service and pushed himself from the packed hay that had been his bed. Reaching for the shirt he had doffed before going to sleep, he found it nearly dry, and the rough fibers scratched as he stretched the shrunken cloth over his shoulders. And though his britches were still damp, they too had begun the shrinking process, clinging tightly to his hips and legs and cutting into his crotch as he walked to where Sagitta and the roan were stalled. The horses turned their heads in brief recognition, then resumed their contented munching of the hay in their cribs, gently whisking their tails as they ate. As he looked them over, he wondered if their feeding was the result of direct order or through the consideration of one of the slaves working nearby. Someone else had cared for the animals before his inspection of them. Fresh ointment covered the sores he had noted yesterday morning. I'se all right and de hosses, dey ez doin' fine. Ah wondahs how Massa Cap'n, be doin'? As he went outside, his thoughts spared him the laughter attracted by his choking garments.

The kitchen door was open, but he knocked respectfully on its frame.

"Who dat knockin'?" Arabella need not have asked had she but turned around.

"Dis ez me. De one whut kum las' night. Some chile say yo' wants me."

"Ah want yo'?" she chuckled, as she continued. "Whuffo' Ah wants yo'?" She looked toward the door and immediately her breasts and abdomen were rocked by laughter. Buck tried to enter into the spirit of her rollicking humor, smiling broadly but quizzically. She wiped a tear with a corner of her apron before saying, "'Pears lak yo' done swapped dem clo'es whut Mah-cus got fo' yo' wif dat chile yo' wuz talkin' 'bout. Come on in de inside an' set on dat char yondah."

He wondered at the change that had come over her since last night, and he sought to hold her to its pleasant vein. "Miz . . . whut dat yo' tole me I'se ter call yo'?"

She liked this show of respect. "Yo' calls me Miz Arabella, jes' lak all de rest ob de Black fo'ks does." Though she meant what she said, she said it smilingly.

He started over again. "Miz Arabella, yo' say somepin' 'bout Mah-cus? An' wha' at ez day?"

"Yo' means yo' doan 'membah dat ole skinny niggah whut took yo' ter de bahn yes'dy evenin'?"

"Ah 'membahs 'im. Wuz dat Mah-cus? Who he 'roun' dis place?"

She placed her hands over the thick layers of fat that covered her hips. "He try ter 'press fo'ks wif his 'po'tance, whut he ain' got none ob. He jes' de doctah's houseboy, all he ez." She turned her eyes toward the deliberate sound of oncoming steps.

Too late, Marcus found he was trapped. Before he could retreat, she was after him. "Whut yo' means by not doin' whut de doctah tole yo'?"

"Whut yo' means, womern?" He tried to hold his poise of superiority, cocking his head to one side.

"Ah means, niggah, dat Ah hud de doctah 'struck yo' ter git dis heah man some dry clo'es. How come yo' dis'beys de doctah?" Her eyes were as gimlets boring into him, and he wilted before their pointing power.

"Ah reckins Ah jes' hab a fo'gittin' spell," he confessed.

She let him stew in his own juice for a few moments before saying, "Soon's Ah fixes 'im some breakfus', an' when he done eatin' hit, I'se 'speckin' dem clo'es ter be ready fo' 'im. Now yo' git outer heah! Yo' done hud de doctah say dis mawnin' dat dis niggah's massa ez quality fo'ks, ain't yo'? Yo' jes' fo'gits agin, an' Ah fo'gits Ah ez a lady!"

After Marcus had made his sheepish exit, Buck asked, "Miz Arabella, how Massa Cap'n? How he doin' dis mawnin'?"

While she answered him, she broke two eggs on the rim of the skillet. "He bad off. He sho' ez. Ah had ter help de doctah an' dat no 'count Mah-cus strop him ter de bed. He dat bad sick. De doctah, he say he lak ter speech wif yo', atter yo' done et." Having given her report on the patient's condition, she switched her subject. "Now dat Ah knows yo' fambly ez quality fo'ks, Ah treats yo' lak quality. But Ah still means whut Ah tole yo' las' night. Yo' stay 'way fum Araminta, yo' heah?"

The mouthwatering smell of ham and eggs had Buck at a point where he would have promised anything she desired. His eyes were glued on the sizzling skillet as he said, "Ah stays 'way, 'way fum her, Ah does."

He treasured the small ring of ham bone after he had finished, storing it between his check and gum. *Dis Arabella, she sho' kin fix de vittles,* he thought. *She a 'li'l extry plump, but dey's jes' dat much mo' ter grab a holt uv. But she li'l older'n me. Now dat Araminta, she jes' 'bout right. She plump lak, but she young. Wondah, kin she cook lak her mammy?*

Marcus was back with some hand-me-downs and the two went to the barn where Buck quickly changed. On their way to the house, Marcus was his old contumelious self as he said sagely, "De mastah say he want ter speech wif yo' when us gits ter de house."

"Miz Arabella done tole me 'bout dat," said Buck.

"She done tole yo'? Dat's mah bizness ter do de tellin'. Ah reckin' Ah speeches wif her 'bout dat! She gittin' kinda uppity heah lately."

Though they passed through the kitchen, Marcus said nothing to her. Rather, he appeared to be leaning away from her as he went by. After he had informed the doctor of Buck's presence and the latter had been ushered into the study, or keeping room, as some called it, Doctor Braxton dismissed him, thus freeing the Negro to sit at the invalid's bedside during the physician's absence.

Buck had never before set foot in such gracious surroundings as he witnessed, once he had left the cooking room. And his out-of-place feeling had induced an attack of nervousness. As he now waited for the doctor to speak, the thick carpeting beneath his bare feet imparted the uneasy sense of trespass.

From above, deep, racking coughs and peculiar rattling noises chopped their way downstairs, battering the quietude of the study. One particularly violent siege caused Buck's head to turn involuntarily and to look anxiously toward its source.

"That's your master, boy. It's in his lungs, and it's very bad. That's why I sent for you. There's a grave possibility that he might die." Braxton paused, evaluating the Negro's powers of comprehension. "Do you understand what I am saying?" Buck nodded his head and he continued. "I believe I know who your master is. I think his name is Mercer, and if it is, I knew of his father who lived in Williamsburg. Now, I want you to think hard. Could Mercer be what you mean when you say Marsar?"

Buck's watering eyes brightened. "Ya, ser. Dat his name! Ah fo'gits it, but Ah 'membahs now. Dat's it!"

"And does he live in Williamsburg?"

"Massa Doctah, Ah jes' cain't call dat ter m' mine. Massa Cap'n', he done tole me, but Ah fo'gits it." The tears made their hesitating way down his cheeks to his quivering lips.

The doctor calmed him with gentle words and then patiently undertook the task of obtaining Mercer's immediate background. He listened attentively as the Negro told of his first meeting with his master at "de place wha' dey makes de salt" (which Dr. Braxton correctly deduced to be Bullitt's Lick), the facts surrounding the unfought duel, their journey to Harrodstown (which name Braxton supplied as Harrodsburg), the tragedy that occurred there, the killing of the Indians, the long journey to the Blockhouse (the only name Buck recalled) and the deteriorating ride from that outpost to Richmond. The doctor noted carefully the Negro's narration of his master's metamorphosis.

He would have talked longer, had not Marcus made his frightened appearance to report what he termed "de death rattle." An expression that alarmed the physician and terrified the already greatly agitated Buck.

Before he went to investigate the character of the crepitation, Dr. Braxton said quietly, "I've got to go upstairs, boy. I'll do my best to save your master. If I can just keep him alive for a week, there's a good chance he'll get well. Meanwhile, I'll give orders for your care. You'll have work to do while you are here, but it won't be too hard. If you aren't treated right, you just come and see me."

Marcus took Buck to the kitchen and, hurriedly leaving him there, hastened to rejoin the doctor. Buck watched his departure and sadly spoke his thought. "Dat Mah-cus look lek a ole black katydid, a-hurryin' his-se'f ter a fun-e-ral."

There was a gale of laughter. Arabella had been listening.

The breakfast Buck had relished so fondly that morning proved to be the last meal he would eat in the kitchen. His idleness had ended also. Most of the time, he did work of odd sorts: mending fences, pruning hedges and weeding the doctor's flower garden, feeding and currying the horses, including Sagitta and his own mount, the white-splattered chestnut. A small part of the time, he labored in the fields. As the doctor had said, the work was not overly strenuous.

He ate and slept in one of the slave cabins, sharing the habitation with four Negro men. One of them, an elderly, white-thatched patriarch named Shadrach was especially nice to him. And it was from Shadrach that Buck learned that Dr. Braxton was a widower whose only child, a little boy, had died of "the sickness" shortly after the death of the wife and mother. He also learned that which he already believed, the doctor was firm, but kind and fair.

Each morning, before starting upon his work, Buck made inquiry of Arabella as to his master's progress. Each evening, he asked her how Massa Cap'n had fared during the day. Sometimes the reports were disheartening, particularly the first few. But lately, she spoke encouragingly, and the depressive fears had lost their control over him. With the release from thoughts of death and its consequences had come pleasant musings, some carnally stained. Arabella stayed in the big house. Araminta lived near him and he had met her secretly. The latest occasion was on a starless night, and they had slipped unnoticed into the barn. When they had come out, there were bits of straw in Araminta's hair. History was repeating itself.

Now that his master was definitely improving, Buck had begun to like living here and he considered himself a part of the community life of his fellow slaves. He shared their mirthful evening hours and there was no sadness. Often he fell asleep to the beautiful harmony of rich voices mingled in song. And the marvelous blessing of the human mind, to remember happiness and forget sorrow, was never more proven than in Buck's naturally forgetful existence. The unpleasant memories were all but gone.

The days wore on, past the week that Dr. Braxton had both hoped for and feared, on to a second week, and then into a third. Buck's visits to the kitchen came only in the morning and Arabella's answer was always the same. "He gittin' bettah all de time." Once in a while she would remind him, "Yo' 'membahs whut Ah done tole yo' 'bout Araminta?" And he would shake his head surely.

*

He awoke to find Marcus standing by his side.

"De Doctah sen' me fo' yo'. Yo' ez ter come 'long wif me." Marcus made the simple summons a portentously ladened edict.

"Massa Cap'n, how he doin' dis mawnin'? He ain' done git mo' sick?"

"Yo' fines out 'bout dat fum de doctah when us gits ter de house," Marcus said gravely. "Yo' follers me," he admonished.

By the time his feet were on the porch steps, Buck was again in the throes of imagined certainty. Massa Cap'n must be dead.

He walked numbly behind Marcus, and their ascension of the stairs made no impression upon him. They stopped at an open door where Marcus bade him wait.

Already, his sensitive nature had yielded to sorrow and the tears had come. When he heard Dr. Braxton say, "Come in here, boy," and he dolefully entered the room. He kept his eyes on the floor fearing to look at the figure in the bed.

"Here's someone to see you who has been awfully worried about you. He's asked about you every single day since he brought you here."

He knew the doctor wasn't talking to him. He slowly raised his head. As if they were out of focus, his bedimmed eyes did not clearly picture what they saw. A beardless, haggard-faced man in the bed. "Massa Cap'n! Yo' ain' daid!" In an instant he was kneeling at the bedside, holding the warm hand against his wet cheek and exclaiming in unbelieving thanksgiving, "Yo' ain' daid, Massa Cap'n! Yo' ain' daid!"

Dr. Braxton's eyes narrowed. "Marcus, did you tell him his master had died?"

"Naw, suh!"

"What did you tell him?"

"Ah jes' tole 'im yo' wants 'im, lak yo' done tole me, Massa."

"Damn you, Marcus! You knew why I wanted him here!" The doctor's face was red. "Now, get out of here! Before I lose control of myself!"

Despite the shocking effect of the ravaging illness, his master looked more like himself than he had before the removal of his whiskers, Buck acknowledged silently. And he felt somehow with their disappearance, the barrier of aloofness had vanished also. This he sensed, for his master did not speak to him. But the feeble light in the sick man's eyes was yet more clear than it had been on the sad morning they had ridden from Harrodstown.

A period of sustained silence ensued after the Negro's outburst of emotion until the doctor said gently, "You can talk to him, boy. But don't expect him to answer. He's too weak. I'll leave you alone with him for a few minutes, then you'll have to leave yourself. Rest and quiet are his chief medicines now."

When Dr. Braxton had gone, Buck eagerly related everything that had transpired since the moment he had first realized his master was ill, that rainy morning on the muddy road to Richmond. The guilty feeling left his heart, after he told of taking the money from the pouch and the purpose for which he took it. He thought he noted a change of expression on the sick man's face, as he recounted its loss. The pallid features eased with his description of Arabella and his mimicking of the black katydid. He did not mention Araminta, skipping over her existence to advise, in glowing terms, as to Sagitta and the roan.

Dr. Braxton made an unnoticed return as Buck was saying, "De doctah ez a good man, an' he done treat me fine. He mak' jes' almos' a fine a massa az yo', Massa Cap'n."

The doctor cleared his throat. "That's about enough for now, boy. You can come back and see your master again tomorrow. Get along now." After the Negro had gone, Braxton remarked to himself, "The tonic benefited everyone. The patient, the visitor and the physician." No, not everyone. He frowned as he remembered the supercilious Marcus.

CHAPTER 85

Convalescence continued to trudge its slow, even way. Elevation of the body in the bed, steps about the room and the paying of their price by a return to rest. Then, sitting up in the chair by the window, and at last the long journey on which the doctor helped him down the stairs. The return of appetite and meals with his physician host. Strolls about the grounds and pleasant conversation with the doctor companion. And always, there was the starting of the day with a visit from the loyal Negro. Throughout it all, Barth's recuperative forces were so intent upon scaling the hill of health they allowed no reflection upon the morose past. Til one morning, after Buck's visit had been concluded, and when Barth and Dr. Braxton were taking their ease upon the stately columned veranda, the doctor sensed a change coming over his patient. He had feared its advent and recognized its ominous significance. For he had been present earlier, when Buck had made the thoughtless reference to "Miz Dracie."

Mercer was as well physically as any physician could have desired. His recovery had been charted in advance, once he had passed the crisis, and his excellent appearance attested the wisdom of Peter Braxton's thorough planning. But what was so readily apparent did not draw the white-haired doctor's concern. His worry centered itself upon that which he could neither see with his eyes nor feel with his hands. He knew that the bodily ills he had cured had found their beginning in a distressed and despondent mind. A mind that had lost all interest in the physical properties under its control. A little while ago, that fountainhead of sickness had been stirred from its dormancy by the Negro's chance remark, and when the lively tone of Mercer's voice had given way to dullness, the doctor realized that the last link in the chain of his patient's convalescence would have to be forged and coupled immediate, or there might result a lasting illness, far more devastating than that which had been overcome.

He had long been aware of the possibility of this undesirable happening, but he had hoped for a greater passage of time before its symptoms made their appearance. Now they were present and he would have to meet them. Until today he had hopefully speculated that the fires of his patient's delirium might have burned the roots of the consuming fires that had possessed his mind. Braxton had been cognizant of the fact that the severity of the illness might, in itself, be a merciful blessing to the overwrought brain, voiding any concentration upon the single, terrible affliction under which it had become accustomed to function. Were the mind to be free of this obsession long enough, the natural healing forces of reason would take command. And though the memory would be permanently scarred, there would no blocking of normal, rational thought. But Buck's untimely words had intervened to threaten his master's mental rehabilitation.

During the long weeks the doctor had spent in constant association with his charge, he had grown to be deeply fond of the man who now sat so quietly at his side, staring into space. For a few moments, he did not disturb the silent soliloquy of the other's thoughts. Then he said to him, "Barth, my old legs are getting stiff sitting here. Come along with me, while I exercise the old bones. I'm in the last score of my life. I'd better make some use of them while I can."

A refusal of the invitation was Barth's desire. But as he roused fully from his abstract state, he smiled his acceptance and rose politely from his chair. "Where shall we go, doctor?" he asked.

Braxton felt encouraged. The first of his diversionary tactics had succeeded. "It doesn't matter, Barth, just so we walk somewhere. And please call me Peter. As I have told you, I become tired of people addressing me always as Doctor or Doctor Braxton. I'm human, Barth. I like the familiarity of the use of my first name by my friends."

"I'm sorry, Peter. I don't know why I do it. I think of you that way, but whether it's the result of my early training to respect my elders—my father was most insistence upon that—or whether it is my sincere regard for your ability, or my deep appreciation of your care and consideration of me, or a combination of all those things, I don't know. Truthfully, I intend to call you Peter, but when I address you, I say Doctor Braxton. Please forgive me."

Braxton laughed. "I'll do it this time, but try and remember it in the future."

"I will, I assure you, Doctor—I mean Peter."

As they descended the steps, both men were laughing.

The year had moved to late September. The morning sun was barely warm, and there was something in its paleness that seemed to spread remorse for the departed summer. The doctor did not press for conversation. It was his plan that there be speech and then time permitted for meditation.

As they approached a grove of perfectly proportioned trees, he spoke again. "Barth, in a few weeks those maples will be the prettiest sight you have ever seen. Some of the leaves will turn golden, others will be purest yellow, and those over to the left—" He indicated their position. "—will be red as wine. This place is pretty in the spring and summer with the flowers and shrubs, but I sometimes think it is even more beautiful in the fall. I surely hope you will stay here long enough to see what magic the first frost will bring."

Braxton's descriptives had brought back memories. "I can well imagine their beauty, Peter. As you talked, I could not help but remember autumn over in Williamsburg. Then the thought came to me that it's just forty miles from here, and I felt a sudden urge to go home. I had not thought of its nearness all the time

I've been here. I suppose that was because it always seemed so far away, when I was traveling toward it—like it would never be reached, I mean."

Braxton was pleased to hear of his companion's yearning, but made no comment, encouraging continuance. However, a moment later he doubted the wisdom of his silence as Barth said, "Peter, ever since I left Harrodstown, I've wanted nothing but to get home as quickly as possible."

The reaching fingers of morbidness had again stroked his brow and the faraway look had returned.

Peter Braxton decided the issue must now be forced into the open so that he might come to grips with it. The preying thought must be conquered. He had no need to study as to what he would say. He had known his words for a long time, ever since he had first asked Buck to tell him about his master.

"Barth," he said, and it was as though he were calling, rather than speaking, to him. "Shortly after Buck brought you to me, I had a long talk with him and he told me many things that have helped me in my treatment of you. For more than a week you were delirious, and through what I had learned from him about you, I was able to separate and classify your ravings, discarding what was purely irrational and remembering that which bordered on fact. I learned of your love for Draice and of the mark the tragedy left upon your brain. I met your friends, some with strange sounding names and stranger habits. I heard of Abe Foster, of Rosie Tindall and Abby. Tom Chism and Mace Hardin were there. And I wondered if Hardin's head had actually been cut off and stuck on a pike, if perhaps it wasn't the wildest sort of fantasy. But I knew its truth after asking Buck about it. The woman named Drusilla was in your mind, and you spoke of her as living, then dead, and as being alive again. Once you were on a raft or flatboat that had nothing but dead men on it. Men named Gibbs and Mallory tried to kill you. Buck was always in your mind. And you talked to him just as you did to the others. I learned of Lucy and her mother and father and of some man whose name I can't recall, but whom you said had been killed by the Indians. He was a friend of yours at Harrodstown. My stomach rebelled when you raved of your encounter with the two savages in the forest. I remember the fierce look on your face as you snarled, 'May God damn you to the lowest depths of hell!' And your incessant screaming of 'Dracie, come back to me!' And the tears that ran down your cheeks as you bemoaned the fact you could not cry. And there was ever so much more that I could not hope to have remembered it all. Oh, yes. There was a man named Grainger whom you linked to Drusilla as being her husband. You called him doctor, and you repeatedly talked of a duel that was never fought." He paused to ask, "Are those names and happenings all true?"

Though he had flinched each time the doctor mentioned Dracie's name, he had listened intently to the entire narration, marveling at the accuracy of Braxton's retentive memory. And he had experienced a strange feeling—as though he were meeting the past face to face. He came from his thoughts when he realized the doctor was waiting for an answer. "They are all true, Peter. But I don't see how you managed to remember them all. It was just like reliving the past."

Braxton smiled. "That's exactly what I wanted you to do, Barth. The chills and fever are gone, and your lungs are clear and sound. I thank God that he has let me help you back to health. But you will have to take over the completion of your recovery. No one can do what needs to be done except yourself."

The doctor purposely detracted from the pressure of Barth's perplexity, exclaiming suddenly, "Look at those red squirrels in those oaks! Did you ever see so many of them in one place? Look at them scamper!"

Peter Braxton knew the success of his strategy when Barth said, "There are a lot of them all right. But will you pardon me, Peter, if I ask you to explain what you meant about me having to complete my own recovery? I thought that had already been accomplished. Tell me what you were driving at."

"To do that, I'll have to tell you some more of what I learned from you when you were out of your head. Other than Dracie, the one whom you seemed to hold in highest regard was someone you called Brother Flinden. I cannot now recall his wife's name, but he had lost her, apparently to the savages. Time and again, you were advising him to accept his loss as being the will of God and not to question that will. If I have marshalled my facts correctly, and if my deduction is accurate, it is my impression he blamed himself. Is that right?"

The answer came quickly. "Yes, that's correct, Peter. Flinden's wife's name was Ursula, and the Indians carried her away. Flinden had been badly wounded by them. He was nearly out of his mind through worrying about her and I tried to bring him back to himself." Reason had sifted his own words as they were uttered. At their conclusion, he knew Braxton's purpose and the understanding to which he had led him so skillfully. "Peter, I see what you mean now. I have been acting the same way that Aaron Flinden did."

"That is true, Barth. And you are the only one who can do anything about it. You must force yourself to accept the fact of Dracie's death. Keep her in sacred memory, of course, but don't let her tragic loss ruin your life. And you must settle the inner conflict between yourself and God. I am a physician, not a preacher. But if I were, I doubt that I could help you. A man must meet his God himself. To be sure, ministers—the thinking ones—might assist him. But in the end, it comes down to man and his Maker. In your case, I believe if you make your peace with God, the grieving sore in your brain will be quickly healed. For, just as you advised Flinden, you must reconcile yourself to his will. You must be your own physician, just as you attempted to counsel Flinden he should be."

"Physician, heal thyself." Barth said the words softly.

Peter Braxton nodded his head. "That is what I wanted you to realize, Barth." He had dropped into a reflective mood and the gentle ease that habitually characterized his features was gone. They walked in silence for a full minute before his face relaxed and he spoke again. "We are going to visit a place that I have never shown you in all our walks together. I had intended to take you there later on. But a little while ago, when your Negro boy, Buck, called Dracie's name and I saw the effect it had upon you, I determined we must make that visit today. Though we may have meandered around a bit, I have managed to control our general direction. When we reach the other side of that little grove up ahead of us, we will be there." He once more lapsed into silence and Barth respected his quiet absorption, wondering what it was the kindly man wished him to see.

They followed a little path that ran between great lilac bushes. And though the fragrant blooms that had adorned the boughs had died with the spring's own demise, Barth could easily picture their prime glory in that lovely season. The path curved, and then he knew where the doctor was taking him. Directly in front of them was a little cemetery, its low walls permitting a view of the three stones, two large and one small, within their confines.

"This is what I wanted to show you, Barth. The place where my two loves lie buried." There was a catch in the old gentleman's throat and his eyes became moist as he opened the grilled gate and said, "Come in with me."

A deep feeling of sincere sympathy seized the younger man. "I'm sorry, Peter. I did not know. How thoughtless it has been of me not to have made any inquiry as to your family. I had assumed you to be a bachelor."

The doctor smiled forgivingly, and the realization came that the tender expression on his features had been shaped by enduring sorrow. Barth noted the fading inscription on the first marker.

VIRGINIA ANNE BRAXTON
Beloved Wife of Peter Braxton
Born, Apr. 21, 1718
Prince William Co., Va.
Died, May 16, 1742
Richmond, Va.

Beneath, it read—

THY WILL BE DONE.

He studied the engraving on the little stone next to it.

WILLIAM LEE BRAXTON
Born, May 23, 1738

So the child had been a boy.

Died, June 27, 1742
Richmond, Va.
Age 4 yrs., 1 mo., 4 days
THY WILL BE DONE.

The concluding line was the same as on the one he had just scanned. The third monument was Peter's, complete except for date of death. And at the bottom, he saw again the four prayerful words of acceptance of God's way: THY WILL BE DONE

He was still contemplating that which he had been reading. The arrangement of the stones—the little boy's between those of his mother and father—suggested the continuance of parental sheltering after the deaths of all three. He was conscious of Peter moving to the side of his wife's headstone before hearing him say, "This is MY Virginia, whom I love so dearly. Her every thought was pure, and her voice was always soft and sweet. You were not there to see your Dracie struck down. And there was nothing you could have done to have saved her. But Virginia became ill right at my side. And though I had medicines immediately available and the knowledge as to their use and administered them promptly and faithfully unto her, she still died. Had you been with me then, you would realize now that savage's tomahawk was a merciful instrument—a misericord— compared to the invisible, tortuous shaft that tore through Virginia's body and brain. I prayed and prayed. But she died.

"The little fellow here—" His eyes were on the small grave. "—could not understand what had happened to his mother. I can still see him running hopefully through the house looking for her. And I can hear his baby voice calling, and I will always remember the pause that would ensue before he called again. And how he would then run weepingly to me and beg me to find his mother for him. I would hold him in my arms and rock him and tell him his mama had gone to heaven. But always, he asked, 'When is my mama coming back from heaven?'

"He did not ask for long. Just a little over a month after she had died, he was with her." He reached down and affectionately patted the top of the little marker as though it were a tousled head.

"Barth, I had saved others who had been afflicted with the same disease, women who never loved and kissed me, children who had never climbed on my lap and hugged me and smeared my face with the leavings of the sweets that clung to their little lips. If I could save them, why couldn't I have kept my own wife and child from dying?" As if in testimony to the infinite depth of his question, he laid his palm on each of the markers, first on his wife's and then on that of his son. Then he walked slowly to the gate and after Barth had passed through, closed it quietly.

They walked in silent meditation until they neared the house. So engrossed had Barth been with what he had seen and heard, the sound of Peter's voice startled him. "I took you there, Barth, because I wanted you to know, and in the hope that perhaps, through that knowledge, your own grief might somehow be helped. Where you lost one, I lost two. And though I know that sorrow is dedicatedly personal, sometimes a sharing of sorrows helps ease their poignancy. As you must now realize, my sadness has never left me. I pray that your grief will age with your years. Mine has not."

They were at the steps. Marcus was waiting for them on the veranda. There were filled glasses on the tray he held in his hands, and when the doctor and Barth were seated, Marcus served them. For a time, neither man spoke, both being seemingly content to sip their drinks as they rested. Then Peter said, "I may be presuming upon both your patience and the privacy of your feelings, Barth, but I would like to say just a little more. Do I have your permission to continue?"

"There is no presumption, Peter. Please do. I think you may have helped me, though to what extent, and for how long, I cannot honestly say."

The doctor nodded his head. "I understand. I groped through the same vale myself. But what I want to say is this. I know you to be inherently a religious man. In your unconscious state, you would frequently quote from Proverbs and Ecclesiastes and from other parts of the Bible. Therefore, whether or not you still believe its words, and I pray that you do, nevertheless, you will be able to understand what I am going to tell you. For nearly a year, I kept asking myself, as you have done, Why? Why? Why? And I still have not found the answer, but I bow to his will. Though I do not know his purpose in taking my wife and my son as he did, I know that he took them for a reason of his own, and I no longer question his doing. But all during that first year after their deaths, whenever I thought of God, I thought of him as having failed me in my hour of trial. Then the light returned to my soul in a strange manner. With Virginia and Billy gone, I found that I had more house servants than I thought necessary. So I determined to sell them. I had always treated them well and I knew that they did not want to leave. But wrapped up in my own troubles as I was, I did not bother to explain beforehand what I intended to do or why I was doing it. When they neared the auction block, they knew my intention. I heard them ask one another why I was going to sell them. One blamed his plight on some displeasing mistake he imagined he had made. Another considered his presence at the block to have been brought about through his failure to do something that I had long forgotten. The other three—there were five all told—just asked. Why? All were grief-stricken.

"They had been called to the block when it happened to me. I suddenly realized that those unfortunate Blacks, over whom I had the power of life and death, were asking the same question I had asked of the one who controlled my fate. I was their master. He was mine. I had not told them, and they had asked, Why? He had not told me, and I had also asked, Why? I quickly withdrew them from the sale and took them home. And they are still here.

"That night, another, more convincing analogy led me to God. My little boy had been on my mind, and I found myself recalling his sweet spirit of obedience. Frequently, I would tell him to do things without my giving any reason for their being done. In most instances, had I tried to explain the purpose he would have not understood. But he always did that which I asked of him. I was his father, and he trustingly obeyed me. It was then that I saw myself as a little child before my heavenly father. The next morning, I engaged a mason to add the last line that you saw on each of the gravestones. I have never questioned his will from that day to this. And I shall never do so again."

The doctor's words had brought to Barth the memory of his own father. The aptness of the simple comparison could not be denied.

Peter Braxton said no more. Shortly, he excused himself on the pretext he had to go into Richmond for a little while. By thus absenting himself for a few hours, he would afford Barth an opportunity for reconciliation.

Barth arose from his chair as Peter was leaving. After bidding him goodbye, he sat down again.

When Braxton returned, a little past noon, he was still sitting there.

When the day was over, Barth excused himself immediately after supper. In the darkness of his room he found light, as he fell to his knees in humble supplication.

That which Reverend Wyeth had prophesied as he stood by the open grave on the frontier had come to pass.

*

At breakfast, Barth told Peter of his decision to depart for Williamsburg later that morning. The doctor expressed his surprise and regret, but did not importune him to stay. He had prescribed for him for the last time. Henceforth, the patient must be his own physician.

Dr. Braxton's surprise was mild, indeed, compared to that which struck the sleep-eyed Buck. For a moment, he was certain his master was funnin' with him, as he used to do. With a grin that disclosed every one of his ivory-like teeth, he asked, "Massa Cap'n, yo' ain' jes' a-foolin', ez yo'?"

"No, Buck, I'm not. Get the horses ready and have them out front as soon as you can. The quicker we start, the sooner we'll get home." Barth turned, as in afterthought, saying in apparent seriousness, "Of course, you don't have to go with me. You can stay here if you want."

Buck made haste to quell the thought in the second of its birth. "Nassa, Massa Cap'n! Dis heah's a fine 'nuf place. De eatin's fine, an' de doctah, he a fine man. But does yo' want ter lebe, Ah lebes wif yo'. Dat's de truf, ef Ah eber done tole it!"

Barth laughed, and Buck knew it was his old Massa Cap'n with whom he would be leaving. Buck managed to sneak a few last words with Araminta. "De place wha' Massa Cap'n libs ain' ver' fah fum dis place. Ah knows he boun' ter come back heah fo' ter see de doctah fo' long." His eyes lit up with another possibility. "Mebbe, Massa Cap'n, he sen' me back heah on his bizness. Does he do it, Ah comes ter see yo' sho'."

Buck steadied the restless Sagitta as his master swung into the saddle and then he mounted the roan. They turned from their farewells and Barth eased his hold on the reins. Instantly, both horses broke into a fast trot down the roadway.

Just as they were being covered by the foliage that arched the curving drive, the doctor suddenly exclaimed, "I knew blamed well there was something I had forgotten to tell him! That young woman whom I met in Richmond yesterday, the one who asked me to remember her to him—who did she say she was? I remember now. She said her name used to be Warren before she married. What was her husband's name anyhow?" He shrugged his shoulders. "It won't make any difference. She said she would see him upon his return to Williamsburg." As though the spoken thoughts had been intended for his ears, Marcus pushed the big lower lip almost to his pinched nose and nodded studiously.

CHAPTER 86

Riding through the streets of the new capital, Barth was impressed once again by the city's thriving appearance. It was as though its activity had increased over what he had observed eight months previously on his way to Kentucky. Of course, he recalled a light blanket of snow covered the city on that occasion, and there would naturally have been fewer people about than on such a fair day as today.

The war had influenced the decision to move the seat of government here from Williamsburg in 1780. Conceding the urgency for its removal as he surveyed the busy scene, he nevertheless experienced a mixed feeling of admiration and envy. The hope that yet lingered in his heart that the capital might be reestablished in his home city, he knew to be baseless. And he considered the fate of proud Williamsburg, whose main attributes had been its fine homes and the social life that had surrounded its former governmental importance. Of the prided twins, only the beautiful residences remained. And some of these had new owners. Other homes were kept furnished and staffed, but their masters and mistresses now spent most of their time in Richmond. During the two years that had intervened, he reckoned fully a hundred residents had left the old capital for the new, and he admitted future years would take from, rather than add to, the already deleted population. And he sadly conjectured that, at least during his lifetime, Williamsburg's peak number of two thousand citizens, counted in 1779, would never again be equaled.

Before the war, no one ever would have entertained the thought that Williamsburg would someday surrender its position of influence to the city forty miles distant. But uncertainty moves with the seemingly certain steps of man, Barth reflected. As the ancient Romans had looked to Rome, so had Virginians viewed their Williamsburg. Spread upon a ridge on the peninsula between the James and York Rivers and partly encircled by Queen's Creek and College Creek, it had been known formerly as Middle Plantation. Still only a grouping of planation dwellings, when it was designated in 1699 as the capital in place of Jamestown, it was then given its present name in honor of William III. After its incorporation in 1722, it became the center of educational and political life. The feet of the mighty had walked the east-west bearing Duke of Gloucester Street that ran a wide, straight, tree-studded course, bisecting the city from the college to the capitol.

His mind reverted to the sixth of May 1776 and the Virginia Convention. He heard anew the great voices of those freedom-loving giants who were both architects and builders of precious liberty. Theirs had been the first forensic deliberation and determination regarding open separation from British dominion. Declaring Virginia to be an independent commonwealth, they had seen to the instruction of their delegates that they propose American independence at the second Continental Congress. Words became deeds of battle, and the revolution was accomplished. Though there had as yet been no signed treaty, he thought that to be only an official formality. But he acknowledged that until the agreement was executed, and respected, the British would continue to inspire Indian attacks upon the frontier. Adventurers would die, and their women and children would die with them.

The old sickness attempted an assault. He saw Dracie's bloodied head and the yawning hole that had claimed her body. But he had conquered. "Thy Will Be Done." As he prayed, he bowed his head in reverence.

The dead past had at last been buried.

*

They had rested comfortably the night before, and as a consequence, this day's ride, though extended, had not proved tiring. There had been merriment along the way, as Barth and his manservant had engaged in lighthearted conversation. And now, as they rode in the dusk, Buck asked the question that had grown most familiar. "How much mo' ez it, Massa Cap'n?" This time the reply was definite. "When we cross that creek up ahead, we'll be nearly there."

Buck now asked concerning that which had occupied his mind ever since he had said goodbye to Araminta and her mother. "Massa Cap'n, does we git dar, does we fine de vittles lak dat Arabella, she kin cook 'em?"

His master smiled. "If they're not as good, they'll be almost as good."

Almost as good would be good enough. He made his next inquiry shyly. "Massa Cap'n, kin Ah ax yo' one mo' ques-shun?" With the nodded approval he asked, "Ez dey eny womerns dar—de plump kine?"

"Why you Black rascal, you!" came the chuckling rebuke. "There are some women, but I better not catch you fooling around them."

The Negro construed the mirthful tone to be more important than the words. He said to himself, "Massa Cap'n, he doan mean whut he say."

*

In Williamsburg, men had taken surcease from the labors of the day and the peace of evening had fallen over the city. He first saw lights in the college building where he had studied in his youth. Then, as if lit by some omnipresent lamplighter, lights appeared in dwellings everywhere, their joyous gleamings interfusing to swell the rapturous passion of his return.

As he traversed the quiet street, he reflected upon the foolish speculation of man, the vain quest of what might have been. His reasoning became, at last, clear, and his conclusions final. That which appears to man to be a coincidence of time and chance is actually a premeditated happening. What might have been, could never have been. Time and chance are mortal, as mortal as the clay that reckons them. That which man considers chance is God's certainty. The past is immutable before its mold is cast.

His mind pondered the future, wondering what new paths in the realm of ifs his feet would be set upon. Of this much he was certain, they would not be paths of chance.

And the light that would shine, or the shadows that might fall, would be ordained. Dictated by the raising or the lowering of the divine hand before the radiant face of God.

*

He was home.

BULLITT'S LICK TODAY

Kahaz and her sister hills stand as before, silently surveying the scene below, part of the vanguard of the vast kingdom of knobs that lies to the south. Their steep slopes are timber covered as in the days of this story of predominant fiction.

During their ageless watch, they have seen the mammoth crash its lumbering way, and the later-coming buffalo, whose hooves paced the ground into trails. The animals of the wilderness were there also in copious numbers. All came to lick the seasoned earth. The Redman made his appearance and satisfied his dual needs of salt and meat. And last in this panoramic parade came the White man, who drove away both Indian and animal from the land, that he might take profit from that which God in his bounty had created for all earthly creatures.

Kahaz breathed the lust-filled, greedy air that rose from those who toiled and brawled on the Salt River plain until the gain disappeared from their ventures. Then, in the year that men reckon as eighteen hundred and thirty, when the fire died under the last kettle, she saw the last, blue swirling whisp as it curled heavenward to join the ghostly legion of flames that had formerly blazed in the valley night.

Today, Kahaz views in the distance the growing community to which Adam Shepherd lent his name—the thriving little city of Shepherdsville. Modern highways wind around the feet of the knobs and through the gaps in their chain, shining like so many silver ribbons in the moonlight. Four or five miles from the bridge-spanned Shepherdsville ford, along a rocky, hillside road, is a small cluster of dwellings, some of them set on stilts. These houses and their quiet setting comprise the town now referred to as Bullitt Lick—all that remains to mark the once populous, busy place where fortunes had been made. It is said that a few of the residents trace their ancestry to some of the original settlers of the region that history passed over so hurriedly, ignoring in its swift flight the importance of the contribution that it made to the early settlement of Kentucky and to the infant nation, now grown so great.

On the plain where, for a span of almost fifty years, lay the center of Kentucky's first industry, plows still occasionally uncover chimney remnants from Saltsburg's cabins. The earth yet retains a grayish cast in those spots where the furnace ash was banked, and metal shards are found sometimes about the sites of the former pits. The wells have been filled long since they were last in operation. But the location of some of the largest of them may be ascertained from saucer-shaped depressions in the area of the former salt lick.

Though all but forgotten in Kentucky's history, and unremembered even by most of those who now live close to where the vanished settlement once flourished, there are some who still remember its existence—those who farm its land. For the sparse vegetation on parts of the land and the scanty production of its gray-white soil will not let them forget that salt once seasoned the frontier and the lives of those who lived in the fair hell that was Bullitt's Lick.

ABOUT THE AUTHOR

Richard Pendleton Watts Sr. was born in 1908 in Louisville, Kentucky, to a middle-class family, who had lived in the area since the early 1800s. He finished first in his high school class, winning a governor's appointment to the US Military Academy, West Point.

At that time, West Point was primarily an engineering school, where officers were required to teach soldiers, among other things, how to compute the trajectory of cannon shot. After failing a third-year calculus class, he was required to fall back to the second-year class. (It was lucky that he didn't finish with those third-year classmates, as most were World War II field officers and more than half were killed.) While at West Point, he learned horsemanship and boxing, which he subsequently taught at Camp Cavanaugh (sic) camp for young men.

He returned to Louisville and entered the School of Law, finishing first in his class. He became a successful independent attorney in private practice. He ran for tax commissioner and won the primary election, but did not win the position in the main election.

Watts joined the Army in World War II but was prevented from overseas duty because of a bleeding ulcer. Because of his law degree, he was assigned to the Military Police, overseeing German prisoners of war at Camp Custer, Michigan. He loved to write and wrote several short stories for Reader's Digest. He died in 1995, at age 86, in Kentucky.

His son, Richard P. Watts 11, fondly remembers the stories his father would tell him. After his father's death, he published Fair Hell at his father's directive to share the story with others.

References

Battle of Little Mountain
> Describes the background that led to one of the bloodiest engagements on the Kentucky frontier.
> https://en.wikipedia.org/wiki/Battle_of_Little_Mountain

The Bloody Year of the Three Sevens
> Refers to the American Revolutionary War year of 1777, when attacks across the Kentucky frontier were encouraged by the British to harass settlements and cause violence for settlers.
> https://www.us-roots.org/colonialamerica/pioneer/chap10.html

Bullitt County History, Time Line Project, Bullitt County Genealogical Society
> This ongoing project places events in chronological order to place events in Bullitt County to what was happening in the state and the nation.
> https://bullittcountyhistory.com/bchistory/timeline.html

Bullitt's Lick Has Salty Past, Charles Hartley, *The Courier-Journal*, September 7, 2014
> This article first appeared in the *Courier-Journal*. It details the history of Bullitt's Lick.
> https://www.courier-journal.com/story/news/local/bullitt/2014/09/06/bullitt-history-bullitts-lick-salty-past/15085367/

Bullitt's Lick: The Related Saltworks and Settlements, Robert E. McDowell, May 7, 1956
> Originally read before The Filson Club, this article was later published in the July 1956 issue of *The Filson Club History Quarterly*. It provides information about Brashear's Station, Bullitt's Lick, Mud Garrison, Dowdall's Station, Clear's Station, Long Lick, Mann's Lick, Fort Nonsense, Parakeet Lick, along with the saltmakers and the extent of the salt trade.
> https://bullittcountyhistory.org/bchistory/mcdowellbullittslick.html

Camp Kavanaugh, Crestwood, Kentucky
> Gives brief history of this campground. Includes photos.
> https://www.facebook.com/liveinoldhamcounty/posts/camp-kavanaughlocated-in-crestwood-camp-kavanaugh-was-founded-by-bishop-hh-kavan/2351330738294341/

Henry Crist and the Battle of the Kettles, Charles Hartley, *The Courier-Journal*, February 12, 2012.
> Describes the May 1788 battle between Indians and a flatboat full of kettles and supplies.
> https://bullittcountyhistory.org/memories/kettles.html

The History of Bullitt's Lick Saltworks, Charles Hartley, The Bullitt County History Museum
> This brief history originally appeared in the Courier-Journal.
> https://bullittcountyhistory.org/memories/licks.html

The History of Louisville, from the Earliest Settlement till the Year 1852, Ben Casseday
> Historical account chronicles the development of Louisville, Kentucky, from its initial settlement through various events and milestones.
> https://www.gutenberg.org/ebooks/38740

How Corn Island Shaped Louisville's Origins, *Kentucky Historic Travels*
Detailed history about Corn Island, the first settlement of Louisville, Kentucky. Shows a drawing by George R. Clark of Corn Island, a plan for the Falls of the Ohio, an image of Fort Nelson, and describes what happened to the island.
https://kentuckyhistorictravels.com/2024/01/13/corn-island-fort-nelson-the-beginnings-of-louisville/

Kentucky Forts and Stations, Kentucky Historical Society
Presents details about more than 150 historical markers located in Kentucky. Includes the name of the marker, the county, the location, the subject, and what's listed on the marker.
https://history.ky.gov/markers/search-results?page=1&count=15

Louisville's First Christmas and the Legacy of Cato Watts, *This Week in Louisville History*
Relates the story of Cato Watts in 1778, along with an image of him.
http://thisweekinlouisvillehistory.culturearchivist.com/2017/12/1225-louisvilles-first-christmas-and.html
https://filson.pastperfectonline.com/webobject/1287EABF-61D5-4374-BE4A-352448869235

Memorial History of Louisville from Its First Settlement to the Year 1896, Volume 1, Edited by J. Stoddard Johnston. "Climatology and Meteorology," Chapter III, Professor E. H. Mark. New York: American Biographical Publishing Co., pages 23-24.
This two-volume history of Louisville includes various chapters of interesting details.
https://www.familysearch.org/library/books/records/item/243062-memorial-history-of-louisville-from-its-first-settlement-to-the-year-1896-vol-1?offset=

Native American Tribes of Kentucky: Forgotten History
Reviews the first inhabitants of Kentucky (about 10,000 BCE) through the Archaic period and the Woodland period. Details are given for Shawnee, Cherokee, Chickasaw, Mosopelea, and Yuchi.
https://www.knahm.org/native-american-tribes-kentucky/

The Revolutionary War on the Frontier, Fort Boonesborough Foundation
Specifically covers the siege of Fort Boonesborough in 1778.
https://fortboonesboroughfoundation.org/html/revolutionary_war_on_the_frontier.html

Salt, A Factor in the Settlement of Kentucky, Thomas D. Clark, May 3, 1937
Originally read before The Filson Club, May 3, 1937. Later printed in 1938 *The Filson Club History Quarterly*.
https://filsonhistorical.org/wp-content/uploads/publicationpdfs/12-1-4_Salt-A-Factor-in-the-Settlement-of-Kentucky_Clark-Thomas-D..pdf

The Wilderness Road's Louisville End, Robert E. McDowell
Gives the history of the Wilderness Road, and the saltworks in Bullitt's Lick. Includes maps.
http://www.anthonyfoster.com/afoster/test/portfolio/digital/web/FV/bc/WT.htm

Endnotes

1. The original name was known as Baird's Town, Beardstown, or Beards Town. It became Bardstown in 1788 when the town was incorporated. Named for the Bard brothers: David Bard obtained a land grant in 1785, and William Bard surveyed and platted the town.

2. Also known as Cahiz Knob or Cahill's Knob, pronounced KAY-hill, it was named for Adam Cahill, who worked in the saltworks in the Bullitt's Lick area. Cahill was lashed to a tree on the knob by Indians and was left for dead. His friends found him alive and that's how the knob got its name. See https://bullittcountyhistory.org/memories/cahillknob.html

3. In the 1780s, as war broke out, salt became scarce and the price per bushel became exorbitant. See Robert E. McDowell, "Bullitt's Lick: The Related Saltworks and Settlements."

4. This is likely an interpretation of the idiom "being led like a lamb to the slaughter," meaning to be led into a harmful situation, acting calmly without resistance. The phrase highlights the vulnerability of the "lamb" being unknowingly led to its demise.

5. The Louis d'Or French gold coin was first minted in 1640 under Louis XIII. The name means "golden Louis" and featured a picture of the king and royal symbols. Its use continued until the French Revolution in 1789,.

6. Refers to the Monongahela River, a 130-mile-long river that flows from West Virginia to Pennsylvania. Redstone Old Fort was built on the eastern shore of the river and was a critical ford site across the river.

7. Named for James Harrod, Harrodstown was founded in 1774. It was the first English settlement west of the Appalachians. It was renamed Harrodsburg in 1785 and incorporated in 1836.

8. Near Harrodsburg, from November 1779 to February 1780, snow and ice covered the ground without any thaw. Known as the Hard Winter, there were strong snowstorms that left up to two feet of snow. In January, the temperature only rose once to 32 degrees F. Rivers, springs, bays, and harbors were frozen. Water was obtained from boiling snow and ice. Wild animals starved and froze in the forests.

9. Friends refers to the Religious Society of Friends, also known as the Quakers. This Christian-rooted movement emphasized simplicity and being guided by their consciences, without the need for clergy. Members refer to each other as Friends after John 15:14 in the Bible: "You are my friends if you do what I command you" (NIV).

10. A small group of Quakers were exiled from Philadelphia to Virginia in 1777 for their pacifist refusal to support the Revolutionary War.

11. George Fox founded the Quaker movement in England in 1647. He was repeatedly imprisoned for his beliefs and for refusing to conform to the Church of England. William Penn was an English Quaker leader who was also imprisoned for his beliefs. He received a large land grant from King Charles II in 1681 and founded Pennsylvania as a haven for religious freedom.

12. During the Battle of Little Mountain on March 22, 1782, Captain James Estill, a militia officer, was killed near Mount Sterling, Kentucky. He led about 40 men to track a Wyandot war party that had attacked Estill's Station. Estill's Defeat was a tragic loss for the Kentucky settlers, and probably could have been avoided except for the actions of one of Estill's officers (William Miller), who ordered a retreat that left Estill's command overwhelmed.

13. The Battle of Fort Duquesne on September 14, 1758, was a British assault by General Edward Braddock on the French fort. After an intense fight by the French and Indians, they were defeated and left during the night after burning the fort. The British and Americans rebuilt the remains and named it Fort Pitt in honor of English Prime Minister William Pitt, who had ordered the capture of the strategic location.

14. George Clear built several cabins about 1780 along the stream that bears his name. He didn't have the land surveyed and ended up losing most of his claims. He left the area in 1783. The area was renamed Hubers (probably from a later settler) and later named Kenlite Station.

15. King Louis XVI of France provided military and financial support to the colonies during the Revolutionary War. He was twenty-two years old and had been king for only two years. He supplied weapons, uniforms, and money. Later he sent France's army and navy.

16. George Rogers Clark led about 175 militiamen on July 4, 1778, to capture Kaskaskia. No shots were fired as the largely French town was sympathetic to the American cause against the British. This was part of Clark's Illinois campaign, a series of engagements that doubled the size of the original Thirteen Colonies.

17. Calomel (mercurous chloride) was a white, tasteless powder used as a purgative, fungicide and insecticide. It was used to treat syphilis, typhoid fever, mumps, diarrhea and sometimes as a teething powder for children. Plasters were a medicated paste (made of herbs, clay and oil) spread on a cloth or piece of leather. They were used for wound protection and to prevent infection.

18. Thomas Nelson Jr. was a Revolutionary War general and also governor of Virginia in 1781 (Kentucky was part of Virginia at that time.) The fort was built in 1781 on the Ohio River near downtown Louisville.

19. Cato Watts, an enslaved fiddler who came to Louisville with the George Rogers Clark expedition, was executed in 1787 for killing his master, Captain John Donne. Watts claimed it was an accident, when he knocked down Donne. But he was tried and convicted of murder. At that time, people of color were not allowed to testify in court, especially in cases involving White people.

20. The term nigger was originally neger (1568, Scottish dialect), a member of a black-skinned race. It was often used to indicate inferiority, but in some cases could be used without deliberate insult. The term later became nigra, a compromise by those who had learned not to say nigger, but didn't want to say Negro.

21. Corn Island, formerly Dunmore's Island, was where the first American settlement was established in Kentucky. In 1778, General George Rogers Clark landed on the island, located just north of Louisville on the Ohio River, with militia and civilian settlers. When Clark's party left, the civilians remained.

22. The Battle of the Kettles occurred in May 1788, when Henry Crist purchased kettles and supplies in Louisville and planned to travel the Ohio River to the Salt River on to his saltworks at Long Lick Creek. After he recovered from the attack, he became a member of the Kentucky legislature and was a member of Congress in 1808.

23. The concept of the benefit of clergy was originally derived from English law that allowed a clergy member to escape a death sentence by being given a lighter sentence from an ecclesiastical court instead of a secular court. It eventually was available to all offenders. In the 1700s, Kentucky was a frontier territory and would have followed English common law.

24. This part of the story is similar to the gruesome end of Micajah "Big" Harpe and Wiley "Little" Harpe, cousins who were notorious outlaws, America's first serial killers. In 1799, Micajah was killed and his head impaled on a pole at a nearby crossroads to warn other criminals. Today it is known as Harpe's Head, a spot near Dixon, Kentucky. Wiley

was executed in Greenville, Mississippi, where his head was displayed.

25. Scottish-born William Fleming studied medicine at the University of Edinburgh and then entered the Royal Navy. He later immigrated to Virginia and served as a justice of the peace in Virginia and Kentucky, briefly acting as governor of Virginia during the American Revolutionary War.

26. Colonel James Harrod—pioneer, soldier, hunter, and farmer—founded Harrodstown, later renamed Harrodsburg. He served in the Revolutionary War and built the first fort in Louisville, Kentucky. He spent some time with the Indians in the area and learned to speak their languages.

27. Under the Virginia Land Act of 1779, Lyne, Trigg, Barbour, and Fleming were appointed as four judges to examine numerous land claims in western Virginia. They were responsible for settling the titles of claimers to unpatented lands. Edmund was a distiller and operated a ferry service and a saltlick in Nicholas County, Kentucky. Trigg, serving in the American Revolutionary War, was killed in an Indian ambush near Bryan Station; Trigg County, Kentucky, was named in his memory. James Barbour was a politician and lawyer in Virginia.

28. Richard Henderson was a land speculator and politician. He founded the Transylvania Land Company to pursue land deals in Kentucky, Tennessee, and Virginia. He later received a land grant in Henderson County, Kentucky. Both the county and the city of Henderson were named in his honor.

29. The Great Grant Deed was the sale of about 20 million acres by the Cherokee Nation to Richard Henderson and Company. The transaction occurred on March 17, 1775, at Sycamore Shoals, Tennessee, and the Transylvania Colony was formed, comprising much of what is now Kentucky. The sale would allow the American westward expansion beyond the Appalachian Mountains. In November 1778, the sale was nullified because Henderson had no legal basis for the purchase.

30. Ann Kennedy married John Wilson in 1759 in Virgina. He died a few years later. In 1763, she married William Pogue. They moved to Kentucky in September 1775. Pogue was shot and killed by Indians in September 1778. In 1779, Ann married Joseph Lindsay. He was killed in the Battle at Blue Lick in August 1782. She was married once more to James McGinty, who died in 1806. Ann died at Fort Harrod in 1815 and is buried in the fort cemetery.

31. The Battle of Brandywine Creek was fought on September 11, 1777, between the Continental Army of General George Washington (14,600 soldiers) and the British Army of General Sir William Howe (15,500 soldiers). After eleven hours of constant fighting, the result was a British victory.

32. A Certificate of Settlement was for Kentucky settlers who made an improvement and planted a crop of corn prior to January 1, 1778. They were given 400 acres of land. A Preemption Warrant allowed a settler to pay for adjoining acreage, up to 1000 acres.

33. A shivaree, or charivari, was a traditional, fun-loving serenade of loud noises (pots, pans, horns, cowbells) for a newly married couple on their wedding night. It was usually meant to be a disruption to the couple's first night together and in return, the couple was expected to provide treats for the community.

34. Femme sole is a legal term for a woman (single or married) who has legal independence. As such, she could legally own property, make contracts, keep her own earnings, get credit, and conduct business in her name.

35. The phrase "you have to eat a peck of dirt before you die" is a metaphor for enduring the unpleasant challenges, frustrations, and difficulties in life.

36. The Wilderness Road was the primary path for settlers who moved into Kentucky in the late 18th and early 19th centuries. It was blazed by Daniel Boone in 1775 through

the Cumberland Gap to the Ohio River Valley. Originally, the road was rough and could only be traversed on foot or horseback. It was later widened to accommodate wagons.

37. Stephen Trigg was a pioneer and soldier from Virginia. He was killed while commanding a group of soldiers in the Battle of Blue Lick, in response to a raiding party of Shawnee Indians, who set a trap that ambushed the group.

38. Daniel Boone was also part of the militia at the Battle of Blue Lick, but he sensed the trap and avoided the ambush. Boone's son, Israel, was killed in the 1782 battle. In 1773, Boone's son, James, was killed when he and others were attacked by Indians.

39. The Blockhouse near Moccasin Gap served as a gathering point for pioneers on the Wilderness Road. It served as a fort where people could have shelter and obtain supplies while waiting for a large group to travel safely westward.

www.ingramcontent.com/pod-product-compliance
Lightning Source LLC
Chambersburg PA
CBHW061607210726
48287CB00001B/31